D0458525

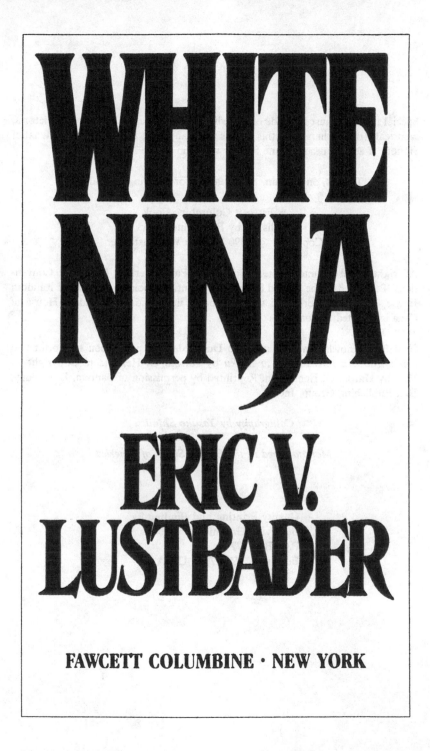

WHITE NINJA

ERIC V. LUSTBADER

FAWCETT COLUMBINE · NEW YORK

Special mention must be made of the editorial contribution of my wife, Victoria, who really outdid herself on this one. Is there anything like an editorial Medal of Honor? If so, she deserves one for her work on *White Ninja*.

Thanks, once again, to my father for proofing the galleys.

A Fawcett Columbine Book
Published by Ballantine Books
Copyright © 1990 by Eric Van Lustbader

Grateful acknowledgment is made to Doubleday for permission to reprint two haiku from *An Introduction to Haiku* by Harold G. Henderson. Copyright © 1958 by Harold G. Henderson. Reprinted by permission of Bantam, Doubleday, Dell Publishing Group, Inc.

Calligraphy by Yasuko Shimizu

Manufactured in the United States of America

Quality Printing and Binding by:
Berryville Graphics
P.O. Box 272
Berryville, VA 22611 U.S.A.

This is for Henry Morrison,
my friend as well as my agent,
without whom . . .

AUTHOR'S NOTE

White Ninja is the third novel in a series—beginning with *The Ninja* and continuing with *The Miko*—about the life of Nicholas Linnear.

All the books are interrelated, but they are by no means interdependent. Still, the novels may be seen as being akin to concentric circles and are meant to complement one another.

The winds that blow—
ask them, which leaf of the tree
will be the next to go!
                    —SOSEKI

He that fleeth from the fear
shall fall into the pit;
and he that getteth up out of the pit
shall be taken in the snare.
                    JEREMIAH 48:44

TOKYO

AUTUMN

He awoke into darkness. Outside, it was noon. In the Kan, a businessmen's hotel on the seedy outskirts of Tokyo, with the steel shutters closed like a raven's claw over the window, it was as black as the grave.

The image was apt. The room was hardly larger than a coffin. The ceiling and the floor were both carpeted in the same deathly shade of gray. Because there were only four feet separating them, any light created an unwholesomely vertiginous effect upon the unwary guest when he awoke.

But this was not the reason why, when rising from the futon bed, Senjin did not light a lamp. He had a far more compelling reason to remain in the shadows.

Senjin thought of his mother as he always did when he was either drunk or homicidal. He'd had two mothers, really, the one who had borne him, and the one who had raised him. The second mother was his aunt, his mother's sister, but he always referred to her as Haha-san, Mother. It was she who had suckled him at her breast when his blood mother had had the effrontery to die a week after he was born from an infection his long labor had caused. It was Haha-san who had cooled his childhood fevers and had warmed him with her arms when he was chilled. She had sacrificed everything for Senjin and, in the end, he had walked away from her without even saying goodbye, let alone thank you.

That did not mean that Senjin did not think about her. With his eyes open he remembered venting his anger against the white, marshmallow-like softness of her breast, of her giving while he took, of his overstepping his bounds time and time again, and of her loving smile in response. He hit out, wanting only to be hit back in return. Instead she drew him again into the softness of herself, believing that she could swallow his rage in the vastness of her serenity.

He was left with this dream, like scoria upon the blackened side of a long-exhausted volcano: Senjin watching while Haha-san is repeatedly raped. Senjin feeling a kind of despicable satisfaction that borders on rapture, and which, without any physical means, rapidly brings him to a powerful climax.

For a long time Senjin watched the milky beads of his semen slide down the wall. Perhaps he dreamed. Then he turned onto his back and got up. In a moment he was dressed, moving as silently as a wraith. He did not bother to lock the door behind him.

Late afternoon. In the street the sky was the color of zinc. It was as dense as metal, as soft as putty. Industrial ash turned the air to syrup. White filter masks were much in evidence, not only among the cyclists whirring by, but also over the mouths of pedestrians fearful of lung damage.

Daylight had torn the neon night down, but what had it replaced it with? A colorless murk, aqueous and acrid, the bottom of a sunless sea.

He had many hours to kill, but that was all right. It was how he had planned it, emerging from an anonymous lair, traveling solely by foot, also anonymously, creating a path through the maze of the city only he could know or follow.

Despite his surroundings, he felt galavanized, ten feet tall, monstrously powerful. He recognized the signs, as familiar and comfortable as a well-worn shirt, and he smiled inwardly. He could feel the slender bits of metal lying along his bare flesh beneath his clothes. Warmed by his blood-heat, they seemed to pulse with a life of their own, as if his burgeoning strength had infused them with a kind of sentience. He felt like a god, an heroic avenging sword sweeping through Tokyo, about to excise a disease that was rotting it from within.

Down narrow streets he went, a man of silence, a singular icon of brutality and death. He crossed puddles of stagnant water from which arose like a miasma the stench of fish innards. Like oil slicks, they threw back the rainbow colors of the fluorescent dusk.

It was evening by the time he made his way toward the doorway of The Silk Road. It was festooned with multicolored neon, garish plastic flowers and cheap glitter tacked against faded crepe paper. Seen from a distance, the entire entrance was made up to resemble the inner petals of an enormous orchid or, if one's mind ran to such images, a woman's sexual organ.

Senjin passed through the glass doors into a space filled with reflected light. It was like being inside a prism. Revolving disco lights refracted blindingly off walls and ceiling, both covered in mirrored panels. The result was as momentarily disorienting as had been Senjin's coffinlike hotel room. He felt at home here.

American rock music was playing at such a volume that the speaker diaphragms were taxed to their limit. The result was a thick, heavy sound, furry with bass and electronic distortion.

Senjin walked across the black rubber floor, identical to that used in children's playgrounds. He passed a bar consisting of columns of colored water bubbling through plastic tubes. The top was Plexiglas.

He caught the eye of the manager, who turned away from him, hurrying to the sanctuary of his office deep in the back of the building. Senjin found an empty table stageside and sat down. He waved away the waitress as she began to weave her way toward him.

Senjin looked around him. The club was packed, mostly with businessmen out on their companies' expense. The atmosphere was dense with the fumes of cigarettes, Suntory scotch, and the sweat of anticipation. Senjin's tongue emerged from between his lips, licked at the air as if tasting the mingled scents.

The minuscule stage before which Senjin sat was teardrop-shaped Plexiglas, one of several on three different levels. The revolving disco lights spun off the scarred surface of the Plexiglas, sending distorted rainbows sparking through the club.

Eventually the girls emerged. They wore oddly demure robes that covered them from throat to ankle so that they had the aspect of oracles or sibyls from whose mouths the fates of the men in the audience would soon be made manifest.

Apart from their faces, one could not see what they looked like at all. One had, rather, to trust those gently smiling faces that looked like neither angel nor vixen, but were suffused with such a maternal glow that it was impossible to find them intimidating or frightening. Which was, of course, the point. Trust me, those expressions said. And, automatically, one did. Even Senjin, who trusted no one. But he was, after all, Japanese and, whether he chose to believe it or not, he was in most ways part of the homogeneous crowd.

Senjin concentrated his attention on one of the girls, the one closest to him. She was as startlingly young as she was beautiful. He had been unprepared for her youth, but far from disconcerting him, her age somehow heightened his own anticipation. He licked his lips just as if he were about to sit down to a long-awaited feast.

The music had changed. It was clankier now, more obviously sexual in its beat and in the insinuation of the brass arrangement. The girls simultaneously untied their robes, let them slip to the Plexiglas stage. They wore various forms of street clothes, most of them suggestive in one way or another. Strobe lights flashed. In unison the girls began to strip, not in any western bump-and-grind fashion, but in a series of still-life tableaux, freeze-frame images held on the video of the mind. The poses, as the garments came off, were increasingly wanton, until, at length, the girls were naked.

The music died with most of the light, and Senjin could hear a restive stirring in the audience. The scent of sweat outmuscled all others now.

The girl in front of Senjin had flawless skin. Her muscles had the firmness, the roundness of youth. Her small breasts stood out almost straight from her body, and the narrow line of her pubic hair would have revealed more than it concealed were it not deftly hidden in shadow.

Now the girl squatted down. In her hands were fistfuls of tiny flashlights imprinted with the name of the club, The Silk Road. She offered one to Senjin, who refused. But immediately there was a mad scramble over his back, as the businessmen lunged to grab flashlights from her hand.

When the flashlights were gone, the girl bent her upper torso backward until her nipples pointed up at the mirrored ceiling where they were replicated over and over. The bizarre image looked to Senjin like the statue he had once seen of the teat-bellied she-wolf who had suckled Romulus and Remus.

Balancing herself on her heels as deftly as an acrobat, the dancer began to part her legs. This was the climax of her act, the *tokudashi*, colloquially known in leering double entendre as "the open."

Senjin could hear the clickings all around him as the tiny flashlights came on, insect eyes in a field of heaving wheat. Someone was breathing heavily on his neck. He was sure that every man in the club was concentrating on that one spot between the girls' legs. The flashlight beams probed into those inner sanctums as the girls moved about the stage, keeping their legs remarkably wide open. It was a discipline to walk this way, as difficult to master as diving or golf, and no less deserving of admiration.

Senjin watched the muscles in the girl's legs bunch and move as she slowly scuttled around the entire perimeter of the stage as easily as if she were a contortionist in a circus. All the while, her face was as serene and in control as if she were a queen or a goddess under whose spell these mortals had come. As long as she held her legs apart for the most minute inspection, this girl—and the others above and around her—maintained a magnetic power as hard to explain as it was to define. Senjin, totally uninterested in that spot of female sexual potency, wondered at its hold over others.

The lights came up abruptly, dazzlingly, breaking the hushed, florid silence. The rock music blared anew, the girls reclothed in their robes, once again mysterious, their faces now devoid of any emotion or involvement.

But Senjin was at that moment too busy to appreciate the dancers' splendid manipulation of emotions. He was already wending his way through the red-lighted warren of the club's backstage corridors.

He found the cubicle he was looking for, and slipping inside, melted into the darkness. Alone in the tiny space, he set about taking inventory. Against the rear wall he found the window, grimy and paint-spattered with disuse. It was small but serviceable. He checked to see if it was locked. It wasn't.

Satisfied, he unscrewed the bare bulbs around the large wall mirror. There were no lamps or other sources of illumination in the room. He reconsidered and screwed one bulb back into place.

When Mariko, the dancer who had been the object of Senjin's attention, walked into her dressing room, she saw him as a silhouette, as flat and unreal as a cutout. The single bulb threw knife-edged shadows across his cheek. She did not, in fact, immediately understand what she was seeing, believing him to be the image on a *talento* poster one of the other girls had put up in her absence.

She had been thinking about power—the kind she possessed here, but apparently not elsewhere in her life. There was a paradox lurking somewhere within this synergistic puzzle of power, but she seemed at a loss to discover what it was or, more importantly, how it might help her attain a higher status than was now accorded her.

She had yet to learn the secret of patience, and now she never would.

Senjin detached himself from shadows streaking the wall as Mariko opened the door. He was against her, pressing himself along the entire length of her as if he were a malevolent liquid poured from the shadows.

Mariko, still half stunned that the poster image had come to life, opened her mouth to scream, but Senjin smashed his fist into it. She collapsed into his arms.

Senjin dragged her into a corner and pulled apart the flaps of her robe. There was now a small blade, warm from his own blood-heat, lying in the palm of his hand. He used it to economically shred her clothes, denuding her in precise, coordinated quadrants. Then he arranged the strips just the way he wanted.

For an instant Senjin's baleful eyes took in the full measure of this glorious creature, as if fixing an image in his mind. Then he knelt and swiftly bound her wrists above her head with a length of white cloth. He tied the other end around a standpipe, pulling the cloth tight so that Mariko was stretched taut.

He withdrew an identical length of cloth, wound it around his own throat, slipped it around the standpipe, calculated distances, knotted it tight. Then he unzipped his trousers and fell upon her flesh without either frenzy or passion. It was not easy to effect penetration, but this kind of grinding pain acted as a curious spur for him.

Senjin at last began to breathe as hard as the men in the club had done during Mariko's act. But he felt nothing from either his or Mariko's body in the sense of a sensual stimulus. Rather, he was, as usual, trapped inside his mind and, like a rat within a maze, his thoughts spun around and around a hideous central core.

Flashes of death and life, the dark and the light, interwove themselves across his mind in a flickering, sickening film that he recognized all too well, a second deadly skin lying, breathing, with malevolent life just beneath his everyday skin made of tissue and blood.

Unable to bear the images and what they symbolized any longer, Senjin dropped his upper torso and his head. Now, with each hard up-thrust inside her, the noose was pulled tighter and tighter around his throat.

As he approached completion, his body was deprived of more and more oxygen and, at last, sensory pleasure began to flood through him as inexorably as a tide, a thick sludge of ecstasy turning his lower belly and his thighs as heavy as lead.

Only at the point of death did Senjin feel safe, secure upon this ultimate sword edge, this life-death continuum made terrifyingly real. It was the powerful but tenuous basis on which Kshira, Senjin's training, was built. At the point of death, he had learned, everything is possible.

Once one has stared death in the face, one comes away both with one's reality shattered and with it automatically reconstructed along different lines. This epiphany—as close as an Easterner will ever come to the Western Christian concept of revelation—occurred early in Senjin's life, and changed him forever.

Dying, Senjin ejaculated. The world melted around him and, inhaling deeply from Mariko's open mouth, he gathered to him the susurrus unique to every human being. Greedily, like an animal at a trough, he sucked up her breath.

He rose, unwrapped with one hand the cloth from his throat as, with the other, he mechanically zipped his trousers. His expression was empty, eerily mimicking Mariko's expression when, at the end of her show, she had faced her audience.

Now that the act was over, Senjin felt the loss, the acute depression, as pain. He assumed one must necessarily feel incomplete when returning from a state of grace.

His hands were again filled with the slender bits of steel that had lain like intimate companions along his sweaty flesh. What he had done with Mariko's clothes, Senjin now did to her skin, shredding it in precise strips, artistically running the steel blades down and across what had once been pristine and was now irrevocably soiled. Senjin chanted as he worked on Mariko, his eyes closed to slits, only their whites showing. He might have been a priest at a sacred rite.

When he was done, there was not a drop of blood on him. He withdrew a sheet of paper from an inside pocket and, using another of his small, warm blades, dipped its tip into a pool of blood. He hurriedly wrote on the sheet, THIS COULD BE YOUR WIFE. He had to return the tip to the blood twice in order to complete the message. His fingers trembled in the aftermath of his cataclysm as he blew on the crimson words. He rolled the sheet, placed it in Mariko's open mouth.

Before he left, he washed his blades in the tiny sink, watching the blood swirling in pink abstract patterns around the stained drain.

He cut down the length of cloth that had bound him to the standpipe. Then he went to the sooty window and, opening it, boosted himself up to its rim. In a moment he was through.

Senjin rode a combination of buses and subways to the center of Tokyo. In the shadow of the Imperial Palace he was swept up in the throngs of people illuminated by a neon sky, clustered like great blossoms swaying from an unseen tree. He was as anonymous, as homogenous within society as every Japanese wishes to be.

Senjin walked with a step dense with power yet effortless in its fluidity. He could have been a dancer, but he was not. He passed by the National Theater in Hayabusa-cho, pausing to study posters outside, to see if there was a performance that interested him. He went to the theater as often as possible. He was fascinated by emotion and all the ways it could be falsely induced. He could have been an actor, but he was not.

Passing around the southwestern curve of the Imperial moat, Senjin came upon the great avenue, the Uchibori-dori, at the spot which in the

West would be called a square, but for which there was no corresponding word in Japanese. Past the Ministry of Transportation, Senjin went into the large building housing the Metropolitan Police Force. It was, as usual at this time of the night, very quiet.

Ten minutes later he was hard at work at his desk. The sign on the front of his cubicle read: CAPTAIN SENJIN OMUKAE, DIVISION COMDR, METROPOLITAN HOMICIDE.

Under the knife, Nicholas Linnear swam in a sea of memory. The anesthetic of the operation, in removing him from reality, destroyed the barriers of time and space so that, like a god, Nicholas was everywhere and everywhen all at the same moment.

Memory of three years ago became a moment of today, a pearling drop of essence, distilled from the blurred seasons passing too swiftly.

Nicholas spreading his hands, palms up. *I look at these, Justine, and wonder what they're for besides inflicting pain and death.*

Justine slides one of her hands in his. *They're also gentle hands, Nick. They caress me and I melt inside.*

He shakes his head. *That's not enough. I can't help thinking what they've done. I don't want to kill again.* Voice trembling. *I don't believe that I ever could have.*

You never sought out death, Nick. You've always killed in self-defense, when your insane cousin Saigo came after us both, then when his mistress, Akiko, tried to seduce and kill you.

Yet way before that, I sought out the training, first bujutsu, *the way of the Samurai warrior, then* ninjutsu. *Why?*

What answer do you think will satisfy you? Justine says softly.

That's just it, Nicholas cries in anguish. *I don't know!*

I think that's because there is *no answer.*

Swimming in the heavy sea of memory, he thinks, But there *must* be an answer. Why did I become what I have become?

A flash of spoken word, uttered long, long ago: *To be a true champion, Nicholas, one must explore the darkness, too.* Immediately, he rejects the remembered words.

He sees the stone basin in the shape of an old coin that lies within the grounds of his house. He recalls, in a starburst of memory, taking up the bamboo ladle in order to slake Justine's summer thirst. For a moment the dark belly of the basin is less than full. Then he can see, carved into its bottom, the Japanese ideogram for *michi*. It symbolizes a path; also a journey.

His journey out of childhood and into the ranks of the ninja. How rash he had been to rush into that hideous darkness. How foolhardy to put himself into such moral peril. Did he think that he could learn such black, such formidable arts without consequence? A child, unthinking, unknowing, hurls a stone into the middle of a pristine, sylvan pond. And is astounded by the change in the pond's appearance because of that one act. All at once the calm, mirrored skin of tree and sky is shattered as ripples advance outward from the trembling epicenter. Image of tree and sky waver, distorted out of reality, then disintegrate into chaos. And down below, the mysterious fish, hidden in veils of shadow, stir, squirming toward the surface.

Was it not the same with Nicholas's decision to study *ninjutsu*?

He floats. Time, like sensation, is wholly absent, banished to another, weightier realm, but recalling *michi*, he thinks of the stone basin on the grounds of his house northwest of Tokyo. Before it was his, it had belonged to Itami, his aunt; Saigo's mother. In his battle with Akiko, she had sheltered him, had aided him, and he had come to call her Haha-san, Mother.

Itami loved Nicholas, even though—perhaps partly because—he had killed Saigo, who had stalked Nicholas, murdering Nicholas's friends as he had come ever closer to killing Nicholas.

Saigo was totally evil, Itami says. *There was an uncanny purity to him that in other circumstances might have been admirable. I wished him dead. How could it be otherwise? Everything he came in contact with withered and died. He was a spirit-destroyer.*

If it had been the same with Akiko, Saigo's lover, she would surely have succeeded in destroying Nicholas. But her purity of purpose, her flame, had encountered Nicholas's spirit, and had flickered in its power.

Akiko, as part of Saigo's continuing revenge, had, through extensive plastic surgery, taken the face of Nicholas's first love, Yukio. But against her will, Akiko had fallen in love with Nicholas. Because of her vow to Saigo, she was trapped into seeking Nicholas's death, and in the end Nicholas knew he would have to kill her in order to save himself. But as he had confronted her, he had wondered whether he could bring himself to kill her, for she, too, had engendered strong, dangerous feelings in him.

Even now, suspended in nothingness, he is not certain of what he would have done had not the gods intervened. The earthquake that hit north of Tokyo opened up the ground on which Akiko stood. Nicholas tried to save her, but she slipped away, down into the darkness, down into the shifting shadows beneath the rippling crust of the earth.

I am not proud that I destroyed Saigo, your son, Nicholas says.

Of course not, Itami says. *You acted with honor. You are your mother's son.*

Itami is eighty when this exchange occurs, three years ago, an hour before the gods will take Akiko to their bosom in the center of the earth. Six months later Itami is dead, and Nicholas, weeping at her funeral, thinks of cherry blossoms at the height of their ethereal beauty, falling to the ground, where they are trampled under the feet of gaily scampering children.

Sadness, unlike sensation, remains with him, bending his inner gaze to the slowly beating heart of his tiny daughter, blue-skinned, as fragile and translucent as a Ming vase. Kept alive by tubes and pure oxygen for three cruel weeks while she struggles valiantly to cling to what fragment of life was willed her, she finally expires.

As if in a movie, Nicholas watches in mute despair Justine's mourning. He had not thought it possible for a human being to shed so many tears. For months her anguish is absolute, blotting out the entire world around her.

And how does Nicholas mourn? Not with tears, not with the self-absorbedness of body and spirit that the mother—within whose body the new life grew, and who already shared with her that mysterious, intimate bond, soul abutting soul—must most wickedly shed like a serpent's dead skin. He dreams.

He dreams of vapor curling. Lost, no direction home, he falls through vapor. Gravity drags at him with such an inexorable pull that he knows he will drop a great distance. He knows that he had just begun to fall. And, knowing that with absolute certainty, he wants nothing more than to stop falling. And cannot. He falls. He screams.

And awakens, his body coiled and sweat-soaked, and cannot return to sleep. Night after night bolting awake, licking his salty lips, staring at the ceiling, at the vapor curling.

Nicholas had come to Japan with Justine's father to merge their computer-chip manufacturing arm with that of Sato International. Now, in desperation, Nicholas throws himself into his new work, the reason he has stayed on in Japan after Akiko's death. The hellishly complex merger has been consummated, and the business of the chip manufacturing has to be coordinated with Sato International. Nicholas and Tanzan Nangi, the vast conglomerate's head, have become friends.

Together they are manufacturing a revolutionary computer chip, known as a Sphynx T-PRAM, a totally programmable random-access memory chip. The ramifications in the computer industry of such a discovery are staggering—and so have been the profits. IBM has tried to deal itself in, offering the services of its infinitely expandable research and development department in exchange for the chip's secret; similarly, Motorola has offered them a lucrative partnership. But the chip's design is strictly proprietary, and, to Nicholas's and Nangi's surprise, no one has come near to duplicating the amazing chip.

Nicholas and Nangi have decided to go it alone.

With Justine so withdrawn, Nicholas spends more and more time with Nangi, and he supposes it would have continued that way for a very long time had it not been for his headaches. Not the headaches, really, so much as their cause: the tumor.

It is benign, but because it is growing, it needs to be removed. This cause for alarm is what breaks their dead daughter's spell over Justine. Finding she is still needed, Justine returns to life. Waiting for the results of the tests, the operation, the two of them find a new intimacy. But, Justine tells him, she it taking precautions. She is not yet ready to return to the psychic ordeal of pregnancy.

The anesthesia is like a carpet upon which Nicholas walks in slippered feet, in a direction unknown to him. In that sense it is like life, and unlike *michi*, the path, also the journey, which are known.

Nicholas, gazing upon the angelic face of his daughter, who lives again and forever in the theater of his mind, for the first time openly wishes to abandon *michi*, his path, his journey. He wishes to change his karma. In the past, he has bent his fate as if it were an alder staff. But now he wishes to break it in two, turning it into an instrument of his own will.

This is what he longs for as, with an open heart, he tries to capture the spirit of his dead daughter, to observe her in the same manner in which he monitored her slowly beating heart. To gather to him like tender blossoms the pitifully few days of her life in order to know what made her strong, what made her cry, what caused her to laugh.

But it is impossible. Even floating godlike in othertime, otherplace, the essence of her passes through his trembling fingers like grains of sand disappearing into the heart of the desert. And here, in front of only one witness—himself—he does what he could not do for three years.

He weeps bitter tears for her . . .

He awoke to a whiteness so pure that for a moment his blood seemed to congeal, thinking of vapor curling, falling without end, dropping like a stone down a well.

His scream brought the nurses running, their rubber-soled shoes squeaking on the polished linoleum floor. It brought Justine awake with a start, her heart lurching because she had not even been aware that she had fallen asleep at his side, holding his hand. She had done that unconsciously, the pad of her thumb against the branched blue vein on the back of his hand, feeling the slow pulse of blood there as, three years before, she had listened for the slow pulse of her doomed daughter's heartbeat.

The nurses brushed Justine away, not with any animosity, but with the cool indifference born of efficiency which was so much more difficult to bear, since they were making it perfectly clear to her how useless she was now.

Nicholas, in the frantic thrashing of new consciousness, had torn out both the IV drip and the catheter. The nurses clucked over him, whispering to him in Japanese, which, in three years, Justine had only managed to learn on a rudimentary level. She found herself resenting the added intimacy of these young Japanese women who bathed him, shaved him, and took care of his bowel movements.

She stood in a corner, a larger figure than any of the nurses, trying to peer over their shoulders, terrified that something untoward had happened to Nicholas, angry that she was reduced to standing helplessly aside.

What if he should die? She clutched at her throat as her heart turned to ice. It was winter; there was snow on the ground. She had not taken off her coat, even though it was warm in the room. Justine was always chilled now.

Dear God, save him, she prayed. She was not religious, did not even now know whether she actually believed in God. But for now she could do nothing more than pray, which at least held a measure of solace because it was something only she could do for Nicholas, and she held that knowledge close to her as a child does her teddy bear when night brings moving shadows close to her bed.

"Is my husband all right?" she asked in halting Japanese.

"There is no cause for alarm," the woman Justine identified as the head nurse said.

Hospitalese was the same the world over, Justine thought. No one offered an opinion on anything, ever.

As she watched the nurses go about their arcane ministrations, she wondered what she was doing in Japan anyway. In the beginning she had readily agreed to staying on here. It was, after all, what Nick really wanted, and in any event, her boss, Rick Millar, had wanted to open a Tokyo branch of his advertising agency. It seemed perfect, like the happy ending of a novel.

Reality had turned out to be something quite different. For one thing, she was a foreigner, and opening a business—any business—that was not wholly Japanese-owned was a formidable task. In fact, looking back on it, Justine recognized that she would not have been able to open the agency in the first place had it not been for the influence of Tanzan Nangi and Nick.

She was amazed at how much power Nick had here. After all, he was a foreigner as well. Except that the Japanese she had met treated him with the deference they reserved only for their own kind. It was partly Nick himself, of course, but the respect also came because he was the Colonel's son.

Colonel Denis Linnear had commanded a section of the British forces in Singapore during World War II. It was there that he had met Nicholas's mother, Cheong. After the war he was assigned to General MacArthur's SCAP occupation headquarters staff in Tokyo because of his expertise in understanding the Japanese mind.

The Colonel had been an extraordinary man, and the Japanese had recognized this quality in him. Their ministers had gravitated to him as moons will to a planet. When he died, his funeral was as well-attended as that of a Japanese emperor.

For another thing, she was a female, and no matter how much was written concerning the strides women were making in Japan, they were still treated as second-class citizens. They were tolerated in the workplace, but advancement was all but unheard of. The fact that she, a woman, was heading up a company made hiring all but impossible. No Japanese man of any talent would apply for a job, because he couldn't take the venture seriously, and she quickly found out that when she hired all women, she got no clients. No one would take the agency's products seriously. Within eighteen months she was out of business.

"Sorry, kid," Rick Millar had told her over the phone. "I know you did your best. Not to worry. Anytime you want to come home, you've got your old job back. Good V.P.'s are hard to find."

Home.

Staring into Nick's pale face—what she could see of it through the mysterious and intimidating swaths of bandages—Justine knew that she wanted to go home.

BOOK I

TWILIGHT
USUAKARI

荷明

Through the shutters it came,
autumn's own shape:
the warp of the candle flame.

—RAIZAN

TOKYO/EAST BAY BRIDGE

SUMMER, PRESENT

Tanzan Nangi, chairman of Sato International, could pinpoint the onset of the attack almost to the second.

In his offices at the summit of the striking, triangular Shinjuku Suiryu Building, fifty-two stories above the thrumming hive of downtown Tokyo, Nangi stared out at the concrete and glass skyrises. His gaze also took in the potted plant on his windowsill, with its deep green leaves and its tiny purple buds: a dwarf purple-gem rhododendron. The first blooms of summer. He had noticed their budding this morning just at the moment of attack.

As it happened, Nangi had been accessing data from his computer terminal when the virus began to unspool. Somehow it had been injected into his company's mainframe, entwining itself throughout the software systems until a prearranged trigger released it and it began to eat Sato's core data.

Even as he dialed his computer technicians on the intercom, Nangi watched in horror as the data that had been coming up on his screen began to unravel, turning into some alien gibberish that was useless to him or, as it turned out, anyone else in the company.

The technicians were at a loss as to how to combat the virus. "It's a nondiscriminatory borer," they told him, "which means that it constantly mutates. Even if we pinpointed its weakness at any one moment in time, by the time we could implement a formulaic antidote, the virus would already have mutated into something else."

"How did it get into the system?" Nangi asked. "I thought we had a foolproof, state-of-the-art antivirus security lock on the system."

"We do," the technicians informed him. They shrugged. "But hackers have an infinite amount of time and a seemingly inexhaustible hunger to crack security locks."

Nangi was about to make a caustic remark concerning the technicians' hunger, when the data he had been accessing began creeping back onto his screen. Quickly he scrolled through it, verifying that it was intact. Then he began accessing other data at random.

After that, he let the technicians take over. To everyone's relief, it was soon determined that the software programs were back on line. The virus had disintegrated. Nangi counted them lucky on that score. On the other hand, their core data had been penetrated. Nothing had been accessed, so a professional data raid was discounted; the hacker theory was probably the right one. Still, Nangi had been disquieted. Even now the computer security system was being overhauled. Nangi could not risk the network being compromised again.

The virus attack had occurred first thing this morning. The day had gone downhill after that.

Now Nangi curled his gnarled hands around the jade dragon head of his walking stick until the flesh went white. Blue veins like ropes filled with sailor's knots pushed the tissue-thin skin outward.

Behind him the weekly meeting of Sato International's senior management continued with its agenda. Suggested by Nicholas, this meeting was concerned first with synopsizing the division-heads meeting that had taken place the day before, and second, with aligning the division successes, failures, and needs in with the *keiretsu*'s—the conglomerate's—overall goals, which had changed drastically ever since they had won the right to manufacture key components for the production model of Hyrotech-inc's so-called Hive computer, which was now only in prototype. The prospect of burgeoning profits was not the only benefit of this deal; it was the enormous face Sato International gained—the only Japanese company to be involved in the HIVE project.

Nicholas, Nangi thought. It had been Nicholas who had negotiated the deal with the American firm, Hyrotech-inc, designated by the federal government to manufacture the revolutionary new computer.

But Nicholas's contributions went far beyond the Hyrotech-inc deal. Before Nicholas's involvement in Sato International, Nangi had been aware of the need to integrate all of Sato's *konzern*—that is, the conglomerate's individual companies—into a smoothly working whole. But it had been Nicholas who had pointed out that this could and should be taken a step further, integrating division schedules at the home office in Tokyo.

In a way, Nangi had realized, this had been a very Japanese idea, because it gave each division a heightened sense of being integral to the whole. Within three months of inaugurating the new meetings, Nangi had been gratified to see a twenty-percent increase in productivity among his division heads. He had been well pleased, and in an extraordinary gesture, had shared this pleasure with Nicholas.

He had taken Nicholas out to his favorite restaurant, a place so expensive that it was virtually a private club for the highest echelons of the industrial sector—no minister of Japan's omnipresent bureaucracy could afford its prices. But food was not the reason one went to this restaurant —it was the atmosphere: discreet, exclusive, confidential, perfect for long, drunken evenings.

For a Japanese to allow a Westerner to get drunk with him was a rare privilege indeed. For a people so studiously rigid in their social behavior, going on drunks was almost the sole source of release. It was felt that when drunk, a Japanese could say anything—express feelings normally taboo, become maudlin, sentimental, even cry—it was the liquor, after all. Everything was acceptable, and all lapses were forgiven.

It had been in the middle of his drunk with Nicholas that Nangi had begun to understand the qualities that men older than he had seen in Colonel Denis Linnear, why Nicholas's father had not been considered an *iteki*—a barbarian—like all the other men in the American occupation forces. Colonel Linnear had been special—and this quality of being attuned to the Japanese psyche, while still being Western, was present in Nicholas as well, never mind that he was half Oriental, half English.

Tanzan Nangi, hero of the war, until ten years ago vice-minister of the all-powerful MITI, Ministry of International Trade and Industry, then founder and chairman of the Daimyo Development Bank, which ultimately owned Sato, and now head of Sato International, never thought that he would love a Westerner. Frankly, he had not thought such a thing was possible. But he saw during that long night that, without quite knowing it, he had come to love Nicholas as one normally only loves a son.

Nangi, one of a handful of the most powerful men in Japan, felt no shame in this love. Nicholas possessed great *hara*—the centralized force so prized by Japanese. He also was an honorable man—Nicholas had proved this to Nangi three years ago, when he had done all in his power to protect Seiichi Sato, Nangi's long-time friend, and when he had refused under torture to reveal the secrets of Tenchi to the Russians. Tanzan Nangi knew that Nicholas's heart was pure. This was the highest honor a Japanese could accord another human being.

Nangi had, as was proper, showed little outward concern when Nicholas had gone into the hospital. But it had been a great blow to Nangi, both personally and professionally, to have Nicholas so rudely taken from him. Justine had not understood his actions, of course, believing that, like hers, his place was at Nicholas's side. This misapprehension on her part had put quite a strain on their already fragile relationship. It saddened Nangi that she could not see that the way he could serve his friendship with Nicholas best was by managing Sato International to the best of his abilities. With Nicholas incapacitated, it was Nangi's duty to the company to shoulder both men's jobs to keep the *konzern* running smoothly.

It saddened Nangi, too, that Nicholas should be married to someone like Justine, who was clearly unable to comprehend the subtle nuances of life in Japan. It did not occur to him to examine his responsibility in Justine's education.

Now, as Nangi stared out his office window, unmindful of the meeting's babble going on behind him, he felt a terrible foreboding, as if the computer attack had been an omen, a change in the wind. Because now he could feel a typhoon on its way, dark and malevolent and intent on his destruction.

In fact the analogy was quite literal, because the typhoon was specific; the force had a name: Kusunda Ikusa.

The call had come just an hour ago. An hour and a lifetime, Nangi thought. Now everything had changed. Because of Kusunda Ikusa.

"Mr. Nangi? This is Kusunda Ikusa." The voice had come down the telephone line, hollow and impersonal. "I bear greetings from the new Emperor."

Nangi had gripped the phone tightly. "I trust his Imperial majesty is well."

"Well enough, thank you." There was the slightest pause to indicate that the pleasantries were at an end. "There is a matter we wish to discuss with you."

By "we" Nangi was unsure whether Ikusa meant the Emperor himself or the group called Nami. But then again it was said that Nami—the Wave—carried out the new Emperor's will. Its members had certainly done so with the old Emperor, up until the moment he went to his final, glorious reward. Nami, it was said, was the true heart of Japan. It knew the will of the Japanese people far better than did any prime minister or any bureaucratic ministry. Nami defined power in Japan, but that did not mean that Nangi had to accept its ideals.

Nami was composed of a group of seven men—all of whom had ancestral ties to those families that had been most influential in Japan before and during the war in the Pacific. They were neither businessmen nor politicians. Rather, they saw themselves as above such mundane concerns.

Nami was interested only in the overriding directive of *makoto*—ensuring that the moral and ethical purity of heart of Japan was kept intact. But Nami's rise to power was itself an example of how purity could be compromised. During the early eighties Japan's roaring economy was based to an overwhelming extent on the worldwide success of its exports —cars and high-tech hardware and software. Four years ago, however, the yen began to strengthen to such a degree that Nami became alarmed. They saw—quite correctly—that a stronger yen would make exports more costly, and therefore the breakneck rate of exports necessarily had to fall.

In order to avoid any resulting precipitous drop in the Japanese economy, Nami had recommended the creation of an artificially induced land boom inside Japan. Nami reasoned that switching the base of the country's economy from an external source to an internal one would insulate Japan from the coming export shock.

And while they were proven right in the short term, the danger was now increased that the boom could go bust overnight. Nangi distrusted artificial means to any end. What could turn an economy on its ear overnight could itself be displaced just as quickly. Japan was now sitting on the economic equivalent of a sword blade.

If Nami's climb to almost unimpeachable power had come with the unqualified success of the land boom, it was consolidated earlier last year with the death of the old Emperor. No one trusted a successor to be able to keep the Emperor's image as the son of heaven alive.

But Nami's direct involvement in the affairs of the country was ominous. In Nangi's opinion, its rise hid a cabal of grasping, power-hungry individuals who had allowed their power to warp the true meaning of *makoto*; namely, purity of purpose. On the contrary, *makoto* had made the members of Nami arrogant, blinding them to national problems and the flaws of the Japanese as a whole. Overbearing arrogance and self-delusion were very much American traits; the fact that they had rooted themselves so firmly in the center of Japan was of great concern to Nangi.

And now that the new Emperor needed guidance, Nami's power had at last come to the fore. The Imperial succession, though it had been a media event of unprecedented proportions in Japan, was of little concern to Nami, as was the new Emperor, Hirohito's son. After the old Emperor had died, it had been Nami that, in the shadows behind the Imperial throne, had really succeeded the son of heaven.

And while Westerners saw the Emperor as a mere figurehead, wielding only ceremonial power, as did the Queen of England, Nangi knew differently. He knew that the Emperor's will defined the word power.

"Of course, it will be my privilege to serve the Emperor's will in any way I can," Nangi said, almost by rote. "Would you care to meet me at my office? I have a free hour tomorrow, if it would be convenient. Say, at five in the after—"

"This conference is of the utmost urgency," Ikusa broke in.

As an ex-vice-minister of MITI, Nangi knew the ministry code words; he had used them once or twice himself, in an emergency. Now he knew two things of vital importance: this was not a social call, and it presaged some dire crisis. But for whom? For Nami or for himself?

"I will neither come to your office nor will I suggest that you come to mine," Ikusa said. "Rather, I can offer a relaxing hour at the Shakushi *furo*. Are you familiar with this bathhouse, Mr. Nangi?"

"I have heard of it."

"Have you been there?" Suddenly, like a gap opening in an opponent's armor, the strain in Ikusa's voice was evident to Nangi.

"No."

"Good," Kusunda Ikusa said. "I myself have never visited it, but I will meet you there at five tomorrow, since that is also a convenient time for me." In the interval Ikusa created, Nangi noted the other man's insistence at dominance. At this early stage it was an ominous sign. Ikusa broke the silence. "I wish to underscore the need for absolute discretion in this matter."

Nangi was offended, but kept his tone of voice clean of emotion. There were other ways to make the affront known and, at the same time, to begin to test the mettle of this man. "I appreciate your obvious anxiety," Nangi said, knowing that Ikusa would hate himself for having betrayed even a glimmer of tenseness. "Rest assured I will take all required precautions."

"Then, at this time, there is nothing more to say. Until five." Ikusa broke the connection, and Nangi was left wondering whether his choice of rendezvous venues was deliberate. Shakushi meant a dipper or a ladle, a typical name for a bathhouse where one was soaped and rinsed with ladled water. But Shakushi had another meaning: to go strictly by the rules.

Cotton Branding, walking down the wide, scimitar-shaped beach, dug his toes into the wet sand each time the chill surf lapped over his ankles.

A salty wind was blowing. With a spiderlike hand he wiped an unruly lock of thin, sandy hair out of his eyes. Somewhere behind him he heard the *thwop-thwop-thwop* of the helicopter rotors, that most familiar harbinger of summer on the East End of Long Island.

Branding was a tall, stoop-shouldered man in his late fifties with pale blue eyes dominating a face whose obvious lineage more or less paralleled that of the Kennedys. He possessed the open, almost innocent look—much like an actor on a billboard in the heartland—of the American politician. He wore his authority openly, like a soldier's medal, so that anyone seeing him pass would say: there goes a power broker, a deal maker.

He was perhaps less handsome than he was attractive. One could picture him commanding a fast sloop out of Newport, head into the rising wind, knowing eyes squinting against the sun. But he exuded a unique kind of scent, a precious attar, which was a product wholly of power. Lesser men wanted to be near him, if only to stand in his shadow, or, like Douglas Howe, to bring him down to their level. Women, on the other hand, wanted only to be a good deal nearer to Branding, snuggling into his warm skin, the better to inhale the intoxicating aroma of supremacy.

But as must be the case in the modern world, to a great degree Branding owed his power to his friends. While he had many acquaintances among his political brethren, his true friends resided in the media. Branding cultivated them with precisely the same fervor that they pursued him. He was, perhaps, aware of the symbiotic nature of the relationship, but he was a politician, after all, and had willingly dived into a sea of symbiosis when he had entered his first election campaign.

The media loved Branding. For one thing, he looked good on TV, for another, he was eminently quotable. And, best of all, he gave them the inside stories—their lifeblood—as they were breaking. Branding was savvy enough to make them look good with their producers or their editors, which in turn made the producers or the editors look good with the owners. In return, the media hounds gave Branding what he needed most: exposure. Everyone in the country knew Cotton Branding, making him much more than New York's senior Republican senator, chairman of the Senate Fiscal Oversight Committee.

In one sense Branding was unaware of the breadth of his power. That is to say, he was unused to taking full advantage of it. His wife Mary, recently deceased, had been especially fond of pointing out his devastating effect on women when he walked into a crowded Washington room. Branding never believed her, or perhaps did not want to believe her.

He was a man who believed in the American system: executive, judicial, legislative, a careful counterbalance of powers safeguarding freedom. He understood that in becoming a senator he had put one foot into a kind of professional Sodom, where colleagues were regularly indicted for all manner of fraud. These people disgusted him and, as if he saw in their heinous behavior a personal affront to his unshakable faith in the system, he was quick to hold news conferences vilifying them. And here, too, his ties with the media gave him an enormous advantage.

Influence peddling, on which he was regularly quizzed, was another matter entirely. The very threads of the legislative fabric of the American government were woven into the pattern of barter: you vote for my bill and I'll vote for yours. There was no other way to do business on Capitol Hill. It was not the way Branding himself would have chosen, but he was nothing if not adaptable. He believed in the innate good he was doing— not only for his own New York constituents, but for all Americans. And although he would never openly admit to thinking that the ends justified the means, that was, in effect, how he had chosen to live his professional life.

This strict, almost puritan morality was, after all, the genesis of Branding's antipathy toward his fellow senator, Douglas Howe, chairman of the Senate Armed Services Committee. It was Branding's opinion that ever since Howe gained that lofty position, he had been throwing his weight around not only the halls of Congress, but the Pentagon as well. But this was apparently not enough for Howe. It was said that the senator had meticulously gathered sensitive intelligence on the private lives of a certain number of generals, and from time to time exercised this extortionate control over them. The abuse of power was, in Branding's mind, the most heinous crime of all, and as was his wont, he had spoken out on more than one occasion against Howe's misuse of the public trust.

Mary, of course, had counseled a more diplomatic course. That was her way. Branding had his. When they had quarreled, it had been around their differing approaches to life.

Still, Cotton Branding had always strived to keep the professional and the personal separate. Now Douglas Howe had closed that division, threatening to lead Branding down a treacherous and potentially disastrous road.

Howe was using his own public forum to denounce Branding and the work Branding was doing with the Advanced Strategic Computer Research Agency. Lately the verbal fight had turned dirty. Allegations of cover-ups, misuse of the public's money, fraud, and boondoggling were becoming the norm; the two were rending each other limb from limb, and privately Branding had begun to wonder whether either of them would survive.

Within the past two weeks he had come to the conclusion that in this instance Mary had been correct. Accordingly, he had cut back on the public speechifying, concentrating his efforts on another front. He and his media cronies had gotten together in private in an effort to amass a case against Douglas Howe's misuse of the public trust.

Howe and Mary: they were the only two people Cotton Branding had thought about for months.

Until Shisei.

He had met her—could it be only last night? he asked himself incredulously—at one of those innumerable social gatherings that for many formed the structure of summer on the East End. Inevitably, Branding found these fetes to be boring. But in his line of work they were strictly de rigueur, and it was at these times that he missed Mary's presence most keenly. It was only now, in her absence, that he recognized how palatable she made these masques.

"Masque" was Branding's private, ironic name for these summer parties. They were affectation personified; evenings where appearance was all, and content virtually nil. If one looked smashing, if one was seen talking to the right people when the photographers came, that was all that mattered, save if one boorishly abrogated social custom, say by bringing an undesirable such as a commercial literary figure or a Jew.

These Draconian requirements left a bitter taste in Branding's mouth, and often when he would get fed up or one too many drinks would loosen his iron-bound superego, he would confess to Mary that he would dearly love to hold one of his famous press conferences in order to expose what he called "this medieval infrastructure."

Always, Mary would laugh in that way she had, defusing his righteous anger, making him laugh along with her. But during his infrequent black moods, when he was off brooding on his own, when he had to resist following his father's besotted fate, he longed to have that righteous anger back and was secretly and ashamedly angry at her for having robbed him of it.

The masque at which he met Shisei—or, more precisely, when he became aware of her—was a morbid affair attended by people compelled to talk at length about their memories of Truman Capote in commemoration of his death. Listening to their anecdotes—meant to be funny, but which in fact were merely sad—Branding felt relieved that he had never met the author.

Still, for Branding the time had not been ill-spent. He had invited two of his best media friends—Tim Brooking, New York's best investigative reporter; and one of the on-air personalities of the TV networks' most popular investigative news show—and the three of them had talked on and off about the state of electronic journalism.

These were evil times for television news divisions, brought on by the demise of the television networks, sold to nonmedia conglomerates eager to increase profit margins whatever the cost. The networks had only themselves to blame, the on-air personality lamented. With cable and VCR use eroding their Nielsen numbers, they had turned more and more to independent producers to supply programs. More and more, the local stations controlled what went on the air. Quiz and info-tainment shows such as *Entertainment Tonight* were far more lucrative than network news shows during the hour before prime time. Further, satellite feeds picked up by local news, and the increasing prominence of Ted Turner's CNN all-news cable network, were making the three network news shows redundant. As of now, they all knew, not one network maintained an investigative news team for its nightly broadcasts, and foreign bureaus, once the pride of American TV, were being closed as fast as was practical.

As they spoke informally, it occurred to Branding that they were looking at him in a certain way. With a start, he realized that there was about their manner to him the same deference he reserved for the President of the United States.

Branding felt warmed, honored. He was well aware that one basis of his friendship with these men was their mutual usefulness. On the other hand, he was not so naive that he couldn't tell the difference between these serious newsmen and the majority of their brethren, who were too lazy, bored, or stupid to know what journalism was all about.

Branding's mother had once said to him, *Choose your friends with care. These are the people who will talk about you most.* Branding had never forgotten those words.

At last the topic reached the real reason for their meeting: the continuing "field research" into Howe's professional conduct. Branding knew that he was on thin ice, that he was using up hard-won favors in order to keep the informal investigation going. There was, as yet, no hard evidence, and the on-air personality—the more impatient of the two—wondered aloud whether there ever would be.

Branding, who had just flown in from Washington after addressing the National Press Club, assured them that there would be. He also spoke to them about his favorite topic—the one he had spoken of in his address—the Hive Project.

At Washington's Johnson Institute a team was putting the finishing brushstrokes on Hive, the advanced strategic computer that Branding's ASCRA bill would fund over the next five years. The Hive Project was a revolutionary kind of computer that could reason, could create strategies. Branding hoped to install the Hive in every government agency: National Security Council, CIA, FBI, Pentagon, and so forth. The advantages of using such a system, which was far beyond anything any other nation had achieved, would be immediate and staggering, not to mention the ramifications for national defense, as well as for a comprehensive antiterrorist response and controlled tactical forays into the Middle East or elsewhere, if the need arose.

Now, Branding's people had given him some information. Someone had been nosing around the Johnson Institute team members, appropriating without permission computer records of their private lives—bank accounts, loans, that sort of thing. To Branding this smacked of Douglas Howe. He told the newsmen that if he could link the unauthorized computer snooping to Howe, they would have a basis to go forward. The two men concurred. Branding could see the greed filling them; they could already see the scoop playing out in their minds.

The masque wound down, and so did the men's discussion. It wasn't until much later in the evening, after the three had split up, that Branding caught sight of Shisei.

She was standing against the marble fireplace in the living room, and Branding remembered thinking how like marble her skin was. She wore a clingy, black sleeveless blouse, and silk trousers of the same color. Her startlingly narrow waist was cinched by a wide crocodile-skin belt with an enormous matte red-gold buckle sculpted into what appeared to be a free-form design. Her tiny feet were enclosed by high-heel crocodile shoes. It was not a typical East End summer outfit, and therefore Branding liked it and her. He remembered thinking: this woman's got guts. Not only for her sense of clothes style, either. She wore her glossy black hair long on top, in an ultramodern sculptured manner. A short fringe across her wide forehead was dyed a shocking blond.

When he was closer to her, he saw that she wore no jewelry—not even earrings—save for a square-cut emerald ring on the middle finger of her right hand. Either she wore no makeup or it had been applied so skillfully that it was invisible.

For a long time Branding studied her face. He fancied himself a student of the human condition, therefore faces were important to him. He saw in Shisei something remarkable. Though her body was that of a mature adult, her face, a perfect oval, had an odd purity, bordering on innocence. Branding was at a loss to understand why until, with an unsettling lurch, it occurred to him that she had the kind of androgynous perfection of beauty only a child could possess.

Watching her, he was reminded of a night when his mother had taken him to see *Peter Pan* on Broadway. How enthralled he had been with the young, dewy perfection of Mary Martin, how secretly ashamed he had been of that feeling because she had been playing the part of a male, albeit a magical one.

Now, in this restored Revolutionary farmhouse in East Bay Bridge, he felt anew that odd, almost compulsive quickening of his blood that was so disturbing, and all the more intense for that forbidden component.

It was not merely the youth—Branding was as sexually unmoved by young girls as he was by homosexuals—but rather what that dewy freshness represented, a kind of ultimate, malleable state. Though he did not yet know it—and perhaps never would—Shisei's face, in the flicker of a heartbeat, by turns encompassed all that the female represented to the male: slut, virgin, mother, goddess.

Who could fail to fall in love with one such as she? Certainly not Cotton Branding.

"Is it possible we haven't been introduced?" he said in his most affable tone of voice.

Shisei looked at him with the wide-apart eyes of a fawn. "Anything's possible. But you look to me like an old friend." She told him her name.

He laughed. "I believe I would have remembered that."

She smiled, as if drawn in by his ironic amusement. "Then I must be mistaken," she said. "Perhaps it's because I have seen you on television. I feel as if I already know you, Senator Branding." Her voice was light, musical, and it pleased him, despite an accent so heavy that he had at first thought she had said, I feel as if I already own you.

"Call me Cook," he said. "All my friends do."

She looked at him quizzically, and he laughed. "It's a nickname," he said. "I grew up in a large family. We all took turns with the chores, but I was the only child who enjoyed cooking or was any good at it. I kept that chore, and got the name."

A band was playing, out on the brick deck, amid the Tuscan terra-cotta pots filled with Martha Washington geraniums and globular English yews, and they went out into the star-filled darkness. The night was typically wet but, because of a breeze, not uncomfortably so.

"Do you think," Shisei asked as they danced, "that these are desperate times?"

The band was playing a tune Branding did not recognize, something with a sinuous beat. "Desperate in what way?"

She smiled sweetly, showing him just a bit of her tiny white teeth. "One need only look to the Middle East, to Nicaragua, to the Midwest here in the States, where it is said another dust bowl is forming, or to the oceans here and in Europe, where it is no longer safe for fish to live or for humans to swim. Already I have read a dozen reports about restrictions on consumption of seafood and fish."

"You're talking on the one hand about ideological antipathies, and on the other about ecological catastrophes," Branding said. "The only thing the two have in common is that they've been part of our world virtually since the dawn of time."

"But that is my meaning," she said. "Desperation is only dangerous when it is looked upon as commonplace."

"I think you've got that wrong," Branding said. "It's *evil* that is most dangerous when it becomes commonplace."

"Are we speaking practically," Shisei asked, "or morally?"

Her body had become entwined with his, and Branding felt her flesh through her thin clothes. He was especially aware of the muscles of her legs and the heated juncture of her thighs as she rubbed against him like a cat.

He looked down at her, was struck again by the innocence of her face. Its sunny, careless expression belied her body's actions. It was as if he held two people in his arms, one who existed before the dawn of sexual desire, the other rapt in it.

"I suppose I was speaking theoretically," Branding said a bit thickly. "Real life has proved that evil is always banal."

Shisei put her head in the hollow of his shoulder, the way a child might when she is tired or in need of affection. But she was not a child. Branding felt with a start the hardness of her breasts. The erotic charge was like an electrical current running through him, and he missed a step, almost stumbling over her tiny feet.

She looked up into his face and smiled. Could she be laughing at him?

"As a child," she said in time to the music, so that she might have been singing, "I was taught that banality was in itself evil, or in any event, not acceptable." A light sheen lay along the skin of her arm, like the dew on the geranium petals. It seemed to Branding to highlight the tender firmness of her flesh. "There is a Japanese word—*kata*. It means rules, but also the proper form to maintain. Do you understand? Banality is outside *kata*, not of our world."

"Your world?"

"In Japan, Senator, training is everything. *Kata* is all. Without them both, chaos would surely ensue, and man would be little better than the ape."

Branding had heard many stories of Japanese prejudice but had never thought much of them. Now, hearing that bias firsthand, it rankled. He was a man who disliked prejudice in any form—it was one of the reasons he disliked this crowd, why he had had so many bitter fights with his father, the blue-blood Brahmin, and why, after college, he had never returned home. It was in his nature to struggle against such ignorance.

"Surely you mean laws," he said, attempting to understand her. "Laws are what make mankind civilized."

"Mankind," she said, "enacts laws to suit individual purpose. *Kata* is equal among all Japanese."

He smiled. "Among all Japanese, perhaps. But not among all people." He realized too late that his tone as well as his smile was the kind he used when, years ago, his daughter said something amusing but essentially foolish.

Shisei's eyes sparked, and she broke away from him. "As a senator I assumed you would be sufficiently intelligent to understand."

Branding, standing with her on the patio with couples in movement all around them, was all too conscious of the stares they were getting. He held out his hands. "Let's dance."

Shisei studied him, unmoving. Then she smiled, as if having taken in his embarrassment, she had been amply repaid for his unintentioned insult. She moved smoothly, effortlessly, into his arms. Again Branding felt the heat of her body insinuate itself erotically against him.

The band had switched to the kind of smoky ballads Frank Sinatra loved to sing.

"What kind of music do you like?" Shisei asked as they slowly circled the patio.

He shrugged. "Cole Porter, I suppose. George Gershwin. As a kid I used to love to hear Hoagy Carmichael play. Do you know 'Sweet and Low Down'?"

"I love Bryan Ferry, David Bowie, Iggy Pop," she said as if he had not answered her. "Am I going too fast?"

He knew what she meant. "I've heard of them," he said, somewhat defensively.

"Energy," Shisei said, "is the kick I need with my champagne."

He studied her face and, feeling his heart beating fast, wondered that his adrenaline had started running. It was after midnight, a time by which he would have normally said his good-nights and been driving back to his wind- and salt-weathered house on Dune Road, bored and slightly depressed, as if contact with these people was somehow pernicious. He found much to his surprise that he had no inclination to leave.

He wanted to continue dancing, to keep her in his arms, but she said, "I'm hungry."

The clams casino and the lobster had already come and gone. They picked over what was left: cold charcoal-broiled chicken, slightly limp salad, corn on which the butter had congealed.

Branding watched with fascination as Shisei ate like a little animal, hunched over her plate. Her long gold-lacquered fingernails speared into the flesh of chicken and corn. She ate quickly, economically and voraciously. She seemed to have forgotten his presence, or the presence of anyone else, for that matter.

When she was done she sucked the fat and juices off each slender finger in turn, her full lips distended outward. It seemed such a blatantly sexual gesture that Branding was taken aback, until the innocence and unselfconsciousness of her expression reassured him. Shisei wiped her mouth on a paper napkin, and her eyes met his.

Branding reacted as if he were a kid caught with his hand in the cookie jar. Then he reminded himself that she could not read his thoughts. He smiled that thoroughly synthetic smile politicians perfect that means nothing to them.

"When you do that," Shisei said, tossing the crumpled napkin aside, "you look as stupid as a puppet."

For a moment Branding was so stunned he could think of nothing to say. Then, angry, he flushed. He set his plate aside and got up. "You'll excuse me."

She reached out, took his hand in hers. "Are you so easily driven away? I would have thought that a senator of the United States would be open to the truth."

Gently but firmly he unwound her fingers from his. "Good night," he said in his frostiest tone.

Now, the morning after, as he strolled down the beach, his feet already numbed by the Atlantic, Branding tried—and failed—to turn his thoughts away from Shisei. He wondered if he would ever see her again. He thought he recognized something dangerous, perhaps even destructive in her. But there was something delicious in that knowledge as well, like standing at the edge of an abyss or playing chicken in a souped-up hot rod. Coming closer than anyone else to disaster and dancing away unharmed was, after all, the object, the trophy of excitement he—and other teenagers like him—had tried to hold on to for as long as possible. Like Peter Pan desperately trying to hold on to his reckless youth.

Oh Christ, Branding thought. What in God's name is happening to me?

But he already knew that it was nothing in God's name.

Justine, coming out onto the *engawa*, said, "There's a letter for you. It's got a Marco Island, Florida, postmark. I think it's from Lew Croaker."

Nicholas looked up from the patch of ground where he had been watching the afternoon shadows creeping along the ground. He took the letter from her without any expression.

"Nick?" Justine sat beside him on the Japanese porch. She did not touch him. "What is it?" Her eyes changed color, from hazel to green, as they often did in times of emotional stress. The red motes in her left iris were fired by the sunlight. Her long legs were crossed at the knees, the dark mane of her hair swept back across her shoulders. Her skin was creamy, as lightly freckled as a teenager's. Her nose, slightly too wide, gave her character, her plump lips adding a note of sensuality. The years had been kind to her; she looked very much as she had on the day Nicholas had met her ten years ago on the beach at West Bay Bridge on the East End of Long Island, when she had been a lost little girl. Now she was a woman, a wife; briefly, a mother.

Nicholas passed the letter back to her, said "Read it" with such a total lack of inflection that another flood of anxiety washed over her. Ever since he had come home from the operation at the hospital—nearly eight months now—he seemed a different person. He did not like the meals she prepared for him with what she knew were his favorite foods; his sleep patterns had changed. Always a sound sleeper, except after the baby had died, she often heard him up and pacing the floor at three in the morning. Worst of all, he had not worked out, even minimally, since recovering from the operation. Instead he came out on the *engawa* each day and sat, staring into the dust, or he drifted through the gardens with a blank expression on his face.

At one point she was so concerned that she phoned his surgeon, Dr. Hanami. Nicholas saw the doctor, who had removed the tumor, once every two weeks, and he assured her that there was nothing organically wrong. "Your husband has sustained a major trauma, Mrs. Linnear," Dr. Hanami had said with the surety of God. "Nothing permanent, I assure you. It is not caused by his anti-seizure medication. Whatever your husband is going through is temporary and purely psychological. His powers of recuperation are quite remarkable. Whatever this minor problem is will pass in a matter of time."

But Justine knew better. She knew how much psychological stress Nicholas could take, since she had been with him through the time Saigo had stalked them both. She knew how well-prepared Nicholas had been for that stalking and assault, and how cleverly he had managed to outmaneuver Akiko, Saigo's former lover. An operation was hardly enough to cause this reaction in him.

Justine slit open the envelope, unfolded the typewritten letter. It was from Croaker, Nicholas's best friend. Lew Croaker had been a detective lieutenant in the NYPD when Justine met him. He had been assigned to the mysterious murders that Saigo had been committing. A year after Nicholas had killed Saigo, Croaker had come to Japan to help his best friend Nicholas in apprehending a Soviet agent who was after Tenchi, Tanzan Nangi's ultrasecret oil-drilling project with the Japanese government. In fierce combat with a particularly powerful agent, Croaker's left hand had been severed. Since that time, Nicholas had been racked by guilt, feeling that Croaker would never have been there except for him. Justine knew better, just as she knew that Croaker did not blame Nicholas for what had happened. Nicholas, so Eastern in so many ways, was in this instance terribly Western.

" 'Dear Nick and Justine,' " she read. " 'Greetings from Marco Island. I suppose you're wondering why we're not still in Key West. Well, the simple truth is that I got bored at the End of the Line. That's what the natives call Key West. It's a strange place, even for Florida, which is a goddamn weird state any way you slice it. You've got to be a serious drunkard or a real dropout to stay there. So, we left.

" 'Here on Marco Island the fishing's fine and Alix is becoming an expert with marlin. I've bought a little boat, and we've been chartering it out. Making a living at it, too, though I doubt I'll ever get rich. On the other hand, I've busted so many boats out here trying to smuggle coke into the country, the Coast Guard's given me honorary commander status. Once a cop, always a cop, I guess.

" 'I keep waiting for Alix to tell me she misses New York and the modeling scene, but she hasn't—at least up till now.

" 'Nick, my new hand works! That doctor you set me up with at Todai Med Center in Tokyo was a whiz. I don't really know what it is on the end of my left wrist, but it's amazing! It works so well, in fact, that Alix has taken to calling me Captain Sumo.

" 'The strength in this new hand is awesome! It took me nearly two months before I could control the power in it. Another four months and

I got dexterity. It seems to be made of a composite of titanium, graphite, and some kind of polycarbonate, all wrapped up in an airtight sheath. I'm only sorry you and Justine were away when I was in Tokyo getting it put on.' "

Justine paused here, risking a glance at Nicholas. When they had gotten back from their trip to Bangkok, where several of the Sphynx components were being manufactured by a Sato International subsidiary, she was furious that they had missed Croaker's visit. Hadn't Nicholas known, she wondered, when his friend would arrive? After all, Nicholas had been the one to set Croaker up with the surgeon at Todai. Then she had wondered whether Nicholas had purposely taken them on the Bangkok trip at just that time. She had begun to suspect that he did not want to see his friend—and certainly had no desire to look at some prosthetic that would remind him of his guilt.

" 'Anyway, enough about me,' " Justine continued reading. " 'What's with you two? I trust you've gotten over your rough time.' " Justine stopped, unable for a moment to continue. She became aware that Nicholas was looking at her, and she made herself smile as naturally as she could.

She cleared her throat, dropped her gaze to the letter. " 'I can't believe it's been months since I last wrote. Can't believe that we haven't seen each other in years. Any chance you can take time out for a vacation? I know a great boat you can stay on, and Alix would love to see you. How about it? Best, Lew.'

"You know," she said tentatively, "this sounds like a great idea."

"What?"

"Taking Lew up on his offer. I think it would be terrific to get back to the States for a little while." She had said nothing to him about her own increasing desire to return to America. "We could fish, swim, relax. Just laugh and have fun. And we'd be with good friends." She poked at the letter with her finger. "I don't know about you, but I'd like to see for myself why Alix is calling him Captain Sumo."

It had been meant as a bit of levity, something to break his morbid mood, but she knew as soon as she said it that it was a mistake to refer to Croaker's new hand. Nicholas flinched as if she had struck him, and he got up and went into the house.

For a moment Justine sat staring straight ahead at the shadows of the huge cryptomeria that had for so long entranced Nicholas. Then, very carefully, she folded Croaker's letter and slid it back into its envelope.

Inside the house Nicholas stood in front of the open *fusuma*, the sliding doors leading to his workout room. He was a formidable, almost intimidating figure: wide, powerful shoulders above the narrow hips of a dancer and the long sinewy-muscled legs of the serious athlete. His face was rugged, angular, handsome and magnetic without being in any way classically beautiful. His eyes were long and upswept, testament to his Oriental blood. His cheekbones were high, his chin solid and as Western as his English father's had been. His thick black hair now had traces of silver through it which Justine loved. He had about him both a sense of quiet and of danger.

He almost passed by the doorway, then Lew Croaker's words came back to him. One-handed Lew. *Stop it!* he told himself irritably. You have more than enough on your mind without playing guilt games with yourself. In the back of his mind was the thought that this form of guilt was peculiarly Western, and he despised that in himself. He wondered whether his father, the Colonel, had ever felt this Western.

In a way, Justine was right. What had happened to Croaker was his karma. But she was also wrong. Because Nicholas knew that somehow he and Lew Croaker had been born under the same sign. Their karma were inextricably entwined. Like Siamese twins, what happened to the one seemed to affect the other. He did not think it a coincidence that Croaker's letter should arrive at just this moment.

Reluctantly, Nicholas went into the workout room and put on his black cotton *gi*. It seemed a lifetime since he had had it on, and it felt oddly uncomfortable. As if that were some kind of omen, he shivered. What was the matter with him? Nothing felt right.

The workout room smelled of straw and slightly of stale sweat. Nicholas saw the padded pole, the hanging rings, the wooden floor-to-ceiling trellis he had made himself, bolted to one wall, and the rough-hewn crisscrossing wooden beams above his head through which he used to climb, swing, and hang by his crossed ankles.

He closed his eyes, trying to conjure up the numerous times he had been in here, practicing the complicated exercises associated with his martial arts specialties, aikido and ninjutsu. He could quite clearly remember being in here, working up a sweat, but he could not, *could not for the life of him*, recall what it was he had practiced. Christ, he thought, abruptly exhausted, it's not possible. This cannot be happening. But it was, and a curious dread crept through him, a thief stealing his resolve.

His knees grew weak and he had to sit down. Slumped against the padded pole, Nicholas remembered the last battle as one does a spectacular but long-gone lover, with an awe tinged by the suspicion that memory had distorted its import, magnifying its significance.

He remembered the pain that Koten—the Japanese sumo, the Soviet agent who had cut off Lew Croaker's hand—had inflicted on him using the *dai-katana*, the Japanese longsword his father had given him on his thirteenth birthday.

Nicholas feinted right, then came in beneath Koten's guard. But the sumo let go of the dai-katana *with his left hand, slamming the forearm into Nicholas's chest. Nicholas hit the floor hard.*

Koten laughed. "I didn't hear you scream that time, barbarian, but you will soon." The dai-katana *swooped down, its finely honed tip splintering the polished wooden boards at Nicholas's feet.*

Koten laughed again as Nicholas came at him, a human mountain attacked by an insect who possibly could sting, but nothing more.

He countered Nicholas's oshi, *using the hilt of the sword, instead of, as Nicholas had expected, returning* oshi *for* oshi. *He felt the crushing blow on the point of his shoulder, felt the resulting grinding of bone and the audible pop of dislocation. Pain ran like fire down his arm, rendering his right side totally useless.*

"This is what Musashi called Injuring the Corners, barbarian," Koten gloated. "I'll beat you down in small strokes. I'll make you scream yet."

He ran at Nicholas, feinting with the long sword, employing oshi *now to throw Nicholas hard onto the floor. He knelt over him on one knee. The blade sizzled downward, cutting a vicious arc through the air.*

Desperately, Nicholas twisted, raising his left arm so that it broke inside Koten's upraised arm, deflecting the blow out and away from him. But because of the injury to his shoulder, he was unable to complete the suwari waza *move.*

Instead he was obliged prematurely to release Koten's arm to deliver an atemi, *a percussive strike, with his left elbow. He heard the answering crack as ribs caved in beneath the blow.*

Koten cried out, twisting his body up and away, at the same time slashing back toward Nicholas's body with the sword.

The steel blade was Nicholas's first priority. He made contact with Koten's forearm, gliding his left hand along the flesh. At the bottom of the wrist he broke inward, twisting. The bone snapped.

Now they were even, in a way; Koten was obliged to drop the two-handed grip on the sword, his right arm hanging loose and ungainly at his side.

But his second attack could not be stopped, and he used a shoulder throw to Nicholas's right side. This time Nicholas cried out. He rolled away, scrambling, directly into a powerful tsuki *that forced all the air from his lungs. His head went down and he began to wheeze reflexively as his lungs tried desperately to regain the oxygen denied them.*

A second vicious tsuki *to his sternum rocked him backward. In an instant Koten's massive bulk was over him, his weight pressing on Nicholas's chest, further denying him air. Bile rose into Nicholas's throat. This was the enormous danger in* sumai—*the form of battle sumo of which Koten was a master. Its territory was in bringing the superior weight to bear in an area close to the ground, increasing the strength of the* sumai *warrior exponentially.*

Koten brought the bright blade point against Nicholas's black cotton gi. *Koten leaned forward, bringing pressure down onto Nicholas's chest. Beginning the first cut, skin rupturing, peeling back like the rind of a fruit. Blood welling, dark and hot.*

Nicholas's mind was screaming for surcease. Reaching back for the "no mind" of the Void, he allowed the organism to work on its own. His left arm shot straight up, the fingers together and as rigid as any sword blade ever forged. Into the soft spot of flesh joining Koten's chin and throat.

Nicholas struck as he had been taught kenjutsu, *as he would have done a sword strike: with all his muscle, mind, and spirit. He thought not of Koten's flesh but rather of what lay beyond it.*

The kite *struck through flesh and cartilage. The sumo was dead before sensation could reach the brain and register.*

Afterward, exhausted in spirit, sick at heart at what the violence in his life had engendered, Nicholas had taken the *dai-katana* and thrown it into a lake not far from where he now lived. It had vanished immediately, taking with it the last vestiges of a life he was determined to leave behind.

Now Nicholas ripped apart the black cotton of his *gi*, feeling with his fingertips the raised horizontal scars on his chest, proof of the wounds he had received from Koten. For without that assurance, surely he would have thought this memory nothing more than a dream.

Abruptly, he heard a sound in the room, and his head snapped up just as if he were expecting an attack from an enemy.

He saw Justine walking barefoot across the tatami mats toward him. He said nothing as she crouched beside him. Her eyes searched his dark face, but she did not touch him.

"If you are in such pain," she said softly, "the least you can do is let me help you."

He was silent for a time. "There's nothing you can do," he said finally.

"You mean there's nothing you'll *let* me do."

His head was down, his face in the shadows he created.

"You're being foolish, Nicholas."

"Since you're so sure of yourself, so be it, then."

Justine sat back on her heels, contemplating him. "You helped me when I was in pain. Why won't you let me—"

"It's not the same."

"Isn't it?" She shrugged. "Well, maybe not." She touched him now, her fingertips on his forearm for just an instant. "You know, Nick, for a long time after . . . the death, I had no interest in sex. Well, that must have been fairly obvious."

"Neither of us were prepared to go on that way then," he said.

She waited for a moment, to let him know that he must allow her to finish. He knew from experience how difficult it was for her to speak her mind, or her heart, in personal matters. She said, "My abhorrence of sex —well, not sex so much as the ultimate fruit of sex, that it had brought us such pain instead of joy—lasted longer than it should have, longer than was normal."

She caught the look in his eye and said, "Yes, Nick, I knew what I was doing—what I was doing to the two of us. But, you see, I couldn't stop. In retrospect, I think it might have been a perverse kind of penance, a feeling that crept over me, a malaise. I was certain that after what happened, you would no longer find me attractive. No—" She put her hand over his mouth. "There's no need for you to tell me otherwise." She smiled. "It's all right. Really it is. Whatever I did, I did to myself. You were not a cause; you were only affected. I'm sorry about that." She settled nearer to him. "I wish . . . in a way, I wish we could go back in time, so I could deal with my own pain more effectively, and not allow it to spill over. I—"

"You had every reason to feel as much pain as you did," Nicholas said.

She looked at him oddly. "What about *your* pain, Nick? She was your baby, too." She said it quietly, and had not meant to inject an accusatory note into her voice.

"I don't want to talk about it. Whatever I feel about her is private."

Justine was taken aback. "From me? I'm your wife, Nick!" She was dimly aware that her voice was rising, but she could not seem to stop herself. "We made our daughter together. She was *ours*."

"It does no good to belabor the obvious."

Justine's anger abruptly burst through. "Oh, stop it! It's so unreal, the way you are able to suppress everything. Love, hate, resentment, anger. What did you really think about me when you saw me wallowing in my self-pity day after day? Surely, from time to time, you must have been angry, hurt at my closing you out. And speaking of that time, I don't even know what you felt after the baby died. You never cried—at least not in my presence; you never talked about it, even when I got up enough courage to bring up the subject. Did you bury it so deeply inside you that you now feel nothing at the passing of that tiny spirit?"

"I see," Nicholas said, "that you've returned to your habit of playing judge and jury in condemning me."

"No, damnit! I'm giving you a chance to explain yourself."

"You see?" he said more easily than he felt. "I am, in your eyes, already guilty, because in order to calm you down I now have to explain my actions."

"I'm perfectly calm!" Justine shouted.

"Your face is red," Nicholas pointed out.

"Go fuck yourself!" She jumped up. She began to walk out of the room, then turned back to him. "You engineered this fight. I want you to remember that!"

Their gazes met, and Nicholas knew she was right. Why couldn't he bring himself to tell her how he felt then—when their daughter had died —or now?

And suddenly he knew, and the knowledge, like a stone lodged in his throat, made him break out into a sweat. It was because he was afraid. He was afraid of the fear that was like a living thing growing inside him.

Senjin Omukae picked up the phone and sent for Sergeant Tomi Yazawa. While he waited he lit a cigarette and, inhaling deeply, blew smoke at the ceiling. He stared out the small window of his cubicle at the ancient Imperial castle where the Tokugawa shoguns had commenced the longest and surely the most paranoid suzerainty in Japan's history, approximately 250 years.

On the other hand, the Tokugawas had been canny rulers. Aware that they must ruthlessly destroy any hint of rebellion against their rule as near to its infancy as they could manage, they conspired to import from China a form of Confucianism suitable to their needs. This branch of religion stressed duty and loyalty above all other traits. Initially, in its purest Chinese form, this meant loyalty to one's father and mother, but the Tokugawas, like most Japanese, could not resist tinkering with the original product. The result was that duty and loyalty came to include one's shogun—namely, the Tokugawas themselves.

If this was a self-serving revision, it was not wholly so. Senjin knew that before Ieyasu Tokugawa, the first shogun, Japan was a wholly feudal nation, prey to constant internecine warfare between regional warlords known as *daimyo*. Ieyasu Tokugawa changed all that, uniting by blood and battle an entire nation, and thus immeasurably strengthening it.

But on the other hand, Japan's absolute dependence on the rigid caste system began with the Tokugawa shogunate, who saw this, too, as a way of effectively controlling the majority of the population.

In a way, Senjin mused, not for the first time, the Tokugawas were control freaks. Just like me.

He heard a discreet cough, and swiveling around to face the door to his cubicle, he saw Tomi Yazawa standing on the threshold. He beckoned. "Come in, Sergeant." It was Senjin's habit never to refer to any of his staff by their name, only by their rank. To his way of thinking, it gave him the proper degree of control, while making it clear to his people where they stood not just with him, but within the family of the police department.

"How are you progressing with that murder-rape case? Mariko something."

"Poor abandoned thing. No one at the strip club seemed to know her last name," Tomi said.

"Quite so." Senjin did not ask her to sit down. It was his feeling that subordinates should stand in his presence. He drummed his fingers on the top of his steel desk. "Have you any progress to report?"

"No, sir."

"None at all?"

"I know you have read the master file as well as my weekly updates."

"And the message found on the corpse, 'This could be your wife'? Have you made any progress with that?"

"Some. I've determined that the victim was unmarried, and that she dated. Her men friends never came to the club, and in interviews with the other dancers it became clear that Mariko had no confidantes there. In fact, the dancers did not much care for her. They said she thought that, essentially, they were dirt. Mariko was apparently filled with high-flying dreams."

He grunted. "She was in the wrong business, then."

"Apparently so, sir."

Senjin regarded Tomi Yazawa. She was a small, powerful woman, yet with all the requisite female curves. She had a strong face, dominated by large, glossy black eyes, more uptilted than most. Her hair was long, also glossy under the office lights, pulled back tightly from her face, wrapped in an elaborate knob atop her head. Senjin knew from experience that she was very smart, which was why he had assigned her to Mariko's murder. If she didn't find anything, no one would.

"It's been, what? Eight months? I think it's time to close the file on the Mariko murder," Senjin said.

"Sir, may I point out that I have been the only officer assigned to the case." Tomi was staring at a point on the wall approximately a foot above and to the left of where Senjin sat. "I know what it's like to be alone in the world. The victim Mariko may seem like no one to you, to the department, but she was a human being in many ways no different from me. I would very much like to continue on the case until it is solved."

"The Metropolitan Police Department does not care what you would like, Sergeant," Senjin said. "It has its procedures and its manpower problems irrespective of your desires." He watched with satisfaction as a deep flush crept up Tomi's cheeks. "Do I have to remind you who it was who allowed you these months free reign on a homicide we both suspected was unsolvable from day one? Be grateful for the time I have given you on your own private crusade."

"Yes, sir," Tomi said. "I appreciate your understanding. It's just that when she was alive, Mariko had no one to help her. I wanted her to know that she had someone now."

"You've done what you could, Sergeant. You have your duty now."

"Yes, sir."

Senjin suddenly stood up, moved so that he was directly in Tomi's line of sight. "The men don't like me much, do they, Sergeant?" he said.

"Sir?"

"Is it my age?" Senjin asked in a tone of voice that precluded an answer. "In just over six weeks I will be twenty-nine. Am I too young in their eyes to be commander of the homicide division?"

"Age is irrelevant to talent, sir."

Senjin was looking directly into Tomi's eyes when she said this, and he had a sudden premonition. He had the uneasy sense of having allowed another predator into his territory, and he wondered whether he had misjudged Tomi Yazawa's intelligence. Senjin prided himself on not underestimating his enemies. But then again, this detective sergeant was not his enemy. At least, not quite yet.

"Is it their perception, perhaps, that despite the department's findings, I lack the talent to run this division, Sergeant?"

"No, sir, it isn't."

Senjin nodded. "Now we're getting somewhere." He waited a moment. "Well, speak your mind, Sergeant. There are only the two of us here."

"What about listening devices?"

Senjin cocked his head and smiled to himself. Yes, he thought, she's not only smart, she's quick. He liked that. It was going to be a treat running her.

Senjin came around from behind his desk. He stood so close to her that he could hear her breathing, smell the perfume of her skin. "There are none in this cubicle." He searched her eyes. "Are there any on your person?"

"I'm clean, sir."

"Well, then," Senjin said, "by all means proceed."

Tomi took a deep breath, but the intake of oxygen seemed to do little good. His proximity had flustered her. She had suddenly become very aware of him as a human being—a *male* human being. She liked watching him from a distance. Up close, he had the effect of making her feel drunk. Her nostrils flared, filled with his musk. With an effort she pulled herself together. "Begging the commander's pardon, does he know the origin of his name, Omukae?"

Senjin grinned without warmth. "Pretend I don't."

Tomi nodded. "An *omukae* is a messenger from another world. A kind of demon."

"Or an angel."

"Yes," Tomi said, trying to get moisture into her mouth. "Or an angel. But either way, an *omukae* is not of this world." By "not of this world," Senjin knew she meant Japan. "It is the opinion of some of the staff that the commander . . ." She paused, mired in the rigid social structure that made it something of a sin to criticize one's superior.

"Yes, Sergeant," Senjin said in a voice of steel. "As I have said, you have my permission to speak your mind."

"It is the opinion of some of the staff," Tomi began again, "that the commander sometimes performs his duty as if he were, indeed, an *omukae*. As if he cares more about himself than he does the division or the department itself."

"Tell me, Sergeant, is that your opinion as well?"

Tomi was disconcerted. This juxtaposition of formal conversation and close proximity, intimate eye contact, was leaving her breathless. Don't let him see—"To give you a perfectly honest—"

"Wait," Senjin said sharply, silencing her. "That was an unfair question. I withdraw it. You see, Sergeant, you and I share something. We are, each in our own ways, outcasts in the department. The series of unfortunate and untimely deaths of division commanders combined with the rapid advancement of my career in the field to bring me into prominence in Homicide. Perhaps unwanted prominence, as far as some are concerned, hm?"

Tomi said nothing. She was immensely grateful that her commander had omitted discussing her own plight inside the department, knowing that they both understood its inherent nature. She was also thinking of the incident that, as Senjin had indicated, had brought him into prominence. For months a clan of particularly homicidal Yakuza seemed to be operating right under the noses of the Tokyo police. All efforts to apprehend the members of this clan had been unsuccessful.

Until Senjin Omukae had gone clandestinely undercover. Clandestine, meaning unknown to the department. He had discovered an astonishing web of graft, extortion, cover-up, and ultimately, murder being perpetrated by certain officers of the homicide division who were conspiring with the *oyabun*—the boss—of the Yakuza clan. Senjin had, virtually single-handedly, brought them all down.

The department owed him an enormous debt. Because of his work, the affair was handled internally. The intrusive media never got wind of the scandal, and thus no further loss of face was incurred. As it was, Tomi knew, many resignations were tendered within the department.

Senjin broke away from their intimate orbit, went back behind his desk. Tomi felt a mixture of relief and loss, which further disturbed her.

Senjin thought a moment, pulling languidly on his cigarette, which was almost finished. "Individualism in the pursuit of justice," he said at length, "is no longer a social crime. That is *my* considered opinion, and you are free to repeat that to the staff."

Senjin took a last puff, ground out the butt in an ashtray. "But since you've brought up the subject, I might as well enlighten you. Our duties here are varied, but more or less our most vital function is to keep Tokyo as free as possible of terrorist incursion. Unless you were asleep through your orientation courses, you know that terrorists don't think like the rest of our citizenry. They act in a chaotic fashion; they are anarchic—which means that they think like individuals. My duty—*our* duty, Sergeant—is to apprehend these terrorists before they can do any damage. I have found that by far the best way to do this is to learn to think like one. And my record—and the record of this division since I joined it five years ago—bears out the wisdom of my strategy." His gaze met Tomi's again. "Have I made myself clear?"

"Perfectly, sir."

"Good," Senjin said. He swung away, stared out the window again. "Now that the Mariko case is closed, I have another assignment for you. Have you heard of a man named Nicholas Linnear?"

"Yes," Tomi said. "I think everyone in Tokyo has."

"Not just in Tokyo," Senjin said cryptically. He turned to look at her. "Well, Linnear-san is your new assignment. Surveil him at close range. Protect him."

"Sir?"

"Wipe that look of astonishment off your face, Sergeant," Senjin said, approaching her again. "This morning we intercepted a coded Red Army transmission. Twenty minutes ago the code was broken. Here's the message." He handed her a sheet of flimsy, and when Tomi reached for it, her fingers brushed his. Momentarily their eyes met. Then, hurriedly, Tomi concentrated on reading the message typed on the paper. While she was doing that, Senjin went on. "It seems as if Linnear-san is the target of a Red Army termination directive. As you see, he is scheduled to be assassinated in one week's time."

The Shakushi *furo* was in Roppongi, that glittering section of Tokyo where the foreigner could feel not quite so alien and any Japanese over the age of eighteen was distinctly uncomfortable. The bathhouse was, at least by Tokyo standards, not far from Nangi's office, along a side street bristling with avant-garde cafés and discos which by midnight would become the throbbing heart of the city. On the corner, across the street, was an audio-video department store whose fifteen-foot windows were made up entirely of synched television screens on which a pair of talentos were posturing in the manner that these days passed for a performance. Talentos were that peculiar form of modern-day Japanese media star who had many talents but were master of none. They were like fads in clothing and hairstyle; they came and went in the blink of an eye.

Inside the bathhouse Nangi bought a numbered key on an elastic band, then proceeding to the interior, began slowly to undress. This was not as easy for him as it was for most people. During the war something had happened to the nerve synapses in his legs, making their movement jerky, seemingly semicoordinated. Using his dragon-head cane, he carefully lowered his whippet-thin body onto the polished wooden bench that ran in front of the line of metal lockers.

As he undressed he wondered how Kusunda Ikusa would react to his face. No doubt Ikusa had been fully briefed. He would know about Nangi's right eye, the lid forever frozen half open over a useless orb, clouded a milky blue-white. He might even have been shown a photograph of Nangi's face. But it would be that first moment when Nangi peered with his good eye into Kusunda Ikusa's face that Nangi would know what this man was made of, and whether he could be bested in a psychological contest.

Nangi sat very still for a moment. He longed for a cigarette. But on the day Seiichi Sato had been buried, Nangi had given up smoking. Not as a penance, but as an eternal reminder—like a flame above a brave soldier's grave—of his friend's spirit. Every time he longed for a smoke, he remembered Seiichi all over again. It had been Seiichi's older brother who, during the war, had sacrificed himself to save Nangi. Now, with Seiichi dead, no one other than Nangi himself knew that, not even Nicholas.

Nangi remembered the Buddhist ceremony, hollow for him, said over Seiichi's grave, necessary in this land of Buddhists and Shinto spirits. He remembered saying a silent prayer in Latin as the joss sticks were lighted and the priests began their singsong litany.

Afterward, emptying his silver cigarette case into a nearby trash bin, Nangi had taken the train back into Tokyo, and had found himself at his church instead of at his office.

The war had changed Nangi in many ways—it had lost him an eye, the full use of his legs; it had cost him his best friend—but no outcome was more profound than his conversion to Catholicism. Drifting alone on a raft in the middle of the Pacific, with the sight of Gotaro's death still a fresh wound in his mind, he had cast about for solace and had found his own spirit wanting. God was not a concept recognized by either Buddhist or Shintoist, but God was what Nangi had needed during that time, and it was to God he had prayed. After the war the first item he had sought out was a bible.

Years later, when Seiichi's funeral was over, Nangi had entered his church, sat in the confessional.

"Forgive me, Father, for I have sinned . . ."

He had felt calm then, composed. He had been sad, but God was with him, and he took solace in that thought. But sometimes, as now in the steam-filled bathhouse, Nangi had his doubts. He did not know whether Catholicism had made him stronger or weaker. It was true that in times of trial his faith in God had buoyed him. But at other moments, as now, he had begun to be concerned by his reliance on the rote of Catholic litany, the adherence to the gospel according to Rome. These things, too, had taken on a hollow ring. On the one hand, he understood that part of his faith meant subservience to God's will and to the dictates of the Church; on the other hand, he sometimes felt much as a self-aware addict does, faced with the ascendancy of the outside force of the drug, that his own will was slowly seeping away. This frightened him.

What was worse, he felt constrained from confessing his doubts to his priest. That alone, he knew, was a sin in itself. But he could not bring himself to admit to his failing, not with the doubt inside him that it *was* a failing at all. Did this mean that he had failed God, or that God had failed him?

He did not know, and, often now, he wondered if there was any difference between the two possibilities. In his confusion, he found it impossible to take communion, and this further increased his sense of isolation, of an almost Roman foreboding, a perception of a moral twilight falling upon him and those around him.

Nangi's good eye refocused on the closed metal door in front of him. He brought his mind slowly back into the present. He centered, breathing deeply, knowing that he would need all his resources to face Kusunda Ikusa successfully.

Naked, Nangi turned the key in the locker, slipped the key around his wrist. He leaned more heavily on his cane than he might normally have were he not in a public place. He had learned long ago that a clever man could derive indirect benefits from his physical disabilities. The war hero was still a powerful image in Japan, and Nangi had put himself into the habit of exploiting every advantage he could.

His good eye, in its odd triangular setting, blazed as he set off down the humid, tile-lined corridor. The floor was composed of wooden slats beneath which drains set in concrete leached away the water. The sound of his cane striking the slats echoed in the hallway.

Inside a small chamber a young woman took Nangi's cane and, as he sat beside a steaming tub, knelt to ladle water over him while another young woman soaped and scrubbed his body with an enormous natural sponge. He was sluiced with deliciously hot water.

Cleaned—purified, the Shintoists would say—Nangi was helped to his feet, given back his cane, and directed out the other side of the room.

Kusunda Ikusa was waiting for him.

Nangi was stunned. He had been unprepared for how young Ikusa was. Certainly under thirty, a mere baby by Nangi's standards. Could one so young truly represent Nami and, by extension, the Emperor of Japan?

Perhaps Ikusa had once been a sumo. His thickly-muscled legs were bowed beneath the weight of his wide frame. Great rolls of pale flesh cascaded in widening layers from beneath his arms to the tops of his thighs. But for all that, he seemed as deadly and streamlined as a bullet.

His head was hairless, dark and stippled over the sections of scalp where hair would have been. He had tiny, feminine ears and the kind of bowed mouth one often found on simpering geisha or female impersonators. But the coal-black eyes set like gems in that wide, suety face seemed to generate beams of invisible light that probed the darkest recesses of the soul. He possessed great *hara*—great inner strength—and Nangi was instantly wary of him.

"Tanzan Nangi, it is an honor to meet you," Kusunda Ikusa said with a slight formal bow of his head. "I bring the presence of Nami. When I speak it is with the voice of Nami, all as one."

This ritual greeting was delivered in a deep, almost grating voice, oddly inflected with the singsong tempo of the Shinto priest.

"Kusunda Ikusa, it is an honor to meet you," Nangi replied in kind. "The presence of Nami is felt, its voice heard."

Kusunda Ikusa nodded, satisfied that the preliminary rituals had been properly observed. He lifted an arm dense with muscle and fat. "I have reserved a private space so that we may speak freely."

He led Nangi into the pool area, an enormous place with an overarching ceiling dim with height. The pool was echoey, filled with hushed, murmuring voices which were nonetheless thrown back and forth in the space by the curved, tiled ceiling and walls.

Ikusa stopped at a small alcove. Tiny, pale green wavelets licked at the green tiles. Seven feet into the water a pebbled glass screen had been erected. Light passed through this translucent barrier, bringing with it anonymous shadows moving slowly, somnolently, in the enormous pool beyond.

Ikusa slipped effortlessly into the water, and Nangi, placing his cane on the tile beside the pool, climbed in with some difficulty. Nangi wondered whether Ikusa's choice of venue was deliberate. Nangi had to put his physical disability on public display.

For a time they floated in the deliciously warm water, shedding like dead skin the memory of the frenetic world outside. Here they were at peace, enwombed in the buoyant water. This was, at any rate, the atmosphere that Ikusa apparently wished to manufacture.

Nangi closed his good eye and, gripping the side of the pool, thought of nothing. He did not open his eye or focus his mind until Ikusa cleared his throat.

Then he saw those laser-beam eyes contemplating him, and he blinked as if he could not bear their scrutiny. Reflected light coming off the water in patches illuminated Ikusa's face as if it were a screen upon which sun and clouds chased one another in ever-changing patterns.

And, indeed, it was a kind of screen, reflecting more than light. Nangi knew that he would need to read that face if he were to hold his own in this conference.

"Nangi-san," Kusunda Ikusa began, "Nami wishes to speak with you concerning a matter of the utmost urgency."

"So you indicated in our telephone conversation," Nangi said neutrally.

"Nami has some concerns—some significant concerns—regarding the way you run your business."

Nangi showed nothing on his face. "I was not aware that Nami had any reason to scrutinize Sato International."

"Two events made it necessary," Ikusa said. "The first is your involvement in Tenchi. The exploratory oil-release program is government-sponsored, so it is natural that Nami should be involved."

When Nangi saw that Ikusa was not immediately prepared to continue, he closed his good eye again, as if he were alone, relaxed and meditative. He did not care for the way this meeting had begun—there was already an accusatory tone in Ikusa's voice, nonspecific, and therefore particularly offensive. Now Ikusa was deliberately baiting Nangi by failing to provide the second reason for Nami's interest in Sato International.

It occurred to Nangi that, from the first, Ikusa's tactic had been to provide offense. What did he mean to gain by this? Was it merely an attempt to establish control, a sense of territory? Or was there another, more sinister motive?

Nangi cleared his mind, aware that one could spend all one's time asking questions, when what he needed to do was to watch Ikusa, listen to him as Nangi sought to draw him out. Only then would the answers come.

"Three years ago," Ikusa said at last, "the Tenchi project came within a hairbreadth of being compromised by the Russians. Since then Tenchi has yielded significantly less than had been initially projected."

Nangi stirred the water. "True enough. But in the first place, it was Nicholas Linnear who almost single-handedly kept Tenchi's secret from the Soviets. In the second place, we have found that the shale at the bottom of the ocean near the Kurile Islands is significantly more dense than is normally found offshore. Our geologists are now convinced this is so because of the large number of earthquakes here. The makeup of the underlayers of shale is quite different."

There was silence for some time. The moving shadows painting themselves across the pebbled glass screen were diffuse. Combined with the soft lapping of the wavelets, they provided a kind of sensory film onto which one could imprint one's own interpretations.

"Nami has read your geologists' reports," Ikusa said in a tone that implied disapproval.

Nangi was aware that he was being baited again. Ikusa had made no allegations against either Nangi or Sato International. Nor, Nangi suspected, would he. Did Ikusa know anything? Nangi asked himself. Or was he on a fishing expedition? That would explain the baiting. Lacking anything of a substantial nature, he might be relying on Nangi himself to provide Nami with any evidence of wrongdoing.

"Then," Nangi said, "Nami knows that we are making every effort to bring Tenchi up to full capacity."

"Tenchi," Ikusa said languidly, "is just part of the issue." He paused, beating the water in front of him with his feet, so that ripples spread outward. When they reached Nangi, he said, "The *origin* of Nami's concern—'anxiety' would not be too strong a word under the circumstances —lies elsewhere."

He only had to be patient, Nangi knew, and Ikusa would tell him the real reason for this meeting. Nangi had secrets—deeply buried, it was true, but he was still vulnerable, as everyone who harbored secrets was vulnerable. Despite his best intentions, Ikusa's form of interrogation was seeping into him. He knew he must redouble his own efforts not to let his own anxieties do Ikusa's work for him.

Nangi speared the other man with his good eye. "Whatever it is you need to know," he said, "it is my wish to provide."

"Even though your own personal philosophy does not often run parallel with Nami's?"

"I know where my duty lies," Nangi said evenly. "In the same concentric circles where every Japanese's duty lies. Emperor, country, company, family."

Ikusa nodded. "There can be no doubt," he said. "But in what order, one wonders?"

Nangi said nothing, aware that Ikusa was waiting for Nangi to indict himself.

Ikusa said, quite disrespectfully, "If your heart is pure, Nangi-san, you have nothing to fear."

Nangi saw that this was to be a trial by fire. He also saw that mere neutrality on his part was not going to work; Ikusa was too smart for that. Nangi knew that in order to draw the other man out, he needed to go on the offensive. But this tactic was a double-edged sword; it was, in itself, fraught with danger, and it could be just what Ikusa wanted, for the more Nangi spoke, the more he revealed of himself and his own strategy.

"Public sincerity," Nangi said, after some deliberation, "is no substitute for nobility." He was tired of being the subject of discussion. "*Iji o haru* is perfectly fine," he said, using the Japanese term for sticking to one's position even after it has been proven wrong, "for sixteenth century Tokugawa *ronin* or romanticized Yakuza, but in this complex present, I have found *iji o haru* used, more often than not, as a subterfuge to grab a handful of personal power."

Ikusa blinked, clearly surprised by Nangi's forceful attack. He knew perfectly well that Nangi had just now put into question not only his, Ikusa's, motives, but the motives of Nami as well.

"Nami is beyond both criticism and reproach," Kusunda Ikusa said rather stiffly.

"Betrayal," Nangi replied carefully, "is never sacrosanct. It must be ferreted out wherever its insidious roots take hold."

Kusunda Ikusa stirred and, for an electric instant, Nangi thought he was going to be attacked. Then the big man settled back in the water. Wavelets from his agitation reached the edge of the pool, splashing water onto the tile surface of the lip.

"True," Ikusa said, "betrayal at any level cannot be tolerated." And Nangi noted with some satisfaction the strangled tone of his voice. "And that is why we have met, why we are here now."

"Betrayal." Nangi rolled the word around in his mouth as if it were a wine whose provenance needed deciphering. He was wondering whose betrayal Ikusa meant, and what that betrayal entailed. He did not have long to wait.

"Nami's concern," Kusunda Ikusa said, impaling Nangi with his stare. "lies with your *iteki* partner, Nicholas Linnear."

Beyond the translucent glass screen, now beaded with moisture, shadows continued to move, their indistinct outlines a perfect counterpoint to this strange meeting.

Very carefully, Nangi said, "Nicholas Linnear is the subject of Nami scrutiny?"

"Just so," Ikusa said, a trifle pompously. He had meant to shock Nangi with his statement, and now that he had been assured that he had succeeded, he was again on solid ground. He liked that, and Nangi made a note of this weakness. "You must understand, Nangi-san, that for a decade Nami has chafed beneath the harness the Americans—and, indeed, the world—have placed around our necks. Over and over we have been reminded that we are a defeated, an impoverished country. Is this not a form of brainwashing? And what happens when even the strongest man is a victim of decades of forced indoctrination? He begins to believe what he has been told to believe. That is what has happened to Japanese of your generation."

Kusunda Ikusa lay in the water, huge and as bloated as a toad gorging itself on insects. His youth seemed somehow obscene to Nangi, as if in Ikusa the opportunity for experience and learning was wasted.

Ikusa continued his monologue. "But people such as myself—members of a younger generation—have grown up knowing only a Japan with a vital economy, an ever-strengthening monetary unit. Now the tables are turned, Nangi-san. Now it is we who are invading America, buying up real estate, record companies, banks, electronic businesses. It is the Japanese who are, in effect, keeping afloat an America that is awash in fiscal debt. For years we have bought their government bonds. Now we are snapping up their corporate bonds, and very soon we will own these corporations as well. In all areas, we see a distressing lack of quality in American products. The world which, I have read, once laughed at a Japanese-made product, now laughs at American-made items. I have been told that the Americans taught us everything we know about engineering and quality control. I find that difficult to believe."

Ikusa's face trembled with a kind of inner rage, as if he himself had been personally insulted by these world events, as if he were outraged Japan. "America, it is true, still possesses an awesome array of natural resources, which we will never have. And the might of their military forces is terrifying. But ask yourself, Nangi-san, is America the same nation that occupied us in 1946? No. Illiteracy and crime are problems that increase with each year. America is now struggling with the downside of mongrelizing its population. Its open-door policy to immigrants will be its ultimate undoing. Fiscally, it has a debt it cannot possibly support. Bank failures are on the increase and, as we know, they create a snowball effect. America is a country in serious decline."

Nangi said, "Even granting that all you say is true, I cannot see what any of it has to do with Nicholas Linnear."

Ikusa grunted, and his great body heaved, setting a fresh set of wavelets in motion. "Nicholas Linnear's parentage may be English and Oriental, but he is an American now. One, I might add, with ties to the American intelligence community. Never forget that he was employed by a major American spy apparatus when he was captured by the Russians and tortured."

Ikusa paused here, allowing the last word to hang in their air as if it were an accusation.

Nangi said, "Linnear-san endured much pain and suffering in order to keep the secret of Tenchi safe from the Soviets."

Ikusa smiled, as if he had expected this response and was gratified that it had been spoken. "Your loyalty to this mongrel is well-documented, Nangi-san."

Nangi sat very still. He had to use every ounce of his self-possession to keep from making a rash statement that might, in Ikusa's eyes, condemn him. "As I told you," Nangi said in a calm voice, "I know where my duty lies."

"Americans," Ikusa said as if Nangi had not spoken, "are masters of lies and deception. When they are your enemies, they defeat you; when they are your friends, they exploit you."

Nangi, listening closely, knew that Ikusa had moved from the general to the specific: he was speaking about Nicholas.

"The merger between Sato International and Tomkin Industries never should have been allowed." Kusunda Ikusa's head moved in small increments, taking in not only Nangi, but the surrounding environment as well. "For one thing, Tenchi is too vital to Japan's future security and independence from foreign sources of energy. I need not remind you that the fact that Japan has been totally dependent on others to provide fuel has made us terribly vulnerable. This was the spur for Tenchi's creation." Ikusa's questing eyes had settled upon Nangi again. "Another reason why the merger was a mistake is that your company, Nangi-san, is privy to too many secrets—industrial, governmental, even military—to have an American so intimately involved. You have already put us in peril. It is unreasonable to think that you can continue in this vein."

Nangi said nothing, though he now knew what was to come. Let Ikusa say it out loud, he thought. I will not help him in any way.

"Nami believes that this unsafe association with the American—both business and personal—must be ended," Kusunda Ikusa said. "The sooner the better."

Nangi said nothing. Apparently, Ikusa felt it advisable to speak for him.

"You have thirty days to dismantle the merger between Sato International and Tomkin Industries. But I will insist that all Tomkin personnel be immediately excluded from any and all involvement in Tenchi. This, of course, includes Nicholas Linnear."

Nangi felt as if he had been handed a death sentence. "What about the Sphynx computer-chip *kobun*? That is our first full joint venture with Tomkin. It is they who brought us the Sphynx T-PRAM technology. The profits are enormous."

"The *kobun* will naturally have to be dissolved," Ikusa said, his eyes again on the environment.

"Without Tomkin's involvement," Nangi said, "we will be left with nothing. The technology is strictly proprietary."

Kusunda Ikusa's eyes slid toward Nangi. "If the Sphynx T-PRAM chip is as profitable as you claim," he said, "you'll find a way to, ah, appropriate the technology."

"I will not steal from my friend."

"I believe," Ikusa said slowly and carefully, "that you need some time to think this through." He lifted a hand, almost in benediction. "You need to see clearly who your friends are."

Nangi was silent. He felt impaled upon a rock, waiting for the carrion birds to arrive to pick his bones clean.

Ikusa said, in what in anyone else would be construed as a benevolent tone of voice, "You have already said several times that you know where your duty lies, Nangi-san, so, at this juncture, there seems no need to remind you." Nevertheless, Ikusa did. "Duty to one's Emperor, one's country, one's company, one's family. That is the proper order." Ikusa closed his eyes, as if at last he could enjoy the heated water. "Do your duty, Nangi-san. Nami—and your Emperor—command you."

Cotton Branding awoke with a strong sense of sexual tension. He had an erection that even urinating couldn't dissipate.

He had dreamed of Shisei.

Of music and her legs and especially what was between them. They had made love dancing to the music, circling the formal brick patio while the band watched. Branding flushed as the dream came flooding back to him. He doused his head in cold water, as if that would drive away the wanton images.

He thought of his wife Mary, just two months dead, seeing again in his mind the footage of her being pulled out of their collapsed Mercedes, hit head-on by an eighteen-wheel truck that, out of control, had jumped the divider on 295 into Washington. The on-the-scene television reporter had said that the police had to use acetylene torches to get her out of her twisted metal and glass coffin.

Branding, hanging limply over the custom sink, gagged, vomited up what little was left in his stomach from last night. That did it for his erection. The dream, too, was gone.

He took a shower, then dressed in seersucker shorts, an emerald polo shirt, and huaraches, he padded into the kitchen. The room was huge, as was every room in the house, and, though it was still early, filled with brilliant light. Out the window, across the dunes, the blue Atlantic curled and sucked at the beach.

Coffee had been made automatically by some West German machine Mary had ordered from the Williams-Sonoma catalogue. Branding had never seen the sense in it, but this morning he was grateful for its presence. He put a frozen croissant into the microwave and, when it was warm, dropped it onto a paper plate.

He went out onto the deck, and while he sat sipping and nibbling, stared at the extension phone. Above his head gulls wheeled and cried to each other. He tasted neither the coffee (which was quite good) nor the croissant (which was not). He was thinking about whether to call Tippy North, the masque's hostess, to ask her if she knew Shisei's phone number or even her last name. It had been three days since he had met Shisei; an eternity.

At that moment he heard the front doorbell ring. He looked at his watch. It was barely eight o'clock on a Sunday morning. Whoever it was must have the wrong house. He continued to stare at the phone, no longer concerned with the charade of eating. The doorbell rang again. He ignored it. He was in no mood for company, and furthermore, whoever it was had a hell of a nerve bothering him at this hour.

Gulls dipped low along the shoreline, and mist lay close in the hollows between the dunes, waiting for death by sunlight. If he squinted he could see the dried remains of a horseshoe crab, its black prehistoric shell looking ominous on the clean white sand.

He heard footsteps on the wooden stairway up from the beach, and he turned his head. Someone was coming toward the house along the walkway the DEC had made him build across the dunes in order to preserve them.

Sunlight struck the figure as it emerged from the mist. The light fell obliquely, burnishing the figure as well as blurring its outline. At first he thought the person was nude. Then, as it drew closer, he saw that the figure wore as skimpy a bikini as he had ever seen. Really, the figure was all flesh.

It was Shisei.

He was so stunned that he did not answer when she said, "Why didn't you answer the bell?"

It was as if she had walked right out of his dream.

"Cook," Shisei said. "You said I could call you Cook."

"Did I?" Already it seemed as if he had violated a sacred trust. Thinking of his ongoing senatorial war with Douglas Howe, he knew that he should have nothing to do with this woman. Yet he did not send her away. Instead he devoured her with his eyes.

Seeing the look on his face, Shisei extracted a white cover-up from the multicolored hemp satchel she carried, slipped it on.

Branding discovered that his need for her was so powerful it was akin to the ache one develops from an animal bite. He felt red and sore, filled all over again with the wretched pangs of yearning he had experienced as a teenager.

"Is there any more coffee?" Shisei said.

An oval of sand clung to her calf, a contrast to her smooth skin, which was somehow so erotic that Branding almost doubled over with the ache in his lower belly.

"I'll get you some," he said thickly.

When he returned she was draped over a chair she had brought to a position directly across the pebbled-glass table from his. He handed her a cup, sat down. Her unbuttoned cover-up had fallen open. Her body was absolutely hairless. There was something eerily fascinating about the endless expanse of cool, tan smoothness. She was, so exposed, even more of a child. Like almost all Americans, Branding equated body hair with maturity.

And yet, at the same time, she was much less the child. The bikini was three minuscule triangles of gold and chocolate animal-striped spandex. Everything underneath was as good as revealed. The shape of her body had nothing behind which to hide, and it was impossible to pretend that there was anything girlish or immature about it.

"I'm surprised to see you," he said.

Her eyes, as dark as the coffee she was sipping, regarded him openly. "I wanted to see where you live. It will tell me much more about you than you could yourself."

He noticed that she said nothing about how the evening at the masque had ended. It was clear she had no intention of apologizing. "Why are you so interested in me?"

"That is a suspicious question."

"I'm not suspicious," Branding said, not altogether truthfully. "Merely curious."

"You are powerful, handsome, intelligent," Shisei said. "Why shouldn't I be interested?"

"My wife is dead sixty days."

"Why should that make a difference to either of us?"

"Besides anything else, there is a period of mourning to be observed." With the politician's glibness, he returned one of her own terms. *"Kata."* The proper form. "And I am currently in the middle of a life-and-death struggle with Senator Douglas Howe. He's smart and unscrupulous, and he's got smart and unscrupulous people around him. That's bad enough. But even worse for me, he has a great deal of money and influence behind him. I can't afford to give him any ammunition with which to smear my name."

Shisei smiled and nodded. "I understand." She put down her empty cup and rose to leave. "Thank you for the coffee and for your frankness."

He had been wrong. Her skin was not like marble. It was like the first golden peach of summer, one that you could not wait to bite into, to taste the sugary, perfumed flesh while the sticky juices ran down your chin.

Impulsively leaning forward over the glass table, Branding took her hand. "Don't go," he said, astonished at what he was proposing. "Stay awhile."

. . . *took two hours to untangle the victim from the mass of metal,* the reporter was saying again, inside Branding's mind, as the television camera tracked in for a close-up—a close-up of Mary. *His* Mary. Dear God!

He closed his eyes. Stop this, he reprimanded himself. What good does it do? Mary made that same trip religiously twice a week all year long. How could you have prevented it? How could you have protected her? The answer was that there was nothing he could have done. Which was, of course, what made the guilt so excruciating. Often he felt crucified by it.

"I'll stay, if you like." It was, from Shisei's throat, purely a neutral statement.

He dropped his hand from hers. "I'll leave it up to you."

She strolled along the old-fashioned wraparound porch. It was the place that Mary had loved the best, the one she had designed with the architect. Every eight feet massive wooden pillars rose up to reach the overhang, which served as an exposed deck from the second floor.

Suddenly curious, Branding said, "You never told me what you do."

"I'm a lobbyist," Shisei said. "I work for various international environmental groups."

Thinking of all the lobbyists honeycombing the Washington political arena, he said, "That must be tough work."

She smiled. "It's impossible, really. But someone's got to do it. Anyway, we Japanese have a long history of championing lost causes."

She put her arms around a pillar, swung herself off her feet in startling mimicry of what Mary used to do when she was happy with her charity work or satisfied with an important bill's passage.

Branding stood up, following Shisei down the porch. He watched her, a puppy at play, her face relaxed and unconcerned, and he was filled with an odd joy that was tinged with the kind of wistfulness one feels on the first crisp day of autumn. It was, in fact, such a strange emotion that Branding mentioned it to Shisei.

She stopped as if he had physically grabbed hold of her. On bare feet she came across the porch to where he was standing. "In Japan," she said, "everyone waits for three days in April, for the cherry blossom viewing. During that time the air is suffused with their perfume. Some go to the parks and the countryside on the first day when the cherry blossoms are in the first blush of youth. Others go the second day, when the vigor of the mature blossoms are at their height. But everyone goes the third day, when, like heavenly rain, the blossoms begin to fall. We watch them drift to the earth so that we may not forget the fleeting nature of all of life's most beautiful creations. We feel both elation and sadness. In Japanese it is called *mono no aware*, the pathos of things." She touched him. "Now, I think, you have felt the same thing."

Branding did not wait for nightfall to take his cherry blossom to bed. Indoors, with the backwash of the hazy day turning the room incandescent, her eyes were glittery. Shisei approached him and slowly undressed him. He did nothing, urged to momentary passivity by her eyes and, possibly, something in her manner.

With agile hands she peeled off his polo shirt, unbuttoned his shorts. Now he was naked and she was not. Branding found that he liked it that way, drinking in her bareness while imagining what those tiny covered bits of her looked like.

He could see the outline of her nipples, but he did not know their color or texture. He could see beneath the spandex the shadow of the vertical crease he ached for, but he did not know its true shape. There was so much to learn, and so little time before the fragrant petals dropped to the earth.

She stared at him in much the same way a man will drink in the sight of a naked female form. Branding had never before seen a woman do this. He felt excited by it, and wondered how some women could be so offended by being considered sex objects. He found the experience egoexpanding.

Shisei stared into his eyes, compelling his attention. She was very close to him; he thought he could feel her heat, remembered the press of her mount against him as they had danced, and got hard. Then he felt her fingers on him, enclosing him. Her fingers did not stroke him. They squeezed him; he got bigger and bigger.

"You're ready," Shisei said. "So fast." She said it in a way that made Branding's mouth water.

She shrugged off the cover-up, stepped out of her bikini, and Branding drank her in as she had, moments before, done to him.

"Turn around," he said thickly.

But Shisei shook her head, advancing on him. Now he felt her against him without any intervening material. She lowered her head, sucked on a nipple, and he gave out a little gasp as a line of pleasure traced itself from chest to groin. Then she climbed upon him, entwining herself about him as if she were worshiping a giant phallus. Branding groaned.

They made love to music by Grace Jones, an album that Branding's daughter had left behind one summer. He had never listened to it, but Shisei found it in among the George Shearing and the Bobby Short records and put it on. The singer's voice was by turns as soft as the inside of a fruit, as hard and shiny as chrome on a sports car.

Branding had never made love to music; Mary had needed undisturbed quiet in order to relax sufficiently for sex. He found the music at once exhilarating and disturbing, almost as if he were making love to two women at once—or, more accurately, as if they were making love to him, one with her mouth and her sex, the other with her voice.

Then, sweat-sheened, Shisei sank all the way down on him, and he forgot about everything else.

Afterward, he said with an ironic smile, "I wonder what would have happened if you'd found a David Bowie album instead of this one by Grace Jones." He was exhausted; she was amazingly dexterous, extraordinarily powerful. He felt as if he had just spent two hours working out at a gym. It was, he thought, a delicious kind of exhaustion.

"I masturbate to David Bowie," Shisei said. "Do you masturbate, Cook?"

"That's an odd question." He was astonished by her power to shock him.

"Do you think so?" she said. "Why? It is merely a parameter of what makes you you—one of many."

He sat up, swung his legs over the side of the bed, determined to break the mood. He was uncomfortable when she spoke like this, with the cutting directness of a child. But she was not a child. "Here in America," he said, "it is not something easily spoken of."

"Not even among man and wife?"

"We are not man and wife, Shisei. We are strangers." And then, because her penetrating gaze compelled him, he added, "Sometimes not even among man and wife."

"That is senseless," she said. "It is natural, like the naked body. Like sex. And yet Americans are ashamed."

"From what I understand, there are many subjects not openly talked about in Japan."

"Shall we speak about all of them now?"

Branding did not believe her. "What about *kata?*"

Shisei moved on the bed, taking between her calves the printed top sheet, flicking it onto the stained wood floor. "I have been taught that if something is beneath the ice, if you sense it but cannot see it, it is still there, moving, disturbing the currents." She opened her thighs, redirecting Branding's gaze. She arched her back. "Come here, Cook. I do not think that I have finished with you—nor you with me."

When Justine stormed out of Nicholas's workout room, she went into the kitchen. It had been close to dinnertime, but she had realized that she could not remember what it was she was going to prepare. Besides, she had not been hungry, and as for Nicholas, she had thought, if he's hungry, let him get his own dinner.

Having come to that conclusion, she found that she was no longer comfortable anywhere in the house. She went outside, down the *engawa* steps, past the huge cryptomeria. In the last of the light she wandered the grounds, until she found herself at the stone basin where, more than three years before, Nicholas had taken her on their way to this house.

I'm thirsty, she had said then, and she was thirsty now. She stopped, took up the handmade bamboo ladle, drank from it. She stared down into the bottom of the basin, made out the Japanese character for *michi.* A path; also a journey.

Was her destiny here, in Japan? Was that the only direction in which her path lay, the sole destination of her life's journey? Could such a thing be possible? She had always thought that life's journey had many paths, a multitude of destinations. Well, then? But she tried to imagine her life without Nicholas, and all she felt was a terrible loneliness that she knew she could not bear. Living somewhere apart from him would be torture, she knew, because her mind and her heart would always be wherever he was. She did not want to live the rest of her life as an emotional cripple.

But on the other hand, she knew she could not continue the relationship as it was. She had relied on Nicholas. He was her anchor, her safe haven, especially here in Japan where she knew no one and, moreover, was increasingly coming to feel that she was unwanted. In the beginning everyone was friendly—no, she corrected herself, *polite* was the right word. Every person Nicholas or Nangi introduced her to was so damn polite Justine couldn't stand it. No one could consistently be that polite, she suspected, and really mean it. And yet Nicholas had repeatedly told her that the virtue of sincerity was extremely important to the Japanese.

What, then, was she missing? Was she crazy in her belief that she would never be allowed into the inner social circles of even Nicholas's closest Japanese acquaintances? She did not think so.

Again she felt as if she were missing something vital, some kind of Rosetta stone which, once deciphered, would explain the unexplainable Japanese to her.

And now Justine understood that she needed Nicholas's help more than ever. She could not allow him to push her away. She had to persevere. She knew in her heart that whatever difficulties both of them might encounter, they could survive them only if they stuck together and did not tolerate this eerie estrangement in their relationship.

Justine allowed herself one brief moment to feel the fear that her estrangement from Nicholas engendered in her. Then she did her best to clamp it off. She listened, instead, to the sounds of summer all around her.

In a moment she had drunk her fill. She replaced the ladle on the stone basin, and immediately the carved *michi* disappeared. Justine turned and went through the twilight, taking a different route back to the house.

Inside, she heard Nicholas in the workout room. She could hear his deep exhalations as he hit the padded pole over and over again with knuckles as hard as steel.

She exhaled deeply, as if she had been holding her breath for a long time, felt how much tension she had been holding in her upper body. For months she had ached with worry for Nicholas. She passed by the workout room now and thought, Everything will soon be all right. He's starting to get back to his old self.

Nothing could have been further from the truth, however. Nicholas knew it the moment he threw the first of the aikido *atemi*. It was clumsy, out of skew, the result not only of being rusty, but of something more pervasive, something sinister.

The unthinkable had occurred. Nicholas had suspected it months ago. Now he was sure.

In the first few weeks after the operation, there had been a great deal of pain. Out of reflex Nicholas had sought to dissipate it through his martial arts training. There was a way to open, internally, the endorphin channels in order to clamp down on the brief, immediate pain one experiences in hand-to-hand combat. For more lasting pain, such as he had, there was another way.

Getsumei no michi. The Moonlit Path. Akutagawa-san, one of Nicholas's *sensei*, had said: *In* Getsumei no michi *you will experience two immediate insights. One, all sensation will gain in weight and significance. You will, in effect, simultaneously see the skin and what is beneath it. Two, there will be an awareness of light even when there is none.*

What Akutagawa-san had meant, Nicholas had learned, was that *Get-*

sumei no michi allowed him to combine intuition with insight. He could hear lies spun in the air; he could make his way through the most labyrinthine enclosure blindfolded. *Getsumei no michi* was a return to man in his most elemental state, long before the layers of civilization accreted, stifling his primitive power.

But *Getsumei no michi* was much more. It was, in effect, a haven, the source of Nicholas's inner strength and resolve. In *Getsumei no michi* all things were made clear to him. Without it he was far worse than deaf, dumb, and blind. He was defenseless.

When, in pain in the hospital, he had sought surcease in *Getsumei no michi*, he had found none. His connection with that mystical state was not only severed, but his knowledge of the state itself was gone altogether. It was not a question simply of memory. Nicholas could remember what *Getsumei no michi* was, could even conjure up what it had felt like to be there, and that proved the most painful realization of all. A person born blind looks upon life differently than one who has had his sight taken from him. Cruelly, Nicholas was aware of what he was missing, and the knowledge ate at him like acid.

Still, because he had been so weak after the operation, he could not know for certain if the damage were irreparable until he returned home and began his twice-daily workouts. Physical proof was required that he had been reduced to the status of mere mortal. Which accounted for his moods, his anxiety and his sleepless nights. Quite simply, he was terrified to confront the truth. As long as there was a shred of hope that he was wrong and in time *Getsumei no michi* would be returned to him, there was something to hold on to. But after the first *atemi* was struck, when he would know absolutely whether or not he had been abandoned, he knew that there would no longer be room for hope, only reality.

Now it had happened; his worst nightmare come true. He was like a man naked beneath a blinding sun with no protection, nowhere to run.

He had never been aware of how he relied on his godlike state until it had been stripped from him. How dull and uninteresting real life seemed with its reliance on the five underdeveloped senses.

Who knew how long Nicholas would have continued to sit on his *engawa* contemplating light and shadow, refusing to come to terms with his fate, had not Lew Croaker's letter arrived, had he not asked Justine to read it, and she not been curious about Croaker's new hand.

That had cut it. In the face of what his friend had gone through, and was still dealing with, Nicholas felt abject and foolish for putting off what he knew was inevitable.

He had gone into his workout room and, staring hard at the padded pole, had begun his preliminary breathing exercises, had, without thinking, assumed the ready position, and had struck out.

The first *atemi*, the basic percussive blow of aikido, was struck. And it was as if he were a rank beginner. The form remained, ingrained in his musculature, but there was nothing behind it: no conviction, no mind-set, no purity of purpose. Instead Nicholas's mind was a chaos of conflicting thoughts and images deflecting and reflecting off one another in wild concatenation.

Nicholas, mechanically striking the padded pole over and over, was in shock. He could not quite believe it was happening. *Getsumei no michi* gone. His mind no longer part of the benevolent Void, emptied in order to absorb fully each clear thought, but rather, a babble of mutually antagonistic currents, each seeking its own independent end.

And that was how Justine found him, collapsed onto the tatami mats, his chin lolling on his sweat-streaked chest.

He heard her enter, heard her little gasp of horror, and lifting his head, he saw the look of pity in her eyes and could not bear it.

"Get out!" he shouted. And, because he had unconsciously used *kiai*, the samurai's war shout, Justine felt as if she had been physically assaulted. She recoiled, reeling in bewilderment. "Get the hell away from me!"

When Tomi Yazawa shut the door to Commander Omukae's office behind her, she was trembling. She stood still for one long moment, composing herself. The realization that she had revealed, to a man she did not know well, more than she had revealed to anyone else in the world, shocked her. More, it shamed her. No matter that Senjin Omukae had given her permission to speak; she should have kept her mouth shut. Why, then, had she spoken? And why had she spoken the truth instead of a well-crafted, face-saving lie?

Tomi did not know, but she suspected that her weakness of resolve had had something to do with Commander Omukae's beautiful face. She shuddered as she recalled the moment when he had stood up, moving into her line of sight. She knew then that he had trapped her as surely as if he were a hunter with a snare. She had had no recourse but to look directly into his face for the whole of the interview.

The experience had been terrifying. She had felt somehow naked—obscenely, glowingly naked—beneath his penetrating gaze. And although she had fully meant to create some kind of fabrication to answer his questions, she found as she was about to speak that she could not. It was as if Commander Omukae possessed an invisible hand that had entered her mind, drawing out from her against her will that which he wanted to know.

And yet . . . Tomi was racked with guilt. Commander Omukae was her champion in the police department, which certainly did not appreciate a female moving through the ranks of its detectives. Were she a man, Tomi knew, she would already have made the rank of lieutenant, would already have been leading her own squad. This was part of what Commander Omukae had meant when he had said, *We are, each in our own ways, outcasts.*

The fact she was on important assignments at all was due entirely to Commander Omukae. He, of all the officers of superior rank that she had encountered, treated her as an intelligent human being. He had even praised her work once or twice, the last time not more than a month ago, when her diligent surveillance had at last paid off and they had taken down a major importer of MAC-10 submachine pistols for the Red Army.

Before that there had been the female terrorist who was about to board a Korean Air flight at Narita Airport armed with plastique explosive. Tomi had taken her into custody in the ladies' room at the very last minute. The knife wound Tomi had received during that fracas had been superficial, nevertheless, Commander Omukae had put her in for a valorous commendation. No matter that his recommendation had been turned down, Tomi thought, as she walked thoughtfully back to her desk.

Commander Omukae was her champion in the department, the only male she thought knew her worth. And yet, Tomi was deathly afraid of him. Why? For one thing, he was not like anyone else, and that, to a Japanese, was a concept filled with suspicion. In Japan everyone strove to be anonymous, to be a part of the crowd. Everyone wore the same colors, black, shades of gray, shades of white or cream. Only when one dressed on formal or religious occasions in traditional Japanese attire was any hint of color permitted. Everyone strove to do his best for his country, for his company. This was not, as Tomi once heard a Westerner describe it, self-sacrifice, but rather, duty. Every Japanese understood the nature of duty, that without duty life would be chaotic and, therefore, meaningless.

Every Japanese save Senjin Omukae. And the Red Army terrorists, of course. As she blindly shuffled her paperwork back and forth over her desk, Tomi contemplated the link Commander Omukae had made between his thinking and that of the Red Army. It was interesting—intriguing, even. But Tomi suspected that there was more to the way he saw life than merely putting himself in his enemies' shoes.

That was also part of what he meant by, *We are, each in our own ways, outcasts.*

She recalled her early life, the rigorous training her mother had put her through. For as far back as she could remember, Tomi had been in charge of washing the rice. The first few times, when she had allowed several grains to escape her control and slide down the drain, her mother, watching her like a hawk, had pulled her roughly from the sink and spanked her.

When she was older she was always the last to eat. Her father, silent and inattentive at the table, and her older brother, arrogant and aloof, would invariably receive the major portion of food. Afterward, her mother and she would finish whatever remained. There was rarely enough to satisfy the two of them.

Once when she was especially hungry after dinner, Tomi had asked her mother why they must eat this way. Her mother said, *Be content with what you have. Your father and brother work hard all day. It is our duty to see that they are strong and fit for their work. We women do nothing but sit at home all day. What need do we have for much food?*

Tomi remembered one evening when she had suggested to her mother that her brother help them out in their kitchen chores, which were so numerous, Tomi often found herself overwhelmed. Her mother was horrified at the thought. *Goodness,* she had cried, *what puts such thoughts into your head? If we allowed such a thing, the neighbors would assume that our habits were so poor and slovenly that we needed male help.*

The male presence in Tomi's farmland household was massive, hovering over every hour of the day, occluding even days shining with a sparkling sun.

When Tomi was *tekireiki*—of marriageable age—she was in Tokyo, at school. One evening, as she was preparing for her final exams, she received a call from her brother. Tomi's father had died some years before, and her brother was now the head of the family. In many ways he was far worse than Tomi's father had ever been. Whereas the father was merely content to keep the family together and running efficiently, the brother was interested in exerting control. Tomi had taken the call with a sinking heart. Her brother informed her that he had selected a suitable husband for her and that she was expected home as soon as possible in order that the particulars of arranging the wedding could be properly and formally effected.

Tomi knew that she had come to a nexus point in her life. She understood that what she said to her brother would change her life forever. She struggled with her inner demons. As if it had a will of its own, her mind scrolled back over the strict training her mother had given her, and she felt her resolve weakening, the desire to give in to the authority figure, to submit to the structure of life, almost overwhelming her with its brute force.

Then she saw the face of her mother, time-worn and pale, rarely smiling, certainly never laughing. And Tomi knew that her mother had never really lived. Rather, she had expended her life in the service of her family, a slave to the unending demands of her husband and her son, hemmed in by the constant criticisms of her neighbors and relatives. Tomi saw that she would rather slit her wrists than carry on that tradition.

So she said into the phone, "I am not coming home." She had dropped the receiver into its cradle and run for the bathroom, making it just in time as her dinner came spewing out of her mouth.

Later, after cleaning herself up, she had crawled weakly into bed and had sat for the rest of the night with the covers drawn up to her chin, the lights on in her room, shivering uncontrollably, as if she had the flu.

It was this irrevocable break with her family—with her *life*—as traumatic for a Japanese as the loss of a leg or an arm, that had come to mind when she was summoned to the crime scene at The Silk Road. Seeing poor, pathetic Mariko and what had been done to her by an unknown hand had touched Tomi in her innermost depths. During the ensuing months of meticulous investigation, Tomi came in some curious way to see her as a kindred spirit, less lucky by far than she, yet so similar that Tomi was driven to find her murderer.

She opened Mariko's file, went through it for what seemed the thousandth time. Who had done such a terrible thing to the poor girl? What kind of mind was capable of such bestiality?

Tomi tried in the manner of Commander Omukae to put herself in the mind of the murderer, but she found herself incapable of conceiving such a warped mind-set.

She continued to turn the pages of despair, Mariko's despair. So many mysteries here, and she had no solutions for any of them. Who killed Mariko? Why? What did the bloody note, THIS COULD BE YOUR WIFE, mean? Who was it meant for? The police? Who else was expected to find her? Was there any significance to the forensic report of tiny flakes of rust found in the wounds of the girl's thorax? Did Mariko have a current boyfriend, and if so, who was he?

Now her commander had ordered her to end her investigation, to label the case: DEAD, UNSOLVED. Tomi did not think that she could do that. Mariko's untouched face stared accusingly up at her from the grisly forensic photos. Was this inhuman mutilation all that would be left of Mariko? It wasn't fair or right.

Duty, Tomi thought grimly as, wiping away an errant tear, she closed the file. She entered Nicholas Linnear's name into her computer terminal, and in a moment the pertinent data appeared on her screen. She tapped out a request for a hard copy, and the printer went to work. She hardly glanced at the sheets as they emerged, merely folded them and put them into her handbag.

Tomi knew that she had to come to grips with her turbulent feelings for Commander Omukae. She saw his face, saw again the interview in his office, and knew what a botch she had made of it. If only she had said something intelligent to him. Something . . .

Tomi put her head in her hands. She had been fighting the realization ever since she had first seen Senjin Omukae, but now she could not deny the attraction she had felt for him from the beginning. And hadn't he revealed something of himself to her? *We are, each in our own ways, outcasts.* That, she knew, was a singular occurrence. What did it portend?

She felt again his presence close and quick in front of her, smelled again his male musk. Those eyes upon her, raking at the core of her, stirring her depths. He had, in one breathless moment, ripped through the fabric of her life, to gaze upon her secret and vulnerable underside. A shiver raced down her spine.

Tomi knew that she was in love with Commander Omukae. Which was too bad for her, because she knew that within the code of the department there was nothing either of them could do about it. Having once been trapped by life, she had thought that she had been clever enough to escape. Now Tomi found herself trapped again.

For a long time after Justine stumbled out of the workout room, Nicholas did nothing. He closed his eyes, slept, dreamt. Nightmares stalked his uneasy, sweaty sleep. Helpless, chained to a rock, gimlet-eyed cormorants wheeling and crying above his head alerted him to imminent danger. Then he could dimly see the outline of his death as it approached like a sleek ship over the shining sea.

At last, toward dawn, he rose and, unable even to bring himself to speak to Justine, confronted his nemesis, the padded pole. He eyed it as if it were his most implacable enemy, and indeed, for this moment it was.

The face of Akutagawa-san swam into his mind. *The moment you begin to hate,* the *sensei* had told Nicholas, *is the moment you will lose* Getsumei no michi.

He was on a hillside shrouded in mist so thick that day had become night. Somewhere ahead of this young Nicholas was a steep precipice tumbling down a rocky scree to the valley floor. It had taken them six hours of arduous climbing to reach this spot. One false step and Nicholas knew that he would fall head over heels until either his head or his back broke upon the spine of the rocks far below.

I can't see, this young Nicholas thought, and yet Akutagawa-san has told me that I must walk this ridge. *Find* Getsumei no michi, the *sensei* said. *Find the path and you will not stumble or fall.*

So, with terror in his heart, the young Nicholas had set out, carefully putting one foot in front of another. There was a metallic taste in his mouth, and his heart was pounding with such force that for a moment he could hear nothing else.

Then, gradually, he began to hear other sounds: the rushing of the wind, the sighing of the tree branches above and behind him. The caw of a kite, circling the sky, riding the currents.

And, abruptly, he could see the bird through the mist, through the opacity; not the creature itself, really, but something akin to its shadow against an unseen sun. His head lifted as *Getsumei no michi* allowed him to "watch" it soar.

And now he could feel the currents and eddies of the wind just as if they were an ocean's tide. And learning this sculptured landscape, he discerned just where the edge of the ridge rippled and curled, where gnarled tree roots thrust up from the eroded cliffside to trip an unwary traveler, where a stoat crouched, caught trembling between the rim and the two humans.

Clouds were coming, and he turned his head, aware that rain was not more than fifteen minutes away. He walked along the snaking ridge, more sure of his footing than if it had been a crystal-clear day. And he told Akutagawa-san everything he saw and sensed and heard. He had felt like a god, but this he had kept from his *sensei*, because it smacked of ego, and the essence of all martial arts involved an egoless state.

Getsumei no michi.

I can remember this, Nicholas thought now. Why can't I remember what to do? Don't think, he told himself. Don't ask questions that you can't answer. Clear your mind of all extraneous thought. Now let go of the hatred of your memory loss. Let *haragei* show you *michi,* the path, the Way to *Getsumei no michi.*

He again took up the ready position, this time painfully aware that he did not understand what he was doing, that his mind, cluttered and uncentered, was merely following the lead of his body.

He raised his hands, aligning his fingers into position, and struck out. Again and again he hit the padded pole, his mind afire with a mounting despair, knowing that he had no idea what he was doing. He stopped and, panting, stood staring at the space in front of him as if it, too, had turned against him.

He heard his mother, Cheong, saying to him, *You must learn to allow things to seep in, to come into your bones in their own time. Patience, Nicholas. This is perhaps difficult for you. Your father makes it so. He is patient and impatient. Very inconsistent, yes. This is strange to me.*

Patience. Yes. Be consistent.

Once more he set himself, and without giving himself time for second thoughts or doubts, he struck the padded pole. Pain flared, emanating from his hands all the way up his arms, but he continued to strike out, harder and harder, with a kind of desperation as he felt his strength waning, forgetting even his mother's wise counsel, until he was doing nothing more than flailing ineffectually at his own inner demons.

Gasping for air, the sweat running off him in streams, he at last collapsed upon the tatami mats and, hugging the padded pole to him, began to weep.

When Nangi returned to his office the morning after his meeting with Kusunda Ikusa, he listened to their conversation all over again. Settling down behind his desk, the skyline of downtown Tokyo glowing like a lambent forest in the early summer sunlight, he unscrewed the top of his cane. The carved dragon's head came off, revealing the workings of a minirecorder.

He took the microcassette from the interior of the cane, put it into the office stereo system. Soon the voice of Kusunda Ikusa came through the speakers, talking of Tenchi and Nangi's duty to betray Nicholas Linnear.

Nangi sat back in his swivel chair, fought the urge to have a cigarette, and thought of his friend Seiichi Sato. Sato had been a fighter, a fiercely loyal friend and implacable enemy. For the first time it occurred to Nangi how alike in many ways were Seiichi and Nicholas.

Nangi knew that he could never have betrayed Seiichi.

He tapped his forefinger rhythmically against his lips as he listened again to everything Ikusa said, not merely the words, but the inflection, the intonation as well, in order to glean every drop of information from the meeting. Others, at one time or another, had tried to extort Nangi. All had failed. But Ikusa was another matter entirely. Ikusa was Nami, and Nami was, for better or for worse, Japan.

Nangi felt locked within a cage. In order to get out, he knew, he would have to use the one door. But to do that, he must betray Nicholas Linnear.

The taped conversation was over, and silence fell like an ominous shadow across the room. Nangi took the tape from the recorder, pocketed it. Then he rescrewed the head onto his cane and left the office.

In the street he found a public phone, dialed a number and deposited the correct change. After one ring a recorded message came on. Nangi let it run its course, waited for precisely three seconds, then said one word into the receiver mouthpiece. He hung up.

He waited five minutes, during which time two people wanted to use the phone. Nangi, his finger on the pips, pretended to speak into the dead receiver. The people went away.

He let go of the pips, dialed the same number. It rang three times, then a human voice answered. Nangi did not give his name, and he was not asked for it. He spoke an address into the receiver, hung up. Then he went back to his office.

Nangi spent much of the day with his technicians, sharing their frustration as they failed to gain any headway in deciphering the nature of the mysterious virus that had attacked Sato International's computer banks. He wished vainly for Nicholas's insightful advice, mourning the loss as if it were a death in the family.

Late in the afternoon, Nangi left the office, went crosstown. He remembered the Akihabara district of Tokyo with great fondness. In the ashen days following the end of the war in the Pacific, a raging black market had sprung up here, and people who were clever and audacious had made fortunes virtually overnight. This was where Nangi had started his new life, before he learned the discipline of *kanryodo*, the way of the Samurai bureaucrat.

Today, Akihabara was a living monument to Japan's postindustrialist economy. Shops, jammed along both sides of the narrow, winding streets, bristled with electronic hardware of all shapes, sizes, and functions, most of them manufactured expressly for export.

Postpunk models with spiked hair and painted faces glowered and sneered out of massive posters that hawked the latest compact-disk player or stereo component. On massive TV screens American women rolled their eyes in ecstasy at the sound of the newest, lightest-weight headphones or portable cassette deck, caressing these electronic marvels as if they were lovers. A cacophony of disparate rock and pop songs emanating from open doorways and stalls fought with colored digital displays for attention along the jammed streets.

Akihabara was steaming with people. Which was, of course, why Nangi had chosen it. There was no chance of being overheard—either accidentally or deliberately—in this fantastic fever-pitched madhouse.

Nangi saw the Pack Rat lounging against a display-packed window. He was watching David Bowie pitching a soft drink on a large-screen TV. The scene changed to show the ecstatic face of a female talento, a perfect image, a new-wave silicon and gallium icon.

The Pack Rat felt Nangi's approach without having to look. He was a tough-looking character, short, dark, with a pockmarked face and a heavy jaw. He was known as the Pack Rat because he accumulated contacts and intelligence like others acquired artifacts. He was a man Nangi had known for many years and trusted implicitly. The Pack Rat was unlike many of the others of his dubious profession: he was not a mercenary, hiring out to the highest bidder. One did not have to look over one's shoulder when one hired him.

The Pack Rat liked Nangi. But even more, he admired him. Many years ago Nangi had saved the Pack Rat's sister from a serious altercation with the head of a Yakuza clan. The Pack Rat owed Nangi *giri*, a debt he could never repay.

As Nangi came past him, the Pack Rat detached himself from the window. Soon, however, he had pushed ahead of Nangi, and taking his unspoken cue, Nangi followed the Pack Rat through a torturous circuit of the district. Nangi lost count of how many times they doubled back on themselves, ducked in and out of shops.

At last the Pack Rat turned and grinned at Nangi. They slowed their pace. Together they strolled the streets.

"I've been here awhile," the Pack Rat said, "seeing if the environment needed cleaning out." He meant he had checked to see if Nangi was being followed. "It did."

Nami.

"I know the source," Nangi said.

The Pack Rat tensed. "Is there any immediate danger?" Which meant, Should I find the man who followed you and take him out?

"Not yet."

The Pack Rat had stopped for a moment, as if he were interested in a shop-window display of portable computers. Nangi knew better. The Pack Rat knew that after the last fifteen-minute mad dash, Nangi needed a breather. The Pack Rat was courteous.

"How may I be of service, Nangi-san?"

Nangi waited until he was ready to move on. Considering Nami's attempt at surveillance, he did not want to talk, even on these crowded streets, unless they were in motion.

When they had gone a couple of blocks, shouldering aside a host of Germans intent on buying everything in sight, Nangi said, "We had a serious incident this morning. Our computers were compromised by a virus."

The Pack Rat was surprised. "I brought you your system of computer encryptions. I thought it was totally secure."

"And it was," Nangi said, moving nimbly through the throng. "Until today." As they moved he handed the Pack Rat a 3½-inch floppy disk. "This is a record of the attack."

The Pack Rat pocketed the disk with the ease of a maître d' accepting a tip. "I'll get right on it."

"I know you will. Even though I have others working on this aspect, they do not have your wealth of resources." Nangi's cane tap-tap-tapped on the pavement. "There's something else, even more urgent, that I want you to concentrate on. Kusunda Ikusa."

The Pack Rat whistled a little tune. They paused at a stall and he pointed out some items that blinked and flashed, as if he and Nangi were prospective purchasers. After a moment they pressed on.

"First of all," the Pack Rat said, "I want to make certain I heard you right."

"If you're thinking Nami," Nangi said, "you did."

They passed a flock of black-leather-jacketed kids in 1950s American hairstyles, complete with Brylcreem and duck tails, dripping metal chains and looking cocky. Clouds of cigarette smoke wreathed them. The two-way flow of pedestrian traffic parted on either side of them, making of their group a kind of island of curiosities.

The Pack Rat said something to them as they passed, and the rockers laughed, giving him thumbs-up signs.

The Pack Rat said to Nangi, "Do you want the target researched? Catalogued? Indexed?"

"No," Nangi said. "I want him compromised."

The Pack Rat evinced no surprise. "Do I have a time limit?"

"Yes," Nangi said. "Yesterday."

The Pack Rat grinned. "Now that's a job to cherish."

When Senjin Omukae moved, he moved like the sea. He had a way about him that was as sinuous as if his bones could bend instead of break. Women especially noted this, if not consciously, then with a part of their mind still attuned to atavistic behavior. Men only said that Senjin was dangerous, but women saw in that danger another dimension, one to which they were attracted, perhaps despite themselves. There was a kind of freedom in being so close to danger, as well as a heightened sense of awareness. They saw more, tasted more, felt more, and they fell in love with that supraclarity, mistaking it for a love of Senjin himself.

For his own part, Senjin did not mind. In fact, he did not make a distinction between the two kinds of love. Love was for him, in any case, a counterfeit emotion, fraught with self-deceit and laden with a treacherous passion that inevitably led to greed, jealousy, and envy.

Senjin laughed. Had he been a bit younger, he could imagine himself a talento, hawking Hitachi or Mitsubishi software, smiling vacuously out at the adoring population glued to their twenty-four-inch cathode-ray tubes, dancing when he was told to dance, singing meaningless pop songs in front of thousands of screaming adolescents, being interviewed by NHK-TV in a series of prime-time programs as eagerly anticipated as the latest soap opera.

He had the kind of face that ad agencies and conglomerate executives fell all over themselves to find, market, and exploit: handsome, lineless, with a hint of the feminine in its softness of angles in jaw and brow.

These qualities did not make him any less attractive to the opposite sex. Quite the contrary, Senjin possessed that confluence of features most admired in doomed Japanese heroes down through the ages.

His girlfriends had been many and varied, but they all shared one experience. They had been taken by Senjin to the Kabuki theater to see *Musume Dojoji.*

Musume Dojoji was Senjin's favorite play, one which he watched with a mixture of fascination and terror, precisely the kind of attraction-repulsion one feels upon seeing a particularly bloody accident. Wishing to avert one's head, one stares instead, mesmerized, even while one's stomach turns queasy.

Musume Dojoji spins the legend of Kiyohime, a bewitching demon woman, who falls in love with a young Buddhist monk. He is torn by his attraction for her and his vows of celibacy. He deflects her attempts at seduction, first in subtle ways, then, as her pursuit becomes ever more determined, in more overt ways.

Finally he flees his town altogether. But Kiyohime will not be denied, and she pursues him, using various magical means to keep him in sight. At last, she turns into an enormous serpent.

The priest, now filled with fear at this supernatural adversary/lover, takes refuge beneath a gigantic bell under which he believes he will be safe.

Instead, the serpent Kiyohime slowly encircles the bell with her oily coils. Enraged that she cannot get to the priest, she rears up and, spitting demonic flames that eat metal, sets fire to the bell, incinerating the would-be lover who had so ill-advisedly spurned her.

Senjin would sit through each performance of this Kabuki play as if for the first time, gripped in the maw of a sickening exhilaration/horror as the hideous denouement approached.

Afterward he would take the woman he was with out to a lavish dinner of *fugu* or Kobe steak, during the course of which he would explore with her the psychological aspects of the play.

It was *Musume Dojoji*'s psychological undertones—or, rather, Senjin's interpretations of them—that most fascinated the doctor. He was, Senjin thought, in many ways like Senjin's endless parade of girlfriends—becoming increasingly fascinated by Senjin's obsession with Kiyohime.

"The demon woman," Dr. Muku said, "is a familiar figure both in our mythology and in our psyches. It should not be surprising that your, er, subject is fixated on such a creature."

Of course, Dr. Muku did not know that Kiyohime was Senjin's own obsession. Senjin had come to Dr. Muku in his official capacity in an attempt to, as he told the psychiatrist, "obtain a clear psychological profile on a suspect in a multiple-murder case." He had given Dr. Muku a fictitious name for his "suspect." He needn't have bothered. Dr. Muku was not interested in identities; he was interested in, as he put it succinctly, "the pathology of crime."

But, of course, Senjin was acutely aware of identity. His initial contact with the psychiatrist had been via the phone. That had been several years ago, when Senjin had been working a difficult serial murder case. Always, his meetings with Dr. Muku were, at the psychiatrist's behest, utterly private.

"I hope you won't take offense, Commander, but I would rather you not enter and exit this office through the waiting room," Dr. Muku had said during that initial phone conversation. "Some of my patients are unnaturally sensitive. Your police aura might disturb not only them, but unnerve my staff as well. Far better that you use the back door to my consultation room which lets out directly onto the outer corridor. That way, we will be assured that no one will see you and, perhaps, mistake your presence."

Now Senjin took full advantage of his previous relationship with Dr. Muku, day after day spending an hour with Dr. Muku—much as a patient would—spinning, as if he were a Kabuki playwright, concentric circles composed of lies and the truth, or subtle combinations of the two, until even Senjin himself often could not distinguish between the two.

This subconscious and unwitting playacting, of course, suited Senjin's lifestyle. He had built his existence using subterfuge upon subterfuge, manufacturing flecks of artifice as if they were bricks, glazing them with the colors of his imagination, firing them in the kiln of Kshira.

What better—and dangerous—way to recreate the skein of his life, a movie filmed for an audience of two, than to speak of it in the darkness and the light of this psychiatrist's office?

"The demon woman," Dr. Muku was saying now, "is, in a very important sense, a figure of innocence."

"Innocence?" Senjin echoed, despite himself. He laughed. "I don't see how my suspect would see her as 'innocent.' "

"Well, of course *he* wouldn't see her as innocent," Dr. Muku said. He was a small man, as compact as a rubber ball, and seemingly as malleable. He had the wide, open face of a child. His salt-and-pepper hair was long and rather wild, as if, as part of his morning ablutions, he spent five minutes in a wind tunnel. He wore old-fashioned, round wire-rimmed glasses that magnified raisin-colored eyes. "He would see her as wholly evil. But, you see, that is part of his problem."

Senjin lighted a cigarette. "How so?"

Dr. Muku shrugged. "Clearly, the subject has lost sight of reality. His senses tell him only what he wishes them to tell him. It is as if he has put a filter on them; as if real life is too frightening or complex for him to interface with without this filter of his own design."

Senjin was inwardly amused by the frailty of Dr. Muku's reasoning, built as it was, assumption upon assumption, on lies masking as truth and vice versa. "Tell me," he said, "how do you come to this conclusion, Doctor?"

"It is simple, really," Dr. Muku said. "To you and me, the concept of the demon woman of which Kiyohime is an excellent example is not so black and white." Dr. Muku chuckled. "Or, in this case, entirely black." He settled his hands across his pudgy stomach. "The truth of the demon-woman myth is this: man sees her as so frightening because when he first sees her, she has the aspect both of his mother and the mother of his children. It is only when he tugs upon her loving, maternal mask that he comes upon the face of the demon woman." Dr. Muku lifted a finger. "However, the psychoanalyst knows that the aspect of the demon woman is, in its own way, also a mask. And the most interesting thing is that *this* particular mask is entirely the creation of the man himself. It is something that *he* desires; that, in fact, he cannot do without. It is, as Yukio Mishima has told us, a reflection of the male's unceasing sexual passion."

Senjin almost laughed in Dr. Muku's face. Did he know how foolish he sounded? Senjin thought not. Dr. Muku was all too wrapped up in Dr. Muku as teacher, as healer.

In order to encourage the doctor, Senjin nodded his head, murmuring empty words of praise as he had once done to his Kshira *sensei*. After all, Dr. Muku thought of himself as a master of psychology, and, at least for the time being, it was to Senjin's benefit to feed that perception.

On the other hand, Senjin did not want Dr. Muku to have an easy time of it. "Pardon me for interjecting this," he said, "but the suspect has shown no signs of violent sexual behavior."

"If he hasn't as yet," Dr. Muku said sagely, "it is only a matter of time before he does. A man so obsessed with the concept of a demon woman must of necessity harbor a deep and violent antipathy toward women. This would, from his point of view, be most satisfactorily transmitted in a sexual manner."

"He wouldn't just kill them?" Senjin inquired.

"No. Killing is too final, too abrupt to satisfy his rage. He would first need to mutilate his victims in some way—perhaps even in a variety of ways. I would be very much surprised if rape was not among them."

Senjin kept nodding and smiling. But in the pit of his stomach something cold and hard was forming. Dr. Muku no doubt would have perceived this sensation as rage. But Senjin knew it was something altogether different. Something entirely outside Dr. Muku's ken.

Branding lay upon the rumpled bed. His body felt heavy with lust, his head light with abandon. While his body was for the moment sated, he found that his mind was not. He watched through eyes slitted by dusty late-afternoon sunlight and lust as Shisei climbed naked off the bed.

For a moment she was silhouetted against the light, and he saw the kind of aura one looks for in eclipses. It was as if the very sun itself was her core, and for the first time he understood the true meaning of the word radiant. As she turned, the light slid across her like honey. Her luminous eyes, for the moment lighter than the black they had been, paler certainly than the surrounding shadows, reached him where he lay spread-eagle, and he felt paralyzed both by excitement and by fright.

Cotton Branding did not want to take his eyes off her. He had never felt such power being exerted by one person over another on such an intimate level. It was one thing to squeeze out one's influence—either gently or crushingly, as the circumstances dictated—quite another to find oneself in the jaws of such a magnetic whirlpool.

And then—just like that—Shisei smiled, and all the shuddering intimations of power were whirled away on a froth of lightness, innocence, and healthy curiosity, so that Branding was left breathless, doubting anything dark and sinister had ever existed.

Shisei, in her open cover-up, sat in a straight-backed chair, her legs demurely crossed, just as if she were fully clothed and this were a business meeting. She sat with her forearms lying along the black wooden arms of the chair, and, even now, with the oblique sunlight spread along their slender lengths, he could discern no hair whatsoever, not even the pale down of youth.

"Shisei," he said, and still smiling, she turned her head toward him. A thick shaft of the sunlight slipped around the curve of her high cheekbone as if she were being painted by an artist instead of being illuminated by the ending of the day.

Then, in a movement so innocent it startled him, she put her head back so that he was able to see as an unbroken line the soft underside of her jaw, the hollow of her throat, the abrupt thrust of her breasts. It was a gesture fraught with intimation, a gesture that was erotic and primitive, a kind of unmasking, revealing an intimacy that went beyond lovemaking, which as Branding well knew, could be as impersonal as getting a haircut. It was the kind of gesture that one jungle cat makes to another, an exposure of a vulnerable spot, an ultimate acquiesence that said on a subliminal level, Here, see how deeply I am in your power.

And in that breathless moment Branding knew that he wanted this woman more than he had ever wanted anything in his life.

He recalled, like the flash from a gemstone held to the light, a moment from his childhood that had been with him, moving beneath the ice of his memory, made shadowy by time. But the presence of Shisei negated both memory and time, and Branding saw in her eyes his past being resurrected like a ghost at a feast.

He had been raised on Beacon Hill in Boston, scion of his father's vast banking fortune. His mother Bess was, in Branding's memory, a somewhat intimidating figure. Because she could not completely control her husband, she controlled her sons with a severity none of them forgot.

The times and her husband's will demanded that she could no longer be puritan in the strictest sense of her forebears, and she resented it. She was deeply, almost obsessively, Godfearing, and Branding remembered being dragged off to her Presbyterian church every Sunday to hear fire and brimstone sermons concerning man's innate sins emanate from the mouths of bearded ministers of considerable ecclesiastical rank. She insisted that he read the Bible over and over until he could quote entire sections to her on demand.

One day, when he was thirteen, his mother handed him a book. Its title was *Wonders of the Invisible World*, and its author was Cotton Mather. Written in 1693, a year after the Salem witch trials, in which Mather was involved, it was an eerie tome discussing satanic possession.

When he had finished the book, his mother sent for him. Holding him by his arms, she had peered deeply into his eyes and had said, "The world is Satan's playground, Cotton, never forget that." She was the only one who called him Cotton, not Cook. After all, it was the name she had given him. "Work hard, never indulge to excess, above all, be disciplined. Stay on the narrow path that God has ordained for you, and you will be safe. Stray from the narrow path, and all the good that I see within you will wither and die."

Now, staring into Shisei's charcoal-gray eyes, with the heat of summer billowing into the bedroom, Cotton Branding thought again of his mother and of the narrow path. How lucky she would have considered herself to have died before he had chosen politics as his career. She had been so certain that he alone, the firstborn of all her sons, would fulfill her dreams and become a man of the cloth.

Well, Branding thought now, perhaps she wouldn't mind his choice of careers, after all. He was railing against injustice in his own way. And, working in Sodom, he had resisted all temptation to wander from the narrow path.

Then he looked at Shisei and thought, How can I keep our relationship a secret?

Night had come at last.

St. Theresa's, the only Roman Catholic church in Shinjuku, was situated four blocks west of the Meiji-dori, on a side street just off the Okubo-dori.

It was, Nangi thought, still an impressive sight amid the clean-lined sky-rises, the gigantic neon signs of modern Tokyo; perhaps even more impressive because of its location in the midst of a concrete and steel forest.

Inside, it was cool and dim and quiet. The light, falling through the arched, stained-glass windows, seemed to echo in the vastness. Somewhere above his head the choir was practicing, the young, sexless voices like a star shower against a night sky.

Day into night, Nangi thought. *Now I lay me down to sleep . . .* The cutside world—and the inherent secrets it keeps—is, for the moment at least, at bay. *And pray the Lord my soul to keep.*

He turned, dipped his fingers in the font, crossed himself. He knelt at a pew in back, staring at the space, hearing in the pauses between the sporadic choral singing, the muffled footfalls, a fragment of hushed conversation, all quickly snuffed out, the silence of God.

He discovered, to his dismay, that there was no solace for him here. He had sinned; he could not take communion. He was cut off from God and the peace of spirit His protection provided.

Instead he found the grinning face of Kusunda Ikusa hovering in his mind, like a spectre or a projection. Those laser eyes seemed to have followed him all the way into the sanctity of St. Theresa's. *Do your duty, Nangi-san. Nami—and your Emperor—command you.*

That meant betraying Nicholas. But Nangi owed a debt to Nicholas that he could never adequately repay, not only for the suffering that Tenchi had caused him, but also for protecting Seiichi Sato from Akiko for so long. And yet, as Kusunda Ikusa pointed out, Nangi's primary duty was to his Emperor, and by extension, his Emperor's emissary, Nami.

It was at this moment, while Nangi was thus engaged in this moral tug-of-war, that Justine entered the church. She had considered how best to contact Nangi. Visiting him at the office, or even calling him, seemed too public to her, and to disturb him at home seemed to Justine beyond the bounds of their uneasy relationship.

She had known about this church, of course, from Nicholas, and it had been Nangi himself who had, in some nearly forgotten conversation, spoken of his ritual visits to St. Theresa's.

Desperation, Justine thought as she glanced around the interior, gave one all sorts of previously unrevealed powers. Like dredging up the subject of that discussion. And desperation most closely defined her current state of mind.

Heartsick at being shut out of Nicholas's life, she had at first retreated to the opposite end of the house. She wanted to stand up to Nicholas, to make him see how wrongly he was behaving. After all, she told herself, she had done so before. But that had been at home in America. Here, in Japan, she found that she had lost her equilibrium, that without Nicholas as her anchor, she lacked the strength to battle on alone.

In the middle of the night, with the rhythmic sounds of Nicholas working out wafting eerily through the house, Justine had considered leaving Japan in the morning.

The pain she felt now, cut off from everything she loved, everything familiar, was like no other she had known. She fought down like unpalatable medicine her anger at Nicholas, unable to come to terms with the helplessness she felt. Here in Japan all her inadequacies, imagined and real, were magnified. And she was in Japan because of Nicholas.

She knew that her love for him was unshakable, but she also realized that she could no longer endure her own torment and guilt concerning their daughter's death while battling with Nicholas.

She felt beset by foes she could neither see nor understand, and the instinct to flee was enormous, but there was terror in that as well, because it meant running out on Nicholas, and she could not imagine trapping herself in such a betrayal. She felt ensnared in a situation that was rapidly spinning out of control.

Long into the waning night she had wept bitter tears, for herself, and for Nicholas.

When dawn had at last come, Justine knew that she was incapable of running away. Under the present conditions she was also incapable of sticking it out here alone. She needed advice, and she needed it from someone who knew Nicholas as well as she did, someone who could guide her through the deepening maze of Japan. There was only one person she could think of who fit those requirements: Tanzan Nangi.

Nangi became aware of someone slipping into the pew next to him. As a matter of course he turned to look at who it was. He was stunned to see Justine.

"Mrs. Linnear," he said, his eyes quickly downcast so that she would not see his shock. "I did not know that you were Catholic."

"I'm not," Justine said, and then bit her tongue. Too late, she realized that Nangi had been giving her a face-saving way of explaining her presence here in church. Of course, he had recognized the real reason she had come, but in Japan one never spoke of real reasons. One was too busy saving face. "That is—" she began again, then faltered. "Well, the truth is—" She stopped again. One never spoke the truth in Japan. Or, if one did, it was cloaked in such a way that it could be interpreted six other ways.

"Please forgive me. I am just finishing my prayers, Mrs. Linnear," Nangi said, bowing his head.

Justine, about to say "Oh, I'm sorry!" clamped her jaws shut. Nangi was giving her time to collect her thoughts, to reapproach him in the proper manner, to regain the face she had lost. Justine was grateful to him. She realized, perhaps belatedly, that her wanting to meet Nangi here was not merely a matter of convenience. She recalled how she had prayed for Nicholas at the moment when he had come out of the anesthetic. If she did not believe in God, how could she have prayed to him? And, further, how could she have derived any measure of solace from prayer? Justine was coming to suspect that she was not the agnostic that she had all along believed herself to be. Now, beside the silent, prayerful Nangi, she bowed her head, too, asking silently for help and for strength.

By the time Nangi raised his head, Justine was prepared. "Nangi-san," she said, forsaking her American inclination to address friends by their first name, "in the past we have often not seen eye to eye."

"I don't think this is so, Mrs. Linnear."

That damned politeness. "This, I admit, has been mostly my fault," Justine persevered. She knew she had to go on, that if she stopped for any reason, she might lack the courage to see this through to the end. "I do not understand Japan. I do not understand the Japanese. I am an outsider here; a foreigner."

"You are the wife of Nicholas Linnear," Nangi said, as if this was all she needed to be.

Listen to me! she wanted to scream. Instead she took a deep breath, said, "Nangi-san, I wish to learn. I wish to work hard at an elementary level."

Nangi seemed uncomfortable with this idea. "This is not necessary, Mrs. Linnear. You are already well thought of."

Justine said, "I wish, as a child must, to become recognized in this society."

Nangi said nothing for a time. The choir practice was finished. He could hear the faint rustlings and whisperings of the children as they departed. In the nave, to one side, candles were being lit. Echoes came to him, as soft as raindrops.

"Change," Nangi said at last, "is often for the best if it has been preceded by thought."

"I've thought about this a lot."

Nangi nodded. "Have you discussed this with your husband?"

Justine sighed inwardly. Sadness gripped her heart. "Nicholas and I have not spoken much lately."

Nangi's head swung around until his good eye was upon her. A Westerner would have said, Is anything wrong? Nangi said, "I have spoken very little to Linnear-san myself. He seems somehow . . . different. The doctors . . . ?"

Now Justine sighed out loud. "The doctor is useless in this situation. He says that Nicholas is suffering from a kind of postoperative stress syndrome. I don't believe he has grasped the nature of the situation."

"Which is?"

"I don't know," she confessed. "At least, I'm not sure. But Nicholas's black mood seems to stem from his inability to practice his martial arts."

Nangi involuntarily sucked in his breath. Dear God, he thought, protect us now. Through his shock, he felt insinuating again that terrifying premonition of an oncoming storm, malevolent, sentient. He remembered all too well his perception of a moral twilight falling upon him and those around him. "Are you quite certain of this, Mrs. Linnear?"

"Yes," Justine said without hesitation. "I saw him in his workout room. He was unable to function."

"Was there a physical impairment?"

"I don't think so, no."

Nangi appeared to take her at her word, and now Justine could see the distress in his face.

She was about to say, What is it? Then began to think furiously. "Are we thinking along the same lines?" she said.

"Perhaps. In the martial arts, Mrs. Linnear, the mental often controls the physical. If one's mind is not properly attuned, aligned, or trained, one cannot master the martial arts. This is difficult for many Westerners to comprehend." He gave her a small smile. "Forgive me, I mean no offense. But you said that you wished to learn. What I say is most basic, and that is part of its power."

He paused a moment, as if collecting his thoughts. "When one first begins martial arts training, one is more often than not given the most menial tasks to fulfill. Day in, day out, the novice often feels that his life is filled with drudgery. Some students, disillusioned, give up their training. The others—the ones who will eventually go on to become *sensei*, masters themselves, learn patience and humility. Without these qualities no form of martial arts skill is possible.

"But the mental aspect goes far deeper, and in Nicholas's case, it becomes everything." Justine noted Nangi's switch to using Nicholas's Christian name, and wondered what it meant. "You see, Mrs. Linnear, your husband is one of those rare people who have mastered *Aka-i-ninjutsu*. He is what we call a Red Ninja. He has learned the good side of this specialized martial arts discipline."

"You mean, there are other forms of ninjutsu?" Justine asked.

Nangi nodded. "There is the Black Ninja, the Red Ninja's opposite side. Saigo was a Black Ninja. He practiced the *Kuji-kiri*, the Nine Hands Cutting. A kind of magic."

"Like his hypnosis on me."

"Precisely." Nangi found himself hoping that her basic knowledge of what Nicholas was would help her accept without fear what he had to tell her now. "But the *Kuji-kiri* is only one of many dark and deadly Black ninjutsu." Shadows fell away from Nangi's face as he turned more fully toward her. In this light the deep lines time and the war had etched into his face were more prominent. "Nicholas has mastered *Getsumei no michi*, the Moonlit Path. It is a mental discipline that is both his gateway and his solace, his strength and his refuge. You said before that you did not believe that Nicholas had a *physical* disability resulting from his operation."

Justine felt the fear crawling like a serpent in her stomach. But, too, she felt curiously empty there, as if the serpent had no substance, but instead belonged to another, less substantial world. "What are you saying?" she whispered.

"If one is trained in *Getsumei no michi*," Nangi said, "and one day one reaches for it, and it is no longer there . . ." He paused, as if unsure how to proceed. "The magnitude of the loss, Mrs. Linnear, would be incalculable. Consider the simultaneous loss of all your five senses—sight, hearing, taste, smell, touch—and you will have some measure of what the loss of *Getsumei no michi* is like. But only a measure. It would be more. Far more."

"I cannot imagine such a thing." Justine was sick with shock. "Is this what has happened to Nicholas?"

"Only he can tell us, Mrs. Linnear," Nangi said. "But I pray with all my heart that it is not so."

"After Lew Croaker lost his hand," Justine said, "I had the feeling that Nicholas was intent on putting aside his interest in ninjutsu. Isn't it possible that that phase of his life is ended?"

"It will end," Nangi said, "only when he is dead." He pressed his hands together almost as if he wished again to pray. "You must understand that ninjutsu is not something one just decides one day he will learn. Similarly, it is not a plaything that one can pick up and put down at a whim. It is certainly nothing on which one can turn one's back. Ninjutsu is, rather, an integrated way of life. Once entered, it can never be renounced."

Nangi turned more fully toward her. "Mrs. Linnear, you no doubt have heard or seen the word *michi*."

Justine nodded. "It means a path or a journey."

"In a sense," Nangi said. "*Michi* can also mean duty. So when one speaks of *michi* as a path, it is a path off which one steps only at the most extreme peril. *Michi* is, in effect, life's journey. Once begun, there can be no turning back."

"But surely one is free to change one's life."

"Oh, yes," Nangi said. "But always within the confines of *michi*."

Justine's heart seemed made of lead. "You mean that once Nicholas chose to be a ninja, it was for life?"

"Perhaps ninjutsu chose him, Mrs. Linnear." Nangi's face seemed sad to her. "We must not discount that possibility. And, if this is so, then Nicholas's *karma* still lies ahead of him."

"Why should this be so? How does ninjutsu come to have so much power over a man?"

Nangi pondered how he should answer her. He decided on the truth. "Ninjutsu is an ancient art," he began. "Older even than Japan itself."

"The Japanese did not create it?"

"No. We Japanese are not good at creating. Our forte is in refining. Our language, much of our culture, has its origins in China. We took the Chinese language, for instance, pared it down, made its ideograms more streamlined. That is Japanese. So it is with *ninjutsu*. Its origins lie somewhere in China, although to my knowledge no one knows precisely where it comes from or from what *sensei* it developed. *Ninjutsu* is most likely a synthesis of many ancient disciplines distilled down. Refined. Its extreme age is, for one thing, part of its power. For another, the element of mysticism involved makes it a life's work." He showed her a small smile. "One couldn't, to give a Western example, imagine Merlin renouncing his work, becoming a farmer instead of a magician."

Justine did not feel at all reassured. On the contrary, she had begun to feel chilled. "Perhaps if we were to learn more about the origins of *ninjutsu*, we could understand it better. We could help Nicholas."

"But that is impossible, Mrs. Linnear. You are asking to know the unknowable."

Justine felt as if they were all in a maze. She reasoned that there had to be a way out. "You have mentioned Red and Black *ninjutsu*, whose strictures are, as you've said, more severe than even the Catholic priesthood." Justine studied him. "Maybe Nicholas could change from Red to— Are there other forms of *ninjutsu*?"

"No." Nangi seemed about to go on, then hesitated.

Justine sensed something. "Perhaps a student should not be given too much knowledge at once," she said, learning from him just by watching him. "But a wife has certain privileges a student does not."

For a moment Nangi seemed very old. He was thinking that perhaps he had underestimated her, after all. By the force of her intellect and her intuition, she had come to the heart of the matter. He nodded, and his face was once more in shadow. "Very well," he said. "I spoke the truth when I said that there were only two forms of ninjutsu, Red and Black. However, there is a term, *Shiro Ninja*. It means White Ninja."

The silence stretched out for so long that Justine found herself compelled to say, "White Ninja. What is that?"

"That," said Nangi with great pain, "is a ninja who has lost his powers." He did not, as yet, want to tell her all of it, that for *Shiro Ninja* the loss of his powers was secondary to his loss of faith. That was something to which Nangi could relate.

Justine thought she was beginning to understand Nicholas's recent behavior. "Could this be why Nicholas has chosen to shut me out?"

"It is likely," Nangi nodded. "For someone such as Nicholas, *Shiro Ninja* is his worst nightmare come true. At such a time as this, he would not want you close to him."

"Why not? I could help him. He's so alone now, drawn into himself."

Nangi's eyes seemed restless, roving the nave, the lines of dark wooden pews. "Please try to understand, Mrs. Linnear. He would be vulnerable to assault. Naturally, he would not want you near him at a time like this."

"Assault?" Justine felt the serpent of fear uncoiling, slithering. "Saigo and Akiko are dead. Who would want to harm him?"

Nangi said nothing.

Justine, her nerves at hair-trigger level, sensed something. "What aren't you telling me? Nangi-san, please tell me. I must know. My life is disintegrating and I don't know why. Do you?"

Nangi stared at her out of his good eye, his gaze steady. "Mrs. Linnear, *Shiro Ninja*, White Ninja, is a wholly *created* state. Do you understand me? It is a subtle kind of attack. An ultimate attack by someone proficient in *Kan-aka-na-ninjutsu*, Black ninjutsu."

"Then there *is* someone out there; another enemy. A Black Ninja *sensei*."

Nangi's good eye closed for just a moment. "Even Black Ninja *sensei* do not have sufficient knowledge to induce *Shiro Ninja*, Mrs. Linnear."

Justine could barely speak. A terror such as she had never known before had enwrapped her in its coils. She shivered, as if with the onset of winter. "Who then?" It was a whisper, hoarse and constricted.

"It is not to be spoken of," Nangi said. "It is a *dorokusai*, a thing reeking of slime."

"What is that? For God's sake, Nangi-san, tell me!"

"Patience." In an extraordinary gesture, Nangi put his hand briefly over hers. "Let us find Nicholas, Mrs. Linnear. Let him tell us what has happened. If he is, indeed, *Shiro Ninja*, then you will need to know everything."

Cotton Branding and Shisei ate lobsters he cooked on the gas grill, stir-fried vegetables that Shisei sizzled in an electric wok she found, a salad of local greens, and thick chunks of Italian bread. She arranged it all so artfully it made Branding want to take a picture of it. The stunning visual display somehow made the food taste all the better.

They went through a six-pack of beer, and he was returning to the refrigerator for a second six-pack before he realized it.

Branding knew that he was besotted—with sex, with food, with the beer—but mostly with Shisei. He did not ever want her to leave. He thought that he might be content going with her from bedroom to kitchen and back again for the rest of his life. It was a dream, of course, but a happy dream, an ecstatic dream, and Branding reveled in it.

They spoke of many things. Branding, lolling on the great porch, feeling the wet mist rolling in off the water, hearing it muffle the constant pounding of the surf, contrived to speak as little as possible. He was fairly far gone, but not so far that a tiny central piece of him had stopped testing her.

During all this long afternoon and evening, Branding, happier than he had ever been since the early days of his marriage to Mary, before the birth of his daughter, whom he loved but who created with her dyslexia an unimaginable chaos and grief, had been more or less waiting for Shisei to bring up the topic of his work and, especially, his upcoming political battle with his personal nemesis, Douglas Howe.

Shisei was, frankly, too good to be true. The fact that she had come into his life at just this moment had embedded itself in his psyche and, like a pearl growing inside an oyster, had festered, prodding him back to reality when the dazzling sheen of his ecstasy had begun to wear off.

It was no wonder that he was becoming paranoid. Branding suspected that Douglas Howe, and Howe's dogged persistence in opposing Branding's ASCRA bill, was finally getting to him. Acting on the findings of a five-year report commissioned by the Washington-based Johnson Institute, the Defense Department's Advanced Strategic Computer Research Agency had petitioned Capitol Hill for a four-billion-dollar funding over five years in order to finance the Hive Project. Branding, as chairman of the Senate Fiscal Oversight Committee, had been the first to see the report, and the first to act on it.

The Hive Project involved constructing a computer that was based not on a single processor, like conventional computers were, but rather on an interconnecting neural network of a complexity not unlike that in the brain of a bee—hence the project name.

This computer would, in effect, be able to think. Using radar, sonar, and Loran, it and subsequent versions—so the Johnson Institute report showed—could distinguish between friend or foe; it could choose a weapon's path and change it instantaneously to suit incoming intelligence from the field; it could recognize, and respond to, human speech. The applications seemed endless.

Douglas Howe, chairman of the Senate Armed Services Committee, was dead set against Branding's ASCRA bill. His argument was that he did not want to foster another disaster on the order of the recent Artificial Intelligence Initiative. Four hundred million dollars had been allocated for a fever-pitch run at constructing a "cognitive artificial brain." So much money had been dropped in the researchers' laps at once that they did not know what to do with it, and consequently, great chunks of the funding disappeared down an unknown drain. But Branding knew that Howe's reasoning was only skin deep.

The fight, which had long been simmering, now threatened to boil over into what many people on Capitol Hill saw as a personal vendetta, as Howe sought to destroy or, at the very least, cripple Branding's enormous influence in the Senate. This influence was now symbolized by the ASCRA bill.

The increasingly bitter conflict had become something more than Democrat versus Republican or even liberal versus conservative. It had about it now something of a pitched battle, with the combatants dug in on both sides, armed to the teeth, and determined that only one would survive the final assault.

But Shisei had continued to surprise him, just as she had ever since they had met at Tippy North's masque. Rather than ask questions about his work, she spoke of those subjects about which she seemed the most passionate: ecology and sex. Branding, beginning to understand Shisei's personality, saw that she was obsessed with health: a healthy world, a healthy life. To her, a vigorous sex life was as integral to a healthy life as eating the right foods or daily exercise.

And again Branding was struck by the essentially childlike qualities lurking beneath the woman's glowing skin. She possessed a kind of naiveté—a straightforwardness of purpose—that to Branding was as exciting as it was refreshing.

From inside the house George Shearing interpreted "Mood Indigo" in a typically lush arrangement. Branding's eyes closed dreamily. He half heard Shisei say she was going to take a shower.

He felt her passing by him. Then he was alone on the porch with the night, the sea, and the music. He inhaled deeply of the heavy, salt air, luxuriating in its purity.

George Shearing disappeared in mid-note, and a moment later Grace Jones's sinewy vocals were imprinting themselves on the even-tempoed surf. Branding was reminded of the long afternoon's session of ecstatic lovemaking. Surprisingly, he felt himself stirring, becoming aroused all over again. He imagined Shisei's body spread upon his bed, and he felt lust clotting his veins as if it were a drug.

He rose, aware that his loose white cotton trousers were already tented at the crotch. He pushed open the screen door, and Grace Jones's voice washed over him. Memories writhed in his head.

He went past the kitchen, through the living room, down the hall. The music followed him, twisting along the corridor as if it were his companion. He could hear the sound of the water spray, and opened the door to the bathroom.

It was steamy and hot inside. Branding undid his trousers, stepped out of them. He stripped off his voile shirt. He could see Shisei's body, a dark shape moving behind the translucent shower curtain. Her back was to him, her arms upstretched into the curving spray, her hands encircling the shower head as, before, they had encircled him.

He was very hard. He could feel the throbbing between his legs, and sucked in his breath. He felt like a sex machine. He felt twenty-five again.

As he watched Shisei washing herself, Branding smiled, remembering that she had not wanted to turn her back to him, that now he could take her from behind, coupling as animals did, as Branding had never done with his wife or with any of the women he had been intimate with before Mary.

He was trembling with desire, fired by the sight of her, hazy and indistinct behind the thin curtain, one filmy layer, a storm of painted violets swaying, rivulets of water running through them . . .

Branding grasped the shower curtain and, in one quick gesture, drew it aside. And stood transfixed, staring at Shisei's back.

It was one of those moments in one's life that did not last more than a tenth of a second but which seemed to last a lifetime—image imprinted upon the retina, burned upon the brain for all time. It was akin to the moment when Branding had learned that his daughter was dyslexic; when it had become clear to him that Mary, the woman he loved, did not particularly enjoy sex. They were infinitesimal moments in one's life—yet charged with such power that they irrevocably changed one's life.

And like all such moments, this one was chaotic. Branding stared at Shisei's back, at, more properly, the perfectly hideous detailed tattoo, there, of a spider. It was gigantic, covering the entire area of her back, the obscene cluster of eight red eyes atop its small head, the two pairs of spread appendages from which venom is secreted to paralyze and liquify its prey, its eight hairy, articulated legs stretching from one shoulder blade to the other, from the top of one buttock to the other.

And then Shisei reacted. Her head jerked around, looking back over her shoulder. Her torso moved, and with the play of her back muscles, the spider moved, dancing in nauseating cadence to the sinuous drift of Grace Jones's vocals.

Branding screamed.

I must be going crazy, Tomi thought. With the night had come the rain, like a curtain coming down on the last tableau held by actors upon a stage. It was a red rain, or a blue rain, depending on which glowing sign one was passing.

Masses of umbrellas held at an acute angle to keep the wind from inverting them clogged Tokyo, turning the streets into fields filled with disquieting black flowers, storm-tossed, beading moisture down the stretched nylon and rice paper.

Headlights washed like klieg lights across these thick swaths of living matter, highlighting faces and hands as if they were segments of one vast millipede making its laborious way across the city.

Tomi, on her way home from work, ducked into a brilliantly lighted pachinko parlor. Her feet and legs were wet, and she was tired of being herded into puddles by the twists and turns of the ceaselessly moving millipede on the streets.

She had tried to find Nicholas Linnear's whereabouts. She had first phoned his office at Sato International, but they had no idea where he might be. His home number went unanswered. She dialed Sato International again, asked to speak to a vice-president. This time she learned the cause of Nicholas's absence, and on a hunch, asked for the name of his surgeon. Then she called the surgeon's office and had a bit more luck. They informed her that he had an appointment with Dr. Hanami at ten the next morning. Tomi had decided to meet him there.

In truth, however, Nicholas Linnear was not uppermost on her mind. Senjin Omukae was. That individual was rapidly assuming dominance over the policewoman, and this fact in and of itself was disturbing to Tomi. If only that were the end of it, she felt perhaps she could, in time, handle what seemed to her a dereliction of her duty.

The fact that her individuality was asserting itself over the figure of Senjin had her really frightened. Senjin Omukae was not only her commander, and therefore forbidden, he was Senjin the individualist, the Opaque Man. This was his nickname among those outside the homicide division. He was—other than heroic—an unknown quantity. He was feared; even, it was rumored, by those who had elevated him to division commander.

That she should be drawn to this man was a source of growing unease for Tomi. Which was why, on this rainy night, she decided to go see the Scoundrel.

The Scoundrel, otherwise known as Seji Hikoko, was her best friend. They had met in school, and it had been the Scoundrel who had supported her when she had made her traumatic break with her family, with her entire way of life. In this way, he was like Senjin. He saw and appreciated her for what she was, not merely a woman to be kept in her place. In response, it had been Tomi who had tutored the Scoundrel in his advanced-level philosophy tutorials when he was in danger of failing those courses.

As a result, there was an intimate bond between the two that Tomi had never had with anyone else, even—especially!—a member of her own family.

The Scoundrel had a *usagigoya*—literally, a rabbit hutch—what Japanese called a modern Tokyo apartment: tiny, cramped, virtually airless. Still, it was a place to sleep.

The Scoundrel's *usagigoya* was in Asakusa, where he often rubbed elbows with Kabuki actors and sumo wrestlers. It was Tomi's favorite part of town, but it made her melancholy as well, for it reminded her of her lowly station in life. As a police sergeant she could not afford to live here, even in a place as minuscule as a rabbit hutch.

The Scoundrel was home. But then, he was always home at this hour, tinkering with his portable computer terminal, which now ran two to three times faster than it had when he had traded for it. The Scoundrel never bought anything when he could barter for it. In the privacy of his home he liked to improve upon what others did. In this way he could assert his genius without exerting ego. It was a Zen exercise, Tomi knew, a way to achieve the same kind of mind/no mind she strove for in her martial arts training. Hers was the more physical discipline, she knew, but hardly the more demanding.

She heard the careening music of Billy Idol as she went down the hall. And when the Scoundrel opened the door, the blast of rock 'n roll almost bowled her over.

"Good God, how can you think with all that sound and fury?" she yelled, putting aside her umbrella and her shoes.

"Because it signifies nothing." The Scoundrel grinned, pulled her inside, shut the door behind her. "I can concentrate with it on."

The music boomed from a pair of three-thousand-dollar speakers the Scoundrel had souped up, and Tomi felt as if she had encountered a g-force liftoff. She had to brace herself against the kineticism. She felt trapped within a huge pachinko game.

The place was, as usual, a mess. Masses of computer hardware were strewn like corpses upon a battlefield in seemingly random piles across the floor, the chairs, the small sofa, the top of the VCR. The TV screen was filled up with the image of Harrison Ford prowling the futuristic Los Angeles cityscape, searching for murderous replicants in *Blade Runner*.

The stereo glowed with a profusion of red and green pinpoints, waxing and waning with the volume of Billy Idol's vocals. And, like Billy Idol, the Scoundrel had dyed his hair platinum. It stood up from his scalp like a bristly forest, longer on top, shorter on the sides. He was, like Tomi, in his early thirties. But while she had matured from the wispy teenager she had once been, he had retained the reedy, almost unformed shape of youth. He was like an oversized exuberant puppy, sloppy in his habits but lovable for all that.

Tomi stood making puddles on the floor, but the Scoundrel did not seem to care. There were times when Tomi needed to escape from the real world, filled with male pressure, constant fear of censure and loss of face. Here she could hide out amid the clutter and the chaos and the Scoundrel's eternal high spirits. She would help him with whatever projects he was working on, and feel useful and appreciated. But tonight she needed to think, so she prevailed on him to take a break and come out with her for dinner.

They went where they always ended up, Koyanagi, their favorite *shitamachi*, an old-style businessman's restaurant, where they invariably ordered *unagi*, the broiled eel, which was the house specialty.

"What were you working on at the apartment?" Tomi asked when they had settled in and had their first gulps of Sapporo beer.

"Oh, you know me." The Scoundrel flashed his boyish grin. "Always fooling around. I'm working on a borer, a computer software program that penetrates into other programs encoded for security."

"Don't they already have things like that?"

"Hackers, yeah. There are some nasty ones around. And if the government finds who's using them, they throw 'em into jail until the next world war." He grinned again. "But the one I'm working on is different. I've named it MANTIS, which stands for Manmade Nondiscriminatory Tactical Integrated-circuit Smasher."

The Scoundrel's grin widened at the blank look on her face. "The essence of the long name is that MANTIS is *adaptable*, meaning it can, in its own way, think. Every locked program has its own individual defense, so normally if you wanted to break in, you'd have to contour a specialized program. My borer is set up to attack *any* defense, and get through."

Tomi laughed. His genius often stunned her. "You'd better not let the government know what you're up to."

"Nah. There's zip chance of that," he said around a gulp of beer.

"I don't get it," Tomi said, intrigued. "You work for Nakano Industries, one of the largest electronics designing and manufacturing *keiretsu* in the country. The government must oversee Nakano the way they do all the major corporations."

"Oh, they do. The MITI people are always over for meetings." The Scoundrel paused as he craned his neck, peering around the restaurant. The gesture was such an outlandish parody of a spy at work that she giggled. "The fact is," he said, returning his gaze to her, "that my boss is head of the advanced research and development department at Nakano. The stuff we're doing is so theoretical, he tells me that the MITI people leave him alone."

The Scoundrel finished his beer, ordered refills for them both. "My boss is a vice-president at Nakano. I've been working for this guy for a year and a half now. He reviewed my file, picked me out of the engineering section, interviewed me over the course of a week. I must have passed some kind of test he was putting me through. Anyway, six months ago he agreed to let me work on this borer project I dreamed up, which is anything *but* theoretical. In fact, it's just about ready to roll now." He grinned. "I'm not really supposed to tell anyone anything about it, but I don't think that includes you."

That was just like the Scoundrel, Tomi thought, making up the rules as he went along.

"Hey," he said suddenly. "Remember when I was promoted out of my engineering department?"

"How could I forget?" Tomi said, laughing. "I threw you a party that lasted the entire weekend. Remember that woman from my office who told ghost stories all night?"

"Are you kidding? I'm lucky I remember my name after that blowout. We did in a case of Suntory scotch, didn't we?"

Tomi nodded. "Among other cases." She was smiling. "Those were the days."

The Scoundrel, downing his Sapporo, watched the smile fade from her face like the color out of a cherry blossom. "I see you've got weight tonight." To him, weight was synonymous with sadness, lightness with happiness. "If that's the case, you've come to the right boy. What's hung the stone around your neck?"

"Around my heart, more like it," Tomi said.

"Ah! *L'affaire d'amour. Bien!* Please explicate your predicament, *madame.*"

Tomi couldn't help but smile. "Is everything a joke to you?"

"Sure. Life's a joke, Tomi. Or have you been too busy to notice?"

"I guess lately I have."

He winked. "We'll soon put you right. Now give it to me straight. Don't hold anything back. I can take it. I promise I won't faint."

This was just what Tomi had wanted. But now she hesitated, wondering whether it made sense to tell the Scoundrel about Senjin Omukae. After all, this was very serious business to her, while to the Scoundrel it was already *l'affaire d'amour*, a situation of which he was more than likely to make fun.

"All right," he said, crossing his arms over his chest. "I can see those two vertical lines above the bridge of your nose. I know you well enough to know that they only come out when you're really concerned. So no jokes." He gestured. "Cross my heart."

Tomi was immediately relieved, and she launched into her tale of attraction and uneasiness, of confused emotions, of the attendant submergence of her policewoman persona, and of her fear of the moral repercussions.

When she was finished, she watched the Scoundrel's face for any sign of what he thought. But he had his face buried in his beer glass and she could tell nothing.

At last the Scoundrel said, "You obviously want my advice, so I'll give it to you, though I don't think you'll like what I'm going to say." He drained his glass. "It's very simple. Forget this guy. From what you've told me, he's not for you. But even if he were, he's your commander. The situation's so dangerous that the risk of going further's not worth it." He put aside his empty glass. "Now I'll shut up, we'll eat dinner, and you can digest what I've said along with the *unagi.*"

As she ate, Tomi tried to sort out her feelings. She knew that she should have been relieved by what the Scoundrel had said. She recognized in his counsel an echo of what a part of her had suspected all along. The best course was for her to bury her feelings for Senjin Omukae, to continue with her life as if he were merely her commander.

But Tomi felt no sense of relief, only a growing despair. For now, as the Scoundrel had clarified the situation, she knew that she would not take the best course, that her path lay in another, darker, less understandable direction.

If she had been the kind of woman to bury emotions she felt deeply, to allow herself to live a life acceptable to those around her but not to herself, she never would have hung up the phone on her brother. The dutiful sister, she would have bowed to his wishes, returning home to marry the man he had chosen for her.

But she was not one to go blindly where an outdated notion of duty would heartlessly thrust her. At the terrifying moment of her break with her family, she had promised herself that from that moment on she would be true to herself and to her own wishes. That must become the meaning of her life, or else her grand gesture, rejecting the traditional life, would have no meaning.

"I wish I could take your advice," Tomi said.

The Scoundrel shrugged. "Advice is cheap, even here where everything is expensive."

"I know. But I value yours."

He leaned forward. His face was unusually somber. "Then take my advice, Tomi. Go out. Have a fling. You deserve some fun." That grin flashed again, lighting up his face. "You're far too serious for your own good."

She put her hand over his. "Thanks, Seji. You're a good friend. Your heart is true."

The Scoundrel, perhaps embarrassed by the compliment, slid his hand out from under hers. He studied her darkened face. "Come on," he said, spilling yen onto the table, "I know a club in Roppongi where they don't allow either day or night to intrude on the nonstop festivities. We'll dance, get drunk, and say to hell with everyone!"

Tomi, laughing again, let him lead her out into the rain- and color-swept night. For the moment, at least, she could allow her anxieties to wait in abeyance while she floated in the Scoundrel's never-never land.

Cotton Branding sat naked and shivering on the edge of the porcelain tub, his head in his hands. Shisei stood in front of him, dripping water onto his bare legs. Behind him the shower rattled the plastic curtain with its painted violets so that they appeared to dance as if in a wind.

"So," Shisei said, "now that you have seen all of me, you are like the rest. Your desire has turned to disgust."

"That's not true."

"If you could only see yourself. You can't even look at me."

It was the contempt in her voice that broke the spell of horror that had enveloped him. He raised his head, stared at her. "Nothing has changed, Shisei."

"Oh, please. Spare me your politician's easy lies. I see your face. Everything has changed."

"Not everything," he said. He rubbed his hands one against the other, as if needing to warm them before a fire. "Give me a moment. Please." He stood up. "We've startled—maybe even frightened—each other. The least we can do is retire to neutral corners before we come out for the next round." He gave her a wan smile. "And perhaps there won't be a next round."

Shisei gave a little shiver, and he reached past her, handed her a towel. "Thank you," she said. She wrapped it around herself, letting the moisture soak into the absorbent cloth.

Branding turned off the shower. He said, "I think I've had all the shocks I care to have in one night."

"The shock," she said sadly, "is what most people feel. But it isn't all. The tattoo revolts them."

Branding registered surprise. "If you care what other people think, then why did you have it done?"

She looked at him for a moment. "I'm cold," she said. "I want to put some clothes on."

He handed Shisei her cover-up, but she said, "No. I want something of yours."

He went and got one of his pajama tops, gave it to her. That was all she needed; it came midway down her thighs. She buttoned it, her gold nails shining. The shoulders hung off her in an endearing fashion.

As if the enormous house had suddenly become too small, or still retained the detritus of the recent emotional conflagration, they went outside.

They stared out into the night. The Atlantic crashed all around them, and periodically the doleful foghorn from the nearby lighthouse intruded on the pull and suck of the surf. For once, the gulls were quiet, walking stiffly along the beach, peering here and there for the last morsels of food of the day.

Above their heads the sky was perfectly clear, strewn with glittering stars, hard, bright, piercing the canvas of the heavens with their blue, yellow, and white light.

But off to the south the horizon was cluttered with a long cloudbank, which Branding estimated must stretch for several hundred miles.

Now, as they watched, lightning began to flicker and spark within the clouds. Seen sometimes as fiery, jagged flashes, sometimes as great flowering bursts illuminating sections of the cloudbank, the heat lightning played out its stunning silent concerto across a keyboard too vast to comprehend.

This exhibition of nature's handiwork was humbling, indeed. For Branding it served to put into perspective human concerns and anxieties, which seemed in comparison both fleeting and inconsequential.

After a time the cloudbank relapsed into darkness; the show was over. They went back inside.

They sat on the down-filled sofa, low lamplight spilling warmly across them. The eerie revelation of a while ago seemed not to have happened, or to have been something they had imagined.

The shock was gone. And in its place, what? Branding knew he very much wanted to find out.

He had poured out snifters of brandy for them both, and they sipped slowly, deliberately, silently understanding that they needed to rescue their equilibrium.

Shisei's hair, shining and still damp, reminded him of a mink's pelt, close and soft and precious. The fringe of blond color above her eyes made her seem at this moment somehow more vulnerable. Then, like a shock of cold water, he remembered the spider etched across her back, and he thought, This is a different kind of mink.

"Shisei," Branding said, before she had a chance to speak, "I don't want to be like all the others."

For a long moment she said nothing. Her eyes, dark as night, held steady on his. "Is that the politician or the man talking?" she said finally.

"The man, I hope. I want it to be the man," Branding said truthfully.

Shisei briefly closed her eyes. "And I want to believe you." She put her snifter down. "You scared me, Cook, when you came in on me like that. I wasn't prepared. The truth is, I hadn't yet thought of a way to tell you—or to show you all of me."

"Is all of you so terrible?"

Shisei snatched up her brandy, and Branding caught a hint of the vulnerable woman she was so afraid of revealing. "You tell me," she said.

"The *image* is a terrifying one." He caught the momentary flash of anger in her eyes as she glanced at him, then away. He was reminded of his daughter when she was a child. She had often looked at him that way when he had said no to her. But it passed, and her love for him would always prevail.

"I don't care for spiders," Branding went on. "I don't know anyone who does." He slowed his pace, understanding that he needed to feel his way in the face of this unknown, for his sake as well as for hers. "But on the other hand, it's a tattoo, a work of art." He saw her shudder. "And because it's on your body, I admit I'm intrigued. Will you tell me how it came to be done? It must have been a project, tattooed over a period of time."

"Two years," Shisei said, as if this were a fact to be proud of, as if this were the only aspect of the existence of the spider to which she could point with pride.

"A long time."

He had meant it as an assurance. But hearing his words, she put the snifter to her lips, drained all the brandy at once. She swallowed convulsively, almost choking on the fiery liquor. Her eyes watered and she wiped them with the heel of her hand. "Oh, God, Cook, you don't know how long."

"Was it painful?"

"My soul hurt for years afterward," Shisei said. "The other pain was nothing. It disappeared like mist in sunlight."

"I want to know what happened," Branding said.

"We have already established that many topics are taboo." Shisei poured herself more brandy, drank more slowly this time. Then she said, "Cook, what did you do after your wife died, when you hurt so much you thought you'd never recover? Didn't the emptiness make the days endless? Didn't you wait in the night for death to come, didn't you hear it breathing close beside you, see its red eyes like lamps hanging in the blackness? And didn't, oh, once, twice, didn't you long to tumble into the oblivion death held in its hand like a prize?"

Branding was taken aback by the extremes of her emotions. He knew that she was describing herself, not him. He had never felt such utter despair as she described, even after the initial shock of Mary's death had worn off. And now he supposed that, at least in part, this is what had triggered his guilt. But he knew that how he answered Shisei was very important. She appeared on the verge of opening up, and he knew that he possessed the power to push her one way or the other.

"The human condition is such that life goes on, no matter the depths of despair into which one is plunged," Branding said. "I did . . . To be perfectly frank, I'm not sure what I saw or heard after Mary died. I only know that I see the car, upside down and still smoldering, I see her body on a stretcher, a blanket over her head. I hear a TV commentator speaking about her death in the same clipped, detached phrases he spoke of Vietnam casualties and the death of American Marines in Beirut. I keep thinking that death should not be degraded by being made impersonal or reduced to its lowest common denominator."

Shisei sighed, and it was as if the last hour had not occurred. "You will not forsake me, Cook, the way the others have," she said. "I know that now." She put her head against the sofa back, and she seemed once more so much the little girl that Branding felt his heart pounding. He wanted to take her in his arms, to protect her, to tell her everything would be all right.

But he knew that he would do nothing of the kind. He could sense that the two of them had reached a kind of shared nadir, and like two motes suspended in fluid, the next moment would tell in which direction they would spin.

"You can't know what that means to me, Cook." Her fingers were lost in her hair, pulling it hard, as if the pain were also part of her penance. "I have been . . . treated poorly; I have been abused. I have loved, and have been punished for that love."

Branding stared at her as if seeing her for the first time. She was like an iceberg. He was wondering just how much of her was hidden below the surface of a dark and stormy sea.

"You've survived, Shisei," he said. "In the end, isn't that what's important?"

"Have you ever been imprisoned?" Shisei said, as if to tell him that he knew nothing about the condition of her life. "I have." She lifted her arm over her head, pointing to the creature that had become a part of her. "This spider is my penance—and my reward."

Branding was once more trying to fathom the nuances, the facets of her personality he could from time to time glimpse like the heat lightning they had seen tonight. "Shisei," he said, "I don't understand."

But she was already bent over, weeping into her hands. And when at last he heard her voice, it caused a shiver to run down his spine.

"Cook," she whispered, "I pray to God that you never will."

Tanzan Nangi lived in an uncommonly spacious wooden house that dated back to the turn of the century. It had been built for the most famous Kabuki actor of his time, and only because the actor's son had fallen into disrepute had it come into Nangi's hands.

The impressive, wide-eaved structure sat amidst an extravagant garden of ornamental cherry, dwarf maple, and cryptomeria trees. Flat stones, some great, some small, were set into the earth between fern, sheared azalea, and purple gem rhododendron, creating a serene environment. Inside, the main passageways between rooms were glassed in so that one could feel, even in the most inclement weather, in the midst of the garden.

Nangi sat alone, staring through the glass at a gibbous moon that plunged in and out of indigo clouds.

The house was silent all around him; it smelled of cedar and lemon oil. Nangi, sipping green tea that he had brewed himself, was sunk deep in thought. He was rerunning his extremely disturbing conversation with Justine Linnear. He had to admit that he was grateful to her. In brashly coming to see him, she had forced him to face what he was coming to conclude was a baffling and thoroughly terrifying situation.

If Nicholas was, indeed, *Shiro Ninja*, it meant that he was under attack. By whom, and for what reason? Nangi had told Justine that even a Black Ninja *sensei* lacked the ability to create *Shiro Ninja* in an adept such as Nicholas. Now Nangi shuddered at the thought of what concentrated evil might be out there in the night, crouching, readying itself for the kill. If, as he was beginning to suspect, that kind of elemental power were arrayed against them, then only Nicholas could save them. Yet according to Justine, Nicholas was without his powers.

Instinct told Nangi to retreat. A general who finds himself facing an army of superior strength retires from the field of battle because the safety of his forces is paramount. He must either retreat or discover another, unconventional path to victory because a frontal assault will clearly end in disaster.

Nangi heard a small sound behind him, but he did not turn around. The faint scent of night-blooming jasmine infused the room, and he filled another celadon cup with tea.

With a rustle of silk, Umi crossed the tatami mats. Now, without a sound, she knelt beside him, accepting the offering of the green tea. Nangi was aware of her huge dark eyes watching him even as she sipped.

Umi said, "It was cold in bed without you beside me. I dreamt that the house was inhabited by a storm, and I opened my eyes to find that I was alone."

In the almost-dark, Nangi smiled. He was used to the poetic way in which Umi spoke. She was a dancer, and whichever medium she chose to express herself was bound to be rife with layers of meaning.

"I had not meant to wake you," he said. He understood by her use of the word "storm" that she had felt the agitation of his spirit.

She put her hand on him. Umi, whose name meant the sea, thus calmed him, bringing him back to that low place inhabited by water, where one can think, one can gain power in the shadows and the silence.

Nangi said, "Music heard so deeply that it is not heard at all, but you are the music while the music lasts."

Umi, very close to him, said, "When I was fifteen you gave me a book by T. S. Eliot. I had never before encountered a Western mind that intrigued me or was filled with such light. I remember that quote from the book you gave me."

That was typical of Umi. She learned everything; she forgot nothing. Though she was only twenty-four, she was far wiser than women three times her age. She was a student who, without being aware of it, had become a master. That was also typical of Umi. She was egoless, could therefore absorb philosophy on the deepest level, incorporating it into her spirit, widening the breadth of her power: the width of a circle. Umi was a *sensei* of myth, the mystical and the Tao. The life-force of the universe was in her heart.

Umi took his hands in her own, placing them palms down. Nangi felt the warmth seeping out of her like the crack of light from a window in a solitary house encountered by a winter wayfarer when night comes down.

She was so beautiful—not only her face, but her body as well, slender, graceful, sinuous and strong like a young tree that had survived winds, rain, and snow.

"There is darkness here," Umi said, "beyond the night." Gripping each of his fingers in turn, she said, "Emptiness and chaos. The stability of the world is threatened. The Spider Woman calls, and the axis wobbles. Ice comes."

Nangi knew that she was speaking of part of the Amerindian Hopi myth of creation—the death of the Second World, before the creation of this one, doomed to an eternal ice age by the Spider Woman, who sings the Song of Creation, because of the unremitting evil of its inhabitants.

If the Spider Woman called, it was because of the existence of inordinate evil. This was what Umi meant. Nangi's skin began to crawl. It was true, then, an enemy of extraordinary malevolence had targeted Nicholas. Fear burst full-blown like a bomb blast upon his consciousness. He wanted to pray to God, but he could not. He was cut off by his own sins, incapable of finding exculpation. He realized, with a start, that he had been rendered as powerless as Nicholas. The loss of his faith was a devastating blow that he had pushed into the background because of the current crisis. But now he realized that it was part of the crisis.

Dear God, he thought, we are lost.

And as if hearing his silent voice, Umi said, "Though the Way is known, the many sin, living as though they had a different wisdom of their own."

The Way meaning the Tao. Hearing echoes of Heraclitus in Umi's words calmed Nangi, reminding him that the knowledge of the ancients was available to him. Thinking of Heraclitus, he thought, too, of Sun Tzu, *The Art of War*, Yagyu Munenori, the synthesis of the sword and the mind, *ichiri*, the One Principle, the mind-set one must use when one cannot retreat in the face of an attack; the synthesis of the universe: the Tao.

In this manner he conquered the chaos in his mind that the fear had engendered, brought himself back into focus. It was not only *Shiro Ninja* with which he had to contend, Nangi thought. His entire business partnership with Nicholas was threatened by Kusunda Ikusa and Nami. Now he wondered whether the two attacks were separate and distinct or whether they were a clever, concerted assault from two different directions.

Paranoia or truth? Nangi, spangled in silver moonlight, sitting close to the sea, knew that he would have to find out.

The next day Nicholas went to see his surgeon. He took the train southeast into Tokyo, because he did not trust himself to drive, and he certainly did not want Justine to drive him, although part of him, perhaps, longed for just that.

He had spoken briefly to Nangi, explaining that he had made an appointment with the surgeon for later that morning and, depending on how he felt afterward, he would either come into the office or not. Nangi's extreme solicitousness had set Nicholas's teeth on edge, another bad sign of his deteriorating emotional state.

The early morning mist rolled in heavy, oily undulations, inundating the green mountainsides. The landscape was, otherwise, a blur, the result of the train's speed and Nicholas's fatigue.

The gentle vibrations lulled him, the far-off train whistle a melancholy reminder of his youth in a Japan struggling to overcome its shame at having lost the war and in being remade in the image of the United States.

The soft song of the rails reminded him of the lullabies his mother used to sing him when she took him on trips by rail to visit his aunt Itami. Cheong considered Itami her sister, even though Itami was, in fact, the sister of Cheong's first husband, a Japanese officer killed in Singapore during the war. That was how Cheong and Colonel Denis Linnear had met: during the war in Singapore. The Colonel had saved Cheong's life, and had fallen in love with her.

A time of danger, long ago and far away. But Nicholas held that spoken-of time close to him, as if it were a magical talisman with which he could ward off the despair rising inside him.

But it was no use. His anger and his anxiety overflowed the inadequate vessel into which he placed it. He had misjudged its size as well as its strength. He wanted to be calm for this interview, to use patience, his mother's gift to him, in order to learn what he could about his loss of memory. He did not want to jump to conclusions, but sitting in the chill air-conditioned train, shivering with the onset of anger adrenaline, he was afraid that he already had.

Tokyo was silver and gray. Fog enshrouded the vast neon corporate logos and advertisements in Shinjuku until their manmade reds, greens, and blues were the color of ash. The sky-rises seemed cut off at the knees, as stubby and discolored as an old man's decaying teeth.

Dr. Hanami's office was on the twentieth floor of an enormous sky-rise complex complete with Plexiglas walkways and indoor gardens. Opposite his brushed bronze door, in fact, three black and white rocks rose from the sea of a small pebble garden.

Nicholas waited thirty minutes in a room lacquered a glossy gray. He sat upon a gray tweed couch at right angles to six matching gray tweed chairs and across from the receptionist's gray metal desk. On the walls were two contemporary lithographs clumsily playing upon the delicacy of traditional *ukiyo-e* woodblock prints, combining them with images of the West: the Statue of Liberty, the front end of a vintage Corvette, a hamburger dripping ketchup. Nicholas hated them.

He got up, strode nervously to the window. Shards of the city could be seen through vertical gray metal blinds. He could not see the streets. The fog had left a film on the glass, which turned a lurid rainbow hue in the dull, shadowless light. He stared out across the plunging vertical canyon between the buildings. The flourescent lights in the windows of a nearby sky-rise burned through the haze with the lambent glow of an acetylene torch.

Nicholas heard the receptionist call his name.

Dr. Hanami was a small, dapper man in his early fifties. He sported an immaculately groomed mustache, and his iron-gray hair was shiny with cream. He wore a white medical smock, open over a gray pinstripe suit. His office was thick with cigarette smoke.

He took a last drag, stubbed out his busily burning butt in an overflowing ashtray, and waved Nicholas to a seat. He was punctilious about conforming to Nicholas's wish that he not smoke in Nicholas's presence, but he seemed unaware that they often spoke through a noxious pall. After his visits to Dr. Hanami, Nicholas invariably threw his clothes in the hamper as soon as he got home.

"So," Dr. Hanami said, "how's it going?" He said this in English. Dr. Hanami, who most often lunched on Bigu Makus from the local McDonald's, fancied himself a student of Americanisms.

Nicholas, slumped in a chrome and gray rubber chair, stared at him.

Dr. Hanami played with his pewter lighter, turning it around and around between forefinger and thumb. "I notice," he said, "that this isn't one of your regular visits." He opened Nicholas's chart, scanned the pages. "Everything looks just great here. The X rays, the lab tests. Couldn't be better." He looked up. "Is there a problem?"

"Yes," Nicholas said, resisting the urge to leap out of his seat. "You could say that."

"Um. And what form, may I ask, is this problem taking?" Around and around went the lighter, its dark pewter face catching the light of the overheads.

Nicholas, unable to bear sitting for a moment longer, sprang up. With a great clatter that startled Dr. Hanami, Nicholas pulled aside the metal blinds, pressed his face against the window glass. It was still as foul as a petrochemical furnace out there; he could not get the burned smell out of his nostrils.

"Tell me, Doctor," Nicholas said without turning around, "have you ever been to Nara Prefecture?"

After a moment's silence Dr. Hanami said, "Yes. Four years ago, I took my wife for a week's vacation to a spa in Nara. Hot mineral baths."

"Then you know how beautiful it is there."

"Yes, indeed. I often find myself thinking that we ought to go back. But, of course, there's never any time."

Nicholas turned around; there was no point staring into that soup any longer, prolonging the agony. "Doctor, have you ever wondered what life would be like if you suddenly could no longer perform an operation?"

Dr. Hanami looked puzzled. "Well, naturally, when I retire, I'll have to give this up—"

"No," Nicholas said, his impatience betraying him, "I mean now. At once. One moment to the next." He snapped his fingers. "Bang!"

"I can't say that I—"

"Well, the beauty of Nara, Doctor, where I studied martial arts for so long, is what I cannot live without. Not the beauty you and your wife see when you go to take your waters. Not that that beauty is inconsiderable. No, I'm talking about the beauty I've learned to see through *Getsumei no michi*. Do you know it? The Moonlit Path."

Dr. Hanami nodded. "I've heard of it, of course. But I didn't know . . ." Something either in Nicholas's face or his bearing caused the surgeon to pause. "You're very different today," he said. "What has happened?"

Nicholas, feeling the pounding of his heart, sat back down facing Dr. Hanami, but this time he was perched on the edge of the seat, leaning forward so that his head and upper torso crossed the intervening space between them. He was aware that his body was very tense. He rubbed his palms together, appalled that they were sweating.

"You asked what the problem is, and I'll tell you," he said into Dr. Hanami's face, the emotion bubbling up now, so that he knew he could no longer control it. He pointed to the side of his head, still healing from the operation. "I can't fucking remember any of my martial arts training. It's gone, vanished, just as if it had never been there. I was up all night thinking about how this . . . impossibility could have happened. And again and again I came back to the same answer, Doctor. The only answer that makes sense." He was up on his feet now, his corded arms gripping the edge of Dr. Hanami's desk. "You and your trusty little scalpel did it to me. You took too big a slice out of me, or maybe you nicked some adjacent tissue, I don't know which. But what I *do* know is that my memory is gone, and you're to blame."

Into the ringing silence Dr. Hanami said in Japanese, "Perhaps some tea is called for."

When faced with a crisis, Nicholas thought, fall back on the old traditions. The rage was so strong inside him that he was trembling. He watched Dr. Hanami ring through on his intercom, order the tea. When it came, on a black lacquer tray, the surgeon dismissed his receptionist, set about brewing the tea himself; taking pinches of the cut green leaves, dropping them into the boiling water, using the reed whisk at just the right speed to stir up the froth, turning the tiny porcelain cup around and around to ensure an even distribution.

There was something soothing, even comforting about the process. Its orderliness, its lack of spontaneity, its formality, even its stylized movements, served to bring a sense of normalcy—of the patient procession of past to present to future—firmly into focus.

Nicholas felt himself relaxing, the enormous tension that had built up overnight dissipating like air leaking from a punctured tire. He sank back by degrees into the chair.

At that moment Dr. Hanami served him the tea. When they had both drained their cups, the surgeon said, "Now, from the beginning, tell me everything."

"I want to talk about some details of the subject's history that have, until now, eluded me." Dr. Muku said this as soon as Senjin sat down.

It was unlike Dr. Muku to seize the initiative in these psychoanalytic sessions. Senjin was like those strange and eerie fish that live near the bottom of the sea, that see without light and, often, without eyes. He knew without having been given any visible sign that Dr. Muku was coming close to the truth.

Senjin was quite certain that the psychiatrist had begun to suspect that there was no psychopathic "subject" and, further, that this mythical "subject" was, in fact, Senjin himself.

There were, of course, dangers inherent in his knowledge. But even had Senjin suddenly stood up and confessed everything, Dr. Muku would be helpless to do anything about it. Certainly, he was constrained by the dictates of his profession from divulging anything they had discussed. Senjin had made it clear in their first session that whatever information exchanged hands was strictly confidential and could not be repeated outside the confines of the room in which they met.

Dr. Muku had readily—if, in retrospect, somewhat foolhardily—agreed, as Senjin suspected would be his wont. Now the relationship between them had taken on a new and, to Senjin's way of thinking, exciting dimension. There was a subtle struggle for control forming between the two of them, a kind of skirmish line as yet amorphous and, therefore, mutable.

It was akin to living on the edge, the length of cloth twisted around Senjin's neck, being pulled tighter by Dr. Muku's pudgy hands as the two men drew closer in a deadly dance. Senjin felt himself growing hard. A pulse in the side of his forehead beat a hasty rhythm with the heating of his blood. This kind of lethal game was what he lived for.

"For instance," Dr. Muku was saying, "what kind of upbringing did the subject receive? Was his family life normal?"

"What do you mean by 'normal'?" Senjin could not keep the sneering tone out of his voice. "Doesn't psychology shun the term 'normal' as being false?"

"Psychology might," Dr. Muku said in an assuring tone, "but psychotherapy may not. It all depends." He provided Senjin with a smile so contrived that, as far as Senjin was concerned, he might just as well have said, *You should know. You're not normal, are you, Senjin-san?* "Of course," Dr. Muku went on amiably, "you're right. In the abstract—that is, statistically—there is always a norm. However, the real world is quite different. Still, it is often the case that psychosis has its roots in early family life. And here, for the purpose of our discussion, we may use the word 'normal,' because I would be willing to bet that our subject did *not* have a normal upbringing."

Senjin sat forward. "In what way?"

Dr. Muku shrugged. "Perhaps his mother was a whore, or he believes that she abandoned him in some way. This would account for his obsession with Kiyohime and the demon woman." Dr. Muku shrugged. Because they were sitting in the small, close room, facing one another, and because Dr. Muku's back was to the window, his face was in half shadow. In that soft light Dr. Muku's face seemed made of putty. "Our subject could even have harbored incestuous feelings toward his mother. That kind of guilt would be too heavy a burden for a child's developing psyche to bear. It would be natural for him to 'get rid' of those unwanted feelings by projecting them outward, away from him, by turning them into something else—namely, the innate evil of the female. He would conveniently believe that his mother caused, by action or word, those taboo sexual feelings." Dr. Muku's eyes glittered behind his round glasses. "Is any of this making sense? Does it have a familiar ring?"

"How would I know?" Senjin said blandly.

"Well, you are far more familiar with the subject than I am."

"Am I?" Senjin raised his eyebrows. "I'm beginning to wonder if either of us know him sufficiently."

Dr. Muku shifted in his chair. "What makes you say that, Senjin-san?"

"Well, for one thing, the mystery of sex. That is, the suspect hasn't, to my knowledge, raped any of his victims."

"Yet they have all been women, his victims, yes?"

"Yes," Senjin lied.

"All young. All beautiful." Dr. Muku was nodding at the appropriate visual prompts Senjin was giving him. "Well, he must have come close. Very close. It is just a matter of time before he spills his seed over them." Dr. Muku pointed, as if Senjin were, indeed, the subject. "You see, our friend must feel that the act of ejaculation is akin to pulling the trigger of a gun. He'll see his ejaculate as the bullets."

Senjin sat very still. "You're very sure of yourself, Doctor."

Dr. Muku shrugged again. "Nothing is sure in my field, Senjin-san. One tries merely to make the proper educated guesses. Like a detective, I carefully walk amidst the rubble of a ruined psyche. I imagine that my modus operandi is quite similar to yours at a murder site. We are both looking for clues that will allow us to piece together the whos and whys that led to tragedy. And in order to solve the mystery, don't you sometimes take a leap of faith or two?"

Senjin recognized the direction in which this was going. Not only had Dr. Muku begun questioning him, instead of the other way around, but the psychiatrist was also bringing Senjin himself directly into the conversation. *We are both* . . . and *don't you sometimes* . . . This methodology was part of the clever interrogator's procedure of involving his subject in the interrogation in order to elicit truthful answers to his questions.

Senjin said, "I have found that the leaps of faith of the kind you describe are best left to films and novels where an author controls the destiny of all the characters."

Dr. Muku cocked his head, looking at Senjin quizzically. "But is it not the same here in real life? Life controls our karma. Surely our destiny is not in our own hands."

Senjin smiled. The balance of power had begun to shift, if ever so subtly. The more Dr. Muku continued in the interrogation, the more sure of himself he became, the more he revealed of his own strategy and the less threatening he became, the less control he maintained over the situation

It was time, Senjin thought, to further enlighten the doctor. "Muku-san," he said, "have you ever heard of Kshira?"

"No. I don't believe I have."

"Kshira is a form of physical and mental discipline," Senjin said. "But it is more encompassing than even a philosophy. It is its own reality. Kshira is the language of the sound-light continuum."

Dr. Muku blinked. "The what?"

Senjin lit a cigarette, but he didn't seem to draw on it deeply or often. "The sound-light continuum," Senjin repeated. "You have no doubt heard of *ki*, the underlying energy of all things—humans, animals, the sea, the forests, the earth itself. Well, the Kshira *sensei* have made a remarkable discovery, and it is this: that there are different forms of *ki*.

By recognizing them, and harnessing them in series, an engine of enormous psychic and physical energy is created."

Senjin could see that Dr. Muku was skeptical. That was hardly surprising. When it came to the human mind, Dr. Muku was locked within the severely limited framework of modern analytical thought. He was, to Senjin's way of thinking, a pathetic cripple, unable to comprehend anything save what he had been taught at school.

"The thing about Kshira," Senjin said, suddenly leaning forward, "is that it is infinitely malleable." He took a puff on his cigarette and it began to sizzle, bursting with an odd blue-white incendiary glow.

Senjin's left hand covered Dr. Muku's face before the psychiatrist had a chance to react. Senjin's thumb lifted Dr. Muku's glasses off the bridge of his nose. The metal slid in the sweat sheen breaking out on the psychiatrist's forehead.

Then Senjin jabbed the glowing end of his cigarette directly into Dr. Muku's left eye. His left hand, fingers spread like a spider across the doctor's face, held Dr. Muku implacably in place.

Dr. Muku's arms flailed at Senjin as the phosphorus-impregnated cigarette burned even more deeply into his eye socket. He began to wail, an eerie, stifled sound that was more a vibration emanating from his throat.

Watching him as if he were an electronic image on a TV screen, Senjin smiled. "The 'subject,' " he said in Dr. Muku's ear, "has not killed only women. Young women, beautiful women." He was throwing the psychiatrist's words back at him. "You were wrong, Doctor. About me. About everything."

There was a smell in the room, emanating from Dr. Muku, and Senjin's tongue appeared between his parted lips, curling slightly, questing for more of the scent. It was the stench of death.

Senjin shifted his gaze, staring into Dr. Muku's wildly rolling right eye. Tears were streaming from it, and with one finger, Senjin wiped them away. The pupil was dilated, as if the psychiatrist were an addict. Senjin wished that Dr. Muku could tell him what the pain, the fear, were like. Surely his analytical brain could make sense of the chaos, could separate the rage of sensation into easily recognizable components.

"Muku-san, what is it?" Senjin asked. "What is happening to you?"

There was an entire world in that one teary eye, defined by agony, detailed with the increments of knowledge at the approach of death.

Then the eye fixed on something even Senjin could not see.

Dr. Muku, burning still from the phosphorus embedded in his skull, lay slumped against the back of his chair. He looked quite relaxed now, Senjin thought.

Senjin reached past the body, jerked open the drawer of the wooden side table. He grunted, extracting the mini tape recorder. The reels were slowly churning, faithfully recording every word, every sound uttered in the room. Senjin had suspected that the doctor had begun taping their sessions as soon as Senjin had given him enough clues for him to form his opinion that Senjin and the "subject" were one and the same.

Senjin depressed the stop button, pocketed the device. Then he looked at Dr. Muku. "You'll never know how wrong you really were," he said.

With slitted eyes he looked into the blinding sun of his memory, remembering each aftermath of the Kabuki play, *Musume Dojoji*. How he would treat his dates to an expansive dinner, encourage them to dissect the psychological motivations of the two major characters. And how, sated on these odd appetizers, he would then proceed to the main course, the slow, aching, erotic discipline of murder.

Senjin pulled the curtains on that lambent sunlight, bent, hefted the corpse onto his shoulder. In a way, he thought, it was a pity that Dr. Muku could no longer answer him. But then again, Dr. Muku still had another—more important—service to perform.

Clearly, Dr. Hanami did not believe him. Nicholas had finished his account, starting with his vague feelings of unease in the hospital after the operation, his trying and failing to stem the postoperative pain, to the events of the last twenty-four hours, which proved conclusively that he had lost the use of *Getsumei no michi* and every other aspect of the martial arts he had painstakingly learned over the years.

Dr. Hanami had sat back, steepled his fingers, and said with absolute finality, "But my dear Mr. Linnear, what you are suggesting is patently impossible. You may well *think* that you have, as you say, lost these admittedly remarkable abilities, but let me assure you that you have not."

He extracted a set of X rays from Nicholas's file, turned and snapped them into place against a pair of light boxes mounted on the wall behind his desk. He switched the boxes on. "See here"—he pointed to a shadow —"is where the tumor lay, along the second temporal convolution, just above the hippocampal fissure. You can see its outline here." He switched his attention to the second X ray. "Now here we are after the operation. As you can see, there is a perfect fitting of the folds. The surrounding area was left absolutely undisturbed. Of this there can be no question, Mr. Linnear. None at all."

"Then what happened to me, Doctor?"

Dr. Hanami considered this for some time. Very deliberately, he switched off the light boxes, pulled the X-ray film down, slid them back into the folder. Then he closed the file, clasped his hands over the top. "It's difficult in these cases to be certain, but it seems to me that we could begin by asking not what happened to you, but rather, what *is happening* to you." Dr. Hanami smiled encouragingly. "After a major operation of this nature it is not at all abnormal for the patient to believe that some part of him has been excised along with the nonbeneficial tissue." He drew a small pad toward him, scribbled a name and a phone number. He ripped off the sheet, gave it to Nicholas.

"What is this?"

"Dr. Muku is preeminent in the field of psychotherapy, Mr. Linnear. His office is right across the—"

"That's what you think I need?" Nicholas said, incredulous. "A psychiatrist?"

"Given your present emotional state, I think it would be highly bene—"

"You haven't gotten it yet, have you, Doctor?" Nicholas was livid. "Someone—maybe it was you—did something to me while I was on the operating table. For Christ's sake, tell me what happened!"

"Linnear-san, you must calm yourself," Dr. Hanami said, resorting once again to age-old rituals in order to quell the modern demons that seemed to have invaded his office. "These outbursts will do no one any good, least of all yourself. When you have returned to a state of serenity, you will be able to see everything in its proper light."

"You're not going to tell me, are you?"

"Linnear-san, I assure you there is nothing more I can tell you." He glanced again at Nicholas's file, as if to give added weight to his words. "Your operation was successful in every way. As for your claim, I can find no medical reason to—"

Dr. Hanami stopped. He looked up, realizing that his patient was already gone.

Nicholas had lost faith. He saw in a flash of terrible clarity that all his training had been in vain. He saw that without *Getsumei no michi* he was nothing. His spirit, diminished because he had been denied his ultimate place of refuge, of intimacy with the world around him, of strength, was withering. Cut off from the kind of communion with the universe that had sustained him through his most painful ordeals, which had nourished him during his brief stab as a family man and a businessman, he felt like the lone survivor of a shipwreck, cast upon a hostile and alien shore.

He thought of his mother, Cheong, and knew there was only one thing for him to do now. His mind flew back in time to the dreadful autumn of 1963, when he had fallen hopelessly in love with Yukio and had, thus, incurred the wrath of his cousin Saigo.

Nicholas, Cheong had said to him, *your grandfather, So-Peng, was a very wise man. It was he who said one is never truly alone in Asia.* Cheong had drawn out a box made of copper. Nicholas had seen it once before, when his father had shown it to him, a legacy of his grandfather, So-Peng. On its enameled and elaborately lacquered top was a fiery, scaled dragon entwined with a rampant tiger.

Carefully, almost reverently, Cheong had opened the box. Inside were four rows of glittering emeralds, fifteen in all.

You are free to use six of these emeralds, she had said. *To convert them into money if your need is sufficient. Originally there were sixteen. One was used to buy this house.* She had taken a deep breath. *There must never be less than nine emeralds in here. Ever. No matter the reason, you must not use more than six.*

As you know, Nicholas, my father, So-Peng, gave your father and me this box when we left Singapore. It is a mystical box. It has certain powers. She had paused, as if waiting. *I see you're not smiling. Good. I believe in the power of this box, the nine emeralds, as did So-Peng. He was a great and wise man in all things, Nicholas. He was no fool. He knew well that there exist on the Asian continent many things that defy analysis; which, perhaps, have no place in the modern world. They relate to another set of laws; they are timeless.* She had smiled gently. *So I believe. If you believe, then the power will be there for you when someday you need it.*

Nicholas believed in the legacy of his grandfather, the power of the fifteen emeralds in the mystic box. He had put away the treasure, secreting it within his house when he and Justine had returned to Japan. For while he had no intention of ever using the emeralds, he wanted them near him, could feel their pulse in his heart as one feels sunlight warming one's flesh.

Cast adrift, Nicholas knew that he had to get home as quickly as he could. Now he understood that the time had come to put the magic of the emeralds to work.

He had lost faith. Now he understood, and the terror flooded fully through him. It was not merely that he had lost his ability to find *Getsumei no michi,* not merely that he had lost his memory of his ninjutsu training. He had lost faith in everything he had believed in.

There could be only one explanation for that: *Shiro Ninja.*

It was clear that if he was indeed *Shiro Ninja,* Dr. Hanami had not been responsible for his loss of memory; it was not a medical problem at all. He almost turned around then, so he could apologize to Dr. Hanami, but he was too wrapped up in his own fear.

Somewhere in Tokyo he had an enemy, one of such power that it beggared the imagination. Who could it be? Why had he been rendered powerless through *Shiro Ninja*?

Nicholas, shivering, imagined himself amid the vapor of his recent nightmares, and shuddered. He imagined that the emeralds' magic could save him from drowning in that colorless vapor. Falling and drowning. Part of him, perhaps, even suspected that his grandfather So-Peng had known this day would come and had prepared him for it by ensuring that he would receive the box, just as once the Colonel and Cheong had received it.

So-Peng. Cheong had told him so much about her father, yet increasingly now, when Nicholas thought of him, he realized how little he knew of the man and his life. Much less than he did about the Colonel's English parents—his father, a middle-class London banker, level-headed, honest, content; his mother, a wealthy Jewess who, despite her money, was never accepted in English society, dark-haired, green-eyed, tempestuous, curious, and very smart. She had had two sons, one of whom, William, had died of smallpox. Three years later, in the winter of 1915, she had given birth to Denis, Nicholas's father.

Nicholas was so wrapped up in his thoughts of the past that he failed to see the young woman heading into Dr. Hanami's office as he left it. They hit head-on, even though she tried to step hurriedly back. Startled, Nicholas automatically apologized, began to move toward the elevator bank.

"Linnear-san!"

He turned, found the woman following him. "You are Nicholas Linnear."

There seemed no interrogative in her inflection, but he said yes just the same.

"Hello. I'm Tomi Yazawa. Detective Sergeant with the homicide division of the Tokyo police." She flashed him her credentials, which he studied with the kind of amused curiosity he normally reserved for outlandish headlines in tabloids.

"Good morning, Miss Yazawa," he said. "How is it you know who I am?"

"I'm looking for you, Mr. Linnear."

"Indeed. Well, perhaps some other time. This really isn't the best—"

The elevator doors opened and Nicholas got in. Tomi followed.

"Ah, persistence," Nicholas said. His mind was far away from Tomi Yazawa and what she might want of him. Whatever it was, he decided, it could wait for a more propitious moment.

"Persistence is a required course at the academy," Tomi said.

If Nicholas recognized this as a joke, he gave no sign of it. All he wanted to do was get down and out of there.

"I appreciate that this may not be the best time for you," Tomi said, "but I must talk with you immediately."

Nicholas discovered that he was gripping a piece of paper in his left hand. He uncrumpled it, saw there in Dr. Hanami's hurried scrawl the name and phone number of Dr. Muku, the psychiatrist, which the surgeon had given him. He wondered briefly why no address had been included. Then he saw the suite number and realized that Dr. Muku must have his offices in this same megabuilding. Cozy, he thought. How many patients did the two cross-pollinate? He imagined the two doctors as tennis players, sending their patients back and forth across the net, picking up finders' fees with every swing. With an angry growl he mashed the paper into a ball, flung it against the brushed bronze of the elevator wall.

"Mr. Linnear—"

The doors opened on the enormous lobby dominated by a sculpture composed of black rock, waterfall, and foliage, and Nicholas strode purposefully out.

Tomi bent, snatched up the crumpled slip of paper. She had just a moment to glance at what was written in it before she hurried out after him. She caught up with Nicholas near the automatic doors. They were glazed a soft bronze color so that the sunlight coming through them was devoid of heat.

"Mr. Linnear, please—"

"Some other time, Sergeant Yazawa." Nicholas went through the doors.

Out on the street Tomi said forcefully, "I must speak with you on a matter of life or death, Mr. Linnear. Your life. Your death." This gave him pause, and she took advantage of it. "I wanted to tell you in a more politic manner, but you leave me no choice. According to a communiqué we intercepted and decoded late yesterday, you have been marked for assassination by the Red Army one week from today. I have been—"

Tomi broke off as a scream reverberated against the mammoth facade of the sky-rise. An instant later the sun was momentarily blotted out as a shape hurtled to the sidewalk not ten yards from where they were standing.

"Jesus!" Nicholas breathed. "A jumper!"

Tomi had broken away from him and was threading her way through the already gathering crowd. Nicholas went after her, saw her kneeling by the side of a male figure. He had landed on the small of his back, and his spine and legs were broken in so many places that his shape had already ceased to resemble anything human. Blood seeped along the sidewalk in a spiderweb pattern radiating out from the broken body. Bits of glass shimmered on the concrete, here and there pink and red and dark brown.

Gingerly, Tomi reached out, turned the head toward them. The back was completely smashed in, but the face, though bloodstreaked, was recognizable.

"God almighty!" Nicholas said, and Tomi looked up.

"Do you know this man, Mr. Linnear?"

Nicholas nodded. "That's Dr. Hanami, the surgeon who operated on me." He looked up, could see the darkness like an open mouth where the window to Dr. Hanami's consulting office had been.

Tomi and Nicholas pushed their way through the gesticulating mob. Inside the building Tomi showed her credentials to a uniformed attendant, told her what had happened, to call the police. Then they took the elevator up.

"By all rights," Tomi said, "you shouldn't be coming with me. We have no idea what happened up there."

Nicholas said nothing, looked at her.

"He could have jumped," Tomi went on. "Or he could have been pushed."

"Why would someone want to murder a surgeon?" Nicholas asked.

"A grudge for malpractice?" Tomi shrugged. "Why does the Red Army want you dead?"

Nicholas continued to look at her. "You tell me. I haven't the faintest idea."

"I'm allowing you to come with me," Tomi said, continuing a previous thought, "because I have been assigned as your bodyguard. I'm on the scene of a potential crime, so I've got to respond. You've got to accompany me."

"Otherwise you would have stopped me?"

"Yes," Tomi said. "I would have stopped you."

"How?" Nicholas leaned toward her. He was not in the mood for either idle bluffs or for tough talk from someone he didn't know.

The doors opened and they raced across the hall to Dr. Hanami's office suite. They burst through the door to confront the white-faced receptionist who stared wide-eyed at them. She had her arms around a hunched woman, obviously a patient, who was sobbing in great, inconstant gasps.

"I've called the police," the receptionist said to no one in particular, but she nodded as Tomi identified herself. She pointed to a closed door to her right. "In there. The doctor's inner office."

"Who was the doctor's last patient?" Tomi asked.

"Well, he was," the receptionist said, pointing to Nicholas.

"Was anyone with the doctor after Linnear-san left?"

"I don't know," the receptionist said. "The doctor asked me to leave him this hour free."

"You saw no one go in there after Linnear-san left?"

"No."

"Stay here," Tomi said to Nicholas.

"Like hell," he said, but seeing the gun in her hand, he kept well back.

Tomi turned the knob, threw the door wide open. Wind rattled the vertical metal blinds that had been ripped from their bottom moorings. To the left of the window was Dr. Hanami's paper-strewn desk, his high-backed chair turned away from them as if he had leaped from it to the window. They saw that a side chair, leaning up against the sill, had been used to break the glass of the sealed window.

"Well, one thing we know," Nicholas said. "It wasn't an accident."

Tomi went across the small room to the door on the opposite side. "What do we have here?"

She put her gun up, jerked the door open. "This leads right out into the hallway," she said, peering out. "If Dr. Hanami was murdered, this was how his murderer got in and out without being seen by the receptionist."

Tomi closed the door, went over to the shattered window, looking for blood, a note, or any other sign that might tell her whether Dr. Hanami's death had been a suicide or a murder. She stared out the ruptured window at the vaporous city below. "God, it's a long way down."

"Sergeant."

Tomi started at Nicholas's voice, which was not loud but nevertheless got her attention. She looked in the direction in which he was staring. From this angle she could see Dr. Hanami's high-backed chair in profile. There was a hand lying along the armrest.

Tomi took three quick steps, spun the chair around to face them. They saw a small, roly-poly man of middle age in a gray pinstriped suit. His long, unruly hair stood up from his scalp as if he had been delivered an electric shock. Wire-rimmed glasses were perched on his pale forehead as if he were plunged deep in thought.

Tomi could not help but let out a gasp as the corpse's one blackened, ruined eye socket stared blankly at her.

"Jesus," Nicholas said, "who the hell is this?"

"What the hell happened to him?" Tomi was peering at the lethal wound. "This is horrific." Close to the corpse there was an unmistakable smell of roasted flesh. "He was burned with something small and very hot."

"It must have had penetrating power," Nicholas said.

Tomi moved back, took a pencil off the desktop, used it to lift up part of the corpse's unbuttoned jacket. Carefully, she extracted a wallet from the corpse's breast pocket. Dropping it on the desk, she opened it with the pencil point.

"Dr. Jugo Muku," she read from a driver's license. She looked up. "Wait a minute!" She took out the piece of paper Nicholas had thrown in the elevator and which she had picked up. Unfolding it again, she said, "Linnear-san, you had Dr. Muku's name when I first met you." She looked at him.

"Dr. Hanami give it to me," Nicholas said. He was staring at the mutilated face of Dr. Muku. "He was under the impression that I needed psychological help."

"There's a phone number here," Tomi said. "And another number, but no address."

"It's a suite number," Nicholas said. "Dr. Muku's office is in this building."

"I think we ought to take a look," Tomi said. She went back past the window. As she did, she noticed something on one of the remaining shards of glass. She moved closer, stared hard at it.

"Linnear-san," she said in a breathless voice, "what color was Dr. Hanami's hair?" There had been too much blood and spattered brains to make such a determination from the corpse.

"Gray," Nicholas said, coming closer. "And he used some kind of hair cream." He was looking at the spot that had caught Tomi's attention. Several strands of iron-gray hair, wet-looking, clung wretchedly to the sharp point of a glass shard. "It looks like his."

"Which could mean," Tomi said, "that he went through the window headfirst. No one would do that, even a suicide."

"You mean he might have been thrown."

Tomi was busily gathering the evidence into a glassine envelope. "It's looking more and more likely. Then there's Dr. Muku's death to con—"

She looked up as a shadow registered on the extreme periphery of her vision. She stared, open-mouthed, as if she were in one of those dreams where unthinkable calamity is about to strike and, shouting a warning, one finds that one's voice is gone.

The black form had coalesced into a distinct shape: that of a human figure. It was clothed completely in matte black, so that Tomi could not see even its face. It rose up from outside the bottom lip of the window. Her brain was frozen in shock. The figure was on the *outside* of the building.

Such a thing was impossible, Tomi knew that. And yet her brain was reacting to what her eyes were showing it. The figure appeared in a split instant. Tomi felt her heart give a painful lurch. She felt as if she were in an elevator in free-fall. Her stomach dropped, her bowels turned to water.

Even so, as the figure was silently swinging in toward her, part of her mind had given instructions for her right hand to grab her pistol, bring it up.

Time ran abruptly out. The figure crashed into her with such force that it drove all breath from her lungs. She flew backward with barely a sound, tumbling over Dr. Hanami's cypress-wood coffee table, dislodging its heavy glass top.

The top of her spine slammed against the side wall, her head snapped back and blue lights flashed, a jolt of pain causing her to cry out at last. But that sound was drowned out by the shattering of the tabletop. Groggy and nauseous, Tomi tried to get up, fell heavily back. She was fighting just to breathe.

All this had taken no more than a second or two. Time enough for the old Nicholas to have turned, assessed the situation, and begun a tactical strategy against the unknown assailant.

But this was another Nicholas entirely. His mind, unfocused, without the ability to "sink in," without his beloved *Getsumei no michi*, was unable to react in any meaningful or coordinated way to the attack on Tomi.

He understood that whoever had murdered Dr. Muku had probably thrown Dr. Hanami out the window. He understood that this individual had been hanging outside the shattered window, clinging to the concrete and steel of the sky-rise's skin like a fly. He suspected, further, that from the deliberateness of the attack on Tomi, the murderer seemed to have been waiting coolly for them.

There was nothing wrong with Nicholas's capacity for *reasoning*. It was his ability to translate the reasoning into action that had been taken from him.

Now he confronted the black-garbed figure and knew that he faced a ninja. Only a ninja could have planned out and executed two such bizarre murders. Only a ninja could have clung to the sheer side of a building twenty stories up, swung in through a shattered window, taken out a trained and armed police officer with such ease.

Nicholas felt a resurgence of the cold fear slithering in his gut. It could be no coincidence, he knew, that just when he had lost his powers, he was confronting another ninja.

It was true, then. He was *Shiro Ninja*. Defenseless and under attack. Which meant that this figure was more than a ninja. Far more and far less.

Nicholas said a silent prayer.

The figure, which had been momentarily still and silent, erupted into a fury of motion. Dimly Nicholas recognized that this was something he had once been able to do.

He tried to prepare himself for the coming attack as best he could, but the figure was upon him before he could get his mind to function properly.

Pain exploded along nerve meridians in chest, abdomen, and pelvis, and like a line of dominoes beginning to fall, Nicholas felt first one section, then another paralyzed by short, vicious blows to various nexus points. The pain was not localized to the target of each strike; because of the nature of the blows, it ripped through the interconnecting nerve network within his body.

His muscles bunched and knotted, betraying him at every turn, spasming with the bursts of nerve pain, overlapping so that they began to have a cumulative effect on him, magnifying exponentially their debilitating impact.

The assault was methodical, almost scientific in the way it dissected his body into quadrants. Nicholas knew without being able to do anything about it that he was being put out an inch at a time. To achieve victory was one thing; this was quite another. It was a clinical demonstration of total domination. Nicholas's spirit withered in utter despair at both his helplessness and the hopelessness of his plight. Unable to turn his back on *ninjutsu*, how was he ever going to live *Shiro Ninja*?

The answer was, of course, obvious. He wasn't going to live. He was going to die.

This was the ultimate lesson of this unrelenting assault.

Tomi was against the side wall, the effects of the figure's initial attack wearing off. Gasping, trying to shake off the dizziness that had gripped her, she became aware that she no longer held her pistol.

She was aware of the figure's attack on Nicholas, and desperately she searched for her gun. She found it lying on the floor several yards away from her outstretched right hand. With a pain-filled groan she pushed herself from the wall, began to crawl toward the gun. Her hand touched it, then closed around the grips. An instant later she was pointing it at the back of the figure's head. She was about to pull the trigger when she realized with a sickening lurch that she was aiming at Nicholas.

"Shit," she said under her breath, and trying a bluff, shouted, "Get off him or I'll shoot!"

The figure turned so that Nicholas's head and upper torso were between him and Tomi. "Go ahead." It was a rasp of a voice, a chilling sound much like fingernails being scratched down a blackboard. "Shoot me. Or will it be him?"

Tomi got a sudden intuition that made the short hairs at the back of her neck stand up. She knew the figure was laughing at her behind his mask.

Then she saw the glint of a tiny blade at Nicholas's throat. "Put down the weapon," the raspy voice said, "or I'll kill him now." As a demonstration of his determination, he drew blood.

Tomi put down her gun.

"Kick it away from you," the voice instructed.

She did as she was told, and was instantly sorry. She saw as if in slow motion the figure release Nicholas. It rose up eerily, spectrally, just as it had from beyond the window. Without appearing to have moved at all, its shape ballooned out.

Tomi realized that it crossed the space between them in some manner totally unknown to her. She felt herself drawn up by a power beyond her comprehension. Then the top of her head was jammed against the wall. Her cry of astonishment and pain was swiftly cut off as she lost consciousness.

The figure dropped her in a heap and turned. Nicholas was crawling toward where Tomi had kicked her gun. It was a measure of his extreme despair that he had forsaken the arsenal of weapons within himself in an effort to lunge at a mechanical one.

In one fluid motion the figure lifted Nicholas as easily as an instant before it had lifted Tomi and threw him headlong across the room. Nicholas crashed into the desktop, sliding across its surface, his near-paralyzed body collapsing onto the floor between the desk and the ruined window.

The figure came around the desk, moving easily, deliberately, but without hurry. It picked Nicholas up and headed with him toward the window.

Nicholas divined his intent and did the only thing he could. He spread-eagled his body in order to stop the figure from maneuvering him through the opening of the window.

He could hear the figure laughing. It was an awful sound, like a mass of pinpricks on the skin. "Do you think that will save you?"

Nicholas gave a low groan as a high-percussion blow landed on his right shoulder. His arm went numb, dropped to his side. With the next blow to his left shoulder, Nicholas bit his lower lip to stop himself from crying out with the pain. His right leg was next, then his left leg. He was going through the window.

Still, he struggled, as the organism must when it senses the end of its existence being thrust rudely upon it. Numbed as he was, Nicholas flailed and thrashed, struggling inch by inch to hold on to the window frame.

Using his shoulders and buttocks, he wedged himself in, defying the figure to push him through the last part of the opening. Heavy strikes landed on his upper arms, his thighs. He ignored them, set his mind on remaining immobile.

Then he was struck on the side of his head, close to the spot that was still healing. It was too much. His body, stretched beyond its tolerance, slumped in the aperture, and he was pushed all the way through.

The sky-rises of Tokyo, smoky and somehow unreal, were tilting, coming up to meet him. Nicholas could feel his heart thumping heavily in his chest. The roar of his pulse was like the sighing of the wind in his ears.

For what seemed an endless moment he hung suspended twenty stories above the street. He could imagine the next instant, the plunge through the air, tumbling slowly head over heels, the pavement rushing up to meet him. He would be inside his recurring dream, falling through the vapor, endlessly falling. Only this time he would not wake up.

Staring down into the heat of Shinjuku, Nicholas heard the last pitiful cry of his daughter. He prepared himself to die.

Then, almost before he knew it, he was pulled back inside the building. The figure's hooded face was very close to his. "If you die now, if you die too easily," the figure said, "you will never understand. And with comprehension will come the certainty of despair. That will crush you far more thoroughly than defeat ever will."

The figure delivered a blow, short, concise, and accurate, to the side of Nicholas's neck.

Vapor curling like an adder's tongue, hiding in its midst secrets too horrifying to endure.

Blackness.

After a brief stay at the hospital, after giving as complete a statement to the police as he could muster, after Justine had arrived with Nangi, she white-faced but with her panic, thankfully, under control, after spending a restless, pain-laced night in the hospital, after deflecting for the moment Justine and Nangi's queries, Nicholas came home.

He had seen Tomi in the hospital, discovered that she was just badly shaken up, that the CAT scan had shown no sign of concussion in her as it had done in him.

Because of the mild concussion, the hospital had insisted that he stay a week to receive a battery of further tests and to be monitored. Nicholas insisted on leaving right away. They compromised with an overnight stay, during which he was given a second CAT scan. Apparently, that had shown no further complications, because Nicholas found himself home by noon the following day.

Justine said that Tomi had already been in to see him twice while he had been asleep. She had told Justine to call her when she got Nicholas home and that she would come out to see him.

At home he went straight into his workout room. With an effort that set his head pounding, he pushed aside the padded post. Beneath it he took up a tatami mat, used his fingernails to remove a small door set flush with the underfloor boards.

Beneath was a small steel-reinforced chamber that Nicholas had built himself just after he and Justine had moved in. Now he lifted out a copper box. On it was lacquered the brothers dragon and tiger, the gift that his grandfather So-Peng had given to Colonel Denis Linnear and which now belonged to Nicholas.

With trembling fingers Nicholas opened the box. Inside were sixteen indentations in the dark blue velvet, one for each mystic emerald. One emerald had been used by the Colonel to buy his house in Japan.

Remember, Nicholas, he heard his mother say to him, *there must never be less than nine emeralds in here.*

"Ahh . . ."

There was such relief in Nicholas's voice that Justine came running. "Nick, what is it?" she asked. "What's happened?"

"The fifteen emeralds are still here," Nicholas breathed. Then he looked up at her, as he locked the box away. "Justine, you must never tell anyone—not even Nangi—what you have just seen. These emeralds are special—mystical. They are a legacy from my grandfather So-Peng, and must never be used or spoken of." He pushed the tatami back into place, drew the post over them. "Promise me, Justine!"

"I promise."

Nicholas rose, a bit unsteadily, the words of his attacker echoing inside him, *If you die now, if you die too easily, you will never understand.*

Why didn't he kill me when he had the chance? Nicholas asked himself. What fate has he saved me for?

SINGAPORE/PENINSULA MALAYSIA

SUMMER, 1889

So-Peng, Nicholas Linnear's grandfather, was born into a family of undistinguished Chinese merchants, hard-working men who nevertheless toiled their entire lives beneath the frustrating weight of ill fortune.

His mother was something else altogether.

So-Peng's family had been in Peninsula Malaysia, it was said, since the 1400s, trading variously in silk, tortoiseshell, and ivory. Early in the 1800s they had moved to Kuala Lumpur, on the peninsula's west coast, attracted by the breathtakingly quick fortunes to be made in the newly opened tin mines. The vast sums of money they made were soon gone, as they gambled, made incautious investments, or were swindled outright.

Still, they persevered, a virtue that must have been in their genes because it was passed down to So-Peng.

So-Peng had spent the first ten years of his life near Pahang, on the east coast, where his father was then involved in importing silks and black teas from China. So-Peng, however, had little interest in being a merchant and none at all in being burdened by ill fortune. He was far more clever than his father and his uncles, almost as quick-witted at nineteen as his mother was at thirty-four.

So-Peng was so like his mother, Liang. She had been a child bride, had borne him when she was but fifteen. No one knew her origins—whether she was Hokkien like So-Peng's father, whether she was Chinese at all, fully Chinese, or, as was sometimes said, Sumatran. She never spoke of her origins and, out of respect, So-Peng never asked her, though he often burned with curiosity.

So-Peng's mother was very smart. She knew everyone of importance everywhere the family lived for more than a few weeks, and what was more important, these people often owed her favors. So-Peng knew that she had saved his father from absolute insolvency more than once by her rather miraculous intervention. She managed to do so, moreover, without causing her husband any loss of face.

By 1889, when he was nineteen, So-Peng had accomplished many things. He was, for instance, proficient in an astonishing array of Asian and ancient Indo-European languages and dialects. Having spent his upper school years in Singapura, the Lion's City, as Singapore had been named in 1100 A.D. by lords of the Srivijayan empire, he had the advantage of not only the best teachers in Malaysia, but also the best opportunities that the labyrinth of backstreets overflowing with canny Chinese, Malays, Indians, and Sumatrans could offer.

He had worked on the city's docks, in its wholesale markets, its bars, restaurants, and hotels, had even shipped out for six months on one of the new steamships that had more and more been replacing the merchant clipper ships ever since the Suez Canal had been opened in 1869, cutting down on the distance between Europe and Asia. He had immediately grasped what others would not for some time: with the advent of the steamship, Singapore would burgeon in importance as a major port. Hitherto, the settlement had been wholly dependent on the winds for its naval trade. January and February brought the northeast monsoon winds which were favorable for the junks from Siam and China. Six months later, in the autumn, the winds shifted, bringing the boats from the subcontinental Malay Peninsula. Ships under their own power would free Singapore from the whims of the weather; trade could continue the year round.

So-Peng had, in other words, tried his hand at many jobs, and had become master of none. At nineteen, in fact, though his mind was full of knowledge, he had no profession and, what was worse, he was penniless.

His fondest memory of his childhood before he had moved with his family to Singapore was of warm May nights when he and his best friend, a Malay named Zhao Hsia, would sneak out of their houses and rendezvous to sit amid the foliage ringing the beach at Rantau Abang.

So-Peng could clearly see the host of stars, blue-white, blue-green, and red, strung across the heavens. The two boys were enveloped by them as completely as they were by the croaking of the tree frogs, the cries of the night birds, the incessant clicking of the insects, the stirring of the palm fronds.

Before them starlight and—if they were lucky—moonlight as well, illuminated the churning surf, and farther out, on the South China Sea, they could see the winking lights of swift ships bound southeast for Borneo or northwest for Thailand.

But as much as they loved this spot in the night, So-Peng and Zhao Hsia had not come to the beach to stare at the stars or the passing boats. Neither had they come to swim.

Soon their gazes lowered from the star-strewn sky, moved closer than the silvered wavetops, the shadowed troughs of the South China Sea. They watched, instead, the progress of the surf as it rolled up onto the dark beach, retreating only to return again, an indomitable force—the creator—upon the sand.

And from the saltwater they at last saw emerging the black, humped shapes for which they had been waiting. The shapes were enormous as they detached themselves from the waves. The surf churned all around them, and they left this, too, in their wake. As So-Peng watched, he seemed thrown back a million years to another age, another time. He whispered to them in Vedic, a language so ancient that he was certain they would understand it.

Within the sheltering sands the shapes ceased to move. Soon, above the hiss and suck of the surf, beyond the insects' drone, the boys could hear the peculiar sound of sand being stirred and moved.

So-Peng and Zhao Hsia waited, learning patience. For this was the end of May, the beginning of giant tortoise season. The boys were here clandestinely. The tortoise of this region was much prized by the Malays and the Chinese for a number of reasons, not the least of which was that the animal's domed carapace was a lucrative source of revenue exported out of the peninsula. What the boys were here to do was strictly forbidden—haram, Zhao Hsia, who knew many Muslims, would say, although this was civil custom and not religious law. If they had been caught, they would have been thrown into prison, and So-Peng suspected that not even his mother would be able to intervene successfully on his behalf.

There were already tortoises on the beach. So-Peng and Zhao Hsia looked at one another. They were physically ill-suited as friends. So-Peng was already tall, towering over the chubby Malay with a sinewy grace that seemed all the more pronounced in Zhao Hsia's presence. But they shared a daring and an unquenchable curiosity that transcended dictates and custom. They were natural explorers, drawn together by their fascination of the different and the bizarre.

Slowly, the boys crawled out from the shelter of the foliage, snaking their way along the sand on their bellies. When they came upon a tortoise, Zhao Hsia touched its horny carapace. So-Peng, fascinated, watched in the dim starlight as its head and legs withdrew into its shell, rendering the fiercely protective creatures harmless. Then they turned the tortoise over and took its eggs.

Back within the chittering shadows of the ferns and fronds, they carefully cracked open the eggs, drank the viscous insides. They smacked their lips, making contented noises as they gorged themselves on this forbidden delicacy.

When So-Peng was almost eleven he and his family had moved to Singapore. Afterward he often wondered what had happened to Zhao Hsia and whether the two of them would ever lie again in the unquiet darkness of Rantau Abang, waiting for the forbidden to come their way.

In Singapore's wide-open atmosphere, it was perhaps surprising that So-Peng had never been involved in anything illegal. What was even more surprising, however, was that it took the murders to bring So-Peng to his true vocation.

Two shipping merchants were murdered within ten days of each other. It was during the height of the summer, the hottest in recent memory, when the sun, white and bloated, simmered even the normally cooler Singapore quayside. The ocean lay flat and listless; not a breath of air stirred on its own, and the breezes created indoors by the ceiling fans moved like sludge against a pier piling.

The murders horrified a community normally inured to death. The British authorities said it was the work of smugglers involved in their internecine warfare. Because the murders occurred on the fourth and the fourteenth of the month, and four was the number of death, the Chinese were certain that the murders were some form of retribution by relatives for the victims' past sins. Revenge was the motive given by the Malays as well, who pointed out that a pig's foot was found in the mouths of both Muslim victims—pork is strictly *haram* to Muslims. But they were just as certain that the murderers were Western because it was their opinion that no Muslim, and certainly no Buddhist, would so profane the strictures of religion.

Liang, So-Peng's mother, had another theory entirely. She had seen the curious eight-pointed metal stars that the police had extracted from the throats of the two corpses, and one night at evening meal she put a name to their murderer: tanjian.

Tanjian, she said, had no god, followed no religion, and thus had no compunction about behaving blasphemously. Tanjian, she said, created their own laws, adhered to their own peculiar dictates which deviated radically from those of society. They were, she said, kingdoms unto their own selves, harnessers of the night and of every evil thing that made their home in the darkness.

All this talk was meant, of course, to frighten So-Peng's brothers and sisters. Liang possessed the very yang—that is, male—quality of using fear as a way to discipline her children. She was more involved in her children than she was in anything else, which was, So-Peng supposed, a direct result of having married a man such as his father. He had no interest in his children save that they were the inevitable result of the sex act, in which he appeared to have a great deal of interest.

When So-Peng was alone with his mother, she said to him, "Now nothing will keep them from their studies."

"You mean all that about the tanjian was a lie?" So-Peng asked.

"It was not a lie," she said. "Neither was it the truth."

So-Peng thought a moment. "Is this a puzzle?"

She smiled at him, an expression filled with pride. "You are so grown-up," she said.

She left him to go to her own chambers. Alone in the kitchen, So-Peng considered what she had said, and as he restlessly wandered the house, he considered the nature of the puzzle she had left for him. Their house was large, in a wealthy area of the city, for his father, at Liang's urging, had two years ago invested in a new firm that had begun to import rattan, black pepper, and giant nutmeg from Borneo. The venture had so far proven highly successful.

After a time the silence in the house proved oppressive. Outside he heard young voices raised in anger, and passing through the garden, he went out in the street.

He saw two of his younger brothers and several of their friends facing off against one another like two armies on a field of battle. Between them a small yellow dog stood, yelping, its bony hindquarters quivering, its tail tucked between its legs.

One of So-Peng's brothers had a firm grip on the ruff of the dog's neck, unmindful of its obvious terror. He kept pulling the unfortunate animal toward his side of the street while one or another of the other boys tried to drag the dog to their side.

"This is our dog!" So-Peng's brother said defiantly.

"No, it's ours!" the most aggressive of the other boys cried. He had a flat face that reflected his anger like a mirror.

"We found him first," another of So-Peng's brothers said hotly. "He belongs to us."

"You found him near our house!" the flat-faced boy shouted, growing ever more angry. "That makes him ours. And it makes you thieves!"

"You're the criminals!" So-Peng's brother said, heaving on the panting dog. He pointed to dark scars upon the creature's flanks where the fur had failed to grow back. "Look how you have mistreated him! You are hateful!"

"We hate you more!" the other boys shouted.

Watching the intensifying fight, So-Peng felt himself grow unutterably sad. To others, perhaps, the incident might appear trivial, quickly forgotten. But So-Peng saw in this childhood acrimony the seeds of something far larger. He recognized the universal, inevitable conflict of man, the image of the eventual usurpation of the world by those not content with what they had, or those too poor to have anything of their own. The need for conquest had risen full-blown out of innocence like a Hydra in a glade of dancing poppies. The long march into the night of the spirit had already begun.

So-Peng advanced upon the opposing would-be armies just as fists began to shake, stones picked up from the gutter. In a moment the former friends would surely come to blows.

Reaching in between the boys, he seized the cringing, whimpering dog, the only truly innocent party in this dispute. He picked it up, cradling it as he stroked its quivering flanks. In a moment its head turned and it began to lick his hand.

"This animal belongs to neither of you," he said.

"But, brother—"

So-Peng's fierce stare cut off his brother's protest.

"We want him!" cried the flat-faced boy. "He's ours!"

"And what would you do with him," So-Peng said, turning on the lad, "beat him some more?"

"I never beat him!" the boy said in that defiant way children have that makes it clear they are lying.

"But you kicked him," So-Peng said, reaching briefly out to touch the boy with his spirit. "You punished him just as your parents punish you. Is that not the truth?" He watched as, tongue-tied, the lad merely hung his head.

"You see?" So-Peng's brother said triumphantly. "We were right!"

"And what would *you* do with the animal?" So-Peng asked his younger brother.

The boy shrugged. "Keep him. Let him go. I don't know. What's the difference?"

So-Peng said, "Did you think of how you would care for him?"

"Care for him?" So-Peng's brother wrinkled his nose in confusion. "He's just a dog."

"Look at him. He's frightened and in pain, just as sometimes you are. How can I expect you to understand. You are all too selfish, thinking of yourselves and nothing else. None of you deserve his friendship or his love." The contempt in So-Peng's voice was so evident it penetrated their childish shells.

"What will happen to him?" the flat-faced boy asked.

"I will take him away," So-Peng said.

"But we're used to having him around," the flat-faced boy said.

So-Peng said nothing, continued to stroke the dog's flanks. The animal put its head on his arm, sighed contentedly, closed its eyes.

"I don't want him to go," the flat-faced boy said suddenly. "I think— Hey, we can take care of him."

"Yeah," So-Peng's brother chimed in. "We'd *all* take care of him, wouldn't we?"

"Yeah!" they all cried.

"Maybe we could train him or something," another boy said.

"Like a watchdog!" another of So-Peng's brothers continued.

The boys were together now, milling in the street, excitedly discussing their plans for the dog. So-Peng put the animal down. It sat, staring at him, its tail wagging.

Suddenly, the boys turned to So-Peng. "What do you think?" the flat-faced boy asked him.

"It isn't up to me," So-Peng said. "He isn't my dog."

"Well, he isn't ours either," So-Peng's brother said.

"Do you have to take him away?" the flat-faced boy said. With the anger dissolved, his face reflected only his tremendous need for love and attention.

So-Peng smiled. He patted the dog's head. "Maybe I could leave him here—just for a while—to see how you do with him."

The boys clustered around the dog, stroking its head and flanks. Its tail wagged faster and faster.

The flat-faced boy came up to So-Peng. "We don't really hate each other, Elder Brother," he said, using the Chinese honorific. "That was just talk."

So-Peng took the boy's fist, opened it up. The stone he had picked up when the threat of violence was in the air rolled into the street.

"Words," So-Peng said, "are often only the beginning."

"I would not have thrown the stone, Elder Brother."

So-Peng knelt down next to the flat-faced boy. "I know that you would not have wanted to."

After a time the flat-faced boy said, "I think I understand."

So-Peng looked at the flat-faced boy. He did not need his power in order to know what the boy needed. It was so basic. "When I was your age," he said, "I longed for an older brother to talk to. Alas, I had none."

"Oh, I know what you mean!" the flat-faced boy cried. Then, as he was about to go on, he lapsed into silence.

So-Peng rose. "Next week I'll need some help on a job I'm working on weekends. Think you'd be interested?"

The flat-faced boy nodded eagerly. Once more he was too overcome to speak.

"I'll come for you in the morning—early."

"There'll be no need, Elder Brother," the flat-faced boy said. "I'll be here at sunrise."

So-Peng laughed. "An hour after will suffice."

So-Peng went back through the gate. The garden was empty and still. Wondering where his mother was, So-Peng reached out with his mind. When he found her, So-Peng gasped. He felt waves of what he could only suppose was panic emanating from her.

He went immediately into the house, to the bedroom she shared with her husband. She was packing her bags.

"Where are you going, Mother?"

She whirled around. There was color in her cheeks, and she brushed several stray strands of hair off her face. She was an extraordinarily handsome woman, powerful of visage, rather than merely beautiful. Her long, narrow head was faced with high cheekbones and oddly deep-set eyes. Her ears were small and were of some pride to her, as were her feet and hands, which were delicate and tiny and very capable.

"A tortoiseshell was cracked in a fire, the pieces read by a *fengshui* man. It was foretold that you would come to me here," she said, looking at him gravely. "If you did not come, I would know that the *fengshui* man lied, that you were not the chosen."

So-Peng looked at her quizzically. "What do you mean?"

She gave him a sudden, dazzling smile. "Let us go elsewhere to discuss this," she said.

She led him outside to the garden, which she knew would be deserted at this time of the evening. They entered Singapore's soft amethyst twilight. The rank scent of the mangrove swamps to the north mingled with the cloying attar of the flowers, hung in the heavy, breathless air. In the distance dogs barked at the encroaching shadows. One by one the streetlights were being lit by a dark-skinned Malay boy on a ladder, whose glossy head So-Peng could just see over the brick wall.

Liang and So-Peng sat across from one another on lacquered rattan chairs.

"When you were still inside me," she said, "I could feel you reaching out to me, not with your hands, but with your mind. I saw colors—*your* colors, the shadows of your still-forming mind. After you were born, I experienced this phenomenon more strongly, and I knew that you had inherited my gift. Thereafter, I encouraged this gift inside you, exercising it, you might say, allowing it to grow as you grew."

"I remember," So-Peng said. "It was a link between us that no one else could share. I could speak to you without opening my mouth, and hear your response without using my ears."

Liang sat in a very yang manner, in a way that So-Peng's father should have sat and didn't. It was as if *she* owned the house and everything in it. So-Peng, observing this, realized that he would not be surprised to find that this was, indeed, the case.

"You are still young, So-Peng," Liang said, "but now circumstance has forced me to impart to you—I pray not prematurely—the full truth behind your gift. You may think now that it is a blessing, but it can so easily turn into a curse. Used for the wrong reasons—greed, envy, lust—it can be a force for great evil. Allowed its freedom, it can come to dominate your life. You must know that you cannot see into all other minds as you do into mine—or I into yours. The link is the key; two people, not one, are required. Do you understand me?" Liang waited for his affirmative nod. "Your gift may be used on its own—as no doubt you have already discovered. But it can be a trap, leading to arrogance—once you come to rely too heavily on your gift, you will blind yourself to the instances when it gives you a false reading or no reading at all. You will begin to tell yourself what you want to hear, not what your gift allows you to see and hear."

Outside in the street, beyond the garden's brick wall, So-Peng could hear the clip-clop of a horse-drawn carriage, the brief chatter of voices. This intrusion of the banal seemed to lend Liang's words even more weight, as a black velvet background will enhance the glitter of a diamond.

He rose, wandering close to the wall. He put his hands out, pressed them against brick and climbing vines. He began to understand now why as a child he had been reluctant to use his gift, why he had always felt as if he carried a burden within himself that weighed upon his mind, a profound enigma.

Liang, aware that her son's spirit was too restless to be contained within the sanctuary of the garden, suggested that they take a walk. They went silently through the teeming streets until they came to Queen Elizabeth Walk and the harbor.

Liang watched her son for some time. At length she responded to his silent question.

"I cannot tell you where I am going, So-Peng," she said, "only that I must go."

He was thinking of the puzzle, that her leaving must be part of it. If he solved the puzzle, he thought, perhaps she would not have to go.

They stopped by an iron railing that protected strollers from a fall into the water from the high embankment. So-Peng leaned upon the black rail, staring out at the patterns the flames of the streetlights made upon the surface of the harbor.

"Who are the tanjian?" he asked.

Liang smiled. "Why do you think I would know that?"

"Because I think you know *what* they are."

The reflection of the flames on the water seemed like spirit lights, and in this close and magical atmosphere So-Peng could imagine emerging from the harbor the merlion—half-land beast, half-sea creature—that was said to be Singapore's protector.

"I imagine," Liang said, "that you have heard all the stories about my heritage. I am, or I am supposed to be, Malay, perhaps part Malay, part Chinese—Hakka, Teochew, even Sumatran. The truth is"—she looked at her eldest son—"that no one knows me."

"Not even father?"

She laughed good-naturedly. "*Especially* not your father."

Liang had three basic qualities from which all the ruffles and furrows of her personality stemmed. She was giving, she was sympathetic, and she was self-controlled. Years later, when his studies were more complete, So-Peng would discover that, as far as the Tao was concerned, these qualities could be reduced to a single syllable, *Da*. And *Da* was the voice of God.

"I never rail against the gods," Liang said. "Neither do I blame those around me if they have sinned or are evil. It is my children whom I care about, and it is you, So-Peng, whom I care about the most."

A small boy emerged from the crowd along Queen Elizabeth Walk. He ran to the railing, stuck his head between the ironwork to stare down into the water.

"Do you know that you came to me full-grown in a dream on the day before you were born?" Liang said. "I saw your face, I spoke to you, I knew your heart. That is how I know now what course your life will take, just as I know my part in it."

The small boy climbed up the railing in order, So-Peng supposed, to get a better look at something he had seen in the harbor. So-Peng thought again of the legendary merlion of Singapore, and wondered if that was what the boy had seen.

He returned his attention to his mother, who said, "Now is the time when you must put all your energies into learning, so that by the time you are thirty you will be secure in your career. So that at forty you will have no more doubts about the world. So that at fifty you will know the will of heaven. So that at sixty you will be prepared to heed it. So that at seventy you will be able to follow the dictates of your heart by traveling the path of the righteous."

He looked at Liang. "How am I to accomplish all this, Mother?"

"That is entirely up to you," she said. "But I will tell you a story that may be of some help to you. In Zhuji, the village in northeast China where I was born and brought up, there was a temple inhabited by the most peculiar monks. They claimed to be descendants of Chieh, the terminator—or so he was called by many, a monarch so degenerate that he single-handedly caused the destruction of his dynasty, the Hsia. This was a very long time ago, nearly two thousand years before Christ, as the Westerners reckon time. Chieh, it is generally thought, undid all the good accomplished by the Yellow Emperor, who ruled nine hundred years before him.

"The monks were unconcerned with how the world at large viewed their infamous forebear. They were practitioners of Tau-tau, a composite form of martial arts that they contended was created by the decadent king, Chieh. They were known as tanjian, the walkers in stealth.

"These tanjian monks worshiped no god, save if you believed that Chieh was a god. Some did; others still do." Liang paused, as if she wanted to gauge the effect of her words on her son.

"How did you come to know so much about the tanjian monks?" So-Peng asked.

"I knew them well," she said, "because I lived with them." She was watching her son's eyes, reading him. "My father was a tanjian monk."

They heard a tiny shout. The small boy, who had been attempting to walk atop the highest rail, had slipped, toppling into the harbor waters where the calm surface belied the strong, swirling currents.

People came running, but it was a long way down. They began to signal frantically to a lighter. But it was still quite a way off and it was clear from the boy's thrashing that he could not swim.

So-Peng climbed up onto the railing, preparatory to jumping in, but his mother put her hand on his arm, restraining him with her typically firm grip. "It is too dangerous," she said.

"But Mother—" He saw the look in her eye and fell silent. He felt the whisper of a wind, cool and invisible as it rippled out from his mother's mind.

Liang was now concentrating fully upon the thrashing child. So-Peng thought for an instant that he saw her eyes glowing, but perhaps it was merely the reflection of the streetlights.

In the harbor the child who had been struggling unsuccessfully to keep his head above water now burst upward as if held by an underwater hand. He looked about him, terrified and at the same time filled with a kind of wonder as he bobbed upon the surface, immune to the treacherous currents.

So-Peng was aware of a thin line of perspiration rolling down the side of Liang's face. His own mind was vibrating in the backwash of her powerful aura.

The lighter, close now, slowed, and one of the crew threw a line to the child. A moment later the child had been pulled to safety. The crowd that had gathered on the quay broke into spontaneous applause.

Liang turned away, allowed whatever breeze there was to dry the sweat on her face. She seemed very calm, and So-Peng was aware of an unnatural stillness enfolding them as if in a healing blanket. They sat on a backless stone bench, and Liang closed her eyes.

He should have been stunned at what his mother had just done, but he wasn't. He remembered a time many years ago when one of his younger sisters had fallen gravely ill. The doctor had come, had done what he could, and had left shaking his head. So-Peng recalled him saying in a whisper at the door, "She will surely die. Make her comfortable, and pray. That's all you can do now."

Of course, thinking about it, there was no way that So-Peng could have overheard the doctor's words. What he had picked up were the reverberations of those words in his mother's mind.

Then he had watched as Liang had knelt beside the sickbed and, taking her daughter's tiny hand in hers, had grown absolutely still. There was a clock upon the mantel at Liang's shoulder, and So-Peng was sure that for the first time and only time it had failed to sound the passing of the hour. He had felt the house bathed in concentric circles of warmth and light, and had felt his mother's spirit expanding.

Later he had been sure that he dreamt the episode, but the next morning his sister had awakened from her high fever. Her eyes were clear, the marks upon her skin already fading. Liang, still clutching her daughter's hand, had slept through that entire day.

So-Peng took a deep breath, exhaled it slowly. He needed time to comprehend the merging of past and present, to let the scattered pieces fall gently into place.

"You recognized how the two merchants were killed," So-Peng said after a time, "because of your father."

Liang opened her eyes. "Your grandfather," she said, and it was as if that were a veiled reminder. She nodded. Her eyes seemed luminous, reflecting not only the streetlights, but the last of the pellucid light in the sky far above.

"Tau-tau," she said. "Those throwing stars are made only by tanjian. The other things, the days on which the merchants were killed, the pigs' feet in their mouths, were nothing more than ruses meant to confuse the authorities. Traditional tanjian tricks."

"Is my gift . . ." So-Peng paused because this was difficult to ask; an affirmative answer would hurt him deeply. He began again. "Is my gift part of Tau-tau?"

"No," Liang said at once. She felt the tension drain out of him. "That was handed down from my mother, who was not tanjian born."

"What are tanjian doing here in Singapore?"

"Tanjian are by nature wanderers," his mother said. "Many emigrated to Japan three hundred years ago. Tanjian are never satisfied, always hungry for new territory. Perhaps that is because they have nothing of their own."

"What do you mean?"

Liang sighed. "Tau-tau is in a way a nihilistic discipline. Tanjian are pitiless, incapable of feeling emotion as you or I know it. As a result, they have no possessions, and are envious of those who do. Also, they are infiltrators. They hire themselves out to do the dirty work others are too honorable or too cowardly to perform themselves. This Tau-tau teaches them."

Perhaps So-Peng heard something in his mother's tone, or again in the cast of her features. In any event, he felt compelled to say, "None of these are the reasons that the tanjian are in Singapore." He knew that this was the truth as soon as he said it.

Once again he felt the expansion of her spirit, witness to its breathing, as enormous as if the earth itself were inhaling and exhaling.

"So-Peng," Liang said at last, "when you came to me in my dream before your birth, this was what you said to me, 'None of these are the reasons that the tanjian are in Singapore.' Your father and I were not in

Singapore then. We were outside Kuala Lumpur, at the tin mines. I had had no thought of moving to Singapore, and after the dream, I had no intention of ever coming here."

"What happened?"

She smiled. "Life happened, So-Peng." Her eyes seemed limpid, as if they had somehow taken on a quality of the water beside which she and So-Peng sat. "And, in time, I realized that I was not to be merely a creator of life, but a transmitter of knowledge as well. I realized almost as soon as I got here that it had not been coincidence that I had been born into a tanjian family and that years later I would give birth to you. It became clear to me that the two were connected. I feared that connection, dreading the moment when you would say those words to me, 'None of these are the reasons that the tanjian are in Singapore.' "

His mother put her head down. Years later So-Peng would remember that the city seemed to have grown still all around them. As familiar as he was with Singapore, he found that an impossibility. Yet this is what his memory told him.

"No," Liang said, "none of those are the reasons the tanjian are in Singapore. The reason they are here, So-Peng, is to bring me back to my family in Zhuji."

So-Peng was silent for a long time, and Liang said nothing in order that he might best absorb what she had told him. At last So-Peng rallied his spirit from the shock it had received. He said, "But why would the tanjian kill two merchants? You did not know them."

"Don't make the same mistake that everyone else has made," Liang said. "It isn't *who* the tanjian have murdered, but *how* they have been killed. The method announces the tanjian presence here. It is a warning to me to obey or die."

"You mean they took two lives merely to frighten you?"

"That is the tanjian way," Liang said.

So-Peng was now so stunned that he opened his mouth, shut it without having said a word. His mother looked neither directly at him nor away from him. She seemed waiting for him, reluctant to continue until he had gathered himself.

From some hidden inside pocket Liang produced a small, black velvet box. She held it in the palm of her hand as if it were a star from heaven.

"Open the box, my son." She intoned this as if it were a religious act, part of an ancient rite that needed completion.

So-Peng, his heart hammering in his chest, did as she bade. Inside the box he saw rows of gems.

"Sixteen emeralds," Liang intoned in the same peculiar, almost singsong tone of voice, "one for each principle of the Tau-tau, one for each founding member of the tanjian. It is said that their essences have been contained in these stones, sealed away at the moment of their deaths."

So-Peng looked at the gems as if they were alive, as if at any moment they would bite his head off. He said, "These are what the tanjian want." It was not a question.

Liang nodded. "They want me back, they want the emeralds back. It is one and the same. The emeralds are mine; we cannot be separated. They are sacred. Their care is my sacred trust. They have power beyond mere monetary value. Here is the very essence, the heart and the spirit of Tau-tau. Here is good and evil, my son. Look upon the varied faces, learn to differentiate between the two. With these stones in your possession you cannot help but live the life of the righteous."

"But what do the tanjian want with them, Mother?"

"As I said, both good and evil are contained here: the spirits of the original tanjian monks. Some were good, others evil. The current tanjian, corrupted by their poverty, warped by their own shifting sense of morality, seek to loose the evil, use its ancient power for their own ends. In so doing, the good would be destroyed forever."

Liang's face had grown dark, disturbed as if by a flux only the two of them could detect.

"You see, there exists within these mystic sixteen gems a kind of equilibrium. Should their number be depleted, fall below nine, the equilibrium would begin to erode, and the evil, no longer held in check, would begin its ascent to power."

In the tiny flames from the streetlights the stones looked dull and black, or devoid of any color at all, so that there was about them an air of brooding menace.

At length So-Peng tore his gaze from the emeralds. Looking into his mother's face, he said, "The tanjian would actually kill you, one of their own?"

"I renounced their way of life when I ran off with your father," she said. He listened for a hint of sadness in her voice, found none. "He is still handsome, your father. In those days, how much more so he was! He was a high-liver. He must have just made an important deal, because he threw money around. I liked that, I suppose. But I liked the idea of getting out of the temple even more. I felt stifled there; I was never born to be a tanjian woman. And your father was completely unlike the tanjian men I had grown up around, whom I had grown to despise. He was so kind, so genuine—of course, that's why he continually loses all the money he earns."

Her smile was wistful, as if she looked upon her husband as an over-grown child, a delightful blessing who, like a tender flower, nevertheless required constant attention. "But I was afraid of my father's wrath—and rightly so. He would not have allowed me to go had I asked him. So I didn't; I just left with your father, who knew nothing of this, of course. I have made certain that he still doesn't. Poor man! What would he make of it?"

Liang looked at her son, saw not herself but her beloved husband mirrored in those features, as the moon is reflected in the water. "What I did was unheard of. How many laws of Tau-tau have I transgressed? In the back of my mind I knew that I would have to pay for those sins. But another, stronger, part of me hoped that that day would never come. Now it has."

"Which is why you must go."

"I cannot endanger my family," she said simply.

So-Peng said, "If you go there will be no family."

She was silent for some time. "But you see, my dearest, I have no other choice."

So-Peng thought, She is right. But I do have a choice. He was also dimly aware that she was withholding something vital from him. "Tell me everything you can about the tanjian," he said.

Liang gave him a small, sad smile. She shook her head. "What I have already told you is far too much. The danger is too great."

"What if you go and the danger is still present?" So-Peng said.

"Impossible," his mother said. "As soon as I return to Zhuji, the danger will no longer exist."

Then, with the direct prescience of youth, So-Peng said, "What if you are not all the tanjian want?"

Liang had begun to tremble. "We will not speak of this!" she said sharply. And then, in a softer tone of voice, "Do not allow your imagination to get the better of you. If you rely overly on your gift now, it will surely fail you."

So-Peng bowed in obedience. "I am sorry, Mother," he said. "Nevertheless, I still believe that knowledge is strength." He lifted his head at what he judged to be just the right moment. He had learned this trick from her, and it worked. Their eyes locked, but there was more that passed between them.

In a moment Liang nodded. She began to speak, telling him every bit of lore and strategy she knew of the tanjian and Tau-tau. It was quite late when she was finished.

As children, So-Peng's brothers and sisters always obeyed their mother. So-Peng did more: he listened to her. So it was that when she revealed the background concerning her past and the philosophy of Tau-tau, So-Peng decided that in order to save both his mother and the family, he needed first to explore the dark. Because there is where he would find the tanjian, the harnessers of the night and of every evil thing that made its home in the darkness.

The way into darkness, he quickly discovered, was twilight, and twilight was synonymous with deceit, within which were always elements of the truth. One could not be truthful and explore the dark, rotting corners of the world. Truth was not the currency of evil, which inhabited the darkness like a bed of thorns in a woodland glade. Neither were lies. In order to negotiate these treacherous byways one needed to speak neither one, but like an incantation, an arcane combination of the two.

So-Peng went to see his cousin Wan, who cleaned the floors in the offices of the British chief of police. Wan, needless to say, knew everything that went on within the police precinct, which was quite a bit more than the chief of police knew.

Wan said, "Why do you ask about these murders, cousin? They are very bad business. Even the British are reluctant to investigate. They would prefer to let the past be the past. The British are afraid. Now I am afraid."

Nevertheless, Wan let So-Peng see everything the police had amassed concerning the incidents. So-Peng concentrated on his reading so as not to allow Wan's extreme anxiety to affect him.

"It mentions weapons called, for a lack of a better term, throwing stars," he said to Wan. "Are the police holding them?"

Wan nodded, showed them to So-Peng, who gave them only a cursory look, though he was extremely curious about them. He returned to the report, asked Wan several meaningless, misleading questions, then gave him back the report. As Wan went to put it away, So-Peng palmed one of the throwing stars.

Now that he knew as much as the police did about the murders, So-Peng felt he was as prepared as he ever would be for Nightside.

Nightside was only an approximate translation of the patois word, part Malay, part Hokkien dialect. It was an area of town shunned by the ruling British, rarely frequented by the Babas, as the Straits Chinese born in the settlement of immigrant parents were called. The Babas, with an eye to the future, were far more respectable than were their forebears, who had endured unimaginable hardships, being brought to Singapore in the holds of clipper ships, being imprisoned there until the cost of their passage was paid for by those who promised to employ them. Subsequently, they toiled eighteen hours a day to pay off that heavy debt whose amount increased with each day's interest.

Nightside was the province of the *samsengs*, professional criminals breeding in the dark underbelly of Singapore. These unwholesome denizens were utterly contemptuous of Western law. They committed murder, extortion, robbery, and burglary with such regularity that these crimes were to them the equivalent of a nine-to-five job.

Because So-Peng knew all this, he determined that Nightside would be the logical place to begin his search for the tanjian. Nightside was a place along the docks. It was filled with godowns—warehouses—bars, and clubs open until dawn. Here liquor and opium vied for prominence among a population that had little thought of tomorrow. They were a godless bunch, the Nightsiders, the concept of belief in anything excoriated by a life without either hope or purpose.

Into this pit of evil stepped So-Peng, weaponless save for his quick wits and the knowledge he had gotten from his mother, the facts he had gleaned from the police files.

At first, at bar after bar, he was left alone, as if he were some dimwitted Baba who had wandered into Nightside by mistake and would soon disappear of his own accord.

When this did not occur, he garnered somewhat more attention, and when he began asking questions concerning the whereabouts of the men who had murdered the two merchants, he became the object of considerable curiosity and speculation.

A *samseng* named Tik Po Tak, the leader of one of the innumerable Chinese tongs, took particular interest in So-Peng. Tak was a thickset man in his early thirties, a former *sinkeh*—an indentured immigrant— who had seen his two older brothers die of cholera in the hold of the Chinese junk that had brought them to Singapore on the wings of the monsoon winds.

Tak himself had emerged from that disease-ridden ship thin and tubercular. He had worked night and day to pay off the enormous debt he had incurred for not only his own passage, but that of his dead brothers as well.

Within two years he had paid off the debt and, a free man, he had entered Nightside. There, he had bought a weapon with the remainder of his money, had returned to the pepper plantation on which he had toiled for twenty-four months, and had killed his former employer.

He was a famous figure around Nightside, and he was much feared. He also had amassed the most powerful tong in the Crown Colony, as the British called Singapore in those days. Rather than being intimidated by the local British police, Tak had made a deal with them—a kind of mutual nonaggression pact. The British did not hinder his affairs to any major degree. They did not dare.

When he had been a *sinkeh*, Tik Po Tak had been a brash young man, willing to take appalling risks for the sake of honor and freedom. In So-Peng he no doubt saw an image of his younger self, and therefore his interest was piqued. On the other hand, he was wary. His truce with the British was at best brittle, and it would be correct to say that Tak was uneasy around them. In his opinion, any people who were more concerned with telling the truth—and, thus, giving offense—than they were with saving face were simply not trustworthy.

Tik Po Tak sent One Eye Yan across the barroom to speak with So-Peng. In that way he might observe the young man's actions, reactions, and manner from a distance, the better to judge whether So-Peng was what he claimed he was or a spy sent into Nightside by the devious British.

One Eye Yan was a massive man with a notoriously incendiary temper who could intimidate the bravest British officer. But Yan had his orders, and Tak had no doubt that he would do what he, Tak, wanted him to do.

Yan said to So-Peng, "Why are you here in a part of Singapore that does not belong to you?"

So-Peng looked at this giant of a man who was of approximately the same height as he but was perhaps twice again as heavy. "I am looking for men who have committed murder," he said.

Yan laughed. He brandished a long, dirty knife in So-Peng's face. "Then you've come to the right place." He watched So-Peng's face as he turned the blade of the knife this way and that. "Which murders?"

"The Muslim merchants who were found with pigs' feet in their mouths," So-Peng said at once.

One Eye Yan grunted. "Why do you want to find these men?"

"I wish to talk with them," So-Peng said.

Yan grinned as he put the filthy blade to So-Peng's neck. "Your search has ended," he said softly. "I am one of them." He leaned into So-Peng's face. "Speak."

So-Peng did not move. He knew that this giant was not a tanjian; he did not have the sense of menace about him that Liang had described. There was nothing mystical about this one-eyed man. His character was simple, straightforward. So-Peng knew that this did not make him any less dangerous.

With that in mind, So-Peng knew that the matter of his reaction now was extremely important. "If you are who you say you are," he told the giant, "you will know my name."

"Is that so?" Yan said. "Why should I know you? You're just a stripling."

Using his gift, So-Peng reached out, touched Yan's spirit with his own, enfolding it in a sense of truth. Straightforward adversaries demanded straightforward measures.

Yan grunted, took the blade from So-Peng's throat. "Aren't you afraid that they will kill you as well?" he asked. "Murderers are notoriously indifferent about their victims."

"Not these murderers," So-Peng said with such absolute authority that for a moment Yan was taken was aback.

He peered more closely at So-Peng. "You know the identities of these men?"

So-Peng nodded. "Yes."

"Can you prove it?"

"Yes, I can."

"Come with me," Yan said. He led So-Peng to the back of the bar, where Tik Po Tak waited in the shadows. So-Peng stood until he was invited to sit down. He shared a drink with Tik Po Tak without knowing the man's name. That was all right, he decided. On that score, the two of them were even.

"I understand that you are looking for the men responsible for the two recent murders," Tak said when they had both drained their glasses.

"That is correct."

"There are elements within Singapore who believe that I murdered the two merchants."

"Why would they think that?" So-Peng asked.

"Because I am Tik Po Tak, and I had business with those two merchants."

"Opium business?"

Tak squinted at So-Peng. Beneath the table he had drawn a small-caliber pistol which he had aimed at So-Peng's stomach. "What is your name?" he asked tightly.

So-Peng told him.

"My business is no concern of yours, So-Peng," he said.

So-Peng shrugged, his nonchalant attitude belying the hammering of his heart. He could feel Tak's distrust; it was like rubbing up against a rusty scow. "If it was opium trade, I could understand the British believing you had the two merchants killed." He had read Tik Po Tak's name as a prime suspect in the material Wan had showed him at police headquarters. He fought down an urge to reassure Tak that he was who he said he was, knowing instinctively that that would only make the *samseng* more suspicious.

"Tell me," Tak said, hunching forward, his hands out of sight beneath the table, "am I who you are looking for?"

"I am looking for Chinese known as tanjian," So-Peng said. "They are monks of a sort, who possess remarkable skills. To them killing is a way of life; this is their Tao. The tanjian worship death." His eyes met Tak's and he put his spirit into his gaze, projecting it outward. "They are the ones who murdered the merchants, not you. Will you help me find them?"

"Monks who kill?" Tak was still skeptical, though So-Peng could sense a growing interest. "Who has heard of such a thing?"

"I have," So-Peng said. He sensed that Tik Po Tak had reason of his own to find the murderers. "I will know them when I see them," he said. "It seems to me that you have the physical means to find them."

So-Peng was proposing a partnership, and Tak knew it. On the surface it seemed ridiculous, a mere lad of unknown—and suspect—origins offering an alliance with Singapore's most powerful *samseng*. Still, Tak said, "Tell me more about these—tanjian."

So-Peng related more or less what his mother had told him. He did not, however, include his mother's, or his own, connection.

"Why do you want to find these tanjian—assuming, of course, that they exist at all?"

Now So-Peng was faced with a fundamental dilemma. Truth or fiction, which should he choose? He decided to stick to the twilight, where he suspected Tak had also chosen to dwell. He began to speak but at the last instant stopped. Something in Tak's eyes hinted of discernment, and so So-Peng told the truth, recounting his mother's fear, his own desire to protect her. He withheld any mention of his own or his mother's gift.

Tak was silent for some time, digesting this. "How will you recognize these tanjian?" he asked abruptly.

So-Peng did not know. He said, "I have seen them before," while projecting that same sense of truth he had directed at Yan.

Tik Po Tak had remained at the summit of Nightside's underworld through rock-hard determination, an iron fist, and the unbending rule of never entering into a partnership. Alliances inevitably led to a sharing—and therefore a diminution—of power. And power was something Tak had been born understanding.

And yet there was some quality in this lad that drew him. It was not merely that in order to maintain face in Nightside, Tak must avenge the death of his business associates, not merely that the lad had knowledge that Tak could exploit, although surely that must have been part of it. It was the sense that So-Peng possessed a talent that could prove enormously profitable. Tak saw that unless he took So-Peng under his wing, someone smart would, and that would be bad for Tik Po Tak.

"We want the same thing," Tak said warily. "Perhaps we can do business." He was aware that So-Peng had not inquired as to why Tak wanted the murderers found. This impressed Tak; it was his experience that partners were inordinately nosy. He was convinced the lad was far wiser than his years would indicate. "Meet me here tomorrow at first light," he said, terminating the meeting abruptly.

The next day, brutally steamy and uncomfortable even by Singapore standards, So-Peng traveled with Tak to Choa Chu Kang village, north of the Colony.

"Do you know how to handle a rifle?" Tak asked So-Peng.

Here there was no use lying.

"Well, no matter," Tak said. "I will teach you." This, in fact, gave him pleasure. Tak, who had two wives and seven children, was nevertheless unused to quick wits and unlimited aptitude in the young. He found his children stupid, lazy, and altogether a disappointment.

He liked teaching So-Peng to shoot, and was oddly proud of the lad's almost instinctive skill. On the other hand, he was suspicious of it.

It was a good thing that So-Peng learned to use the weapon quickly, because by midday they were on a tiger hunt. The violent carnivorous cats were unhappy with the encroachment of civilization on their territory. Already this year almost three hundred people had been killed in tiger attacks on the outskirts of Singapore.

Tak was affable, even loquacious. This was a side of the *samseng* that So-Peng had not seen before, and he was fascinated. Tak managed to introduce his young ward to everyone in the party. They were friendly, spending time talking to So-Peng, asking him questions, answering his in turn.

Tak introduced So-Peng to a Western man of pleasant mien named H. N. Ridley, who Tak said would stalk with them. The two men seemed to know each other well. It seemed odd to So-Peng that Tak would befriend a Westerner, and his consternation increased when, during a rest break, he discovered that Ridley was the director of the Singapore Botanical Gardens.

"I'm a flower fancier," Tak said, laughing.

What could the two men have in common? So-Peng wondered. Immediately he corrected himself, and asked, What was it Ridley had that Tak could exploit?

He pondered this question while the party moved out, the Malay dog handlers first, fanning through the jungle, the dogs straining at their leashes.

So-Peng had heard that the government had put a bounty on every tiger head brought back to Singapore, but he suspected that this group would have gone hunting merely for the excitement and the sport of it. The atmosphere among the party was nothing short of that of an exclusive men's club. Among the Chinese there was intense gambling, not only on how many heads the party would bring back, but also what time the first tiger would be spotted, killed, as well as what time the party would bag its last animal.

So-Peng was very excited. While Tak and Ridley spoke idly of rumors making the rounds of the Colony, So-Peng was watching the dogs—or at least the one closest to them—a saluki. This animal was far smaller than So-Peng would have imagined would be used to hunt such large beasts. It was brindled black and white with quick, inquisitive eyes and large, triangular ears.

The tiger must have been downwind, because it came gliding through the thick underbrush on the saluki's left without so much as a rustle. So-Peng had swung his rifle around and, as the tiger leaped for the dog, jerked the trigger hard. His rifle went off with a terrible roar. Unprepared for the recoil, he was thrown backward, his rifle pointing skyward.

Tak whirled, squeezed off two accurate rounds. The result made it seem as if the dog, tiny by comparison with the giant cat, had shrugged the larger beast off its back.

The dogs were howling. Everyone ran, converging on the spot where the tiger lay on its side, panting, eyes rolling. So-Peng arrived in time to see it lift its noble head and roar defiantly at those who had brought it down. Tak reloaded, put a bullet through its right eye.

The brindled saluki sat, panting and bleeding, by the tiger's side. The poor wounded beast howled as best it could along with its brethren, and it resisted its handler as he dragged it away from the kill to administer to it.

Tak walked over to where So-Peng stood staring at the tiger. Its death seemed an ominous foreshadowing.

Watching So-Peng's reactions, Tak nodded to himself. He pointed to the Malay dog handler, said, "Desaru owes you much for saving his dog's life. Those animals are difficult to train, very hard to replace." He went to where So-Peng had dropped his rifle, returned with it. "You did a good job," he said, handing over the weapon. Two of the Malay boys stayed with the kill while the rest of the party prepared to move out.

As often happened after an early kill, for a long time nothing occurred. The day wore on, hot and intensely humid. A spattering of rain fell and then was gone. So-Peng watched the sunlight evaporating the precipitation off the wide leaves and fronds.

For a while Ridley walked side by side with So-Peng, speaking easily and lightheartedly. The answer to what Tak wanted from Ridley appeared gradually and was simple enough. According to Ridley, a rather gentle man, astoundingly intelligent for a Westerner, Tak had been donating money to the botanical gardens, in return for which Ridley was experimenting with growing poppies.

So-Peng could see what Tak was up to. If he could get Ridley somehow to adapt the flower to this area, Tak could cultivate the opium crop himself, cutting out all the middlemen who cut into his profit margin.

"It's a fool's dream, really," Ridley confided in So-Peng during the long, tedious afternoon. "The *papaver somniferum*, or Eurasian poppy, is a delicate creature. For one thing, it craves the coolness one finds in these parts only in elevations between one thousand and fifteen hundred meters. It is impossible to get it growing here at sea level, and any attempt at hybridization mucks about with the end product—opium."

"Have you told Tak this?" So-Peng asked.

"No," Ridley said immediately. Then, appalled, he said, "Good God, I hope you won't tell him. The fact is, the bulk of his donations have gone to a new project I've been interested in for a year now. I've imported seedlings of the Para tree from England. These were smuggled illegally out of the Amazon River basin—do you know where that is? I'm not surprised. South America. The other side of the world.

"In any event, unlike the Eurasian poppy, it appears as if this climate and soil are perfect for the Para tree. If this proves true, the effect on Singapore will be—well, I can't really imagine it. Quite remarkable, at the very least.

"I've mentioned the Para to Mr. Tak, but he seems to have other matters on his mind. Growing it would be easy for him; he's got acres and acres of land to the north of Singapore."

"Why would he want to grow this tree?" So-Peng asked.

H. N. Ridley looked at him. "Have you ever heard of rubber?"

"No," So-Peng admitted. "What is it?"

Ridley told him. To So-Peng, what he had to say was far more interesting than the brace of tigers the hunting party took.

The tiger hunt was a way for them to move northward without causing any undue talk.

"If these tanjian were actually in Singapore," Tak said to So-Peng, "I would have known about it. That means they're out here in the jungle with the tigers."

So-Peng nodded. "From what I understand, that fits their elemental philosophy." He had not said anything about his talk with Ridley, preferring to keep his information to himself until a propitious moment. In life, So-Peng knew, one not only had to cross bridges, but one had to cross them at the proper time.

"It also means they'll be far more dangerous," Tak warned. "In Singapore I control virtually everyone or know someone who does. We would have a much easier time of it."

To So-Peng's surprise, they did not head into the jungle when the hunt broke up. Instead, they trekked for just over an hour through mangrove and thick forest palms until they emerged on the bank of a wide, meandering, muddy river. A slim sampan was waiting for them. Surrounding it were three heavily armed men who bowed when they saw Tak approaching. He stepped aboard the boat, checking the provisions himself. Apparently satisfied, he waved So-Peng aboard, and casting off the lines, the three men leaped into the sampan as it nosed out from the shore. At the rear of the boat, one of the men had a coal fire going. An iron wok was beginning to sizzle.

"What river is this?" So-Peng asked.

Tak said, "The orang asli have named it, but I don't know what it is." He was speaking of the original people—the natives—of the peninsula. "It doesn't matter. It will get us where we need to go."

The man in the stern produced food—drunken chicken, strips of meat boiled in *shao shing*, the yellow rice wine that was a Shanghainese favorite, served cold with broad, pungent sprigs of fresh coriander. In a moment the wok was emptied, filled again, and Tak and So-Peng were delivered of baby eels sauteed in sesame oil; crisp baskets of deep-fried yam noodles.

Tak talked animatedly as they ate. As he spoke it gradually dawned on So-Peng that he had passed some kind of test that Tak had devised for him. He thought back to the people he had been introduced to on the hunt. Each of them, though polite, had seemed eager to know about him, almost as if they were quizzing him. And, indeed, So-Peng now realized that that was precisely what they had been doing.

When he thought about it, it was not so surprising. People in Tak's position had a right if not a duty to be skeptical of everyone with whom they came in contact. Tak's only fear was from infiltration from the police or from a rival tong. Tak had, in effect, passed him around to all those in the hunt party who could identify him as something other than what So-Peng had claimed to be.

"These two merchants," Tak was saying now, "were something special to me, and everyone knew it. They had the fastest fleets, the trained personnel, the desire to take risks that I required. It is clear to me that whoever murdered them—the tanjian, you say—did so at the behest of someone with whom I have done business. We had a disagreement about six months ago, and he vowed to get even. Now he has, and I cannot let his challenge go unavenged."

Hearing this, So-Peng was about to say that this could not be so, since his mother was certain that the tanjian had murdered the two merchants as a warning for her to return to her family, but instead he bit his tongue. It was clear to him that Tik Po Tak was far from a fool. If he believed that the murders were meant to teach him a lesson, So-Peng could not discount that possibility. Then who was right about the motive for the murders, Tak or Liang?

"You were very quick with your reflexes," Tak said, returning to the subject of the tiger hunt. "Desaru owes you; he will not forget."

"I had some practice," So-Peng admitted. "Some years ago I made money by bagging those giant rats that were gobbling up the Colony's cats. Remember? The governor put a bounty on their heads. One week I brought in twenty. They made a good deal more noise than the tiger."

"You heard him anyway," Tak said, missing nothing, "when Ridley and I did not."

"Well, I have not lived in Singapore all my life," So-Peng said, judging the time was right to divulge this information. "My family moved around a lot, and I spent time on both coasts of the peninsula."

Tak laughed. "So you know the jungle better than I."

So-Peng told him the Malay name of the river they were on, then immediately regretted it; Tak might think him devious.

"Do you also know where we're going?" Tak asked seriously.

So-Peng shook his head. "I'd need second sight for that," he said.

"I know someone who has second sight," Tak said. "I consulted him before we set out." He spat into the muddy water. "He said I would not return from upriver."

"Yet you chose to go anyway."

"Chose?" Tak seemed surprised by the word. "Face dictated that I must go. These merchants were like part of my family. Also, I was waiting for a sign." He pointed at So-Peng. "You are the sign, lad. You know the murderers, these tanjian. I no longer feel like an eagle in the dark. You'll see them before they see us."

So-Peng felt his bowels turn to water. He was angry at himself for inflating his value to Tak. He had told the *samseng* that he had seen the tanjian and could thus identify them. Now Tak was counting on him to provide the edge in a showdown between two powerful enemies. So-Peng was in the middle of a war from which it was impossible to extricate himself.

Yet he knew that he could not confess his error in judgment—not now, after he knew what was required of him. All of a sudden he found that his cynical feelings about Tak had dissipated. Tak had revealed himself as a man who believed in his ideals and was willing to die for them. So-Peng thought that no better definition of a hero existed.

It was, perhaps, not surprising that Tik Po Tak should have such a profound effect upon So-Peng. After all, the boy had grown up in a family where his father was all but completely absent. That So-Peng should wind up admiring this man with the iron will and compelling personality was, in retrospect, inevitable.

Children from a kampong they passed swam out into the river, laughing and splashing at the garfish which could swim atop the water for minutes at a time. Two enterprising lads swam alongside the sampan until one of Tak's men shouted a warning in Bahasa, pointing to an oncoming crocodile. The kids shouted. So-Peng could see their eyes rolling in fear, and he was reminded of the mortally wounded tiger before Tak shot it through the eye. The children turned, trying to head for shore, but So-Peng, watching the crocodile overhauling them, did not believe they would make it to safety. The crocodile, close now, opened wide its greedy jaws.

One of Tak's men reached for a rifle, but So-Peng put his hand on the barrel, saying, "The blood will only attract more animals."

Leaning over the side of the boat, So-Peng ripped off a thick branch, and launching himself into the river between the terrified children and the crocodile, he jammed the branch into the mouth of the crocodile. Immediately he swung aboard its back, riding it as it thrashed. Behind it the river was turned into a froth by its whipping tail.

The children, seeing this display, began to laugh, swimming to shore, pulling themselves up the embankment, standing, dripping, pointing, and laughing as they nonchalantly peeled giant leeches off their bodies.

Tak pulled So-Peng back aboard the sampan, and the boat moved on.

"Where did you learn that trick?" he asked.

So-Peng, thinking of Zhao Hsia, laughed. "I'm glad it worked," he said. "When I was a boy my best friend used to do that with crocodiles larger than this one. He had a knack with animals. Not like second sight, but similar, I suppose. They would not harm him." He shrugged. "Perhaps he hypnotized them."

Tak was staring upriver at the Gunung Muntahak mountain, rising in blue haze out of the emerald and khaki jungle. "I could use your friend's powers on this journey," he said. Then he turned and smiled at So-Peng. "It is good that you are here, lad. Not many Chinese are familiar with the Malay east coast. It is my great good fortune that you came to me at just this moment."

Within a stand of huge Tualang trees they saw a brace of scaly pangolin, overseen by a family of raucous gibbons, swinging from branch to branch. Kingfishers, hornbills, and sunbirds flitted and stalked along the river and its steep embankments. Sunset was approaching.

There were few cooking fires in the kampongs, for this was the beginning of Ramadan and, for the Muslim Malays, the next thirty days were reserved for fasting and for prayer.

"I chose this time well," Tak said as the sampan nosed into a natural cove in the right bank. "In Ramadan the spirit may be strong, but the flesh is weak."

They crept ashore, under cover of the swiftly encroaching night and the chittering of the nocturnal insects. Fireflies glittered in the gathering dusk and, here and there, birdwing butterflies as large across as So-Peng's head made their last foray of the day. They went as far as they could, then made camp without a fire, settled down for the night.

At first light they set out. Tak led them down a jungle path, winding and circuitous. There were many breaks, and the path was overgrown with palm and fern, so that intuition—or perhaps memory—played as great a role as jungle lore in divining the way.

However, it was So-Peng who pointed out that several of the clumps of fern were unattached. Rather, they had been purposefully placed in order to obscure the path in as natural a manner as was possible.

"Is this your enemy's doing?" So-Peng asked.

"I don't think his people are that sophisticated," Tak said, shaking his head.

They pressed on, strung out in single file: two of Tak's heavily-armed men, then Tak himself, So-Peng, and the last of the men, the one who cooked for them.

The foliage, thick, wide, beaded with moisture, held all manner of treasures: a multitude of insects, tiny jeweled snakes, green and blue tree frogs, small multicolored birds.

The days were always more quiet than the nights, but just as dangerous. Spitting cobras, krates, and vipers whose bites were powerful enough to paralyze a man within seconds were much in evidence. Once, the lead man stopped, pointing at a great creature coiled around the bole of a tree by the side of the path. It was a reticulated python which looked to be longer than the height of five men.

Just before midday Tak called a halt and they hunkered down in place for a light meal. So-Peng, who was nearest the cook, helped pass the fruit down the line of men: rambutan, which were similar to litchi, and the sweet-sour mangosteen with its pure white flesh. It was said that one told seasons in Singapore by what fruit was on sale there.

So-Peng was opening the last of his mangosteen when the white sections were suddenly, startlingly spattered with deep red. So-Peng smelled the sickly sweet stench of fresh blood, and out of the corner of his eye saw the cook crumple over as if he had fallen asleep.

Except that the middle of the cook's chest was rudely split by a gleaming steel object, eight-pointed, buried halfway into flesh. So-Peng recognized it immediately as a tanjian throwing star.

So-Peng grew very still. He felt his spirit contracting into an opaque ball, keeping to the low ground, staying invisible. The hairs at the back of his neck stirred; he was acutely aware of his vulnerability, his utter helplessness. He waited for the soft whirring of the throwing star, the sharp bite of steel blade burying itself in his back. He willed his mind to think of nothing. Afraid to move or to make any sound, So-Peng clandestinely watched the cook die.

All was quiet around them. The men ate, unsuspecting. So-Peng acted accordingly, so as not to differentiate himself from them.

He believed he knew what the tanjian were up to. His mother had emphasized their dependence on strategy, and he knew that he must bank on that dependence, turning it to his advantage, transmuting the tanjian strength into a weakness. He could not do that by offering himself up as a target. Sick at heart, trembling in fear, he obediently ate his last mangosteen, speckled with the cook's blood.

At length So-Peng rose, went off the trail to urinate. Afterward, instead of returning directly to the party, he struck out in a direction that ran roughly parallel to the jungle path they had been following.

He had been at this for perhaps ten minutes when he heard a voice calling softly, "Don't move."

So-Peng froze; he dared not even look around. Now he felt something on his back. As it began to undulate, silently tracking obliquely across one shoulder to his waist, he began to understand.

He waited patiently. In a moment he sensed someone approaching him from the side. So-Peng relaxed his muscles. There was a quick movement, no more than a blur, then he felt the weight off his back, heard the swish of the knife through the air, turned and saw the viper's head severed from its writhing body. Black venom squirted onto the jungle floor, absorbed by the thick mulch.

So-Peng looked into Tik Po Tak's eyes. "What do you think you're doing, lad?" the *samseng* said. "You could've been killed."

"I was looking for the tanjian in the trees," So-Peng said, watching Tak wipe down his knife. "The cook is dead."

"I know. I got the men under cover, then I went looking for you. I thought you'd been killed as well."

"The tanjian are here," So-Peng said. When Tak said nothing, he went on. "The cook was killed with the same weapon as the two merchants in Singapore—a throwing star."

Tak was scowling. "You knew this and you made no outcry?"

"If I had," So-Peng said, "I would have been the next to die. I did not know from which direction the star had come, but I knew I was being watched."

As he moved through the jungle, he avoided a spot where the sun dropped almost straight through a small gap in the jungle canopy, golden instead of luminescent green.

"We are being stalked," So-Peng said as they returned to the jungle path. He had made his circuit, had seen no one. Still, he fingered the throwing star hidden in his trousers, the one he had purloined from the police office in Singapore. "I believe the tanjian mean to kill us one by one until you are the last remaining member of this party."

The silence stretched on so long that Tak was forced to say, "And then?"

"I don't know," So-Peng confessed. "Perhaps they will seek to take you apart in front of your enemy."

Tak looked at So-Peng. "Second sight says that I will not return from here," he said. "That future, I believe, is but one of many. Now we must prove that it is the wrong one."

"We cannot remain on the path," So-Peng pointed out.

"No, we must head directly into the jungle."

"How well do you know this area?"

Tak spat. "Maybe better than the tanjian, though not as well as the man we have to get to." He eyed So-Peng. "Do you have an idea?"

"Maybe," So-Peng said, "but I need height for it to work."

Tak smiled, pointing almost due north. "There," he said, "not a mile away are the Kota Tinggi waterfalls. They are over one hundred feet high."

So-Peng nodded. "They'll do."

Tak and So-Peng returned to where the men squatted under cover, and headed out. Less than a mile, Tak had said. Still, So-Peng thought, considering the numerous skills of the tanjian, that could seem like a day's march.

The second man went down at precisely the moment when So-Peng heard the deep rumble of the falls. An outflung arm flared across So-Peng's vision like the wavering of a battle standard. Moving, he shouted in Malay patois, a dialect he and Tak had agreed upon for future communication, rather than a Chinese dialect, which might be understood by the tanjian.

The three of them hurried onward toward the falls, zigzagging as best they could. The terrain began to change, first subtly, then more obviously, as they approached the lowest level of the falls.

In the first of the rocks surrounding the falls, the last of Tak's men went down with a throwing star in the back of his neck. As they had agreed, Tak ascended the wet rocks, heading directly up the left face of the cliff.

So-Peng hoped that the tanjian would be filled with their recent accomplishments and so could be taken off guard. So far as they were concerned, their strategy had been wholly successful. This was what was crucial, and as he climbed above and to the left of Tak, So-Peng thought it a shame that two men had had to die in the furtherance of this fiction. He would have much preferred to go after the tanjian after the first attack, but that would have proved foolhardy and, no doubt, fatal. They had obviously held the high ground, and as his mother had explained to him, they were masters of their environment, learning to blend in to their surroundings. He would have had no chance at them back on the jungle floor.

Now he was taking the high ground. Now, like the field mouse fixed in the pupil of the eagle, he was about to fix the tanjian in his mind. Soon their image would appear in his eyes.

As he ascended, the water, white and fuming, bellowed in his ears. Birds flew at the level of his shoulder, then moments later soared below him. When he looked down he could see now and again Tak's black hair bobbing in among the rocks and spume, a tiny boat trying to find safe harbor in a storm.

So-Peng paused and, setting his back firmly against the rocks, closed his eyes.

Was it the fear engendered by the tanjian or the arrogance inside himself that caused him to ignore his mother's warning not to rely upon his gift? At that moment who could say? In any event, he sought to find that secret place in the center of him from which point his psychic link with his mother had been born. Then, as he had seen her do, he expanded his spirit outward, breathing in the sky.

It was a heady experience. He felt the wind against his mind and, rising, the salt spray of the South China Sea far away. He could see the stars burning in the heavens beyond the sunshine, could begin to feel the currents of unseen particles filling the vast trenches between the stars.

Below, he ranged across the tumbling arc of the waterfalls, fascinated by the continuous outpouring of kinetic energy, wondering like a child if he could find a way to tap into that elemental source.

It was then that he felt the wall. Featureless and grim, it rose up around him, blotting out first the stars, sun, and sky, then the wildly rushing water, even the rock face upon which he now crouched, trembling and terrified, his arm over his eyes.

He had disobeyed his mother. He had chosen to abandon the low ground where he could use his gift in obscurity. In thoughtlessly expanding his spirit, he had announced himself as clearly as if he had shouted "Here I am!" at the top of his voice.

Because a link had been forged. Not with Liang—she was many miles away. But with another who possessed the gift!

In the moment when their spirits touched, So-Peng gave up his anonymity. But in return he learned a great deal. For one thing, he now knew that there was only one tanjian who had been stalking them. He knew where that tanjian was, and most terrible of all, he knew his identity.

Hearing his name being called, So-Peng took his arm away from his face and rose in time to see the tanjian appearing through a narrow defile in the rocks not more than six feet away.

So-Peng looked into the face of Zhao Hsia, his childhood friend.

At that instant Zhao Hsia laughed. "Not merely your childhood friend," he said in a voice grown deep through the years. "Your half brother."

Seeing the look on So-Peng's face, he smiled. "It is clear that Liang never told you. She was married before she met your father, wed to the tanjian monk our grandfather chose for her."

"Was it you who killed those two merchants in Singapore?" So-Peng asked. He was still half in shock at discovering the true identity of Zhao Hsia.

Zhao Hsia shook his head. "Originally, I was with another tanjian. We were meant to scare the merchants so that they would work for Tik Po Tak's enemy, not with Tak himself. My friend does not have my temperament. When the merchants refused to leave Tak's employ—well, the persuasion got out of hand. I tried to stop him, but it was too late. The merchants were already dead. I regret that sincerely."

So-Peng wanted to believe him.

"Tell me," Zhao Hsia said. "I have not seen our mother in many years. How is she?"

"She has been well," So-Peng said, still trying to discern truth from fiction. "But the tanjian presence in Singapore—the murders—have upset her terribly."

"Then I will have to speak with her," Zhao Hsia said, "to pacify her fears." He took a step up the rocky slope. "Tell me, have you seen the box?"

"What box?" The trip-hammer beating of So-Peng's heart almost made him trip over the words. As it was, the lie felt squeezed out of him like a pip from a fruit.

"The one containing the emeralds." Noting So-Peng's puzzled expression, Zhao Hsia went on. "The sixteen emeralds, you idiot. The energy of the tanjian. Our sacred history is engraved upon their facets, although no one but a tanjian monk can see the writing. The emeralds are encased in a small velvet box. Have you seen it?"

"No."

"I would know if you were lying," Zhao Hsia said, and So-Peng felt again the cool, featureless wall enclosing him for an instant.

"Why would I lie?"

Zhao Hsia's expression was contemptuous. "Because evidently you are our mother's son, devious, depraved. Just as I am my father's son, a true monk of Tau-tau, schooled in all its disciplines."

So-Peng, his heart in his throat, thought it interesting that Zhao Hsia could not tell that he was lying. Was this, too, part of his gift? he wondered.

"You have the gift," So-Peng pointed out. He thought he had discovered something, a glittering rent in the apparently seamless wall. He struck out at it to see if he could prize it open. "The gift comes from mother. Like it or not, we are both her sons."

Abruptly, Zhao Hsia's demeanor shifted. His mask slipped off his face and the hate appeared, as stark and powerful as theatrical makeup. "Do not speak to me of Liang," Zhao Hsia said tightly. "She despised my father, she despised me just as she despised the tanjian way of life. So she ran away. She broke the law of Tau-tau."

"Then it's true," So-Peng said, struggling not to be overwhelmed by the brilliant light flowing out from the wall's rent. "You've come to take her back to Zhuji."

Zhao Hsia threw back his head and laughed. "Not her, my friend. I've come for you!"

So-Peng was so stunned that all he could utter was, "Me?"

"You have the gift, just as I do. That gift is revered by the tanjian; its uses are limitless when it is harnessed to the discipline of Tau-tau."

"I have no wish to be harnessed by anyone or anything."

So-Peng thought frantically—how could I have been so blind as not to see the connection between my gift and Tau-tau? And he asked himself why his mother had lied to him about the connection. She had lied, too, about Zhao Hsia's mission. What else had she lied about? What if everything Zhao Hsia accused her of was true?

"Then you are a fool." Zhao Hsia's face was like rubber, stretching into the aspect of utter dismay. He was an actor upon a sunlit stage. "Don't you understand? Your potential, like mine, goes beyond anything yet imaginable. But you are undisciplined, untrained, unfocused. Tau-tau can change all that. It can give you the power of dreams!"

So-Peng now realized what his mother had been hiding from him. She had known all along what the tanjian wanted—of course she would know, he was her son! She had understood that it was So-Peng's and Zhao Hsia's karma to meet like this. She had done her best to prepare So-Peng, to have the meeting occur on neutral territory where So-Peng would have at least a semblance of a chance. She had known that his gift was raw, untrained, unfocused, as Zhao Hsia had said. Just as she knew that Zhao Hsia's gift was already in harness to Tau-tau.

"I will not return to Zhuji with you," So-Peng said, sealing his karma, and Zhao Hsia's.

"Would you leave me no choice, then?" Zhao Hsia asked. His voice was sincere, laced with regret. But beneath that glossy surface So-Peng felt the emanations of exultation, and his spirit recoiled in horror.

"Weakling!" Zhao Hsia cried. "Remember how we stole the tortoise eggs. It was only after Tau-tau that I understood the magnitude of our sin. We stole the tortoise's future, So-Peng. Just like Liang did. She robbed me of my future—just as she robbed you of yours—when she stole away into the night. I needed her and she was not there. You needed the tanjian community and she withheld it from you. It is she who is the evil one! It is she who must be punished!"

Like a wave inundating the shoreline, reality wavered, and So-Peng saw the world woven for him by the words of the tanjian. Zhao Hsia's hate became his hate; Zhao Hsia's sense of abandonment became his.

"She did not tell you about your heritage. It is your birthright, So-Peng! It was her duty to tell you. But she didn't, did she? Did she tell you that she stole the sacred emeralds from our grandfather? I imagine not. He wants them back, So-Peng. He needs them. They are the source of his power. It is said that these sixteen emeralds were the prize possession of Chieh, the terminator, from whom our grandfather is directly descended. It is said that their power kept Chieh alive for decades after his contemporaries had perished."

So-Peng felt an urge to hurl epithets in Zhao Hsia's face, to tell him what a liar he was. But he said nothing, knowing that any such words would give him away. Zhao Hsia would know that Liang had the emeralds, and this, he knew, he must never reveal.

"It must be so," Zhao Hsia was saying. "Even now Grandfather grows ill and weak, the life draining out of him. Without the emeralds, Grandfather will perish." He was inching closer, sidling up the rock face toward So-Peng. "Liang knew that, yet she took them anyway. Now her punishment is at hand."

For an instant the two boys' personalities merged, and So-Peng caught a glimpse of the terrifying entity thus created. He felt a lurch, as if the earth itself were shuddering at such an abomination.

Then he saw Zhao Hsia, the surrounding rocks, heard the churning of the waterfall beside and below him, and he knew how completely he had been deceived. He also had a firsthand glimpse of the awesome power of Tau-tau. Had it not been for his gift, he would have been hypnotized by the speech, would have been convinced that Liang was indeed evil incarnate.

With a crystal insight he understood that he was the only thing standing between his half brother and Liang's death.

Palming the throwing star from his pocket, he threw it at Zhao Hsia's head. Zhao Hsia did not move his upper torso, but rather lifted his hand, catching the whirling weapon out of the air.

"You do not know how to use this, brother," Zhao Hsia said. Like a conjuror he twirled the deadly thing between his outstretched fingers. "It cannot harm me. *You* cannot harm me." He was grinning now. "But thrown by a true tanjian, it can kill you." All at once the star was on his fingertips, poised, waiting. Sunlight glinted blindingly off its razor edges, as if the weapon could gather in that solar power.

"As I told you, brother," Zhao Hsia said, "you leave me no choice." He twisted the star. "Here is your karma."

At that moment So-Peng felt a presence behind him. He willed himself not to turn around, not to move or to think about the presence. Tak had been quite clever. He had used the sound of the falls to mask his approach, coming upon Zhao Hsia from the only direction possible—by keeping So-Peng's body between him and the tanjian.

Now everything happened at once, and like a glass ball in which was embedded a tiny scene, the snow falling as it was shaken, the present became the future, and that future was changed forever.

Tak emerged from behind So-Peng's right shoulder and, in a blur, lunged for Zhao Hsia. So-Peng, too, was moving forward. He saw the glint of the knife blade emerging out of Tak's extended right hand. At the same moment he heard the whir, like a mosquito in his ear, and he caught Tak's ankle with his foot.

The star whirred past Tak's head. Tak, sprawled headlong across the rocks, swiped with his right arm. The knife blade cut the skin of Zhao Hsia's calf just as So-Peng reached him.

The moment they came together, So-Peng knew that it was a mistake to grapple physically with his half brother. While So-Peng was quite strong, he had not been trained in Tau-tau, and strength alone was not enough.

Caught unprepared for the nature of the assault, So-Peng felt himself bound to Zhao Hsia. He tried to strike out with his balled fists, his knees, toes, and heels. All to no avail. Zhao Hsia either deflected the blow with his body or twisted so that So-Peng painfully struck rock rather than flesh.

Out of the corner of his eye So-Peng could see Tak rising, pulling a pistol from his belt. But the two boys were so inextricably entwined that Tak could not venture a shot without the possibility of shooting So-Peng.

So-Peng tried now to pull himself away from his half brother, but as if sensing the danger to himself, Zhao Hsia kept him tight against himself. At the same time he managed to enclose So-Peng's throat in his fingers. He began to squeeze.

So-Peng fought back as best he could, but he knew it was fruitless. Zhao Hsia would never release him, and would most certainly kill him.

So-Peng's mind was in panic, searching this way and that for a way to survive. There was none. He knew he was going to die.

And with that knowledge he let himself go, relaxing into the very core of himself, until he discovered that place his gift had given him, and allowing that place to speak in the rustling of a tongue more ancient than any other, he discovered what he must do.

Using the weight not only of his body, but of his spirit as well, he offset their combined center of gravity. He leaned into Zhao Hsia instead of pulling away from him. He pushed hard with his spirit.

He heard the call of a bird in flight. He heard the rumble of the water, felt the first chill splash of the rushing water as it churned over the rocks.

Then they were spilling past the rocks, into the water itself. In that last moment of coherent thought, So-Peng was sure he heard Tak cry out.

Then the two struggling boys were cast into the falls. As So-Peng's gift had shown him, the churning water acted as his ally, breaking Zhao Hsia's desperate hold on him. So-Peng gasped, and water filled his mouth and throat. He began to choke.

Restless water, bellowing like thunder, overflowing with energy, carried them both down.

BOOK II

MIDNIGHT
SHIN-YA

How often the fear of one evil
leads us into a worse.

—NICHOLAS BOILEAU-DESPREAUX

ASAMA HIGHLANDS/WASHINGTON/EAST BAY BRIDGE/ TOKYO/THE HODAKA

SUMMER, PRESENT

*T*anjian."

They all froze at Tanzan Nangi's one spoke word.

"That doesn't sound like Japanese," Justine said.

"It isn't," Nicholas told her. "It's Chinese, I believe."

Tanzan Nangi nodded gravely. "You're quite right." He addressed Justine, but it was clear he was speaking for Nicholas's benefit as well. "You asked me before about who could create *Shiro Ninja*. Now that it is clear that this is what has happened to Nicholas, I have no choice but to tell you."

"No!" Nicholas fairly shouted this.

Nangi said, "If there is love between you, surely she must be told."

"It is because of that love that I want her kept out of this," Nicholas said, blind to the pain he was causing Justine.

"Love is sustaining," Nangi said simply. "Cutting yourself off from it is but one manifestation of *Shiro Ninja*." He waited long enough for this to sink in, then said, "The attack of *Shiro Ninja* is beyond a Black Ninja's skills. It is beyond even a ninja *sensei*'s scope." His good eye glittered. "It is the domain solely of the tanjian."

Tanzan Nangi, cognizant that Nicholas had just returned home from the hospital and would fatigue easily, wanted to get right to the point. "There is no doubt that the creature you and the policewoman encountered at the doctor's office was a ninja." Nangi was watching Nicholas carefully. "Are we agreed on this?"

Nicholas heard himself say as if from a great distance, "Yes. A ninja."

"Could you by any chance discern his *ryu*?" Nangi meant his school. For a ninja of Nicholas's skill, it was not difficult to discover where another ninja had been trained by how he moved, which strategy he employed, even the weapons he chose to use.

"No," Nicholas said, sick at heart.

Nangi nodded. "This is yet another manifestation of *Shiro Ninja*."

When Nicholas said nothing, Nangi went on in a more urgent tone of voice. "You must come to terms with the fact that you are *Shiro Ninja*, that you are under attack, and that your adversary is an adept in Tau-tau."

"There is no evidence," Nicholas said carefully, "that either Tau-tau or tanjian exists or ever existed."

Nangi took out a cigarette, lighted it.

"I can't abide cigarette smoke," Nicholas said. "You know that." Even to his own ears, his voice sounded peevish.

"I know what I see," Nangi said evenly, "and so do you." He took another puff, let out the smoke slowly through his nostrils. "Will you stop me from smoking?" He grunted in disgust. "Look at you. You can't even get out of bed. You are attacked by a ninja. Without *Getsumei no michi* you cannot discern his origin, let alone battle him one to one. Only by the grace of God are you alive now to tell us of the encounter." He squinted through the smoke. "How much more evidence do you require?"

"Get out of here!"

Justine cringed as Nicholas shouted at Nangi. Perhaps that was the trigger. This colossal breach of faith in his friend cleared Nicholas's head for a moment; he understood then what Nangi had done. What had it cost Nangi, Nicholas thought guiltily, to smoke after three years of abstention? He had broken his vow for Nicholas, a vow that meant a great deal to Nangi. The anger Nangi had quite deliberately engendered in him had sprung the gate that Nicholas had been holding fast with all his spiritual might.

Because as long as he denied *Shiro Ninja*, he could deny that anything was wrong with him. To accept its existence was to admit that his life had been turned inside out. That, worse, he might never be the same man again.

But *Shiro Ninja* was real; all he had left were the emeralds. Nicholas knew that he must do everything in his power to keep So-Peng's precious magic—arcane and distant—out of the hands of his enemy.

It was odd, now that he thought about it, just how far removed his life had been from those invaluable gems. Only now that they were threatened could Nicholas recognize what they meant to him, although he still had no idea of their function.

And Nangi was right: Nicholas almost wept at how helpless and weak he felt. Another wave of despair swept over him. *The certainty of despair will crush you far more thoroughly than defeat ever could.*

"I am sorry, Nangi-san," Nicholas said. "Please forgive my bullheadedness."

Nangi stubbed out his cigarette. "There are times when fear can devastate even the most stouthearted." He leaned upon his dragon-headed walking stick. "Before you can learn to walk again," he said, "you must accept that you are a cripple. *Shiro Ninja* has done this to you. And behind *Shiro Ninja* is a clever, deadly foe."

"Tanjian," Nicholas said.

Justine said, "Just what is tanjian?"

Nangi waited for Nicholas to answer, but when it was clear that he was not going to speak, Nangi said, "Quite simply, some believe that tanjian were the precursors of ninja; that the arcane discipline of Tau-tau is the origin of *ninjutsu.* But Tau-tau is far more primitive, therefore more powerful in ways a refined discipline such as *ninjutsu* cannot be."

"Tau-tau is heavily laced with magic," Nicholas said.

"Magic?" Justine echoed.

"Like the kind Akiko possessed," Nangi said carefully. "Many sects of *ninjutsu* employ some forms of minor magic or quasimagic, sleight of hand, hypnotism, and the like, relics of Tau-tau adulterated by generations of verbal translation, by time itself and by Japanese culture. Tanjian are different. Their discipline has remained intact, pure and primitive as it once was. Their magic is quite real, quite potent. Akiko was a *miko*, a sorceress. It is clear that she was trained in elements of Tau-tau."

"She was no tanjian," Nicholas said.

"No," Nangi agreed. "But the ninja you encountered two days ago certainly is."

"Whoever this tanjian is," Justine said, "he is after Nicholas. Does anyone know why?"

"The shadows inherent in *ninjutsu*," Nangi said, "create their own danger."

Seeing Justine's lost look, Nicholas said, "What Nangi means is, the attack might not be personal at all. Being *Aka-i-ninjutsu* makes me something of a target." That made him think of something, and he said to Nangi, "That detective-sergeant, Tomi Yazawa, told me of a supposed threat on my life from the Red Army."

"What was this," Nangi said, "some kind of rumor?"

"She said that her department had intercepted and decoded a piece of hard intelligence."

"You cannot fight the tanjian alone and unarmed as you are," Nangi said.

"I know that," Nicholas told him. "In fact, I've known ever since I suspected the loss of *Getsumei no michi* what I must do. It's just that—" He turned to look through the window at the grounds he loved so much. He could feel his aunt Itami's spirit very close at hand, and took what courage he could from its aura. "—I've put roadblocks up to deflect my every step."

"Or someone else has done it for you," Nangi observed. He stamped the end of his walking stick on the floor. "This Red Army message is obviously part of the tanjian tactic of sowing confusion. The Red Army has no reason to harm you."

"I know that," Nicholas said.

Nangi's hard stare penetrated the haze of aftershock. "Now tell me what strategy you have devised."

A week later, as he ascended, the breath in his throat growing cold, Nicholas had cause to remember that conversation. It gave him some measure of spiritual comfort, something he was very short on. He blocked out the howling of the wind as he made his laborious way through calf-deep snow. This high up his breath condensed in front of his face, misting his vision. It was still summer, to be sure, but up here in the Asama *kogen*, the highlands of the northern Japanese Alps, it was always cold.

He adjusted the straps of his backpack and, despite his physical aches and pains, continued his ascent. It was his spiritual pain, far more severe than any his body felt, that drove him onward.

Upon the spine of Asama-yama, a mile and a half high, he paused within the lee of a mighty outcropping of striated gray granite. He put his back against the rock, cheered by its eternal presence, its elemental strength. He squatted down, scooped a handful of snow into his mouth, let it melt slowly. He chewed on a strip of dried beef.

He was more tired than he could have believed. The trek up the face of the mountain had taken an inordinate physical effort. Normally, such a journey would be nothing more than moderate exercise for him.

But these were not normal times, and he was not the Nicholas Linnear of old. He understood that he would have to get used to that painful reality. Still, he was only human, and once, on the high ridge of Asama-yama's southern flank, he almost broke down, feeling an overwhelming urge to weep in fear and frustration. But that would have been self-indulgent, or worse, self-pitying. He had no room in his new life for such treacherous emotions; they could only undermine his resolve to enter into battle with the tanjian despite being *Shiro Ninja*.

Nicholas, coming off the spine of Asama-yama, began a long, loping descent into a bowl-shaped alpine valley studded with larch, snow-white birch. Here and there he could see a peach tree, remarkable in such a climate.

He looked back down the path he had come. Far below, where the last of the roads ended, he could make out several villas, stone and wood structures fixed into the side of the mountain, where the rich of Tokyo made the eighty-mile weekend journey northeast from the metropolis.

It was not a villa that he was looking for, but rather a castle. As he searched for it, he thought of Akiko, Saigo's lover, then his. The *miko*.

It was Akiko who had described the castle in Asama to Nicholas. She might have learned *Kan-aku na ninjutsu* with Nicholas's cousin Saigo, at the *ryu* in Kumamoto, but it was here in the Asama *kogen* that she had learned *jaho*, the magic of the *miko*.

Then, coming down off the ridge, Nicholas saw it: Yami Doki castle, the Kite in the Darkness, where dwelled Kyoki, the master of *jaho*. Kyoki, the only man who could save Nicholas from *Shiro Ninja*, because Kyoki was tanjian.

Akiko had told Nicholas about Kyoki during her last hours on earth. She had felt compelled to describe him in such detail that Nicholas was certain he would recognize the tanjian on sight. Akiko had studied with Kyoki for seven years. That had been during the 1960s. He was then, according to her account, in his forties, relatively young to be the master of such powerful arcane disciplines.

Akiko had never used the word tanjian to describe Kyoki. Nicholas doubted whether he had told her what he was. But from what he had taught her, it seemed clear enough to Nicholas that Kyoki was tanjian. His physical description—a savage Mongol face, more Chinese than Japanese—gave added credence to this theory.

Nicholas had to believe now that Kyoki was tanjian: it was his only hope.

Catching sight of the castle, still standing, looking exactly the way Akiko had described it to him, he felt a surge of faith that here was where he would be healed. He was coming closer to discovering what arcane power So-Peng's emeralds represented. Here was where he would be restored to life; *Shiro Ninja* would be banished.

It had begun to rain. The fine needles of the alpine firs swayed in the swirling wind, and the larch leaves, showing their silver undersides, danced as if in response to a choreographer's tutelage. The sky was oyster-white, and the air was fecund with the scent of mulch. Great drifts of blue-gray fog billowed over the sloping volcanic shoulder of Asama-yama, obscuring for minutes at a time entire sections of the valley.

Pushed by the winds through the mountains, the rain was falling in an almost horizontal plane. Nicholas hunched his shoulders, pulling up the Gore-Tex collar of his alpine parka, fastening the snaps across his throat. He was cold and wet, in need of shelter and rest.

In this atmosphere Kyoki's castle at times appeared to wink in and out of existence, at others, to fade completely into the mist-shrouded landscape within which it was set. It had seemed close enough when Nicholas was picking his way down the rubble-strewn slope of Mt. Asama. But now in the valley itself, the perspective changed, and Nicholas could see that he had farther to go than he had at first believed.

He thought about his encounter with the ninja—the tanjian—in Dr. Hanami's office. Tomi Yazawa had thought this had been the assassination attempt ordered by the Red Army. Nicholas did not. As Nangi had said, it was likely that there would be no assassination attempt at all, that the Red Army had no interest whatsoever in Nicholas Linnear. He could not think of a single reason why they would want him dead. Yet there was a deeper mystery to be solved: why hadn't the tanjian killed him when he had had the chance?

If you die now, if you die too easily, you will never understand, the tanjian had whispered in Nicholas's ear.

Understand what?

Nicholas had no idea. He tried to put out of his mind the feeling of utter helplessness he had experienced in the tanjian's grip. It was as if his body, ready and able to respond to the challenge, had been waiting for the proper commands from his brain. They had never come. Why?

With an effort, Nicholas pulled himself back from the abyss of despair. He found that he was panting, the breath blowing through his nostrils as if he were a frightened animal. Appalled by this lack of control, he took slow, deep breaths, trying to center himself. It was no good. Anxiety continued to swirl through his spirit as the mist advanced across the valley.

At last he came to the castle. Soon he would see Kyoki; soon *Shiro Ninja* would be just a memory, a bad dream dissipated by Kyoki's *jaho*.

The castle was nestled behind a rise strewn with mountain laurel and oak. It dominated a glen, a private sector of the alpine valley, from which it overlooked Asama-yama, as well as much of the entire Hida Range.

The views from its upper-floor windows, Nicholas saw, would be spectacular.

The entire fence of vertical iron bars appeared to be something from medieval times. The high, carved wooden gate was unlocked, and Nicholas entered.

Inside the compound it was very still; the restless wind coming in off Asama-yama was nowhere in evidence.

The front door, which should have been locked, was not. Nicholas pushed it open. On the threshold of Kyoki's domain he paused, listening to silence inside the castle. He could smell wood smoke, aromatic with balsam, undercut by the bitter scent of charcoal, residue of years of fires. As he walked in, other smells that he could not immediately identify swirled around him like the mist coming off the shoulder of Mt. Asama, like the fearful vapor through which he kept falling, falling . . .

At that moment he thought of Justine, and the memory was like a knife in his heart. He missed her with an intensity that he found almost insupportable. Another wave of despair washed over him with the knowledge that he would never be able to return to his old relationship with her while he was *Shiro Ninja*. The thought gave added urgency to his mission: find Kyoki, convince him to use his tanjian magic to undo what tanjian magic had created.

Although it had been utterly still in the grounds outside the castle, inside a chill wind blew through the stone corridors, the oversized chambers. Someone had been cooking recently, and the remnants of a balsam-log fire lay in the great-room hearth. Shadows lay everywhere, seeming to Nicholas like spectators at the theater, eager for the denouement. Or perhaps, he thought, it is only I who am anxious to get this over with.

He went through chamber after chamber, found them empty though not unused. In the Room of All Shadows, where once Akiko had knelt to meditate on her *jaho* lessons, the flickering flames of slender white tapers cast shadows as sharp as knife blades into every corner of the chamber.

Upstairs Nicholas entered a singular chamber whose ceiling was arched. Tatami mats covered the floor. It was divided by a traditional Chinese moon gate, and Nicholas nodded in recognition. Tanjian was, after all, originally a Chinese discipline.

The room had about it the air of great antiquity, as if it had existed long before the rest of the castle, as if by his magic Kyoki had transported it here from another place, another time. Of course, nothing of the sort was possible, Nicholas told himself. There must be a limit even to Tau-tau.

The scent of lit joss sticks was so thick it was cloying, clinging to the back of his throat, choking him. Coils of the aromatic smoke lay on the air like sleeping serpents. Nicholas went across the chamber. The stone walls were unadorned, and there were few pieces of furniture. A dark wood *tansu* chest stood against one wall, stark and majestic, surrounded by space.

Just beneath the moon gate was the demarkation between two tatami, and Nicholas, about to go through the gate, paused. Still in the first half of the chamber, he knelt down, stared at the black borders of the two straw nuts. Unlike the usual close abutment, he saw a space of perhaps a sixteenth of an inch between the mats beneath the moon gate. Immediately he looked up, located the hairline slit in the underside of the gate.

He looked around the part of the room he was in, took up a floor pillow, braced himself, thrust it through the moon gate.

With a faint hiss a blade blurred down, bisecting the pillow. As the blade whirred back into its hidden niche, Nicholas somersaulted through the opening.

He was about to make a quick circuit of the chamber, but instead stood as still as a statue. In a moment tiny, violent quiverings broke out just beneath his skin. He felt sick to his stomach.

He had found Kyoki, the tanjian.

Kyoki lay spread-eagled in a far corner of the chamber. There was so much blood that for a moment Nicholas could not understand how he had failed to smell the stench. Then he remembered the lit joss sticks.

Slowly, as if in a dream, he approached the corpse. He stared in horrified fascination. Kyoki's skin had been detached in precise strips, every inch of his body laid open. The skin, like ruddy streamers, lay in a pinwheel pattern, radiating out from the central core of the corpse.

The tanjian's face was unmarred. Nicholas had no trouble identifying Kyoki from Akiko's description—it was as if he had not aged at all from the time he had trained her.

This close, the stench of death was apparent. Nevertheless, Nicholas squatted by the corpse's side. A despair he had never known before overwhelmed him. Kyoki had been his only hope, and now that hope had been denied him. What was he to do now? Was it his karma to remain *Shiro Ninja* until his unknown adversary came to kill him?

No, no. It could not be. His hands at his sides curled into fists. He fought against the hopelessness of his situation. But then a new dread wormed its way into his psyche. Kyoki had been tanjian, a master of Tau-tau. And yet he had been skinned alive. By whom? Who could have such power?

We have no power if we cannot use our imagination, Kansatsu-san,

Nicholas's first ninja *sensei* had told him. *Just as we know that the mind-body continuum maintains a balance inside the human shell, so we have learned that power and imagination provide the Way inside the human mind.* Kansatsu-san, small and intense, tranquil as a stone amid a leaf storm. Black eyes shining in Nicholas's mind, his words playing the chords of memory. *Others teach that being excessive is the same as being inadequate. These* sensei *do not possess imagination, which is synonymous with excess. Yes, it is true that in the mind-body continuum excess is to be avoided. But the power-imagination continuum is different; it presents us not with a whole new set of laws—which would be impossible to absorb, since we obey the Way—but with no laws at all.*

Now we can understand the origin of chaos, because in the power-imagination continuum chaos can reign. This is the side of unbridled power. But imagination keeps chaos in check, knowing that power with too little imagination is disastrous not only for the perpetrator, but for those around him as well.

Never forget, Nicholas, that ninjutsu *is in the realm of the power-imagination continuum. Those who abuse its teachings are* dorokusai, *warped beyond redemption, and must be destroyed.*

With a shiver of precognition, Nicholas knew that it was such a one—a *dorokusai*—he had encountered in Dr. Hanami's office. If that was the case, even with So-Peng's emeralds, without *Getsumei no michi* Nicholas knew that he had no chance to survive.

Douglas Howe, chairman of the Senate Armed Services Committee, stood on crowded Wisconsin Avenue, in Chevy Chase, just outside the Washington, D.C., city limits. As he glanced around the posh neighborhood, his car, a sleek, dark blue Lincoln Continental, slid to a stop in front of him and he climbed in. The Lincoln took off.

Howe slipped the gift-wrapped package onto the backseat, said one word, "Nora's," to Michael, his chauffeur/bodyguard. As the big car slipped through the late-morning Washington traffic, Howe settled back in the leather bench seat. A letter faxed from his office was waiting for him, and he pulled it out of the portable machine's slot.

He turned on a light, slipped on a pair of half-lens glasses and began to read. The words meant nothing to him. His mind was still on the size-four Louis Feraud suit—mid-tone speckled gray wool with a fox-trimmed peplum, harbinger of the new fall collection—that he had just picked up. He had picked it out last week, and in his absence, it had been put on the seamstress's torso he had had Saks Jandel make for him in lieu of tedious fittings. He had heard that Jack Kennedy had had one made to fit Marilyn Monroe's figure, using it to buy her occasional presents of a jacket, a dress, or a suit.

With an effort, he concentrated on the memo. It concerned the number of new Navy transport carriers to be alloted in next year's military budget. Howe scribbled his comment in the margin, initialed it, sent it back by fax to his office, put the glasses away.

Truth to tell, it was not precisely the Louis Feraud suit that was on Howe's mind, but rather, what the suit represented: not so much a present, but a bonus for a hazardous job well done. Not that he knew for certain yet what the final outcome would be, but it was good to be prepared.

The Lincoln Continental pulled into the curb on R Street. Douglas Howe fleetingly felt as he opened the door that in leaving the Louis Feraud suit on the seat, he was leaving a part of himself behind. Immediately he overcame this weakness and emerged into the glorious Washington sunlight.

It was exceptionally hot and humid, nothing new for summer in the city on the Potomac. But Howe was, as usual, crisply, sharply dressed in a single-vent charcoal pinstripe suit of a superb tropical-weight worsted, brilliant white shirt hand-loomed for him from Egyptian cotton, and a dark tie of rich silk in a thoroughly subdued pattern, so as not to take anything away from the exemplary cut of the suit.

Howe was a slight man with fine sandy hair above the high, domed forehead of the deep thinker. His face was odd, compelling, with its pointed chin, sunken cheeks, and round blue eyes that burned with a luminous intensity. He was not a handsome man, yet he was so totally at ease with people that no one had yet commented on how much his face resembled that of a weasel.

Howe was greeted by Nora's smiling maître d', shown to his usual table in the far corner, where he commanded a full view of the room.

Within moments a Bloody Mary made to his specifications appeared. Howe took a long swallow, allowed himself the luxury of one long circuit looking around the restaurant. He nodded to several people he knew or who fancied they knew him. The room was already three-quarters full. Within ten minutes, he knew, there would not be a seat free.

He glanced at his Polo watch. Twelve twenty-eight. Brisling had precisely two minutes to walk through Nora's door and sit down at his table. Two minutes and counting.

Actually, Howe couldn't care less about Brisling or the news that he would bring. Brisling would no doubt be so anxious to relate it that he would not even wait a civilized amount of time until a drink was brought and consumed in quiet reflection.

All things considered, David Brisling was the perfect assistant. He was smart enough to accomplish most assignments on his own, but stupid enough for Howe to control him utterly. He was, Howe thought, like an idiot manqué, something Howe might have concocted in his laboratory had he been a genetic engineer in the twenty-first century.

Thirty seconds to go, and there was David Brisling, hurrying by the maître d'. In another life, Howe thought as Brisling was shown to his table, his assistant might have been a CIA agent. He was thoroughly nondescript, a man of middle America, made of solid stock. Salt of the earth.

David Brisling sat and, without a greeting, said a bit breathlessly, "I think I've got the answer."

"Hello, David." Manners were of the utmost importance to Douglas Howe. To him, they were synonymous with breeding, and since as a son of farmers he could never have the one, he was damned sure he would have the other.

Only rarely did it occur to him that part of his abiding enmity for Cotton Branding stemmed from the fact that the other man had everything that Howe coveted because he could never have it: Branding came from the right family, had graduated from the right school, had the right friends, the right contacts, and had entreé into the right clubs, the inner circles of power open to only those elite few born to money and to old-line families. These people—like Branding—had everything laid out for them from the moment they were born, while poor slobs like Howe had to slog uphill for every crumb, to curry favor to get even a brief moment of recognition. But the doors—the important doors to power, to the inner circle—were always closed.

Brisling nodded to Howe, fluttered some papers. "I think we've got what we wanted out of the Johnson Institute study." He was speaking about the feasibility study that would give the go-ahead to the Hive Project: four billion dollars of the government's money down the drain because of Cook Branding's damnable Advanced Computer Research Agency bill. Chasing after the Holy Grail of a thinking, interactive computer, no matter its theoretical benefits, was all well and good for some privately funded organization. But to involve the government—to waste the taxpayer's money on what, in Howe's opinion, was nothing more than a pipe dream, went beyond the ludicrous—it was unconscionable.

"Read these."

Howe, reluctant to put on his half glasses, said, "Just give me the digest version."

What Brisling had unearthed were several questionable affiliations among two members of the fifteen-man Johnson Institute research team, including the director, Dr. Rudolph. This was just the kind of breakthrough Howe had been praying for: a way to derail the passage of the ASCRA bill. He knew he needed more facts, that he should hire a team of investigators to get them. Two factors dissuaded him. The first was that he did not want to involve himself personally in this investigation, in case it somehow backfired. Plausible deniability was, since Irangate, the watchword in Washington. The other was that he was innately impatient.

Patience was one of Cook Branding's virtues, and since Howe could not discover within himself that particular resource, he hated Branding all the more for possessing it. It was Branding's strategy to wait for his adversary—whomever that might be—to make a mistake, and then to pounce on it. It was a strategy that could only be successful if employed by a man who was both patient and faultless. For such a man, it proved a potent strategy, indeed. But should that man with the spotless reputation ever stumble—and should that stumble be brought into the public eye—then that man's position would not only be jeopardized, but his entire career would come apart.

Such a man, in Douglas Howe's opinion, was Cook Branding. And Howe meant to ensure that Branding would stumble hard.

Howe tapped the Johnson Institute flimsies. He smiled, said, "I've got to admit that you've done your job well, David." Pitting Brisling against Branding was like letting loose a trained flea to bring down a raging bull. Which was perfectly acceptable, Howe thought, as long as the flea did not become aware of its status. He handed the flimsies back to his assistant. "Keep these," he said. "Add them to the Branding file we've been amassing. And make certain the file's in a safe place. It's now strictly Eyes Only."

Brisling nodded, pocketed the flimsies.

"Now I want you to find a way to work with this information. Dig deeper into the private lives of these scientists, see which ones will be most vulnerable to coercion." Seeing the look in Brisling's eyes, he added reassuringly, "Don't worry, David. This is for a good cause. What we're doing here will be ultimately redeemed when the ASCRA bill goes down to defeat."

At that moment the maître d' bustled up, plugged an extension phone into a nearby jack. "Telephone call for you, Senator Howe," he said, placing the phone on the table.

Howe put the receiver to his ear, said "Yes?" into the mouthpiece.

"Have you begun to eat yet?" Shisei said from the other end of the line.

Howe smiled just as if she could see his expression. "No," he said. "In fact, I'm contemplating a fast."

"Fasting is my favorite purgative," Shisei said, but he already knew that.

"Where are you?"

"In a phone booth," she said, meaning the line was secure.

"How is your particular meal coming?" Howe asked her.

"Splendidly," Shisei said.

"Good. I want you back here in forty-eight hours."

"But you told me—"

Howe replaced the receiver in its cradle. He called for the waiter and, without bothering to ask Brisling if he was ready, began to order lunch. He had forgotten all about his resolution to fast.

Tomi Yazawa got to headquarters late, as she had since being released from the hospital. Someone was sitting beside her desk when she approached it. One of the uniforms told her that the man, Tanzan Nangi, had been waiting for her for over an hour.

She stopped at the communal hot plate, brewed two cups of tea, brought them over to her desk. She bowed as she introduced herself, apologized for keeping Nangi waiting. He accepted her offer of the tea, and they both drank in silence. Nangi inquired as to her health. They drank amid more silence.

After the requisite time, Tomi said, "How can I be of service, Mr. Nangi? Your insistence on waiting makes me think your mission is urgent."

"I believe it is," Nangi said, "but not in the way you mean. While Mr. Linnear is recuperating, I would very much like to gain as much information as is possible about the man you encountered in Dr. Hanami's office."

Tomi frowned. "But surely you've talked to Mr. Linnear. He must have provided you with the facts."

Nangi nodded deferentially. "I have, of course, talked to Mr. Linnear regarding the incident. However, he was still somewhat in shock. Besides, he is not an individual trained to respond to memory the way a police officer—a detective such as yourself—is."

Tomi said nothing for some time. She watched Nangi for some sense of what he might be after. Failing to find any clue in his words or his expression, she said, "May I ask to what use you will put this information?"

"I intend to discover the whereabouts of the individual."

"Don't you think that is best left to the Metropolitan Police, Mr. Nangi?"

"Not necessarily," Nangi said. "This individual is a ninja. Furthermore, I believe that he is tanjian. Are you familiar with the term, Detective Yazawa? It is said by some that the tanjian were the precursors of ninja. They are adepts at arcane arts we cannot even imagine."

"Come, come, Mr. Nangi."

"Think back to the attack on Mr. Linnear and yourself, Detective Yazawa. Was there anything unusual about it? Were you overpowered with great difficulty or with relative ease? Think back to how the two doctors were murdered. Was there anything unusual about the methodology?"

"It was all unusual," Tomi admitted. "But that is nothing new to me. I think you would be surprised at the oddities that cross my desk every day. It's part of the job, Mr. Nangi." She picked up a folder, opened it for him. "Look at this, for instance. A sad and bizarre chronicle of Mariko, a dancer at The Silk Road—you know, one of those *tokudashi* parlors. She was a young, beautiful girl—once. Now look at her." She pointed to the forensic team's brightly-lit photo's of Mariko's flayed corpse.

Perhaps because of her mood, or because she thought it preposterous that this lame, one-eyed gentleman should profess to want to track down her suspect, Tomi had picked this dossier—which despite Senjin's orders, she had been reluctant to file—in order to shock him.

To her surprise and subsequent chagrin, Nangi did not blink or flinch from the grisly photos. Instead he pointed to a section of her initial report.

"What is this?" he asked.

"Oh, it's a transcription of a handwritten note we found stuffed into Mariko's mouth. It said, 'This could be your wife.' It was written in her blood."

"May I see the original?"

Tomi shrugged, flipped to the end of the report where the meager pieces of evidence were affixed in appendices. She handed him the sheet of paper, watched in mounting fascination as he turned the paper this way and that.

"There are holes in the sheet," he said.

"I know that."

"What I mean is, the paper was slit as the words were being written."

He pointed. "You see here . . . and here, on the downstroke. Interesting. One can see immediately that this was not written with a brush. Now it seems that a normal stylus was not used either." He looked at her, his one-eyed gaze momentarily disconcerting her. "I believe that the same instrument used to skin this girl Mariko was used to write these words."

"Yes?" Tomi could not see where this was leading.

Nangi put the paper carefully on the desk. "Don't you see?"

"See what?"

He was silent for a moment, then he said, "Tell me, Detective Yazawa, what meaning does this sentence, 'This could be your wife,' have for you?"

"It is a message," Tomi said. She had gone through this so many times, she spoke almost by rote. "Obviously for someone connected with Mariko."

"Someone? Who?"

"We've . . . never been able to ascertain his identity. Clearly, though, it was someone Mariko was . . . seeing."

"Ah," Nangi said. "Now I see it all."

"See what?" Tomi continued to be bewildered.

"A moment ago you called this bloody scrawl a message."

Tomi nodded with the certitude of her police training. "And so it is."

"No," Nangi said. "It is a warning. 'This could be your wife' is written in blood, using a steel blade. What do you suppose is meant? The threat is there, and it is more than implied. I think—my apologies for saying this—that your focus has been wrong. The dancer, Mariko, is merely the victim in this crime—not the focus. Consider. Mariko was not killed in a fit of rage or jealousy. Her death was a calculated chess move—one part of a larger whole. This warning, 'This could be your wife,' was meant for only one person. *He* should be the focus of your investigation, Miss Yazawa. Mariko was just a pawn used to put pressure on this individual. Why?"

Slowly Tomi placed the blood note back into the dossier, closed the file. She was angry. Not with Tanzan Nangi, who had, after all, only pointed out the truth. She was angry with herself for not having seen what was, in retrospect, the obvious. She had been so wrapped up in the plight of poor, pitiable Mariko that she had failed to catch a glimpse of the larger picture. She had injected a piece of herself into the puzzle, turning the objective into the subjective.

In showing him the Mariko case, Tomi had planned to reveal to him his folly at trying to play detective. Instead, he had reversed her strategy, effectively convincing her of his intelligence and insight.

"As you wish," Tomi said softly. Her aikido *sensei* had taught her to have respect for those who could beat her. She gave a little bow. "What is it exactly that you wish to know?"

Nicholas had known about the tanjian since he was a young boy, he had merely repressed their existence out of a deeply-rooted sense of self-preservation.

Years ago, when he was young, Cheong had said to her son, "Nicholas, my father, So-Peng, had many children. But, oddly, they were all male. I was three when he adopted me. I would have, in any case, felt special among all those males—there were seven brothers—but So-Peng made me feel special all by himself. He was a most unusual man."

Nicholas listened with heightened attention. He knew by now that his mother was the master of the understatement. For her, "most unusual" was the ultimate superlative.

"Your grandfather was educated in many different places. He had schooled in Singapore, in Tokyo, in Peking. He spoke with an astonishing fluency every language and dialect extant in Asia.

"By the time I came to him, he had been a copra merchant in the Maldives, where he made his first fortune, and spent most of it battling the rhinoceros hunters in Borneo and the pirates in the waters off the Celebes; he had drilled for oil in Kalimantan, where he had made his second fortune; he had mined coal and gold in Sumatra, and owned virtually all the rubber plantations there, as well as extensive forests of teak, sandalwood, and ebony north of Singapore.

"But above all, he had a capacity for *understanding*. This was what made him truly unique. He did not view women as slaves or as inferior beings. As I was growing up I attributed this to his being so well-traveled. But when I was an adult, I realized that his understanding had evolved from within. He would have had it had he stayed in Singapore all his life.

"My education came mainly from him. The schools were inadequate where we lived, and in any case, So-Peng had his own curriculum to teach me. I could ask anything of him and he would gladly tell me. But one day I remember asking why all his children were males. He said nothing, but his face grew sad and lines I had never noticed before appeared.

"Many months later he said to me, 'We are in a battle, you and I. To you, Cheong, I give everything of true worth. Not my oil fields or my rubber plantations or my export business or even my real estate. These are of no lasting import, and therefore can easily be managed by my sons, who are all clever and good judges of character.

" 'This battle we are engaged in will continue long after we are both dust. This is as it should be. It is, in any case, karma. Once I had daughters and I thought that they would join me in this battle, but now, sadly, they are gone. But I have you. You are my joy and my savior. You will continue the battle, as will your child.'

"I was a young girl. His words terrified me. 'But Father,' I said, 'I wish to have many children. I am sure—I can feel it—that whomever I marry will want many children as well.'

"And So-Peng said, 'You will fulfill your duty, Cheong. You will bear a child. You must content yourself with that, because he will be the one. The battle begun so long ago will end with him.'

" 'He will be victorious against the tanjian?' I asked him.

" 'That I cannot say,' So-Peng told me. 'It is not for human beings to know such outcomes in advance, even human beings such as we.' "

Her words had terrified Nicholas. "Why are you telling me this, Mother?" he had cried.

Seeing the look of fright on his face, she had pulled him close to her breast, rocking him back and forth. He could hear the beating of her heart, feel her warmth seeping into him, dislodging terror's grip upon him. "To prepare you, my darling," Cheong had said, "for the coming storm. I want you to have every advantage I can give you."

All this Nicholas remembered as he stared at Kyoki's corpse. He could not pull himself away from the grisly sight. A bad sign, he knew, a further disintegration, slipping deeper into *Shiro Ninja*. Nicholas had had the crazy notion that if he stayed close to Kyoki, somehow, even in death, the tanjian could find a way to save him.

Madness.

Nicholas knew it was madness, yet he still clung to the insane hope of resurrection and salvation by proximity. Then, as if in a dream, he caught a glimpse of himself kneeling like a penitent beside the flayed corpse with its fastidiously arranged, sickening banners of skin. It was such a demented tableau that he knew he was truly lost.

He bent over until his forehead touched his thighs. His mind could not encompass the wretchedness of his situation. Without *Getsumei no michi* to guide him, he was directionless. It brought up another memory inside him, of Kansatsu-san, his first *ninjutsu sensei*.

Nicholas had been pitted against his cousin Saigo in a match at the *dojo*, Kansatsu's ninja school. The first time they had met, Nicholas had defeated his cousin. Because Saigo had been at the *dojo* longer, was more advanced, that defeat had caused him to lose face not only with his fellow students, which was bad enough, but with Kansatsu as well.

This affront Saigo could never forgive. And, forever afterward, he was scheming to humiliate Nicholas. Then Nicholas's father, Colonel Linnear, had murdered Saigo's father, and the generations of revenge had been sealed in blood. So much time spent toward one end.

Like the dark side of the *Go Rin No Sho*, the Book of Five Rings, Miyamoto Musashi's ancient guide to martial arts that Kansatsu had Nicholas study when he had first come to the *dojo*. When Kansatsu had asked what he thought of the philosophy, Nicholas had said, "There is a dichotomy. On the one hand, it is clear that its purity is its ultimate purpose and its ultimate strength. On the other hand, the philosophy has about it the air of a monomania. And there is something intrinsically dangerous in that."

Nicholas did not know it then, but he could have been talking about Saigo.

Kansatsu-san, his short, bristly hair already white, though he could not have been more than forty, taught Nicholas *haragei*, the forerunner to *Getsumei no michi*.

There was a bond between them, but it was no doubt an odd one. Nicholas had been bested by Saigo in a demonstration of the lesson of *Uteki*, the Raindrop, a particularly nasty method of disabling an opponent from a prone position in such small increments that he is not aware of its effects until its accumulation disables him.

Afterward, the *dojo* otherwise empty, Nicholas had been summoned to Kansatsu's study. He had expected a *sensei* sympathetic to his feelings not only of loss, but of humiliation at being defeated by his cousin, who openly mocked him.

Nicholas could still taste like ashes the bitterness he had felt when Kansatsu had exhibited no sign of being aware of Nicholas's bruised emotional state.

Instead the *sensei* had embarked on a philosophical discourse that, at the time, Nicholas felt had no relation to what he had just gone through.

The darkness and the light, Kansatsu told him, *are not, as everyone would have you believe, two sides of the same coin. The darkness and the light are two separate spheres. They are akin to parallel rungs of a pair of ladders that have come very close to one another. At a point in time it becomes extremely easy to move from one to the other. What makes the darkness and the light different is that they are governed by different laws. And it seems to be that only those who cling to the darkness, who have*

*learned how to manipulate it—and are thus manipulated by it—under-
stand that.*

Kansatsu, in the darkness, like a kite in a field or a bat in the rafters.
*You see, Nicholas, those in the light are not without flaws. Many believe
that their virtues hide their flaws. Others are prideful of their mastery of
the light, absolutely certain of their place in the world above those in the
dark. That is their sin. Pride is the downfall of all heroes, Nicholas. If you
retain nothing else of what I teach you, make sure it is this.*

Now Nicholas knew that much of his despair was rooted in his pride.
Despite Kansatsu's lesson, he had fallen into the trap of the prideful.
Thinking himself a hero, he had gradually become like an addict, dependent on that concept. Now that he had been stripped of his powers, he
could no longer be a hero. With that crutch gone, he had been plunged
into the abyss. Falling through the vapor. Falling, endlessly falling . . .

Nicholas raised his head and, with a concerted effort, moved away
from the final remains of Kyoki, the tanjian. He turned his gaze away
and began a thorough search of the rooms.

He had no idea what he was looking for. Perhaps he was, after all, still
clinging to the absurd notion that Kyoki could be of help even in death.
Whatever the motivation, he was determined not to leave the castle without having explored every avenue. Tanjian were said to be clannish in the
extreme. If Kyoki had any friends—or family—surely they would be
tanjian, too. And possibly there would be some evidence of them in this,
Kyoki's private chambers.

He went through Kyoki's desk, through another *tansu* in this part of
the chamber. Above it was a hanging scroll of fine calligraphy that said,
"Thunder/On a clear day/Brings thoughts of homecoming."

An eighteenth century lacquer writing box lay atop the *tansu*. Nicholas
opened it, took it apart. He was not admiring the exquisite workmanship,
but examining each component. A ceramic vase, devoid of flowers, nothing inside when he turned it upside down save a tiny dried leaf. Still, he
lit one of the candles he found inside the *tansu* so that he could examine
the inside of the vase. It was innocent.

Nicholas placed the candle in a stone holder atop the *tansu*, bent to
examine the chest's interior for any sign of a false bottom or compart-
ment wall. There was nothing.

With a deep sigh he shifted his gaze. Above the *tansu* the calligraphy
scroll seemed to float on the stone wall. But now something had caught
his eye. Was it a discoloration in the scroll? But surely it had not been
there moments before.

Nicholas studied it more carefully, bringing the candle closer to the paper. And, with mounting excitement, saw that the heat from the flame had caused a chemical reaction to occur. Lettering hitherto invisible was appearing, superimposed upon *kisho*, the ideogram for homecoming.

Nicholas read, "Genshi, my brother. The Black Gendarme. The Hodaka."

And he thought, Dear God, not the Gendarme. But, of course, it had to be. The Black Gendarme was where at the age of fourteen Nicholas Linnear had died.

"Before I allow you to interrogate me," Tomi said to Nangi, "I want you to understand that I don't believe a word you've told me regarding your interest in the murderer of Dr. Hanami." She raised her hands. "That's all right; I don't suppose I have to know. But I know enough about Nicholas Linnear to know that he has the kind of mind that would remember as much if not more than I do about the attack."

Nangi nodded. "I apologize for that, but what I said concerning Linnear-san's shock is the truth. I'm sure he remembers in detail his encounter with the tanjian. But he is currently in no shape to be of use to me."

Recalling Senjin's order about finding out Linnear's whereabouts, Tomi said, "Are you currently in contact with Mr. Linnear?"

"No," Nangi said.

"Do you know where he is?"

"No."

Tomi looked skeptical. "Nangi-san, I must tell you that there is still a good deal of concern for him inside the department because of this Red Army threat."

"Forget the Red Army threat," Nangi said. "That was just a ruse used by the tanjian to direct our attention away from the true threat."

"My boss did not think it a ruse. The threat came directly from an intercepted, decoded Red Army communiqué."

"I have no doubt that it appeared genuine," Nangi said. "Nevertheless, I believe that your superior—what is his name . . . ?"

"Captain Senjin Omukae, Commander, Homicide Division."

"Well, I believe that in this case Captain Omukae has been misled. There is no reason for the Red Army to want to assassinate Nicholas Linnear."

Tomi thought a moment. "Tell me, Nangi-san, assuming you know where Nicholas Linnear is now, would you tell me?"

"My dear Detective Yazawa," Nangi said, "I thought you had agreed to tell me what you can about the tanjian."

Tomi shook her head. "I would very much like to come to some kind of accommodation." She smiled sadly. "You must understand that I am running an investigation. If you have any information pertinent to this investigation and I think you're withholding it, I can cite you, designate you a material witness, even declare you a suspect. In which case, I guarantee that you would be spending a good deal more time answering questions in this building than you would care to do."

"Besides anything else," Nangi said, unperturbed, "I am in negotiations with Kusunda Ikusa. I don't think Nami would care for my incarceration, your investigation notwithstanding."

They stared frostily at one another for some moments. At length Tomi said, "Okay, we've crossed our swords and where has it gotten us? Obviously, we each have something that the other wants."

Nangi nodded. "That is clear enough." This was a difficult moment for him. It would be a mistake, he knew, to let her know just how crucial it was for him to gather information on the tanjian. On the other hand, he suspected that he would lose her—and whatever knowledge she could provide him with—unless he made it clear to her that he was not going to withhold information.

"What I know is this," Nangi said. "The tanjian may have some connection to Nicholas Linnear, who, as I am certain your computers have told you, is a ninja. The tanjian are ninja of a sort—a very specialized and dangerous sort. Their arts are at once more primitive and more powerful even than a ninja's. A tanjian is a more dangerous foe than one can imagine."

Nangi paused to allow Tomi to come to terms with the reality he was presenting before turning that reality subjective. He said, "I suspect—but do not know for certain—that this tanjian is someone from Linnear-san's past. If this is so, you can see the urgency in my discovering his identity. Revenge is not so easily accomplished. The death of Linnear-san is obviously not the tanjian's immediate objective, though I believe it to be his ultimate goal. If I can learn his identity, I have a chance to figure out what his strategy is and how best to counter it."

Tomi digested all this. "If I had not encountered this tanjian myself," she said, "if I had not heard what he said to Mr. Linnear, I would find your story too fantastic to be credible." She watched Nangi as she would a rival in a sharpshooting contest. "All right, I think we have a treaty of sorts," she said. "And I'll take what you've told me about the tanjian's ruse under advisement. I already have too many dead ends on my calendar to add another one, especially one that concerns the Red Army. That's really Commander Omukae's specialty." She settled herself more comfortably behind her desk. "More tea? No? Then, what can I tell you about the attack that Mr. Linnear hasn't already told you?"

"Did you see the tanjian's face?" Nangi said.

"No."

"Was he a man or a woman?"

"Man."

"Is that a guess, an impression, or a fact?"

Tomi thought a moment. "I first became aware of him as a shadow. He came through the window as if he were shot from a bow. He must have been hanging on just outside, and the way he levered himself up and in—that kind of power—he was a man, no doubt about it."

"What happened then?"

"I pulled my gun—or tried to. He slammed into me so fast, so incredibly fast! I hit the wall, I was groggy, but I saw that it wasn't me he was after, it was Mr. Linnear."

"Is it your impression that he could have killed Linnear-san?" Nangi asked.

"Yes."

"But he didn't."

"No."

"Have you any idea why?"

"He seemed—I don't know, not to want to, is the best way to put it—as if it were too easy, as if he didn't want it to be over so quickly."

"Again, is that an impression or did something specific happen?"

"Well, I was unconscious for a time. But I remember opening my eyes for a moment, seeing him drag Mr. Linnear back from the open window. He said, 'If you die now, if you die too easily, you will never understand.' "

Nangi sat completely still. "Are you certain of what you heard?" he said at last.

Tomi nodded. "I remember because there was more he said, but that's an impression. I was trying to get at my gun and I think I was slipping back under. I could hear a sound, like a buzzing or muffled laughter. By then I was putting all my energy into trying to get the gun. But the pain came back, and then I don't remember anything else until I woke up in the hospital emergency room." She was trying to read Nangi's face. "Do you know what the tanjian meant?"

Nangi did not, at least not in any specific way. But the evidence was mounting. The possibility that the tanjian had a long-range strategy was now a probability. And the strategy made chilling sense.

How Nangi missed Nicholas's expertise in strategy. Without Nicholas, the threat of the Sphynx computer-chip *kobun* became far more acute. The fate of the entire Sato International organization was in jeopardy. Nangi needed Nicholas's agile mind in this crisis. But Nicholas had been neatly put out of the way. He wasn't dead; but he was worse than dead: he was alive but powerless and unreachable. It could not be coincidence, surely.

Nangi knew that neither he nor Nicholas could successfully fight the tanjian alone. They needed each other, but the tanjian's strategy, *Shiro Ninja*, had torn them apart: Nicholas was useless to Nangi in his current state. And, with each passing hour, the threat of Sphynx was growing.

At that moment, Tomi looked up, startled. "Commander Omukae!"

Senjin, who had come to drop off several files with her on his way out of the office, bowed stiffly, almost formally. He repeated the process when Tomi introduced him to Nangi.

"These dossiers require your immediate attention," Senjin said to Tomi. "Please have your comments ready by the morning's meeting."

Nangi, watching the two of them, saw in their interaction layers like nacre on the inside of a pearl's shell. He saw in Senjin Omukae a diffidence he found odd in a Metropolitan Police division commander. Too, there was a disturbing lack of *hara*, of intrinsic energy within the man. It seemed to Nangi almost as if Omukae were deliberately masking some essential part of himself.

But for the moment, Nangi was more concerned with Tomi. There was no doubt that the abrupt, chaotic splintering of her own spirit was caused by Omukae's presence. It occurred to Nangi then that the two were hiding something—perhaps a romantic entanglement. This forbidden possibility would explain both of their extreme subsurface reactions.

Senjin politely said goodbye. When he had left, Tomi said, "What are you thinking?"

It took a moment for Nangi to get back on the track they had been pursuing. Interesting, he thought. Obviously Omukae has had an affect on me as well.

With an effort, he redirected his mind back to Nicholas and the tanjian. "The murders of the doctors have more questions hanging over them than there are answers," he said. "For instance, it seems clear that Dr. Hanami was killed in order to get Nicholas back to that office. But why was Dr. Muku murdered? Where does he fit in?"

"Perhaps he overheard the first murder being committed, or—"

"Did the two doctors know one another or have any patients in common?"

"Several," Tomi said. "Apparently, Hanami referred a number of his patients to Muku for psychological counseling before and after surgery. But there's nothing there. I checked them all out myself."

"Then it would be safe to assume that the tanjian is the link between them. He knew them both."

"Or," Tomi said, "the tanjian knew only Dr. Muku. After all, if he was after Mr. Linnear, he would have little difficulty in finding out that Dr. Hanami was Mr. Linnear's surgeon."

"Too much talk," Nangi said, rising. "Too much speculation. Right now there's nothing solid to go on. Therefore, we've got to find something solid."

"If this tanjian is only half as clever as you claim," Tomi said, "he'll have already erased every trace of himself."

"Perhaps," Nangi said. "But I think it's time we discovered just how clever he's been."

Shisei did not want to leave Cotton Branding, but she was used to being in chains, and, dutifully, she obeyed. It would have been unthinkable not to comply. Suffering was nothing new to her. On the contrary, suffering had been her constant companion ever since she could remember, as basic a part of her life as breathing or eating.

She contrived a story concerning her work. She did not want to suggest that he accompany her back to Washington. It would be far better for their relationship, she knew, if he came upon that idea on his own.

So it was that when she returned to their table at the Lobster Roll, the open-air restaurant in Napeague where they were having lunch, and sat down opposite Branding, her features had taken on the aspect of worry coupled with a newfound concentration.

Her frown was enough to compel him to say, "Is something the matter?"

"My office wants me back in Washington."

"When?"

She was careful not to look at him. "Tomorrow—at the latest."

She allowed the silence to spread like a stain upon the afternoon. She picked at her fried clams. In truth, she had little appetite. But she was also glad of it, because she knew that Branding would see. He noticed everything about her. He followed her moods as others studied the phases of the moon, with a rapt concentration she sometimes found frightening.

Her fright stemmed not—as it would in others in her position—from the degree of attention he accorded her. She was accustomed, one could

even accurately say most comfortable, with radical extremes both in emotional makeup and in psychological need. The basis of her fright was the
degree that she had come to rely on his involvement in her. She could not
quite believe in its reality, therefore her addiction to it was altogether
dangerous. Hung up on an illusion, Shisei felt weak, vulnerable. This was
what she had for so many years been trained to do to others. Tables
turning. The sensation of inhabiting an inside-out world was eerie, disturbing.

Branding finished off his beer, said, "Aren't you hungry?"

She smiled, pushed her plate across the table. "Here. You eat them."

Her eyes followed the orbits of his hands, watching his fingers move as
he picked up one curlicue of fried clam after another. Shisei propped her
head up on her fists. "I love to watch you eat," she said.

"You do?" He seemed surprised, as if no one had ever said such a thing
to him before. "Why?"

"Eating is primitive," she said. "Like fucking. Do you know how
much you can tell about a person by the way they eat? It's like seeing a
film of their childhood, how they were brought up."

"Oh, yeah?" He was clearly skeptical. "And how was I brought up?"

"You loved your mother," she said. "I imagine that she ate just the
way you do, with precise, pleasurable bites. Your father was either indifferent about food or liked drink more."

Branding felt a tiny ball of ice congeal in his lower belly. Immediately
he stopped eating, and Shisei laughed. "You look like you're being scrutinized by a psychiatrist," she said.

"Anything more?" he said tightly.

"Mmm, yes." Shisei went on as if she weren't aware of his tension.
"You have at least two brothers or sisters. I know that not only because
you like to share, but also because of the manner in which you share. You
must have been the oldest child."

"I was," he said, staring at her. "And everything else you said is more
or less true."

She smiled. "I never fail."

"You're not psychic?"

She heard the faint interrogative inflection. "No," she said, because
that was what he wanted to hear. "Just a keen observer of the human
condition."

"Well." He wiped his lips with a paper napkin to give him time to
recover. "Now you know a good deal more about me than I do about
you."

She shook her head. "That's not true. I don't know one secret of yours, but you know my only secret." He knew that she was speaking of the gigantic spider spread upon her back. It was hard, seeing her in clothes, to believe that the tattoo was actually there, pigmenting her skin in many hues.

"But I know nothing about it, or how you got it."

"It's time to leave," she said quickly, slipping her gaze away from his.

"Shisei." He put his hand over hers, staying her. "I'm sorry if I've upset you."

"Cook." She turned her hand over, pressed her palm into his. "Nothing you could do could upset me." She looked into his eyes, as if studying something there only she could see. "If you want, I'll tell you all about it," she said. "When I return from Washington."

Branding did not want to wait an indefinite amount of time. In fact, he found that he did not want to wait at all. "When will that be?"

Her silence gave him the answer he had been dreading. "I have an idea," he said. "Why don't I cut my vacation short? I'm getting restless. Besides, it would do me good to get back. The people at the Johnson Institute have been clamoring for me to see their new advances on the Hive Project. There are some bills that need my attention. And there's a State dinner for the West German chancellor at the end of the month. It's one of the most important of the endless political affairs that keeps Washington spinning on its axis of power."

"But what about Senator Howe? You said that he might somehow use our relationship against you."

Branding, leaning across the table, put a forefinger against her lips. "Leave Senator Howe to me," he said.

Shisei, relaxing inwardly as well as outwardly, smiled.

Tanzan Nangi had listened to the recording he had clandestinely made of his conversation with Kusunda Ikusa at the Shakushi *furo* so many times he knew every word, every subtle intonation by heart. As he stood in the rain, at the edge of Ueno Park, waiting for Ikusa to arrive, he played it yet again in his mind.

He had come to the park several minutes early in order to reacquaint himself with the curving paths, the bowing cherry trees, the ordered rows of azalea and dwarf rhododendron, so that he could sink in, feel that this was familiar territory. Often, such attention to detail was all the edge he required in an adversarial situation.

He tried to blot out the fact that Kusunda Ikusa was unlike any adversary he had ever faced, and to concentrate on what lay before him. In the intervening days between meetings, Nangi thought he had found a way out of his dilemma. But he also knew that he would have to be clever indeed in order to give himself that slim chance for success.

He saw the bulky figure of Ikusa gliding along the slick sidewalk as effortlessly as if he were a slim man. Nangi spent thirty seconds working on slowing his heartbeat and increasing the depth of his breathing. It was crucial now to have his mind absolutely clear.

The two men bowed, exchanged the ritual greeting that with this man so set Nangi's teeth on edge. Ikusa had had no real reason to go through this formality a second time except, Nangi thought, if he were using it as another deliberate provocation.

Their umbrellas bobbed in unison as they moved off through the park.

"We can change venues," Ikusa said amiably, "if you would prefer."

Nangi did not care for the veiled reference to his disability. He said, "I enjoy the rain. It renews flowers that summer's heat has beaten down."

Ikusa nodded as if acknowledging a well-placed return of service on the tennis court.

"I wanted to speak with you about a situation that has arisen since our last discussion," Nangi said.

"Does it concern the *iteki* Nicholas Linnear?"

Now, as he was about to take his first step upon this dangerous path, Nangi felt his heart skip a beat despite his careful preparations. "Only indirectly," he said. "Once I have severed our ties with Tomkin Industries, I am going to need help in running the Sphynx computer-chip *kobun*."

"If you're asking for my advice," Ikusa said, "close it down."

"Oh, I would," Nangi said. If he had been walking through a mine field he could not have been more cautious. "In fact, that was what I had in mind. I felt you had given me no choice."

"You are quite right in that assessment."

"Toward that end," Nangi went on, "I had a final audit begun on the *kobun*'s books. I discovered that this year's projected revenues are astronomical."

At this crucial junction Nangi fell silent. A pair of businessmen, as identical as ravens, hurried by, perhaps ruing their decision to take a shortcut through the park.

"What kind of numbers are we talking about?" Kusunda Ikusa asked, a sleek-skinned shark, rising out of the depths to take the bait.

Rain poured off the perimeters of their umbrellas, bouncing against the hard concrete of the path they had chosen. Nangi gave him the number upon which he had previously decided.

Ikusa blew air out of his thick pursed lips. "It would be against sound business principles to close down such a profitable enterprise."

"That thought occurred to me," Nangi said humbly. "But what am I to do? Nicholas Linnear's people have all the expertise. You tell me that I must do without them." He shrugged. "I have my duty to perform, no matter how odious I might find it."

Ikusa's mouth curled into a sneer. "Your confusions of feeling are of no concern to me. But profits are. It would be foolish to terminate the Sphynx *kobun.*"

"How, then, am I to proceed?" Nangi asked.

The big man considered the problem for a moment. Nangi could feel the rumbling of his spirit as it sought a solution. He remained quiet, seeking the low ground, where he waited as still and patient as a fox who has sighted its prey.

"This is what I propose," Kusunda Ikusa said. "Wait until you have hired Tomkin Industries' key people away from Linnear, then sever the merger. That way you will be able to continue to manufacture this extraordinary chip on your own."

Nangi arranged his expression to indicate that he was giving this ludicrous idea serious thought. He would no more entertain the idea of betraying his friend than he would of foisting on him the termination of their merger.

"There is merit to what you have suggested," Nangi said, "but with your permission, I would like to provide an alternative." He took the other man's silence as an affirmative. He said, "Leave Linnear and his people in place—for the time being. This alleviates the possibility of bad blood and reprisals in the courts, which could tie up profits from the Sphynx *kobun* for many years." He let Ikusa digest that before continuing. "Instead, I propose another merger: Sphynx with a *kobun* outside my own *keiretsu,* a company that has the management expertise in chip manufacture. That way their trained personnel can gradually learn the ropes of the T-PRAM process without arousing suspicion."

"What about Linnear? He can't possibly let this go by without comment or some kind of protest."

"When he questions the merger I will simply tell him that with the increased revenue and demand, we've got to expand immediately. As long as I assure him that his profit percentage won't be diluted, he won't care."

"I don't like the idea of Linnear staying on." Ikusa's tone was so firm, so belligerent, that for a moment Nangi suspected he had failed. Then Ikusa said, "In order for your proposal to be acceptable, Nami would have to pick the electronics firm. That way we could be certain of the loyalty of those being introduced to its design and manufacture."

"Here I have anticipated you," Nangi said. He produced from his jacket pocket a folded sheet of paper. He handed it to Ikusa. "I have taken the liberty of drawing up a short list of firms I thought would be appropriate."

"I don't think Nami would approve of your dictating the parameters of such a search," Ikusa said.

Nangi shrugged. "I understand. Perhaps, though, you could look at the list and tell me where I have made a mistake in judgment."

This appealed to Ikusa's ego. He dropped his gaze to the list. He went through it three times before he said, with some apparent surprise, "As it happens, there is a firm here that Nami would find acceptable. Nakano Industries is on Nami's own list of clean *keiretsu*. If you can convince the chairman of the merits of the merger, Nami would not oppose such a venture."

Thinking, I've won, Nangi said, "Perhaps, Ikusa-san, it would not be inappropriate for you to have a word with Nakano Industries' chairman."

"As it happens, Ken Oroshi is an acquaintance of mine," Ikusa said. "We play golf together several times a year." He nodded thoughtfully. "I'll see what I can do."

They were approaching the far side of the park. Nangi could see a black Mercedes glistening in the west, waiting for Ikusa. The big man turned to Nangi, said, "I may have misjudged you, Nangi-san. Your proposal was well thought out. It pleases me. Nami approves of your actions. It is grateful for your loyalty."

With that Ikusa moved swiftly away. It was not until he had climbed into the Mercedes and the car had disappeared into traffic that Nangi, breathing an inner sigh of relief, allowed himself to feel the elation of a difficult victory painstakingly won.

Justine lay on her back staring at the pattern the shadows of the trees made on the beamed ceiling. There seemed at this time of night, the first lonely beachhead of morning, an entire world alive in the hills and valleys above her head. In the old days of the Tokugawa shogunate, Nicholas had once told her, ninja hired by the shogun himself to enforce his will—even if it went counter to the tenets of *bushido*, the Way of the Samurai—hung in the rafters very much like these, waiting for their victims to fall asleep. Then, like silent bats, they would drop to the tatami mats, draw a silken cord around their victims' necks, or, rendering them unconscious, would sling them across their backs, making off with them.

That was seventeenth century Japan. But some things, Justine was learning, did not change here. That was the essential difference between Japan and America. In America *everything* changed constantly.

Here ninja still existed. Justine ought to know. She was married to one. Nicholas.

That name was enough to set her crying. Wiping the tears from her cheeks, she sat up and, pulling the covers around her chin, cursed herself for her essential weakness. Her father had wanted sons. Instead his wife had borne him two daughters. If I had been born male, Justine thought, perhaps I would not be so weak. But that in itself was a weak thought. Even Nangi—a Japanese—had told her as much.

She had come to cherish their twice-weekly lessons on the society of Japan. It was Nangi who described to her how Japanese women held the purse strings in the family, even to doling out weekly spending money for their husbands; how it was the mother-in-law who dominated family life, lording it over her son's wife and children; how it was the geisha who afforded many of Japan's most powerful and influential men their only opportunity to get drunk, turn maudlin and irrational, to weep upon a female breast as they once had when they were infants. It was the geisha, too, Nangi informed her, who listened with complete objectivity to knotty problems inherent in momentous state and industrial deals, and who offered clever advice to the same clients who cooed at their breasts.

Slowly she was coming to understand Japan and, with it, the people who inhabited the islands. She was both grateful to Nangi and amazed at his sensitivity to her insecurity. Even if he was playing Professor Higgins to her Pygmalion simply because she was Nicholas's wife and he had a duty to make her comfortable, she knew that could not be all that motivated him. Seeing him praying in church, she had realized how she had underestimated Tanzan Nangi. He was filled with the kind of Christian charity that was all too rare even in America. To find it here in this alien landscape was a godsend.

She knew that Nangi and his cherished lessons were all that was keeping her here now. Nicholas was gone—God only knew where or for what reason. He had tried to explain it to her, but she could not understand what he was saying, as if she had lost the ability to decipher English. She knew only this: there had been an attack on him, and it would not be the last. But by whom?

A tanjian.

The word sent slivers of dread down her spine. Nicholas and Nangi had said that Akiko had been a kind of tanjian, but that this one—this *dorokusai*—was far more powerful.

"Oh, Nicky," she whispered, "how I pray that God will watch over you and keep you safe."

She went to church now because suddenly even Nangi and his lessons were not enough to make her feel safe. Something had happened.

Often she would see Nangi there, for she had chosen to attend services at St. Theresa's, though there were certainly other churches that were nearer. Mass was a kind of return for her to the days when as a small child her mother would take her. She had never felt anything then but a kind of protective warmth, and later she understood why. Her mother had taken her and her sister Gelda out of a sense of hollow duty, rite by rote, because this was how *her* mother had brought her up. Justine's mother had felt nothing for the mass or for the presence of God, and her children had eventually followed in her footsteps.

Now, in this ultimate crisis, Justine had returned in order to find some solace in the rituals that God decreed His children should follow. But she had found none. Church was as closed, as cold and incomprehensible to her, as it had been when she was a child.

Often she found herself inattentive to the service; she wanted only to slip into the pew beside Nangi and whisper in his ear. She desperately needed to talk to someone, but she could not bring herself to talk to him.

Here in Japan, with the darkness holding the light at bay, with Nicholas in the gravest danger, alone with her private fears, Justine had nothing to hold on to.

Fear and her memories of Nicholas before he had gone off into the Alps. After Nicholas had described how he must find the *sensei* who had trained Akiko, who he now believed to be tanjian, after Nangi had gone, there were just the two of them alone in the old wooden house.

Nicholas and Justine. And the tension between them, rising like a phantom or an animus in the gathering dusk.

They had looked at each other.

"Are you hungry?" Justine asked.

He shook his head. "How do I look?"

"The truth?" When he nodded, she had sat on the edge of the bed. "You look like hell, but you also look beautiful."

He had closed his eyes then, as if her words had a physical presence. "We have some unfinished business, don't we?"

"I don't think that's important now. What you've just—"

"No." It was his hand on her arm as much as his exclamation that stopped her. "It *is* important. Justine, ever since I suspected that something was the matter with me—that I might be *Shiro Ninja*—I've been so frightened, so obsessed by the fear, so terrified that by being close to me you would become in some way contaminated by it, that all I could think of was pushing you away, of keeping you clear of the disaster zone."

"Oh, Nicky," she had said, her heart breaking, "it was what you did—distancing yourself from me—that frightened me most. All this other stuff—the magic, the tanjian, the *Shiro Ninja*—I can take." She had rushed on, not wanting to give herself time to consider whether or not she was telling the whole truth; because if, as she suspected, she was as terrified as he was over this attack, it would do him no good to know it, it would only reinforce his intuition to keep her apart. And that, she knew, she could not tolerate. "All that matters is the two of us. Whatever happens, we have each other. You're enough for me, darling, you always have been, you always will be."

He had kissed her then, and she had been so grateful to feel his arms once again around her that she had wept. They had not broken the kiss even when Nicholas had drawn her fully onto the bed, even when his nimble fingers had unbuttoned her blouse, unzipped her jeans.

She had spread her legs on either side of his hips and, feeling his hands come up to cup her breasts, had settled over him. He had groaned deep into her throat.

Their lovemaking was long, slow, ecstatic. Justine kept delaying her orgasm, not wanting the pleasure to end. Nicholas had ended it for her. His release had triggered her own, and she had gasped, her eyes squeezed shut, feeling only him inside her, around her, below her, knowing that for this moment all she wanted to feel was him, only him.

And how she missed him now. Justine, in their bed, rested her cheek on her upraised knees, rocking herself back and forth in that gray, vulnerable time of night when one is ultimately, inescapably alone.

But she wasn't alone, and this frightened her. She was terrified of her fright and what it might portend.

She could feel the seed stirring inside her, or imagined that she did. Dutifully, stoically, she got up, administered the self-pregnancy test she had given herself several days before. Five minutes later she had the results, the same as the first test she had given herself when she had returned from her doctor's visit and he had told her the news.

She stared sightlessly at the slip of paper: positive. She was pregnant. When in God's name had it happened? Of course she knew. She and Nicholas had made love so infrequently since his operation, she could count the number of times. Her doctor, an American, part of her ever so tenuous lifeline in Japan, had laughed at her shock. "It only takes one time, Justine," he had said jocularly. "I thought you learned that long ago."

If only Nick were here now, Justine thought in anguish. I could talk to him, explain my terror away. She shivered as if freezing, because she knew that part of her almost desperate longing for him now was the fear that Nicholas would not return from the Alps, that this tiny life would be all she would have of him. And the terror came again, almost overwhelming her this time.

How unfair of him to leave her this way, disappear into the night. Hadn't she always been there for him, right by his side when he was most vulnerable? But men expected that from their women; did that mean women had no right to expect the same consideration from their men? Were the roles of the two sexes so immutably different?

She hated Nicholas now for abandoning her when she needed him the most. She could not help it, just as she could not stop the tears from forming, from flowing down her cheeks. I can't make it alone, she thought. My world is breaking apart, spinning out of control.

Her mind was filled with funeral orations, the cloying scent of checkerboard bouquets of flowers, the smell of rain in the air, and newly-turned earth, gleaming caskets being lowered into the ground, *ashes to ashes, dust to dust*, the muffled sobs of the mourners, death hanging in the air like a suffocating shroud.

She tried to turn her mind away from death and could not; could not stop the prayer from forming on her lips.

"Dear God," she whispered, "save me from myself."

Douglas Howe had a residence on Seventeenth Street in the heart of the northwest district of Washington. It was a Federal-style building of four stories. The first floor served as offices, the second as quarters, when needed, for visiting notables. The third and fourth floors were devoted exclusively to Douglas Howe.

The residence, which was now worth a small fortune, was just down the block from the Corcoran Gallery of Art, whose glorious facade was eternally guarded by its brace of sleeping stone lions. The Corcoran was once described by Frank Lloyd Wright as "the best-designed building in Washington." As such, Howe had decided that it was a fitting place to be near, both chic and immune to the incomprehensible whims of Washingtonian fashion.

Shisei approached Howe's residence with a good deal of trepidation. Her time with Cotton Branding had made her feel a good deal less san-

guine about what she had been hired to do. Only once before had she
been affected by a man in the way Cook Branding affected her—and that
time clearly did not count.

Shisei had been trained to emit emotion much as a television set emits
images: in order to attract the attention of others. To accomplish such a
feat with any degree of success, one had, of course, to train oneself to feel
nothing. Objectivity rather than subjectivity was the rule—the law.

With Branding, Shisei had crossed the line, broken the law. Unwittingly at first, to be sure, but cross the line she had. Now she was entangled in her own emotions, and that was dangerous—especially with
Douglas Howe, to whom emotions were like poker chips to be hoarded
and used at the proper moments.

An aide opened the door to her knock and, recognizing her, ushered
her into the library which abutted Howe's office suite.

"The senator will be with you shortly," the aide said, before leaving
her alone with the great minds of man's history. She idly let her fingers
play along the expanse of leather-bound spines. She took out a volume of
Nietzsche, read passages at random, thinking of the apologists for Na-
zism plundering poor Nietzsche, a man who denounced as pernicious the
state—especially the German state—warping his concept of the moral
superman into their physical one.

Shisei knew that she had picked up the book in order not to think of
Cook Branding. It was Branding, she thought, who should have a taste
for Nietzsche, because the two were such pure moralists. But Cook was
horrified by the German philosopher's search for moral perfection, believing that such perfection belonged solely to God. In this way, as in a
surprisingly large number of others, Cook was quite Eastern. The Japanese, too, knew that perfection was beyond the human condition, preferring the myriad pleasures afforded by the journey to the anticipation of
the journey's end.

Then she came across a sentence that startled her. "All idealism is
falsehood," Nietzsche wrote, "in the face of necessity." This was quintes-
sential Douglas Howe. It reminded her of a quote from the French philosopher of materialism, Denis Diderot, that was one of Howe's favorites:
"There is no moral precept that does not have something inconvenient
about it."

She put the book back, searched in vain for the Tao. In truth, she had
not expected to find it. She had too firm a grip on Howe's psyche to
expect that he would be open to the mystical Tao. Yes, Nietzsche and
Diderot were more his meat, solid, definite, Western—most of all, ra-
tional and pragmatic.

She turned at the sound of a door opening and saw David Brisling, Howe's assistant. "The senator will see you now." Brisling's voice was cold, aloof.

Shisei smiled her actor's smile. Everything, she thought, was simple when I felt nothing. Amid the brambles of her newly-exposed emotions, possibilities multiplied like reflections in facing mirrors.

She was wearing a short white silk skirt, a sleeveless black crepe de chine blouse with a high mandarin collar. Around her waist was a wide velvet belt with an oversized red-gold buckle in an abstract shape. Brisling looked right through her.

Howe was waiting for her in his office. It was teak-paneled, with brass lamps, a large, overly masculine leather club sofa against one wall, an overly large carved English walnut desk behind which stood a matching credenza. A pair of black antique English chairs lurked like guardian Sphinxes. An excellent Robert Motherwell painting hung on the wall above the sofa.

Shisei duplicated Howe's dazzling hollow smile, reflecting it back at him, just like a television image. And like a television image she came across the room, kilowatts in her eyes.

She made certain the door into the outer office where Brisling had retreated in glowering silence was left ajar. She sat in one of the black English chairs, sorting out in her mind what it was he needed to hear, what she wanted to reveal, most importantly, how much she needed to tell him in order for him to be satisfied.

"You're late," Howe said without consulting his watch. "I expected you sooner than this."

Shisei shrugged. "When one is involved, one's time is not one's own."

"Save the act for someone who'll appreciate it. How deeply is Branding involved?" Douglas Howe said in the same tone of voice he used to order one of his staff to get a Joint Chief on the phone.

"He's in love with me," Shisei said truthfully. "He is fascinated by me, consumed by me." Her eyes glowed until they were almost the color of prehistoric amber.

"But does he trust you?" Howe asked.

He knows how to get at the heart of the matter, Shisei thought. She said, "Trust does not come easily to a politician, especially one who is locked in a life-and-death battle with his worst enemy."

Howe scowled. "Does he suspect that I hired you?"

"He does not suspect me, no," Shisei said, again truthfully. "But the possibility has crossed his mind."

Howe's scowl deepened. "How do you know that?"

"He told me."

"He told you?" Howe was incredulous. "Then he's an idiot!"

Shisei said nothing.

Howe tapped a pen meditatively against his lips. "In which quarter does he plan to attack me?"

"I don't know."

"What have you been up to, then?"

"The creation of an obsession," Shisei said, "is accomplished only with patience and determination. No one responds to haste; they mistake it for insincerity."

"That's unhelpful," Howe said sharply. "Time is the one commodity I have very little of," he said, busy chewing on his pen. "I hired you to burrow inside Branding, to get me information. I don't give a shit whether he loves you or just has the hots for you, as long as you get me information I can use against him.

"You say Branding is consumed by you. Let me clue you in. While you've been playing Mata Hari, Branding has been a busy little boy." He made her aware that he was throwing her own words back in her face. "He's been burning up the phone lines, calling in markers, political favors; he's made deals all over Capitol Hill. He's blocked me at every turn. He's going to get that fucking ASCRA bill passed, despite my contacts. The Hive Project is very much alive and well and threatening to eat our federal budget whole. Unless you can bring Cotton Branding down by the end of the month, when his bill gets onto the Senate floor, the Advanced Computer Research Agency will have the federal government by the balls, and Cotton Branding will have enough power to run for the President of the United States in two years and win."

Howe was baleful when he was in this sort of mood. He could work himself up into a kind of trembling rage that often required a full-scale explosion to dissipate it.

"Do you know what that would mean?" Only too well, Shisei thought, but, dutifully, she said nothing. "I know how far the Hive Project has come. They've already perfected the goddamned computer. Branding would have the entire government switch over to the Hive computer. I mean everyone: the NSC, the CIA, every fucking secret this country possesses will be in the Hive memory banks.

"Poor blind Branding has become dangerous to the security of this country. He doesn't see the risk inherent in the system, and neither do very many other people. Everything we know, every secret thing we've amassed on foreign powers, on what we're secretly working on, would be fed into the Hive. Of course. It could solve our problems of defense,

create initiatives one thousand times faster than any of our current inefficient think tanks or bureaucracies. But the Hive Project has enormous
drawbacks. No one knows whether it can be penetrated. Its technology is
so new, so revolutionary, that everyone assumes its so-called invulnerable
defenses will be impenetrable. Branding is so sure of the technology he's
championing. But think of what could happen to the United States if a
program run by an unfriendly power could worm its way inside the Hive
computer. It would be a disaster of unimaginable proportions. It would
undermine the very foundations of this country, putting everyone and
everything we stand for in jeopardy."

Howe's eyes were blazing. "Goddamnit, we have to stop Branding!"
His shoulders assumed the powerful, compact hunch of the street fighter.
"God, I hate that monied, privileged bastard! Look what his family has
given him. He's an insider here because he's a Branding, because of his
old-boy contacts. And what am I? The perennial outsider, the poor boy,
the hick farmer's son, the nobody, clawing and scratching for every contact I make." All of a sudden he realized how worked up he had become.
He snapped his jaw shut, whirled, poured himself a shot of Bourbon.
When he turned back to Shisei, he was calm again.

"If only Branding's wife had not died in that senseless accident," he
said. "We would have caught him up in a sex scandal that would have
finished him right now."

Shisei studied him for some time. At length she said, "There's something I need to know. Where is the boundary? How far are you willing to
take this in order to bring Branding down?"

Howe was again shaking with rage. "Isn't it clear to you yet?" he said.
"I'll do whatever I have to in order to destroy him utterly. This isn't a
game I'm playing with Branding. I think you understand."

"Of course."

"Then tell me what it is you understand. Tell me what I want to
know." He leaned toward her. "Enlighten me as to why I should continue to employ you when I have Brisling running an operation to discredit the people at the Johnson Institute involved in the Hive Project?"

Shisei laughed. "That's a dead end. Those people are clean. And if you
manufacture a scandal, Branding will make it backfire back at you."

"Not me," Howe said. "I've distanced myself from the operation. It's
strictly Brisling's baby. I've got plausible deniability."

"Still, you're wasting your time with it."

"I'm not paying you to be a critic," Howe said acidly. "So kindly tell
me how I *won't* waste my time."

Shisei felt nothing. She was comforted by the fact that she had so effortlessly slipped back into her methodology. She no longer felt confused, vulnerable, entangled. Everything was again clear; the normality of the Void encircled her like the arm of a loving parent.

"Well, we agree about one thing," she said. "Brisling's expendable. You know, of course, about the dinner at the end of the month?" She was referring to the State dinner for the West German chancellor that Branding mentioned to her over lunch. "I will make sure Branding takes me." She looked at Howe. "You must do one thing. Convince Brisling that he has to act against me. It won't be difficult; I'll give him an incentive. Do whatever you have to, but make sure he breaks into my house the night of the dinner. I want him in the house just after I leave."

Howe stared at her for a long time. "You'll find the way, won't you? You understand that I must destroy Cotton Branding, Shisei, or the Hive Project will go through." He shook his head. "Christ, but you're cutting it close. The dinner is only a few days away from when Branding's ASCRA bill makes it onto the Senate floor." His low voice was full of menace. "It's my last chance to destroy him."

Howe did not show it, but he was pleased. As usual, he had found that his bullying tactics worked. People did their jobs more effectively, he had found, when they were firmly shown their place. Everyone wanted recognition more than anything else. But if you gave them too much, they became lazy, complacent. You had to keep employees on their toes, keep them in obedience school in order to keep them performing at peak efficiency.

In that light, Howe decided that Shisei had earned her reward. He gestured, and she saw the Louis Feraud suit draped elegantly over the back of a chair. She stared at it, entranced.

"It's yours," he said. "I reward employees who perform for me."

Shisei touched the suit. For a moment she luxuriated in the feel of the superior wool. Then her fingers encountered the fox trim and she experienced a wave of revulsion so powerful that she felt her gorge rise. How typical of this man to buy her so expensive a present because it was what *he* admired, what he thought she should wear. He had, as usual, been oblivious to her own preferences, ignoring her distaste for the killing of animals for such a reason.

She excused herself, went to the bathroom. She looked at herself in the mirror, tried to see herself as Douglas Howe saw her. She thought he might be dangerous if he ever started thinking for himself.

She cursed the day she came to Washington, ingratiating herself slowly into Howe's confidence. Necessity and obligation, *giri*, these were always uppermost in her mind. But too often Douglas Howe had a way of making painful the performance of one's duty.

Unlike Cook Branding.

She had wanted to take this time to figure out why her mind was again filled with Cook Branding. She had returned to that disturbing state of entanglement, her objective edge blunted by emotion. At the sink she stared at herself in the mirror. What is wrong with me? she asked herself.

She pushed the troubling questions aside for the moment, concentrating on how happy she was at what she was about to do. She was committed now; her feet were firmly set upon the path. There was no turning back.

Kusunda Ikusa had a vaguely humiliating weakness for Chinese food; he also had an affinity for a certain restaurant in Shinjuku.

Both facts were in the Pack Rat's computer. When he entered the Toh-Li restaurant at the top of the fifty-story Nomura Securities Building, he was unrecognizable as the man who had met Nangi in Akihabara. The Pack Rat looked every inch the paradigm of ministerial Japan. His dark suit was impeccably cut, his shirt a blinding white, his brogues polished to a mirror shine.

It happened that the maître d' was a friend of a friend, and the Pack Rat was seated at a table just behind the one that Kusunda Ikusa had reserved.

Ikusa was not yet at the restaurant, but a small, powerful-looking man had already made himself at home. He was sipping a martini while reading today's copy of the *Asahi Shimbun* newspaper.

The Pack Rat did not recognize him. It did not matter. The Pack Rat was in seventh heaven. He lived for danger; it was his way of ridding himself of the rigid hierarchical strata of responsibilities that made up life in Japan.

When Tanzan Nangi had given him the directive to compromise Kusunda Ikusa somehow, the Pack Rat had been unfazed. Rather, he relished such an assignment, which carried with it the heavy burden of danger. The Pack Rat was like Atlas: the more weight he was asked to bear, the better he liked it.

When he and Nangi had parted company in the Akihabara, he had spent the next forty-five minutes checking and rechecking the vicinity in ever-expanding squares that eventually took in the entire district. When he was certain that the environment was clean, he had gone to find Han Kawado.

Han Kawado was one of the Pack Rat's most reliable "team members," as he liked to think of them. But the Pack Rat also loved the young man. He had picked Kawado to keep track, as Tanzan Nangi also wanted, of Justine Linnear's movements.

The Pack Rat had found Han Kawado making out the last of his report on the Kawabana affair at the back of the zinc-topped bar in Mama's.

"I'm looking for the key to this guy," the Pack Rat had said to Han Kawado as he slid onto a stool beside him. He was referring to Kusunda Ikusa. "Unfortunately, what I need isn't a key, but a crowbar. Ikusa-san's gate is not to be delicately opened, but pried off its hinges. Only then will one find his weakness."

"Prying is a dangerous activity," Han Kawado had observed. "It's said that Ikusa-san does not even trust his own mother! Can you imagine such a thing!" Han Kawado shook his head.

The Pack Rat was looking at the calligraphy on a scroll hanging behind the bar. *The clouds/With no mortal weight/Disappear like man/ Thought remains.*

Han Kawado had rubbed his face. "What do you know of Kusunda Ikusa's psyche?"

"My computer bank holds facts, not psychology," the Pack Rat had said. "All it tells me is that he's so goddamned virtuous, he's invulnerable to coercion. But I don't need a computer to tell me what I already know of Kusunda Ikusa. He's a young man, an arrogant man, engorged with the aphrodisiac of power. Therefore, he's vulnerable."

Now, a week after that conversation, a week of frustrating surveillance, the Pack Rat found himself here at this Chinese restaurant.

At the moment Kusunda walked through the door, the man drinking the martini folded the paper, put it away in a slim alligator document case. He rose.

The two men greeted each other warmly, and the Pack Rat was indirectly introduced to Ken Oroshi, chairman of Nakano Industries.

"Oroshi-san," Ikusa said, settling in, "how are your wife and children?"

"All are fine, Ikusa-san," Oroshi said. "They send their greetings, and their blessings."

It had been Oroshi, the Pack Rat observed, whose bow had been the deeper. For all of Nami's power, that was unusual in someone of Ken Oroshi's position, who was at least twenty years older than Ikusa. Custom—not to mention etiquette—demanded that Ikusa, as the junior man, bow that much deeper than Oroshi, to show his respect. Instead, the opposite had happened.

The two men began to talk about golf—the Japanese businessman's mania. It had cost Ken Oroshi more than four million dollars to join Koganei Country Club, the most prestigious in the country, where greens fees were three thousand dollars a month, and then it was only because Ikusa sat on the club's owners' committee that Oroshi jumped the one-hundred-plus names on the waiting list.

The conversation drifted on with nothing out of the ordinary coming up. The Pack Rat allowed his attention to wander around the room, which was filled, for the most part, with serious-faced businessmen along with a spattering of tourists: thick-necked Americans and beefy, red-faced Germans.

The Pack Rat's gaze fell upon a young woman—perhaps no more than a girl, really. Though she was dressed in the height of sophisticated, moneyed fashion, her utterly unlined face indicated that she was still in her teens.

She was, like the Pack Rat, sitting near Ikusa's table. Ken Oroshi's back was to her, and once, startlingly, the Pack Rat saw her eyes lock with Ikusa's. Something akin to amusement played like a melody across the girl's face, and she seemed abruptly more grown-up than the Pack Rat had given her credit for. Ikusa's face showed nothing but polite attention directed at Ken Oroshi, but the flicker of his eyes in the girl's direction caught the Pack Rat's attention and he began to study the girl in earnest.

She wore a dramatic black and white pony pattern bolero jacket over a black rayon blouse. She wore a leather skirt of the same color with a wide gold belt. Gold sandals were on her feet.

Her thick, shimmering hair was stiff with gel, her lips small, bow-shaped, glossed a bright crimson. She had the kind of face, the Pack Rat decided, that devoid of its artful makeup would be, at best, plain. In any event, the eyes were filled with life and intelligence, and the Pack Rat noted this because it was more significant than how she dressed or was made-up.

Over steaming platters of gingered fish and abalone in black bean sauce, Ikusa steered the conversation away from golf. "I think I may have the answer to your fiscal problems."

"As long as it will not expose our plight to the public," Ken Oroshi said. "We have gone to great lengths to conceal our difficulties."

"There is cause on both sides for secrecy," Ikusa said, fastidiously extruding a translucent fishbone from between his lips. "This plan will also bring you the most important new technology in computer chips."

"What is it," Ken Oroshi said, laughing, "the Sphynx T-PRAM?"

"Yes," Kusunda Ikusa said. "Precisely that."

Ken Oroshi put his chopsticks down. "Do you mean to tell me that Nami has wrested control of that proprietary technology from Sphynx?"

"Not quite," Ikusa said. "Not yet." He cut himself another thick slab of fish, dexterously maneuvered it onto his plate. "Tanzan Nangi is under some immediate pressure. He must merge Sato International's Sphynx computer-chip manufacturing *kobun*. In the course of these discussions, your name came up as a possible partner. I indicated Nami's acceptance."

"But Nangi-san is not in Sphynx alone. The T-PRAM technology isn't even his. It comes from Tomkin Industries, which is owned by Nicholas Linnear. What about him? I doubt that he will approve the merger."

"Linnear is not a factor in any of this," Ikusa said, shoving the crisp fishtail in his mouth. "Your deal is with Tanzan Nangi."

The conversation then turned to appointments with lawyers, points to keep in mind when drawing up the merger papers, and so on. The Pack Rat's attention drifted back to the girl, who was sipping tea with the avidity of a lioness hunkering down to her fresh-killed meal.

This struck him as odd until he realized that her full concentration was on the exchange between the two men. Even when the terminology became excessively technical and esoteric, her interest never flagged. On the contrary, her face became suffused with the kind of glow normally only stage lights can provide.

Lunch was over, the tea had been drunk, the last pieces of business discussed. The men rose, bowing, but only Ken Oroshi left, hurrying out of the restaurant, his chic document case swinging at his side.

Kusunda Ikusa heaved himself back into his chair, sipped meditatively at his tea. The Pack Rat paid his check and, as he did so, he noticed the girl from the next table get up, start toward the door. Ikusa looked up sharply, a dark look on his face. His eyes flashed as they locked with the girl's.

Was it the Pack Rat's imagination or did the girl hesitate as she passed his table before heading for the door?

Five minutes later Ikusa paid the check and left. The Pack Rat followed.

He momentarily lost Ikusa in the lobby, then found him just outside. He was with the girl from the next table. She was smiling at him as she strode beside him.

The Pack Rat got out the miniaturized shotgun mike he had made himself, got his tape recorder going. Ikusa gave the girl a feral grin, a baring of the teeth typical of a jungle predator.

"I wish you wouldn't persist in doing this kind of thing," he said.

"It's not prudent," the girl said, in a passable imitation of his voice. She swung her head around. "*I'm* not prudent. I have you for that. Yin and yang, Kusunda. We must have a balance."

One thing struck the Pack Rat immediately: how shockingly the girl used Ikusa's first name.

"As far as I can see, there is nothing balanced about this relationship," Kusunda Ikusa said. "It is based on mutual need, and need is never balanced."

"Like riding the back of a dragon."

"You thrive on danger, Killan. Sometimes I think that what you really want when you make these forays is for your father to turn around and recognize you."

The Pack Rat's heart was racing. He could scarcely believe what he was hearing. Ken Oroshi had three children—two boys, aged twenty, and a girl, aged eighteen. The girl, according to the Pack Rat's computers, was named Killan. Now here she was in the flesh, entangled in some bizarre, clandestine way with Kusunda Ikusa. What was going on?

At that moment Ikusa broke away, and without a further word to Killan Oroshi, disappeared into the throng.

Black igneous rock, thrusting skyward in jagged, clawed might. How many eons ago had the earth thundered, spitting in fire and gas? From that raging inferno the Hodaka had emerged to be weathered by wind and snow and ice.

The massif of the Hodaka was perhaps the most perilous area in all of Japan. From Nishi in the west to Oku in the northeast, the Hodaka was a series of razor-thin, serpentine ridges between deep, black ravines crusted with ice and hoar frost over lime-impregnated granite. Fissures created in groaning slippage through the severe winter months crisscrossed the succession of ridges like wounds in the corded arm of a veteran warrior.

The fissured wall known as Takidani, the Valley of the Waterfalls, had developed another name over the years, one which all climbers knew and used in memory of the number of their brethren who had perished in failed assaults: the Devil's Graveyard.

Just beyond Takidani, rising like a brooding giant, remorseless and fearsome, was the Black Gendarme, a veil of absolutely perpendicular igneous rock, veined with black ice. Threatening, intimidating, the Cassandra of the Japanese Alps, it seemed to have been thrust in one culminating upheaval from the center of the earth's core.

It was here that Nicholas had been brought as a teenager by Kansatsusan to complete his training, to prove in Nicholas's mind, at least, that he was better than Saigo.

And, perhaps, this was why he had died upon the Devil's Graveyard, with the Black Gendarme mocking him from its lofty eminence.

He had not learned his lessons well; his arrogance had misled him into believing his mastery of *ninjutsu* was far more advanced than it actually was. His heart had not been pure. Instead of concentrating on reaching the state of mind/no mind that was the Void, the path to understanding, he had been intent upon besting Saigo again.

In a way, he saw now, he and Saigo had been alike in that. Their rivalry had become, for them, a monomania—as the Book of Five Rings had been for Miyamoto Musashi—infusing their study of the martial arts with a very personal motivation. Their hearts had been tainted, then warped by the same sin: hate.

The revelation shook him to the core, making him unsure whether he wanted to see this arduous journey through. In truth he had no idea how long ago the secret message had been written on Kyoki's scroll, or even what it portended. Even if Genshi, the tanjian's brother, had indeed lived within sight of the Black Gendarme, he might well be dead by now.

But Nicholas knew that if he did not go on, he would never know. There would certainly be no salvation for him, and he would lose everything—Justine, his family, Tomkin Industries—because he could detect like a menacing iceberg sliding through the water the slow disintegration of his own sense of himself.

With comprehension will come the certainty of despair.
Shiro Ninja.

The path from Nishi Peak to the Devil's Graveyard was so arduous and hazardous that it had attracted far fewer climbers in recent years, after the disasters of 1981 and 1982, when ten people were lost there. And yet, within the community of professional mountaineers, there continued to be a fascination with the Hodaka and, in particular, with the Devil's Graveyard.

In retrospect it seemed clear that Kansatsu, in selecting the Hodaka as the site of Nicholas's graduation from the *ryu*, had meant to drive out of the boy all thought—conscious and unconscious—of his obsessive rivalry with Saigo. Nicholas could not imagine what other reason Kansatsu-san might have had for choosing it.

The Black Gendarme was a locus of death; it had no place in a teenage boy's life.

It had been December, and even in ultraefficient Tokyo great drifts of snow, charcoaled from soot, rainbow-hued from car oil, lay against the sidewalks.

It had been the coldest winter in twenty years when Kansatsu took Nicholas northeast into the Hodaka. Snow lay hip deep like sand; the mountain had been transformed by nature into a desert of ice. Snow eaves sixteen feet wide overhung the passes and shoulders which they traversed, their breaths coming hard, the hot exhalations crystallizing instantly in the thin, frigid air. The sky, an almost painfully brilliant shade of blue-purple, seemed brittle, little more than an eggshell.

Nicholas had been barefoot because Kansatsu had said, *Ice and the fear of death are one and the same. Once you learn not to feel the one, you will not fear the other.*

Nicholas remembered vividly how clear it had been on their ascent of the Hodaka. To this day he could not fathom where the storm had come from. But the range had mighty canyons, vast peaks like flying buttresses which acted like tunnels, directing the elements, magnifying their force, their virulence. Up here, when the sun shone, its rays could burn the skin off your face and hands; the same was true of an ice storm.

Nicholas had been in sight of the Black Gendarme when the storm hit. He had been perhaps halfway through the program of tests Kansatsu-san had devised for him. Perhaps—this was forever an enigma in Nicholas's mind—the storm itself had been part of the examination.

In any event, a snow eave, perhaps twenty feet in length, was broken off by the rising wind whipping through the canyons between the peaks. Nicholas, who had been fighting just to breathe the thin air that the wind swept away from him, should have felt the solid arc of snow and ice dropping toward him, should have heard the echo of the crack as it was dislodged, even though the wind sucked the sound away into the storm.

The truth was that Nicholas was fighting *haragei*, the sixth sense Kansatsu had taught him to find within himself. *Haragei*, the precursor to *Getsumei no michi*, could be terrifying to the inexperienced. Controlling it was far more arduous than finding it. Nicholas did not fully know himself. Therefore, he was having difficulty manipulating *haragei*; it was, in part, controlling him.

Ice and snow dropping out of the sky crushed him beneath its weight. The storm was upon him, darkness and cold enveloping him all at once. The first thing he did was panic. He tried to breathe, and when he found that he could not, his mind dissolved into chaos.

Like a flash of lightning the panic quickly passed. Silence rang in his ears. He could hear the beating of his heart, the blood rushing through his veins, amplified in the dimensions of his tomb. Curiously, this revived him. I am alive, he thought.

Something—an ancient instinct, he believed—came to the fore, told him to center himself. And with centering came *haragei*. He reached out with his mind, and rediscovered the world outside. Immediately he became aware of Kansatsu's presence and was comforted.

He began to dig. He used his skills. He could "see" Kansatsu pointing, showing him in which direction to dig, just as Nicholas imagined that Kansatsu himself was digging.

There was a finite amount of oxygen in the tomb, and it was fast giving out. Carbon dioxide burned his lungs. His body was on fire. Still he concentrated on the task before him, refusing to be distracted by fear. He did not feel the cold; he was not afraid to die.

The storm hit him square in the face when he emerged like an infant from the egg, the chrysalis, the womb. He gasped, taking in long shuddering breaths as Kansatsu, pulling him free from the pile of ice and snow, wrapped him in his powerful arms and sought shelter beneath a ledge of twisted black rock. . . .

Nicholas, upon the Hodaka again, stared at his nemesis, the Black Gendarme. It was the present, the past merely a vapor drifting above his head, a ragged war banner shredded by the sharp mountain peaks. Part of him could not believe that he was actually here. He had been certain that he would never again set foot upon the Hodaka.

But he was *Shiro Ninja*, and everything had changed.

The sky was an opalescent white, giving the impression that he was inside a mass of cartilage, cut off from the rest of the world or in another world altogether. A distant howling told him that a wind had sprung up; the first drops of rain, fat and heavy, roughly brushed his cheeks like a dissatisfied lover.

Nicholas stiffened. As it had done so many years ago, a storm was approaching. It was at his back, moving swiftly north. There was a crack of thunder, and the shell of the sky was split open by a tongue of iridescent lightning.

In a moment the rain came, part ice, part hail, beating down upon him. He took shelter beneath a ledge of twisted black rock. It occurred to him that this might be the spot where Kansatsu had held him safe and warm so many years ago.

Nicholas shivered. He was unutterably tired. His body ached in so many places he could no longer distinguish individual pain. His head throbbed where the incision had been made, and he unconsciously touched the spot beneath his knit cap. Despite the Gore-Tex parka, his layers of thermal clothing, he was cold. His teeth began to chatter.

He could see nothing beyond his shallow lair. He clung to the side of the Hodaka, at the foot of the malevolent wall of the Black Gendarme, as insignificant as an insect upon an elephant's back. In the face of the soaring majesty of this mountain range, the elemental fury of this storm, he was nothing, less than a speck lost in time, soon forgotten.

He closed his eyes, rocking himself. It would be so easy to sleep now, encysted in the bosom of the storm, curled upon the Hodaka, ancient of the earth, to sleep the eternal sleep, and in such sleep an end to fear, to struggle, to *Shiro Ninja*.

He heard the siren call and part of him responded, edging closer and closer to a surcease for which he surely longed. Death came again to him, as soft and seductive as his first lover, at once a melancholy and exhilarating reunion. . . .

He awoke with a start. His throat was dry and raw, as if he had been breathing sulfur instead of oxygen. He blinked heavily. He could still see nothing beyond the hollow in which he crouched. He could no longer feel his feet. He squeezed his calves, pounded his fists weakly against his thighs. Numb. Totally numb.

Nicholas knew that he was dying. Even if he wanted to get up to run—*did* he want to? where would he run to?—he could not. The storm raged; night came down like a heavy cloak, the darkness of a moonless midnight.

Nicholas knew that if he fell asleep he would never awake. He exercised his mind, dredging up memory after memory, parading them across the theater of his mind, immersing himself in the detail of recall. But he was so tired. His bones ached. He was cold. His eyelids drooped and once or twice his head jerked up, his heart thumping wildly with the knowledge that against his will he had begun to drift off.

He was terrified, not only because he was losing conscious control over his body, not only because he was helpless, but because he knew that part of him welcomed death. He fought against that part of him as, years ago, he had fought against *haragei*.

He thought of Nangi, his friend. He thought of Lew Croaker, the friend he had pushed away because of his own guilt. He thought of his tiny dead daughter, white-faced beneath the plastic tent that had not been able to keep her alive. He thought of Justine, of how much he loved her.

His heart broke then, and he wept bitter, crystalline tears. They froze on his eyelids, his cheeks, his lips. And still they came in such profusion that he might have been made of tears.

At last it was over. A calm after the emotional storm.

Emptiness.

Nothingness.

With his tears still frozen on his face, Nicholas drifted away into sleep. Through vapor he was falling, endlessly falling . . .

Until at last Death came to claim him.

"If virtue were its own reward," Tanzan Nangi said to the Pack Rat, "it would not be a human trait. It would belong solely to the gods."

The noise and lights of the rows of pachinko machines was deafening. All the better for them; the Pack Rat knew it was safe in here.

"I was speaking just now of Kusunda Ikusa."

Nangi nodded. "And so was I. If Ikusa seems virtuous, it is because it will prove useful to him."

"Not to Nami itself?" the Pack Rat asked.

"We must examine most carefully the motives of those near a nexus of power who profess too easily to pure altruism. One suspects anything in a pure form, but most of all virtue, which is not natural to man and which does not come to him without a struggle."

Outside, in the dazzling Ginza, it was raining. Here, in the Twenty-Four Hour pachinko parlor, all was the same as it always was, day or night: bright with garish neon colors, humid, dense with the sweat of human emotion. The place never closed, which was why, the Pack Rat had said, he liked it. He came here often, Nangi knew, playing pachinko while he worked out problems in penetration, surveillance, and so forth. The nuances of his tradecraft.

"I have passed on your computer record of the virus attack to an associate," the Pack Rat said.

"It is most frustrating. My people have gotten nowhere," Nangi said.

The Pack Rat nodded. "Then identifying the source of the virus has become my sole responsibility. But I must tell you, Nangi-san, it is proving to be a difficult problem to solve. Its architecture is wholly alien."

Although there were a number of pachinko machines free, the Pack Rat was waiting for a specific one. Pachinko, something of a national craze in Japan, was similar to American pinball, but played on a vertical field. It was a decades-old game, but as with almost everything, the Japanese liked it best in its current high-tech form. Some of the newest machines were equipped with tiny televisions so the player could keep up with his favorite shows while scoring.

"I always play that one," the Pack Rat told Nangi, pointing to the sixth machine in the seventh line. An old lady was on her last game; she must have been there for hours, moving from machine to machine.

"Is Justine Linnear being guarded?" Nangi asked as he watched the Pack Rat prepare to play. Curiously, the Pack Rat had bought only one token from the cashier at the front of the parlor. Nangi wondered whether the Pack Rat was that good. Winning would give him free tokens from the machine itself.

The Pack Rat put his hands on the machine, nodded. "As you requested. I've put my best man, Han Kawado, on it. Please don't worry about her."

"It is a precaution only," Nangi said. "I have no idea yet what this *dorokusai* is after, but one cannot be too careful. I want full security maintained."

The Pack Rat nodded. He began to play. He won the first game, but not by much. His score only netted him a single token. He began a second game. "Getting back to Ikusa," he said. "Seeing him and Killan Oroshi together, I can tell you firsthand there is nothing virtuous about their relationship."

Nangi grunted. "So much for protestations of the absolute."

"And there's something about Ikusa's relationship with Ken Oroshi. Oroshi, the elder by twenty years, genuflected in front of Ikusa."

"Oroshi's company, Nakano Industries, is in desperate financial straits," Nangi said.

"Yeah. I'd heard that."

"You're among the few who have," Nangi said. "Oroshi's moved heaven and earth to keep it secret. Frankly, I don't know how he's kept the company going this long. All he's got there now is a superior research and development department. I would give my left arm for some of his resident geniuses. That's what gave me the idea when Ikusa started to squeeze me. That's primarily why Nakano was the one firm on my list I was hoping Ikusa would pick. After we merge, I'm going to exercise my right of stock option immediately. Then I'll own Nakano. I'll have expanded, acquired key personnel, gotten three thousand square feet of prime laboratory space, something the Sphynx *kobun* desperately needs. And the best part is that I'll have done it for virtually no money."

The Pack Rat said, "Pardon me, but what do you need me for?"

"Insurance," Nangi said. "I am not about to underestimate Ikusa-san. I want no interference from him or from Nami once I begin."

The Pack Rat lost the second game. Nangi saw his expression, said, "What's troubling you?"

"Killan Oroshi's not what I had expected. She's not a pawn, more of a wild card. I can't tell whether her actions are unpredictable or premeditated."

"Why should this concern me?"

"I'm not sure," the Pack Rat admitted. "Perhaps it's as you suspect, nothing but an indiscretion on Ikusa's part. He thinks she's having the affair with him to spite her father who she clearly despises. But I wonder. I wonder whether it's she who's playing the great Kusunda Ikusa for a fool."

"That would, indeed, be interesting," Nangi mused. "But for this kind of investigation one needs time, and I have very little of that before I sign the merger papers with Nakano. Ikusa has worked more quickly than I had imagined. Already the contracts are with my lawyers. Continue the Ikusa surveillance. This tidbit about Ken Oroshi's daughter is interesting, but that is all. I need something with which to destroy Ikusa's reputation —not his friendship with Ken Oroshi."

"Ikusa doesn't gamble," the Pack Rat said. "He owes no debts, he takes no bribes, he gives his advice freely. He's unmarried. He's a prudent man."

Nangi shook his head. "Do not make the mistake of confusing *tatemae* —the facade—with prudence," he said. "Kusunda Ikusa is clever; he covers himself in virtue as a squid ejects ink into the water. But for whatever reason, he has formed this liaison with Ken Oroshi's daughter. This is not the act of a prudent man, but a man so in love with power that it has warped his judgment."

The Pack Rat reached around to the side of the machine, did something Nangi could not see. A small door opened and the Pack Rat extracted a couple of tokens. So that's his secret, Nangi thought. He cheats. "Still," the Pack Rat said, closing the door, beginning his third game. "I've got a feeling we're missing something important, or looking at the situation from the wrong end."

"With the recent death of the Emperor, Nami's power has grown tenthousand-fold. They have become a danger to Japan. This coercion they have me under is proof of that. It is Nami, ultimately, whom I must discredit," Nangi said. "If we bring Ikusa down, Nami will follow."

"Are we doing the right thing?" the Pack Rat said.

"As far as Nami goes," Nangi said soberly, "it exists neither for Japan nor for the Emperor. It was created in the minds of men, and there is where its true power resides. It has no real function other than to raise its members to power. It is the guardian of this power and nothing more. But time passes, and it seems to me that that empty power—that talismanic facade—needs to be fed. The warp of the flame is never so extreme as when it exists for itself and not to light the way for others."

"Yet the topmost ministers, the business world's most influential chairmen, acquiesce to its wishes."

Nangi grunted. "Such is the hypocrisy of the modern-day society in which we live. Men fear the unknown, and Japan without the old Emperor is a question mark. Nami seeks now to capitalize on the insecurity of the nation. They are predators who know well the stench of the rotting flesh upon which they feed."

The Pack Rat watched the tiny steel ball-bearing rocket around the vertical pachinko field. "Perhaps you're right, and Nami is our ultimate target," he said. "But right now I feel as if I can't get to that until I've unraveled the mystery of Kusunda Ikusa and Killan Oroshi."

"I won't tell you how to do your job," Nangi said, "but have a care, Pack Rat. Nami is extremely dangerous. They are a law unto themselves. Remember, I need you beside me, not dead in some alleyway."

The Pack Rat won big. He was on a roll.

David Brisling watched Douglas Howe on the phone in his office, and felt a sharp stab of jealousy. That damned Japanese bitch, he thought. Nothing has been the same around here since she squirmed her way into Howe's inner circle. He tried to stem the wild burst of envy he felt, but blurted at Shisei when she emerged, "Why wasn't I at that meeting? As operations deputy, I should have been involved."

"Why don't you ask your boss?" Shisei said tartly. She turned her kilowatt smile on Brisling, held up the Louis Feraud suit. "Did you see what Dougie bought me? It must have set him back a fortune." She laughed to see Brisling's face flush. "The problem with you," she said, "is that you're a wuss. I can't imagine what your function is." She stuck her face in his. "Why *does* Dougie keep you around? For laughs?" Her smile deepened, changed subtly. "Or maybe it's just to bring his suits to the cleaners. Face it. You're a little boy in a man's world, and you always will be." She laughed as she left him standing there, white and trembling.

Howe, who was on the phone with General Dickerson, his stooge at the Pentagon, beckoned for Brisling to come in. He cupped his hand over the speaker. "I need you to do something for me."

"What is it?" Brisling snapped. "You need me to go to the cleaners?"

"What?" Howe's head came up. "General," he said into the phone,

"I'll get back to you." He cradled the receiver, said to Brisling, "What the fuck're you talking about?"

"Nothing," Brisling said sullenly. "Just something the Jap bitch said." He watched Howe emerge from behind his desk, reach for his jacket. Phones were ringing in the ready room, fielded by Brisling's cadre of assistant secretaries.

"Come on," Howe said. "I've got to get to S One to see Stedman." He was talking about John Stedman, currently the most senior senator on the Hill. S1 was Stedman's hideaway office in the Capitol Building. Ever since the dawn of the republic, the seventy-five hideaways were the most precious perks in Washington. "Life begins at S Forty," Howe often said, because he didn't have one. But Cotton Branding did, because of his prestige, his contacts. Another unhealed wound in Howe's flesh, another inequity for which he despised Branding.

"Forget Shisei," Howe said in the car as Michael, his driver, pulled out into traffic. "She's not your concern."

"That's what you always say. You know she calls you 'Dougie'?"

"Does she?" Howe stared at his assistant. "It's a joke, David. She's pulling your goddamned chain." He shook his head. "Jesus, sometimes I can't believe you."

"Still. I want to know what her status is around here." Brisling's jaw was firmly set and a vein pulsed in his temple. He could not believe how deeply Shisei had gotten under his skin. He had resented her from the moment Howe had started using her, and that resentment had steadily percolated. But the way she had talked to him just now had been the last straw. It was inexcusable.

"Shisei's a servant, David"—Howe shrugged—"just like all the other dedicated, patriotic servants I employ to help me navigate the perilous waters of Washington." There was a smirk on his face; privately, he was amused by Brisling's obvious jealousy.

"Leave that bullshit for the press," Brisling said hotly. "She's nothing like the rest of us, and you know it."

"Yeah," Howe said with a peculiar combination of satisfaction and malice, "her pussy's prettier than all of you put together." He was fed up with Brisling's whining. In fact, the only thing that was keeping him from firing Brisling was plausible deniability. Brisling was a born pawn. When his usefulness is at an end, Howe decided, he's out.

Howe picked up his mobile phone, spoke to General Dickerson for several minutes. Then, because he was in the mood to have some malicious fun, he leaned over, said in a conspiratorial whisper, "I'll tell you a secret, David, sometimes her pussy is smarter than the whole bunch of you." He laughed so hard he had to wipe tears out of his eyes.

"Your jokes aside," Brisling said somewhat stiffly, "I don't trust her. For the life of me, I can't understand why you do. I've seen her twist you around her finger when you thought the opposite was happening. You set out to use her, which is okay, but this has turned into something else. She's gotten under your skin, into your blood. I see the presents you give her whenever she does a job for you. I think you want her, and that's all that's on your mind when you're with her. *That's* power. *That's* control."

"Are you finished?" Howe said. He was angry now. Who was this little pissant to tell him what was what? Shisei was right about Brisling, he was eminently expendable. He reined in his emotions with a great force of will. "I just sent the bitch off to make sure Branding takes her to the gala State dinner for the German chancellor at the end of the month. There I will ruin him forever. So forget your little operation at the Johnson Institute. I have something else for you.

"You hate Shisei's guts, you think she's affecting my judgment. Maybe you're right. I think it's time we found out the truth about her." He smiled warmly, settled his features into a mask of confidentiality. "I'm giving you that job, David, because I know I can trust you. I happen to know that Shisei keeps her intelligence notes at home, in her bedroom. Wait until the night of the dinner, when we know she'll be out with Branding. Just after she leaves, find a way to get those notes."

"But . . ." Brisling's face showed his concern. "You want me to break into her house?"

Howe raised his eyebrows. "David, I don't know what you mean. Use your own initiative—that's the way to get ahead in this city." He stared out the window at the passing parade of Washington's monuments. They all seemed to be saluting him. "It seems to me I'm giving you what you want most: a chance to prove to me what you're really worth."

He swung around, cultivating his avuncular look. "You've always found my advice helpful to you in the past, haven't you? I took you out of the Senate cloakroom, made something out of the young drone you once were. That's because I saw the potential in you." The benevolent smile broadened as he slipped an arm around Brisling's shoulders. "Listen to me, David. You're going places. Today, my director of operations. Tomorrow—well, who knows?"

And Death had a name.

Nicholas opened his eyes, staring up into a face he had been certain he would never see again.

"Kansatsu-san?" His voice was a dry, reedy rasp. "Is it really you? Am I dreaming? Am I dead?"

"You are not dead," Nicholas's first *ninjutsu sensei* said. "Neither are you alive. Yet."

His face—which was all of him Nicholas could see—was exactly the same as the last time Nicholas had seen it, in the winter of 1963. Impossible, Nicholas thought. But his thoughts were hazy, half formed, still partially encased in ice.

"Where are we?"

"In Limbo," Kansatsu-san said. "My home upon the Black Gendarme."

"A house? Up here?" How odd my voice sounds! Nicholas thought. How hollow, how timbreless.

"Though Limbo is my home," Kansatsu said, "it is a retreat. Think of it as a monastery, a holy place of serenity and of strength." He peered down at Nicholas. "Isn't that what you need most now?"

Nicholas tried to nod his assent, fell asleep instead. He dreamed of the Black Gendarme, rising from the center of his soul.

Two weeks after they returned to Washington, Cotton Branding took Shisei with him to the Johnson Institute. It was the first time since he had been back that he had been able to break away from his duties on the Senate floor.

The Institute, the ne plus ultra destination of the best minds graduating from MIT and Stanford, owned a large red-brick building constructed at the turn of the century in the Georgian style. It was essentially a country house that now sat in the center of Washington, on Devonshire Place, just a block from the Connecticut Avenue Bridge with its gigantic Art Moderne urns.

That a structure originally built for displaying works of art was now used for highly advanced and elaborate laboratory facilities perhaps said more about the capital than a year's worth of speeches in the Senate.

Though the mansion was still beautiful on the outside, all its interior charm had been lost in the renovation. Still, as far as Cotton Branding was concerned, the Johnson Institute was the center of the world, as beautiful as any museum he had been in or contributed to.

He was here to see the latest demonstration of how far the Hive Project had actually come. It was meant only for him, since this phase was still in its embryonic experimental stage. Yet Shisei was with him. He was proud of the work being done here, saw it, perhaps, as a reflection of his own efforts, the fruit of his hard work.

They entered the long, echoey marble foyer where a formidable state-of-the-art security network had been installed. Shisei gave the attendant her vital statistics, full name, date and place of birth, place of employment, watched in fascination as the young woman typed the information onto a computer screen. There was only a fractional hesitation, then the printer began spewing out hard copy, including a facsimile photo of Shisei. The computer operator handed the hard copy to a uniformed officer, who scanned it, then scrutinized them. He nodded, indicated that they should step through a metal detector. They were asked to empty their pockets. Shisei's handbag and the contents of their pockets were X-rayed. In addition, Shisei was made to hand over her jewelry to be analyzed by a spectrometer.

They were fingerprinted, then directed to look into the eyepiece of a great, arching machine so their retina patterns could be photographed—and in Branding's case, compared with those on file. Then they spoke in turn into a grill so that a sophisticated computer could record and store their voiceprints.

At length they were given laser-etched tags to wear, each imprinted with an invisible one-time-only code.

"Is that all?" she asked ironically as they passed through into the Institute proper.

Branding smiled thinly. "If you come back next month, they'll take blood as well," he said. "I understand they're about to perfect instant DNA identification."

Dr. Rudolph, a tall, whip-thin man with a pencil mustache and high-arched eyebrows, was waiting for them just past the next computer-operated checkpoint. His bald skull gleamed in the overhead illumination. A brim of salt-and-pepper hair hung down over his ears and the nape of his neck. Shisei thought that he had the air of a man who bred dogs or roses in his spare time: meticulous, patient, gentle. He peered at them as if they were laboratory subjects, quickly shook their hands with a dry, firm grip. He nodded absently as Branding introduced Shisei.

"Do you smoke?" Dr. Rudolph asked. "No? Good. No smoking of any kind is allowed here."

He turned and led them down a quiet corridor. Shisei thought the subdued light and acoustically-muffled carpet were more appropriate to an executive suite.

Dr. Rudolph opened a door, ushered them into what looked like a boardroom. The space was dominated by an oval mahogany table around which high-backed chairs were arranged. On the table, in front of each chair, were a glass ashtray, a copper-colored water carafe, two glasses, pad and pencil. In the center of the table, where a floral arrangement would otherwise be, sat a sleek black oblong box made of ABS plastic. On its face were three rows of color-coded buttons and toggle switches.

"Sit," Dr. Rudolph said laconically.

Shisei looked around. She saw that one wall of the room was entirely composed of a clear plastic sheet on which had been etched a detailed Mercator projection map of the earth. In all other respects the room was nondescript. She had expected a laboratory, and was slightly disappointed.

"As you know," Dr. Rudolph began, "the Hive Project is involved in constructing an altogether new form of artificial intelligence. There have been attempts before this. Indeed, other projects are going on even as we speak. But, sadly, all are doomed to failure. All except the Hive. This is because true artificial intelligence is impossible utilizing conventional computers. While these clumsy machines may be programmed to aid in disease diagnosis or the like, outside the laboratory they cannot reliably perform even routine tasks involving movement and recognition. Simply put, computer processors, even a series of linked processors, executing one preprogrammed task at a time, cannot achieve a useful kind of artificial intelligence.

"For that, one needs a brain, and what is a brain but billions of neurons—the human equivalent of processors—running a multiplicity of tasks simultaneously. This has been our goal here, to accumulate and store information much as humans do, as a pattern of interconnections that can be accessed all at once. Hence the name Hive Project, because our 'brain' has the approximate complexity of a bee."

Dr. Rudolph rubbed his hands together. "Enough talk. I brought you here, Cook, for a demonstration." He nodded at the plastic object in the center of the table. "Would you take the remote?"

Branding did so, then passed it to Shisei. "I think I'd prefer my friend to participate in the demonstration," he said.

Dr. Rudolph nodded. "As you wish." He pressed a stud and the lights went down. Simultaneously, as if it were a Broadway stage, the map of the world began to glow. Then several spots began to pulse. "We are in the war room below the White House," he intoned. "Our DEW-line defense has automatically come up in response to the firing of several ICBM's"—red circles blinked, moving toward the United States—"from three different locations." Yellow lights flashed to indicate the launch sites. They were in Siberia, the USSR's southwest coast, Shisei saw.

"You want me to figure out a defense or offense with the help of the Hive computer?" Shisei asked, looking over the array of buttons and switches on the black box.

"No," Dr. Rudolph said, "you have in your hands the Russian initiative. Of course, you will be aided by conventional computers. You will even get their advice on the box's printout screen. But you will decide how and when to launch the second and, if you survive, the third launch waves."

"If I survive?"

"The defense of the United States is now in the hands of the Hive computer," Dr. Rudolph said. "World War Three has begun."

The red dots indicating the Russian missiles were more than halfway to their targets. Now she could see, arcing to meet them, green blips. Soon there were a series of yellow explosions as the first wave of missile strikes was detonated in the atmosphere.

Shisei asked for computer advice even as she launched a second wave of missiles, double the number of the first launch. She glanced at the wall map in time to see clusters of green dots moving toward the Soviet Union: American missiles; the Hive computer had successfully defended America, and was now retaliating.

She punched the button for missile identification, got it, asked her computer to match a defense. She waited impatiently as the green dots streaked ever closer to impact. She sent bombers aloft, dividing them into four sectors, separating them. But already she could see the orange lights of American fighters launched off aircraft carriers, rushing to intercept her bombers. The Hive computer was doing all this, thwarting her at every turn? Impossible!

Again she asked her computer for advice, then, desperately, deployed her fleet of atomic submarines, punched up the Soviet automatic defense net against the American missiles. Identifications were flooding in, too many for the computer to handle, too many for her to defend all at once. Her computer managed to detonate some in the atmosphere, but one by one she saw her launch sites impacted, destroyed, or crippled beyond use. Before she knew it, American stealth bombers had decimated her subs. Then Moscow was wiped out and she had only a minimum number of bombers left. She was sweating. What was there to do?

"Had enough?" Dr. Rudolph's voice echoed hollowly in the room.

"Yes." Shisei's voice was hoarse. She thrust the black box from her.

"But how convincing can this be? I know next to nothing about missiles and defense systems. The Hive knows everything there is to know."

"The Hive computer knows as much as the computer at your disposal," Dr. Rudolph said. "Which, I might add, is an accurate simulacrum of the Kremlin's supercomputer."

"But the difference is . . . astounding," Shisei said.

"Like pitting modern-day man against a dinosaur in a game of intelligence." Dr. Rudolph nodded. "I couldn't agree more." He rubbed his hands together again. "Was the demonstration a success, Cook?"

Branding was beside himself with delight. He had it all in the palm of his hand now. The Hive computer on which he had staked his career was a reality. Rudolph and his staff of geniuses had taken it out of the realm of theory, taken it further even than the first primordial jury-rigged experiments. Branding had been in on the Hive's first bleating squalls; encouraging, to be sure, but this was a full-fledged success. It had spoken in sentences, paragraphs, volumes. The Hive brain was here, now, and it was his. "You tell us, Shisei," Branding said, too overcome to say more.

"I'd . . ." Shisei seemed a little stunned. "Would it be possible to actually *see* the Hive?"

Dr. Rudolph looked at Branding. "Cook, it's up to you. She's your guest."

"All right."

The Hive computer itself was housed three floors down, beneath even the old mansion's sub-basement. Rock had been blasted away to make room for the shielded laboratories. But when Shisei saw it, she could not believe her eyes.

"Why, it's no larger than my pocketbook," she said. "This can't be it."

"But it is!" Dr. Rudolph was beaming. He pointed to a copper beryllium object that was a three-dimensional octagon. "This is the Hive computer. Your adversary during our simulation of World War Three. You see, the Hive is well named. It's really a multibrain, a new form of intelligence. It's not compartmentalized, as we humans like to think of everything being, but rather is made up of many inputs working at once, in concert. We've mastered a revolutionary technology to make it so. These resonant tunneling computer chips are constructed not of silicon, not even of the newest hyperfast conductive alloys, indium phosphide and aluminum gallium arsenide. We're beyond even that technology. The Hive runs on multilaser computer chips. You see, what we've accomplished is to find a way to send coded light signals through chips at a rate of ten billion times a second. There they are converted to electronic signals via a monocrystalline diamond layer. The result is a chip that not only processes data at mind-boggling speed, but also insulates the data from the massive heat buildup such high-speed work would otherwise generate. In short, the speed of this Hive brain makes that of even the fastest of the conventional supercomputers seem annoyingly slow."

"So I had no chance against it," Shisei said.

"Not even George Patton at the helm would have a chance," Dr. Rudolph said.

"But if it's so good, so fast, and can reason, plan strategies and such, why isn't it being used now?" Shisei asked.

"This demonstration was just that," Dr. Rudolph said. "It was in a controlled environment over a short space of time. There are still problems, applications we have to work on. And, of course, in some areas the Hive is still incomplete."

"Aren't you afraid that someone will tap into the Hive brain?" Shisei asked.

Dr. Rudolph beamed at her. "Ah, no. Besides the security network you yourself have experienced—which, I might add, is only a fraction of the external shell security, as we refer to it—the Hive brain has been programmed with its own *internal* policing system designed to eradicate any form of intrusive or destructive virus program, as well as to deny any attempt at unauthorized usage. I assure you that Cook Branding's baby is quite safe."

"The Hive computer is *your* baby," Branding said to Dr. Rudolph. "I'm only godfather to its birth and development."

"Thank you, Cook," Dr. Rudolph said. "Come. I have some coffee brewing in my office. I'd appreciate a moment of your time to go over the revised estimates for next year's budget requirements."

"Shisei?"

"Coming, Cook." She was still staring at the amazing computer that thought like a brain. She took a step to follow the two men and her right heel gave way. She stumbled, went down on one knee. "No, no." She waved away their help. "I'm okay. I'll just have to go barefoot."

She slipped off both shoes, turned away from them a moment, and as she did, palmed a tiny cylindrical object she slipped from the center of the broken heel. For just an instant her hand slid beneath the table upon which the Hive computer rested. Her heart beating fast, she felt the coated plastic cylinder adhere to the underside of the table just beneath the octagon of the Hive. Then she was turning back to them, saying, "Oh, coffee. How wonderful. I'm dying for a cup."

———

Late in the afternoon Tomi Yazawa returned to police headquarters. She had spent the entire day interviewing Dr. Hanami's and Dr. Muku's assistants, lab and X-ray personnel, anyone with frequent contact with either the offices or the doctors themselves. She also went over the appointment books for the previous six weeks. She was searching for some clue to the identity of the man who had murdered Hanami and Muku.

It was clear to her by the manner of the doctors' deaths that their murderer had been known to them. This was, perhaps, more apparent in the case of Dr. Muku, because he had been killed at close range without a struggle. Tomi could not imagine anyone—even the frightening figure that had attacked her and Nicholas Linnear in Dr. Hanami's office— breaking into Dr. Muku's office and shoving a phosphorus cigarette into his face. Phosphorus was what the Medical Examiner's lab report had found traces of in Dr. Muku's eye socket. The intense flash of heat had, in the M.E.'s words, "burned through the orb, the external and internal recti, the optic nerve, the lesser wing, the sphenoid." In other words, it had penetrated all the way into the brain, causing death by flash-searing the organ.

In the assistant M.E.'s estimation—and in Tomi's as well—one not only had to be very close to the victim in order to inflict death in this bizarre manner, but also to take the victim completely by surprise. Dr. Muku's clothes were not torn or even wrinkled, his office was in immaculate condition. There was, in sum, no evidence of a struggle. Ergo: Muku knew his murderer. Assumption: Hanami knew him as well.

Tomi spent the remainder of the afternoon in tedious phone work, trying to get a line on Hanami's friends and associates, trying to match them up with Muku's to see if there might be an overlap, a common ground from which to proceed. She had also asked for reports on the two men's families, not that she thought she might find something, but because she was well trained and was meticulous in her investigations.

All she knew so far was that Muku had been a widower and that Hanami was survived by his wife. According to Hanami's widow, they had been happily married. Neither doctor had progeny.

When Tomi's call list gave out—she was unable to reach more than a third of the people on it—she went to see Senjin. She needed advice on how to proceed. Besides, records showed that he had consulted Dr. Muku several times concerning suspects since he had been in the homicide division.

It was early evening. Most of the day watch had already gone, and the building was palpably quieter. Senjin, however, was in his office.

" 'Psychopathy is not the face of evil,' Dr. Muku once told me," Senjin said in response to her first question. " 'It is, rather, the beam emitted from a long-forgotten lighthouse. Loneliness is the only companion a psychopath is able to tolerate.' " Senjin nodded. "Yes, I remember Muku-san well. It is more than a pity that he is dead, it is a tragedy for the department. Because of his insights into the criminal mind, I was able to identify, isolate, and track down Kuramata, Shigeyuki, and Toshiroh, three of our most wanted terrorists."

"What was he like?" Tomi asked.

"Muku-san?" Senjin's forehead creased in concentration. "Well, it is hard to say. He was brilliant, of course, but also, I would say, introspective. He did not actively seek the limelight; he was not, I would judge, a good public speaker. But, of course, he was by nature essentially a thinker."

"From what I've been able to gather, he didn't seem to have many friends."

"Frankly, I'd be surprised if he had any," Senjin said. "Muku-san, though brilliant, was opinionated, often quite stubborn. I doubt very much whether he'd have made an acceptable friend."

"Is there anything else you can tell me?"

Senjin had come out from behind his desk. "On a related matter, Nicholas Linnear has not returned to Tokyo?"

"Not to my knowledge," Tomi said. "In a way, I'm relieved. No one knows where he is. Surely he's safe from whatever attack the Red Army had planned for him."

"Let us hope so," Senjin said. "Though I am not as comfortable as you are with him being outside the scope of our watchful eye, and I would think it rather important that you locate him as soon as possible."

He was standing so close to her, she could feel him against her breasts. Tomi began to burn. She took a shuddering breath, taking his scent into her lungs, enjoying it as if it were nicotine-laden smoke. But she was ashamed, not because of her erotic thoughts, but because she had not immediately stepped away from him; this was not seemly behavior in public. She did not move.

"How are you feeling, Tomi-san? You took quite a beating."

She felt a little thrill pass down her spine as he used her first name. This, too, was unseemly behavior, impolite in the intimacy it implied. Tomi found that she was not offended.

"I am feeling fit enough," she said, aware of the slight tremolo in her voice. "Except for some aches here and there." She was having trouble catching her breath. "I've had several nightmares." Her heart was hammering in her throat. "Nothing hard work won't cure."

"I see that I've been correctly worried about you." Senjin put one finger beneath her chin, lifted her head up so that he could stare into her eyes. "You are such a dedicated officer."

When he touched her, Tomi felt her knees go weak. She prayed that she would not collapse. Had the office gotten abruptly hot? Then she ceased to breathe at all as his head came down and his lips grazed the side of her neck. Tomi's lips parted and her eyelids fluttered. She heard him whisper her name as if from a great distance.

Then she heard him say, "Come with me." Automatically, she obeyed, allowing him to steer her out of his office, down the half-deserted corridor and into a utility closet.

He shut the door behind them. Dim aqueous light filtered through a tiny window of translucent glass high up in one wall. Tomi felt shelving behind her back, pressing into her calves. Senjin was tight against her. With the two of them in there, the space was so tiny there was scarcely room to move, and none to turn around.

"Wh-What's happening?" Tomi asked, though her body knew, just as it had known of this inevitable end from the moment Senjin had come around from behind his desk.

She felt his lips on hers, felt her own mouth opening, almost dying of pleasure when their tongues met, searched, entangled. My God, she thought. It's happening and, oh, oh, I want it to happen.

Slowly she felt her skirt being lifted, felt his hands upon her thighs. Then he had sunk down on his knees. Tomi was so stunned that she could not utter a sound, not even the sob she felt welling up around her heart as his mouth sought out the spot between her thighs that most yearned to have him.

Tomi felt as if she were slowly slipping into a bath, her skin frictioned by heat, her muscles relaxed by heat, her bones melted by heat. Her mind was awash as if with a drug. Dimly she remembered how often she had dreamed of this moment, never truly believing that it would ever be made real. And those dreams, like images perceived in dusty light, in a mirror cracked and peeling, added an almost insupportable weight and urgency to the moment as reality merged with fantasy. How many nights had she lain sleepless, sightless, touching herself in a sad mockery of how Senjin was touching her now, imagining that he was beside her, above her, in her? Those imaginings were all here with her now, a surrealistic pillow on which to rest her slowly working hips.

She felt a lightness of spirit in the tiny, stifling closet. The smell of sweat—her sweat, the smell of arousal; her arousal, the smell of sex—her sex was like the most delicate of perfumes, a mingling of scents that created a whole she breathed in with each shuddering breath, expelled with each muffled moan, each tiny cry of delight.

Until, her hips working faster and faster, the entire universe seemed to implode inward. She gripped Senjin's sweat-soaked head, pushing him against her with great force, floating down from the heights slowly, slowly. And when she thought it was over, she was wrong, because he was fully against her, his heat overwhelming, and then he was in her, and the sensation made what had come before as nothing.

Tomi needed more of his flesh. She tore frantically at his tie, unbuttoned his shirt all the way down to his navel. She licked his neck. She felt abraded skin as if from a wound, kissed it tenderly. Sweat ran into her eyes.

She wept into his chest as he thrust into her, thrusting back at him, biting his salty flesh as she encircled his hips with her legs, and in the claustrophobic space there was only the two of them, and then just one, aflame, melting, fused.

When it was over Tomi tasted his blood on her lips. She lay against him, encircled by his arms, encircling him with her legs, content just to listen to their two disparate heartbeats thumping in the darkness and the heat. She could not breathe, but she liked that, too. It was as if the engine they had created had sucked all the oxygen from the environment. She felt a pulse beating madly in the side of her head, and knew that whatever else might happen, a part of him was now hers, an emotion, a sensation, perhaps something altogether more ephemeral than that, who knew? This was not a time for definitions or even for absolutes. It was a time of mystery and an acceptance of the unknown, acknowledging not only its existence, but the idea that it existed wholly without answers.

And then like a thief in the night the thought came: what have we done?

She broke away from him; it was as if they had been pressed together with glue. Tomi found that she was panting as she voiced her question to herself, "What have we done, Omukae-san?"

"Perhaps," he said, "we have saved each other."

In the intimate space, under the intimate circumstances, it was such a shocking reply that she blurted, "What do you mean?" even though a secret part of her knew very well that he might be right.

"It is no secret that you have been unhappy, Tomi," he said gently.

"How did you . . . ? But I have told no one!"

He ignored her outburst. "And I . . . ." He gave a little laugh. "Of Omukae the stone there is little known, neh? That is because there is precious little to tell. My life is hollow, empty, meaningless save for my work." He reached out to touch her, an electric contact, like a quick burst of lightning. "Now I feel as if the universe has caught up with me at last. The stars shine in my corner of the world. There is a moon . . . even, I think, a sun." He sighed. "Tomi . . ."

"I— No!" She broke away from him and, with a little cry, thrust open the door, gasping in the cool air-conditioned air of the corridor as she ran out.

In the ladies' room she washed up, splashed cold water on her face. She did not look in the mirror, as if she suspected that she might see his face instead of her own reflected there.

She was struck dumb by the thought of being involved with a man such as Senjin Omukae. While her attraction had been kept in the realm of fantasy she could ignore the implications of someone who lived by his own rules, who lived most uncomfortably within the rigid societal restraints of Japan.

It is no secret that you have been unhappy, Tomi. She heard again his voice echoing in the darkness, coiling around her throat like a plait of her own hair. How had he known? It *was* a secret, or so she had thought.

The reality shook her. How easily he seduced me, she thought. How well he must understand the desires of my spirit. How easily I can be led astray by him. I have sinned once, but not again. Does he understand how he has humiliated me by making me feel pleasure in such a proscribed act?

Probably not, she decided. Senjin Omukae was a loner, at his core a kind of rebel who, if brought into the full spotlight of his peers, would never be tolerated. This was why he was feared rather than admired by those in power in the Metropolitan Police Force. They chose to look the other way at Senjin the man because Senjin the homicide-division commander was so useful to them. And what if one day that changed? Tomi thought with a shudder. He would have nothing; he would be nothing.

She closed her mind to her newfound terror, rushed out of the ladies' room as hurriedly as she had entered it.

It happened that Kusunda Ikusa worked late every Thursday night. As such, that was the one night that the Pack Rat had not kept strict watch on him—there didn't seem to be any point to it.

Now he saw the enormity of his mistake. It was past nine o'clock and Ikusa was still in his office. Everyone else had gone home but lights were still burning in Nami's suite.

The Pack Rat was already inside, having entered the building during the afternoon as a civilian engineer, disappearing into the upper floors without a trace.

From his vantage point he saw Killan Oroshi coming before Kusunda Ikusa did, and he began to set up his electronic "ears." Killan, wearing a suede skirt that came barely halfway down her thighs, a cream-colored silk blouse, patent leather boots, and a floor-length python-print coat of some shiny synthetic, pushed open the door of the suite Nami used in the Nippon Keio Building two blocks off the Meiji-dori, in Nishi-Shinjuku, and went directly into Ikusa's office.

Outside, Tokyo shimmered like a jewel suspended in amber. Dusky lights glowered in the darkness like a beast's lambent eyes. Microscopic particles of petrochemical detritus hung in the air, outlining Shinjuku's massive office towers with Seurat's impressionistic brushstrokes. It was art, after a fashion, if only a postmodern one that deserved the name industrial pointillism.

Kusunda Ikusa was not working; he was waiting for Killan. He put aside papers he had not really seen for hours.

"Why do you insist on being so foolishly indiscreet?" Ikusa asked as she came through the door.

"If my father knew about us he'd have a heart attack, for sure," Killan said. A kind of beatific smile suffused her face. "That would be nice."

"Don't be ridiculous," Kusunda Ikusa said. "It would be nothing of the sort."

"You don't have to live with him," Killan retorted. "He hates me almost as much as he hates Mother."

"You're very precious to him."

Killan gave Ikusa a twisted smile that somehow made the Pack Rat's stomach contract. "You'd like to think so because that's why you fuck me."

Ikusa said, "Your sense of humor sometimes fails you, Killan."

The smile became more twisted, and now it was disturbingly knifelike. "But I wasn't joking. Of course you knew that, Kusunda. You know everything."

"What is it I see in you, Killan?"

The girl reached beneath his desk. "You know." She looked like she was manipulating something. "You know."

"Yes," Ikusa said thickly after some time. "You are so very bad for me. How is it I know that much yet I can do nothing about it?"

"Do you really want an answer," Killan Oroshi asked, "or is this another of your rhetorical questions?" When he made no response, she went on, "You love fucking me because you're fucking my father at the

same time. That's it, isn't it?" She shook her head, her expression perfectly sincere. "No, I'm wrong, or at least that's not all of it." Her features softened like wax, her lower lip jutted out; her tiny tongue appeared
as if she were about to suck up a savory sweet. "The fact is, I'm the only
one who can seduce you, Kusunda. You spend all your time lording it
over others, and that's a strain. Oh, I know it's a strain you'd never admit
to. But that's one of the beauties of our relationship. You don't have to
admit anything to me. You don't need a priest and I have no aspirations
to play the role."

The Pack Rat could see the fullness of knowledge throbbing behind
her eyes, and he wondered whether Kusunda Ikusa yet knew what he
had gotten himself into.

"You can seduce me because I allow you to."

Killan laughed. "That's not seduction," she said. "You're talking
about a business deal." She shrugged. "Forget it. I don't care about your
weaknesses, Kusunda, either real or imagined. You're like a dream to me,
or a vision I conjure up in a marijuana haze. I don't care about you at all.
I do what I do because of my father. I fuck you because it would literally
kill him if he found out that I spread my legs for you. I scheme with you
because the schemes appeal to my sense of disorder, because I am the
outlaw my father is not and never could be. The Americans say I have
balls, Kusunda. My Japanese revolutionary friends say that I have an
overwhelming desire for change. What do *you* call it?"

It seemed as if Ikusa was faintly amused by Killan's monologue. Certainly he was not bored by it, and now the Pack Rat was sure that he was
underestimating her. Kusunda Ikusa's black eyes gleamed with a kind of
inner insight as she recounted the litany of her philosophy, as if her
words had the power to illuminate a hidden part of himself.

Listening to Killan Oroshi, the Pack Rat was reminded of a line from
the English poet, Algernon Swinburne, "Change lays her hand not upon
the truth." But he thought that these two would-be revolutionaries,
oddly entwined, could hardly understand what Swinburne had in mind.

"I would call it *tatemae*," Kusunda Ikusa said. "The facade that
talentos use so artfully on television or on the stage. Ten thousand people
become caught up in *tatemae* at once. We Japanese are, after all, fetish-
ists, worshiping the facade, some symbol to which we may attach and
defuse our fears, to which we may humbly dedicate our lives."

"Like the Emperor." Now Killan's eyes were alight. She had a talent,
the Pack Rat observed, for turning even the most clever response back
upon itself so that it served her own purpose. But she also spoke as no
other eighteen-year-old that the Pack Rat had known. But then, he re-

minded himself, she fancied herself a revolutionary, and a successful revolutionary's sense of oration and theatrics was highly developed. "No one knows more about the Emperor than you do, Kusunda. When I am near you I feel so close to him."

"Stop it!" Ikusa snapped. "You are making a mockery of the sacred."

Clearly Killan had reached a nerve, and such was her personality that she pursued her advantage to the limit. "Who says that the Emperor is sacred? You? The other members of Nami?"

"The Emperor is descended from the son of heaven."

Now that she had successfully drawn him into untenable philosophical waters, it was clear to the Pack Rat, if not to Ikusa, that Killan was determined to undermine his position. "Now who's using *tatemae*? You are better than any talento at *tatemae*. The myth of the god-king is ancient, universally revered. It is also, as you well know, an empty talisman that you have seen fit to use to compromise the spirit of the people."

Kusunda smiled. "Now you sound merely foolish. If this were true, what would you be doing with me?"

"You know, Kusunda. I am as apolitical as you are political. That is the only aspect of balance we have in our relationship."

"I would have thought apolitical was the wrong term for you," Ikusa said. "You are a nihilist. A black-draped sibyl, a *futurisuto*."

"Oh, if only you'd call me that while we're fucking!" Killan said.

The Pack Rat could see that Ikusa's tack with her expletives was to ignore them. He pulled her against him. She seemed lost against his massive bulk. The Pack Rat averted his gaze but did not stop the recorder as they made love.

"*Futurisuto* instead of angel," Kusunda Ikusa said afterward. "I will never call you angel again."

Killan Oroshi laughed as she dressed. "That will suit me just fine," she said. She put on her coat. Ikusa did not move or make a sound.

When Killan left, the Pack Rat decided to follow her. She took him crosstown, into the Asakusa district. Into an anonymous postwar building made of ferroconcrete, made up of *usagigoya*, tiny rabbit-hutch apartments.

The Pack Rat watched as a thin young man with hair the color of platinum opened the door to her repeated knocking.

"Killan!" he cried, clearly delighted.

"Hello, Scoundrel," Killan said, closing the door behind them, shutting the Pack Rat out.

When Tomi went to interview Dr. Hanami's widow, she asked Nangi to come along, and was pleased when he accepted her invitation. Tomi found his comments and opinions insightful rather than intrusive. More and more she was coming to see that he was a natural detective: his intense curiosity combined with his sense of detail and the analytical bent of his mind. And he had become her only ally in the murder of the dancer, Mariko. He seemed as fascinated by the case as Tomi herself was. Besides all that, Tomi liked him.

Haniko Hanami was a tall, slender woman of imperious mien. She came, so she told them with no humility, from one of the oldest Samurai families in the north of Honshu. She wore a magnificent silk kimono which, by its workmanship, appeared to be at least fifty years old. A scattering of flowers crisscrossed its deep blue background. Golden threads winked and shone as she moved.

She had entered into marriage with Dr. Hanami and, according to her, had an ideal marriage until his untimely death. This was all she would say, no matter what questions Tomi tried. Clearly, she did not like anyone prying into what she considered her private life, and she resented the intrusion even from such a commonly acknowledged authority as the police. Almost everyone in Japan cooperated with the police. Why wouldn't she?

"If you don't mind, Mrs. Hanami," Nangi said when the silence had taken on the aspect of a stalemate, "might I have a chair? Often my legs do not allow me to sit in the traditional fashion."

"Of course. This way, please." Haniko Hanami led them into a room furnished in the Western manner. She studied Tomi as Nangi sat down, careful not to cause him any embarrassment should his legs inadvertently give out.

When he was comfortably seated, she said, "Is the pain bad?"

"Bad enough, sometimes."

She nodded, kneaded her hands. "I suffer from arthritis," she said mournfully. "Now it is not so bad, save in the morning when I wake up. But in winter . . ." She clucked her tongue against the roof of her mouth.

"Winter is the worst," Nangi agreed.

Tomi watched the growing rapport between them with something akin to awe. The angry, sullen Haniko Hanami who had met them at the door had disappeared. In her place stood this suffering old woman.

"Is your pain bad now?" Mrs. Hanami inquired.

"I have perhaps overwalked today," Nangi admitted.

"Then I have just the thing to help you." She rushed out of the room, returning within moments with a jar, which she held out almost shyly to him. "This is what I use on my hands. It works very well. My husband made it."

Nangi took the jar and, much to Tomi's astonishment, rolled up his trouser legs and began to apply the ointment. "This way?" he said.

"No," Mrs. Hanami said, "this way." And kneeling beside him, she dipped her fingertips into the ointment, began to massage it into his calfs precisely as if she were his mother. "There," she murmured. "There, there."

When she was finished, Nangi thanked her, helping her to her feet. She was blushing.

"I am old and childless," she said wistfully. "This is all I am good for now." She brightened somewhat. "Still, it is good to be useful in any way one can, *neh*?"

"Indeed," Nangi said. "Since my retirement some years ago, I, too, seek to be of help to others. Which is why I am here today." He leaned on his cane. "Mrs. Hanami, it is important that we ask you some questions. Whoever killed your husband has killed before. Without doubt he will kill again. Do you see how vital it is that we find this person?"

This was more or less what Tomi had said to Mrs. Hanami at the beginning of the interview. But that had been before Nangi had adroitly found the key to her spirit. Tomi continued to marvel at the man.

"I understand," Mrs. Hanami said as she rose. "Shall we go outside? There is so little sunshine these days, only industrial haze, one must take every advantage of it." She led them out onto a stone porch that overlooked a jewel of a garden. She led then down a path of flat blue-gray river rocks artfully laid to seem naturally scattered.

"My husband, as you no doubt already know, was a perfectly brilliant surgeon. His hands were like those of a master sculptor, and he obsessed over them. He used more hand cream than I did."

She confessed this as they sat in a tea room across the lush but tiny garden from the main house. It was redolent of dried grass, spice, and wood smoke.

"He never used soap on his hands at home. Indeed, I often thought he had a phobia against it. Of course, that could not be so, since he obviously used soap when he scrubbed up for an operation. Still, he was nervous if he caught even a hint of chapped skin on the backs of his hands. He had the hands of a teenager, of a girl, really."

Initially Tomi was surprised, not to say shocked, by these revelations unseemly told of the dead, and she found herself feeling a growing antipathy toward the woman. But she soon came to realize that Haniko

Hanami needed to unburden herself of secrets she had too long carried unaided in her breast, and Tomi's heart softened in acknowledgment of her plight.

Whatever faults Haniko Hanami might have, making tea wasn't one of them. Tomi watched, entranced, as the older woman deftly turned the ash whisk to create a froth the palest shade of green imaginable.

"Well, he was a wonderful surgeon," Mrs. Hanami said, "but as a husband he was something less than that." She paused for a moment to take more tea, and seeing her thin face above her lifted hands, the tiny cup, Tomi was given a startling glimpse of the coquette she once must have been. "I had wanted so much from this marriage," she said. "I had such high hopes. Well, perhaps that was a mistake. But I didn't know my husband very well at the time we were married. Apparently I never did."

"Why do you say that, Mrs. Hanami?" Nangi asked.

Haniko Hanami sighed. "My husband grew tired of me over the years. When he was younger, he liked an assortment of women. Later on, there was only one." She looked at them in turn. "Lack of stamina, or perhaps a sense of—what shall I call it?—stability." She sipped tea. "You may think that an odd word for an adulterous liaison, but in my husband's case it was accurate, I assure you."

"Do you know what it was your husband wanted?" Nangi asked gently.

"Wanted?" Mrs. Hanami blinked. "Why, yes. I'd have thought it obvious enough. He did not want to die. Or, I suppose more accurately, to get old. The parade of women assured him of new faces—and bodies—that, for him, never aged. His women were like a mirror into which he could look, seeing with absolute assurance the man he had once been."

"But somewhere that changed," Nangi said.

"What?" She appeared startled, as if he had interrupted a private meditation.

"He went from many to one, you said."

"Oh, that." She nodded. "I believe this one was very young, her flesh very firm. Lately my husband had begun to long for more. Perhaps he had come to see the parade for the charade it really was. Perhaps he needed to hold youth in his hand in what would have been for him a permanent way."

Nangi said, "Was there ever any talk of divorce?"

Mrs. Hanami gave a startled little laugh. "Oh, my goodness no. It is clear you never knew my husband. There was never a hint of that, and there never would be. My husband had no idea that I knew of his liaisons. He would have been mortified had I been cruel enough to tell him that I knew."

"Why *didn't* you tell him?" Tomi asked in the same gentle tone of voice Nangi was using.

Mrs. Hanami's eyes opened wide. "But why would I? We loved each other."

Into the silence that had wrapped itself around them, Nangi said, "About this last girl your husband was seeing. How do you know she was very young and very firm-fleshed?"

"Well, she was a dancer, wasn't she?" Mrs. Hanami said.

"You *knew* who your husband was seeing?" Tomi said.

"Not who, dear," Mrs. Hanami said. "What." She was perfectly composed now, the mask she had presented to them on their arrival firmly back in place. It was forged of pride, Tomi saw, a family pride of Samurai forebears, a procession of centuries. Nowadays, Tomi thought, that ironbound tradition must be difficult to shoulder.

Haniko Hanami rose and, with the grace and bearing befitting her station in life, crossed to a dark wood tatami chest. She opened a top drawer, took out something, came back to where they were sitting. She held out her hand, opened it up like a chrysanthemum budding.

"I found this in one of my husband's suits when he came home very late one night," she said. "I went through it while he slept. I felt I deserved that much."

Tomi and Nangi looked at what she displayed. It was a tiny plastic flashlight. Along its side was emblazoned the name of the *tokudashi* club that Tomi had come to know so well, The Silk Road.

Kansatsu said, "I have been sought, I have been defeated, I am now forgotten." He was sitting cross-legged on the floor of the great room of the stone structure he had created in the shadow of the Black Gendarme. "You asked, Nicholas, why I am here in the Hodaka, and this is my answer. Now tell me why you are here."

"Tell me first if I am dead," Nicholas said. "I have no idea if this is some afterlife."

Kansatsu cocked his head. "Do you believe in an afterlife, Nicholas?"

"Yes. I suppose I do."

"Then this is an afterlife." Kansatsu waited a moment. "This is what you make of it, Nicholas. After a time, you will give it your own definition."

"But am I dead? Did I freeze to death on the Black Gendarme?"

"That question has no relevance here," Kansatsu said sternly. "As I said, it is you who must make the determination. Is this life or death?" The ageless *sensei* shrugged. "I no longer seek to differentiate between the two states."

"But surely you can tell me if I still live? Is this a dream?"

"When you understand how useless these questions are, Nicholas, you will have the answers you seek."

Nicholas quieted his racing heart. He no longer felt chilled or numb, but his body still ached and, touching the side of his head, the scar of the incision was as evident as ever. I must be alive, he reasoned. But reason seemed a stranger in this land.

"You did not seem surprised to see me," Nicholas said.

"Why should I be?" Kansatsu said. "You have come here to me many times."

"What? I haven't seen you since the winter of 1963, and I'm certain that I've never been here in this house before."

Kansatsu looked pointedly at the plate in front of Nicholas. "You haven't finished your meal," he said. "I suggest you do so. You will need all your strength soon."

"I know," Nicholas said. "If I remember correctly, the descent of the Hodaka is every bit as exhausting as the ascent."

"I was not speaking of the physical," Kansatsu said.

Nicholas looked from his enigmatic face to the bits of food on his plate. He ate. He slept. And dreamed again of the dominance of the Black Gendarme . . .

. . . This recurring image so disturbed him that when he awoke he described it to Kansatsu.

The *sensei* was silent for some time. At last he stirred himself. But his voice was slow, surreal, as if he had been roused from a dream. "Why does this image disturb you so?"

"I don't quite know," Nicholas admitted. "Perhaps it has to do with the emeralds, my grandfather's legacy."

"Is that so?" Kansatsu's eyebrows lifted. "Explain."

Nicholas did, telling him about the box with the fifteen emeralds, about how his mother, Cheong, explained to him that he could use the gems in whatever way he saw fit, with only one caveat: he must never allow the number of stones to drop below nine.

"Did your mother tell you what would happen if this occurred?"

"No," Nicholas said. "Do you know what these emeralds are?"

"Perhaps I have heard something of their existence," Kansatsu said. "But I had no idea that you possessed them."

"They are very powerful."

"Yes. Extremely."

"But in what way?" Nicholas asked.

"In the Way of Tau-tau," Kansatsu said.

"But what have I to do with Tau-tau?" Nicholas asked.

Instead of answering him, Kansatsu said, "The *dorokusai* will want the emeralds. Where are they?"

"Safe enough," Nicholas said.

"Are they with you?"

"No. I didn't think that being *Shiro Ninja* I could adequately safeguard them."

Kansatsu nodded, was quiet for some time after that. At length he said, "You have been here some time now. I expect you are strong enough for us to begin." He was dressed in a black cotton *gi*, the costume of the martial arts *dojo*. "When I sent you to Kumamoto those many years ago," Kansatsu said, "you believed that it was to confront your cousin Saigo. I imagine you have believed that self-deception until this moment. Well, you were young then. And just because you are supremely talented does not mean that you are capable of fully *comprehending* that talent.

"Of course, I know this because I have had this conversation with you many times."

"Why do you keep referring to how often this has happened before?" Nicholas asked. "It's happening now, for the first time."

"Time," Kansatsu observed, "is somewhat akin to the ocean. There are tides, currents, eddies which at certain nexus points overlap, creating a kind of whirlpool of events that repeat like ripples until, having spread sufficiently outward, are spent upon a rocky shore."

"You have a strange concept of time."

"On the contrary," Kansatsu said, "it is *you* whose concept of time is strange. But then, that is to be expected of someone who still sees a difference between life and death. Coming to grips with this illusion is the same as recognizing the Ten Oxen, the stages of Zen enlightenment. Do you remember, Nicholas?"

"Of course. One begins by searching high and low for the ox, one finds it, ensnares it, tames it, rides it back into town only to find that the ox never existed, that it was a part of oneself, a part cut off, lost, confused."

"Does that remind you of something?" Kansatsu asked.

"Nothing that I can think of," Nicholas replied.

Kansatsu turned, took an iron pot off the hibachi stove sunk into the floor. He poured them both tea. It was the bitter, dark red tea of northern

China known as Iron Dragon. "Listen to me, Nicholas," he said. "I sent you to Kumamoto in the winter of 1963 to find the ox."

"But I confronted Saigo and he defeated me."

Kansatsu nodded. "And in so doing he defeated me as well. That was meant to be. One month later I left Tokyo for good and came here to fulfill the last of my three stages: to be forgotten."

"I never forgot you, *sensei*."

"No. You were never meant to. And that is why you have come."

"As I have said, *sensei*, I am *Shiro Ninja*," Nicholas said. "I came to the Black Gendarme seeking a path to salvation. I thought Akiko's *sensei*, Kyoki, would help me because I suspected that he was tanjian, but I discovered him dead, flayed alive in his castle in the Asama highlands. Then I discovered that he had a brother. His name is Genshi."

"I know," Kansatsu said. "I am Genshi, Kyoki's brother. I am also Kansatsu. I have many names."

"You . . ." Nicholas almost choked on his words. "You are tanjian?"

"Before I answer you, you must understand that your spirit is entangled. You are driven by fear. An exhaustion of the soul has made it impossible for you to distinguish between good and evil."

"Yes," Nicholas said. "I understand. *Shiro Ninja* has ensnared me."

"*Shiro Ninja*," Kansatsu said, "was only able to work on you because you have hidden your true nature from yourself. You are still searching for the ox, Nicholas, unaware that the search is counterproductive because the ox does not exist."

"What are you saying?"

"Remember the winter of 1963, Nicholas," Kansatsu said. "In Kumamoto when you believe your cousin Saigo defeated you, took Yukio, the girl you loved, away from you."

"I believed it happened only because it happened," Nicholas said.

"Again, you are thinking of the ox when the ox doesn't exist," Kansatsu said patiently.

Nicholas looked at him. "I don't understand."

"No," Kansatsu said. "You are not yet strong enough. Sleep now."

. . . "I am lost, *sensei*," Nicholas said when he awoke.

"Outside," Kansatsu said, "you will gain strength."

"I am glad you are here to guide me," Nicholas said, pulling on his waterproof hiking boots, bundling himself in his Gore-Tex parka.

"Your spirit is still entangled," Kansatsu said, leading the way out onto the Black Gendarme. "No one can guide you."

"It is night." Nicholas was surprised.

"This time, you slept all night and all day. Did you dream of the Black Gendarme?"

"No." But Nicholas had the sense that Kansatsu already knew that. "I dreamt of bulrushes. I was searching for something. I can't remember what it was. Then I found footprints in the black marshy earth. When I knelt down to examine them more closely, they spoke to me. The voice was like the trilling of a nightbird, almost a song. And then the bulrushes and the marsh were gone. I was back in Kyoki's castle, passing through the moon gate in his study."

"What did the voice say?"

"I can't remember," Nicholas said.

"Was the voice my brother's voice?"

"Not his," Nicholas said, "but the source was close." He was moving with some difficulty and great effort across the blistered rock wall. "Perhaps," he added hopefully, "I have succeeded in banishing the image of the Black Gendarme from my dreams."

"Would that be a good thing?"

"Of course it would!"

"Have you so quickly forgotten that your spirit is entangled, that you cannot distinguish good from evil?"

It was then that Nicholas noticed that Kansatsu was wearing nothing more than his light cotton *gi*. "Aren't you cold, *sensei*?"

"Is it cold out?" Kansatsu said unconcernedly. He gestured to indicate that Nicholas should take the lead. "I hadn't noticed."

The icy wind whipped through the canyons, ravines, the sheer, glassy walls of the Black Gendarme. Drifts of dry snow crunched beneath their feet as they followed a narrow winding path up the nearly sheer rock face. Now there was nothing at all but the rock face, vertical, glasslike, supremely forbidding. Nicholas began to climb, digging his fingertips into barely seen fissures, hauling himself up. He grunted with the effort, his breath coming in animal pants.

"When I dream of the Black Gendarme rising like a specter from the center of my spirit," Nicholas said, resting for a moment as he clung precariously to the rock face, "I awake full of anxiety and fear."

Kansatsu did not answer, and Nicholas turned his head to find that he was alone on the Black Gendarme.

Shisei lived in a brownstone just off Foxhall Road in Georgetown. It belonged to one of the main benefactors of her environmental lobby, but she was rarely in it, preferring St. Moritz in the winters and Cap Ferrat in the summers. She had sumptuous villas in both, caring more for Europe than her native Washington.

Shisei lived in the house alone. Every Wednesday a couple came in to clean and, if she wished, cook food for the week, as they had for the past eighteen years.

The downstairs was all carved paneled walls, painted *boiserie*, ornate marble mantels upon which rested eighteenth century French bronzes, ormolu-mounted Chinese porcelain, among other priceless knickknacks. But upstairs, the bedroom Shisei had chosen was relatively simple. It overlooked a small but exquisite garden overseen by a Japanese gardener who loved his charges as he did his children. Sunlight filtered through the tall honey locusts rimming in gold the peonies and azaleas.

Coming out from the bathroom barefoot, Shisei went to her closet, rummaged behind the boxes of shoes she had piled up, pulled out her equipment. She set her portable computer on the small French desk, plugged it in, set up the telephone modem. She sat down, inserted a specially modified RCA jack into the back of the computer, wrapped the featherweight headset around her head.

She began the access procedure not by using the keyboard but by speaking into the microphone of the headset. The powerful computer hummed along to her complex instructions. As it did, the screen went dark, then began to brighten as streams of characters began to fill it. At last she downloaded the MANTIS program from hard disk memory. There it sat in the center of her screen, pulsing like a dark, dangerous jewel.

Shisei took a deep breath, spoke into the mike. The computer accessed the phone line and she gave it a number. A female voice answered on the second ring.

"Johnson Institute. How may I help you?"

Shisei hit the ENTER key on her computer. The Institute operator heard only a dial tone; but Shisei was inside, connected to the Institute's phone lines via her computer, its modem, and the program activated in the small cylinder she had secreted beneath the desk where the Hive brain sat. The cylinder was her link, via the phone lines, to the Hive computer.

Shisei wiped a drop of sweat from her forehead. Her shoulders were hunched, her eyes staring at the screen as she checked and rechecked. It was time.

She spoke a code into her mike, then hit the ENTER key again. The version of the MANTIS virus program she had been given was released, transmitted instantaneously through her linkup to the Hive brain.

She could see on her screen the two interfaces—the honeycomb gridwork of the Hive brain and the spirals of the MANTIS virus—beginning to merge. She saw the spirals breaking down the gridwork, sector by sector, as the virus began to mutate, feeding on the Hive security program, and she began to exult, thinking, It's working. It's going to work.

Then something happened. The honeycomb gridwork began to phase in and out of focus. At first Shisei thought that there was a malfunction in the linkup—a phone man working on the lines in the area would do it —but her computer told her otherwise. Everything was secure. She stared at the screen. Now the gridwork seemed to have quadrupled, sextupled, on and on, until it filled up the screen, and the virus, overwhelmed, self-destructed as per its built-in instructions. In an instant there was no sign it had ever existed. A heartbeat later the Hive gridwork was back to normal. Shisei dissolved the link. What had happened?

Then she remembered what Dr. Rudolph had said about the construction of the Hive brain. Not only was its design radically different, but its components, its transistors, were unique, perhaps a thousand times faster than the standard silicon chips. That's how the Hive overcame the virus. Its security program ran at such hyperspeed, it overwhelmed even a virus that could feed off it.

Shisei sat back for a moment, digesting the entire event, reviewing every instant in her mind. Then she shut down the computer and picked up the phone. She had some calls to make.

Nangi waited until the last minute, risking being late, waiting for the Pack Rat to call or to walk through the door to his office. When neither happened, Nangi put on his hat and walked out the door. His lawyer was waiting for him. When they got to the street, the lawyer opened an umbrella.

It's always raining lately, Nangi thought. He was unconcerned by the Pack Rat's failure to get back to him. It would have been nice to go into the meeting with some ammunition, but it was hardly a requisite. Nangi lifted his head up to the rain and laughed silently.

His car took them the half mile to the Nippon Keio Building. Before he got out he called Tomi, set up a time that evening for them to meet at The Silk Road, when everyone they would need to interview would be there. He sat still for several moments, hoping that the Pack Rat would catch up with him. Perhaps he prayed. He spoke with his lawyer about several last-minute matters, then they emerged from the car, went up to Nami's offices.

Kusunda Ikusa had suggested his offices as a neutral site for the merger signing. They were all waiting for him in the big conference room: Ken Oroshi, Ikusa, the lawyers.

The deal was, on the surface, simple, but in fact it was extremely complex. It had to accommodate clauses that Ikusa insisted on; it had to include the clauses Nangi needed to complete his subsidized takeover of Nakano Industries and their priceless R&D department.

Everything was in order. Nangi, Ikusa, and Ken Oroshi chatted informally like the best of friends while the lawyers pored over their arcane wordings, nit-picking each other to death.

Tea was served on an enormous silver tray, out of English silver cups. Ikusa led the conversation, discussing green fees at his golf club. This is all nonsense, Nangi thought, but it is worthwhile nonsense. Like being in the dentist's chair, the pain is a necessary evil.

In fact, his mind was not fully focused on the signing. He was thinking of Tomi and of Mariko, the dancer who had been raped and flayed at the *tokudashi* club, The Silk Road. What was the connection between Mariko's and Dr. Hanami's deaths? Was he Mariko's last lover, the man for whom the message "This Could Be Your Wife" was meant? If so, if the *dorokusai* had also murdered Mariko, then it was clear that he had coerced Dr. Hanami into doing what to Nicholas? What had happened to Nicholas that Nangi did not know about? He burned to find out the answer; he worried about Nicholas as if the younger man were his son.

At length the lawyers called to their respective clients, who looked over the contracts one last time.

Then the two principals, Nangi and Ken Oroshi, signed the merger papers. Kusunda Ikusa, looking smug, bowed to both of them, presented them with small gifts. The Sphynx computer-chip-manufacturing *kobun* and Nakano Industries were now one.

The Kan, the businessman's hotel on the seedy outskirts of Tokyo with which Senjin was so familiar, had a health service that hotels in the better districts did not provide. It was not a spa, not a masseuse, not a gym. It was a sensory-deprivation tank.

The tank was one third the size of the Kan's coffinlike rooms. It was filled with water at blood-heat temperature. Slipping naked into its depths, Senjin felt nothing. Nothing at all.

A net suspended him at a level so that only his nose and lips were above the water. When the lid came down, he heard nothing, saw nothing, felt nothing. Neither was there anything for him to smell or to taste.

His mind was cut off, set adrift—inasmuch as modern-day man can be—from his body.

Without a shell to bind him, Senjin floated in the Void. His childhood *sensei* would have been appalled at his practice of sensory deprivation, which no doubt they would have viewed as an artificial stimulus, a path but not the Path, and therefore strictly forbidden.

But for Senjin nothing was forbidden. He had passed beyond such delusory boundaries the moment he had outgrown the pedantic philosophies of his teachers, the moment he had begun to formulate his own philosophy, his own Way. He had been pursuing this singular Path for years now, and in so doing, his power had been growing.

Once he had the nine mystic emeralds in his possession, he would become unstoppable. Even those tanjian masters from whom he had learned the last esoteric nuances of Tau-tau would not be able to defy him.

They had believed that their lessons would irrevocably bind him to them. This had been the way of Tau-tau for centuries, part of the reason for its continued survival, a clever mechanism embedded in the very heart of the basic twenty-four principles.

Others, before Senjin, had defied the code of Tau-tau. All had suffered greatly for their transgression—Senjin knew this because their sorrows had been told to him and to his sister when they were young. It had become part of their training, a subtle warning, as if even then their tanjian *sensei* might have suspected that they would seek to follow in those foolish footsteps.

And Senjin had. Not without terrible suffering, of course, bitter years of struggle, but this had been expected. Yet he knew that with the emeralds in his possession, the suffering would cease. He would be the first to have broken with the traditions of Tau-tau and been truly free.

For it would be he, now, who would rule the tanjian elders, dictating his own law to them as they had once inflicted their antiquated canon on him.

Freed of this weight, floating in nothingness, Senjin could now think about his mother—his true mother—whom he had never known, and whom he hated. Into his mind swam the directive of a poster put up in the subway station near his Metropolitan Police office. MARRIAGE IS DUTY, screamed the headline. THE ULTIMATE ACT OF FILIAL PIETY. To disobey this imperative, the poster implied, was to dishonor one's parents, who still, in one family out of two, chose the mates for their children.

Senjin had never married. He had always felt it was a slap in the face of his mother—the mother he never knew. That it had broken the heart of Haha-san, his aunt who had raised him, was of no interest to him. Haha-san was of no moment; his mother was.

Floating in the nothingness that was water at blood-heat, Senjin remembered the photograph of his mother Haha-san had once given him as a keepsake; "a method," she had said, "of keeping your mother alive."

Senjin had stared at the black-and-white image for some time, trying to find even a minute speck of himself in that plain, expressionless face. Finding none, he had taken a knife and had carefully cut the image into ribbons. Where his mother's lips pressed together in a tight, unrelenting line, he had left intact a central core the size of a dime. He had placed the photo in the bottom of his dresser drawer beneath a meticulous stack of snowy white undershorts, which he wore once and then threw away.

Senjin had never loved anyone—certainly not his mother. Love had about it a certain morality that even marriage did not, a morality that he despised.

But he did not need love; he had had something else far more precious.

Once, Senjin had regularly merged with his sister. (Oh, how painful it was to think of her!) They inhabited each other's spirit, closer than two human beings had ever been. Now she was gone, and there was an emptiness in Senjin's spirit he was driven to fill. To try and try again—and to fail. But try he must, for it was an emptiness so terrible that its dark heart had inured him to loneliness even while it was turning his heart to stone.

And why not? Everything else in what humans laughingly called society was monstrous: grotesque, pointless, suffocating.

He recalled Haha-san taking him to a movie in which he saw a white-faced, expressionless young woman being prepared for the marriage ceremony in very much the same way as the Christian knights of medieval England had been dressed by their squires for battle.

Trussed tightly into restricting layers of cloth before the heavy, armorlike wedding kimono was wrapped around her, the young woman stoically endured the ceremony and its aftermath with a bravery Senjin found as admirable as it was foolish. Why didn't she kill her lout of a husband, he wondered, at the moment of painful penetration? Why had she allowed herself to be violated by desire and custom?

Senjin, too, had been trussed tightly into restricting layers—the strata of Japanese society. He despised those restrictions because they represented both the definition of his world and the limitation of his power. All that Senjin had needed to create his Path was a starting point. His *sensei* had obliged him, unwittingly giving him this and more, a foundation from which to work. His extraordinary mind had accomplished the rest, grasping what they had not, plumbing the unknown depths, forging a new spirit, reshaping himself into an image cast in his mind at the moment of his birth, his consciousness bursting into the world like the blazing trail of a comet.

The Tau-tau training of his childhood and adolescence had not been enough for Senjin. In teaching him what they knew, his *sensei* had inadvertently exposed to his restless mind the limitations of their magic. In being made aware of the limitations, he had automatically taken a leap of faith, going beyond the boundaries of Tau-tau. And he had found another world.

It was based upon the ancient principles into which Tau-tau tapped, but it used them in a wholly new way, a way of which only Senjin could possibly conceive.

Senjin had come to his tanjian *sensei* through Haha-san, who, thinking that she understood the nature of his melancholy, had done her best to discover some way in which to motivate her "son." She had, in fact, correctly recognized the scope and depth of his intellect, and was certain that only Tau-tau would be a strong enough discipline to challenge him, sustain him, and, ultimately, contain him.

Being tanjian was a matter of bloodlines. One could not learn Tau-tau without being of the blood, and tanjian blood was passed down through the mother.

This was another reason why Senjin hated his mother. She had had the effrontery to bequeath him a legacy even though she had abandoned him. It had taken all of Senjin's skill not to master Tau-tau (which had come easily to him), but to mold it into something he could find useful.

Senjin had grown up with dogs, or so it seemed to him, and that, too, he laid at his mother's feet. If only she had lived, if only she had not abandoned him, casting aside her sacred duty to keep him safe from harm.

But she had been weak; she had allowed her life to come to an end, cowardly wriggling out of her responsibilities to him. From the day he became aware of her sin against him, of how wickedly she had robbed him, Senjin had like a tireless stoker fed his hatred with the singular obsession of someone fearful that without constant attention it would in time fade like memories.

Haha-san had been a tanjian *miko*, an adept at a certain kind of magic. But she had been bound up in obedience. Often Senjin wished only one thing in life: to cut her free of her moorings, to beat out of her the obedience that defined her life. To make of her something she was not and never could imagine being.

The first time this happened was when he came upon her fresh and dewy after her bath. She had turned her back to him, demurely slipping a cotton kimono around her shoulders. But not before he had had a glimpse of her naked torso.

Senjin was twelve when this occurred. He had not seen her naked since he was six, when he still took baths with her, and sometimes, when he was frightened or was awakened by a nightmare and was allowed into her bed, where he fell back to sleep with his arms around her.

He was aroused not only by Haha-san's naked torso, but by how she had deftly turned her back on him in a gesture that was as coy as a coquette's. He burned then to press himself against the suffocating pillows of her white breasts, to expel his breath into her, to slide into her warmth, to be intoxicated by her intimate scent.

But this was all fantasy on Senjin's part. It could never occur because of Haha-san's chasteness, which came not from any philosophical, religious, or sociological strictures, but simply because she was following the dictates set down for her by her mother. As far as Haha-san was concerned, these laws were carved in stone, so inviolate that Senjin could never even know whether in her heart she wished to join with him in sexual congress.

When, years later, he entered his first woman, he found that only through thinking of Haha-san could he find release. Yet thinking of his surrogate mother enraged him. Inevitably this led his mind back to his real mother, and his rage would become uncontrollable, overtaking him like an eighteen-wheel truck bearing down upon a tiny car, swallowing him whole.

Death and the imminence of death was all that could satisfy him then.

The slight ammoniac smell caused him to reach up, crack the lid on the sensory deprivation tank. He could feel before he saw it the slick, viscous strings of his semen crisscrossing the water that lapped at his belly. Sliding his fingertips along the velvet length of his still quivering erection, Senjin sighed in contentment.

Naked, Shisei lay upon her stomach. Sunlight, slanting in through the bedroom window in Branding's Georgetown town house, struck the giant spider's carapace, firing the colored ink embedded beneath her skin. It was the last day of the month, almost high summer.

She stirred, luxuriating in the feel of the bedcovers, and the insect stirred to life, articulating its hairy legs with the rippling of her muscles.

The rhythmic expansion and contraction of the cephalothorax, the eight ruby-colored eyes alight as if with intelligence, completed the illusion.

Cotton Branding watched with a combination of fascination and horror. He reached out as if in a dream, his hand upon the spider, feeling only Shisei's warm skin. The feeling was eerie, like the fly in the depth-perception test optometrists gave kids, which appeared three-dimensional until you tried to grasp its wing.

"You promised to tell me," Branding said, "how you got the spider."

Shisei turned over and the creature was gone, like that, a door banging shut. Her clear skin, her firm flesh, was burnished in the early morning sunlight.

"Why can't you see me tonight?"

"I have to work," Branding said. "As long as you've brought me back to Washington, I've got to attend this State dinner for the West German chancellor. Don't be upset."

"But I've already made plans. Dinner at The Red Sea, then home for some dancing. I went to the record store yesterday and spent a fortune on music for us."

Branding smiled. "It sounds wonderful, but tonight it's just not possible."

"How long will you have to stay? I'll wait up for you. We'll dance when you get home."

He saw the need on her face, and marveled at its childlike quality. "All right," he said. "I'll do my best to be home by midnight. But if I'm not, go to bed."

She reached up, locked her hands behind his neck, drew him down to her. Her body writhed up against his in an almost uncontrollable spasm, or so it seemed to Branding as his mouth was filled with the taste of her.

But he could not imagine making love to her again without knowing the origin of the spider tattoo. "Tell me," he whispered in her ear. "Tell me the story."

Shisei broke away from him long enough to search his eyes with her own. "You really want to know, don't you?"

"Yes."

"Even if it means being shocked. Even if it means that afterward you might come to hate me."

"Shisei," he said, moving against her, "do you believe that I could hate you?"

"Hate and love, Cook, are often so close that one cannot tell them apart."

"Trust me," Branding said. "I know the difference between the two."

Shisei closed her eyes. For a moment he could feel her breathing, his own body rising and falling upon her own. Somewhere in the house a phone was ringing. He ignored it, letting the answering machine do his work.

"Tell me," he urged her. "I want to know." He understood that in a basic sense that was a lie, or, at least, not the whole truth. He *needed* to know how she came by this strange and eerie device, as others need to know by word or deed that they are loved.

Branding wanted to understand this enigmatic creature who had so captivated him, not only because he would then be closer to her, but also because he clearly recognized the enigma as her ultimate protection. And he knew that he would never pierce to the core of her until she revealed to him the secret of the spider.

Shisei took a deep, shuddering breath. "Like everyone else," she said at last, "I was born of the union of a man and a woman. But unlike most people, I never knew my parents. The family who raised me cared nothing for me. Had they shown me any emotion, even cruelty, I would have been grateful. As it was, I grew up feeling nothing. I did not understand emotions save the most basic one: fear. I ran away from the family and, as far as I know, they did not try to find me. When I was hungry I sought out food; when my bladder was full, I urinated in the shadows; when I was tired, I sought out shelter. I was an animal, nothing more. I was, in essence, a blank canvas."

Shisei moved, and each time she did, Branding was suffused with her scent, a spicy musk that made him dizzy.

"Karma is unfathomable, but sometimes it is also strange," Shisei whispered. "A man found me. He was an artist, but he did not put paint on canvas. He did not chisel figures out of stone or with a blowtorch bend metal into sculpture. He was a tattoo artist."

"He drew the spider," Branding said.

Shisei gave him a sad smile, brushed a lock of hair back from his face. "Life is so simple for you, Cook. Things happen and there is a reaction, a direct consequence, like a theorem in physics."

"You met an artist and he saw in your body the perfect canvas for his art. You *are* perfect, Shisei. You don't need me to tell you that."

She stirred restively, as if she could not bear the weight of his words. "The spider was the greatest tattoo he had ever produced, the pinnacle of his art," she said. "In that you are right."

"And the rest?"

"The rest is unknown to you." Shisei's body was slick with sweat. "And now, as you wished, you will hear it."

Branding had sudden misgivings, as if he had come too near the fire and was suddenly in danger of being burned.

Then it was too late, because Shisei was saying, "The artist's name was Zasso. Zasso means 'weeds' in Japanese, so it must have been a name he had taken rather than been born with. It was a kind of political declaration typical of artists who, by necessity, live apart from the rest of mankind.

"Zasso, as I came to find out, loved the theatrical. Artifice was his first line of defense against the world, which he considered to be hopelessly entangled in its own entrails. He often referred to people on the street as cattle grazing in a field. They had, he maintained, no more conception of what was important or beautiful than did a cow.

"Beauty—or the pursuit of it—was Zasso's life study. He was an aficionado of *matsuri*, which is a kind of phenomenon one can find in Japan either on the theater stage or in the whorehouse bed. It is wholly Japanese, meaning one must view it on many levels. Most often it involves the sort of brutality for which we Japanese are justifiably infamous. In the old days, however, it was different. The *matsuri* was performed in every village of the country. It began as a primitive tribal ceremony, a dance of chaos. Our novelist, Yukio Mishima, once called the *matsuri* an obscene attempt to join humanity and eternity. But I think he was afraid of the implications, that through chaos man had the potential to be godlike. Mishima abhorred chaos."

"As do we all," Branding said.

Shisei's golden nails scored white lines in his flesh. "No," she said. "Not all."

"You know what I mean."

"No," she said, "I don't." Her nails dug into him further. "Tell me, Cook, if I hurt you with these—really hurt you—will you love me or hate me?"

"That's an odd question."

"Nevertheless, I want you to answer it."

"But why would you want to hurt me?"

"That's not the question."

"I don't know how I would feel," he admitted.

"How easily love can be turned to hate. How fragile is existence, that it can be instantly turned inside out!" Shisei's eyes were glittering, catlike. "Now the doorway to chaos has been opened. It would take only the smallest nudge to loose it completely."

"You're not taking into consideration the psyches of human beings,"

Branding said. "The essential fairness of the vast majority of them keeps chaos in check."

"You were right about one thing," Shisei said, abruptly switching topics, "Zasso was attracted to my beauty. He presented himself as a kind and compassionate benefactor who understood my state and wished to, as he said, 'save me from the life that had been thrust into me like a knife.' "

Shisei was trembling. Branding held her close. "I don't want to go on," she whispered. "Oh, Cook, please don't make me."

"I can't make you do anything you don't want to do," Branding said. He thought he could feel her suffering almost as if it were his own. "But I think it would be beneficial for you as well as for me if you told me what happened."

"Cook, I—"

"You need to unburden yourself," Branding said gently, in his lust for forbidden knowledge imagining himself a priest-confessor, uninvolved in the emotions being invoked. "This incident isn't a scar, but an open wound. It requires healing."

"Is there no other way?" She said in a small voice.

"No."

Shisei closed her eyes, and he wiped the sweat from her face. "It's all right. You can tell me."

Her eyes flew open, and he thought he glimpsed a dark-red flame flickering within them. Then she said, in a hissing exhalation of breath, "Zasso was an artist, a connoisseur of beauty and of pain. He became my jailor, my tormentor, my demented lover. I had no choice. I had to submit to everything. The moment I stepped across his threshold, I became a prisoner."

"Of course you mean that figuratively," Branding interjected.

"No. I mean prisoner in the literal sense." She saw the look on his face. "I knew this was a mistake."

"I'm sorry," he said. "It's difficult absorbing everything you're telling me."

Shisei's eyes were focused inward, and as she began to speak, Branding could almost feel the past being resurrected. "Zasso debased me so that when he exalted me he would know from what abominable depths he had raised me up. And with each further debasement, he said to me, 'I am saving you.' "

"You mean he raped you?"

"I was ten when Zasso found me. I suppose that carnal desire was a component of the 'radiant beauty' he saw in me. But not right away; I was still too unformed, too far from the ideal into which he was determined to fashion me." Shisei licked her dry lips. "No, he treated me like an animal. 'You are a creature of the streets,' he said to me. 'Some wild thing. It is my duty to train you.' He made me crouch in a corner. When I moved it was on all fours; when I ate it was from a bowl he put on the floor; when I urinated or defecated I did so on sheets of newspaper. He insisted I speak in grunts and barks. 'Animals have no knowledge of civilized language,' he told me."

Branding was horrified. "It's sick," he said. "Why didn't you escape?"

"It was impossible while he was with me," Shisei said. "And when he was gone, he chained me up."

"But surely you must have tried to get away."

Shisei let out a breath, and he felt her beginning to tremble. "You still don't understand, Cook. Without him I had nothing. I would have been lost. I might have died."

"But, my God, Shisei, how he treated you! How you must hate him!"

"How easy life must be for you, Cook," she said sadly. "Everything is either pure or perverted."

"Well, there's no mistaking what went on between you and the tattoo artist." His voice was righteous, filled with moral outrage.

"But that's the point, you have no idea what went on between us. Zasso saw me in the street and recognized in me a perfection he had been seeking all his life."

"You're wrong," Branding said. "He thought he could *make* you perfect. But perfection is God's province, not man's. The fact is, this man needed you. What he did to you was a consequence of his own inner perversion, nothing more. He did to you what his own demons forced him to do."

Shisei, looking into Branding's face, was reminded of the quote from Nietzsche she had discovered in Douglas Howe's library. "All idealism is falsehood in the face of necessity." And for the first time she came face to face with doubt, the lurker in the shadows, the enemy.

What if Branding was right? she asked herself. What if her whole life was a facade of that perversion, if her karma were not in fact her own, but one she had been duped into accepting? A chill raced through her. It would mean that her whole life was a lie. She used her discipline, turned her mind away, unable to face the horrific possibility.

"How does this story end?" Branding asked her.

She put her face into the hollow of his shoulder. "Cook," she whispered, "I want you in me. Now." When she felt him hesitate, she said, "I need to know that you still love me, that you'll love me when all this has been said, when you know what I have been and what I am."

She felt his powerful body fit against hers, covering the shadows that pooled in the dells of her flesh. She was wet, and he entered her easily. The pleasure began to pool in her lower belly, and she gasped. She kissed his shoulder, shuddering. Then she said, "When Zasso 'saved' me from degradation, when he judged me purified, ready, he said to me, 'I have performed the *matsuri*. Now it is time to transform you into the Dread Female of Heaven, to make you into that which pleases the gods.'

"He lay me down on a straw pallet and began his masterpiece. He did not chain me up after that. He did not have to. And each day, he would work on my back, giving painful birth to the giant spider.

"When, after two years, he was finished, Zasso believed that he had transformed me, that the soul of the spider had sunk into me as his inks had, that he had conferred on me a kind of godhood, or"—she shuddered —"something far more frightening. Zasso said to me, 'Now you may stay or go, it makes no difference to me. You are no longer human. You are a weapon. The Dread Female of Heaven, the demon woman who destroys all men she entangles in her web.'"

There was silence for a time. Then Shisei, feeling him slipping out of her, clutched Branding. "Don't leave me, Cook! Oh, please!"

"Is this what you believe, that you are a demon woman?"

"Dear God, if you leave me now I'll die!"

Branding, attuned as he was to her, felt the fear emanating from her in waves. "I want to know if you believe this nonsense." He seemed angry.

Shisei was bewildered. "It's not nonsense. It's Shintoism."

"No," Branding said firmly. "It's the product of one man's sick mind, that's all."

To contemplate such a thing, Shisei knew, was to look into an abyss beyond understanding. It was to contemplate the thought that her life was a hideous parody, warped beyond all comprehension. The product, yes, of one man's mind.

"Cook," she gasped suddenly, "I want to be with you tonight. I cannot stand the thought of being alone. Take me to the dinner with you."

Branding looked at her. He had been certain that knowing the origin of the spider tattoo would unlock for him the mysteries of this fascinating, enigmatic woman. But now he became aware of the many layers of mystery that overlaid Shisei's personality. Perhaps he would never be able to understand her fully, but that knowledge only drew him on, a seductive siren's song as ancient, as irresistible, as the one that had lured Odysseus.

"Oh, God, Cook!" Shisei was crying.

Nicholas thought, I have dreamed it all: my rescue, the warm house, Kansatsu-san. Panic gripped him in its icy fist and he shuddered. A blast of wind hit him full on and his rear foot slipped off the rock groove. He could feel his position deteriorating. If he fell off the Black Gendarme, he had no way of knowing how far he would drop. Mist occluded his vision. He could not see Kansatsu's stone house built into the side of the rock. There was no trace of Kansatsu himself, and Nicholas was frightened that the bone-chilling cold had combined with his deteriorating condition to make him delirious. In that case, there was no Kansatsu, no warm house on the mountainside that would provide him with shelter, no salvation from *Shiro Ninja*.

Falling, endlessly falling . . .

Desperately he reached up, feeling with his fingertips for purchase, but the rock had turned to glass. He encountered only layers of black ice which, indifferent to his plight, shrugged off his grip.

He could not see: snow, lying long in the dark hollows of the Black Gendarme, swirled up by the wind, blinding him. He could not hear: the howling of the wind in the crags was incessant. He could not feel: the cold penetrated his gloves, numbing his fingertips. In the thin frigid air he could smell nothing, not even himself or the matted fur collar of his parka. He opened his mouth, put his lips against the stone, trying to taste the minerals which would tell him where the Black Gendarme was most solid, where there were dangerous fissures that might crack beneath his weight. He sucked on the dark granite but he could taste nothing. Now, with *Shiro Ninja* blocking his sixth sense, he was truly defenseless.

He clung to the rock face like a fly on a windowpane, with a blind tenacity that came solely from instinct. But the wind was increasing in intensity, its gusts raging, scouring all in its path. His foot slipped again and he almost pitched headfirst into the abyss. It was at precisely that instant, with the sensation of being jerked awake, that Nicholas knew that he was not ready to give up.

I am strong, he thought. I am weak. It isn't that the two are indistinguishable, it is that they don't matter. And then he understood what Kansatsu-san had said about life and death. They did not matter.

This is what mattered: the Darkness.

His heart hammering painfully in his chest, Nicholas looked into the Void. He was so far up he could not see the base of the Black Gendarme. He was terrified, but he knew that this was what he had to do. The Path lay in only one direction. Or, all directions were the same. They led to this terrifying place. The Black Gendarme. They led to this moment in time.

Then the wind, howling in fury, tore him free from his tenuous grip upon the rock. In a sense, perhaps, he let go. He would never know.

Into the abyss he fell. Falling, endlessly falling . . .

Justine was on her way to church, backing her car out of the long driveway to her house, when she almost ran right into a man on a bicycle. He had appeared out of nowhere, emerging, it seemed, from the thickets lining the road.

She braked hard as, startled, he swerved into a stand of cryptomeria. He lost his balance, was flipped head over heels into the underbrush.

Justine said "Oh, God" under her breath, put on the parking brake and jerked open the car door. She ran to where the cyclist was lying, knelt beside him. She could see that he was conscious, said a little prayer for that.

"Are you all right?" she said in passable Japanese.

The cyclist nodded, immediately groaned, rubbed the back of his head. He got up slowly, and Justine rose beside him. He was a relatively young man, handsome, smooth-skinned, with the kind of face Justine had seen many times on Japanese TV and posters. There was something slightly feminine about the fullness of his lips, the flare of his delicate nostrils, but this merely made him seem gentle, in need of help. He wore black shorts, a loose short-sleeved white shirt, American sneakers.

He bent to pick up his bicycle, gave another little groan, and Justine instinctively reached out to steady him. He looked at her sharply and she dropped her hand, abruptly remembering the Japanese prohibition against members of the opposite sex touching in public.

She wondered what she should do. Obviously, the man was shaken up —at the very least—and it was her fault. She was at once wary and eager to do the right thing, to not walk away from an incident she had caused. Then she understood that she was thinking like an American. Here in Japan there was so little crime that one did not worry about strolling around any area of Tokyo at night. Tokyo was perhaps the safest city in the world, and the Japanese thing to do, of course, was to offer the cyclist rest and some tea. It was the polite, the civilized way to act.

"I-I'm sorry," she said, flustered. "Would you like to come up to the house for some tea? I live right here."

"Thank you, no," the cyclist said. "I'm all right."

The denial was also the Japanese way. The polite, the civilized way to act.

"It would be no trouble at all," Justine said. "In fact, it would make me feel a good deal better. Don't you think we should make sure you aren't really injured?"

He turned to her, nodded somewhat stiffly. "How can I refuse such hospitality?"

He followed her at a sedate pace up the driveway.

"Why don't you make yourself comfortable on the porch," Justine said. "I'll bring the tea out."

"I guess I am a bit more bruised that I thought," the cyclist said. "Perhaps there are some pillows inside I could use."

Justine hesitated only a moment. "Of course. It will be more comfortable for you inside."

They removed their footwear in the small stone-paved entryway, and Justine placed them within the bamboo cabinet against the wall. She led them into the living room.

The cyclist said nothing until the tea had been brewed, served, and they had both finished a cup. As Justine was pouring more tea, he said, "You have a beautiful home."

"Oh, but it isn't much," Justine said in ritual response. "Are you feeling better?"

"Much better, thank you," he said.

"I wonder if you speak English. It is easier for me."

"But of course." This elicited a smile from him. He really was quite handsome, quite striking. "It would be my pleasure, Missus—"

"Oh, I forgot," Justine said. "My name is—" She had to stop herself from giving him her Christian name. That would have been most impolite. "Mrs. Linnear."

"I am Mr. Omukae," Senjin said. "I think we found the worst possible way to meet, don't you?"

Justine laughed, grateful that he could speak lightly of her almost hitting him with the car. "I'm afraid so. I can't think why I didn't see you until the last minute."

"The driveway bends and so does the road," Senjin said diplomatically. "It is difficult to see traffic coming from that direction. If I may make a suggestion . . ."

"Yes, of course."

"A mirror hung on that large cryptomeria would show you enough of the road to give you warning."

"Why, that's a wonderful idea," Justine said. "Thank you, Mr. Omukae."

"It is my pleasure," he said around his teacup. He looked around. "This is a large house for one person," he said.

"Oh, I don't live alone," Justine said. "My husband and I live here."

Senjin sipped his tea. "What does your husband do, Mrs. Linnear?"

"He runs my father's company. It's diversified: computer-chip manufacture, steel, textiles. My husband's taken it a step further, into advanced computer research." She cocked her head. "And what's your line of work, Mr. Omukae?"

"Oh, I'm afraid it's nothing so innovative or interesting as your husband's," Senjin said. "I'm a bureaucrat. I work at the Industrial Location and Environmental Protection Bureau, in the safety section."

"That sounds interesting enough," Justine said.

He gave her an odd smile. "Actually, it's quite dull."

When he got up, she said, "If you don't mind me saying so, Mr. Omukae, you certainly don't look like a bureaucrat. My husband studies the martial arts, and your body is much like his. It looks like a well-tuned instrument."

He turned, gave her a little bow. "Since you are Western I can assume that is a compliment," he said. "Cycling is a hobby almost anyone can benefit from. But to me it is more. It is a sport; an obsession, perhaps, one could uncharitably say. Did I say that right? I am often not certain of my English."

"You said it better than most Americans would have."

"Thank you, although I'm sure you are merely being polite." That smile came again. "My obsession keeps me fit in mind as well as in body. I find that my obsession is akin to meditation: it is in constant motion, providing a cleansing of the spirit."

"The way you put it," Justine said, "I could use an obsession like that. Too much time alone with nothing to do, nowhere to go, breeds its own kind of inertia, which seems at times impossible to break."

Senjin nodded. "If I were your husband I would not leave you alone so often."

"His . . . work is often difficult, demanding," Justine said, abruptly annoyed at having to defend Nicholas to a stranger. Didn't Japanese have better manners?

"Of course," Senjin said. "That is most understandable. Life is never perfect. One must often make sacrifices." He shrugged. "This is natural; it is to be expected."

Justine, close to him, was suddenly curious. "What is it, I wonder, that

I see behind your eyes?" She was stunned that she had spoken in such an intimate way to a virtual stranger. What, she wondered, had made her do that?

Senjin looked down into her Western face. "What do you mean?"

She hesitated a moment, but found that she could not help herself. She felt abruptly light-headed, the pulse of her heart like a drumbeat in her ears. "Despite what you've said about your English, you're very self-assured in any language. I can tell that just by the way you move." Startled by her own revelation, she blurted, "It's uncanny. You remind me so much of my husband."

"Thank you, but I am sure it is merely your imagination," Senjin said, with that note of humility only the Japanese can project.

His face in the waning light had the aspect of a statue of a hero long forgotten. There was about him a blend of the stoic and the melancholy that pulled on Justine's heartstrings.

"One learns in America," Justine said, "never merely to *accept* an unpleasant situation, but to strive to overcome it."

"Unpleasantness, Mrs. Linnear, is an inescapable element of life. The Japanese understand this implicitly."

She watched him as he slowly circled her. "Surely suffering is a natural part of life. But do you really believe that unpleasantness is natural? That it must be accepted?"

"Oh, yes," Senjin said. "Unpleasantness is essential to existence. Perhaps I should say *human* existence to be perfectly correct. By unpleasantness I mean pain. Without pain, Mrs. Linnear, there can be no pleasure, certainly ecstasy would be entirely unknown, because there would be nothing with which to contrast it. Do you see this?" He was smiling, but in a wholly different way. This was not the smile of the open innocent, but the knowing expression of a worldly man.

"Of course you have followed me so far. But there is more. Much more. Because it follows that pain can in itself be pleasurable. It can, in fact, provide a release of a magnitude never touched by ecstasy. You do not believe me? I can see that you do not. How can I persuade you save by example."

Alarmed, Justine said, "Just what are you talking about, Mr. Omukae?"

The cyclist gave her a small bow. "Call me Senjin," he said, taking her hand in a very Western gesture. "We are on sufficiently intimate terms to use our first names, don't you think, Justine?"

"Was I ever outside?" Nicholas asked. "Did you lead me there?"

"You were outside," Kansatsu said. "Yes."

"But you were with me, I know that. I just couldn't see you."

"You were alone, Nicholas," Kansatsu said. "Just as you are alone now."

"I don't understand."

They sat in a plain stone-walled cell within Kansatsu's monastery, just within the circumference of illumination from several fat votive candles. The light seemed ancient, given a three-dimensional quality by the scent of the burning candles.

"Remember," Kansatsu said, "you have come many times to my retreat here on the Black Gendarme."

"Did I also jump many times?" Nicholas asked. "Did I let go many times?"

"Ripples," Kansatsu said, "spreading outward until they are spent upon the shore."

"I let go," Nicholas said. "In some point in time I let go."

"But you did not fall," Kansatsu said, "as you were afraid you would."

"No," Nicholas said, wonder still in his voice. "I hung in the Void, above the abyss that still terrifies me. All around me was the Black Gendarme, below and above. I was separated from it yet a part of it. It was as if I could fly."

"Or suspend gravity."

"What happened to me, *sensei*? Please. You must tell me. I am in an agony of knowing."

"Find the answer, Nicholas. My answer will not be yours. Think."

"I found . . ."

"Go on."

"I found the Darkness."

"Yes," Kansatsu said. "This is what I meant you to find when I sent you to Kumamoto in the winter of 1963."

"Instead, I confronted Saigo."

"Forget the ox, Nicholas. The ox does not exist. I sent you to confront yourself."

"No!" he shouted. Darkness was turning by degrees into light. But Nicholas was sickened by what was revealed.

"Think of the Darkness," Kansatsu said. "There is only one law, one Way. You gave yourself up to the Darkness, and it protected you. The Darkness is what you have shunned for all your life. You have always known of it, Nicholas. You have chosen to turn away from it."

"If what you say is true, that you sent me to confront myself, it would mean that Saigo and I are the same. He is me; I am him." He thought in terror of Saigo's enormous capacity for depravity and evil. "That cannot be!"

"Ah, but in a sense it is!" Kansatsu said. "And now you have the proof. Think back: it was your *mother* who explained the legacy of your grandfather's emeralds to you, your mother who was tanjian just as your grandfather was, your mother who passed her gift and your grandfather's legacy down to you."

"But even though she was his favorite," Nicholas said, "my mother was adopted by my 'grandfather.' No one knew where she came from."

"That was what she told you," Kansatsu said, "and no doubt there is much truth to the story. However, I would wager that your grandfather —if no one else—knew precisely her origin. And she became his favorite because he was tanjian and so was she. He could not pass down his gift through his genes, I'll put another wager on that; the wife he took was not tanjian. But your mother was, and he saw in her the cycle renewing itself, and he loved her all the more for what she would provide for him."

Nicholas stared at Kansatsu. Chunks of memory, stories of her past Cheong had told him in his youth that heretofore had made no sense, were now dislodged, rising, coming together into a recognizable whole.

Kansatsu accurately read Nicholas's expression. He said, "Think back: you found the Darkness even though you are *Shiro Ninja*. This is impossible. Yet it has happened. You *know* that it has happened. Take no one else's word for it but your own. The Darkness is the Way. It is that part of your true self that up until now you have not been able to face.

"Now you know the whole truth." Kansatsu's face was shining, lit by something more than the candles' glow. "Nicholas, you are tanjian!"

Justine felt a sudden, almost painful stab of fear. "How do you know my first name? I haven't told it to you."

Senjin watched her in the last of the light. "Pain and pleasure. This is the way my mind works: on all possibilities at once. Or is it the only possibility?"

"Who are you?" Justine's voice was tight. She was thinking, How do I get to a phone? Who do I call? Is there a 911 number in Japan? My God, how little I still know of everyday life here. "You're not just a cyclist I almost hit."

Senjin advanced on her, said, "I am alone. I have chosen to be alone."

The taste of brass was in her mouth, a storm was brewing in her heart, and she tried to move away from him, as if she might free herself from a kind of palpable magnetism that seemed to have gripped her, to suffuse her with a frightening lassitude which increased the closer she was to Senjin.

Her cheeks were hot. "I . . . was thinking of my husband."

"Were you? Are you certain of that?"

Justine looked up into his long, black eyes. She glimpsed an animus, iridescent as the scaly side of a fish, that drew her to its center like Theseus in the Cretan labyrinth, where crouched the Minotaur, breathing, waiting, patient as a god.

His eyes, as large as moons, seemed to burn with a cold light. Justine could not avert her gaze; in a moment she did not want to.

"I take no wife," Senjin said. "I will have no family of my own."

"So instead you live your solitary life, drifting like a cloud above the jam-packed earth."

"I think I know your meaning."

"You're so terribly alone. How do you stand it?"

"When I was a child I was always lonely," Senjin said. "I cried often, and was ashamed of my weakness. In time I overcame that."

"And that's your answer?" Justine said incredulously. "You see loneliness as a character flaw?"

"Certainly it is not a virtue," Senjin said. "What else can it be?"

"It is, I think, the pain behind your eyes." They were so close that she was breathing him in like the scent of an exotic orchid, blooming in the night. "It's a scar on your soul."

"Japanese do not believe in a soul."

"Your spirit, then." Justine knew that she should move away from him now, this instant, because she felt as heavy as lead. She recognized with a start the taste of brass in her mouth as lust. "I know you have a spirit if not a soul."

"My spirit is pure," Senjin said. "It is without emotion, therefore it requires no solace." He put his hand gently over hers. For a moment Justine was paralyzed. Fantasy had now begun to spill over into reality, and the sudden presence of the two, as disparate as oil and water, made her feel queasy. She had no feeling in her legs, and she leaned against the wall, feeling its coolness against her burning skin.

"Justine?" Using her Christian name again, as intimate as a caress. His lips close to hers. Night coming down, a pull like the tide. Desire, mindless, savage, burning like a jewel at her throat.

Dear God, she thought, what's happening to me?

_____

"No!" Nicholas cried. "I can't accept what you're saying! I can't be tanjian!"

"You are what you are, Nicholas," Kansatsu said. "Karma. There is nothing I or even you can do about it."

"I refuse to accept my karma. I reject any notion that I am tanjian. It simply cannot be!"

"Think of the Darkness," Kansatsu said. "Remember what it felt like to hang suspended above the gorge."

"It didn't happen!" Nicholas shouted. "I dreamed it! I must have! Or I am dead. I died upon the Black Gendarme, as I suspected earlier."

"You are alive, Nicholas. But the truth is that before this is over you may wish that you had died there."

"Stop talking like that!" Nicholas was so agitated that he could not sit or even stand in one place. He paced back and forth like a wild animal made suddenly captive. "I have no wish to hear any more of this!"

"On the contrary, that is your only wish now," Kansatsu said with great patience. "It is why you came here, why you risked a perilous journey in your currently fragile physical state."

"I am *Shiro Ninja!*" Nicholas shouted in anguish and in fear. "Why do you talk when you can act? You can save me. Use Tau-tau. Undo what has been done to me!"

"Don't you understand?" Kansatsu approached Nicholas, his aura, dark, iridescent blue-green like the body of an insect, preceding him. Nicholas shrank from him.

"Why should you fear me?" Then Kansatsu straightened. "It is not me you fear, Nicholas. It is that part of yourself lying long buried in the center of your spirit. Is it so hideous that you must fear it so?"

"I don't know what you mean," Nicholas said, his misery clearly etched on his face.

"But you do," Kansatsu said. "The Darkness is your friend, Nicholas. It saved you when the wind tore you off the face of the Black Gendarme. Why can't you believe your own senses?"

"It was a dream, I tell you! What I saw, what I felt—it couldn't have happened!"

"That way lies madness," Kansatsu said. "Your senses are all you have to rely on."

"But I *can't* rely on them now. I am *Shiro Ninja!*"

"You are still Nicholas Linnear," Kansatsu said. "Nothing will change that. Your spirit abides, Nicholas. It is indomitable. Only your own mounting fear can crush it."

"The fear entangles me, *sensei,*" Nicholas whispered. He shivered suddenly and his teeth began to chatter furiously. "It will not let go its hold."

"No!" Kansatsu said so sharply that Nicholas started. "It is you who are holding on to the fear. This fear is known and therefore can be handled. This other fear—the fear of the Darkness, of your heritage and all it implies—is the unknown. Better by far the former than the latter."

Nicholas drew his legs up to his chest. He trembled as if he had the ague. "I am afraid, *sensei*."

"Of what?"

"What if I *am* tanjian?"

"If that frightens you, Nicholas, let yourself feel the fear. At least give yourself that much freedom. Reach out once again and touch the Darkness."

"I can't. I seem paralyzed."

"If you feel up to it," Kansatsu said softly, "tell me what happened to my elder brother, Kyoki."

Outside, a storm was whistling through the ravines and narrow gorges on the approach to the Black Gendarme. Hail rattled against the thatch roof of Kansatsu's monastery. Real time had seemed to vanish, retreating down a well of gravity that kept the two of them in an orbit all to themselves.

Nicholas told Kansatsu what had transpired from the moment he saw Kyoki's castle to the moment he left. When he was through, Kansatsu said, "How long do you think my elder brother had been dead when you discovered him?"

"Half a day. Perhaps less than that. Six hours."

"Tell me, Nicholas, who knew you were going to the Asama highlands?"

"Only my wife and my close friend, Tanzan Nangi."

"Do you trust this Nangi?"

"With my life," Nicholas said.

Kansatsu fixed him with a stare. "It may yet come to that. I advise you to choose your words—and those you trust—most carefully."

"I stand by what I said."

Kansatsu said nothing.

Nicholas, growing anxious, said, "What are you thinking, *sensei*?"

"He must be an individual of enormous personal power, this murderer of my brother. He got to my brother before you could talk to him, so he must have known where you were headed. How was that accomplished? Did someone tell him, your wife, your friend Nangi? Or did he already know?"

"What are you saying," Nicholas said angrily, "that Tanzan Nangi, with whom I have trusted my life, who is so crippled that he must walk with a cane, this man could be a *dorokusai*, a tanjian fanatic?"

"Someone managed to breach the castle's defenses," Kansatsu went on as if Nicholas's outburst had not occurred, "to defeat my brother, a tanjian adept. We do not know how that was accomplished, either. Yes, there are many mysteries here that must be unraveled."

Thinking Nangi was right, Nicholas said, "One thing is certain: my enemy is a *dorokusai*."

"Oh, yes." Kansatsu nodded. "All things are possible in this universe, Nicholas. Even the unthinkable: the existence of a *dorokusai*, the most feared of tanjian. As you must know, a *dorokusai* is a loner, a rebel who has deliberately turned away from the discipline of Tau-tau—from *all* discipline. He is the master of deceit and disguise. Often, he appears in a benign guise. Always, he is not what he seems."

Here Kansatsu paused, and it seemed to Nicholas that he had at last answered his question.

"A *dorokusai* inhabits his own universe," Kansatsu continued. "He has created his own laws—his own Way. Even the tanjian *sensei* fears the *dorokusai*, because he has such power that he cannot be killed—he must be destroyed."

"What is the difference," Nicholas asked, "between death and destruction?"

"That is one of the reasons you have come to me," Kansatsu said. "It will be the last lesson I teach you, Nicholas. But know this: if you begin your lessons here, then you choose to place yourself squarely in the Path this *dorokusai* is bent on pursuing."

Nicholas considered this. "I have already been placed in the *dorokusai*'s path," he said at last. "My only choice is whether to fight or to die."

"If you have found the conviction," Kansatsu said, "then reach out. Find the Darkness again. It is your special friend."

There was a silence of such duration that the light changed in the chamber before Nicholas gave a sharp cry. "I felt it," he whispered. He was covered in sweat but was no longer trembling. "I felt it."

"Hold out your hand," Kansatsu said. When there was no response, he said again, "Nicholas, hold out your hand."

Slowly, Nicholas extended his hand until it had crossed from the light into the shadows on Kansatsu's side of the chamber.

Kansatsu touched the tip of his forefinger to Nicholas's. "Here is your fear. Touch it, breathe it, own it. Understanding will come only in this way."

After a time Nicholas said, "The fear comes from inside myself, not from the Darkness." His voice was filled with a kind of wonder.

Kansatsu said, "Now your spirit hangs suspended over an abyss just as, before, your corpus was suspended over white snow, gray ice, and black rock." He waited a moment, then said in an entirely different voice, "Tell me what you are thinking at this moment."

"I don't want to believe that I am tanjian," Nicholas said. He took a deep breath. "I'm afraid that if I do, I'll be no better than my cousin Saigo, whose spirit was warped and corrupted by the evil inside him."

"Is that what you believe, that the Darkness is evil?"

"Isn't it?"

"I admit that it has the potential for great evil," Kansatsu said. "The *dorokusai* who pursues you is ample evidence of that. But that is not all the Darkness is. The universe, Nicholas, is neither good nor evil; rather, both moral extremes exist within it." Kansatsu's voice was soft, a tide calming the racing of Nicholas's terror-driven heart. He kept the physical connection between them. "This was one of the first lessons I taught you, remember? It is the most essential of all the truths.

"The same is true of the Darkness. It, too, is a universe, but because it is one of almost limitless power, its potential is often abused, corrupted. That is the nature of power.

"All power is transitory. In its ephemeral nature lies its infinite malleability, and its potential to warp the spirit of human beings. If you touch it, you will not die. But you *will* change. In what ways even I cannot say."

"I am afraid to change," Nicholas confessed.

"If you do not change," Kansatsu said simply, "I cannot help you. If you do not change, the *dorokusai* who pursues you has already won. You will never be able to use the emeralds your grandfather bequeathed you. You will remain *Shiro Ninja* forever."

Nicholas was shaking as if with a fever. The minutes stretched on, building an agonized silence. At last, slowly, Nicholas bowed his head.

Kansatsu closed his eyes. He seemed to resume breathing after a very long time. "All right, then," he said. "The first thing you must do is to learn to speak all over again. You must learn to think in a new language. It is called Akshara, the language of eternity."

"It is part of Tau-tau?"

"It is the very essence of Tau-tau," Kansatsu said. "Without Akshara nothing else is possible." He looked at the whiteness of Nicholas's face. "Tell me, Nicholas-san, are you afraid?"

"Yes, *sensei*." It was a hoarse whisper. The fear was coming in a flood, but then Nicholas realized that Kansatsu had called him Nicholas-san, and he could breathe again.

"Good," Kansatsu said. "You should be frightened now. Your spirit is through being suspended. The time has come to plunge yourself into the abyss."

Nangi and Tomi arrived at The Silk Road after midnight. The tokudashi parlor was packed with sweating businessmen, a colony of milling ants, dressed alike, wreathed in acrid cigarette smoke.

Tomi paused for a moment, fascinated by the expression on the men's faces, replicated over and over. She knew what they were watching, knew what was in their minds, and she marveled at the power behind that one image. She wondered whether women could become so obsessed over one portion of the male anatomy. She did not think so. Women were not so much involved with the physical as they were with the emotional. Not that they couldn't be sex-driven, but certainly not in the way men often were.

Mega-amplified music almost blasted them back to the entryway; the strobes came on, momentarily blinding them. Tomi blinked, flashed her credentials at the bouncer. She had to shout to be heard over the music.

She led Nangi around the perimeter of the main club room, past a stained and greasy cardboard sign marked NO ADMITTANCE.

The warren of corridors was like a catacomb carved from the earth. Nangi followed Tomi as she wended her way past identical-looking doors. The corridors were shabby, the walls filthy, paint peeling, air vents clogged with soot and grime fluttering feebly. Bare light bulbs hung on twisted lengths of flex from the exposed sockets in the blackened ceiling.

Tomi paused at a door. She had to pound on it in order to be heard over the rock music. She heard a response and opened the door. Inside was a tiny room furnished with a slab dressing table, a mirror surrounded by several lights, one cane-backed chair, a rusty sink. A young woman in a thin, ratty robe stood staring at them.

"Oh, it's you," she said in a dull voice, and turned away from them to apply makeup. She watched their reflections warily in the mirror.

"Atoko," Tomi said, "this is Mr. Nangi. He's a friend of mine." She turned to Nangi. "Atoko shared Mariko's dressing room with her. She found the body." Then turned back. "We'd like to ask you some questions."

"About what?"

Tomi slipped a photo of Dr. Hanami out of her pocketbook, placed it on the dressing table in front of the girl.

Atoko glanced down at it, said, "Who's this?"

"I thought you could tell us," Tomi said.

Atoko shrugged, went back to applying her makeup.

Nangi, with his limp exaggerated, walked over beside the girl. He reached up, plucked a photo stuck between the mirror and its frame.

Atoko said, "Hey!"

Nangi allowed her to take the photo from him. "Your brother or a boyfriend?"

Atoko pushed her lower lip out sullenly, stuck the photo back in its niche.

"You know," Nangi said, "I had a sister once. She had a lot of boyfriends when she was young. Just about your age, I should think. How she loved the boys to come around! How she encouraged them! Not, I think, with any evil intent. She was a good girl. She just enjoyed their company so." He took several limping steps away. "Sometimes, though, she would get into trouble."

Atoko cocked her head in his direction. "What kind of trouble?"

Nangi looked at her, as if startled that she had actually been listening to him. He waved his hand. "Oh, well, sometimes another girl's boyfriend would be sweet on my sister. Not that my sister did anything to encourage them. Oh, my, no. It just happened." Nangi gingerly took another step. "But her girlfriends never understood. They blamed her, of course, because they could not bear to blame their own boyfriends."

"But that's exactly what happened!" Atoko exclaimed. She put down her eyeliner, stared at Nangi. "Mariko and I were such good friends until . . ." Her eyes lowered and she pointed to the photo of Dr. Hanami. "Until him."

"He preferred you to Mariko?" Nangi asked.

Atoko nodded. "For a time. Then he switched back and forth, without us at first knowing. In the end I think he believed he was in love with Mariko, but by then it was too late. Mariko wanted nothing more to do with me." There were tears in Atoko's eyes; she would not look at herself in the mirror. "Poor Mariko, she was a good girl. She didn't deserve . . . Oh, damn!"

Nangi and Tomi exchanged glances, and Tomi went to hold Atoko while the tears streamed down her face.

"I'm all right," Atoko said at last. She took a handful of tissues, dabbed at her face. "Oh, shit, I can't go on stage like this." She began to cry again. "I thought I was finished grieving for her."

Nangi waited a moment, then said, "Can you tell us anything about the man in the photo Detective Yazawa showed you?"

Atoko shrugged. "What's there to tell? He was a rich guy who loved to cheat on his wife. I got the impression that he liked being around us because we were young. He soon grew tired of me. But in a way it was different, I think, with Mariko."

"Different in what way?" Tomi prompted.

"Like I said, he thought he was in love with her."

"Do you think he'd do anything for her?" Nangi asked suddenly.

Atoko paused in reapplying her makeup. She stared into the mirror at nothing, at the past. Then her eyes cleared. "You know, the funny thing is, when he was with me, practically all he talked about was his wife. I think he would have done anything for *her*."

"Was he here the night of Mariko's murder?" Tomi asked.

Atoko would not meet her gaze. She nodded at last. "I lied about that. I . . . was ashamed of how my friendship with Mariko had ended. I . . . didn't want to talk about it. I didn't want anyone to know." She took a deep breath. "But, yes, he was here that night. He had a date with Mariko. I saw him, his face white as milk as he rushed out of her dressing room. I heard him vomiting in the alleyway outside. That's when I went into Mariko's dressing room and . . . found her." She bit her lip, looked away from them. "I'm sorry. I should have told the truth from the beginning." Her eyes met Tomi's in the mirror. "I'm a good girl."

Justine was staring into Senjin's lambent eyes. It was like staring into the night sky, strewn with mysterious stars, filled with shadows whose shapes so familiar in daylight had taken on hidden meanings, extracted from the depths of her own imagination.

Tau-tau, and more than Tau-tau, the forbidden magic of the *dorokusai*, was at work here. She could not know, and if she had known, she would not understand.

Senjin, the vampire, continuing what Haha-san had begun, was doing to Justine what he did to all his women—what he had done even with Dr. Muku before he had plunged the phosphorus-laced cigarette into his eye socket, into his brain—he was sucking out of them their life, seeking as he did so the key to them (the key, had he but known it, to himself): their secret fears, their humiliating weaknesses.

Justine, taken out of time by Senjin's conjuring, looked down upon her life, observing, much as Nicholas had many months before while undergoing his operation.

Now she did Senjin's bidding, as Nicholas had while Dr. Hanami's scalpel had probed his brain for the tumor.

"Where does your husband keep the box, Justine?" Voice like a silken whip, urging her to speak. "Where has he hidden the emeralds?"

Justine knew—or, in any event, she remembered Nicholas frantically rushing into the house, digging beneath the floorboards, seizing the box. His sigh of relief when he opened it. How could she forget? But there *was* something she was forgetting. What was it?

"I'll take you," Justine heard herself saying. "Come with me." Taking his hand, her body filled with an energy that made her teeth chatter.

She showed him the spot in Nicholas's workout room, showed him how to push aside the post, how to unearth the box. Just as Nicholas had . . . what was she forgetting?

Senjin brought up the box into the light. He realized that his hands were trembling. At last, he told himself, the emeralds! The last link with Eternity, for which he had been searching, it seemed, all his life. Ever since, at least, he had been told of the mystic emeralds' power and what it could unleash.

He opened the box and gasped. Six emeralds, only six. Where were the other nine? He needed nine. His hands scrabbled over the dark blue velvet, tearing it into shreds. Six were not enough; in fact, as he knew, the number could be quite deadly. But not for him.

He scooped up the emeralds, put the empty box back in its cache.

Senjin turned to Justine. He could see the Tau-tau imprisoning her, coloring her eyes, making her do what he ordered. "Where are the other emeralds?" he said sharply. "There are only six here."

"I don't know."

Senjin studied her bewildered face. "Are you certain? Think hard." But she must know. Some part of her perhaps had seen or heard something, a tiny incident that she could not connect with the disappearance of the remaining gems. He would have to find out, look into her mind, dig deep, as a surgeon might, for what he was looking for.

"I am," Justine said. "I don't know. I thought they were in the box. I saw them in the box when Nicholas—" She stopped abruptly.

"What is it?" Senjin asked. "Go on."

"I—I . . ." She grimaced suddenly, put her hands to her temples. "Oh, my head hurts!"

Senjin knew immediately what was happening. Some deeply buried part of her was fighting him, resisting this direct approach. Perhaps Linnear had told her directly that she must never reveal the emeralds' hiding place. That would be enough to set up the moral conflict. He decided to try another approach. After all, he had the time. And, in any case, it might prove interesting on other levels.

He pocketed the emeralds, put the workout room back in order. Then he took her out of there, out of the house entirely. On the *engawa* the night had settled in. The cicadas were buzzing and, here and there, fireflies danced among the cypresses and the cryptomeria.

"Talk to me," Senjin said to Justine. "Tell me about yourself; tell me what you can't tell anyone else. Above all, I want you to remember."

Justine sat on a cedar lounger Nicholas had made just after they had moved in here. It was her favorite spot, looking out as it did on Nicholas's garden.

"When I came here to Japan, I loved it," she whispered. "Why not? It was exciting, exotic. I was filled up with the unfamiliar sights, smells, sounds of the country, and that was enough to sustain me. A year later I seemed to hit a wall. I had taken care of setting up a household in a foreign land, or so I thought. My husband hired a Japanese woman to help. I became pregnant. It all seemed to be on track. But it wasn't. It was terribly, terribly wrong. I missed my family and my friends. There was no one here but my husband and *his* friends. They weren't enough, and then my daughter was born and I lost her. I became negative about everything. Now I hated Japan; now all I could think about was going home to our house on the ocean in West Bay Bridge on Long Island. Oh, how I longed to be there! How I long to be there now!"

Justine was trembling with the force of the emotions these memories were exacting from her. She felt a need to catch her breath. But she suspected that if she stopped, she would not finish, and now she needed to do that more than anything else, because that was what Senjin was willing her to do. "Then old disturbances I thought I had successfully dealt with when I was younger began to resurface and I felt as if I were back where I had started so many years ago."

She felt now as she had felt then, a resurgence of the past, the ripping asunder of the fabric between past and present, the rushing of something hidden overtaking her.

"When I was much younger," she continued, "and also at a low point in my life, I turned in desperation to analysis. I hated my father for paying no attention to me, for despising my weak-willed mother. I needed someone to talk to, someone who could set me straight." She looked at Senjin Omukae. "I suppose you wouldn't understand."

"There are many psychiatrists here in Japan," Senjin said noncommittally.

Justine rolled her head away from the moonlight. "The doctor I saw was a woman. She looked like a dark-haired gypsy. I felt embarrassed coming to her, the rich lapsed Catholic, emotionally bankrupt, my pockets bulging with money. Funny. I remember what I was wearing on my first visit: a Mary Quant miniskirt and polka-dot blouse I had just brought back from a shopping spree in London. Afterward, looking at myself in a full-length mirror, I was so appalled, I showed up the next week in jeans and a work shirt, and never let Honi see me in anything else again."

Justine paused. It was hard work dredging up the past, facing up to the unhappy, spoiled brat she had been. She had never even spoken of this to Nicholas. How was it, she asked herself, that she was able to confess her sins to this man? Then the question slipped, unanswered, from her drugged consciousness.

"Honi wore huge silver earrings from Mexico, multicolored peasant skirts woven in Guatemala. She was totally unconcerned with how she looked, and I learned by example. She taught me to look inward at those dark, dank places inside myself I would rather ignore. It was hard work —at times impossible, I thought. Many times I broke down and sobbed, unable to go on. But Honi was always there, and her strength eventually became my strength, as if she were an empath, able to draw the inner pain out of me and into herself.

"She had an infinite capacity to absorb pain, like an icon or a saint. Often, when I was with her, I thought of myself in church, my idealized church which accepted suffering rather than displaying it in numbing profusion. I thought of Honi as a nun in a holy order, myself as a novice who must pass test after test in order to prove herself worthy.

"That was my problem, you see—I could never think of myself as being worthy of a decent relationship. Loving someone else and being loved in return was simply out of the question. But gradually I came to see that Honi loved me. She saw all my flaws, digested all my sins as I disgorged them. And still she accepted me. Still she loved me.

"What a revelation that was! Of course, at first I couldn't—or wouldn't —believe it. But Honi wore me down. I came to her like a wild animal intent on gnawing itself to death. She taught me not to bite myself, then she healed my self-inflicted wounds.

" 'I will bear the weight of your sins when you cannot,' she told me. 'Justine, it's important for you to realize that you're not alone anymore.'

And, of course, I thought, where's the catch? What does she want from me?

"Honi was the only person in my life who wanted *nothing* from me. She loved me so that I could learn to love myself." She turned her head back. "Do you love yourself, Senjin? It seems to me that you don't. It seems to me that you're too involved with the mechanics of keeping your environment in check. Nicholas is the same way. He melts into the darkness, he treads silently, at times I am certain that he has stopped his breathing. He has mastered all these things, yet he is not the master of himself. I sense the same thing in you, Senjin, am I wrong?"

Senjin said nothing.

"Being with you is like being with my husband. Can you tell me how that is possible?"

Senjin knew but he would never tell her. Instead he reached out for her. He had known that this evening would turn interesting.

Justine felt suspended above an abyss, entangled in her own roiling emotions. She felt Senjin's touch like an electric current surging through her, and she thought in disbelief, This is not happening, I cannot feel what I am feeling, my body is betraying me, just as I am betraying Nick. She felt as if she had a fever, her legs weak, her lungs raw, coherent thought as distant and unreachable as a star.

Moonlight drifted like lace through the trees. I should be alone, waiting for Nick to return, she thought, but I'm not. I'm with this strange Japanese man and I want him against me, on me, in me.

Justine wept into the soft, fragrant hollow of Senjin's neck as she clung to him, as he lay her on the porch, bound her wrists and her ankles. Her mind was on fire, but it could not match the heat of her body.

Senjin felt the heat as if it were emanating from a forge. This moment was very sweet for him. He had dreamed of just this triumphant moment, a transcendent experience, surely.

"I promised you an example," he said, "of the mingling of pleasure and pain. The oneness."

At that moment a twig snapped. They both heard it and, startled, Justine's eyes sparked. Her chest was heaving, and he could see the fear-lust like a drug dilating her irises. He wondered what his own eyes looked like, and was glad he had no mirror in which to look.

He put one finger across his mouth to stop her from talking. He signed to her to stay silent, then went without a sound off the *engawa* into the swath of pebbles, the border of the front garden.

Anyone else would have made noise, weight crunching down on the pebbles, but Senjin seemed to have no weight. Justine watched him gliding across the garden and saw in him once again an aspect of Nicholas that made her desperately uneasy.

She was shaking from the cool night air and the release from forces so unknown and intense that they seemed to stop the normal functioning of her mind. She felt them even now, though they were less intense, like the tendrils of a dream that entangles you in its mood throughout the day.

If she had expected to be free from them the moment Senjin left her, she was wrong. There was about her the sense of lying in a hammock, swaying rhythmically in erotic indolence. She lay as if entranced, glutted with the throbbing of her body, rolled on her side, staring at the spot where Senjin had blended into the darkness, waiting for him to return as if he, not Nicholas, were her husband.

Han Kawado cursed himself. Crouching in the bushes beside the Linnear house, he drew a long, thin-bladed knife. He had done some work on the hilt so that it was covered with a dark abrasive material that would not slip or twist at a crucial moment even in the sweat of fear or the flow of blood.

Fear was what Han Kawado felt now. His mind, numbed by the long hours of surveillance, had begun to slip into a twilight fugue. Memory had merged with the present, and his wife, dead now six months, had been reborn in his mind. She had died suddenly while Han was off on a job for the Pack Rat. The doctors who attended her last hours had assured Han that had he been with her when she was stricken, he could have done little to prolong her life. A massive heart attack was like an earthquake, they told him, one had but to assess the damage in retrospect. *Karma.*

So they said. But Han could not help but blame himself. Because of the nature of his work, he was hardly home, and then it was apt to be for odd hours, the sporadic day or so. In retrospect, he realized that he loved his work more than he had ever loved his wife. That was *his karma*, knowledge that he could not allow himself to forget, a kind of legacy from his wife, a justification, however tenuous, for her death.

And ever since, he was conscious of how alone he was. Previously, he had chosen to live his life in this manner, a shadow man, lurking in the night, inhabiting a nether world forever apart from the bulk of mankind. He wore his solitary life like a badge of courage, certain of his heroism. Now his aloneness preyed upon him, withering his spirit as time lined his skin. At times he felt older than his own father, survivor of Bataan and of Hiroshima.

Still, surveillance work was the only thing he knew; and he was good at it. He had taken the Linnear job when the Pack Rat had offered it. But the hours were long. They weighed upon him mercilessly. His legs were stiff, the joints painful from holding one position for so long.

Han had been witness to everything: the almost collision, the talk over tea, the enigmatic seduction on the *engawa*. Tiredness and his guilty thoughts had conspired to make him careless. He had moved to get a better view of Senjin tying up Justine, had not looked where he was putting his feet, and *snap!* A dry, dead branch had cracked beneath his weight.

It was impossible to judge just how loud the sound had been to others or to know how disastrous his misstep had been. He had no clear idea who the Japanese cyclist was or what his interest in Justine Linnear might be. His job was to report to the Pack Rat any suspicious contact Justine had with anyone outside a circle of people he had been briefed on.

Perhaps, he thought now, as he crouched in the thick darkness, I should have reported this contact immediately. But he dared not leave Justine alone with this unknown man until his identity could be cross-checked. Now Han braced himself for the worst. If no one came looking for him, so much the better. But his instincts were too sharp to rely on a chance. He had to assume that his misstep had been heard. If the man named Senjin Omukae had any designs on Justine Linnear, he was sure to be suspicious and would want to check out the sound.

Well, Han thought, let him come. He strained for any hint of approaching noise, hefted the knife. I'm ready for anything. Then something as hard as steel was across his windpipe and he could no longer catch his breath.

Senjin had ceased to breathe in the normal sense. Instead he inhaled and exhaled tidally so that there was no rushing in his ears, no discernable throb of his pulse. In this way he heard far more than any other human, more even than most animals.

He found the man hidden within the underbrush. This proved no great difficulty for him, though by the manner in which he had secreted himself, Senjin could tell that the man was a seasoned professional in matters of surveillance. Any normal man—or even a team of men—would have overlooked him.

But Senjin was not a normal man. Senjin scented him first, the sharp man-odor wafting his way mixed with the soft-edged scents of camellia, jasmine, and pine, and knew that he was being spied upon.

Senjin heard the spy's breathing within the gentle sigh of the wind, between the infrequent hoot of an owl. Senjin stood still as a rustling overhead in the branches of a cryptomeria momentarily disturbed his concentration. Then, glancing upward, he saw the owl's great wings, black sails in the moonlight, dipping down, impaling a trembling vole in its talons, settling back in the cryptomeria to begin its nocturnal feast.

Senjin felt a special kinship with the owl, as he did with the cryptomeria. Both were sentinels as well as symbols of the solitary existence of the warrior, the last bastion against decay.

Scenting blood and then the sharp man-odor, so out of place in this environment, reminded Senjin of what he must do. He moved on.

He stole up behind where the man crouched in the underbrush, hidden, so he thought, in dense shadow. Senjin slipped one arm around the man's throat.

"Who sent you?" Whispered into the spy's ear. "Why are you here? Who are you working for?"

The man said nothing, and Senjin repeated his questions, inflicting a great deal of pain as his free hand hit a series of pressure points on the spy's body.

Senjin had very little time—something the spy knew—and so was at a disadvantage. He needed answers to his questions, but unable to get them, he progressed to the next logical step.

His eyes closed to slits. Only their whites showed. A beat became palpable, a dimple in the fabric of the night. He plunged the stiffened fingers of his free hand through the man's eyes. The spy's body gave a powerful galvanic leap like that of a bucking bronco. Bunched muscles spasmed, then all at once let go. There was an abrupt stench, and Senjin stepped quickly away, letting the corpse fall into the bushes. He went hurriedly through the man's pockets, taking anything he thought might give him some clue as to the man's identity, what he was doing here, or who sent him.

Then Senjin went back to where Justine lay, bound, on the porch.

Her drugged eyes opened, her irises huge. "Where did you go?" she asked.

Senjin said nothing. He wound a silken cord around her neck.

The horned moon, melon-colored, bloated as it neared the horizon, seemed alive, malevolent, a mute, unforgiving witness to what was about to take place.

"The sex act," he said, "can often be cruel, brutal, inhuman. It can so easily become a weapon. Some speak of it as rape, not the act of love. But love and sex are so far apart that they're not in the same lexicon."

"Sometimes," Justine said, her lips opening. "Only sometimes."

Senjin looked directly into her eyes. "But sex is only interesting when it is used as a weapon," he said, thinking more about himself, about this moment, suspended in time, than he was about the missing emeralds.

There was blood on his hands, blood in his nostrils. The proximity to death, the act of killing, made him feel more alive than ever, close to the edge where eternal mystery reigns, where the end becomes the means to controlling the destiny of others, and in so doing, of ensuring his own destiny.

He began to tighten the cord around Justine's neck.

"You look like someone I should avoid at all costs," Kusunda Ikusa said, eyeing Killan Oroshi as the Pack Rat began to record. They were in Ikusa's office in the Nippon Keio Building in Nishi-Shinjuku.

Killan laughed. "I always try to read your mind, if not your heart."

He swung his chair around to face her. "Every once in a while it occurs to me that I should kill you before you have a chance to destroy me."

"Perhaps one day you'll try," Killan said, apparently unfazed. "It would be fun to play that game with you."

Ikusa scowled. "Death is no game, Killan. No matter what I do, I can't seem to make you understand that."

"Oh, I understand, all right," she said. "I just don't give a shit."

"One day," Ikusa said, "you'll see that it's the same thing."

Killan Oroshi dropped her coat onto Ikusa's desk, took a chair near him. She was facing the large window behind his desk, and she said, "Tokyo is like the sister I always wanted and never had. I don't think I could survive without her wildly beating heart: the postpunks strutting their stuff in Ueno, the eternal electronics bazaar in Akihabara, the city of neon signs and deified symbols that mean nothing at all. Japan is the land of the empty hand, of the primitive, the sexual throbbing just beneath the obsessively ordered surface. Welcome to the future: the postatomic society."

Kusunda Ikusa watched her with the gravity of an incumbent politician observing his rival's election campaign. "It is a pity you were born a woman," he said. "You have such a male mind, and worse for you, a man's ambition."

"Ambition—or the lack of it—is my father's ruination," Killan said. "I have to make up for that lack. He never would be dependent on you if he'd had an ounce of conviction. He let others talk him into deals that destroyed Nakano's reserves. Then his only recourse to bankruptcy and seppuku was Nami."

"He could count himself lucky that Nami's Chiyoda Central Bank stepped in, lending Nakano Industries enough capital to get itself back on its feet."

"With *your* policies implemented by *your* officers."

Ikusa shrugged. "You yourself have recounted the bad deals."

"Not my father's fault!" she cried. "Others made those decisions."

"Sometimes, it's possible to forget just how young you are," Ikusa said. "Then you make a naive statement like that. One would almost think you love your father, rather than hate him. He was the chairman of Nakano, Killan. His was the ultimate responsibility for all decisions implemented by the company."

"You ruined Nakano. Broke it into fragments."

"Did you expect us to throw good money into a situation that was fast deteriorating? We had to protect our investment. That meant getting rid of the old regime, installing a new one."

"Handpicked by Nami."

"We knew what we wanted of Nakano when your father came to us," Ikusa said. "It was a business deal, plain and simple."

Killan laughed. "There's nothing plain and simple when it comes to Nami."

Again Ikusa shrugged. "Think what you will. The outcome will be good for you. I promised you a position of importance within Nakano in exchange for your help."

"But I don't want that." Killan got up, stood in front of Ikusa. Though she was dwarfed by his bulk, she was not overwhelmed by it. On the contrary, by the way in which Ikusa gave her his attention, her eminence seemed to grow within the confines of the office. "I want to be inside Chiyoda."

Kusunda Ikusa laughed. It was a heavy, rumbling thing not so much different than the sound presaging an earthquake.

Killan's expression appeared cast in granite. "It is a mistake to mock me," she said.

"Oh, Killan, I do not mock you." Ikusa wiped his eyes with a sausage-like finger. "I am merely astounded by the scope of your ambition. Every time I think I've calculated your limit, you step past it."

"I'm only making the logical choice," she said. "Nakano is nothing. Not now, anyway. It's a shell that Nami has filled up. It doesn't interest me. Why should it? Chiyoda is where all the money, all the action's at.

Chiyoda, as a central bank, owns many conglomerates because it holds their purse strings. Chiyoda is where the power resides, and I want in."

Kusunda Ikusa ran a finger along the line of her jaw. "Even though you speak like an adult, in some matters you are only a child," he said at last. "I can't fault your mind. But you must accept that there's more information than you or even your father know." He grunted. "Now that the merger of Nakano and Sphynx has been effected, we have moved into our end phase. The shell of Nakano will begin to fill up, not with personnel, but with intelligence, the greatest intelligence-gathering network the world has ever seen. And it all emanates from what you quite rightly call the shell.

"Nakano is research and development, that is what we left when we began to dismantle it as Chiyoda's money began to be used. We used your father's company as bait, Killan. Even he never understood.

"We wanted—needed—Tanzan Nangi's Sphynx technology. But how to get it? Nangi had made too many fail-safe provisions against a takeover; he could not be coopted, the damnable man is incorruptible. We had to catch him unawares. So we set the Nakano shell with its legendary research and development department as bait. Then I applied pressure on Nangi.

"The result is the merger between Nakano and Sphynx. Nangi believes he will exercise certain options to take over Nakano. He wants their R and D as much as we want Sphynx. But he won't get them. Instead, we'll own Sphynx, and that will be the end of Nangi. The warrants he will exercise are worthless because, as of a week ago, the R and D department was moved from Nakano Industries into a semidormant subsidiary not covered by the warrants. That was all right with Nangi because as far as he knows, the subsidiary owns only rusting refineries in Kobe."

The Pack Rat's hands were trembling. Ikusa had set a trap for Nangi all along! He double-checked his recorder to make sure he was getting every word they spoke. He wanted to get out of there immediately, get this information to Nangi, but something made him pause, his sense that Killan Oroshi was more than either he or Kusunda Ikusa knew. She had a part to play in this drama, and he was determined to discover what it was.

Kusunda Ikusa laughed. "Be patient, Killan. Be content with the post I have secured for you at Nakano. You'll find an outlet there for all your restless energy. Chiyoda will always be there. Besides, isn't there a risk? I wonder what your revolutionary friends would say when they found out where you'd be working. No doubt they'd believe you'd been coopted by the establishment."

"Fuck them," Killan said. "They've become boring, anyway. They're little people with minds as dogmatic as those in the establishment they hate so much—the same establishment that feeds and houses them, I might add. Of course, they don't recognize the irony of that—or the hollowness of their so-called philosophy. They want to bring down the establishment by violent means, but what do they mean to replace it with? They can't tell you because they don't know."

"You're so young," Ikusa said, "to understand so much."

"We're both young, Kusunda. That's *our* curse, isn't it? Another thing to bind us together so we can gather the courage to ride the dragon's back."

"Come here." Ikusa gestured.

"Not yet," Killan said. "Be patient." Mocking him. "I want what I want, Kusunda."

"I cannot get you inside Chiyoda," Ikusa said. "Not yet."

"All right. I can accept that. What I can't accept is a shitty publicity job at Nakano."

Kusunda Ikusa sighed. "What would make you happy?"

"For the time being? Though it's a secret to the outside world, I know the emphasis you're putting on new product development. That's the new thrust of Nakano—you want to go head to head with Sato International. A formidable task, since Sato is number one in its fields of electronics, computers, and chip manufacture. I think you're going to need all the help you can get. I want to be involved in the battle."

"But Killan, you are no scientist."

"No, but I know how to reach people. If I can work with the Nakano R and D staff, I can devise the best ways to market Nakano's arsenal of upcoming products."

Ikusa thought for a moment. "Your suggestion has merit," he said at length. "I will take it up with Nami."

"Which means you'll set it up," she said.

"You give me credit for wielding more power than I do," Ikusa said, but he was chuckling, obviously pleased.

"You know I'm right." Killan slipped onto his lap. The chair squealed beneath their combined weight as slowly it turned. Ikusa held the girl to him, his face lost in her hair.

In this position, the Pack Rat could look directly into Killan's face. He saw that her eyes were open, burning with a hatred so intense that it made him shudder. And then he understood that it was not hatred of Killan's father that he saw filling her eyes, but her hatred of Kusunda

Ikusa. She was still the dangerous revolutionary at heart, despite the convincing lies, the show of disaffection.

He remembered Ikusa's words, *Every once in a while it occurs to me that I should kill you before you have a chance to destroy me.* The Pack Rat now knew what Kusunda Ikusa obviously did not: this was Killan Oroshi's goal.

In Mariko's bleak dressing room at The Silk Road, Tomi said to Nangi, "This is where she was found, where she was tortured, raped, and ultimately killed."

Nangi crossed the room with some difficulty. It was late, and his leg was giving him some pain. "Right below this network of pipes?"

"Yes."

"The murder occurred some months ago."

"Almost ten. But it seems nothing much has changed since then. The girls are superstitious. No one's willing to use this dressing room now."

Tomi watched as he looked upward, something she had never done. He seemed to be examining the pipes.

"Would you do me a favor?" he asked. "Get down on the floor in approximately the same position in which you found Mariko."

Tomi did as he asked. To do so she had to slither herself between his legs.

Nangi said, "Was there any evidence that Mariko was either tortured or raped elsewhere in this room before being dragged over here?"

"None," Tomi said. "It all happened here, where we are."

Nangi nodded, as if satisfied with something. He tapped a point on a horizontal pipe with his cane, extended the cane down until the tip almost touched her. "This point is just about where your neck is. You are more or less the same height Mariko was, aren't you?"

"Yes."

"I don't remember seeing any neck bruises in the photos of Mariko's corpse."

"You've got an excellent memory," Tomi said, impressed all over again. "There weren't any."

Nangi moved the cane over, began tapping the pipe rhythmically now. "It is also approximately where the neck of the person who tortured and murdered Mariko would be when he was raping her."

"That's logical," Tomi said. She was at a loss as to where this was leading.

Nangi had his free hand beneath the pipe. He kept tapping the pipe with the head of his cane, then pulled up a chair, lowered himself into it.

Tomi sat up and he poured what was in his hand into hers. Tomi looked at it. It was rust. She looked up at Nangi. "So the pipe is rusty. That's only normal for a dump like this."

"Exactly," Nangi said, "but come here. Look at the spot that was just above your neck."

Tomi rose, stood on tiptoe. "There's no rust there."

"The only spot on the pipe where that's so," Nangi said.

Tomi turned to him. "Do you know what this means?"

"I'm afraid I'm getting to know this murderer far better than I'd like to."

"What on earth do you mean?"

"I've made the connection between Dr. Hanami's and Mariko's deaths," Nangi said. "To understand, you must recall the note found on the unfortunate girl's body."

" 'This could be your wife.' "

"Yes. I told you I thought it was a warning. Now I know it to be a warning for Dr. Hanami. He was being blackmailed by the tanjian, the *dorokusai*."

"Are you telling me that this tanjian who attacked me and Mr. Linnear in Dr. Hanami's office is the same person who murdered Mariko?"

"Tortured, raped, and murdered her, to use your own words," Nangi said. "Yes, that's precisely what I'm telling you."

"But how could you possibly know that?"

"This told me." Nangi tapped the shiny spot on the horizontal pipe. "This was made by a rope, weighted at one end, abrading the metal, flaking off the rust." Tomi remembered the line buried in the forensic report about flecks of rust found on some of Mariko's wounds, specifically around her upper torso. "The *dorokusai* will use a specific methodology, self-asphyxiation, during the sex act."

"But there's no such term as self-asphyxiation," Tomi pointed out. "Long before death, the autonomous nervous system will kick in. The person's grip on the rope will loosen and he will continue to breathe."

"Oh, yes, true," Nangi said. "But even before that happens, the carbon dioxide buildup in the *dorokusai* will bring him close enough to death for him to achieve orgasm."

"It's disgusting."

"It's part of his training. He practices it regularly—not only during the sex act—until it becomes as basic as *aiki taiso* in aikido," Nangi said. "It is another area in which the tanjian are taught to attack the Void."

Tomi hardly heard Nangi now. Something had caught in her mind. She fought to bring it to the surface, but it slipped away from her and was gone.

Nangi, watching the intensity of her expression, wanted to ask her what was on her mind, decided to observe instead.

In a moment there was a knock on the door. Tomi opened it. The owner-manager of The Silk Road stood in the dim light of the busy hallway.

"Back after so long, Detective? This is a surprise. I thought the case had been closed," the man said, bowing with exaggerated humility. "Can I be of service in some way?"

Tomi stepped back, beckoned him inside.

He looked around the room, taking inventory, as if needing to assure himself that they had not appropriated anything. He was a thin, weasely individual with bad breath and an obsequious manner.

Tomi had taken an immediate dislike to him, and nothing about her subsequent relationship with him had changed her mind. In fact, as she studied his anxious face now, a door clicked open in her mind. She began to suspect that there might be something here that she had overlooked, or that had been deliberately hidden from her. Now she thought that Nangi's presence might give her a chance to find out.

"I'd like to ask you a few questions," Tomi said.

"Again?" The weasel made washing motions with his hands. "But of course." He frowned. "But after all this time I can't imagine what it is you expect to find."

"This is Tanzan Nangi," Tomi said, ignoring him. "He's a professor of psychological criminology at Todai." She meant Tokyo University. "He's begun studying the case. Professor Nangi has developed a theory concerning the case that he would like to try out."

She waited until the weasel's oily eyes flicked from Nangi back to her. "How long have you been managing The Silk Road?"

"Six years," the weasel said. "But you already know this, Detective."

"This is for the professor's benefit," she assured him. "And is that the same amount of time that you've owned the club?"

"No, I bought it seventeen months later. But you already know—"

"How did you originally obtain financing for this establishment?"

"But this is all old ground, Detective." The weasel's hands were working overtime, washing themselves. "I obtained a loan from a local bank. As collateral, I put up the assets of my small sales business."

"How long was the dancer, Mariko, working here?"

"Three years, almost," the weasel said. He addressed Nangi now. "She was quiet, a hard worker. And the patrons liked her. She never missed a show, never complained. I have a daughter who gave me more trouble than Mariko ever did."

The three of them waited in the silence of the tiny ferroconcrete room, as small as a closet, as large as a tomb of the wealthy. The muffled rhythmic thump of the electronic bass, the pulsing of an evil heart, was a constant reminder of where they were.

When Tomi could no longer tolerate the oppressive sense of despair inhabiting the room like a *kami*, she said to the weasel, "That will be all."

The weasel looked stricken. "I thought—I mean, I was hoping to witness the development of the professor's theory. After all, Mariko worked for me. She was like family."

Tomi controlled a desire to spit in the weasel's face. She said, "We'll call you if we need you."

When they were alone, Nangi said, "What was that with the professor from Todai all about?"

"I'm not sure," Tomi said. "A hunch, maybe. You stay here, see what you can uncover. I want to see what that weasel's up to. Something in his face when he saw you made me suspicious."

"Haven't you already run a check on him?" Nangi asked.

"Yes, and I found nothing in the police computer. Still, when I saw how he reacted just now, I decided to put him to a test. It's simple, almost crude, but maybe it worked."

She slipped out of the room, feeling an uncomfortable weight lift from her chest. She moved quickly down the warren of corridors. By now she knew her way almost as well as did the girls who worked here.

At the weasel's office she put her ear to the door, but with the muffled thump-thump-thump of the amplified bass she could hear nothing.

She tried the knob but the door was locked. It required nothing more than a paper clip bent just the right way to pop it.

Tomi took a deep breath, swung the door open wide. She saw the weasel on the phone, made a dash across the room. His eyes opened wide and his instant of hesitation was enough to allow her to lunge across his littered desk, grab the receiver before he had a chance to hang up.

"Who were you calling?" Tomi snapped.

The weasel said nothing. His face was pale. She pinned him where he sat behind his desk.

"*Moshi,*" she said into the mouthpiece, but she could hear nothing. She put the line on hold, punched open a second line, dialed the telephone company maintenance shop, gave them her name, rank, and authorization number, told them what she wanted to know.

Within five minutes a technician was back on the line. "The call that was just made from the number you gave me was to the Metropolitan Police."

The ensuing silence was so long that the technician said, "Hello? Sergeant, are you still there?"

"Yes," Tomi said hoarsely. "Yes." Gathering her wits. "Can you tell me which precinct?"

"That's a snap," the technician said. "Uchibori-dori headquarters, the main one." Tomi's offices.

Still in a daze, Tomi thanked the technician, put down the phone. She fought to center herself, but thoughts kept intruding. The weasel had clearly been nervous at her reappearance. And when she had introduced Nangi as a new player in the investigation, the weasel had become positively agitated. Then something he said hit her like a shot: *I thought the case had been closed.* How would he know that? Unless he had some contact with the Metro Police?

Tomi, staring hard at the weasel, said, "Who did you call?"

"My mother."

"Your mother works for the police?"

"Yeah. She's a cleaning lady. She mops out your latrines."

For a long moment Tomi did nothing. Then, in a lightning move, she snatched the weasel up by his lapels, slammed him against the back wall. Glass shattered in the window.

Tomi put her face so close to his, he had trouble focusing on her. "You're going to tell me," she said, "or you won't leave this room."

"Big words," the weasel said.

Tomi jammed him backward so hard he cried out. Blood began to seep out of his suit as the shards of jagged window glass punctured his skin.

"Tell me who you called!"

All at once the weasel began to weep. Sweat slid down the side of his face. "Oh, my God," he whimpered, "I can't. Don't you see, he'll kill me."

"He won't have a chance," Tomi said savagely. The glass sunk deeper into the weasel, and he gasped.

"All right," he said, twisting and moaning in pain. "But you'll have to protect me."

"Who? Tell me?"

"I demand protection!"

"You're in no position to demand anything," Tomi pointed out. "But

I'll see what I can do. Who did you call? Who were you going to tell about Professor Nangi?"

The weasel's eyes almost bugged out of his head. "It's not so easy, damnit!" he gasped. "The bastard's a division commander. He used to come here years ago when he had been assigned this district. He worked out a deal with me so I'd allow him access to my girls, so he could do— ow, God, that hurts!—so he could do what he wanted with them. I—I never—God—I never asked what he did. I didn't want to know. Then this *thing* with—oh, God!—Mariko happened and I was terrified. I didn't want to be implicated in her—"

"Are you telling me that a Metropolitan Police division commander tortured, raped, and murdered Mariko?" Tomi was aware that she was shouting. She didn't care.

The weasel nodded. "Y-yes."

Mariko, she thought, all your life you had no one. Now you have me. Your avenger.

"Who was it? Who killed her?" She was shaking him like a leaf. Bursts of adrenaline surged through her, powering her. And a glimpse into the flash of memory that had been eluding her: dim light, the tiny precinct closet, her body entangled with Senjin's. Her mouth opening onto his flesh. The taste of him and . . .

"Who killed Mariko? Tell me, you bastard, or I swear you won't walk out of this room alive!" A red haze behind her eyes, the memory, slippery as an eel, winking in and out of her consciousness. Nangi saying, *The dorokusai will use a specific methodology, self-asphyxiation, during the sex act. It's part of his training. He practices it regularly . . .*

"Who killed Mariko!" Working the weasel on the rack of the shattered glass fragments. The red haze deepening, Mariko, I have him for you, the memory surfacing, Senjin making love to her in the closet, she pulling aside his tie, unbuttoning his shirt so she could kiss his chest, the flesh of his neck abraded as if by a wound. A wound around his neck.

The dorokusai will use a specific methodology, self-asphyxiation. He practices it regularly . . .

A Metropolitan Police division commander was a tanjian, a *dorokusai*, and dear God, he seduced me in every way it is possible for a man to seduce a woman: he assigned me to a homicide case in which he committed the murder *and* coordinated the police work in its aftermath; he used me as a stalking horse to keep track of Nicholas Linnear when it would arouse suspicion for him to do it himself; he took me like an animal in the office, where even a kiss between colleagues is unthinkable. He made me break all society's rules, all my own rules as well. He made me feel elated

and debased at the same time. He used his dark erotic magic on me to
penetrate my mind and my flesh, to suck himself into me, to use me over
and over again. And I was powerless, as powerless as Mariko must have
been.

Humiliation, rage, fear all combined inside her.

"Who killed Mariko!"

What he did to me. The abraded flesh of his neck. What he did to her.

"Who killed Mariko!"

Used like dolls made of putty he could mold into any shape, Mariko
and I and how many others? My God, how many more?

"Who killed Mariko!"

"Omukae!" The weasel shrieking at her in a potent mixture of terror
and relief. "Commander Senjin Omukae!"

When Killan left the Nippon Keio Building some hours after she had
entered it, there was no question as to what the Pack Rat's next move
was going to be. He followed her. She was the key, he was sure of it, the
enigma whose solution would bring into perspective everything he had
heard up until now.

It was a moon-drenched night, the air unnaturally clear and calm after
the days of rain, gloom, and suspended petrochemical ash. The Pack Rat
encountered no difficulty in tailing Killan as she went across town into
Asakusa, to the Scoundrel's *usagigoya.*

This time the Pack Rat would not be shut out. He had run a check on
the Scoundrel, had found to his intense curiosity that he was a member of
Nakano Industry's research and development department. He was also
Killan Oroshi's friend. What were the two of them up to? It seemed clear
now that Killan had wanted to be at Nakano, not Chiyoda, all along.
Why? The Pack Rat meant to find out.

He scouted the hallway. On one side of the Scoundrel's apartment was
a stairwell, on the other, another tiny apartment. The Pack Rat chose the
stairwell first, finding the common wall with the Scoundrel apartment.
He knelt down, got out his miniature listening equipment. He got nothing. He put his hand against the ferroconcrete of the stairwell wall. There
must be a ton of structural iron in there, he thought, blocking transmission.

He gave it up, went back into the hallway. He listened with his ear, at
the door to the adjacent apartment, then with the electronic equipment.
Silence.

It took him fifteen seconds to get through the lock.

Cautiously, he pushed the door open just wide enough to allow him to slither through sideways. Darkness and the smell of plaster, fresh paint, kerosene. There was debris on the floor, which he could see in the moonlight filtering through the blindless window had been taken down to the rough concrete underflooring. There were no lights, no electricity. Obviously the place was deserted, awaiting construction.

The Pack Rat went to work. Crouching beside the common wall with the adjacent apartment, he put his electronic "ears" on.

Immediately he heard Killan's voice, very loud, filled with the harsh sibilants of the "ears." ". . . telling you, life wouldn't be the same without you, Scoundrel. You're the only person who really sees me. All the women I know despise me, and all the men want to fuck me. Except you. You want to listen to what I have to say."

"And *then* I want to fuck you." It was a male voice, no doubt belonging to the platinum-haired Scoundrel.

Killan laughed. "You're the only one who can make me laugh, you know that? It's a gift, like your genius with computers."

As he had done in the Nami offices, the Pack Rat was taping all this, avidly preserving Killan's aural history as if that would allow him to capture her like a butterfly in a bell jar.

"Look at all this equipment," Killan said. "I sure hope it's going to do us some good. Are you sure this virus-thing is as powerful as you've said?"

"You bet. More. MANTIS, the Manmade Nondiscriminatory Tactical Integrated-circuit Smasher. Not a virus-thing, a borer," the Scoundrel said. "But MANTIS is a unique kind of borer virus. It only attacks computer software programs with virus-prevention encryptions. It actually cannibalizes the software's own security systems, mutating them so that they turn on themselves. The deeper the encryption, the harder my borer works. I've told you, MANTIS is very sophisticated, very experimental stuff."

The Pack Rat heard Killan's laugh. "Listen to you. You're a genius in the lab. But in the real world, forget it. When you first told me about this, you weren't even going to get a piece of the action."

"That's right," the Scoundrel said, sounding defensive. "I was told the MANTIS project was strictly for governmental use."

"And I said, fuck the government," Killan said. "I said, let's take this shit and go private. We'll make a fortune. Do you know how many Western conglomerates will deliver a year's assets in order to get an edge on their competitors? Jesus, the American market alone for this virus will make us millionaires!"

"If we live long enough," the Scoundrel said. "Which we might not. I'm not so sure we're doing the right thing, Killan. This is the real world. Besides, MANTIS isn't perfected yet."

"Real world. My God, listen to us!" Killan said. "Next thing we'll be discussing is getting married, having kids, which brand of diapers and rash ointment to buy. We'll be dead! Or something even worse: entombed by *kata*, the rigid rules of our society."

"Ah, Killan the eternal revolutionary," the Scoundrel said in a gently chiding voice. "Revolutions are great to think about. But they don't exist, not in our world. Anyway, there were only two revolutions that meant anything, one in America, the other in France. The others were jokes, parodies that exchanged one form of dictatorship for another. They don't even deserve the name."

The Pack Rat was paying no attention to the talk of revolution; he let his machines soak up the conversation for him. He was fully concentrated on the fact that this friend of Killan Oroshi's, this platinum-haired postpunk computer genius, the Scoundrel, who worked for Nakano Industries, Killan's father's company, was working on a supercomputer virus. Just the kind that had attacked Sato International's computer banks. Could it have been the Scoundrel's MANTIS being tested out? he asked himself. He knew there were tons of viruses being born daily, but according to Mickey, the expert to whom he had given the record of the virus's attack, this particular one was a mole virus, not a destroyer like most others. Was MANTIS that kind? The Scoundrel had called it a borer. Did that mean it was meant as a communication device? The Pack Rat did not yet know. On the other hand, the Scoundrel was just the kind of genius Mickey had described when she had talked with the Pack Rat about the virus's creator.

The Pack Rat had a weird sensation of déjà vu, as if he had come full circle: Nangi and the Scoundrel's MANTIS; Nangi and Ikusa; Ikusa and Ken Oroshi; Ken Oroshi, Ikusa, and Nangi; Ikusa and Killan Oroshi; Killan Oroshi and the Scoundrel. There seemed a connection to be made in the odd and disparate interlocking of relationships, but, maddeningly, he could not see it. He knew it was there, though, and his heart beat faster. Nangi will know, he thought. He knew he had to get all of this to Nangi right away.

He was concentrating so hard that he at first failed to recognize the blossoming geometric shape cast upon the wall in front of him. Then, with a start, he saw that it was a lozenge of light that could only be made by the hallway light coming into the apartment through the front door.

But he had been careful to close the door behind him when he first entered.

The lozenge of light winked out. Darkness, again, mitigated by blue moonlight. And the Pack Rat knew that someone was in the apartment with him.

He did not move; he scarcely breathed. He slowly pulled the "ears" from around his head, letting the recorder continue monitoring the conversation from the next apartment through its umbilical suctioned to the wall.

His immediate environment was silent save for the tiny noises all apartment buildings manufacture, the sounds of the nighttime street filtered through the cracks between the window sash and the glass. Nothing else.

And yet . . .

The brief crackle of newspaper underfoot, the sound as explosive to his ears as that of a match being lighted in a warehouse full of gasoline.

Hurriedly, the Pack Rat placed his "ears" against the wall, covered the paraphernalia with debris. He moved away from it as a mother wren will from her chicks when she senses danger is near. Her instincts tell her to lure the danger away from her progeny; keeping them safe is her first priority. So, too, with the Pack Rat's recording of events and meetings, the shadow world that Tanzan Nangi had hired him to penetrate and neutralize. He knew that he had to protect his evidence at all costs.

As he moved stealthily across the apartment, he withdrew a dagger with an eight-inch blade whose shape he had designed on the computer. It was thin enough to be easily concealed beneath clothes, yet wide enough to be lethal even on a cut that was slightly off the mark.

Shadows played along the walls and the floor, across the humped shapes of discarded lathe, dried spackling compound, and wallboard, adderlike tangles of wires, exposed phone lines.

The Pack Rat heard it coming long before he saw it. The whistle of air being displaced, and the small hairs at the back of his neck stood up. He knew that sound, and he curled into a ball, launching himself forward, *toward* the direction of the attack, knowing that this was his only hope now.

What the Pack Rat recognized was the sound a *tetsubo* makes when it is wielded. A moment later, as if to confirm his suspicion, the area of the concrete floor on which he had been standing, exploded in a choking shower of particles and dust.

Tetsubo-jutsu was a highly specialized form of the martial arts primarily because the *tetsubo* itself—a solid iron bar, its working end covered with iron studs—was so heavy. The weapon had been developed centuries ago for armored warfare. A warrior would wade into the enemy, swinging the iron bar, opening up their armor or breaking the legs of the mounted enemies' horses.

Nowadays, tetsubo-jutsu was used for only one reason: to crush an opponent. There were no halfway measures with such a weapon.

The Pack Rat came out of his curled position, struck immediately upward. It was as if he had encountered a mountain. It took an exceptionally strong man, an enormous man, to effectively use the *tetsubo*. Without having seen his face, the Pack Rat knew who had followed him from the Nami offices into this vacant apartment: Kusunda Ikusa.

The Pack Rat's blow was deflected, and he found himself thrown hard across the room. He hit the wall with a thud, bounced up immediately. Even so, he could hear the *tetsubo* humming in the air as it headed toward him. He ducked, and a chunk of the wall splintered, showering him in biting bits of lathe and plaster.

To avoid the *suki*, the weaknesses in defense that could result from tetsubo-jutsu, Ikusa had to strike at the Pack Rat quickly and repeatedly. This could be tiring, even for such a sumo as Ikusa.

But the Pack Rat knew that he could not keep up the pace of evasion in such a constricted space. Eventually he would duck the wrong way or make a misstep and Ikusa would crush his skull.

Therefore, he did the only thing he could think of—he got as near to Ikusa as he could manage. He theorized that the iron club would lose much of its effectiveness at such close quarters.

Ikusa's free arm came up, and the Pack Rat batted it aside, struck out with his knife, heard the sound of material being slit, felt the blade bury itself into flesh, and he knew he had a chance.

Ikusa dropped the *tetsubo*, made a grab for the Pack Rat. The Pack Rat was ready for him, drove an elbow inward in a powerful *atemi*. He whirled, crouching down, beginning his circular entering movement, and got his left hand on the iron club. He began the aikido immobilization *jo-waza*, turning outward, back the way he had come, feeling Ikusa's weight coming forward, beginning to unbalance as the Pack Rat used his momentum against him, and the Pack Rat thought, Now I have a chance.

He slid his left leg forward, shifting the axis upon which his body rotated, readying the completion of the *jo-waza* that would hurl Kusunda Ikusa's enormous weight to the floor. At that moment a tremendous blow caught him in the side of his head.

He staggered, his vision blurred. He struck out blindly with his blade, missed, overcompensated, spun helplessly around.

Then he heard the whistle, actually saw the iron bar coming at him, filling his vision. He tried to move his head, but nothing seemed to work.

A crack like thunder from the edge of the world. Time, like existence, as fragile as a candle's flame, was snuffed out.

When Senjin touched Justine's belly with the flat of his hand, he said to her, "You're pregnant, aren't you?"

He might have said, You're dead, aren't you? In fact, for the first split instant, that was what Justine thought he had said, but then she understood that what she was hearing was an echo of her own inner voice.

"Oh, God," she said, collapsing against him, "I lied."

Senjin let go of the silken cord, held her as delicately as if she were as fragile-boned bird with a broken wing. He saw the moonlight, slow and thick, falling across her face, illuminating one by one her features: mysterious eyes, strong nose, high cheekbones, full, partly-open lips; her hair in the semidarkness a shroud rich with promise, below which her breasts rose and fell with her rapid, shallow breathing. The dense moonlight cast purple shadows, creating two other figures on the porch, elongated, humanoid but certainly not human, winged but certainly not angels.

This light had come a long way, slipping through the vast wasteland between the stars, a prehistoric light, though of what alien civilization's prehistory, it was impossible to say. But Senjin recognized this light and the power its properties of immense distance and time represented.

"I've lied to my husband all this time, and I lied to you when I said that I went to see Honi because I hated myself. I mean, I *did* hate myself. That much is true. But that's not all of it, not nearly. I was—how can I put this so you'll understand? I didn't want to grow up. I was afraid of growing up. I had lived my life with a mother sapped of life and of strength. It seemed clear to me that in giving birth to me and to my older sister, my mother had given us the juice of her flesh along with her milk.

"She was dried up, desiccated, devoid of zest. She had bequeathed that to us, had used up her quota of youth and gusto in becoming a mother. She was old before her time, lined, forever tired, forever plagued by vague maladies—headaches, backaches, cramps—that often prevented her from participating in even the simplest family requirements. More often than not she had her meals in her room, which by then was separate from where my father slept—she claimed the weight of his body on the mattress caused her calves to spasm in the middle of the night.

"She rarely attended parties or family gatherings, never made it to our graduations from high school and college, but sent two trusted servants in her stead, as if believing that quantity would make up for her absence. Funerals were, of course, out of the question—they were too emotionally taxing—and she never went near a hospital until the day she died.

"It was as if, along with her drying up, her giving us her life fluids, her capacity to take on obligation had dissolved.

"This, to me, was adulthood—all I could expect in the coming years. Can you imagine how I felt when I thought about having a baby of my own? All I could see in my mind's eye was the image of my mother, gray-faced, bedridden, racked by the kinds of aches and pains women twice her age only start to experience."

" 'You're not your mother,' Honi assured me. It wasn't enough. I worked hard to want to be an adult, a mother, but it wasn't easy. My God, I tortured myself over it for years. I shed so many tears, you wouldn't believe how many. Finally I thought I had it down. I thought I knew that I wouldn't turn into my mother. But then I came here to Japan with my husband. I got pregnant and my little daughter died. I got through the hurt and the guilt just like an adult. I was proud of myself. I stood by my husband when he was in difficulty.

"Then I got pregnant again and everything burst apart. My whole life seemed turned upside down. It was as if I was back in Honi's office, terrified of becoming my mother. I don't know whether I want this baby. I don't know whether I can handle the responsibility. I feel as if I *am* turning into my mother, that I'm simply incapable of doing it—being a mother—and I'm so ashamed and disgusted with myself I can't stand it. And yet I don't want to be like my mother. I don't!"

Senjin, holding her, feeling her racked with sobs, was mute. I hated my mother, too, he thought. Only my sister knew that, and she didn't understand until I explained it to her, not with words, but with actions. My sister is a stubborn, strong-willed woman. So much so that she became used to getting what she wanted. Except from me. I tried to cure her of her excesses. Perhaps I was at least partially successful. But I had to stop correcting her. I saw that if I went too far she would break, rather than bend. I would not change her spirit, though that spirit is imperfect, dangerous even. She is my sister, not my mother. I would have changed my mother if I had been given a chance. My mother, like this woman, was weak, deficient. A cure, no matter how radical, would have been good for her in the end, anyone who knew her could see that.

I think my whole life has been an effort to be strong in everything I do or say or think. I cannot allow myself even a momentary weakness, it's too much to bear, the thought that I'm carrying some of her inside me.

Can weakness be inherited in the genes or passed like poison through the umbilical?

With Justine's lips against his neck, her breasts hard against his muscled chest, her thighs against his leg, Senjin thought he felt nothing, just as he felt nothing when he stared down at the nude body of Mariko, the dancer at The Silk Road, just as he felt nothing when he had sucked the innocence out of Tomi, using Tau-tau to seduce her in the office, just as he felt nothing when he had entered the myriad women who had populated his past like signposts in a distant terrain. Without thinking of Haha-san, he had never felt even a fleeting atom of carnal desire at the touch of female flesh.

He had intellectually savored each coupling with the avidity of a cryptographer tackling a new code. For the rest, the wolf in heat throwing his shaggy head back and howling at the night, there was nothing.

Then he heard, with a start, Justine whispering in his ear, "Save me. Oh, save me," and he began to tremble with despicable desire just as if she had said, Take me.

Because he thought of someone else: his sister, with whom he shared everything of importance: strength, sin, punishment, the terror of weakness, destiny. And a longing that was pain swept over him.

Justine was lying so close to him that he could feel the press of her heavy breasts, feel the accelerated beating of her heart. Her face was upraised to his. Starlight picked out highlights in her hair, the waning moonlight coated the soft flesh of her neck.

That was when, with eyes of copper, Senjin again wrapped the silken cord around Justine's neck, jerking her against him. He captured her hips with his powerful thighs. She tried to cry out but could not. He saw her teeth, white in the moonlight. He imagined blood on them, an animal's mouth thrown back and howling at the soft moon, and knew that he wanted to—*needed to*—make her as much like him as possible, to merge her being into his as he had pathetically tried to do and failed with Mariko when he devoured her susurrus at the moment of her death, as he had tried to do with the other women he had been with. To possess them in as full a meaning of the word as was imaginable.

Because he could no longer possess his sister in that unique way that, for him, filled the dread place inside him where even he would never venture, where pleasure was pain.

"Pleasure and pain, yin and yang, the light and the dark," Senjin whispered hoarsely. "This is the world view, the false reality. Kshira showed me the truth: that pain and pleasure can be one, the width of a circle, and when they are, the result is otherworldly, leading to a state beyond even ecstasy." His breath hard and hot on her cheek. "I promised you an example. I want you to understand. Now . . ."

Senjin pulled up her skirt, roughly ripped her underclothes. The terror emanated from Justine's wide-open eyes, filled her face like a river swollen to a torrent from spring rains. Her terror exuded from her pores like sweat, its peculiar scent making his nostrils twitch, his mouth water.

Senjin was so hard that he could barely feel his member. It was stiff, it was numb; he thought of Haha-san. Now not only Justine. But his sister as well.

His sister and possession.

The cord around Justine's neck was making the white flesh turn red and raw. Her neck began to swell as it bruised, as the blood filled it, as he pulled the cord tighter, as it was further abused. The sight made Senjin dizzy with desire and he almost collapsed into her.

He pulled on the cord, cutting off more oxygen, and her head went back, lolling as her eyes rolled up. Drool spilled from the corner of her mouth, her hips lurched inward against him, against the quivering tip of him.

Senjin was overcome by desire. Never before in his life had its advance been so swift, so overpowering. He was delirious with sensation, about to thrust himself into her when, unbidden, he remembered that he needed her in another way, just as he had once needed Haha-san, and his hot, desperate seed spilled out of him in a paroxysm of need.

Senjin grunted like an animal. His head fell forward onto her shoulder. With a sob he released the cord from around Justine's neck, seeing not her but his sister, Haha-san, his sister, they were all fused in his mind because he needed all three, hated himself for that need.

Then the three images became unstuck, drifted apart. Senjin tenderly kissed the already blackening welt, licking it with his tongue, tasting the salt on her skin, already associating it with her wound, the pain he had inflicted on her.

He held her head as she had before, to take away the pain. "You must tell me," he whispered hoarsely, "I must know what the ninja did with the emeralds he took out of the box." But he could tell that Justine had not heard him, and he put his lips against her ear, said into it, "Think of the ninja, think of your husband in his workout room, with the box in his hands. Now he has the emeralds, you can see them sparkling in the light. What do you see him doing next? Tell me."

Justine, her eyes only half open, her mind benumbed with Tau-tau, said, "I remember . . . something . . ."

"What? *What!*" But Senjin could see it was no good, she would not be able to dredge it up just yet. Not yet.

Staring at her white, sweat-slicked face in the moonlight.

But soon.

Leaving her there, untied in the moonlight, freed, but only for a time.

Shisei, dressed ever so fashionably in the Louis Feraud suit that Douglas Howe had bought her at Saks Jandel, locked the door to her borrowed brownstone just off Foxhall Road in Georgetown, skipped down the steps to the waiting black Jaguar sedan.

Branding himself was behind the wheel. Although he employed a driver to get him crosstown in rush-hour traffic or out to the Pentagon while he was doing business in the backseat, he preferred on off hours to drive himself, taking pleasure in the purr and power of his own automobile.

"You look tremendous!" he said as she slid into the leather seat beside him. "I'll be proud of you."

"What have you planned for Howe?" Shisei asked nervously. "Or for us?"

Branding laughed, swinging out into the Washington twilight. "You must know General Dickerson, Howe's pet dog inside the Pentagon? Woof! Woof! Anyway, just about, oh, twenty minutes ago, while Howe was dressing for tonight's dinner, the general called him at home. But, you know, the funny thing is, there's a guy on my staff who does an amazingly accurate imitation of Dickerson's voice. In any case, whoever it was who called swore that there's a security leak at the Johnson Institute. This information surely set Howe to drooling with anticipation. Greedy people are predictable people.

"The general—or whomever it was—insisted that Howe meet him in the wilds of Maryland where—so Howe's been told—the information is being leaked."

Branding laughed again. "It'll take Howe about an hour and a half to get where he's been told to go—longer, even, since this is his chauffeur's night off and he has to drive himself. He'll wait there, oh, I'd say an hour or so, just to make sure he got the time right, that the general hasn't been detained somewhere. Then another ninety minutes back. By then the State dinner will be over."

It was almost eight o'clock, the worst of the rush hour had dissipated, and the monuments were just being lighted. It was a magical time of day, Branding thought. If you were in New York, you'd be on your way to a

Broadway show; in Paris, strolling down the Boulevard Haussmann to the Opera; in Tokyo, in Roppongi, taking in the fashion show on the street while on the way to a glittering dining spot.

Here in Washington they were heading for the seat of power: the White House. The thought never failed to set Branding's heart to pounding. He wondered whether one day he would sit in the Oval Office after having been elected to the nation's highest office. As he often reminded himself, that was one of the reasons he had gotten into politics in the first place.

He knew that with the success of the ASCRA bill, with the formidable array of strength he had been able to muster, he now had a shot at the next nomination, less than two years away.

"Cook," Les Miller, the chairman of the Republican Party, had told him last night, "I've never seen any one man impact the party the way you have. This bill is just the final touch. Even our most conservative sonsabitches are mighty impressed with you. They've told me privately that they've been aware of you for some years. By God, you've got their full attention now. We're all tired of the man in the White House. This party wasn't founded to be led by a man who's turned out to be more Democratic than most Democrats.

"I can tell you your last speech on the Senate floor had them spellbound. They saw in it, as I did, the new platform fundamentals to return us to being the party of hard, no-nonsense principle. It's not too early to begin thinking about running for the nomination. Right now organization is half the battle. The sooner you give us the go-ahead, the sooner I can throw the full weight of the party machine behind you and get the process going. That's how sure we are of you, Cook."

"Oh, God," Shisei said, "I've forgotten my bag. I always do that. I think it's deliberate. I hate evening bags."

"No problem," Branding said, making a U-turn. "Anyway, if we're late, it will create a bigger splash."

Shisei turned to look at him. "I thought that's exactly what you wanted to avoid."

"Look at yourself, darling," he said. "In that outfit, even a blind man would notice you." He shook his head as he pulled into the curb in front of her house. "Strategy is useless unless it can be changed. And I've changed mine." He saw her puzzled look, kissed her hard on the mouth. "Go on, get your bag. Otherwise you'll never get to see how this evening ends."

Shisei went up her steps, dug in her pocket for her key. She opened her front door and disappeared inside.

In the foyer she put the key in her pocket and removed her high-heel shoes. Then, on stockinged feet, she crept up the stairs to her bedroom.

The hallway on the second floor was dark. The door to her bedroom was ajar, just as she had left it, but a thick wedge of light streamed out into the hall.

Keeping to the shadows close to the mahogany banister, Shisei went silently past the half-open door without attempting to peer inside. Instead she went into the adjoining bedroom, which shared the huge, luxurious bathroom with her bedroom.

She entered her bedroom through the bath. She could look at the full length of the room in this way, saw the vanity closest to her, her evening bag sitting on its marble top, just where she had left it. She saw the drawers to the antique oak dresser piled hastily one atop the other, their contents strewn in a jumble across the Oriental scatter rugs and the polished oak floor.

David Brisling was rummaging in her closet, frantically pushing aside her hanging clothes. Soon, she knew, he would reach her shoes and, behind the carefully piled boxes, her computer, headphones, her entire cache of clandestine equipment.

She went across the room so silently that an animal would not have heard her. But in so doing, her shadow was thrown partway into the closet's interior.

Just as she came upon the figure, it turned. She saw the muzzle of the pistol and Brisling's face in the same instant.

Shisei ceded all conscious control of her body to Kshira: her mind emptied, to be filled with the Void, the sound-light continuum that was Kshira.

Her left foot blurred out and upward even as her upper torso twisted away. Her rigid toes struck the inside of Brisling's wrist at the vulnerable juncture where nerves and veins come together.

Brisling's hand went numb even as his brain, in shock from surprise, gave its sluggish command to his forefinger to pull the trigger.

The pistol flew out of his hand, and Shisei dropped down, cupped her hands and, jamming them under his chin, drove upward with strength emanating from her hips, her lower belly—her *hara*—forced upward into her shoulders, her arms.

Shisei shouted, one quick bloodcurdling cry—a *kiai*, a giving voice to the spirit, more than a battle cry, a martial art in its own right. At the same time, she shoved Brisling's head backward with such force that the top of his skull shattered against the edge of the closet door.

Only then, with the threat ended, did Kshira recede, did the Shisei familiar to Cotton Branding reappear. She blinked once and, within the space of a heartbeat, took in the entire scene, ran through her plan again in her mind. She recalled with delight Branding telling her where Howe would be tonight; it was perfect. Plausible deniability. She could find no flaw.

She picked up the phone, completed her preparations.

Four minutes later she was back in the Jaguar with Branding. "Sorry I was so long," she said a bit breathlessly.

"I was getting worried about you," Branding said, putting the car in gear. "I thought I heard something, I don't know what. I was just about to come in and get you."

"It was nothing." Shisei leaned across, kissed him on the mouth. "My boss called just as I was leaving. I had the answering machine on but I had to pick up." She put her hand on his thigh. "By the way, he says to thank you for taking me to this party. I wouldn't've gotten in otherwise, and I'm certain I can break some new ground with the people who'll be there."

"Good," Branding said, grinning. "Now you can say I've done my bit today for environmentalism."

"It's something, Cook. But don't think it's enough. It won't ever be enough until 'environmentalist' stops being a dirty word in American politics."

Outside the tinted windows northwest Washington, the Washington tourists saw, glittered like a million-dollar necklace. But Branding knew that for the magician's illusion it was. Hidden from sight was the poverty, the crime and unemployment running rampant in the predominantly black neighborhoods. While tuxedoed pols like himself gorged themselves nightly on fine food and power, the real Washington simmered and, like an unwatched kettle, threatened to boil over.

A cop car heading in the other direction, its cherry lights flashing, its siren screaming, gave physical weight to his thoughts.

But for this night, at least, Branding wanted to put all that out of his mind. "How did you get into being a lobby for the environmentalists, anyway?" he asked.

"Murder," Shisei said. She saw Branding looking at her from the corner of his eye. "Too many whales slaughtered by my people. Too many seals clubbed to death on the ice and the beaches. The dumping of hazardous wastes into our streams, rivers, and oceans. The senselessness and evil in greed was never more apparent to me. I wanted—I needed—to do something. It was important to me to know that what I was doing was making a difference."

Branding thought about Shisei's life, how she had been imprisoned, tortured, how Zasso, the mad artist, had attempted to remake her in the image of the demon woman. Branding thought mostly of how Zasso had failed, of how Shisei had overcome her past, becoming a strong-willed woman whose work *did* make a difference in the world. He realized then just how proud of her he was.

The State dinner was one of those affairs where protocol and diplomacy were the only acceptable currency. Branding had both of these to spare, and he was soon one of the few around whom knots of people congregated to listen, laugh, and be seen.

He kept an eye on Shisei as she drifted through the gilt and cream ballroom, a glass of champagne in one hand, talking to one diplomat after another, who listened intently to what she was telling them. They would nod sagely, smile, and in the end give her their cards as if delivering an offering on the altar of a goddess.

An hour after they arrived, Branding drew her aside. He winked. "Having a good time?" he asked.

"Successful," she said.

"I noticed." It was for Branding, too. All the ranking Republicans were in attendance, and they were never far from him, engaging him in conversation, always bringing up the ASCRA bill, pledging their support.

The only sour note was delivered by Tricia Hamilton, the wife of Bud Hamilton, the senator from Maryland, a good friend and often an ally of Branding's. Like a herald announcing the approach of a still distant army, Tricia arrived at Branding's side with a flourish.

"You're my escort into dinner," she said.

She wore a formal silk and crinoline dress that must have cost a fortune but made her look ten years older than her fifty-three years.

Her eyes flashed, and he could see her eyeing Shisei with the kind of predatory avidity raised to a high art by Washington wives.

"What a perfectly lovely girl," Tricia said in a tone that made it sound as if she had said, What a perfect little tart.

Branding laughed, in too good a mood to allow Tricia's bitchiness to disturb him. "She's smart, too," he said.

"I'll bet." Tricia smiled sweetly at him as they headed for the dining room. "That's an interesting suit she's wearing. A Louis Feraud, isn't it?"

"I have no idea," Branding said. "But I like it."

"Oh, so do I," Tricia said acidly. "Funny thing, though. It looks terribly familiar, and I *know* there aren't too many Louis Feraud suits around these parts. I mean, only Saks Jandel carries them hereabouts, and they only get in one in each size. I know because I was there just the other day trolling for a new outfit and, do you know, I believe I saw that very suit there." She pulled herself closer to Branding, hugging herself against him. "Yes, it *was* that suit. I'm sure of it." She looked into his face. "But, do you know, Cook, Senator Howe was buying it. Douglas didn't see me, I'm happy to report, he was in too much of a hurry. A repugnant little man, isn't he, Cook? The thought of him touching me sends shivers down my spine."

Branding said, "Despite what you say about Saks Jandel, that can't be the only Feraud suit in all of Washington. I don't know what you're getting at, Trish."

"Me? I'm just making small talk, Cook."

He tried not to let what Tricia Hamilton said bother him but, despite his best intentions, he found himself brooding over dinner. Afterward, he could not remember what he had eaten or what he had talked about with his dinner companions. The President made a speech, then the West German chancellor, but Branding paid them no attention.

In the car on the way home, he was so quiet that Shisei touched him, said, "Is anything the matter, Cook?"

He thought, then, about asking her where she had gotten the Louis Feraud suit. Had she bought it herself or had it been a gift? He almost did, but at the last instant bit back the words. The fact was that he did not want to hear her answer because the chances were it would be a lie.

"Nothing," he said.

What Tricia Hamilton had told him—her "small talk"—had rocked him. Tricia was a gossip only in the sense that she liked to talk about other people because it furthered her belief that knowing as many intimate things about the power pols put her in the center of things. But she only passed on verified gossip. She wisely let other Washington wives indulge in innuendo and semitruths.

What bothered Branding was that if Tricia said she saw Douglas Howe picking up Shisei's suit from Saks Jandel, that's exactly what happened.

At first he tried to think of an innocent explanation, but soon abandoned the idea as improbable and foolish. Then he began to work out the strategy behind Howe and Shisei as a team, and got nowhere. For the life of him, he could not imagine Shisei's personality meshing with Howe's. Something didn't feel right. Not unless Shisei was the greatest actress on earth.

He pulled up at her house but did not turn off the engine.

"Aren't you coming in?" Shisei asked.

"I don't think so. Not tonight."

In the almost silence of the engine purring there was a gulf between them that had not existed when the night began. The street was quite deserted. Arching streetlights cast pools of diffuse illumination at regular intervals. Shadows from the leaves on the elm trees fell across the long hood of the Jaguar.

Shisei put a hand on Branding's arm. "Cook, what is it? Your entire mood changed during dinner."

He closed his eyes for a moment. "I'm tired. I want to go home."

"Please, Cook," she said. "Come inside, if only for a moment. I can't bear the thought of the night ending here."

Branding waited a moment before turning off the ignition. Inside, Shisei went through the first floor turning on all the lights as a child will ask to be done when awakened by a nightmare. Branding watched her at this ritual with opaque eyes.

"Drink?"

"I'd rather not," Branding said. He had not sat down, was standing in the center of the living room.

"For God's sake, Cook, won't you tell me what you're thinking?"

"I don't know what I'm thinking," he said. "Not yet."

"You want to go," she said. "I can see it in your face. You can't wait to get out of here."

"It isn't like that at all."

"Don't lie to me," Shisei said.

Branding choked on his words. He was furious at *her* accusing *him* of lying. Especially because it was true. "How dare you say that to me, you lying bitch!" he shouted wildly at her. "Where did you get that new suit?" He strode into the hallway.

Shisei's heart thudded heavily. Had he found out that the Feraud suit had been a present from Howe? How could he have?

Branding heard her calling his name, then the phone started ringing. He went out the door. His legs felt oddly stiff, the muscles jumping beneath his skin.

Shisei picked up the phone, shouted "What?" into it, and her breath caught in her throat because she heard her brother's voice.

"Senjin," she whispered, "I thought we had agreed—"

"Our agreement is at an end," Senjin said.

"But you'll put into jeopardy everything we—"

"Quiet!"

"What is it?" Shisei said. "What's happened?"

"Life's happened." Senjin's voice was like an engine about to explode. "The unimaginable has happened. I realize that I need you."

"What do you m——"

"I'm coming," he said. "To Long Island, West Bay Bridge." He gave her an address. "Meet me there."

Shisei was about to reply, but the line had already gone dead. She put down the receiver and shivered. Unconsciously she fingered her emerald ring.

Outside, Branding had gotten into the Jaguar, fired it up. As he nosed out into the quiet street he noticed that his hands were shaking. His heart was beating fast and an anguish he could identify almost as pain racked him. He longed for his wife's counsel; she would know what was right and what was wrong; who was, figuratively speaking, in bed with whom. She always had.

The thought that Shisei had been sent by Douglas Howe to somehow undermine him in order to send the ASCRA bill down to defeat was almost too much to bear. It wasn't until this moment that Branding could admit to himself that he loved Shisei. Almost immediately he realized just how much he loved her. She had penetrated deep inside his defenses, touched the core of him as no one else—not even Mary—had. To find out that it was all a lie was beyond comprehension.

He felt as if his world had been turned inside out, as if the neatly identifiable labels he had prepared for people were useless—worse than useless: false. It was as if he were a child who had been transferred to a new school, only to find that all the lessons he had so painstakingly learned in his former school were incorrect. He felt stupid, naive, betrayed by the very city of power that had pretended to nurture him.

He knew that it was his Puritan blood that made him all too ready to condemn her, to refuse to hear her answers to his questions, knowing that his love for her would make it all but impossible for him to differentiate the truth from the lies.

He could hear his mother's words as clearly as if she were sitting beside him in the Jaguar, one of many physical manifestations of his work in Sodom: *The world is Satan's playground, Cotton. Stay on the narrow path that God has ordained for you, and you will be safe.*

Revolving red and blue lights in his rearview mirror made him start. A touch of a siren and he pulled over. His mind was still full of heavy black thoughts. A Metropolitan Police patrol car, white with the familiar horizontal blue stripe, nosed in behind him. Between flashes Branding could see two shadowed figures in the car behind him.

For a long time nothing happened. Then the driver's door opened and a uniformed cop stepped out. His partner remained in the car.

Branding rolled down his window, heard the cop's footsteps crunching over the asphalt of the street. The cop, all six-foot-three of him, stopped in front of the open window, peered at Branding through mirrored sunglasses. Branding wondered how he could see anything at night.

"May I see your license and registration, please?"

"I'm sure I wasn't speeding, Officer," Branding said.

The cop made no reply, and Branding handed the documents over. He noticed that the cop accepted them with his left hand; his right was on the walnut grips of his holstered service revolver.

The cop signaled to his partner, then said, "I'm afraid I'm going to have to ask you to open your trunk, Senator."

Branding said, "What?"

The cop backed up a step, said, "Please step out of the car, Senator."

Branding got out of the car, walked toward the rear of the Jaguar. The cop was behind him. Ahead he could see the second cop climb out of the patrol car; he held a .12-gauge shotgun loosely in one hand.

Branding said, "Can I at least ask what's going on?"

The cop behind him said, "If you would be kind enough to open your trunk, Senator."

Branding did as he was asked. He opened the trunk, then stepped back. The first cop shone a flashlight into the trunk's interior. An odd, unpleasant sickly-sweet smell erupted into the night.

The cop said, "Jesus."

Branding heard the twin hammers of the second cop's shotgun being cocked as he stared into his trunk and saw the body lying curled in the darkness. Sudden nausea gripped him. The flashlight's beam illuminated the patches of dried blood, the crushed skull, just as it illuminated the corpse's bloodless face.

Branding's mother saying, *Stray from the narrow path, and all the good that I see within you will wither and die.*

God in heaven, he thought, frozen in shock, I know this man. It's David Brisling, Douglas Howe's personal assistant.

Nicholas, high up in the Hodaka, his bearded face rimed with ice, out of time, assaulted the Black Gendarme. He was living his dream in which he was searching among the bulrushes, for what he did not know. He had found footprints in the black, marshy earth: in reality, clues seeded in his memory, recorded, embedded there by his senses. The voice he had heard speaking to him was that of his memory. But with his spirit entangled he had not been able to hear the voice clearly enough to understand what it was telling him.

As Kansatsu had said, it was not *Shiro Ninja* that was entangling his spirit—that was merely a symptom of the disease. In fact Nicholas was already ill, entangled when the tanjian attacked him; he was already susceptible, made vulnerable to *Shiro Ninja.*

Nicholas, with the elementals of Akshara already absorbed, was still *Shiro Ninja.* That was another thing he had been taught. Neither Kansatsu nor anyone else could "cure" him of *Shiro Ninja.*

In fact, there was no cure. *Shiro Ninja* was a delusion that must be healed from inside himself. And yet, his memory of his martial arts training was little improved.

"*Shiro Ninja* is one thing," Kansatsu had said, one evening after lessons were finished for the day. He was examining the scar on the side of Nicholas's head. "This state you find yourself in is quite another."

"But why?" Nicholas had asked. "The main symptom of *Shiro Ninja* is loss of memory."

"That is just it," Kansatsu had pointed out. "Your problem is not *loss* of memory but, rather, an *inability* to get at it. Akshara has begun to disentangle your spirit, yet your memories of *ninjutsu* and *Getsumei no michi* are still unavailable to you. Therefore, I believe now that the cause has an organic component."

"Do you mean my inability to remember is physical?"

"Yes. Precisely. It is my belief that something was done to you during the operation."

A chill went down Nicholas's spine. "You mean the surgeon severed something he wasn't supposed to cut?" The thought of some part of his brain irrevocably maimed was too frightening to contemplate.

"No," Kansatsu had said immediately, as if he had an intimation of the dread creeping through Nicholas. "That would be random, and the chance of him damaging the precise part of your brain dealing with memory retention is so infinitesimal it is not worth talking about." Kansatsu had sat very still. His eyes were black specks, a pair of ravens seen from afar over an autumn wheat field. There was both melancholy and power in such an image. "I am speaking now of something deliberate, Nicholas."

In the stunned silence Nicholas had heard his heart beating, the blood pounding in his ears, a deafening symphony of terror. "But the surgeon—"

"May not have been the actual instrument," Kansatsu had said, interrupting him. "Although it would seem that he must be implicated."

Nicholas had an image of Dr. Hanami's bloody face, his broken-boned body crumpled on the sidewalk.

"The surgeon who operated on me," he had said. "He was pushed from his office window." Then he told Kansatsu everything, from the moment Dr. Hanami pronounced his diagnosis like a sentence, to the battle with the tanjian in Dr. Hanami's office more than six months later.

"Ah, everything is falling into place," Kansatsu had said. He produced an anatomical text, opened it to a section titled, Hemispheres of the Brain. "Let us take this chronologically. According to what you have told me, your tumor lay along the second temporal convolution"—he pointed—"here. Now you will notice that this is just above the hippocampal fissure"—he pointed again—"here.

"Tanjian have known for centuries that the brain is a kind of computer whose myriad functions are precisely divided into well-defined sections. A certain section of the brain, for instance, is involved in the formation and maintenance of memory. This area is relatively small. It resides in what Western science has termed the hippocampus."

"But my tumor was right above the hippocampus," Nicholas had said. "It's becoming increasing likely that Dr. Hanami made a mistake, a slip of the scalpel."

"On the contrary," Kansatsu had said. "Put such negative thoughts aside, Nicholas, and concentrate on the evidence. The hippocampus is so far beneath the area where your tumor lay, it is impossible for a qualified surgeon to reach it accidentally. No. For the hippocampus to be invaded, it must have been deliberate."

Kansatsu had turned to another section of the text. "The hippocampus is crucial to memory, modern science has discovered, because the brain cells there are rich in a peculiar molecule, the NMDA receptor. It is called that because scientists use the chemical, N-methyl D-aspartate, to detect the receptor's presence. The NMDA receptor accepts memories and encodes them into the cells for later recall. This can only be done if the brain's cells—or neurons—are allowed to link up, firing neurotransmitters across synaptic bridges. If something interferes with the synaptic spark, new memories cannot be retained. But, as in your case, if something destroys these cells or interferes with the NMDA receptor, memories already residing in the brain cannot be accessed. The result is what you think of as memory loss but is actually nothing of the sort."

"What happened to me?" Nicholas had asked.

"Here I can only hazard a guess," Kansatsu had said, "but I believe it's an educated one. I believe that while the surgeon was working on your tumor, someone else inserted a suitable object, say an optic fiber, coated with a chemical, an NMDA receptor-inhibitor, into your hippocampus."

"But wouldn't random memories be affected, not just those involving my ninja training?"

"Normally, yes," Kansatsu-san said. "But we are talking now about not only a tanjian, but a *dorokusai.* Just as you are able to inhibit those areas where you feel pain, and not others, so the *dorokusai* was able to interfere with your deepest memories. Besides," Kansatsu added, "your mind has been almost entirely focused on your state of *Shiro Ninja.* I think you will find it difficult, if not impossible, to dredge up certain deeply inlaid memories of your very early childhood."

Nicholas considered this. It was true that many details of his childhood memories were unavailable to him. He knew they were there, but try as he might, he could not bring them into the light of consciousness.

Nicholas shook his head, dismayed. "But Dr. Hanami was right there beside the *dorokusai,*" he said. "He must have known what was happening."

Kansatsu nodded. "This is true enough. But, Nicholas, if what you tell me about him is true, then we must consider the possibility of extreme coercion. Perhaps he was forced to allow this person access to your brain."

Nicholas considered this for some time. "Could the tanjian, the *dorokusai* who attacked me, be capable of such surgical skill?"

"Yes," Kansatsu had said. "Indeed, it is quite likely that such an individual would possess great surgical skill. As a ninja, your own knowledge of anatomy and the workings of the mind and body is quite extensive."

"I couldn't insert a poisoned optical fiber into a hidden area of the human brain."

"Thankfully. You are not *dorokusai.* You do not have such reckless disregard for human life."

Though Kansatsu had begun giving him a mix of natural powders as an antidote to the NMDA receptor-inhibitor, Nicholas was still forced to rely almost exclusively upon Akshara for his mental discipline. It was akin to learning to speak or to walk all over again—so basic, yet so painfully difficult. His brain was like an open book, blank pages ready for the script of the maker's hand. Rapidly, Akshara was filling it, creating its own subtext.

Oddly, his body—not his mind—was his greatest ally in this battle. It was so superbly trained, he found that it could do whatever Akshara asked of it—neither lightning response nor stamina were now problems, and Nicholas was heartened by this change in him from when he first began his journey to find himself.

Then, all at once, as he ascended his nemesis, the Black Gendarme, he felt himself growing heavier and lighter at the same time. He was aware of his body sinking into the rock face, seeping into the minute cracks and fissures so that even a high wind could not dislodge him. At the same time he felt his spirit soaring free. And he was in *Getsumei no michi*! Remembrance flooded him; his body and mind were once again one. Power suffused him. He was no longer *Shiro Ninja*.

The feeling of elation was so overwhelming that Nicholas threw back his head, shouting into the wind, stirring the clouds. The jumble of images inside his mind concentrated, coalesced, resolved themselves into insight.

The footprints among the bulrushes: the voice of his memory. He was back in Kyoki's castle, passing through the moon gate in his study.

What did the voice say? Kansatsu had said.

I can't remember, Nicholas had said.

Was the voice my brother's voice?

Not his, but the source was close.

How close? Akshara gave him the answer: very close. And now the voice spoke to him and he heard every word. It was his own voice saying: *Time.* Like the chiming of a grandfather's clock, like the tolling of a bell, like a shadow emerging from out of the mist. *Time to learn, time to absorb, time to be. This is the end: of fear, of confusion, of death.*

And Nicholas, the wind from the north whistling in his ears, his body charged with the newfound strength of Akshara, thought: Where are you, *dorokusai*? Wherever you are, I'll find you now. I'm coming to get you. I'm coming.

ASAMA, JAPAN/ZHUJI, CHINA/TOKYO, JAPAN

SUMMER 1970–WINTER 1980

Is that all you're going to tell us?" the young girl said.

"You promised to tell us the end," her brother said.

The *sensei* looked at them with some humor. "This is a story that has no end," he said.

"But you promised," the boy, Senjin, always the more impatient of the two, said.

"What happened after they went over the waterfall?" Shisei, his sister asked.

"Ah, the waterfall," the *sensei* said, as if her words reminded him of why they were there, not just there at this moment, but *there* as in on the planet.

He was the River Man. At least that is the only name Senjin and Shisei knew him by, although to his face they always called him *sensei*, teacher. He was father to them, these waiflike twins. He was mentor and companion, tutor and friend. He was Haha-san's brother.

He was, in essence, their universe, and they loved him above all else, even each other.

They knew him as the River Man because that was where he took them to learn, in the depths of a shadowed, leafy valley, by the bank of a wide, snaking river. He was very much at home there, living at times as much in the water as on dry land, as wholly amphibious as the frogs that sunned themselves on the hot rocks of the river, waiting to snatch unsuspecting midges out of midair with their lightning tongues.

"The waterfall was like a star in the sky," the River Man said, "resonating with unimaginable energy, an engine of life and of destruction.

"When the two brothers, locked in mortal combat, were taken over the falls, something happened. The universe shuddered. Perhaps it shuddered at the moment when Zhao Hsia died, his lungs filled with churning water as So-Peng held him with the force of his will against the rocks at the base of the waterfall.

"Or then again, perhaps it shuddered when So-Peng emerged, dripping and gasping, upon the black muddy shore. For he had lived and Zhao Hsia, his childhood friend, had not. So-Peng had had it in his power to save his brother, but he had elected to drown him. He had been judge, jury, and executioner in the trial of Zhao Hsia.

"There was no justice here. At least, none that we can readily understand. Justice, no matter how harsh, must be admired. Anything less is to be reviled—and avenged."

So this is how it began. Amid a sylvan river glade, leafy and green, lush in the fullness of summer's heat. Morality imprinted upon two young, growing minds, so full of trust in a world not yet fully defined. But whose morality did they so readily absorb?

Haha-san had no one but her brother, *sensei*, the River Man. Unlike her sister, the woman who had given birth to Senjin and Shisei, Haha-san had chosen to remain unmarried. She carried with her from childhood a morbid distrust of men.

She did not understand sex, and was afraid of it. She saw in it an innate violence that apparently no one else did. Until, of course, Senjin was old enough to comprehend what he had unconsciously absorbed from her.

Perhaps in her youth Haha-san had been brutally raped. That would have explained her view of sex. However, life is rarely so neat and tidy, and the truth was perhaps far more nebulous: Haha-san had developed this belief somewhere within a childhood she could no longer clearly remember.

What she could remember disturbed her, and her reaction to these surfacing memories, chunks of stinking, rotting debris, was terror. At those times the household would be charged with menace, as if Haha-san's fear was like a drunkard run amok, violence and chaos strewn in its erratic wake.

At other times Haha-san, as if appalled at what she had done, would take the twins to her pillowlike breast, rocking them, crooning to them lullabies in a language they could not yet understand.

This underlying unpredictability characterized the twins' early years. Only with *sensei*, in the sinuously winding river glade, did Senjin and Shisei feel secure.

Is it any wonder that they gratefully embraced the River Man's teachings with a fervor that he found invigorating?

It was only much later, floating free in his sensory deprivation tank in the Kan Hotel in the dingy fringes of Tokyo, using Kshira to place himself out of time, that Senjin came to understand that Haha-san was gifted in just the same way that he and Shisei were gifted.

But Haha-san was in a sense a displaced person. Her parents had been destroyed when the Americans had dropped their atomic bomb on Nagasaki. The doctors said that Haha-san herself had absorbed a lethal dose of radiation. As such, knowing that she was doomed, they contrived through a mare's nest of paperwork to keep her in their laboratories, observing her eighteen hours a day, their chrome and fiberglass instruments monitoring all her vital signs in order to understand better how the radiation broke down the cells, platelets, and tissues of the human body.

This living experiment was not entirely the doctors' doing. On the contrary, it was Haha-san herself who conceived of the idea as if it were a baby in her belly. Immediately following the exhaustive physical examination given to her, as it was to all refugees of Nagasaki, Haha-san approached the doctors. She had heard them in consultation, talking about her case as if the radiation had already robbed her of her hearing. She was ten at this time, in 1945, already old enough to understand her own mortality and what it meant to die, the war accelerating her knowledge in the same way atomic fission accelerated ions.

But it was life that concerned Haha-san. Although her parents and two older brothers had perished, a sister two years her junior was alive, having been out of the Nagasaki area when the sky exploded in light and in death.

Haha-san understood that she was now the head of the family, and as such she needed to take care of her sister. She could not count on the authorities, who were in chaos in the last days of the war.

She knew she needed money, and this was the way to get it. Haha-san sold herself as an exhibit, a living laboratory for the scientists who were so eager to discover the short- and long-term effects of this new radiation that had been unleashed on the world. The money they paid her she turned over to her sister, who, in turn, bought her way into a farming family. Having lost three sons to the war, the farmers were happy to have another body—no matter how small—to help them with their rice harvest.

The experiment was short-lived. After six months, when Haha-san had developed none of the expected signs of radiation poisoning, the scientists abandoned her for more fertile survivors. They believed that their initial findings were wrong, because now they could find no sign of the radiation at all inside her.

Many years later, floating in nothingness, it was clear to Senjin that this manifestation of her gift clearly terrified Haha-san. More, it had traumatized her. She had been prepared to die, and when she had not even become ill, a sickness of the spirit descended on her.

Perhaps she felt that she had deserved to die in the bomb blast. She was, she felt, no more deserving of life than her parents or her brothers had been. On the contrary, she felt inadequate to the task life was presenting her. Surely one of her older brothers would be better equipped than she to care for her younger sister.

And yet she was the one who had survived—oh, no, not merely survived, flourished. For Haha-san emerged from the radiation laboratory rosy-cheeked, strong, with lustrous hair and perfect teeth, and was never ill a day in her life.

That was the course her gift took; her sister's took another path entirely. In fact, Senjin believed that his mother never even knew she carried the gift inside her. It was not her karma to possess it at all, merely to pass it on to her children: her twins, Senjin and Shisei.

It was Haha-san who named them, just as it was Haha-san who cared for them. Their mother had no interest, or she was too ill to be bothered with them. It was as if her life had a single purpose: to give birth to them. After that occurred she, like many insect mothers, perished; in a sense, consumed by her offspring.

If Haha-san had two brothers and both had died, who was *sensei*, her brother? Senjin asked this of Haha-san as soon as he was old enough to grasp the contradiction.

Haha-san laughed. "*Sensei* is my brother," she said. "He appeared on your mother's doorstep a year to the day that she was married. She was already pregnant with you and Shisei. He claimed to have survived the bombing of Nagasaki. He said that he stood at ground zero and was unharmed, that he did it to test himself and the strength of his gift, that if he had not survived, that would have been all right, because it would have meant that his gift was too weak, and he never could have endured the thought that he was inferior among his own kind.

"He said that once he survived, he went to China, to a place known as Zhuji, to study mental disciplines. In Zhuji, he said, he earned the title *sensei*."

Senjin, feeling warm and full of food, for it was near to bedtime, had looked up into her face. "Is it true, what *sensei* told you?"

Haha-san had smiled at him. She smelled of milk and of sugar, a unique scent which was to haunt Senjin for all of his life. "Well, it's not polite to doubt the word of *sensei*," she said. "But I did not believe what he said about the bomb." She shrugged. "Perhaps he hid out in the mountains or he was given a concussion by the shock wave of the blast. I doubt that anyone could have survived at ground zero, but I don't know what the truth is. The other part is true, however. *Sensei* did go to Zhuji to study. That's why it was many years, and your mother and I were in our twenties before we saw him. By then a great deal had happened to him."

What had Haha-san meant by that? What had happened to *sensei* in Zhuji? Senjin tried by various ways to get Haha-san to tell him (it was inconceivable to ask such a question of *sensei*, who was so secretive about his life), but each time, she managed to avoid answering him.

It was then that Senjin learned that he could not depend on any one person to answer all the questions crowding his brain. Haha-san could answer some, *sensei* could answer some others. But, increasingly, Senjin discovered that neither of them could, or would, answer the questions that were most crucial to him.

He told only Shisei what he planned to do—journey to Zhuji. Of course she cried. They had always been together, even—especially—in the womb; the thought of a separation terrified her.

"You're weak!" Senjin yelled at her. "What did *sensei* tell you about such weakness?"

"I don't remember," Shisei said through her tears.

Which made Senjin hit her. He did not mean to, or anyway had not planned to, which was the same to him. It was the first time he hit her, but certainly not the last. Only later, far away from her, across the South China Sea, did he hear in her response an echo of Haha-san's obfuscations. He could not punish Haha-san—well, not yet, anyway—so he had punished her.

Shisei, his twin; his other half. She.

Senjin was haunted by *she*: a maddeningly diffuse femaleness that dominated his dreams, which he pushed from his conscious mind during waking hours. At first he was convinced that this femaleness was the essence of his weak and hated mother, absorbed with her nutrients through the umbilical. Later he suspected that it was that part of Haha-san's gift she found frightening and repulsive, that she had cast off from her. Still later he thought that perhaps this femaleness contained something of both.

It had nothing to do with Shisei; it had everything to do with Shisei. Shisei had absorbed everything he had, in the womb. Like a member of the underground searching for a traitor, he suspected her of inheriting their mother's fatal weakness. This was because he could not bear to suspect himself of such a sin, remembering what Haha-san had said about *sensei*: *If he had not survived, that would have been all right, because it would have meant that his gift was too weak, and he could never have endured the thought that he was inferior among his own kind.* Senjin knew that she could just as well have been talking about him.

He was as vigilant against any sign that he had absorbed his mother's propensity for weakness as the scientists had been with Haha-san in their search for radiation poisoning. In so doing, his attention was elsewhere when he incorporated into himself the River Man's moral universe.

He did not, of course, know that he was doing this; no child ever does. But it happened just the same, because in the end Senjin was as needy as any child is, and he took what he needed where he found it, mindless of the consequences.

Perhaps it is too easy to say that this happened mainly as a consequence of his having no father, but what other explanation is there? It is true that both Senjin and Shisei looked like their father. Their mother had been a pleasant-looking woman, but nothing more. Their father, on the other hand, was, like them, filled with a luminous beauty.

All Senjin had left of him was a photograph. It was now frayed at the edges; it had a center crease, and the lower left-hand corner had been torn away. But it was still his prized possession. It showed a slim, magnetic man in a knife-creased army uniform, the tunic of which was so studded with medals it was possible for the young Senjin to believe it was made out of metal.

What had happened to the twins' father? No one knew. He had been a career military man, had survived the many harrowing battles of the war in the Pacific, as the Japanese termed World War II. His bravery in battle was unquestioned, as was his leadership. He had become invisible to the American war-crimes tribunal, which convened just after the war, so it was clear that he had many friends in high places.

He began flying planes—experimental jets at Mitsubishi and Kodai, gaining a reputation for nerve that nearly eclipsed his wartime climb to glory. He rode at the edge of the earth's atmospheric canopy, nearer to the sun than anyone save Chuck Yeager. Then the American astronauts burst on the world stage, and everything turned to dust.

One day he just disappeared. Perhaps, so brave in battle, he could not bear to be eclipsed in its aftermath. He lived his life near the edge, was not otherwise content. Perhaps he, too, had served his purpose in impregnating the twins' mother, and was no longer needed.

Not true. Senjin and Shisei needed him.

"The waterfall," Senjin prompted the River Man.

"Yes," Shisei said. "What happened after the waterfall?"

The waterfall. To the River Man the waterfall was the apocalypse, the twilight of the gods, Armageddon. It was at once the end and the beginning. Like a nexus point in time, all paths led to the waterfall and away from it.

For many years the twins dreamed of the waterfall as if it were alive, a presence suspended in the twilight of their room.

"It was the *samseng*, the tong leader, Tik Po Tak who pulled the murderer So-Peng from the boiling waters at the base of the falls," the River Man said. "The body of Zhao Hsia, weighted down by the force of So-Peng's projected will, never reappeared.

"So-Peng said, 'The tanjian we both sought is dead.'

"The vile pair returned to Singapore, congratulating themselves on the success of their mission. But everything had changed in the weeks they had been away.

"A rival *samseng* had taken advantage of Tak's absence to stage a bloody coup in Nightside, the area of Singapore where Tak had held sway. And So-Peng's mother was gone. Terrified by the consequences of what she had done, of pitting one son against the other, she had apparently fled into the dense forests of teak and sandalwood far to the north."

That was the end of the story, as far as the River Man was concerned. To the twins, he had merely tantalized them, and they tried in every way they could think of to get *sensei* to go on with the story. It had no ending, he had told them, but they were unsatisfied with such a nebulous answer.

And as far as Senjin was concerned, this was another reason why he was determined to travel to Zhuji. It was in China that he became convinced the end of the story would be revealed to him.

Shisei had other desires. When she dreamed of the waterfall, it was composed not of rushing, turbulent water, but of a forest of bright faces. These faces, all young, all beautiful, were turned in her direction. They were looking at her, not in the way of observing, but with the kind of adoration reserved for celebrities or movie stars. Yet she was neither. But she knew—this was still in her dream—that she required this adoration of the forest of bright faces as a flower needs water or sunlight in order to survive. Without this adoration, there was only an unutterable darkness, filled with fear.

But it was not, as might be supposed, loneliness that Shisei feared—after all, she had Senjin, always and forever a part of her spirit. It was that she would never get enough love.

Senjin loved her; but what about anyone else? Haha-san had nursed her, nurturing her, attending to her basic desires. That was duty; but was it also love?

It was not yet clear to Shisei that Haha-san lived in agony, that this agony determined not only her actions but, far more importantly, what lay beyond the actions. Haha-san's agony was like a living thing, an evil-tempered pet or a revolting disfigurement that Haha-san humped around with her wherever she went.

It was as if this inner agony were Haha-san's own twin, the entity to which she was most intimately connected. It had made of her a freak locked within herself, an automaton subject to irrational bursts of emotional violence.

This violence—a projection of Haha-san's will—took many forms. For Shisei it usually began with an intense itching inside her head, as if a nest of spiders had crawled inside her mind. Then bright flashes of light would blind her, so that in the beginning, before she learned to anticipate this part, she would fall to her knees or, if she were in the middle of playing, stumble painfully against some piece of furniture.

But these preliminary manifestations were nothing compared to what was to come: a re-creation of the horrors of postblast Nagasaki with its stink of burned flesh, its sight of bloated, charred bodies, shrieking wounded, its choking taste of ash composed of human bones and waste, all filtered through Haha-san's disturbed psyche, magnified, warped, embroidered by her own peculiar terror, anguish, and rage.

Think of the worst nightmare monster, then imagine it come to life, stalking you through your house, passing through walls and closed doors, seeking you out wherever you hid. Think of it finding you, entering your mind, filling it with hideous images, impressions of terror, despair, and death.

The children were affected differently by these chaotic disgorgings of psychic violence. Senjin would run outside, enraged that his environment had been invaded. Here was the origin of his demon woman, soft and seductive on the outside, yet within, seething with malefic destructive force. In the rain and the snow he would curse Haha-san and vow some day to wreak a terrible vengeance on her. But Shisei, as if paralyzed by the onset, could not get herself to leave the house. She would lose control over herself, her own essence contracted into a tight ball, as if her will to resist was subverted by her need to submit to what she believed were the definitions of her life with Haha-san and *sensei*. She would cower in her room, trembling in fear as each new assault inexorably sought her out. Her eyes were squeezed shut as she prayed for an end.

She endured the monstrous horrors until the fiery psychic attack subsided and the house returned to a semblance of normalcy, although always she could hear the crockery continuing to vibrate on the open
shelves in the kitchen. For a long time after the attack ended, no one
dared go near Haha-san, not even *sensei*.

Gradually Shisei became convinced that these outbursts, terrifying in
their power and unpredictability, were a result of some failing on her own
part (why else, she reasoned, would they seek her out?), that it was
irrefutable evidence that she was somehow unworthy of being loved.

When Senjin fell ill or was overtired and Haha-san pulled him to her
pillowlike breast, he felt himself unable to breathe, suffocating in her
endless warmth, the smell of milk and sugar. But when Shisei climbed
upon Haha-san's lap, she reveled in the proximity to that slowly beating
heart which put her to sleep within minutes no matter how agitated her
state had been. This inevitable passivity (which came from Shisei's overwhelming desire to please Haha-san and thus gain her elusive love) en-
deared her to Haha-san, who, despite her perseverance over suffering,
must have found Senjin's aggressive squirming at her breast unsettling.
Her duty was to pacify the children, and when she could not, once again
her anxiety blew through the house like a storm.

Ironically, Haha-san's emotional violence led indirectly to the birth of
Shisei's own philosophical outlook on life: the struggle to attain *seishinshugi*, the triumph of the power of the spirit over the physical. Two other
factors influenced Shisei: the fear that she would never get enough love to
survive, and the fact that she was female, therefore inferior to any male.
And it was a male—her twin brother, Senjin—who she was constantly
pitted against in her lessons with the River Man.

At night, pointing over his head, *sensei* would say, "Look there." Obediently, the twins would crane their necks, staring into the star-filled sky.
"You are looking outward," *sensei* would say, "yet what you see is in the
past. That light—all those lights from the stars—is millions of years old.
It took that long to reach us here on this planet. You look outward and
see inward.

"This is the essence of Kshira, the language of the sound-light continuum. It is the opposite of eternity because Kshira is never at rest. Take
the lesson of the stars to heart; it is the essence of everything I will teach
you. The stars are far away both in distance and in time. In a sense, the
two are the same. The past—your past and mine—are in another place as
well as another time.

"It is the same with the days. Man has names for the different days, but Kshira tells us that there is only one day. It returns again and again, and so may be influenced.

"There is a membrane at *kokoro*, the heart of things. It is not an organ that beats thum-thum, thum-thum, as your heart or mine does. It is a field of energy that can be influenced by manipulation of the forces inside ourselves.

"The paths aré twofold: ritual and meditation. Ritualized *actions* and meditative *thoughts*. Both focus energy, harnessing it into a concentrated beam that may be beaten against the membrane of *kokoro*, exciting it, exerting an influence. The paths must be repeated over and over. And the longer these repetitions go on, the more the membrane *kokoro* is excited, the more energy is created."

Firelight played across the River Man's face, making it seem to change aspect with each flicker. "As an example . . ." he intoned, his eyes closing, his face becoming placid.

The twins, with their extraordinary gift, could feel the emanations— much as So-Peng had felt his mother's force—concentric circles of light that were nevertheless devoid of illumination. The atmosphere became heavy, aqueous. The stars still dazzled, but now it seemed to the avidly watching twins that their light was being reduced from a shower to a drizzle.

Abruptly, overhead, the stars winked out, a wind, damp and chill, sprang up and it began to rain lightly. In a moment it stopped. The fire sizzled and cracked as if filled with bones.

The River Man opened his eyes. "You see what Kshira can do," he said softly.

"You made a cloud," Senjin said.

"Now the night is clear again," Shisei said.

The River Man smiled. "I did not make a cloud. That is beyond the powers of any human creature. But Kshira tells us that there are always clouds, even when they are not apparent to the eye. Clouds are part of nature and nature is entirely in flux. Always. Clouds are always forming or dissipating, always there. This is true of everything in nature. One needs but to gather up the requisite energy, focus it against the membrane of *kokoro*, cause an action to gain a reaction."

The River Man stood up. "But I used only thought to generate the energy, one path, and I told you that there are two." He disappeared into the darkness, returning a moment later with a stoat. The twins had seen stoats many times in summer, their thin brown coats unmistakable in the underbrush. Now, in winter, the stoat was covered in a long silky pelt. It was a magnificent creature.

It squirmed in *sensei*'s arms, clearly terrified, until with a twist of his thumb and forefinger he broke the stoat's neck. Then, producing a small knife, he set about skinning it. He did it not as a hunter might, in the most efficient way, but in long, protracted cuts that were so stylized that their ritualistic nature was evident even to the children.

The stoat's skin came off in thin, bloody strips which *sensei* carefully arranged like the petals of a flower. Senjin and Shisei could see that his eyes were almost fully closed; just a thin line of white was visible, and they knew that the meditation, the focusing of energy, had begun anew.

Now the two paths, ritualistic action and meditative thought, were combined, and the twins shivered as they felt the first harsh gusts of the gale whipping the tops of the trees. Leaves spun in the night air, and the tree frogs ceased their croaking. There was no sign of the nocturnal insects: fireflies, crickets, or midges.

The night grew black, as if a vast blanket were being pulled across the stage of the heavens, blotting out the starlight. The rushing of the nearby river coalesced with the rushing of the moisture-laden wind to give the impression that the entire world was suddenly in flux.

A moment later the twins started as a ferocious clap of thunder cracked almost directly above their heads and the world seemed to tremble beneath them. There was no lightning that they could see, but the thunder continued, short and sharp, very close, very loud.

They became aware of a kind of fabric, perhaps the very membrane of *kokoro* that the River Man had described to them, its dark vibrations, like beats upon a drum, the cause of the instability that flooded the sylvan river valley.

It was only when the downpour began that the River Man's eyes opened fully. He grinned at them.

"This is your power," *sensei* said. "The power of Kshira, the Way of the Two Paths."

Time passed, and Senjin dreamed of Zhuji. Soon Haha-san had her own curriculum for them. She began to teach them the strange language that she had used to sing them lullabies when they were younger. It was, she told them, the language of the tanjian.

Senjin now began to see a purpose to his hard, exacting work. The search for the ending of the story of the two brothers, So-Peng and Zhao Hsia, had become a passionate obsession.

The River Man was nothing if not thorough. He delivered to the twins volumes encompassing a broad range of philosophical, theological, moral, political, and ethical thought. These included the great minds of Western as well as Eastern civilization.

The twins, precocious in all aspects of their development, gorged themselves on literature. They continued with their lessons in Kshira. But as for their interaction with the outside world, Senjin soon knew that something was wrong.

He automatically assumed that he would be better at everything than any of the other boys his age. He wasn't, and this crushed him. He could not understand how he could be so smart and so talented in some areas, yet utterly ignorant and inept in others.

Then, during his reading, Senjin came across a volume by the sixteenth century French moralist, Joseph Joubert. In it, he found the way for him —the separatist, the special, the one—to live comfortably in society, side by side with the common man. "Great minds are those that disguise their limits, that mask their mediocrity," Joubert wrote, and from that moment on, Senjin lived his life by that rule.

He ceased to insist on competing in everything, but rather stuck to his areas of expertise and even, on occasion allowed himself to lose in order not to bring too much attention to himself. He discovered, much to his surprise, that he had little desire to become a leader among his peers, simply because they were so uninteresting to him. He would much rather practice his martial arts, read, or discuss philosophy with *sensei*, or debate morality with Shisei.

This last he did with his sister late at night, when they were in bed. Either he would crawl into her bed or she into his. Initially, this was done so they could talk as long as they wished without disturbing Haha-san, who was attuned to their psychic emanations even, it often seemed, in her sleep.

In time the twins came to understand the shared warmth. Senjin found that he liked to be up against her, reveling in the places where women, even ones as physical as Shisei, were soft. For her part, Shisei loved the press of his hard muscles. There was no give anywhere on his body, and she often dreamed of Senjin's form splayed wide to protect her from unnamed dangers. And often when they fell asleep in this way, they dreamed the same dream.

But the warmth was not physical alone. Shisei could feel inside herself a strange sensation, as if someone were massaging her spinal chord and brain stem. Much later she would be stunned to discover this same, peculiarly wonderful feeling flooding through her at the moment of sexual orgasm.

In the warm, formless zone they constructed of their energies, the twins spoke deep into the night of the nature of good and evil. Because they made it so, there was nothing here but their psyches. They created their own colors, generated light without illumination: the heat of the merging of their twin engines.

They were gods without knowing it. Neither good nor evil had yet touched them (so they could view them with a rare kind of objectivity), but these momentous concepts were lurking just around the corner, in the slowly opening doorway to adulthood.

Senjin was of the opinion that good and evil were mutable, defined differently from individual to individual; this, he argued, was endemic to the nature of man. He even likened this to a punishment: the Western concept of original sin, theorizing that at some time far in the past, before original sin, good and evil were immutable.

On the other side, Shisei believed that good and evil were and always would be immutable principles. This, she told her brother in an impassioned tone, was what made mankind mortal, different from the gods or from Buddha, who could indeed perceive good and evil as arcs of light that bent to his will.

"We are humbled by the gods, by nature—even by the animals—who are closer to the spirits, the energy, that animate the universe than we can ever be," Shisei said.

"But isn't that what *sensei* is teaching us, what Kshira is all about?" Senjin said. "Learning to manipulate the energy membrane of *kokoro*."

"That's the problem with you." Shisei said. "You see everything in terms of manipulation. *Sensei* is teaching us to understand our world as we come to understand ourselves."

"You still don't see it," Senjin said. "All understanding is an illusion, the understanding of the self the biggest illusion of all. And do you know why? Because we don't want to know what sightless worms are squirming in the blackness at the heart of our spirits."

"You don't know how wrong you are. 'The beautiful spirits are they that are universal, open, and ready for all things,' " Shisei said, paraphrasing Michel de Montaigne.

Senjin laughed. "The fallacy of that," he said, "is that we are not living in a beautiful world."

"Why is it," she asked, "that you see everything inverted?"

Senjin had no answer for her. Instead, he reached out and touched her. After a time Shisei sighed. "That feels good."

He took one long fingernail, scraped it down the center of her back until he drew blood.

"And this?" he said. "How does this feel?"

Two years later, when he was seventeen, Senjin disappeared. Shisei knew, of course, where he had gone: Zhuji. But she told no one, not even Haha-san, who was frantic with worry, because she knew that if Haha-san found out where Senjin had gone, she would dispatch the River Man to bring him back.

Shisei felt her brother's absence with the keen edge of a blade. Her bed was cold and lonely without the hard metallic circles of his aura surrounding her. Oddly, she felt less innocent with his departure, as if this abandonment were a passage for her from the naiveté of youth to the disillusionment of adulthood.

There had been no adolescence in the twins' development. Their rigorous training, eighteen hours a day, seven days a week, precluded some basic hormonal development as well as effectively isolating them from the normal growth patterns of their contemporaries.

Theirs had been a world apart, an odd kind of paradise where their work was endless and arduous, yet in everything else they were pampered as if they were the sole successors to the Emperor.

Shisei felt her twin's abandonment with as much force as Senjin did his mother's. Shisei did not feel abandoned by her mother. She never thought of her parents at all, or when she did, it was of a couple in a motion picture, with a sense of observation rather than obligation. Besides, she had Haha-san, who was Mother, and the River Man, who was Father.

Still, Senjin's departure shattered Shisei's dream world, and at once she saw how like Haha-san she had become, locked within a hermetically sealed environment, feeding only on herself. This disturbed her. Her pursuit of *seishinshugi*, the triumph of the spiritual over the physical, was perhaps generated by the knowledge of how weak she was. Oh, yes, she had Kshira, and with it she could do many things. But it could not give her brute strength. For that she was, and always would be, dependent on others. She knew that she needed to find a way to do that while keeping to a minimum the risk of being dominated.

In the stillness of the night, alone in her bed, hugging a hull pillow to her breast, she thought of Senjin, her brother, her twin, of how she was dependent on him, of how she wanted to be dominated by him. A single tear trembled in her eye.

If it had not been for the River Man's detailed description of Zhuji, Senjin undoubtably would have ended up in the wrong place. The only

Zhuji that anyone knew about was a town perhaps forty-five miles almost due south of Hangchow, now known by the revolution-obsessed Chinese as Hangzhou.

But this town, engaged in the manufacture of silk and Dragon Well green tea, was in an alluvial plain in the lake country of southeast China, and Senjin was certain that the Zhuji he was searching for was a much smaller mountain village in the northwest.

He finally found the Zhuji of the tanjian in the north of Henan province, in the Taihang Shan, the mountains fifty miles west of Anyang, the cradle of Chinese civilization.

Even the dung-colored mountains here seemed bent and worn with antiquity. Zhuji, carved into the heart of the shan, was filled with temples. Like grains of salt spilled from a shaker, the temples were identical, spread across the slopes of the mountains.

But it was not only the River Man's description that led Senjin to his goal, it was Kshira. Kshira enabled Senjin to "see" Zhuji in the past: over distance and time. And when he came to Zhuji, hidden within the dung-colored mountains of Taihang, he found no Mao jackets, no maddening modern Chinese bureaucracy, no Communist Chinese exhortational slogans, posters, cant, no inefficient government appointed by Peking.

On the contrary, Zhuji seemed encysted in time as well as in the Taichang Shan. The sad-looking, poverty-riven, grimy modern-day China was unaware of Zhuji's existence. It abided as it had for centuries, a cenobitic religious community, wholly self-contained, entirely self-sufficient. The nineteenth and twentieth centuries had not touched it with its coal- and diesel-smeared hands.

Senjin's presence was announced by the steely rings of his aura. The whole of Zhuji knew of his imminence even while he strode through the rough, dusty foothills of the Taihang Shan. As a result, the tanjian elders were already in the village square when Senjin entered it from the east.

They greeted him in the language he had been taught by Haha-san. He was welcomed like a long-lost son because, after all, that was precisely what he was. And the next morning at sunrise he began his formal education in Tau-tau.

The tanjian elder assigned to oversee Senjin's training was named Mubao. He was a tall, willowy man with the hard cast of China's harsh northern steppes imprinted on his face. In the quickness of his eyes, the darting movements of his head, he reminded Senjin of a hawk.

Senjin was ushered into his chamber, a rock-walled cubicle rimmed with soot. A fire was blazing in a rough-hewn hearth, for it was chilly this time of year in the Taihang Shan. Through a tiny glassless window

Senjin could see the cloud-streaked sky, stained red by the advancing sun.

Mubao said nothing. He did not look up. He sat at his bamboo desk immersed in his papers for some time, as if there were no one else in the room with him.

After a time, restless, Senjin stirred. Mubao was up and moving before Senjin knew what was happening. His first instinct was to use his gift, and he sent his dark, metallic aura outward in order to intercept the older man.

Much to his shock, he found that he was imprisoned, encircled by an impenetrable wall, featureless, still as eternity or death. In that moment of immobility, Mubao reached him. Clamping a powerful hand at the base of Senjin's neck, Mubao forced the boy across the stone room, thrusting his head at the fire.

Flames danced before Senjin's eyes, the dry heat and coiling, aromatic smoke threatening to choke him. He felt his face grow hot, smelled something burning, realized belatedly that his eyebrows had been seared off.

At last Mubao thrust his head away from the fire, but he did not relinquish his paralyzing hold. "You come here arrogant, ignorant," Mubao said in his deep, vibratory voice, "ready to use your gift indiscriminately, injudiciously. You are selfish, vain, mistakenly self-assured. You are a danger to us and to yourself. Have you anything to say in your defense?"

The moment Mubao turned him loose, Senjin bridled. The anger gushed through him, a hot and milky substance, as sweet and thick as honey. For an instant he contemplated reaching out with the steely rings of his aura, using what the River Man had taught him to inflict, punishment for his humiliation.

Then, like an animal appearing from the depths of a forest, his instinct for survival surfaced. Senjin knew, without quite knowing how, that were he to use his gift in such a fashion, it would strike only that puzzling featureless wall, rebounding back, disabling him.

Then everything changed. Senjin's aggression dissipated. He averted his eyes and hung his head. "I have no defense," he whispered hoarsely, "in the face of the truth." But it was not humility that had overcome him; it was greed. He wanted the power that Mubao obviously possessed, and he vowed that whatever it took to attain it, he would do.

"That being the case," Mubao intoned, "I now pronounce sentence. You will shave your head, and keep it shaved to publicly show your unworthy nature, until directed to do otherwise. You will work and make your bed in the kitchen, an assistant to the apprentices. You will follow their direction without question. You will perform whatever tasks are set before you no matter how menial for as long as you are in the kitchen or wherever you are directed to go."

"What about my instruction in Tau-tau?" Senjin asked.

"It has already begun," Mubao said.

I will not give in to humiliation, Senjin thought.

And there was a great deal to give in to. The apprentices hated him—he was Japanese, after all. They made fun of him, these stupid boys with their stunted auras and their backward minds. Senjin despised them, all the while acceding to their endless demands on him. They made him handle the rotting garbage, spread animal manure with his bare hands on the delicate plantings in the extensive vegetable and herb gardens. Once they even ordered him to dig a new cesspit, and while he was at it, lined up above him at its lip, urinating on him in concert. Another time, he found a turd in his bed. Routinely, there were insects in his food; he ate them with a great show, relishing their taste as if they were a delicacy.

All this humiliation was meant to make him a better person, but it did not. Senjin was oblivious to the mirror of his self that Mubao was determined to hold up to him. It was as if Senjin were a mythical vampire who had no reflection to be thrown back into his face.

Neither, it seemed, did he have a shadow. The substance of his life at Zhuji had no meaning for him. He might as well have been in prison or in paradise, it was all the same to him. Only his internal questions, ticking like time bombs within his mind, were of any importance. As for the rest, he was as an automaton or more accurately, an exquisitely trained actor whose greatest triumph is the illusion of normalcy his art allows him to create.

So it was that even Mubao, with all his skills and power, was taken in by the master illusionist. He believed, as did all the tanjian elders, that humility was at last coming to arrogant Senjin, that the baseness of his existence in Zhuji was an important lesson well learned.

How wrong they all were, and how ignorant of their mistake they were. Perhaps there was a lesson for them in Senjin's stay. Their own arrogance in their time-honored methods caused them to treat him as they treated all novices in Tau-tau. But Senjin was unlike any other novice who had been born to their community. But the tanjian elders had, over time, become comfortable with their powers, which had stymied even great Mao. How were they to guess that a mere boy could evade their methodology? They had taken a viper into their midst, and were unable to see themselves in the scales gleaming dully beneath his illusory facade.

Senjin rarely slept for more than an hour or two a night. By day he was the willing slave of the kitchen apprentices who hated him. By night he delivered himself up to Mubao or whichever tanjian elder was involved in the different phases of Tau-tau.

It was not Kshira, the form of Tau-tau that the River Man had been teaching him, though to be sure, there were certain similarities. Senjin saw immediately how the discipline, despite the best intentions, had been corrupted by time, the vagaries of oral transmission, the needs and necessities of the Japanese culture.

What were the questions that neither Haha-san nor the River Man could answer, the questions that had driven him to seek out Zhuji and the tanjian? When he had arrived here, Senjin thought he knew: what had happened to the River Man here? Wasn't there more to learn than the musings of dead men which passed for philosophy? Where was the Truth in the world, the answer to the universal questions: why am I here, where am I going, what will I become afterward?

But now Senjin knew that he needed to know more even than that. Why am I rage? he kept asking himself, his hands full of manure. Why am I anger? his mouth filled with beetles. Why am I fury? crouched in the night, his dark, metallic aura clamped tightly around him, a bird with its wings bound.

Neither Mubao nor any of the other elders took the slightest notice when Senjin asked them about the experience of the River Man in Zhuji. He had been scheming for some time to find some way to get them to open up, when an opportunity presented itself from an unlikely source.

There was a strictly enforced ban against the younger males and females getting together save for mealtimes, which were always communal. Still, here and there boys and girls managed their trysts. Senjin could never quite figure out whether these clandestine affairs went unnoticed by the elders or whether the lengths to which the couples went in order to hide their meetings were part of the Tau-tau training.

It happened there was a girl who seemed confused by much of the instruction. She seemed never to understand her lessons fully or to perform to the standards set by the elders. As a result, she was reviled and ridiculed in much the same manner as Senjin was.

Her name was Xu, and she was very beautiful. She had porcelain skin and the face of a doll, almost hypnotic in its perfection. It seemed ironic to Senjin that she was so physically perfect yet so inept at her lessons. Senjin, ever the consummate liar, told himself that he was drawn to her because he adored perfection in any form. He saw himself as a sculptor and Xu a half-formed lump of clay from which he could fashion a masterpiece. The truth was that in this strange community, he could not bear his absolute isolation. Yet he could not admit to himself that this inner pain drove him to seek out someone who was very much like himself: reviled, scorned, a beautiful outsider. And it was his own need for companionship that blinded him to her own weaknesses, which in other circumstances he would have despised. He was aware only of Xu's degradation, and saw in her suffering face his own reflection.

At first he observed her humiliation as the others did, although not enjoying it as they obviously did. But soon her treatment became so painful for him that he was obliged to intervene. He saw the concerted cruelty as a transgression—not against any spoken or implied law of the tanjian, which meant nothing to him—but against his own internal code, which was becoming more manifest to him day by day.

Outside, in the cold surrounding the privies, he watched as Xu was taunted by a group of girls. They began by verbally abusing her. This quickly escalated to pushing and shoving, sending her stumbling over the rocky ground, until she slid into the cesspit he was digging.

Senjin stopped what he was doing. He saw Xu biting so hard on her lower lip that it began to bleed, trying desperately not to cry. She pulled herself into a ball, thrusting herself into the dirt of the pit's side in a pathetic attempt to hide from the laughing, mocking girls.

These girls were now standing at the edge of the cesspit, bending over, hands on their knees, calling out to Xu. One of them spit in her direction; it struck Senjin on the cheek. This made the girls laugh even more.

"Oh, look," they cried, "it's Shit-boy! We didn't see you digging there, Shit-boy!" Tears of laughter streamed down their faces.

Senjin looked down, saw Xu trembling, staring up at the gob of spittle on his cheek. He saw the tears that she had been so valiantly holding back begin to slide down her face. She wept for him where she would not weep for herself.

Senjin closed his eyes, found that place inside himself where dwelled the dark metallic rings of his aura. This place was distant in both time and place, very near the place where the membrane *kokoro* hung suspended. Now Senjin began his repetitions, and soon the energy he emitted began to excite the membrane, setting it to vibrating.

Now he moved his essence outward, grabbing hold of his aura and casting it into space and time. A moment later the earth gave a lurch in the way a wild boar will convulse when a spear is struck through its back.

Senjin heard screaming, a rumble, and opening his eyes, he observed through slitted lids that the ground had given way beneath the feet of the gaggle of girls, so that now they lay in a tangled heap below the level where he stood. They were screaming and crying in terror.

He laughed, threw down his shovel. "Look, Xu," he said, "my morning's work is done. The new cesspit has been dug for me."

Xu was wide-eyed beside him. He leaped up out of the shallow pit and, bending, drew her upward beside him. He watched, content, as Xu lifted up her skirt, squatted, and inaugurated the new cesspit.

Xu, her self-respect restored, took his hand, leading him wordlessly up along a twisting path. Solemn mountain goats, munching tufts of dried grass, observed their ascent with huge liquid-brown eyes. Jackrabbits bounded out of their way, and once, they caught sight of a thick ruddy tail, then a glimpse of a large triangular head as a fox sought to avoid them.

She took him off the path a distance before it petered out on bare rock, and they moved carefully down the scree. Behind a pair of enormous boulders they came upon a small grassy clearing. It was shielded in every direction, utterly private.

"How do you know of this place?" Senjin said.

"I come here when I want to be alone, when I can no longer bear the taunts."

"You won't have to worry about them anymore."

"Oh, no one else would have done that for me!" Xu said, then immediately blushed.

"You could have done that yourself," Senjin pointed out. "You didn't really need me—or anyone."

"Oh, yes. But I do," Xu said. Her eyes darted away at him as she spun around. "It's so beautiful here." She took a deep breath. "The air is so different high up, so sweet, like a baby's smell."

Senjin had other things on his mind. He watched her, wondering how he could change her so that she would reach perfection. But then a sad thought crept into his mind: if he should ever form her into a masterpiece, he would have no choice but to destroy her.

He grabbed her wrist. "Why did you bring me up here?"

"Why?" She seemed confused, as she did when asked to perform with her gift what the elder had just demonstrated. "Oh, to share all this with me."

"Share all what?"

"Well, *this*." Xu threw out her arms to encompass everything around them.

"This patch of dirt and rock looks like every other one."

"No," Xu said, catching his eyes with hers. "This one is different, special. Like you." She took his hands in hers. "Because it's *mine*."

Then, for the first time, Senjin felt her gift. He thought that it must be very weak, although much later, after he had left Zhuji, he began to suspect that perhaps she was expert in shielding the existence of her gift from other tanjian, and he regretted not getting to know her better.

But for the moment, he felt only pity for the feebleness of an aura that needed all this space and solitude to make its presence felt. Still, it was beautiful, as striking as Xu's face, and he surrounded it with the powerful rings of dark steel so that its light would reflect back on itself, better illuminating it. Immediately he saw that Xu had been right: this spot was made beautiful by the projection of her will.

"It is said that you come from Asama." Xu looked up into his face. "Is this true?"

"Yes." He felt the tension come into her frame, and decided to allow her to ask all the questions of him she desired.

"Do you know a tanjian from there known as Aichi?"

"No." But instinctively Senjin knew that he had made a mistake. "What does he look like?" he asked.

Xu described the River Man.

"I know him," Senjin said. "For many years he has been my father."

"Your father!" Xu exclaimed.

Senjin explained how the River Man was Haha-san's brother, and how he had been his first *sensei*.

"Oh, that explains it, then," Xu said. "Why the elders are afraid of you."

"Mubao and the others are afraid of me?" Senjin was incredulous. "Then why did they take me in?"

"They were bound to accept you," she said. "They had no choice. You are tanjian and they cannot refuse you. But coming as you do from Aichi, the man who tried to steal the emeralds of the tanjian—"

"Wait," Senjin said. "I thought the sixteen emeralds had been stolen many years ago by a traitorous woman named Liang."

"There were originally twenty-four emeralds," Xu said. "Eight still reside here. These were the emeralds that Aichi tried to steal."

"What happened?"

"He was caught," Xu said. "He was tried, sentenced, and banished. Now I see that he returned to Asama and has begun teaching his own version of Tau-tau. This is strictly forbidden."

"It hasn't stopped him."

"Obviously," Xu said.

Then something occurred to him. "This law you mentioned, that the elders were bound to take me in. I have not heard of it."

"It exists, I assure you."

Something in her eyes drove him to say harshly, "But that's not all of it." He evoked the projection of his will, just a little bit.

"No," Xu whispered, "it's not all. The law affects only tanjian descended from the prime line."

Senjin was stunned. "Are you saying that I am—"

"You are descended from Zhao Hsia, the martyr who—"

"Was drowned in the falls by So-Peng."

"Yes." Sunlight drenched Xu. Her eyes were liquid. Her face was pure gold. She broke from his grip, moving until she was against his chest.

He felt a stirring of his darkness, the metallic rings that were the projection of his will, which still enclosed her aura. He felt a kind of expansion, a rhythmic pulsing that flooded him with pleasure.

Senjin had already discovered that he could enjoy an odd kind of nontactile sex with his sister. For him, if not for her, it was a game of sorts, of mastery, of dominance. He had loved to feel Shisei's will dissolving beneath the onslaught of his own prodigious aura, his massive coils that encircled hers, until her pleasure was so great that it spilled over into him.

But this was something far different. It was happening to him from the inside out, his coils being manipulated by that which they enfolded, and the intensity was so great that for an instant he was totally disoriented, floating in time as well as in space. He had no control, had ceded all movement to this other will which possessed him utterly, which made even the questions that had burned themselves upon his spirit disappear behind a veil of delight.

When it was over, Senjin was so shaken that he could not stand up. He slid down Xu's form, grasping weakly at her ankles. He closed his eyes and for one brilliant moment he was at peace. Then the questions began to reassert their dominance over him, and he was himself again.

Senjin and Xu never returned to that spot in the Taihang Shan; they never came together in that way again. Perhaps she would have wanted to, but Senjin never gave her the opportunity to suggest it. Part of him reveled in the rape (for there was no other word to adequately describe what had happened), in the kind of wild pleasure she had given him. But another, deeper, more dominant part of him remained so terrified of the experience of ceding all control to another that it would not allow the merging to be repeated.

Three months after coming to Zhuji, Senjin saw that the River Man's

truth was not *the* truth. Three years after that, he discovered that the
Tau-tau truth was also not *the* truth.

Then he thought of Shisei, who he had not thought of in a very long
time. He recalled their conversation when she had asked him, "Why is it
that you see everything inverted?" He had had no answer for her then,
but he suspected that he did now. He longed to drink her in with all his
senses, with his finely-attuned aura, and while thus merged with her, say
to her, "I see everything inverted because I know that in this world there
is no truth, only many supposed truths. Each man has his own or appro-
priates another's, and this is why life is based on conflict."

Three years and three months after Senjin began his work in Tau-tau at
Zhuji, the elders cast the runes. This was a neolithic ritual which took
place over the course of a week. It was a week of constant repetitions,
constant chanting, and Senjin saw in the elders' rituals the increased
excitation of the membrane of *kokoro*, a building of energy that rang in
his ears like a silent shout until sleep was out of the question and every
movement, every gesture, was put toward the beating of *kokoro*.

At the end of this time, the elders met within the center of one of the
stone temples set high up in the side of the mountains. Here a massive fire
had been lit by the women, who tended it constantly. Senjin, when he was
led in, could see the stars through a hole high up in the roof of the room.

Here the elders were hard at work etching runic messages on the inside
of long shards of tortoiseshell. Senjin was reminded of the River Man's
story, of how So-Peng and Zhao Hsia, as boys, had stolen and eaten the
tortoise eggs on the beach at Rantau Abang.

These messages were questions the tanjian elders wished answered
about the future. When they were done with their etching, the week-long
rite culminated with the elders throwing the shards into the fire. The
chanting rose to a crescendo, then slowly subsided.

Afterward, the women were dispatched to retrieve the tortoiseshell
from the ashes of the fire, and by the way each shard had been cracked by
the heat, the elders thus could read the future.

Mubao was brought his tortoiseshell, and he signed for Senjin to join
him. When Senjin had squatted down beside Mubao, the elder said, "This
is your future."

Senjin, staring at the sooty shard of tortoiseshell, could see nothing but
a fine network of cracks bisecting the etched runes. "What is predicted?"
he asked.

"A flood, a torrent, a rage of thunder, a detonation of energy," Mubao intoned. "And after the deluge, *xin*." By *xin* he meant the center or heart of things. *Kokoro*.

Senjin's heart beat fast. "Is this what lies in wait for me?"

Mubao nodded. "In part." His callused thumb rubbed the cracked tortoiseshell. "Death is strong. Its tone permeates the silent echoes we hear and which guide us. Death and more death."

Mubao's thumb paused over one spot on the shard. He looked at Senjin and said, "You must leave here. Our time of the day has passed."

Senjin found it no hardship to leave Zhuji. In fact, he had in recent weeks grown bored with his schooling. He had absorbed everything that Mubao and the other elders had sought to teach him. Now, in his heart, in his own *kokoro*, he wished to teach *them*. They did not know the Truth, but he, Senjin, did. Then, after the casting of the runes, after Mubao had, in effect, delivered his sentence, Senjin understood that they would not understand even if they had given him a chance to tell them what he now knew: that there was no Truth.

It was not that what he had learned was either false or useless. Far from it. But the fact that both forms of Tau-tau were valid and were believed in wholeheartedly, delivered the reality of life to Senjin with the force of a hammer blow.

Nothing was true; nothing was sacred. In that case, there was no Law.

Thus did Senjin return to Japan at age twenty a *dorokusai*. And, to satisfy both his sense of yin-yang and his desire for irony, he became a policeman in the Tokyo Metropolitan Police Force.

He did not return to Asama, to where he knew Haha-san and the River Man were like death, waiting for him. He did not return to Asama, where he assumed Shisei would be waiting for him. It did not matter; they met in Tokyo, on the glittering Ginza, where giant signs of snaking neon advertised the icons of a new age: SONY, MATSUSHITA, TOSHIBA, NEC and CBS/SONY.

They were drawn together amid the winking, blinking electronic jungle, by the concentric circles that had bound them as children, the dark, oiled steel and the coil of sinuous perfume.

Their reunion was a joyous one, though no one looking at them could tell. There was no expression on their faces; everything was internalized. And everything was mended, settled.

Or so Shisei thought.

Senjin moved into his twin's apartment. It was in the most fashionable area of the city. It was huge, filled with Western furniture covered in luxurious, snow-white fabrics. On the way to it that first night of their reunion, Senjin came across three enormous posters with Shisei's face. He saw her on television, singing before a gargantuan crowd of screaming youngsters.

"I'm a talento," Shisei said. "The most successful talento in Japan."

Having been away for some time, Senjin did not know the term.

"I'm a kind of media star," Shisei said. "I sing a little, dance a little, a dilettante entertainer. I give concerts, I'm about to star in my own television soap opera, I do commercial endorsements for all the big companies. Anything and everything. I'm a role model, held up to the hungry public for their inspection and adoration."

"Does it make you happy?" Senjin asked. He was riveted by her image, blue and gold, moving across the screen, caressed by the television cameras. He was certain that the director must be in love with her.

"They're *all* in love with me," Shisei said. "The audience, the crew, the publicists, the corporate executives. *Especially* the corporate executives. That makes me very happy." Her face clouded. "But as wonderful as it is, I know it can't last. A talento must be young, dewy-fresh, virginal. Time is my most vicious enemy."

"But how did this happen?" Senjin asked.

Each wanted to know everything that had happened to the other during the three years they had been separated. In a way, since the texture and complexities of the energies they threw off had changed, they knew. In other ways, they needed to be told verbally. Oddly, they were both reluctant, just as if they were shy newlyweds come to the moment of truth: their marriage bed.

But Senjin, ever the more impatient of the two, was eager to share with Shisei the end of the story of So-Peng that the River Man had begun so many years ago.

"I was right to travel to Zhuji," he told her that night. "They knew what had happened there, and they told me."

It happened, Senjin began, that Tik Po Tak was so incensed by his rival's usurpation of his territory in Nightside that he discovered where the man went to have sex, and invading the brothel just before dawn, he single-handedly slew the man, his three bodyguards, and their lovers while they slept.

At least, this is what the Singapore police thought, and though they had had a lucrative deal with Tak, this bloody carnage he had wreaked was too much even for their avaricious stomachs. They pursued Tak with all of their resources. They were aided in this by the remnants of the slain rival's tong.

Now, it must be remembered that So-Peng had a cousin, Wan, who cleaned the offices of the chief of police. Several days after the hunt for Tik Po Tak was begun, newspapermen, following an anonymous note, discovered the tong's involvement in what was a police murder investigation. The scandal rocked Singapore. The British chief of police, of course, disavowed any knowledge of the involvement of criminals with elements of his department. But the information was too damaging, and he was forced to fire, arraign on charges of misconduct, or reassign, two thirds of his force. This, naturally, left him little time to pursue Tik Po Tak, who eventually returned to Nightside, consolidating his power and then expanding it.

Now, however, Tak was not alone. He had So-Peng behind the scenes to guide him. The tanjian elders at Zhuji say that So-Peng was behind everything. It was he who conceived a way into the closely-guarded brothel, bribing the kitchen staff, who laced the wine drunk by the rival *samseng* and his bodyguards with a sleeping potion.

It had been So-Peng, as well, who had his cousin secrete the incriminating documents in the chief of police's office. And it was So-Peng who applied for the vacancy left by the departing deputy chief of police.

It was ludicrous, on the face of it. After all, So-Peng was only a lad (no older than I am now, Senjin said). But So-Peng was aided by the nature of the emergency in which the chief of police found himself. The chief was under enormous pressure to restore not only order, which a grand show of British soldiers could accomplish, but confidence in his administration. And military might certainly would not do that. Already the governor had met with him twice, threatening to relieve him of duty, sending him back to England in disgrace. Besides, no one else had applied for the job.

The chief of police, desperate, at his wit's end, gave So-Peng the job of deputy, even though So-Peng had not had even one day's experience at police work. But for So-Peng such training was superfluous. He had his extraordinary gift. And he had Tik Po Tak as his staunchest ally.

So-Peng's plan was brilliant. Using the Singapore police, he did Tak's work for him, effectively decimating all of Tak's rival tongs. The other *samseng* could do nothing but acquiesce to Tak's sovereignty.

In this way, inside a week order was restored in Nightside. Within two weeks a suspect in the multiple brothel murders had been apprehended. The major surprise was that it wasn't the *samseng* Tik Po Tak at all, but an overly ambitious member of a rival tong. The evidence against the tong member was overwhelming, and the chief of police and the governor made sure that the murderer's subsequent trial and execution were given maximum exposure. That way the alarmed townsfolk were given a finite focus for their fear and rage.

A month from the day So-Peng was hired, life in Singapore had returned to normal, and So-Peng, at the age of twenty, became the most celebrated man in the Colony.

He had used his gift to bury from sight the murder of his half brother, which he had committed, and the murders he was responsible for planning.

So-Peng had advised Tak to pull his money out of the poppy-growing business. He had, with Tak's money, begun to buy up acres of land just north of the Colony. He hired H. N. Ridley, the director of the Singapore Botanical Gardens, whom So-Peng had met on the tiger hunt Tak had taken him on on their way to find the tanjian who turned out to be Zhao Hsia.

So-Peng set Ridley to work planting his beloved Para trees, and within five years they had the beginning of what was to be the largest rubber plantation in the area. So-Peng quit his civil post to devote himself full-time to his business. He hired the flat-faced boy he had met in the streets near his house. They soon became friends as close as brothers. He allowed his brothers to come and work for him. His father had recently died of dysentery in Java. There was no word about his mother, although So-Peng spent a great deal of money trying to find her.

Time passed, and while the plantation was developing, So-Peng, still using Tik Po Tak's tainted money, bought up other businesses, always at the most strategic time—times of stress for the seller.

He met and married a Chinese woman, and like a machine, she began to drop a female child in his lap every year. But still, it seemed, So-Peng was not content. The tanjian elders say that friction developed between So-Peng and Tak as to how to handle the legitimate businesses. The disagreements became protracted, bitter. Tak wanted out, and apparently So-Peng obliged him.

The authorities discovered Tik Po Tak's bloated corpse floating in the bay one morning. Whatever investigation might have initially arisen was quickly terminated. Even though he had left the police force, So-Peng had maintained close ties with those who had succeeded him. . . .

"But what of the most important part?" Shisei asked. "The tanjian emeralds?"

Ah, the tanjian emeralds, Senjin said. Well, it happens that the tanjian were not idle during the time of their enemy's consolidation of power. They sent out others after Zhao Hsia failed to return. They saw their mistake. They had assumed that the son of the traitor, Liang, would be able to persuade his mother to return the tanjian emeralds she had stolen from her father. They thought that Zhao Hsia would be able to convince his half brother to return with him to Zhuji to properly begin his studies of Tau-tau, as was his right, and duty.

Instead, only death had come of their attempt at forgiveness.

Still, they were loath to assert the full extent of their power. Both Liang and So-Peng were tanjian. Moreover, they were of the prime lineage, and the imperative to keep them alive overrode even the most energetic arguments to the contrary.

So the tanjian elders sent emissaries to find Liang and her priceless cache of power. All efforts failed. They did not find her or the emeralds. So-Peng and the members of his family were watched to see if they had somehow acquired the gems, but there was no sign that they had. The tanjian even kept watch over So-Peng's flat-faced friend, now the foreman of the rubber plantation. They observed as So-Peng's wife died, as he courted and wed a second wife, as she began to deliver sons to him even as, one by one, his daughters died of a virulent plague sweeping the Malaysian peninsula.

The tanjian kept their silent vigil, careful not to interfere, waiting for some sign of the emeralds. What else was there to do?

Zhao Hsia had been telling the truth at the falls. His grandfather, and So-Peng's, was slowly dying an agonizing death. He needed the power of the emeralds, which were like a magnifying glass or a mantra engine: they absorbed energy from the *kokoro* membrane and stored it. Within those emeralds was the energy of the millennia, growing, bouncing from perfect facet to perfect facet, from gem to identical gem, the repetitions expanding like ripples upon a lake.

The number nine was significant since that number of emeralds set up a complex three-dimensional figure whose angular harmonics actually *multiplied* the energy from the *kokoro* membrane. On the other hand, any number below nine would create another figure, whose discordant angles would actually attack the membrane, robbing it of energy and eventually threatening its very fabric. . . .

"What would happen if the *kokoro* membrane were to shred?" Shisei asked.

Senjin looked at her. "Death would happen," he said. "Its tone would permeate the silent echoes we hear and which guide us. Death and more death."

Shisei was seeing someone. It came as a shock to Senjin that time hadn't stood still while he had been away in Zhuji. He was so self-absorbed that it was difficult to believe that events were not held in limbo when he was not there to affect their outcome.

Senjin never said a word against Shisei's boyfriend; he didn't have to. She could feel the oiled steel of his aura darkening like the fall of night, contracting like an adder whenever Jeiji was around.

Jeiji was in his last year of law at Todai, the country's most prestigious university. He was in the top ten in his class. He was the lucky beneficiary of two of the most important bonds in Japanese society—*gakubatsu*, between classmates, and *kyodobatsu*, between townsfolk—his father went to school with the law-school dean, his mother came from the same prefecture in Nara as the head of Tokyo's most prestigious law firm. This man had already pledged to hire Jeiji upon his graduation from Todai. And Shisei was in love with Jeiji. Jeiji had everything, except what he needed most—Senjin's approval.

Jeiji openly adored Shisei. Of course. This was a prerequisite for any relationship she might enter into. The adoration she felt at a distance when the rich spotlights fell upon her must be replicated in more intimate detail, so that she could run her hands over its each and every contour in order to satisfy herself that it really did exist.

Jeiji was made to order for this role. When she had met him, he had been devoted to only one thing: his career. In no time, he had become devoted to Shisei as well. But this was not enough for her. This was perfectly clear to Senjin, although he doubted very much whether it was to his sister. She still saw herself in that exalted virginal state of childhood that existed for them both in Asama; she could not imagine that she had yet within her the seeds of good and evil, let alone the power to wield them. Senjin, of course, knew better.

He watched with studied interest Jeiji's slow slide into wretchedness. Oh, he was sure that Shisei did not fully understand what effect the projection of her will, that seductive coil of perfume, had on someone such as Jeiji. In fact, Senjin became convinced that she did not even know she was flexing her aura each time Jeiji was drawn deeper under her spell.

Jeiji's disintegration—the utter dissolution of his sense of himself—came as a delight to Senjin, especially because he saw the young man as a threat, an interruption of the psychic continuity he sought with his sister. And it pleased his heightened sense of irony that he needed to do nothing but sit back and watch Shisei destroy that which she coveted.

Thus it came as a shock to her when Jeiji was thrown out of Todai for his failure to attend classes, hand in the requisite number of papers,

participate in the highly intensive series of debates on matters of law that
were an integral part of the senior-year curriculum.

Was it possible that Shisei did not understand that her beloved Jeiji
could only be in one place at once, that if he was with her he could not be
at school or studying or writing his papers? Apparently not. And Jeiji,
for his part, had given up all interest in the law. His adoration of Shisei
was now slavish; the more he gave her, the more she wanted.

Senjin observed with fascination her sucking him dry. She was as wanton, as reckless as a whore. She flaunted her gift without even knowing it.
She was as unconscious about this as Haha-san had been about aspects of
herself. The parallel was striking, and the more Senjin thought about it,
the more convinced he was that he must save Shisei from herself.

That was when he decided to kill Jeiji.

Well, not just kill him—that would have been useless; worse, foolish—
but do it in a meaningful manner, a manner that would bring Shisei out
of childhood, that would open her eyes to the reality of what she was and
what her gift might cause her to become. After all, he thought (unconsciously, inevitably taking on the mantle of Haha-san), it is my duty.
Who will take care of her if I fail to?

And what was going through Shisei's mind during this time? Was she
as oblivious to her effect on Jeiji as she seemed to be? Or was she deliberately blinding herself to the truth of her needs?

What she thought of during this time was neither Jeiji nor Senjin. The
impending storm of them both being in her life was beyond her powers of
observation.

Her mind was dominated by the monster of Haha-san—whom she
loved, whom she still considered running to; climbing upon her lap,
pressing her face into the pillows of her breasts to listen to that slowly
beating heart, to close her eyes and to sleep in blissful silence.

And yet, like a scrim pulled across a theater stage, the bursts of Haha-
san's emotional violence followed her, pulsing in the darkness of her
bedroom, filling the end of the night with pieces of the enigma, bludgeon-
ing her with questions she could not answer: How did I fail her? How
could I have pleased her? Does she love me? *Does she love me?*

And each time an unanswerable question assailed her, in reflex she
asserted the sinuous perfumed coils, drawing them ever tighter around
Jeiji.

Long before Senjin decided to kill Jeiji, Shisei was bent on destroying
him, but how could she know that? She would not have believed anyone
—even Senjin, had he been foolish enough to point it out to her—had
they told her. Would she understand that she needed to destroy Jeiji, who

adored her so, in order to save herself from the wintry monster of Haha-san, which still blew through her heart, shutting down a part of her each time it asserted itself? Not yet. But soon.

Senjin determined that if Jeiji's death were to serve a purpose, it would have to serve Tau-tau; it would have to excite the energy at the mem-brane *kokoro*, the heart of things.

As he set to work, it was not lost on Senjin that Jeiji was in many ways the perfect sacrifice. He was, if not a physical virgin, pure in other ways. His adoration of Shisei was without ulterior motive. When Shisei had met him, he had been a rather arrogant young man, as certain of his superiority to others as he was of his place in the world. Shisei's sinuous coils had stripped him of his arrogance, of all artifice, in fact; ironically, at the edge of destruction he was a more virtuous human being.

When Senjin killed him, he was as unprotesting as a lamb. Until the last, he was immersed in his adoration of Shisei, oblivious to any and all unrelated stimuli.

Senjin had spent much time deciding on the moment of Jeiji's demise. But in retrospect he thought that perhaps he had failed to take into account the effect it might have on his sister.

Senjin had a perfect view of working limbs and pumping buttocks as he climbed upon the bed in which they were industriously making love. He would never forget the look in Shisei's eyes when he wrenched Jeiji's head right around, snapping the third and fourth cervical vertebrae. He was reminded of saplings snapping in a stiff wind.

Shisei's eyes were pale—which they always were when she was making love—and they stared into Senjin's with a combination of shock, disbe-lief, and horror. It was this last that, later, made Senjin think that he had made a mistake in his timing.

The truth was, in this he had been selfish, wanting this much for himself, to interrupt forever the one act Jeiji could perform with Shisei that was forbidden him. It was a dream he created out of smoke and spun thought as he pushed Jeiji off Shisei, rising over her so that his shadow fell across her naked body, entering its mysterious hollows as his body could not.

Shisei covered herself as if he were some leering stranger, and this hurt him terribly, so that now he tasted only his own bile in his mouth, and he considered giving it up, throwing away this opportunity to gather power to him, to teach his sister about herself, to force her to grow up.

She spit into his face, and Senjin hit her. Then, because she was becom-ing unaccountably hysterical, he bound her wrists behind her back, her ankles with strips ripped from her own silk pajamas.

The chanting of the ancient runes had already begun in his head. Now he spoke them, the repetitions turning the air dark, setting it to vibrating. He worked to prepare them both for what was to come, as Shisei stared wide-eyed at him, shouted invective at him. That was repetition, too, and served his purpose, so he did not hit her again. Besides, she would soon enough understand what she might have become without his intervention.

This was at a time before he had forged his own blades. He used a factory-made knife, kneeling before Jeiji's corpse and ritually stripping the flesh from it. Shisei's eyes bugged, she made little choked, clicking noises in her throat. Then she vomited. But she could not avert her gaze, could not even voice her opposition to what he was doing.

It had already gone too far. She, too, close to *kokoro*, felt the reverberations as its energy was excited, bouncing off the membrane at the heart of things, creating the presence in the room that was power, that was much more than power, that made them what they were, more than the others all around them.

Gasping, Shisei slipped her bounds and, as if in a fever, extending across the bloody bed, her muscles flexed in spasm, reached out for Senjin.

They had crossed the boundary that separated those who were aware of *kokoro* and those who used it. Yet this was not Kshira; nor was it Tautau. It was something else, something new, something of their own creation.

On that day in 1980 a severe earthquake hit Japan. Tokyo was its epicenter. The violent paroxysm of the earth took seismologists completely by surprise.

Across the ocean in China the tanjian elders, locked away in their sanctum in Zhuji, felt the convulsion at *kokoro* and looked wordlessly at one another.

One, Mubao, especially was filled with dread. He was remembering the casting of the runes and what the fire-induced cracks on the etched tortoiseshell foretold: *A flood, a torrent, a rage of thunder, a detonation of energy. And after the deluge, death. Its tone permeates the silent echoes we hear and which guide us. Death and more death.*

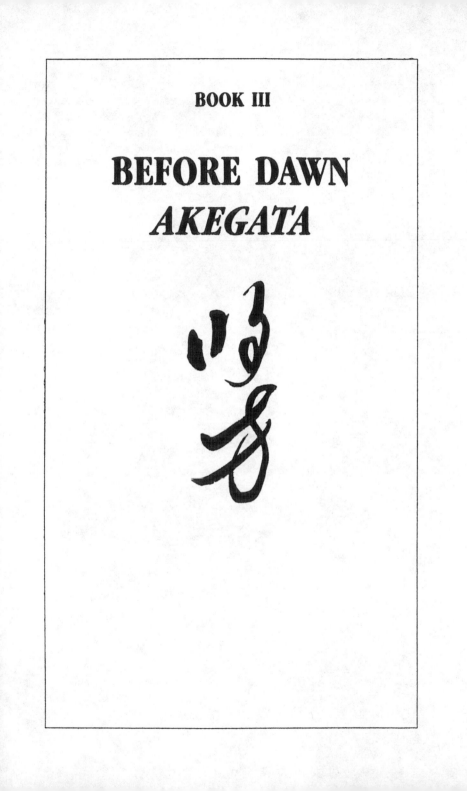

BOOK III

BEFORE DAWN
AKEGATA

*The man who fears nothing
is as powerful as he who
is feared by everyone.*

—FRIEDRICH VON SCHILLER

TOKYO/WASHINGTON/WEST BAY BRIDGE/ NEW YORK

SUMMER, PRESENT

When Nicholas returned home he found that it had been turned into a battlefield. The house and grounds were surrounded by concentric circles of officers from the Tokyo Metropolitan Police Force. They did not recognize him, and so detained him at the outermost ring until someone in a position of authority could be contacted to tell them what to do.

His first thought was for Justine, and his heart froze in his chest. "Can anyone tell me what's going on?" he asked, but they couldn't, or wouldn't. They just stared at him with stony, colorless eyes.

The longer they held him here at the perimeter, away from his house, away from knowing what had happened there, whether Justine was safe or . . . the more agitated he became.

Then he saw Tomi emerging out of the throng of police officers, and he called out to her. She was heading his way, saw him and hurried up.

"Linnear-san?"

"*Hai*. You look surprised to see me, Detective."

"Not surprised; curious. You look different."

He rubbed the back of his hand over his furry cheek. "It's the beard or the windburn."

"And something besides," Tomi said, peering into his eyes. "This is a happy moment. Your coming now must surely be a sign from heaven. Your expertise is sorely needed." She nodded to the men barring Nicholas's way, and they stepped dutifully aside.

"What's going on here?"

"I will take you to Nangi-san," Tomi said. "He's inside the house."

"My wife," Nicholas said breathlessly. "Is she all right? What's happened?"

Tomi glanced at him. "Every bad thing. But do not fear, your wife is unharmed."

"Then she's inside with Nangi-san?"

But Tomi was busy threading their way through the phalanxes of policemen. They went up the steps of the *engawa*, through the door guarded by two officers wearing riot helmets and bulletproof vests and holding machine pistols.

"What is this?" Nicholas asked, indicating the guards.

"It's war, Linnear-san," Tomi said, taking off her shoes. "All-out war."

Nicholas threw aside his muddy, scored mountain boots, shrugged out of his backpack, threw aside his parka, which he had taken off as soon as he had come down from the high altitudes.

"Justine?"

A rice-paper door slid aside and Nangi stepped through.

"Nicholas! Thank God! My prayers have been answered!"

"Nangi-san." Nicholas bowed. The two men embraced one another with their eyes. Tomi had never seen Nangi's face take on such a glow. Watching this extraordinary meeting, she began to understand the singular link between these two men: the closeness between a father and a son.

"Where is Justine? Where is my wife?"

"Gone," Nangi said. "She left eight hours ago for America."

Nicholas, aware of the stricken look on his friend's face, said with a sinking heart, "Why did she leave now? What's happened here? Tomi said we're in an all-out war."

"And so we are," Nangi said. He was leaning heavily on his dragon-headed cane, and Nicholas saw how lined and tired his face looked. Nangi gestured. "But come inside, Nicholas. Umi is here. There is tea and cakes. There is food. Come reclaim your house. We will eat, and I will tell you everything that's happened—at least, so far as I know, which, I readily admit, is not nearly far enough."

Shisei had had only one friend in her life. Kiku was indeed as fragile as the cherry blossom for which she was named—or so it at first seemed to Shisei. Kiku was studying to be a geisha. Shisei had met her in dance class. This had been during the years that Senjin was away in Zhuji. Since dance was one of the fundamental *gei*, or arts, from which the term geisha derived its name, it was not surprising that Shisei should come across geisha students in class.

Kiku had about her a stillness—a sense of a flower preparing to open its petals to the sun, or a bird waiting to spread its wings into the wind— that Shisei admired. Kiku was the best student in dance class. This was, Shisei deduced, because dance was about stillness as much as it was about movement. Like the play of shadows ornamenting an otherwise austere room, stillness augmented the dance steps, set them off, showed them at their most electrifying.

Kiku was able to sit in the proper geisha position—legs folded directly beneath the hips—for many hours with only the slightest, barely discernible movements of her feet (a subtle shifting of her weight) to ease the awful tension that stillness built in muscles, tendons, and joints.

To the extent that Shisei became an acceptable dancer, it was due not to her dance instructor, but to Kiku. In revealing to Shisei the secret of stillness, Kiku taught her a valuable lesson that was to prove useful her entire life. To know when not to move was just as important as to know when to move. Later this ability impressed Shisei's talento managers and, ultimately, her sponsors, the chairmen of Japan's top business conglomerates.

Shisei was thinking of Kiku and stillness when Douglas Howe burst through her door, rupturing the aura of silence and contemplation she had carefully constructed around herself following the phone call from her twin brother, Senjin.

Their abbreviated conversation, like blood poured into shark-infested waters, had disturbed dangerous but up until now controlled elements in her life. The waters, which had been calm, therefore predictable, had abruptly become roiled, menacing, unsure.

Into this potentially treacherous emotional sea walked Douglas Howe. His face was suffused with triumph, his eyes so filled with his delicious victory that he failed to see the tears glistening in the corners of Shisei's eyes.

"I came as soon as I heard! I couldn't believe it!" He was shouting, and his face was florid with his excitement. "This is too good! Too perfect!" He swept her up in his arms, hugging her to him in a grip strong enough to be painful. "Involved in a murder! Oh, Shisei, it's too good, better than I could have imagined! It more than makes up for the goddamned wild-goose chase I've been on tonight." He swung her around and around. "This is what you had planned all the time, isn't it? Jesus God, I swear my luckiest day was the one when you walked into my office!"

Shisei had always known Howe was a pig, but as with all negative facts presented to her, she had filed it away as something she could eventually use for her own purposes. It never occurred to her that Howe's cruelty would affect her personally.

Here was Douglas Howe, gloating and grinning like a monkey over a tree full of bananas. It disgusted her even as it shamed her. There was nothing surprising in his reaction, yet it strengthened Shisei's resolve to tread the treacherous path she had carved out for herself. And she used her anger as a shield against the abrupt turn her life had taken with just one phone call. Senjin was coming; he needed her. What did it mean? Did it put Shisei's own plan into jeopardy? Better not to think along those lines, she knew, or her reserve of courage would dissipate like smoke in summer . . .

Summer. Shisei was once again swimming in the past, in her summer with Kiku, who had dedicated herself to making her life into a work of art. But it was not merely this that attracted her to Shisei. In so early expressing her desire to become a geisha, Kiku was not only embracing a kind of discipline and fealty to duty with which Shisei could identify, she was also exhibiting her own iron will in defying her parents and the collective dictates of a society that decreed that at *tekirei*, the appropriate age, females should find a suitable man to marry. The strength of this defiance was enormously charismatic to Shisei, who in all respects felt herself to be an outsider in a society with a decidedly inward bias.

That Kiku should choose the far more difficult path of dedicating herself to art, so that each movement, mode of dress, gesture, and syllable of speech was painstakingly polished like a facet of a stunning and perfect jewel, meant as much to Shisei as that she was choosing independence over submission. It was further proof to her of the validity of *seishin-shugi*, the triumph of the will over the physical, a philosophy she had embraced since her frightening encounters with Haha-san's emotional violence . . .

"I merely did what you hired me to do," Shisei said with becoming modesty. "What you yourself would have done had you been in the position to do it."

"But you did it so cleverly!" Howe exulted.

"I took my cues from you," Shisei said truthfully. "You gave me everything I needed to do the job well."

. . . The two youths, Shisei and Kiku, regularly spoke for hours of many deeply felt matters. For Shisei these talks, inasmuch as they were able, took the place of her mergings with Senjin.

Nothing lasts in this sad world, Kiku once told Shisei. *The world of flowers and willows that I have chosen is built of illusion, so it makes sense that what matters most to me are taste and style.* So she taught Shisei to revere *iki*, that wholly Japanese form of chic best exemplified by the finest geisha, artful and understated. Again, the stillness amid the movement, the silence amid the noise, the shadow amid the light: all transmogrified their opposites, not only setting them off, but creating something more, a greater whole, an art form that might take a lifetime to achieve.

On the other hand, Kiku, disciplined as she was, was always lonely. She craved a man's company the way most people needed food in order to live. It was Shisei, with her gift, who exposed to her friend the astonishing array of subterfuges young men would use in order to worm their way between a young girl's thighs. Kiku could not, of course, sleep around; even though she was merely a geisha trainee, she was obliged to keep her reputation spotless.

At some point it became clear to both girls that love—the romantic love about which stories were written, songs composed, dramas created —could play no part in their lives if they were to adhere to *seishinshugi* and art, the principles that fired them. Not, they realized one breathless summer afternoon, that these two principles were so fundamentally different . . .

"I'm glad you're so pleased," Shisei said to Howe.

"Pleased?" Howe shouted. "My God, woman, I'm delighted, ecstatic! You've solved all my problems at once! Brisling was expendable. He was never content with what I gave him, he always wanted more. I was setting him up as a buffer. I didn't want to be traced to the investigation I had ordered into Branding's Hive advanced-computer research people at the Johnson Institute."

"Why the investigations?" Shisei asked. Stillness at *kokoro*, the heart of her. A sheet of iron forming, bitter, reflective, the gleaming carapace of a wholly alien creature. The world—her world—turning on the axis of this moment.

"Isn't it clear to you yet?" Howe replied. "I'll do whatever I have to in order to destroy him utterly. This isn't a game I'm playing with Branding. I think you understand.

"I've distanced myself from the operation. It's strictly Brisling's baby. I've got plausible deniability. But that didn't work out. You were right about that, I never should have tried it. Branding got wind of it. This is better—much better! Branding *and* Brisling dealt with in one preemptive strike!

"Forget the environmentalists you work for, Shisei. That mind of yours is wasted there. When the vote for the ASCRA bill is over—and I know it's as dead as Branding's political career—I want you to sign on with me." How easy it was when it suited him to elevate her above the status of slave, Shisei thought. "I could use your talent on a permanent basis. You'll insulate me from any danger; you'll guard my domain like a well-trained mastiff. You'll scare the shit out of anyone who tries to cross me."

And Shisei thought, How dangerous it is to make assumptions. Perhaps I am lucky to have already learned that lesson . . .

There was something else about Kiku that drew Shisei like a magnet. She was aware of it even before the night of the moon-viewing festival when she came upon a delicate-boned young Samurai warrior kneeling on the tatami of the living room of Kiku's house. Her heart seemed to cease to beat, to turn to liquid, to be drained entirely out of her body by the aching beauty of that warrior. That warrior who was Kiku.

Kiku smiled deeply when she saw the look on her friend's face. *This also is a* gei, *an art of the geisha,* she told Shisei. She turned her head this way and that so that the light played across her heavily made-up features. *Do you like it? They say that only women can successfully portray men on the stage because only women have the purity and the perfection required of a hero. Have I done well?*

She had done more than well; she had caused Shisei to fall in love with her. This was another important lesson that Kiku taught Shisei: there is only one thing more important in life than artifice, and that is *kokoro,* the heart of things. To control artifice, to be the master of illusion, is to control the thinking and the emotions of men. This, for a female, was the height of power, the ideal to which one must dedicate one's life. It was, in effect, the ultimate outward manifestation of *seishinshugi,* the triumph of the will . . .

With consummate *iki,* so that even one such as he could not possibly take offense, see through her artful facade, Shisei said, "You don't want me, Howe. Not really." She immediately turned and walked away to make them both drinks. She needed time away from his incessant kineticism to allow the stillness to coalesce again, to accumulate in the dark corners of her psyche, to infuse her with strength, a sense of what she needed, step by step, to do.

"What would you like?" she asked him. "Scotch or vodka?"

"Clear liquor tonight," Howe said, lurching after her. "I can drink more vodka, and tonight while Branding's locked away in a cell, we're gonna celebrate! We're gonna get stinking drunk, because now all my problems are solved!"

. . . Shisei had realized that with her gift and with the doorway Kiku could provide for her, she could become the greatest geisha in Japan. But to what end? The power she could wield—considerable in those circles—was too limited. Her audiences would be too small to satisfy her thirst for adulation. Though she might entertain—and be able, ultimately to influence—the rich and the powerful, these were, after all, only individuals. The stage of the geisha was already too small. Shisei needed to act out her life on a far wider-reaching scale.

And, of course, there was Senjin to think of. In retrospect she saw that he never would have allowed her to devote her life to the willow world. He had a master plan, and she was an integral part of it.

How many times, years later, had he repeated to her, *Shisei, I cannot do this without you,* as if those words, whispered into the delicate whorl of her ear, could ameliorate the pain he was inflicting on her with the bundle of ink-dipped needles that pierced her skin over and over for hours, days, weeks, months on end? . . .

Howe slopped half his drink over his shirtfront in his excitement, and Shisei had to mix him another. In the meantime he had ripped off his stained tie and shirt, and now, bare-chested, reached for his glass.

He was covered in curling black hair, even over his back and throat. Shisei, for whom smoothness of flesh was an ideal, was nauseated. She was reminded of the stoat whose neck *sensei* had cracked just before he had skinned it in thin, delicate strips.

She had never before seen Howe naked, and she wondered why he should want to reveal himself to her, the mastiff, now. It could not be for any sexual purpose, for she knew that Douglas Howe was a man for whom sex's pleasure was defined strictly by the amount of power it gave him. Otherwise, he was content to satisfy himself; who knew better than he what gave him pleasure? He would never take a mastiff to bed; he was too class conscious to ever again lie down with dogs.

Perhaps, she thought, it was her triumph over Branding that gave her, at least for now, a position above the dogs, a kind of status with which Howe would wish momentarily to mingle.

Smiling at his hideous masculine fur, Shisei imagined herself back on stage, swathed in the burning spotlights, aflame with the adoration of young Japan, acting the coquette and then—as the powerful lights turned the amphitheater into a bowl of seething energy, illumined that vast seething throng, their arms outstretched, their faces yearning toward her, toward *her*—and she drawing from them, like milk from an udder, their innocent ardor.

There was a certain pleasure close to her heart in seeing his response, how he melted and strutted at the same time. But he was such a gross, despicable creature that Shisei's secret triumph was demeaned, made meaningless, and she wanted only to be rid of him, to end as quickly as possible this shameful charade she had been dutybound to play.

He finished off his drink, pulled her to him, swinging her around, pushing his face into hers. His breath stank of liquor and decay. She was dizzy from his baseness, faint from his brutality, as if these traits were a kind of radiation he gave off that had begun to affect her in much the same way the atomic radiation at Nagasaki had affected Haha-san.

She gently disengaged herself from his clumsy embrace, said, "Why don't we save this victory celebration until my job is done?"

Howe stared at her. "What do you mean? It's over. Branding's in jail."

"But nothing's been proved yet, and it won't be, until I do my job." She smiled, thinking of the stage where she had reigned until Senjin had come for her. "You want me to finish what I started, don't you? It's what you pay me for. You want it all nailed down, so there's no chance of escape, no way that the outcome can be changed, don't you?"

And Howe nodded, not understanding what he was agreeing to . . .

One day Shisei had gone to Kiku's house and found that Kiku was gone—she had not been in dance class for over a week. There was no trace of her mother and father and sisters, and the family of farmers that now inhabited the house had no idea who had lived there before them— the house was empty when they had moved in three days before. It was as if Kiku and her family had never existed, had been, instead, a figment of Shisei's imagination. This was impossible, but what other explanation could there be? Shisei's dancing instructor ignored her questions about where Kiku had gone, and when she asked Haha-san to make inquiries throughout the neighborhood, Haha-san told her that she could find out nothing of what had happened to the family. But Haha-san had lied . . .

Howe's sweating palms left dark stains on the bartop as he scrabbled for another drink. He was shaking with elation.

Howe began to laugh. "He didn't know what he was up against when I sent you after him. Poor Branding," he said thickly.

Shisei continued to smile at him, the talento again, the perfect icon, as her future, meticulously planned, resolved itself like a reflection in a pool . . .

How had Haha-san lied? She not only knew where Kiku had gone, it was she who had sent her away. Why? Shisei learned this many years later, when it was too late, when her life had already taken too many turnings for it to matter.

But it mattered.

How Shisei wept in the silence and the loneliness of her room, when no one could see, when *sensei* would not scold her for being weak, when

Haha-san would not inquire what was troubling her, pulling Shisei to her pillowlike breast to console her when she did not want to be consoled.

She wanted Kiku.

If, as Senjin later surmised, Haha-san survived by pawning her weaknesses off on them, her charges whom she was duty-bound to raise, to love and sacrifice everything for, then surely she needed to pull them periodically to her breast. For all human life—even Haha-san's—must wither and die without a reciprocity of emotion, even if that emotion be so savage as hate.

And would it not then be understandable that Haha-san would not wish to share her one source of nourishment with another? For this is what had happened. When Haha-san could no longer bear the threat of the relationship forming between Shisei and Kiku, she dispatched *sensei* to rid her of her fear. She had no more thought of Shisei's happiness than she ever had. Only her children's welfare was uppermost in her mind, which is why she sacrificed herself as she did to raise them as her sister would have raised them herself if she had had the strength and the courage.

Happiness did not enter into this equation. After all, Haha-san had no clear idea of what happiness might be. Whatever glimmering of this emotion she might have had as a child had been obliterated by the atomic detonation that had overtaken her and her family at Nagasaki.

In a very real sense, life had overtaken Haha-san before she was ready to accept it. No matter. It had overtaken her anyway, twisting her still unformed personality, lashing her to the unyielding mast of her duty. In the process her heart had turned to glass. And with each agonizing gale of recollection that blew through her, it was shattered into ten thousand fragments.

Shisei, of course, knew none of this at the time of Kiku's disappearance, and if she had, it would have made no difference. She would not have understood, or been able to forgive Haha-san's selfishness masquerading in the guise of altruism. She would have done what she ended up doing, her path had been set, *karma*.

She, like Senjin before her, abandoned the nest, the sanctuary, the prison that had been her world virtually since the day she was born.

And Haha-san and *sensei* were gone from her life. But not forgotten. Never forgotten . . .

Shisei, looking down at Howe, said, "Stay here. I'll get Michael, your driver, to get you out to the car."

But Howe was already shaking his head. "It's Michael's night off." But, of course, Shisei already knew this.

"Well, you can't stay here," she said, bending to lift him off the floor. "I'll take you home."

Nicholas said, "If Justine's gone back to West Bay Bridge, then I've got to go after her." He folded the note Justine had hurriedly left for him. Maddeningly, it said nothing of what had happened or how she felt, just where she was going. It was written as if she did not expect to ever see him again.

Nangi and Tomi exchanged glances. "Until we discover the whereabouts of the *dorokusai*, I don't think that would be a good idea," Nangi said. He had already told Nicholas all he knew: the computer-virus attack on the company's core computers; the suspicions Kusunda Ikusa and Nami had of Nicholas; Ikusa's order to dissolve the Sphynx joint venture, disassociate Sato International with Tomkin Industries; Nangi's idea to bring in another company in order to salvage the merger, the agreement on the floundering Nakano Industries, the signing of the papers in Nami's offices; the Pack Rat's information concerning Ikusa and Killan Oroshi, Nakano's chairman's daughter.

"I haven't heard from the Pack Rat in three days," Nangi concluded. "We have been trying to find him ever since."

"But what happened here?" Nicholas said. "You still haven't told me—"

Nangi gestured. He had already risen. His legs must have been stiff, for he limped more than usual as he led the way outside, around the side of the house. This area among the trees and bushes had been staked off and was being guarded by more Metropolitan Police officers in riot gear.

Nangi pointed to a dark patch on the ground, which had been carefully outlined in lime. He nodded to Tomi, who produced a set of black-and-white prints.

Nicholas took them. They were forensic photos. "Who's this?"

"A man named Han Kawado," Nangi said. "He was one of the Pack Rat's men. Very good. At my request, the Pack Rat had him keep track of Justine—"

Nicholas's head snapped up. "Guarding her."

Nangi nodded. "Even though I did not truly believe she was in any danger, I felt it prudent to—"

"Damnit, what happened here?"

"The *dorokusai* happened," Tomi said. "He was here with your wife. We don't know what happened, except that Han Kawado saw them. The *dorokusai* must have become aware of Kawado." She tapped the photos. "This is the result."

"And Justine?"

"Unharmed," Tomi said. "As far as we can determine."

"What do you mean?" Nicholas turned to Nangi. "Didn't she call you?"

"No," Nangi said. "The first I knew she had left the country was when Immigration informed Yazawa-san."

"Immigration had been alerted some time ago, when we became aware of what now seems to be the bogus threat on your life from the Red Army," Tomi explained. "We wanted as best we could to be able to monitor your and your wife's movements."

Nicholas handed back the photos. "Well, that's it, then. I'm going after her. I've got to know that she's all right. I've got to be with her."

Nangi said, "As much as I sympathize with you, Nicholas, I have to disagree. You know she's headed home to your house in West Bay Bridge. A simple phone call there will ascertain her condition. On the other hand, you're needed here. This is where the *dorokusai* is. This is where the war is. Obviously he was trying to get to you through Justine. Don't you see it's a blessing that she's gone out of the war zone? Do you really want to bring her back into it? Because that is precisely what you will do if you follow her home."

Follow her home. Why did that stick in Nicholas's mind? Oh, Jesus!

He broke away from them, headed into his workout room. He pushed aside the post, knelt as he threw the tatami this way and that. Tomi and Nangi came into the room, stared at him.

He dug down, found the box. But when he opened it, he found the six emeralds gone, their blue velvet bed in shreds.

"Jesus God," Nicholas whispered. "That's what he wanted. The emeralds. Kansatsu was right. He needs them. But what for?" It was clear that the *dorokusai* had somehow gotten Justine to show him where the box was hidden. He did not blame Justine; with the *dorokusai*'s powers, Justine would have been helpless.

Privately, Nicholas thanked whatever forces were looking out for him that he had decided to split up the cache. At least the remaining nine emeralds were safe. For now. With a dismaying lurch he remembered that Justine had seen him wrap the package. Could she have seen the address? Even if she hadn't, she could reason it out. She knew, even if she didn't know she knew, to whom he had sent the emeralds for safekeeping.

Nicholas got up. "I've got to go," he said. "I've got to find Justine."

"Correction," Nangi said. "Your first priority is keeping yourself safe. You won't be able to protect Justine or the company her father willed you if you're dead."

"What does Tomkin Industries have to do with this?"

"Everything," Nangi said. "It's part of the war. It's being attacked along with Sato International, as surely as the *dorokusai* has attacked you."

Nicholas still looked doubtful, and Nangi said, "Hear me out, at least before you decide anything."

Nicholas nodded.

Tomi glanced at the doorway. Several of the guards were close enough to overhear the conversation. "I think we should continue this discussion elsewhere," she said.

Deeper inside the house, in the private areas where not even the police guards were allowed, Umi sat in a six-tatami room. When the three of them came in, she rose, made to leave them to their difficult, painful talk, but Nangi stayed her. "You are needed here," was all he said, and Umi sat back down.

"Even before you encountered the *dorokusai*," Nangi said to Nicholas when they had settled themselves on the tatami, "Umi had intimations of danger. She saw a darkness forming beyond the night. She felt the encroachment of emptiness and an evil so great, it threatened the stability of the world. She heard the voice of the Spider Woman of the Amerindian Hopi. She felt ice coming.

"The Hopi believe that the Spider Woman raises her voice only at the instigation of inordinate evil. In the Hopi myth of creation, the Spider Woman's voice turned the second world—the one before this—to ice in order to destroy its evil inhabitants."

Tomi was fascinated. "What does all this mean?"

Umi turned her beautiful, unlined face toward her, said, "The nemesis of the Spider Woman is awake and active. He threatens the fabric of life. I can hear his footsteps; they are the tolling of a bell."

"Umi feels the *dorokusai*," Nangi said. "She felt him that night; she feels him now. You see, Nicholas, all myth is intertwined like the branches of one tree, old, gnarled, sprung from one source. I suspected then that there was a relationship between the personal attack on you by the *dorokusai* and the imminent raid on Sato by Nami. If you were *Shiro Ninja*, then you were rendered helpless, therefore useless in a coming war. I was right.

"Nami has attacked us—Sato and Sphynx—in your absence. I don't believe that to be a coincidence. Ikusa boxed me into a corner, and I was sure I had found a way to fox him. By taking in failing Nakano Industries, I felt sure I could appease Nami and still keep you as a partner. But the real lure was Nakano's research and development department, which I've coveted for years. I thought I had found a way to gain control of Nakano through the exercising of an obscure warrants clause that was buried in the merger contract.

"Apparently that is just what Ikusa was counting on. Yesterday, I exercised those warrants. What I got was Nakano, all right, but Nakano's now just a hollow shell with nothing of value in it. The R and D department was secretly switched several weeks ago into a holding company that had owned some rusting and outdated oil refineries. That holding company was not part of the merger. I don't own it, and now I never will."

"Then the whole deal was a setup," Nicholas said.

Nangi nodded. "I was in a war and I didn't even know it. Now I understand Nami's involvement in Nakano Industries; it wasn't merely good business practice to bail out a failing company with one asset too precious to allow to fall apart. Nami has used Nakano as bait to snare us, Nicholas-san."

"But you own a majority stake in Nakano now," Nicholas said.

"I own nothing of value," Nangi said mournfully. "In fact, Nakano as Nami has set it up without the R and D department will be in the red this fiscal year for more than four hundred million yen. That, combined with the highly leveraged bonds I had to float in order to buy the worthless warrants, threatens the entire structure of Sato International and, because we are so tightly linked, Tomkin Industries as well. I'm afraid that unless we can come up with a solution, I'll be forced to find someone to bail me out."

"You mean Nami?"

Nangi nodded. "You can bet Nami stands ready, willing, and able to come to my rescue. Except it won't be a rescue, but an out-and-out corporate takeover, just like what happened at Nakano."

"Nonsense," Nicholas said. "You can have access to Tomkin International's assets. We can set up a loan. Structure it—"

But Nangi was already shaking his head. "Don't you think Ikusa's already considered that? There is a MITI prohibition against Japanese companies accepting loans from foreign firms or banks." The Ministry of International Trade and Industry was, along with Nami, one of the two most powerful business entities in Japan, in effect setting economic foreign policy for the country. "Should the borrowing firms default, such an arrangement could lead to foreign takeovers of Japanese companies, something MITI—and, of course, Nami—is adamantly against. Unless we do something fast to stop the bleeding, both our companies are in jeopardy of being targeted for a massive leveraged buyout. Which, I see now, is just what Kusunda was after all along. He wants the secret of the Sphynx T-PRAM computer chip. But it's proprietary, and not even Nami could get it from us. So Kusunda decided to buy us out. Once he owns us, he owns the secret of the T-PRAM." Nangi exhaled deeply. "I am most sorry, Nicholas-san."

"History," Nicholas said, "is only profitable when one uses it as a lesson for the present."

"*Hai.*" Yes. Nangi bowed deeply. He was grateful for Nicholas's understanding. The understanding of a Japanese. "The present is what must concern us now."

"Pardon me, Nangi-san," Tomi interjected, "but there is still the *dorokusai* to consider."

"Yes," Nangi said. "The *dorokusai*. We know quite a bit more about him than we did before you left, Nicholas." He described their tour of The Silk Road and what they had found there—the link between the rape-murder of Mariko, the dancer, and Dr. Hanami, of how they suspected that the *dorokusai* had blackmailed the surgeon.

"You're right," Nicholas said, and told them what he had learned of his condition, of how the *dorokusai* had, in effect, poisoned his brain, or at least one tiny piece of it.

"There's more," Nangi said. "We know the identity of the *dorokusai*. He—"

At that moment a uniformed policeman hurried into the room. So agitated was he that he failed to observe the formalities. Instead he thrust a folded slip of paper into Tomi's hand. When she read it, her face went white.

"What is it, Detective?" Nangi said.

"He's gone, Nangi-san," Tomi said, dismayed.

"Who are we talking about?" Nicholas asked.

"The *dorokusai*," Tomi said.

"His name is Senjin Omukae," Nangi said. "He is a division commander in the Metropolitan Police Force. At least he was up until his encounter with Justine. He did not report for work this morning. Something we don't know about happened—"

"That tanjian is a *policeman*?" Nicholas was stunned.

"Yes," Tomi said. "He was my boss. Which made it easy for him to forge that phony communication concerning your assassination by the Red Army." She waved the message. "Now we know where he's gone.

He was spotted boarding a JAL flight late this morning. He used a phony passport, ID. With his abilities, it wasn't particularly difficult."

"Where was Omukae headed?" Nangi asked.

"The United States." There was a kind of despair in her voice. "New York City."

And Nicholas cried, "Justine!"

The Scoundrel held the artifact in his hand and wondered what he should do with it. He studied it with all the horrified fascination one displays toward a scorpion moving in one's palm.

He thought of the object as an artifact because he had unearthed it, not from an archeological dig, but from the rubble in the apartment next door. He had found blood there, as dark and dry as wine, and bits of matter that might have been bone, but the Scoundrel could not be certain. His field was computers, not anatomy.

He had gotten the idea to take a peek into the apartment the night Killan had come by, when he had heard the loud *thunk!*, a thick, wet sound against the common wall with the adjacent apartment, something he had never heard before yet which seemed weirdly familiar. He knew no one should be in the apartment which was at the moment deserted. The rumor was that a Yakuza *oyabun* had bought the place for his daughter, had ordered extensive renovations, then had a falling out with the contractor. As a result, the apartment, stripped and unlivable, had been lying dormant for more than a month.

Killan had been in the bathroom, so she had not heard the sound, and the Scoundrel had said nothing about it to her. What was there to say? Besides, he needed time to decide what, if anything, he wanted to do about it. So what had made that noise, *thunk!*, a sound not unlike a melon hitting the sidewalk from a height?

A dream had woken the Scoundrel this morning. He did not remember all of it, only the sense of it. *Thunk!* The sound, given weight by his dream, had made him break out into a sweat.

Perhaps it was the dream that, in the end, decided him to take a look inside the apartment. But not until the next day, when Killan was gone, when the building was nearly empty, still as a Western church.

The front door was unlocked, which in itself was odd. The Scoundrel could imagine himself in a film, a detective on an important case: a girl in a black moire dress comes into his office, smokes a cigarette, asks him to tail the man who's been trying to murder her. Now he's trailed the man to his lair. Cue the sound effects, cue the music. Do *not* cue the villain.

Lath and broken sections of wallboard were strewn across the rough concrete underfloor. Bundles of wire starting nowhere, going nowhere, snaked over debris. Old cans of paint, crusted and beginning to rust. The stink of plaster dust—and something more. If this were a film, the Scoundrel thought, squinting through the gloom, this scene would be shot in black and white.

But unlike the hero of a film noire, he was very frightened. The beat of his heart seemed so loud to him that he imagined someone standing in the hall outside could hear it. In fact, he went back through the tiny apartment, peeked out the front door. The silent, deserted hallway yawned. He could not even hear the whine of the elevator. He was alone with his thoughts, frightened by his own imagination. That's what I get for spending my youth in the movie theater, he told himself.

Back in the apartment, he concentrated on the section of the wall from which he had heard the thick wet noise, the *thunk!* that had haunted his dreams last night as if it were a person, not a sound.

The first thing he found was the dark stain: a spidery-looking shape. In its center the wallboard had been smashed inward. He bent closer. On the jagged filaments of the wallboard, and soaked into the insulation behind it, the Scoundrel could see what appeared to be tiny fragments of bone, skin, and some kind of tissue. Someone had been slammed, *thunk!*, into the wall here last night. That was what he had heard: a fight. But here, in a deserted apartment? Why?

There was a great deal of junk piled up against the wall, and the Scoundrel, though he was looking for more evidence of the extent of the fight or who its participants might have been, would have missed (as Kusunda Ikusa had) the tiny tape recorder the Pack Rat had so carefully hidden inside an empty paint can, had he not stumbled over the stubby end of a two-by-four.

The two-by-four barked his shin and turned over the paint can hidden beneath crumpled, stained sheets of last month's *Asahi Shimbun*, and out tumbled the artifact: the miniature tape recorder with its ultrasensitive suction cup for picking up conversations through walls. Staring at it, the Scoundrel thought, through *my* wall. He had scooped up the artifact and hurriedly slipped out of the apartment. But not before checking the hallway again to make certain he was unobserved.

Now, as he remembered once again how he had discovered the artifact and what it portended, the Scoundrel's hand closed around the microrecorder. He knew that he should listen to what was on the tape, but he was afraid. His bosses at Nakano had briefed him, of course, on the astonishingly complex security measures at work in the office. They had similarly cautioned him against taking his most sensitive work—MANTIS—home, where it would not be protected by the Nakano security system. The Scoundrel, staring at the microrecorder now, felt a rising urge to throw it away and forget about it. It made the most sense. After all, what he was holding here was most probably an indictment against himself, a detailing of the many ways in which he had deliberately flaunted the well-outlined security measures he had a duty to uphold. What would his superiors do were they to become aware of his transgressions? They were fanatic about security. Time and again he had heard the phrase, "Breaches of security will not be tolerated at Nakano." The trouble was, he had paid no attention; he had been busy with his work.

Yes, the Scoundrel thought, self-preservation uppermost in his mind, I will dispose of this as if I were a criminal destroying the evidence of his crime. How had he made the jump from detective to criminal in so short a time? he wondered. He was overwhelmed by self-disgust, and he went to throw the thing away, the sooner the better. He was sorry he had ever let his curiosity get the better of him.

Yet when the moment came, he could not throw the microrecorder away. He had to know what was on that tape. Shit, he thought. His finger hovered over the play button, then hesitated. If this recording had been made of him, then his apartment might still be under surveillance.

Stuffing the artifact in his trousers pocket, he went out, losing himself in Tokyo's smoggy sprawl. He was headed for Ueno Park, then thought better of it. If his apartment were under surveillance, perhaps he was as well. It would not do to play the tape in public. Where to go, then?

He had no idea. In fact, he was in a bit of a panic. All of a sudden he had been thrust into the muzzle of a gun. People—he had no idea who—were watching him, bugging his conversations; for all he knew, they were following his every move. Why? Of course it must be the MANTIS virus program. The Scoundrel knew he did not want any part of this. He was a certified genius on the computer, and that was what he wanted to work with. He had already begun to work on the next phase of the program. According to Shisei, the Hive brain was so fast, its internal security program could still overwhelm MANTIS. Laser transistors composed of atomic layers—not of indium phosphide and aluminum gallium arsenide, but of a monocrystalline diamond film—were all well and good for high electron mobility (in fact, he was astounded that the Americans actually had perfected them), but, the Scoundrel knew, under the right circumstances they actually could work to his advantage. The very tunneling effect—turning the electrons that carried the data inside a computer into a light wave rather than separate particles—that made these transistors so fast, could be used to carry the MANTIS spirals more swiftly into its midst. What the Scoundrel had to do was modify his virus program to accommodate the Hive laser chips.

But now consider what he was doing: looking over his shoulder in constant fear that someone was watching him, rather than getting on with his work. He thought about films he had seen, then decided on a course of action.

He spent the next hour and a half doubling back on his own trail, ducking in and out of stores, hurrying down narrow alleys where he had a view of anyone in front or behind him. He used the subways and the buses as well, getting on them and off at the last possible instant.

In the end he was certain that no one was following him, assuming anyone ever had been. Then he headed for Killan's.

Nicholas asked that Nangi go with him to the airport. When Tomi offered to drive them, Nicholas said only, "You're needed here, Detective. You know your duty."

Nicholas had brought up the question of Tomi contacting the New York City police, getting them to detain Senjin at Kennedy Airport, and Tomi had done this. On the basis of the testimony of The Silk Road's owner, there was enough hard evidence to indict him. She gave Nicholas the name and number of the homicide detective she had contacted in New York.

Umi came into the bedroom while Nicholas was hurriedly throwing clothes, passport, money, and other paraphernalia into a carryon suitcase. She said to him, "There are many matters Nangi would discuss with you, but because of matters of propriety, will not. He is of the old school, while I am . . . Well, I understand the old school well, and I respect it. But I see beyond its confines. I see more, but I am less. Do you understand?"

Nicholas paused, several shirts in his hand. "I listen whenever you speak, Umi," he said. "Hasn't this always been so?"

Umi came close to him then, and with her hand on his chin, turned his head to the left, then to the right. "What do I see there, Nicholas? You are different."

"I am tanjian," Nicholas said.

"This has not made you different," Umi assured him. "You were born tanjian, inheriting this from your mother."

Nicholas was startled. "You knew this?" She nodded. "And Nangi?"

"Nangi as well knew."

"And neither of you told me?"

She smiled. "You would not have believed us," she said with conviction. "It was not our place."

Nicholas threw the shirts into his luggage. "Sometimes," he said, "I still don't believe it."

"Being tanjian," Umi reiterated, "is not what has made you different." She was looking into his face in the same way she studied her texts on cultural mythology, with an eerie intentness, as if she were devouring it whole.

"I am stronger now, Umi. Stronger than I've ever been as a mere ninja."

Umi's eyes regarded him directly. "The *dorokusai* is close," she said. "Closer than you believe or can imagine."

"He's already half a world away," Nicholas said, resuming his packing. "I've got a lot of catching up to do."

"Beware. Your new power may at first blind you, until you understand that such power can be a weakness as well. You still have much to learn, Nicholas." Umi watched him at his work, never taking her eyes off his face. "It is useless to speak of distance or of time when one speaks of a *dorokusai*, because one must focus on the power of the mind. And of illusion. Both are trademarks of the *dorokusai*."

"So I have been warned." He was finished. He zipped up the bag, hefted it.

"Do not take lightly this threat to your joint venture," Umi said.

Nicholas smiled for the first time. "Believe me, I'm not. That's why I've asked Nangi-san to accompany me to the airport. I have an idea, but it's very dangerous—not only for me, but for Nangi as well. I want you to know this now. Before I tell Nangi-san."

"I trust you, Nicholas," Umi said. "As does Nangi." That was all she needed to say, and Nicholas was grateful for her support.

"There is something for you to do, Umi," he said. "I may need some help in New York. After I leave for the airport, I want you to make a call for me. Don't use this phone, or yours, for that matter. Find a pay phone and use that. I want you to memorize this." He gave her the Manhattan phone number. "Let it ring for as long as you have to. Whatever you do, don't hang up. Someone will pick up eventually. If you hear a man's voice, tell him, 'Be ready tomorrow.' Exactly that. If a woman answers, say you're a friend of Tik-Tik's. Ask when the man will be in. Get a definite time, and remember to translate it to Japan time. Say you'll call back, and hang up. When you hear his voice, say, 'Be ready tomorrow.' Will you do that?"

Umi nodded. *"Hai."*

Nicholas was grateful again for his network of friends. He turned as he was about to leave. "And, Umi? Don't tell Nangi-san. He'll only worry."

Umi watched him with her intelligent black eyes. He thought she was about to say something, then appeared to change her mind. She bowed, her hands together. "Goodbye, Nicholas-san," she said, using the formal construction, the respectful inflectives.

Nicholas bowed in return. *"Domo arigato,* Umi-san." Thank you.

Justine sat in the third window seat in the giant 747-SP. She stared out the window at billowing clouds, but her vision was turned inward, backward.

What did she remember of her encounter with Senjin Omukae? It might be more accurate to ask what she was allowed to remember. The Tau-tau that Senjin had worked on her still drifted through her mind, keeping her conscious thoughts away from him, from what she had been made to do at his behest.

Instead she thought of her coming to Japan. She felt now as if her time there had been compressed, so intense that she felt as if she had lived a lifetime there, although it was just under four years. She had read, once, an account of a grunt's—an infantry soldier's—time in-country during the Vietnam war, and it seemed to her now that the experience curiously, eerily, resembled her own. In the end both she and the grunt had felt that disorienting compression of time, a lack of community, an acute sense of being overwhelmed by the wholly alien culture—in short, an insidious destabilization of day-to-day life that could, and too often did, lead to the breakdown of reality.

This, Justine assured herself, was what had happened to her. It was why she was flying home now, wasn't it?

All of a sudden her head hurt, and she dug a couple of aspirin out of her pocketbook, stumbled down the aisle to wash them down with the plane's tepid, stale-tasting water.

She returned to her seat, stepping past the child in the seat next to her, settled back down. She closed her eyes and was soon asleep.

She dreamed of Senjin. He was a white tiger stalking her through a sun-streaked jungle.

As a child Justine had always loved the tigers best at the zoos she had been taken to. Despite that, she had never seen a white tiger except in photographs. Thereafter, she had attached a special significance to their splendid coloring: at once more powerful—stark and somehow sad—and less beautiful than their tawny brethren. It seemed to her as if the albino tigers had to give up one thing to gain the other. She thought that was how it was for people, too.

Senjin, the white tiger, came for her. He bounded through the thick tangles of growth that were impeding her flight. He quickly closed the distance between them. When he was close enough to leap upon her, he opened his enormous jaws.

But instead of biting her, he spoke to her. When he did so (did white tigers talk?), it was with Honi's voice. *I will have no family of my own. I am alone. I have chosen to be alone,* the white tiger with the therapist's voice said. The white tiger, its lambent eyes upon her, crouched, breathing, waiting, patient as a god.

And Justine felt only pity in her heart for this great beast, so stark, so sad. *You're so terribly alone,* she said. *Drifting like a cloud above the jam-packed earth. How do you stand it?*

The white tiger's tail went thum-thum, thum-thum, like a heart against the black earth. *When I was a child I was always lonely. I cried often, and was ashamed of my weakness. In time I overcame that.*

A weakness? Oh, no! Justine said. *The pain behind your eyes is a scar upon your soul.* And she wanted to reach out to touch, comfort the beast.

It smiled at her. *My spirit is pure,* the white tiger said. *It is without emotion, therefore it requires no solace.*

But Justine saw through this deception, and she swallowed her fear, went to put her arms around the great beast.

At that moment the white tiger began to come apart. Beneath the mask of the beast stood Honi. She began to say something to Justine, and Justine knew that it was important. She strained to hear. But fissure lines were already forming in Honi's face, and it, too, burst apart to reveal the face of Senjin Omukae. Even in the midst of her dream Justine asked herself, Do I know this man? Have I seen him before?

But before she had a chance to come to a conclusion, the mask of Senjin Omukae began to melt as if it were made of wax, had been held too near the flame of her scrutiny.

And now she could see this creature's true identity, one that it had by deviousness and trickery sought to conceal from her. All else, she knew, had been illusion but this.

She beheld the countenance of her pursuer, and her heart froze in her chest. She felt a scream beginning to form; her throat ached from the effort. She tried to back away but could not move. She knew that she was going to die unless she could move, but there was nowhere to go.

And impaled upon the symbolism of her dream, she started awake. "Huhh!" A great exhalation, an equally great shuddering breath.

"Are you all right?"

"What?"

"You're shaking." A little voice, the girl in the seat next to her, the one who had been reading a book from the moment they had taken off. "Are you sick?"

"No," Justine said, doing her best to smile. She put her head back against the seat. "It was just a dream."

"My mother says not to be afraid of anything you dream," the little girl said. "Is that why you're afraid?"

"Yes," Justine said, her smile a bit brighter. "I suppose so."

The girl rummaged in her backpack, pulled out a candy bar. "Have a Snickers," she said. "They always make me feel better."

Justine had to laugh. "Thanks." She took the candy bar, began to unwrap it. "You know, this looks awfully big for one person. How about we share it?"

"Great!" The little girl squirmed with delight.

Justine, watching the tiny mouth devour the sweet with such unalloyed enjoyment, found that this gave her more pleasure than eating her half. "What's your name?"

"Martha."

"Mine's Justine." She smiled. "I'm glad we met."

"Me, too!" Martha said, licking her lips of the last of the candy bar's chocolate coating.

"You're traveling alone?"

Martha made a face. "My mom's in New York and my daddy's in Tokyo."

"That's a long distance to be separated," Justine observed.

Martha's face fell. "They were separated before Daddy ever moved."

"Oh," Justine said, feeling as if she had stumbled into someone's very private room. "Well, at least you get to see them both. And Japan, to boot."

"Yeah!" Martha brightened. "I like Japan. I've made some friends there. I'm always sorry to leave." But her face told Justine that it wasn't her new friends she was sorry to leave.

"I want to show you something," Martha said, rummaging again in her backpack. She extracted a sheet of heavy paper, rolled and kept with a colored cord tied in a bow.

Martha slipped the cord off, unrolled the paper, handed it shyly to Justine. "I made it myself."

"Why, it's beautiful!" Justine exclaimed. And it was: a painting of the Japanese countryside, primitive and lovely in the candor of its bold, uncomplicated strokes. It captured something about the culture Justine had never been able to put into words. She thought of it as a kind of austerity, but translated through the child's eyes, it became a purity that was, perhaps, closer to the truth.

"I made one like this for my daddy," Martha said. "He was so proud, he put it up right away in his office. This one's for my mom."

"He *should* be proud of you," Justine said, handing it back. She helped the child slip the cord back over the cylinder of paper. "You're very talented."

"Thank you," Martha said. "But I didn't work so hard on it or anything."

"Sometimes very hard things come easily to people," Justine said, thinking of Nicholas, and of how proud she would be of Martha if she were her mother and were presented with this painting. "I think it's wonderful."

Martha squirmed in her seat again as she returned the painting to her backpack.

Justine, wanting to keep her attention, said, "What are you reading? It must be interesting. You've had your head stuck in it all the time we've been flying."

"Oh, it's a book about two girls," Martha said. "One has no friends."

"That's terribly sad," Justine said, meaning it.

"Yes, but it's sadder for the other girl," Martha said. "She has no family. I think that's the saddest thing of all, don't you?"

Justine looked at this little girl, at her freckled face, her innocent eyes, the tiny blue and white outfit she wore—blouse, skirt, shoes and socks— so accurately mimicking an adult's ensemble, and her heart melted. For the first time in many months she touched her belly without any sense of loss, guilt, or anxiety.

One of you is in here, she thought. Growing inside me, being nourished by me. When it comes out it will be tiny and helpless and in need of love. Martha's words, *I think that's the saddest thing of all, don't you?* echoed in her mind.

"Yes," Justine said, meaning it, "you can always make friends—like your friends in Japan; like us. But not having a family is the saddest thing of all."

The Scoundrel listened to what was on the microrecorder while he waited for Killan Oroshi to come home. He had let himself into her apartment, which wasn't difficult for him since he had designed the computer-generated digital locking mechanism that served in lieu of the conventional key and tumbler lock system. "You never have to worry about walking out without your keys," he had told Killan when he installed the new system. "Besides, it's far more secure." Except for him.

White-faced, the Scoundrel went into Killan's minuscule kitchen, poured himself a stiff shot of Suntory scotch while he tried to digest everything he had heard on the tape. Talk about incrimination, he thought. But then, he wasn't the only one incriminated. There was Kusunda Ikusa, as well. Christ!

The Scoundrel downed the liquor, hurriedly poured and drank another. Then he went back to where the tape recorder sat on Killan's free-form ferroconcrete coffee table like a malevolent beast, waiting to be unleashed. He played the whole thing again.

He was sitting, his face in his hands, staring at the beast, when Killan walked through the door.

"Howzit, Scoundrel," she said. If she was surprised to see him, he couldn't tell it. Anyway, they were always popping up at each other's places. "What d'you have there?"

"Our pasts," he said, not taking his eyes off the black metal shell of the recorder. "Also maybe our futures."

He played her the tape.

Killan said nothing until it was over. He could read nothing on her face; it was as if she were dead, or concentrating. Then she said into the silence, "Where in the hell did you get that?"

He looked at her. "Had no idea you were being tagged, did you?"

"Shit, no." She pointed at the beast. "Whose is it?"

He shrugged. "It belongs to me now. I found it next door. In the deserted apartment." He told her of the sound he had heard while she was over, the *thunk!* like a melon hitting the pavement from a height. "Or a man's head being smashed into the wall." He told her what he had found, the dried blood and human matter in the hole in the wall.

"Must have taken a lot of force to do that to a human head," Killan said.

"Yeah. A whole helluva lot." He could see her brain working overtime even as he said it. "Hey," he said, "what're you thinking?"

"I'm thinking about what could have gone on in there—and who could have been strong enough to smash a human head hard enough to break through the wall. Brute strength rather than finesse."

"You mean you know someone who could do that?"

"Maybe," she said. "Yeah." She gestured. "You figure out what you're going to *do* with that tape?"

The Scoundrel said, "I was thinking of giving it to someone I know."

"Yeah? Who?"

The Scoundrel hesitated. He had been dreading this moment. "Tomi."

"Ugh! That bitch?" Killan cried. "No way. I've got a better idea."

"Yeah? Better for me or for you?"

"You're too cynical sometimes," Killan said, sitting down beside him. She smiled. "Are you having second thoughts now, after all this time? Whatever I do, it'll be what's best for both of us."

"I don't know about that."

"Why did you come here, if it wasn't for my help?"

"I needed a safe place to play the tape. I couldn't tell if the surveillance on me was still in force."

Killan looked from him to the microrecorder. "The tape tells us that you weren't the only one being monitored," she said. "In other circumstances I suppose I'd think having my sexual couplings taped was kinky."

"Jesus, d'you think this apartment's being watched?"

"I have no idea."

"I was very careful."

Killan laughed. "Sure. I know you. The last detective."

The Scoundrel grunted, contemplating the beast on the table. "So," he said at last, "what do you want to do with it?"

"Take it to the person who'll want it most."

"Who's that?"

Killan's eyes began to spark, and there was just the hint of a smile on her lips. "Kusunda Ikusa," she said.

The Scoundrel jumped just as if she had struck him with a live wire. "I always knew you were nuts," he said. "But I didn't know until now just how nuts."

"Calm down and think about it," Killan said. "Ikusa will give us everything we want for that tape. And why not? It's bad enough that his affair with me would come out if it were made public, but the evidence of his manipulation of Nakano Industries for his own ends would destroy him utterly."

The Scoundrel got up, paced back in forth in front of her and the dully gleaming beast on the ferroconcrete table. "You know, I remember once years ago when you were just a kid and wanted to hang out with us on the street, one of us dared you to put your hand in a fire. We thought you'd chicken out and we'd get rid of you." He reached out, turned her right hand palm upward. His thumb traced the old raised scars there. "But you called our bluff. And we let you run with us. We called you Bad Company then. But Killan, that was then and this is now. We were all so young, we didn't know any better. Now we do."

Killan, looking directly into the Scoundrel's eyes, said, "How can you talk like that? Or are you blind to how you're being exploited by Kusunda? He's the real power behind Nakano Industries; my father is history. You're being paid shit for your work, and it's Kusunda's doing. You've created MANTIS, and what do you have to show for it? Nothing. Worse, there will never be anything *but* nothing for you. How many times do I have to remind you? You work like a dog for Kusunda. And for what? Who's profiting from what *you* create? Who *should* be profiting from it?"

She gave him a cynical look. "Besides, I *love* those scars. They're a part of me—an *important* part, like a badge or a medal. They say I didn't back down then; they say I was as good as any *boy* on the street, I was as tough, and a whole helluva lot *smarter*."

"Crazier, too."

She laughed. "But I *survived*. It's my karma to survive. I've got the brains to beat them *all*, Scoundrel."

"But Kusunda Ikusa." He shook his head. "He's different. Hasn't it occurred to you that Ikusa might be smarter than you?"

Killan shook her head. "Uh-uh." Then she grinned, in one motion pulled away from him and scooped up the microrecorder. "Trust me." She kissed him lightly on the cheek. "This is our ticket to the promised land. Everything we ever wanted."

The Scoundrel looked down at the empty table. In a moment he said, "I have everything I want."

But Killan was already gone.

The police came for Shisei, polite, deferential, even. She was expecting them, and went with them without fuss. A bearded, porky detective questioned her concerning her whereabouts during the night before. Shisei watched his eyes, which were intelligent and penetrating. He inhabited a crumpled, ill-fitting suit the way other men wore robes; he was comfortable, relaxed. Shisei, dressed in a short black skirt, wide black cloth belt, and a fire-red cap-sleeved blouse, spent some time taking him in.

He was eating a sloppy meatball hero while they talked, but Shisei got the impression this was trapping, like a good actor using a bit of stage business. She wondered whether he was trying to put her at ease or attempting to catch her off guard.

They sat at a scarred wooden desk set in the center of a featureless room painted a dull institutional green. A water cooler stood in one dusty corner, a greasy hot plate with a glass pot of coffee in another. There were heavy metal grills across the windows.

Although the detective, who told her his name was Albemarle, did not say it, it was clear by the direction of his questioning that Branding had given her as his alibi. Albemarle said that the police had received an anonymous tip about the body in Branding's car. Nothing was known about the caller other than he had a male voice. Right now, he said, they were holding Branding for the suspected murder of David Brisling. Because of the much publicized, often rancorous enmity between Branding and Howe, there was cause to question Branding at length. Shisei understood the implication that the police still needed to establish motive and opportunity. Which was why they wanted to question her.

Of course, they would never discover the truth. The call she had made from her house on the night she had killed Brisling had been to a support group whose number she had memorized when she had first been given the assignment to help infiltrate the Hive Project. She had left for them a copy she had previously made of the ignition key to Branding's car.

While Shisei and Branding were at the State dinner, the group had taken the car, deposited Brisling's corpse into the trunk, and driven it back. They had left their car in Branding's parking space so that his car would be just where he had parked it at the beginning of the evening.

Shisei answered all of Detective Albemarle's questions as fully as she was able, omitting only her discovery of Brisling in her house when she went back for her purse. But she did tell him about the oversight because she wanted him to see that she was giving him everything she had. Also, she didn't know how full a statement Branding had made, and there was no point in giving him a discrepancy that he would start thinking about.

"You and Senator Branding are good friends," Albemarle said after a while. He did this while wiping tomato sauce off his lips.

"We went to the State dinner together," Shisei said. "It's not the first time we've been together after business hours."

Albemarle took a long look at her. He grinned, showing a set of broad teeth. "I admire the senator's taste."

"Excuse me, but how is our relationship interesting to you except from a voyeur's standpoint?"

Albemarle laughed to show that he had a serviceable sense of humor, but he sobered up fast. "You're the senator's alibi."

"Are you implying that I would lie for him—out of love?"

The detective shrugged. "It wouldn't be the first time."

"Two hundred and fifty other people saw Senator Branding at the State dinner."

"But according to your statement"—Albemarle's eyes flicked down to the note pad on which he had been writing—"you and the senator arrived at the White House at approximately eight-thirty. Is that right?"

"Yes."

"Well, the doc said Brisling was iced anywhere from seven to nine P.M. That leaves a lot of time before eight-thirty."

She was aware of how long he had withheld that information from her. "We were together from a quarter to eight on."

"Couldn't have taken but, what? Three minutes to murder Brisling," Albemarle drawled. "Give me your best guess. What did Branding do for the other forty-two minutes?"

Shisei could feel Albemarle baiting her. They had come to the crucial time in the interrogation. He was tired of sparring with her. He had taken off his gloves; it was time for her to do the same. "Senator Branding didn't murder David Brisling," she said.

Detective Albemarle's brow wrinkled, the sole sign that she had surprised him. His eyes held steady on hers, as if they could detect a lie at twenty paces. Shisei thought that might be precisely what he believed. "Now how would you know that for a certainty?" Albemarle drawled.

"Why would he carry Brisling's body in the trunk of his car all night? He's not stupid and he doesn't have a death wish."

"He'd want to dump it somewhere. He didn't have time to do it before he went to pick you up."

"You told me he had forty-two minutes."

Albemarle said nothing, but his eyes said he wasn't giving ground—yet.

It's too convenient, too like a setup, Shisei wanted to say, would have said to a detective less discerning than Albemarle. But she had to be careful not to let him see her do too much of his work for him.

She reached into her pocket, drew out an audio cassette. "Do you have something to play this on?"

Albemarle stared at the cassette for a long moment, then, as if making up his mind, he grunted, reached into a drawer of the scarred wooden table, pulled out a tiny tape recorder. "You've been singing for the birdie." He grinned, snapped out a cassette of his own. "I don't trust my shorthand. It's been so long since my Kelly Girl courses."

He inserted Shisei's cassette, pressed the play button.

"Brisling was expendable," Douglas Howe's voice said. "He was never content with what I gave him, he always wanted more."

Albemarle stopped the tape. "Who's this?"

"Senator Douglas Howe."

"Ah." Albemarle nodded.

Shisei liked this man. She didn't have to tell him that Howe was Brisling's boss or that Howe and Branding spit at each other every time they met. He knew all that.

Albemarle's finger stabbed out. "I was setting him up as a buffer," Howe's voice continued, a disembodied voice at his own trial. "I didn't want to be traced to the investigations I had ordered into Branding's Hive advanced-computer research people at the Johnson Institute."

"Why the investigations?" Shisei's voice said.

"Isn't it clear to you yet?" Howe replied. "I'll do whatever I have to in order to destroy him utterly. This isn't a game I'm playing with Branding. I think you understand.

"I've distanced myself from the operation. It's strictly Brisling's baby. I've got plausible deniability. But that didn't work out. You were right about that, I never should have tried it. Branding got wind of it. This is better—much better! Branding *and* Brisling dealt with in one preemptive strike!"

Albemarle stopped the tape. "How'd you get this?"

"I've worked for Howe on and off," she said. "Nothing official. I liked the money, I admit that. But this thing between him and Senator Branding was getting out of hand fast, I could see that. I tried to warn him, to stop him, but he simply wouldn't listen. Howe was obsessed with his feud. All he could think of was destroying Branding. I wanted out before Howe did something really stupid."

"Like murder his assistant and try to pin it on Branding." Albemarle tapped his forefinger against his lips. "What exactly did you do for Howe?"

"When my environmental interests and his overlapped, as they sometimes did, we pooled resources, got bills passed up on the Hill. That sort of thing."

Albemarle nodded. "Go on."

She leaned over the desk, started the tape running again.

"Forget the environmentalists you work for, Shisei," Howe's voice went on. "That mind of yours is wasted there. When the vote for the ASCRA bill is over—and I know it's as dead as Branding's political career—I want you to sign on with me. I could use your talent on a permanent basis. You'll insulate me from any danger; you'll guard my domain like a well-trained mastiff. You'll scare the shit out of anyone who tries to cross me."

The tape ran out, and Albemarle turned off the machine. There was a thoughtful look on his face. "What'd he mean by that?"

"Howe saw me in the same light he saw Brisling. We were dogs to be trained to do his bidding. He's loathsome."

"No. I meant about scaring the shit out of people."

Shisei shrugged. "I know some martial arts. Howe liked that; it made him feel more secure to have me around."

Albemarle grunted again. "I'll say one thing for you, you sure ain't worried about implicating yourself."

"In what?" Her voice was absolutely neutral. Shisei knew to be more careful than ever now. She could see the sheet of ice Albemarle was leading her toward, waiting for her to hit it with her backside.

"You're so good with your hands, so scary, how about you iced Brisling for Howe?"

She made sure her eyes didn't waver from his, but there was nothing aggressive in her look. "Tell me again how Brisling died."

"Something thick and square crushed the back of his head," Albemarle said, as if he were describing the features of a new car. "You know, like you do with an eggshell on the edge of an iron skillet."

"That sounds to me like a crime of high passion, done in a fit of rage, or at least with a sense of premeditated hate," Shisei said. "Besides, I had no motive."

"You told me you work for Howe. You like the extra bread."

Shisei was good at putting venom in her voice. "When I was young, I was used by a man. Abused, you might call it. I vowed then I'd never let it happen again. No one has the right to do that to me. When I realized that Howe was using me, I called it quits." She allowed her face to relax a little. "In any case, I would have been more circumspect in what I did."

"Meaning?"

"Do you know anything at all about the martial arts, Detective?"

"I've taken some karate—the usual departmental thing."

"If you don't mind my saying so, that isn't martial arts. That's putting your hand through a board or subduing a perpetrator."

"Perps're my business."

"But they're not mine, Detective. The true martial arts—the way they should be taught—are eighty percent mental. In any case, they're reactive. I was never trained to be the aggressor. If David Brisling—or one of your street perps—came at me, I'd know what to do to protect myself, but I certainly wouldn't smash the back of his head in. I wouldn't have to work that hard."

Albemarle was silent a long time. He produced a toothpick, began to twirl it around his mouth. Then his finger tapped the tape recorder. "I'll need to impound the cassette. Evidence."

"It's yours," Shisei said.

"When I bring Howe in, I'll want you with me."

"Well." She let something new into her voice. "I wouldn't mind that at all."

When Nicholas cleared Immigration and Customs at New York's JFK Airport, he heard his name being called over the loudspeaker. He went to a courtesy phone and was given a telephone number. He went over to a bank of chrome and graffitied pay phones. He needed to go to the far end of the baggage carousels to do so. He had gotten yen changed to American dollars at Narita Airport. He dialed the local number he had been given.

"It's me," a voice said. "I'm at a phone on the other side of the place. I can see you. No one's tagging you."

"I didn't think it was that kind of situation," Nicholas said. "We can meet."

Nicholas dialed the number Tomi had given him. Homicide detective Mel Branca was working nights, and he took Nicholas's call. "Bad news, bud," he said in a smoky voice. "I met this Japanese yo-yo's plane like Tomi asked me to, but couldn't find the guy. He was on the passenger manifest, all right. I checked that. I even polled the flight crew, but none of them could remember him. The seat assigned to him was filled, though, that's all they could tell me. Best I could do, bud, at such short notice. My in tray's higher than a cokie with a head on."

Nicholas thanked Branca, hung up. He was about to call Justine, at their house in West Bay Bridge, then thought better of it. If Senjin were loose here, there was no point in giving him any advance notice of his, Nicholas's, arrival. But the thought of the *dorokusai* with Justine out in the beach house was almost too much to bear.

Patience, he thought. Your time is coming.

He turned, saw Conny Tanaka striding toward him. It had been Conny who, through Umi, Nicholas had asked to meet him here at the airport.

Conny was Terry Tanaka's older brother. He had been living in Vancouver when Saigo had come to New York in 1980, challenged Terry in Terry's own *dojo*, and subsequently killed him. Afterward, Conny had left Vancouver to get his brother's martial arts school back on its feet. But he had never gone back to British Columbia, preferring the highlighted kineticism of New York. Conny loved to party, but that didn't mean he wasn't serious about business.

"Tik-Tik," he said, taking Nicholas's carryon from him, "I got your message." Only Conny called Nicholas Tik-Tik, because, as Conny had once told him, *You're like a bomb, man, ticking away beneath that ultracool exterior. Nobody has a chance against you.*

Conny had no trouble recognizing him; Nicholas had shaved off his beard thirty thousand feet over the Hawaiian Islands. "What's up?" Conny said now.

"Trouble," Nicholas said as they weaved their way out of the terminal. "A whole bellyful of it." It was already night, the sodium-arc lights bathing everything in their unnatural bluish glow. Windshields were haloed and people's faces looked ghoulish, drained of blood.

Only Conny looked the same, short, squat as a fireplug, muscular shoulders and arms, slim hips. He moved like a dancer with his center of gravity low to the ground. His square, even-featured face, so like Terry's, yet so much more massive, seemed intimidating to those who did not know him. Yet, as Nicholas knew, Conny was capable of great tenderness and concern. It had been his idea to give a third of the *dojo*'s profits to Eileen Okura's family. Eileen had been Terry's girlfriend before Saigo had murdered her.

It had begun to rain. The access road looked filthy, clotted with soggy trash. They crossed it, dodging limos, cabs, and lumbering buses, picked up Conny's battered Buick in the short-term parking lot. "I've got a lot to do and very little time to do it in."

Conny threw Nicholas's carryon in the backseat, fired the engine. "We'd better get rolling," he said.

In the privacy of the car's interior Nicholas turned to Conny. "It's good to see you, Tanaka-san," he said formally.

Conny bowed. "You honor me, Linnear-san." There was a debt that Conny could never repay Nicholas for avenging his brother's death. It was unspoken, and would forever be, but it was always there, cementing the boundaries of their friendship.

"First things first," Nicholas said. "West Bay Bridge. You know where."

Conny nodded as he paid the parking lot attendant, and they joined the line of vehicles on the airport ring road. "Everything's as you left it. It's cleaned every week, and someone comes to check up every other day."

"And my car?"

"I go out and run it myself each weekend," Conny said. "It's in beautiful shape." He swung around a rental car minivan that had stopped to pick up passengers. "I miss that old house. You were smart to buy the place you'd been renting. Bought at the right time, too, when the market was soft. Beach houses are hard to come by now, unless you want to build one from scratch. Then you've got to want to part with two, three million, easy."

"Ouch."

Conny gave him a look. "What d'you mean ouch, man? Did you ever count how many millions you're worth?"

"No." Nicholas grunted. "To tell you the truth, I've never gotten used to the wealth. I'm not entirely comfortable with it."

Conny nodded. "Yeah. Money's got a karma of its own. Well, you've got to ride it like an unbroken stallion."

"Doing my best," Nicholas said as they accelerated, heading east on the Van Wyck Expressway.

The windshield wipers made a kind of music, a rhythmic undercurrent. It wasn't until they were past Patchogue that Nicholas spoke again. "There's some very bad news headed my way. In fact, it's already here. It's the kind I don't want you to touch under any circumstances. The way you can help me best is to stay at the periphery."

"Just how bad is it?" There was no inflection in Conny's voice.

"I'm in a tunnel," Nicholas said, "and truthfully, I don't know if I'm coming out the other side."

"That bad," Conny said. He flashed Nicholas a grin. "It's a good thing you've got friends, man."

"I know."

"But you don't say 'don't touch' to friends, Nick. You don't keep them on the periphery when they can help you stay alive."

"Conny—"

"I'm not about to let you tie my hands behind my back just so I can watch you die."

Not a word was said about Terry Tanaka and the debt Conny owed Nicholas. It didn't have to be. It had its own life in the minds of both these men. *Giri* was never spoken of among Japanese. Everyone knew that it existed along with the air that one breathed, and was just as essential to life.

"Okay," Nicholas said.

Nicholas kept to himself the rest of the way out. When Conny swung the Buick off Montauk Highway into the parking lot of the A&P in West Bay Bridge, he said, "The place looks the same."

Conny trod hard on the brakes. The Buick's headlights illumined empty spaces. "It's not here, man," he said. "Your car's gone."

"That's a good sign," Nicholas said, knowing that Justine must have taken it. "Just drop me off at the house."

"I can hang around if you want."

Nicholas knew what Conny meant, wanting to be there if there was going to be trouble. "You'll be more use to me in the city. I've got a couple of things I want you to do." He handed Conny a sheet of paper folded around an audio cassette Nicholas had taped on the flight over. "Take a look when you get home."

Conny took the cassette and the note as he wheeled out of the parking lot, heading for Dune Road and the Atlantic Ocean. It was late, quiet. Just some kids hanging out against their cars, smoking, drinking, perhaps. But the little town had a peaceful look, like something out of a children's story, waiting for teddy bears to begin dancing along the streets. Nicholas thought of Justine.

He remembered the Christmas they had spent out here just before leaving for Japan. They had needed to be alone, away from the city and, in the aftermath of the holocaust caused by Saigo, everything it had come to represent.

How beautiful the town was, with Christmas trees strung with colored lights all along the streets, a dusting of snow on Christmas morning and then brilliant sunshine, the beach so cold and windy that they couldn't take their usual early walk, so they retreated to the house to drink steaming glass mugs of mulled wine Justine had made while they opened presents. She had given him a watch, the one he still wore now; he had given her a ruby necklace from Tiffany's. He remembered how much time and care he had spent in selecting it for her, the look on her face when she had opened the blue box.

What's happened to us since then? Nicholas asked himself. Where did we get lost inside ourselves? When did we stop being a couple?

"We're here," Conny announced.

The Buick's headlights illuminated Nicholas's car, a 1962 white Corvette with red side scoops. Nicholas had had it completely reconditioned a year after he had bought it, and it ran superbly.

"Hey, someone's in there," Conny said. His voice was wary, and Nicholas could feel the tension come into his frame.

The lights were on in the house, but Nicholas could not see anyone moving around.

"It's okay," Nicholas said, getting out of the Buick. He reached in, pulled out his overnight bag. "Go back home, Conny. You've got a lot to do."

Conny nodded, waited until Nicholas stepped back, then reversed out of the gravel driveway.

Nicholas went up the steps to the house. Behind him the black Atlantic pummeled the shoreline unmercifully. Out here in winter, he knew, the beach could lose two to three yards to the sea and to storms, until spring came and the winds and tides turned more favorable. It was ten to fifteen degrees cooler than it had been at the airport, and he was grateful for the relief from the sticky heat. He was hungry and he needed a shower.

On the porch he used his key without ringing the bell. Despite what he had told Conny, he was cautious. He did not know where Senjin Omukae, the *dorokusai*, was, or even what he really wanted beyond the rest of So-Peng's emeralds.

If you die now, if you die too easily, you will never understand. What had the *dorokusai* meant? Nicholas thought he was closer to finding out.

He crossed the threshold, heard music coming from the stereo, Tracy Chapman singing "Fast Car." One of Justine's favorites. He knew he should relax a bit, but he could not.

He looked around the wide, open living room, dining room, and kitchen. The space looked huge, yawning after so much time in Japan, where everything, it seemed, was in miniature, exquisite miniworlds standing shoulder to shoulder, elbow to elbow, in a land where for centuries chronic overcrowding had been a way of life.

Amazingly, the large fish tank, the demarcation between the living and the dining areas, had been maintained. A trio of lacy angelfish swam regally by, and his ancient whiskered catfish was wiggling up one side, vacuuming algae as he went.

"Gus, old buddy," Nicholas whispered to the catfish. "It's good to see you."

He put his bag down, went silently all through the house. When at last he came to the master bedroom, he found Justine's suitcases opened on the bed. She had not unpacked, but clothes had been laid out. He heard the shower running. In a moment it was shut off.

He stood there in the semidarkness, in his own house, listening to his wife moving about the bathroom. Yet he did not move. It occurred to him that he felt like a stranger here, and the realization saddened him. He had no home, no family. The only thing he seemed connected to was Japan.

He abruptly realized what this connection had cost him, and he wondered whether it was worth it. Japan was his milieu, but it was not Justine's. Until this moment he had not realized what a fundamental difference that could be. Now standing here, alone, in the midst of everything that should have been familiar and comfortable and was not, he could put himself in Justine's mind, see as she saw the alien in the familiar.

At that moment he almost turned and walked away, but he could not. She rooted him to the spot as much as did his anomie, an ironic juxtaposition that he could not yet come to grips with.

Nicholas did not know what to do.

Then the door opened and, in a billow of fragrant mist, Justine came out. She was wrapped in a bathsheet, a towel turbaned about her hair. She stopped dead when she saw him.

"Oh, my God, Nick!"

Then she was in his arms, sobbing, kissing him all over his face, her warm, damp body pressed close to his. He could feel the tremors of her muscles, smell her through the soft scents of the soap and the shampoo and the body talc.

Nicholas, enfolding her, warmed by her, felt his love for her, felt that it had never died. But whether it had merely receded on its own by time and circumstance or he had pushed it away, he could not say.

He recognized that, in a way, his withdrawal from her—indeed, from everyone around him—had been a necessary part of his awakening to his own destiny: the knowledge that he was tanjian. And this thought saddened him in a way he could not fully explain and was, as yet, unprepared to explore.

All he knew was that he was drenched in Justine once again, just as he had been so many years ago, when they had first met along this stretch of beach only a few yards from where he was now standing, their feet wet, their psyches wary, suspicious of each other and any incident that would so wildly, willfully bring two people together with such breathless abandon.

All he knew was that he was whole once more, and a kind of exultation, fierce and undeniable, gripped him, so that he held her to him all the tighter.

"Dear God, I love you, Justine."

And she was crying. "Nick, Nick, Nick," she whispered as if the mere evocation of his name would assure her that he had really returned to her. "I was so afraid that I would never see you again. I—"

"Why?" He pushed her a little away from him so that he could look into her face. He wanted to see, he needed to see that she was all right. "Where would you get an idea that I wasn't coming back?"

"I—I . . ." Justine shook her head, the towel turbaned over her hair coming down around her shoulders, her dark hair, damp, tangled, an erotic web, coming free. "I don't know. I think—"

And he could see it in her eyes, the green hidden and murky in the dominant brown, the red motes in her left iris dull, remote. He could see the Tau-tau lurking there like a spider crouched in its web, and his heart broke, and he had to fight the fear because this was so new to him that he lacked the confidence to know whether he could free her, really free her as he had from the ninja hypnosis that Saigo had once worked on her.

"Someone told you," he said. "Someone put it into your mind." To shock her because he knew this much: that he would need her help, he could not exorcise the Tau-tau on his own.

"Yes . . ." Justine looked bewildered, as if he had pulled her roughly out of a deep sleep. "I remember . . . something." She looked into his face. "Like a dream or a painting in smoke, shimmering, shifting, dancing away when I try to look it full in the face."

He saw the fright steal into her face, darken her eyes, obscure the red motes. "Nick, what's happening to me? I feel . . . I feel like I'm living in two separate worlds. I feel, I don't know quite how to say this, but as if I'm locked up and have been set adrift at the same time. Crazy, huh?"

"Not nearly as crazy as you think," Nicholas said. "Why don't you get dressed, and I'll see what kind of food—"

"Don't leave me." Justine reached out for him. "Please, I—Nick, I don't want to be alone now that you're here. I just want to look at you, touch you. I—It feels like it's been so long since I've seen you, years instead of weeks. I—" She held her head. "I don't know what's happening to me."

"Get dressed, honey," Nicholas urged her. "You'll get cold standing around like that."

Justine smiled, slipped into jeans and a black cotton turtleneck sweater. "Better?" She came over to him. "Nick, what is it? What's happened?"

He put his arms around her. "Remember Saigo? Remember what he did to you, hypnotizing you?" She nodded. "Somewhat the same thing has happened, I think. Though you don't remember it clearly, the *dorokusai* who is after me came to the house in Tokyo. He spent some time with you." He saw the puzzled look on her face. "You don't remember someone new, a stranger coming to the door?"

"No," Justine said. "There was only the cyclist. But I don't remember what happened to him."

"What cyclist?"

"I—Well, I almost ran him down, I think. I was coming out of our driveway and didn't see him. I was lucky and so was he; he just went into the cryptomeria on the other side of the road. He said he was okay but I insisted he come and have some tea." She gave Nicholas a little smile. "I was practicing being more Japanese, thinking to myself his refusals were just his way of being polite. He came, though."

"And then what happened?"

"What?" Justine looked startled. "Oh, I don't know, really. I can't seem to remember. I guess he came with me to the house, had some tea, and left."

"No, that's not all that happened," Nicholas said. "The cyclist was Senjin Omukae."

"Yes. That was his name. I remember that now."

"He's the *dorokusai*, Justine."

He felt her begin to shake all over again. "Oh, Nick." Tears welled in her eyes. "Nick, what's happened? What's he done to me? I can't remember . . ."

"I know exactly what he's done," Nicholas said, although he didn't. "I'll take care of it." Although he had no way of knowing whether or not he could. He wondered, then, how much he could—or should—tell her of his own new circumstances. Would it make her feel more secure or just deepen her fright if he were to tell her that he himself was a tanjian? He did not know.

He led her into the living room, where there was more light and more space. He poured her a whiskey, brought it to her.

"But what has he done to me?" Justine insisted.

"He wants to get to me through you."

She took a sip of the scotch, shuddered. "Maybe he wants me to kill you, like Saigo wanted."

"I doubt it," Nicholas said. "This one wants me all to himself. There would be no satisfaction for him in a murder by proxy."

Justine's eyes were wide and staring. "Nick, do you realize what we're talking about?"

Nicholas knew that he had never loved his wife more deeply or completely than he did at that moment. He kissed her hard on her lips, feeling hers soften, open beneath his. "Don't worry," he said. "Senjin had one chance to kill me, up in Dr. Hanami's office, and he didn't do it.

Good for me; too bad for him. There's an old Japanese saying: If you fail to kill an enemy, you had better dig two graves."

Justine collapsed into his arms. "Oh, God. Death and more death." She put her head against his chest. "Isn't there another way? Oh, there must be." She looked up at him. "Can't we just run away somewhere, anywhere, I don't care where, I swear it, just so long as—" But she stopped, seeing the look on his face, which confirmed her own inner sense.

"No, I see this is the only way now. Because of your life, Nick, and how you've got to live it. All right, then." Slowly she covered his hand with hers. "I accept whatever must be, whatever is to come. Karma. Because I love you and only you." She drew his hand down to her belly. "But I want you to remember that whatever happens, our future—or part of it—is in here, waiting for its time. Promise me you won't do anything to jeopardize that future."

"Justine, are you saying—" But he already knew, could tell with his gift, just as Senjin had, that she was pregnant. "My God, a baby."

"Are you happy?"

"Yes. Oh, yes!" He kissed her. "When are you due?"

"Early in the spring."

"A baby," Nicholas echoed, his hand still on her belly.

"This one we'll keep, Nick." She pressed herself hard against him. "That's my promise to you. This baby will live, grow up, be our future . . . together."

Nicholas picked her up, carried her over to the long modular couch. They lay together, entwined, twinned, each reaching for that part the other had withheld during the past bleak months out of anger, frustration, and fear, but not indifference, never indifference.

Above them, in their floating city, the angelfish rippled their translucent fins, darting serenely in and out of the vertical water plants, while Gus the catfish slept, sated, in his niche between two plastic spars of a mock shipwreck.

The heat rose in them, the same delicious fire they had first felt when they coupled frantically, knowing little about each other except that they burned to be closer than close.

Justine's fingers were already unbuttoning his shirt, pushing it back off his chest and arms. He licked her lips, her ears, and, when he pushed aside the turtleneck, the hollow of her throat.

"I want you."

Nicholas began to lift up her sweater, but she moaned, "No, no, I want you now. This instant." Unbuckling his belt, pushing all his clothes down as he worked at her jeans.

She wore nothing underneath, and he was inside her almost immediately as she urged him on top of her with her fingertips and her thighs. She thrust up hard, once, twice, three times.

"Oh!" she cried, her neck arched, her eyes fluttered closed. "It's been so long." Her hips moved with his, and she grew hotter, her inner muscles working at him frenziedly, her mouth whispering "Yes, yes," almost a religious chant or a prayer of thanks, her hips bucking out of control until he could do nothing else but explode inside her, filled with her, and her with him, all they had now, but everything they ever wanted.

Kusunda Ikusa was in the Imperial Palace East Garden, but he wasn't there to jog. This was the only part of the palace open to the public, filled with traditional flower-bearing shrubs and trees, tiny ornamental buildings as old as the palace itself. From here one had an excellent view not only of the Imperial Palace, but the circular path around it, a favorite track for many of frenzied Tokyo's avid joggers. Of course, they ignored the pall of exhaust fumes from the monstrous convergence of vehicular traffic beyond the moat.

It was just past six on a pink pointillist morning, and Ikusa had no difficulty in discerning Masuto Ishii in the shell-colored haze. Ishii was Sato International's vice-president of operations, a key man in Tanzan Nangi's operation, perhaps even in his strategies, and when he had called late yesterday, Ikusa had immediately agreed to meet him.

Ikusa was wary as he approached the little man, but not as suspicious as he might have been in other circumstances. Normally, Nangi's people were notoriously loyal in a land known for its loyalty. But the Nakano deal, especially the detonation of the bomb Ikusa had left hidden in the contract, had shaken a lot of leaves off the tree. For the first time in its history Sato International was in real trouble. Everyone knew where the trouble came from and what it would take to get rid of it. Ikusa, so secretive before, had wanted this public now; he wanted Nangi's confidence shaken, his people anxious.

So, in a sense, Masuto Ishii's call had not been unforeseen. The one surprise was that it had come from someone so high up in the Sato *keiretsu*, someone so close to Tanzan Nangi. Ikusa was inclined to take that as a very good sign. Over the course of the last several days—ever since he had done away with the man spying on him and Killan—he had allowed his feeling of elation full rein. He was on the verge of obtaining everything he could hope for, everything he ever wanted. The thought sent shivers down his spine.

The two men made their ritual greeting at the break of day, with the city waking all around them. They began their circumnavigation of the garden. Ikusa could feel the nervousness emanating in waves from the other man.

Though he had familiarized himself with all of Sato International's top management months ago, in preparation for his raid, Ikusa had brought Ishii's file up on his computer screen just before meeting him to make certain he remembered every detail.

Ishii had been at Sato for twenty years, and was an integral part of its growth during that time. He was a small, almost tiny man, wiry, with quick, intelligent eyes magnified from behind thick glasses. His only vice appeared to be gambling, an all too common Japanese pastime, as far as Ikusa was concerned.

Ishii was a quiet, family man, but he was by no means meek. There was a story about him that during the communist riots down by the docks just after the war, he had, as a twenty-year-old boy, swung a crowbar into the side of the communist leader's head. "Anyone who wants to overthrow the Emperor has to kill me first," Ishii was reported to have said. The dock workers were back at their jobs that afternoon.

"Ishii-san, it comes as some surprise that you would want to meet with me," Kusunda Ikusa said as they passed a sheared dwarf azalea in full flower. "Aren't I considered by some to be the enemy?"

Ishii responded to his ironic tone with the trace of a smile. "Enemies are often a matter of semantics," Ishii said.

And Ikusa thought, What you mean is a matter of convenience. But he said nothing, confident that he could allow Ishii to do all the work at this meeting.

The day had just begun, and already it was growing hot. Ikusa could see Ishii sweating beneath his dark gray pinstripe suit. The collar of his white shirt was damp.

The little man did not disappoint Ikusa. He said, "May I speak candidly, Ikusa-san?"

"Of course. We are all part of one family now." Radiating benevolence. "There is no difference between us."

"The matter is simple, really. That is, it is a straightforward one." Ishii mopped his perspiring brow with a handkerchief. "It involves money."

Ah, Ikusa thought, seeing the point at which he could ford the stream. He disguised the distaste he already felt for Ishii's weakness of character. "If I can be of assistance."

"I'm afraid I am an inveterate gambler. Often, I regret to say, my desire exceeds my means."

"Have you tried to curb this desire of yours, Ishii-san?"

"Oh, yes," the little man said, mopping his brow again. He could not seem to keep it dry. "Many times. Nangi-san was kind enough to pay for my rehabilitation."

"And yet?"

Ishii shrugged. "I do my best, but I cannot overcome it. No matter how long I stay away—I once abstained for a year—I must go back." He shrugged again. "Karma."

"Yes, unfortunate karma," Ikusa said. He turned a corner, Ishii following as obediently as a dog on a leash. "But, tell me, why come to me? Surely Nangi-san can obtain a loan for you. I assume he has done so in the past."

"Once or twice," Ishii admitted. Now Ikusa could discern a trace of despair in his voice. "Frankly, I was afraid to approach him this time. The recent turn of events has him off balance, angry. But finally I brought myself to ask. Nangi turned me down. He said I had a lesson to learn. I understand his anxiety over other matters, but I feel this was not right. I have been a loyal member of the Sato family for years. It is my life. Now he has turned his back on me when I need his help the most. It is unfair."

"Ah, well, the most accommodating of employers . . ." Ikusa left this thought deliberately open-ended. "And the banks, Ishii-san? Can they not be of service?"

"I need the money by the end of the week, Ikusa-san. No bank will fill a loan that quickly."

They passed beneath the shade of plum tree. "What size loan would satisfy the debt?"

When Ishii told him, Ikusa spent some time pretending to consider. "Well, I think you've acted correctly coming to me, Ishii-san. I'm sure we can work out an exchange of services."

"Oh, Ikusa-san, I would be most grateful, most grateful," Ishii babbled with embarrassing emotion.

Ikusa looked at him out of the corner of his eye as if the little man had dropped his pants and defecated in the azaleas.

They walked for some time in silence. Ikusa watched the joggers on their circuit, their lungs soaking up the carbon monoxide. What possible health benefit could be derived from that? he wondered.

"By the way," Ikusa said, breaking the contemplative silence, "what exactly is Nangi-san thinking? He's lost the heart of Nakano, and he can't sell the worthless shell he's bought so dearly. What is he going to do?"

"Well, it's not just him now," Ishii said. He seemed to be a different person, relieved of the burden of his gambling debt. It was, of course, a matter of face that he should be able to pay on time and in good faith. "He and Linnear-san have gotten together to plot strategy."

"Nicholas Linnear is back?" Ikusa was momentarily so nonplussed by the news that he blurted it out. "That is to say, I had heard reports that he disappeared."

Ishii shrugged. "I don't know about that. But if they were true at all, he's back."

Damnit, how is it I didn't know about this? Ikusa asked himself. And where the hell is Senjin? He was supposed to be taking care of Linnear. If Linnear has returned, he should have informed me. That could be trouble.

"Do you have any idea what Nangi and Linnear are planning?"

"Not specifically," Ishii said. "I do know that a number of MITI officials went to see them yesterday." This could be more bad news, Ikusa knew. Nangi was a former vice-minister of the powerful Ministry of International Trade and Industry. Though MITI and Nami professed to be essentially on the same course, Ikusa knew that this was not always the case. He did not actually know how strong Nangi's ties remained his erstwhile ministry, but Ikusa was not in the habit of underestimating his enemies. Nangi had been in his day a fierce practitioner of *kanryodo*, the art of the bureaucrat. What strings he could still pull were as of now a matter of conjecture.

"Ishii-san," Ikusa said. "If you meet me here at this time tomorrow, I will have your money."

The little man bowed. "*Domo arigato*, Ikusa-sama. I will, of course, sign a note agreeing to any rate of interest you see fit."

"Oh, that will not be necessary," Ikusa said, taking the opening. "This is a matter of trust between equals." He used an inflective, the Japanese equivalent of a wave of the hand. "And as for interest, there will be none." He looked into Ishii's wide-eyed face. "But if I might ask for an alternate form of payment?"

"Anything, Ikusa-san. I am most grateful for your understanding and generosity."

"It is very little," Ikusa said, making the ritual response to a compliment. "This is what you might do for me: when you meet me tomorrow, I would appreciate knowing what strategy Nangi-san has decided on."

At approximately the same time that this meeting was taking place, but in an eastern section of Tokyo, Tomi and Nangi were making their way along the water-slick pavement dockside at Tsukiji, the sprawl of single-story buildings on the bank of the Sumida River, which winds through the city.

Tsukiji was Tokyo's vast wholesale fish market, where more than twelve million dollars worth of fish were sold every day. Today, however, there was something other than fish at Tsukiji.

Using her credentials, Tomi pushed their way through the police barriers, around the Medical Examiner's ambulance. Lights blazed, creating pools across the slick docks. Workers in black slickers and high boots, carrying curved fish hooks and water hoses to spray the lines of fish lying on their sides, gleaming in the hazy morning sunlight, stood around staring, talking among themselves as their open-mouthed catch piled up on the dock.

Nangi walked slowly. He leaned heavily on his cane, and his face was lined and drawn tight by concern. The sky was suffused with the milky light that presages sunrise, the illumination of preconsciousness that gives everything a surreal quality, blurring edges, making definition indistinct.

Tomi stopped at the edge of the indigo river. Boats bobbed at their slips as their cargo was off-loaded to be inventoried, sprayed, priced for the morning's sale.

Nothing, however, was going on. The men on the boats were staring at a mounded plastic sheet spread over a six-foot length of the dock.

"They pulled him out of the Sumida not more than forty minutes ago," Tomi said to Nangi. "That's when I was called." She pointed. "He rose up to the surface, bumped against the side of this boat here. The captain looked over the side, called the police."

With that she gestured, and the plastic tarp was thrown back.

"Dear God," Nangi breathed.

"Is it him?" Tomi turned to him. "Can you make a positive identification?"

"Yes." Nangi had difficulty swallowing. "That's the Pack Rat."

Tomi nodded, as if to herself. She pointed. "I don't know what happened, but you can see where he was weighted down with something, maybe iron bars. That's how they do it."

"Who?"

"Yakuza."

Nangi was bent over the Pack Rat's bloated corpse. "This wasn't a Yakuza hit."

"You seem sure about that."

"I am," Nangi said. "The Pack Rat had too many friends among the Yakuza."

"Where there are friends, there are bound to be enemies," Tomi pointed out. "That's the law of the jungle."

"No doubt," Nangi said. "But look here—and here—these wounds. A blunt and heavy weapon was used." He looked closer. "It seems to me these are the wounds inflicted by a *tetsubo*."

"Isn't that a feudal weapon? If I recall my history, it was used for opening up armor plate and breaking war horses' legs," Tomi said, coming closer. "I've never seen one at work."

"Well, I have," Nangi said. "A long time ago. A real *tetsubo* match isn't pretty. It's a matter of great skill combined with brute strength to successfully wield a solid iron bar mounted with iron studs." Nangi put his cheek against the dragon head of his cane. "Poor boy," he said softly. "It takes a nasty mind to want to use one of these things. You have to want to inflict fatal damage. *Tetsubo* matches are invariably to the death."

"You mean they still exist?"

"You're looking at evidence that they do," Nangi said, straightening up. He had said his goodbye to the Pack Rat. They walked away from the forensic team, so they would not be overheard. "What was found on the body?"

"Not a thing," Tomi said. "He was either carrying nothing or he was stripped before being dumped in the river. My guess is the latter."

"I agree," Nangi said. "Though the Pack Rat was very careful. He would not have been carrying anything but false identity papers, some money. Nothing incriminating that would let anyone know what he was doing."

"He popped up like a cipher, but the description you gave us was what caused the investigating officers to call me," Tomi said. "I'm sorry, Nangi-san."

Nangi nodded. "It's sad. And terribly bad luck for me. The Pack Rat was my eyes and ears inside Kusunda Ikusa's strategies. He gave me only a broad outline of what he had discovered at our last meeting. I'm sure he had so much more." But perhaps it doesn't matter, Nangi thought. He had solved the riddle of Ikusa's raid: to gain control of Sato International and its Sphynx T-PRAM division.

And yet, this was only an assumption. Nangi longed for outside confirmation. If only the dead could talk, he thought bleakly. What secrets would you tell me, Pack Rat, if you could?

Nangi said, "The one thing of interest he did mention was that somehow Killan Oroshi, the daughter of Nakano's chairman, was involved with Ikusa. That struck both of us as odd. She might be the only lead we have left now."

"Detective Yazawa!"

They both turned to see one of the investigating officers gesturing frantically to Tomi. They went back to where the corpse was being loaded onto a folding stretcher, preparatory to being taken away in the ambulance.

"Look at what we found," the officer said. "The man's left shoe must have been ripped off when he came to the surface. Look at the space between his big toe and the others."

Tomi and Nangi bent to look. The Pack Rat, as was his habit, was not wearing socks. His foot was so bloated, one could hardly recognize it for what it was. Taped to the inside of his big toe, lying against the white flesh, was a tiny metal key.

Tomi took out a pocket knife, slit the tape. Carefully she peeled the key off the dead man's flesh, dropped it into Nangi's palm.

"Now," she said, "maybe we have another lead."

"There's no time like the present," Detective Albemarle said. "How about we locate Senator Howe right now?"

Shisei nodded. "Anything you say."

"This is Sergeant Johnson," Albemarle said, as a big black cop joined them on their way outside.

"I remember him from the interrogation room," Shisei said.

"You're quite some woman," Albemarle said as they went down the steps of the precinct house to an unmarked car. It was hot and sticky, with little breeze coming in off the Chesapeake: a typical summer night in the nation's capital. "Still, you sure you're up to this?"

"You want me there, I'm going. It's as simple as that."

Albemarle grunted. "Nothing's ever simple." He pulled out onto the street. "Howe's got some rep when it comes to his people crossing him."

"I'm not crossing him," Shisei said. "I'm turning him in."

That got a smile out of Albemarle. "I'll say this for you, you've got guts. Ain't she got guts, Bobo?"

"Damned if she don't," Sergeant Johnson said from his position in the backseat. Shisei got the impression that he was staring intently at the back of her neck.

Albemarle went on, "I assume you know that Howe has enough juice to pull your career out from under you for what you're doing. Does anything scare you?"

Shisei looked at him in the night.

He drove very fast but not recklessly. Within minutes he pulled up outside Howe's residence on Seventeenth Street in the northwest district.

"Place should be a museum, not a goddamn private house," Albemarle muttered as they got out of the car. Looking up, they could see lights on in the third floor. Albemarle pointed. "You know your way around here, I imagine?"

Shisei said, "I'm familiar with the offices on the ground floor. The senator's private apartment is on the third floor. I've never been up there."

Albemarle grunted as they went up the stone steps. He rang the bell. They waited. When no one answered, he rang again, this time leaning on the bell. Nothing. He turned the doorknob and the door opened inward.

Immediately Albemarle and Johnson drew their guns. "For a paranoid like Howe, this is decidedly not kosher."

"I'd better call for a backup," Johnson said.

"Nix," Albemarle ordered. "This is ours. I'm not in a sharing mood tonight." He gestured to Shisei. "You stay here."

"I want to go with you," she said.

"It's against regs," Albemarle told her, already inside. Sergeant Johnson glowered at her, then followed his boss into the house.

In a moment Shisei followed them.

The downstairs offices were dark. She could see that the two cops had found the curving staircase, went slowly upward. She was a shadow behind them. The second floor was also dark, but now they could see more clearly, as light from the third floor seeped down the spiral stairwell.

"Keep your head down," Shisei, close behind them, heard Albemarle whisper to Johnson before they began to ascend.

Light flooded the third-floor landing, emanating from the open doorway to a room that was obviously Douglas Howe's study. Floor to ceiling bookcases surrounded a pair of facing leather sofas, a matching highbacked chair. A massive antique fruitwood desk and leather swivel chair were set in one corner. A brace of English hunting paintings hung on the deep green walls. Lamps glowed here and there.

An antique Isfahan rug lay behind one of the sofas, but it was now worthless, stained beyond repair with blood and brains.

Senator Douglas Howe half sat at an unnatural angle on one of the leather sofas. His legs were incongruously crossed at the ankles, as if he were in repose, which, in a sense, was the case.

His arms were flung wide as if in shocked reaction. A .357 Magnum lay just beyond the reach of his right hand. There was nothing left of the back of his head. Some of it clung to the spines of books in the cases three feet away.

"Jesus," was all Albemarle said. Then he said to Shisei, "Don't move, and don't under any circumstances touch or move anything."

He went over to the desk, used his handkerchief to pick up the phone. He dialed, using his pen to hit the push buttons. "Bobby? It's Phil," he said into the phone. "Ambulance, full forensics, M.E.'s office and backup." Then he gave the address. "Yeah," he said. "Senator Howe himself. He won't be running for reelection, so for Christ's sake let's keep this quiet for as long as we can before the press starts treading all over us, okay? Who can you get to cover this? Okay, good. Yeah, yeah. And I want you here five minutes ago."

Albemarle put down the phone. He studied Shisei for a moment, just to see whether she was taking her instructions seriously. Then he went and knelt beside Johnson, who was staring at Howe. He peered down at the .357 Magnum, then at Howe's right hand.

"What are you looking for?" Shisei asked.

"Usually these handguns aren't used much, but they have to be kept in working order," Albemarle said.

"There looks to be traces of gun oil on the senator's fingers," Johnson said.

Albemarle stood up, looked at her. "That's crucial to establish, because if Howe fired the gun, it's suicide. If it was put in his mouth, it's homicide. Big difference, especially for me."

"But not for Howe," Shisei said.

Johnson barked a laugh.

"You've got some sense of humor," Albemarle said.

"I wasn't being funny," Shisei said. "Just making an observation."

Five minutes later they heard the sirens and a commotion downstairs. Detectives, uniformed police, a forensics team, a cadaverous doctor from the Medical Examiner's office all trooped into the room. They worked swiftly, efficiently, taking photographs, prints, measurements, statements from Albemarle, Johnson, and Shisei.

Of course, they found Howe's permit for the .357 Magnum. The assistant M.E. said to Albemarle, "This is only a prelim, off the top of my head, Phil, but if this doesn't turn out to be a suicide, I'm a monkey's uncle."

Shisei looked over the scene with some satisfaction. She knew that the doctor's final report would not note anything out of the ordinary, certainly nothing to point to homicide.

The fact that hours earlier she had driven Howe home, had taken his gun out of the drawer in his desk, put it in his hand, shoved the barrel into his mouth, put her forefinger over his, squeezed slowly, until the report of the explosion cracked the silence of the night, would never be revealed. It was nobody's business but hers.

She stood in one corner, out of the policemen's way, waiting patiently for Detective Albemarle to take her back to the precinct. She wanted to be there when they released Branding.

Her work here was almost done, but there was still the question of Branding. Cook, she thought, have you lost faith in me? Do you still love me?

She was impatient now to find out.

Senjin watched Nicholas and Justine making love with the kind of envy one feels for a peer whose ease with other people makes him the constant center of attention.

It was the envy, perhaps, that made Senjin want to kill Nicholas now, to forget his vow, to wreak wholesale vengeance of a sort that would appease his growing appetite for chaos.

He was stopped from exercising this self-indulgence by a new element. Reaching out with the projection of his will, as he had in Dr. Hanami's office, he encountered not that withdrawn, uncertain psyche that had caused him to feel such elation, but a black, featureless wall beyond which nothing was discernible.

Nicholas had ceased to exist, as far as Senjin's gift was concerned.

What had happened? Senjin was certain that he had effectively destroyed Nicholas's one avenue to salvation when he had ritually murdered Kyoki, the tanjian living in the castle in the Asama highlands. But where had Nicholas gone after Asama? He had not immediately returned to Tokyo the broken man, as Senjin had thought he would. Had he gone farther into the Alps? And if so, why?

In the end, Senjin knew, the answers to these questions did not matter. All that need concern him was this new and wholly unexpected element: Nicholas had somehow come to terms with his being a tanjian. For the featureless wall that blocked out any psychic foray was only possible from a tanjian.

That meant that Nicholas knew Tau-tau. Senjin considered. Why hadn't he been told of this? Again, his training told him that this did not matter. He needed to reassess the situation, fashion a new strategy accordingly.

Kshira, the sound-light continuum, teaches: yang, the First Son, inciting motion, light gives birth to fire, and thought gives birth to light; thunder gives birth to sound, and anger gives birth to thunder. Yin: the Mother, yielding, fluid, the earth is the receptacle for thought, the crucible of idea.

One cannot exist without the other, Kshira teaches. But Senjin knew better, for yin gave to yang weakness as well as strength, a weakness Senjin saw as fatal. Thus had he spent so much time in ridding himself of yin: the Mother, yielding, devoted.

He had sought to stop the cosmic order of yin flowing into yang, to still the eternal flux of the two forms of energy. Thus had he become *dorokusai*, the scourge of tanjian.

As he watched from the rafters like a predatory owl in the crotch of a tree, Senjin assumed the position of repose. He watched Nicholas and Justine asleep, entwined, and he thought of himself, as Justine had said, as a cloud drifting above the jam-packed earth, separated from the joy, cares, and desires of those whom he observed. Kshira allowed him to see this, but his own special philosophy made it so.

He inhaled deeply. Death was not in the air. At least, not yet. There were private hells, degradations of the state of being alive that needed to be traversed before Senjin could allow death to come to Nicholas Linnear.

But there was purpose here, and Senjin's nostrils dilated as if he could scent it. Senjin had come for the remaining emeralds. He had hoped that Justine would be able to tell him where they were. But now that Nicholas had appeared, Senjin saw another path, a powerful attack, both a way for him to know if the emeralds were here inside the house and the first hell for Nicholas to inhabit on his journey toward his own demise.

With the stillness of the dead, Senjin left his perch and, keeping to the shadows, went about his business. When he was finished, there was light where none had been before, and there was heat, a warping of the atmosphere, sucking the oxygen out of the house.

A moment after Senjin left, Nicholas awoke with a start. He coughed, his lungs already filling with smoke. Flames licked along the floor, devouring the night.

Killan and the Scoundrel stood on a street corner on the seedy outskirts of Tokyo. Across the dark, infrequently traveled avenue they could see the flickering neon entrance to a dive called the Kan.

"Kusunda said that I should come alone," Killan said for the fourth or fifth time. She stood on one leg, then the other, a sure sign that she was nervous. "Maybe you shouldn't have come."

"I wasn't going to let you do this on your own," the Scoundrel said, also for the fourth or fifth time. Then, "Do you think he'll give us what we want?"

"Of course he will," Killan said, with the wholehearted conviction of the revolutionary. She scanned the sparse traffic in both directions. "What other choice does he have?"

The Scoundrel said nothing, fingering a bulge beneath his nylon windbreaker.

When Killan had played the tape she and the Scoundrel had created from carefully culled excerpts of the tape the Scoundrel had found in the apartment next to his, Kusunda Ikusa had smiled.

"Where did you get that?" he had said.

"It doesn't matter," Killan told him, her voice full of authority. "What matters is I have it. Interested?"

"Naturally." Ikusa's eyes, half hidden in his folds of flesh, regarded her with reptilian solidity.

"Don't you want to know what I want for it?" Killan asked, growing impatient.

"Whatever it is, it is sure to be outlandish." That smile again, as if he did not have a care in the world.

Killan said, "I want authority. Not just an entry-level job at Nakano, not a job in publicity convincing jerks they ought to buy your new products."

"I thought—" Abruptly, Ikusa's jaw snapped shut; he wasn't smiling now.

"The trouble with you, Kusunda," Killan had said, "is that you see me as a female. You make beautiful noises about my abilities, my mind, my ambition, but you always temper that by saying it's a pity I wasn't born a man. Do you understand how that makes me feel, how it shames me? No, of course not. How could you have any idea?

"Well, you're going to understand now, because I'm going to extract a heavy price to save your face. I want a position of authority within Nakano."

"Once a revolutionary, always a revolutionary," Kusunda had said. "Well, I suppose it was inevitable, but I must say you've disappointed me, Killan." He pursed his pouty lips. "On the other hand, I know you now. Like all revolutionaries, you long for the respectability you can by definition never have. Because once you do, you've been coopted by the establishment, you're a part of it, the revolution's washed away on the tide of inevitable change." He made a dismissive gesture. "Take your position, then. Anywhere in the consumer division. Which job do you covet so much?"

Killan had smiled thinly, but the venom so long held in check had come to the surface. "You think you know me so well, but you don't. There's more. I don't want a position in the bogus consumer division you're setting up as a front, but in the area where it's really happening: the R and D. I want a piece of what's going down with MANTIS. Ten percent of profits."

Killan thought she had seen all the blood drain from Ikusa's face. She had so desperately wanted him to ask, Where did you find out about MANTIS? But all he said was an address and a time. "You bring the tape," he said, "and I'll have a contract for you to sign."

It had been that simple.

"What if he doesn't show?" the Scoundrel asked now.

"He'll show," Killan said, moving from one foot to another. "What other choice does he have?"

"We should have insisted on seeing the contract before the meet," the Scoundrel said. "I should have handled the negotiations."

"Are you kidding?" Killan said. "You're invisible in this. I don't want Kusunda to know how I found out about MANTIS. You're my strength *and* my weakness, so stay back in the shadows when we see Kusunda coming. I don't want him recognizing you."

It was now two minutes past the time Ikusa had set for the exchange of documents. A black Mercedes turned a corner, headed their way. The Scoundrel retreated to the shadows. As it came closer, they could see that its windows were heavily tinted.

It was less than a block away. "Here he comes," Killan said confidently. She had stopped shifting from foot to foot.

The Mercedes, very close to them now, abruptly began to accelerate.

"Are they crazy?" the Scoundrel shouted.

The Mercedes jumped the curb, headed directly for them.

"God in heaven!" Killan breathed, rooted to the spot.

The Scoundrel ran at her, grabbed her hard around the waist. At the same time he jerked the bulge beneath his windbreaker. He lifted the pistol as it came free, aimed it at the windshield of the careening Mercedes.

He put two shots into the glass, then they both jumped to avoid the heavy grill. The Scoundrel, his heart pounding so hard he thought he was going to have a stroke, hit his shoulder on the Mercedes' off-side fender as it shot past, then they were both up and running as hard as they could.

They heard what sounded like a crash but they did not stop, did not even turn around to see what had happened. They gained their car, which they had parked out of sight. The gears ground as the Scoundrel hurriedly started up. They shot forward, racing down a deserted street. The Scoundrel was still gulping air. Killan began to cry in terror and relief.

Smoke filled the house. It was so thick, so acrid, that Nicholas knew immediately that the fire had been deliberately set.

"Get down!" he yelled in Justine's ear. "Keep down!"

They were on the floor of the living room, and already the crack and spark of the flames filled the house, eating even the atmosphere. It was impossible to see clearly, and Nicholas had to pause a moment to remember the layout of the house he had not been in for years.

There was a great deal of glass—an easy exit—but getting to it was a problem. Flames were everywhere, and they were in the center of a huge space. But the smoke was as serious a problem: the longer they delayed, the worse it would be for them.

He glanced up. The angelfish, as if sensing the danger or merely feeling the heat, were huddled in the center of the tank, fins rippling in agitation. Gus the catfish was traversing the gravel as if frantically searching for something.

Nicholas took Justine's hand. He could see the fear in her eyes, but also the trust in him. He closed his eyes, went into himself, centering. He found *Getsumei no michi*, that special place where he could see without his eyes, where hidden strategies were eventually made manifest to him. And saw the way out.

"Let's go!" he yelled, leading the way as they sprinted around the sectional, leaping over an easy chair and through a narrow patch of flames. The sudden, sickening smell of singed hair.

Six feet beyond, he knew, lay the sliding glass doors and safety. He rushed them forward, but a sudden sharp crack filled the air.

Nicholas felt the collapse of a wooden joist, eaten through by the ferocious fire. He did not need to see it coming. He jerked Justine sharply toward the kitchen, moved himself. The heavy, flaming joist crashed down, the edge of it slamming into the meaty upper part of his left arm. His skin began to burn, and Justine cried out, wrapped her hands around the spot.

She screamed as an explosion resounded. She covered Nicholas with her body. Glass fragments shot at them as one of the kitchen windows cracked in the fierce heat.

The smoke was much worse now. Justine started to cough, and Nicholas felt her falter. He scooped her up in his arms, leaped over the flaming joist. He turned sideways, crashed through the safety glass of the slider out to the porch.

The night exploded into ten thousand fragments, but the shards were not sharp, and they clattered off Nicholas and Justine like sleet.

On the beach Justine bent over, retching and gasping oxygen into her lungs. Nicholas took slow, deep breaths. *Prana*. He had ceased to breathe in the normal manner the moment he woke up.

He stroked Justine's hair, holding her shoulders. All the hair had been burned off his left arm, but otherwise he was unharmed.

Already he could hear the sirens approaching. A neighbor must have called the fire department. People were rushing along the beach. They brought first-aid kits and blankets, one of which Nicholas threw over Justine's shoulders. Someone put Polysporin cream on his left arm, but other than that, there was nothing to do but watch the house burn. It was wood frame, as were all the houses on the East End of Long Island, and the fire ripped through it with appalling speed.

"What happened?" someone asked. "How'd it start?"

"I don't know," Nicholas said. But of course he knew. He could smell the taint of Tau-tau. Senjin Omukae, the *dorokusai*, had been here; he had set the blaze. Why? To kill them? In such an impersonal manner? Nicholas doubted it. Then what? Nicholas reentered *Getsumei no michi*. Allowed his mind to drift toward the answer. The emeralds! How Nicholas reacted after the fire would tell Senjin if Nicholas had hidden the rest of the stones in the house.

Justine, her head on his shoulder, stood beside him, shivering. He put his arms around her. "Oh, Nick," she said softly. "I can't believe it. It's all gone."

The fire trucks were arriving, the hoses snaking out, connecting up to the water lines, spraying the house from several directions at once. The firemen swarmed, already breaking a sweat. They fought valiantly. But it was useless, Nicholas saw. The fire ate voraciously at the house, seemingly oblivious to the water being poured on it. It was too well entrenched, raging out of control.

"Look out!" a fireman called, as the center roofbeams collapsed inward, sending great gouts of flame shooting skyward, followed by a cascade of sparks and cinders. The gathering crowd oohed and ahhed as if it were the fourth of July. "Everyone stay clear! This is a dangerous area!"

Nicholas, looking sadly at a part of his past, repository of so many memories, knew that Justine was right. It was all gone.

Detective Albemarle opened the holding cell door, stepped back. "You're free to go, Senator. I'm truly sorry for the inconvenience." He shrugged. "We've all got our jobs to do. Sometimes mine's not so wonderful. This is one of those times."

Cotton Branding looked at him silently. He stood, slung his tuxedo jacket over his shoulders. His sleeves were rolled up and his tie and cummerbund were stuffed in his pocket.

He walked out of the holding cell and said, "Will you kindly tell me what the hell's going on?"

Shisei, who had been standing in the dense shadows of the precinct corridor, moved into a pool of fluorescent light. Albemarle had taken her into the precinct through a side entrance because the front steps and surrounding street were brilliantly flood-lit with hastily erected television lights, jammed with press clamoring for news of Branding's status.

Shisei said, "Howe's dead, Cook. He shot himself tonight."

"What?"

Albemarle nodded in response to Branding's look, but he did not say a word.

"Apparently," Shisei went on, "Howe, obsessed with your growing success, decided to do something drastic about it. After a fight with David Brisling which ended in Howe killing him, Howe decided to try to implicate you in Brisling's death."

"Good God."

"That seems to sum it up nicely," Albemarle said. He led the way down the corridor. "There are just some papers for you to sign, Senator, and you can have your personal effects back." He turned. "If you want to call any of your friends in the media from here," he said, "be my guest. There's a whole bunch of them outside. I don't know how you want to handle them, but it's no sweat to get you out unseen, if you want."

Branding nodded. "That's very decent of you, Detective."

They went through the formalities in the privacy of Albemarle's chaotic cubicle. "It may not look like much," he said, "but it's all mine."

"After that holding cell," Branding said, "it looks awfully good to me."

Albemarle left them for a moment to file the forms Branding had signed and to get his things.

Branding and Shisei looked at each other.

"You're all I thought about in there," he said. "I thought I really hated your guts."

Shisei looked at him levelly. "Does that mean you don't now?"

"What do you care?" Branding said bitterly. "You played me for the perfect fool."

"Is that what you think?"

"Oh, please. Don't deny it. It's what I know."

Branding noticed Albemarle standing in the doorway, and he and Shisei lapsed into an uneasy silence.

The detective looked from the one to the other, concerned. "You two having a fight?" He sat on the corner of his desk. "It's none of my business, right?" He slit open the large manila envelope he was carrying, said to Branding, "Make sure everything's there, okay?"

"It is," Branding said shortly, putting away his wallet, keys, address book, and other items returned to him.

"Sign this." Albemarle nodded, as if the preliminaries were over. "Here's what I have to say, Senator. You can take it any way you want or not at all, that's your privilege. This woman's got a lot of guts. I don't know your history, don't want to. Maybe too much water's gone under the bridge." He shrugged. "Anyway, you ought to know. She fought like a sonuvabitch to see you freed. She knew you didn't murder Brisling, and she was willing to put herself in my line of fire in order to help prove it." He spun the sheet of paper Branding had signed onto his desk. "All things being equal, that ought to count for something. At least, that's the way it seems to me." He smiled. "But what do I know, right?"

He got up off the desk. "Good night, Senator, and good luck." At the doorway he turned, "Feel free to use the office. I've got to give a status report to the Indians outside, then I'll be waiting in case you need me to spirit you out. Use the phone, if you want. Dial nine for an outside line. Like I said, it's up to you. Handling the press is your métier."

When they were alone, he and Shisei stared at each other for a long time. When, at length, she saw he had nothing to say, she picked up her handbag.

"Wait a minute," Branding said. "Don't go."

"You said that once before," Shisei told him, "and look at the trouble it got you into."

"What trouble?" Branding said.

When she did not answer him, he picked up Albemarle's phone, got an outside line. He went through his address book, calling all his media contacts either at home or at work. He got them all—a good number were outside the precinct house, linked to their offices, and Branding, by mobile phones. These people never took vacations; they were news junkies, it was all they lived for.

Forty-five minutes later he was finished. "Well, that's done," he said. He called his press secretary, briefed her. "I'll hold a full news conference tomorrow. No, not in the morning. I've given a preliminary statement— that'll have to hold them for the time being. Let's go for the jugular. Yeah, right. Prime time. Take a page from the President's book. And let's do it from S Fourteen." Branding was referring to his coveted hideaway office in the Capitol Building. "Take the cameras inside. We'll make it very personal. You know. The photo op will be irresistible. And priceless. We'll get massive coverage. I'm going to turn this thing right around, make all the points I can and then some. It'll hit the public like Reagan getting shot and surviving. The news of what Howe tried to do to me will make me a hero. Yeah—and Maureen? I want this Washington police detective, Albemarle—" He looked through the papers on the desk. "Philip Albemarle." He gave her the precinct number. "I want him at the conference. No. Up there with me. Shoulder to shoulder. Right. You know the kind of thing. The press will eat it up, see us as brothers, kindred spirits. Right. Okay, do it. See you. And Maureen? Thanks." He put down the phone, sighed deeply. "Long night."

"Where's your lawyer?"

"Oh, he was here through the questioning," Branding said. "When they put me back in the holding cell, he went looking for a judge to sign a writ to get me out. I think he's still looking." He laughed suddenly. "I guess the joke's on him." He got up, looked at Shisei. "You coming, or what?"

Shisei did not move. "I want to tell you what happened."

Branding looked at her. "Why is it I wonder that you feel you have to lie to me?"

"I hate that Feraud suit I wore to the dinner," Shisei said. "I burned it after you left."

Branding said nothing.

At last Shisei lowered her eyes from his. "I don't know," she said in the smallest voice he had ever heard.

"Well," Branding said, "at least that's a start."

This morning Kusunda Ikusa had no time for formalities. He walked up to Masuto Ishii and said, "I have your money." He fairly thrust the thick envelope at the little man. His contempt for the amount of money, so dear to Ishii, was clearly defined by the gesture.

Ishii opened the envelope; they were alone in the Imperial Palace East Garden, so it was all right. "Thank you, Ikusa-san. Thank you." He could not stop bowing.

"Forget that," Ikusa snapped. "What do you have for me?" His nerves weren't what they were yesterday. But then yesterday that stupid spy was on the bottom of the Sumida River. What in the name of Buddha had caused him to surface? Ikusa wondered. Not that the police would find anything on him to link the body to Ikusa, but Ikusa was a believer in omens, and this was an evil one.

"You were right," Ishii said, pocketing the envelope, "Nangi-san is planning to move against you." They began their walk, circumnavigating the garden. It was a brilliant morning, sunshine drenching the last of the night's dewdrops. "To that end he is marshaling all the support he can from his minister cronies at MITI."

"I knew it!" Ikusa said triumphantly. On the one hand, he was dismayed that after so many years of being a ronin, Nangi still had such close ties to MITI. On the other hand, he welcomed a showdown with the ministry. If he were to be honest with himself, this battle had been a long time in the making. Ikusa was well aware of the jealousy many MITI ministers felt toward Nami's burgeoning power. Especially now, since the new Emperor had taken power; he was making it known that Nami's important policy decisions had his imprimatur. This was especially galling to MITI, which had many decades of smooth sailing in ramming its economic policies down the throat of the industrial sector.

Perhaps the time was right for Nami to put an end to the rivalry. After all, no ship of state could be steered successfully by two captains.

Well, all right, Ikusa vowed, if it's a fight Nangi wants, that's just what he'll get. But I have the edge because I've got my pipeline into his strategy.

Ikusa said, "What kind of operation, specifically, is Nangi mounting?"

"I would think financing," Ishii said, struggling to keep up with the huge man. In his mounting fervor, Ikusa had quickened his step. "Judging by the people he's brought in"—here he named four of MITI's top ministers—"that has to be the route he's taking. All of them have ties to central banks. He's going to float his company on their backs."

"And in return?" Ikusa asked.

"It's brilliant, really. He doesn't have to mortgage even one division of Sato International." Ishii took a deep breath. "He's offered them your head."

The key. The key to what? Nangi had no idea.

"The first thing to do is to search the Pack Rat's apartment," Tomi said, ever the methodical detective.

"It would be a waste of time," Nangi said, turning the key over and over in his hand. "The Pack Rat never kept anything of importance at home. It was a matter of security to him, and he never broke his own rules."

"Still," Tomi said, "it would be poor procedure to assume the key didn't fit anything there."

Three hours later they had satisfied themselves that it didn't.

"Phew! This place is a pigsty," Tomi said, looking around the cluttered space.

Outside she said, "There was no evidence that the Pack Rat had a safety deposit box."

"He didn't," Nangi assured her. "In his line of business, that never would have occurred to him."

"Just what *was* the Pack Rat's line of business?"

Nangi smiled. "He was an information gatherer. He was the best at it I'd ever met."

"All right. The key opens nothing in his apartment, it's not for a safety deposit box. That makes sense. Obviously, considering what he did, he'd need twenty-four-hour access to everything important." Tomi shook her head. "So where does that leave us? Running down lockers in every train and bus depot in the city?"

"No," Nangi said. "The key has no number, it can't be to a public locker."

"Then what *does* it open?"

Nangi considered. Something Tomi had said stuck in his head. What was it? Then he remembered, and it gave him an idea. "Come on," he said. "We're going to play some pachinko."

The Twenty-Four Hour pachinko parlor was in the Ginza, gaudy, loud, smoke-filled, open, as its name said, day and night.

Nangi bought a token from the cashier and moved along the aisles of machines. He counted: seventh row, sixth machine. The machine the Pack Rat always played.

It was being expertly played by a kid of about eighteen with a foot-long Mohawk bristle of hair in flamingo colors down the center of his skull, his head shaved on either side. The kid wore shit-kicker boots with spurs, black jeans covered with metal studs, a short-waisted black leather jacket. Lengths of chains appended from the epaulets clinked rhythmi-cally as he worked the levers that flipped the ball bearing through the maze of the pachinko field. The kid won big and was rewarded with a gush of tokens.

"This could take forever," Nangi said.

Tomi flipped open her police credentials, hung them in front of the kid's face.

"Hey!" he said.

"Beat it," Tomi said, "before I run you in."

"Yeah?" The kid sneered. "For what?"

"Your hair's disturbing the peace, sonny," Tomi said, showing him a glimpse of her gun. The kid beat it out of there.

"Okay," Tomi said. "What's up?"

"We'll see in a minute," Nangi said, handing her the token. "Here, go crazy."

Tomi slotted the token, began to play. Meanwhile, Nangi slipped around to the right side of the machine, bent over. There was the little door the Pack Rat had opened to get his tokens. His heart beat a little faster. There was a keyhole in the upper third of the door.

"What are you doing?" Tomi asked.

"When we last met, the Pack Rat insisted we do so here. Partly, it was security. So much noise makes even the most sophisticated electronic surveillance impossible. Partly, it was his hangout. He came here, he told me, when he needed to work out solutions. But he always played this one machine. I wondered why, until he opened a door back here where they keep the tokens."

"Nice little scam," Tomi said.

"Maybe," Nangi said, "it was a lot more than that."

Tomi had said of the Pack Rat, *Obviously, considering what he did, he'd need twenty-four-hour access to everything important.* That was what had jogged Nangi's memory of the Pack Rat's pachinko parlor open all day and all night.

He took the key that had been taped to the Pack Rat's big toe and, reciting a prayer, inserted it into the hole. It fit, sliding all the way in.

Nangi tried to turn it to the right. Nothing happened; the key wouldn't move. His heart sank. Then he tried it to the left.

The door fell open.

Nangi put his hand inside, felt around. And there it was, taped to the metal top of the receptacle that received the tokens. Nangi feverishly pulled it free, took it out and looked at it. It was an audio microcassette.

Jackpot!

Nicholas rocketed west along the Long Island Expressway at ninety-five. Justine was curled in the Corvette's passenger seat, the borrowed blanket still across her shoulders. Every so often, as Nicholas glanced at her, she twitched in her sleep and made a little crying sound. He put one hand protectively on her hip.

It was four-thirty in the morning, the sky the color of the inside of an oyster shell. Clouds along the horizon in the south were tinged pale orange.

Nicholas had the top down. The wind felt good ruffling his hair; it took the stink of the fire out of his nostrils.

He and Justine wore borrowed clothes; everything had been burned in the fire.

Every twenty seconds or so Nicholas glanced at the miniature radar detector hidden behind the Corvette's sun visor, even though he knew its beeping would alert him to a police car waiting to pull over impatient drivers just like him. It gave him something to do beside stare at the ugly, featureless highway.

He made the trip back to New York from West Bay Bridge in an hour and fifteen minutes. Justine woke up as he slowed for the toll for the Queens-Midtown Tunnel.

"What time is it?" she asked, stretching.

"Too early for you to be up," Nicholas said as they entered the tunnel. "Go back to sleep."

Justine rubbed her eyes. "Too many dreams," she said. "Too many ghosts stalking me." She looked over at him. "Nick, I dreamed of Saigo. And then he turned into you."

Nicholas shivered, thinking of Kansatsu-san saying, *The Darkness is what you have shunned for all your life.* And his own answer, *That would mean that Saigo and I are the same.* "This man Senjin is not Saigo," Nicholas said. "I want you to understand something. Saigo was evil. Senjin, this *dorokusai*, has transcended evil—or good, for that matter.

The concept of morality is irrelevant to him. He lives, or thinks he lives, beyond such considerations."

"Which is it?"

They had emerged into Manhattan, and Nicholas headed downtown.

"I'm not sure I know," he said. "But then again, I don't know that it matters. What's important now is what's in Senjin's mind. When I know that, I'll know him."

He went straight down Second Avenue all the way to Houston, then cut west. In SoHo he turned onto Greene Street, pulled up in front of a line of industrial-looking buildings. Up until five or six years ago they had been factories owned by dry-goods manufacturers and other companies of light industry. Now they had been converted into spacious, and all too often chicly-designed, co-op loft apartments.

Nicholas took Justine up to a metal door lacquered a deep sea-green. Punched into it was a vertical line of three Medeco locks, surrounded by thick brass anti-pry-bar plates. Beside the door was a series of buzzers below an intercom grill. High up, Justine could see the glass lens of a video camera.

Nicholas pressed a button that said, enigmatically, Con Tower. In a moment a buzz sounded and the door popped open automatically.

The door closed behind them and they were immersed in pitch-blackness. A minute went by, another. Nicholas did not move, and neither did Justine. She knew better than to say anything. She could feel Nicholas relaxed beside her, and that was enough to reassure her.

Light popped on without warning, and Justine blinked. She saw them surrounded by images of themselves. The hallucinatory, almost vertiginous perspective changed only after a door cut flush into one of the mirrored panels opened inward. Nicholas took her through.

Inside, Justine found herself in a large but warm space. The ceiling was as high as a cathedral's. The walls were curved, creating concave and convex spaces, untraditional, mysterious, which reminded Justine of the hills and dales of the human form. Enormous canvasses hung on some walls, modern paintings of voluptuous sun-dappled countrysides in the post-Impressionist manner.

The space was furnished comfortably and eclectically in contemporary leather, chintzed antiques and functional copies of antiques, none of them Oriental. Scattered throughout were antique Japanese lacquerware, writing boxes. Against one concave wall stood a life-size statue of a Kabuki actor made up as a woman complete with wig and costume. In the center of the room, a large lacquered and gilded wood Buddha sat on an ancient

Buddhist plinth. Oddly, the place was not a jumble, but through some unknown magic, a harmonious whole.

There was a menacing-looking Japanese man standing in the middle of the room. Justine could feel his tension, realized that he was making no secret of it.

"You're here fast, Tik-Tik," the Japanese said. "Too fast."

Then she recognized him. "Conny?" she said. "Conny Tanaka?"

"Hai!" Conny bowed, seemed at a bit of a loss when Justine rushed into his arms.

Nicholas laughed. "You should see your face, Tanaka-san."

Conny groaned.

"This place is new," Justine said. "It's spectacular!"

"You haven't seen anything yet," Nicholas told her.

"Tik-tik?" Conny was scowling. He glanced at Justine. "Don't think I'm not happy to see you." He kissed her, then turned back to Nicholas. "I read what you gave me, Tik-Tik. I'm fast, but I gotta confess, not this fast. Why are you here now, when I didn't expect you for a couple of days yet?"

"The timetable has been accelerated." Nicholas flopped down onto an excellent reproduction of a Louis Quatorze sofa. "The *dorokusai* burned down our house last night."

Conny barked an epithet in Japanese that Justine could not understand. "I'll get tea," he said.

Justine turned to Nicholas. Her eyes were opaque with fear. He could see her trembling. "Why didn't you tell me?"

"There was no point, before," Nicholas said. "What would you have done, except be frightened? You needed your sleep."

"But Nick, how did he know where I was going?" She seemed to be begging him to tell her this was all a lie or, at least, a nightmare from which she would eventually awaken.

"I'm afraid you must have told him," Nicholas said. He was careful not to tell her that he had somehow made her lead him to the cache of So-Peng's emeralds. That bit of humiliation would be too much for her now.

"Oh, my God! Nick, what else did I tell him? I can't remember anything!"

"How can I know that?" he said softly.

Justine's shoulders slumped. She felt abruptly exhausted. It was odd how mentally enervating terror could be, she thought. Then Conny returned with a laden tray, and Justine felt some sense of equilibrium returning.

Each crisis brings its own tea ceremony, she thought. It was very civilized, but it was practical as well. In the time it took to perform the many small but important tasks associated with the ceremony, the spirit could free itself from turmoil, settle in to the accepted pathway of thought that would lead to a victorious strategy.

When the tea had been made, the formalities observed, the tea drunk, Nicholas told Conny what had happened and what he surmised had happened. This was the part Justine was hearing for the first time as well, and she shuddered as if swallowing bitter wine.

"What do you want me to do, Tik-Tik?" Conny asked after Nicholas had finished.

"You're already doing it," Nicholas said, looking directly at him. "But I need cash, credit cards, driver's license, the works. The office can fix all that up for me. There's still a great deal I have to do, and I've got to do it alone. Will you take care of Justine while I'm out?"

"Nick!" Justine cried before Conny had a chance to reply. "I want to be with you. I don't want to sit here feeling useless while you—"

Nicholas came and sat beside her. He took her hand. "Not useless," he said in that tone of voice she knew so well, which she listened to without question. "All of us here have our parts to play. But it is essential that we do play them."

Justine, looking into his eyes, nodded.

"Maybe you lost this guy when you came here," Conny said. "I wouldn't want to try to follow you around town. If you're lost, you can stay lost. Avoid—"

"He'll find me, Conny," Nicholas said. "No matter what I do, he'll get here. It's just a matter of time."

"But we can—"

"Forget about avoiding the inevitable," Nicholas said. "It's a waste of energy, and we're all going to need a lot of that very soon." He hunched closer, trying to ignore Justine's terrified face. "The object here is to play a game. *Our* game. It isn't Hide and Seek, it's Three-Card Monte. Illusion's at the heart of this. We show this bastard a seven of diamonds, and when he's close enough to give us a shave, he finds out it's really the ace of spades."

"The death card." Conny nodded. "It's a good plan."

"It had better be," Nicholas said. "It's the only one that'll possibly work."

Conny cleared the teacups, disappeared behind an antique Japanese screen depicting white herons in flight above a gold and green sea.

Nicholas turned to Justine, stared into her eyes a long time. Then he said, "I wonder whether you know just how precious you are to me."

"Nick, Nick." Justine put her head against his chest. Hot tears welled in her eyes. "I'm so frightened. I feel like I've just gotten you back. Now, knowing Senjin is so close, I'm terrified. I—"

Nicholas put his hand gently over her mouth.

"Shhh. Be still. Be calm. Have faith."

"Memo to myself," the Pack Rat's voice crackled through the microrecorder's speaker. The entry was dated, as were all the subsequent entries. "Re: computer virus attack on Sato. Gave floppy record of attack to Mickey for analysis. Said to call her forty-eight hours . . . Memo to myself: Called Mickey. Right now she's got nothing. Says architecture of virus is like nothing she's familiar with. That's the bad news. The good news is she's hooked, fascinated with the project. She wants to run this sucker down, taken herself off all other private projects. Call daily . . . Memo to self: Called Mickey. Nothing . . . Memo to self: Called Mickey. Nothing . . . Memo to self: Mickey says this virus mutates. From what she's been able to piece together so far, it seems the virus actually *feeds* on the host security system, using it as it adapts to it, to actually penetrate the security to get to the protected files . . . Memo to self: According to Mickey, the virus is not designed to destroy or scramble host programs. It's a mole virus, meant as a communication link between the protected files and the user of the virus. This is getting crazier and crazier. Mickey agrees. She's flipped over this thing, working on it eighteen hours a day . . . Memo to myself: I think Mickey's close to breaking the virus. From data she's rerun from the magnetic copy Nangi gave me, she's certain now the attack on Sato's computer was a test run. She's also fairly certain the virus is not yet perfected. She says she knows one guy—and only one—who could have come up with this amazing supervirus that adapts to different security programs. He's a certified genius, she says and, guess what? He works at Nakano's R and D department. Coincidence? Must call Nangi soonest . . ."

The tape was over, but a kind of energy, invisible, pervasive, filled the room. The first dated entry was the day Nangi had first met with the Pack Rat in the electronic jungle of Akihabara; the last entry was the day before he disappeared.

Nangi sat staring at the tiny black microrecorder. They were at Tomi's office at police headquarters. Tomi was pacing back and forth with so

much agitation that Nangi, despite his preoccupation with the revelations
of the tape, said, "What's the matter with you?"

Tomi gave a sad little laugh. She stared at him. "Nothing," she said
through tight lips, "except that if this Mickey's right, I think I know who
created the supervirus."

Nangi picked his head up. She stopped her pacing, put her hands on
her hips. "Don't look at me like that. I even know what the virus is
called. MANTIS. It's an acronym for, let's see, Manmade Non-some-
thing, Nondiscriminatory Tactical Integrated Circuit Smasher. I think
that's right. According to my friend, it's an adaptable virus. It actually
uses the security program to piggyback into the computer's core. That
word—'adaptable'—is what stopped me cold."

Nangi said, "Your friend created this MANTIS?"

His quiet voice made her wince. She nodded. "His name's Seji Kikoko
but everyone calls him the Scoundrel. He works for Nakano, in their R
and D department. I've known him for years. He's an old, trusted friend.
I'm just—I can't believe he knows what his program's being used for."

"He must." Nangi looked at her. "This virus is so new, so radical, he's
the only one who could possibly evaluate its results."

Tomi nodded. She slumped heavily into a chair, ran her hand through
her hair. She was obviously devastated. "I've got to talk to him, find
out—"

"Not yet," Nangi said.

Tomi cocked her head. "What are you thinking?"

"I'm thinking that at this moment we are in way over our heads,"
Nangi said. "We're in the middle of a conspiracy far larger than I had
imagined." He looked at her. "Now I know what it's like to be standing
in front of a bull's-eye. Nicholas was right. It's one of the things he told
me in the car on the way to the airport. He and I have been targeted for
months. This kind of operation was a long time in the planning."

"But what kind of operation is it?"

Nangi rested the point of his chin on his hands, which were cupped
over the dragon head of his cane. "I'm still not quite sure of its ramifications," he said slowly, "or even its full intent. It's similar to this quite
amazing mole virus. Like the Pack Rat's computer-language whiz,
Mickey: I can see the architecture, but I'm not yet certain of its purpose."

He glanced at his watch, stood up. He pocketed the tape recorder, said,
"Let's go. It's time we started seeing some fruits of our own operation."

Masuto Ishii, his vice-president of operations, was waiting when he
and Tomi arrived at his house. Umi had made tea and sweets for Ishii,

making him comfortable in the nine-tatami room that served as one of the formal rooms.

One entire wall was open to a lacquered wooden *engawa* that led out onto an interior garden. Ishii, who was sipping his tea, staring out at the azaleas and the peonies, scrambled to his feet, bowed deeply, when Nangi entered the room. Nangi made the introductions, as Ishii and Tomi had never met.

Umi came and served them tea, then sat beside Nangi. Nangi said, "What news have you brought?"

Ishii smiled, withdrew a videocassette from a slim briefcase. "It is all here, Nangi-san," he said, offering the cassette with a deep bow. "Just as you predicted."

Nangi grunted, took the cassette, slipped it into a VCR sitting atop a sleek twenty-four-inch TV. The electronic gear came on, and using a remote, Nangi set the tape running as soon as he resumed his place beside Umi.

"Watch closely," he said.

Color bars were replaced by image. Tomi could see immediately that this was no amateur job; it was professional surveillance work all the way.

The image resolved itself. They all recognized the setting as the Imperial Palace East Garden. Ishii came into the frame, and shortly thereafter, Kusunda Ikusa. As with all surveillance tape, this had the date and the running time digitalized in hours, minutes, seconds along the bottom of the frame, so there could be no doubt as to when this was being taped and no allegations of fraud or splicing.

With a sharp gesture, Ikusa thrust a thick envelope at Ishii, who took it. Ishii opened it up in the direction of the camera which, as if on a prearranged cue, zoomed in. Tomi could clearly see the stacks of yen.

The two men spoke for some time, walking around the garden. There was no sound track to the tape. At length Ishii and Ikusa parted. The tape followed Ishii as he got into his car. The car was followed to the other side of Tokyo. The tape stayed with Ishii all the way. He made no stops.

Ishii pulled over on a side street, waited. He looked at his watch. A man came into the frame, opened the back door of Ishii's car, climbed in. The image showed him clearly. He was Catch Hagawa, a well-known bookie, gambling operator. Yakuza-connected.

Hagawa spoke briefly to Ishii. Ishii said nothing, handed over the envelope. It was the same envelope that Ikusa had given Ishii. Hagawa took it, counted the money twice. Then he nodded curtly, stuffed the yen back in the envelope, slipped the envelope inside his jacket. He got out of the car. Ishii drove out of the frame. End of surveillance.

"Good Christ," Tomi breathed.

Nangi bowed to his vice-president of operations. "You did well, Ishii-san."

The diminutive man bowed back, much more deeply. "Thank you, Nangi-san. The integrity of Sato International must be maintained at all costs. An attack against the corporate entity is a personal attack against every loyal employee. I was humbled by your faith in me. Whatever I accomplished is little compared with the tasks facing you."

"Each individual is integral to the whole," Nangi said, obviously pleased with Ishii's reply. "Each contribution, if pure in heart, is equally important. This is the way of Sato International."

Tomi said, "How in the world did you set that up, Nangi-san?"

Nangi turned to her, smiled. "It was Nicholas's idea. Are you familiar with the philosophy behind aikido? Aikido is an art of concentric circles. It uses an aggressor's own momentum against him, pulling him in toward you, instead of the more difficult direction, outward and away.

"We employed the same philosophy here. Instead of fighting Ikusa's attack—pulling away from it to attack him ourselves, we drew him closer to us, we appealed to his essential lust for power, for seeing us utterly defeated. We presented him with a situation of distress." He told her of Ishii's initial contact with Ikusa. "Ishii's history made such a story not only logical, but irresistible to Ikusa, because in Ishii's supposed plight, he saw a way to use Ishii against us. As we suspected, Ikusa wished to use Ishii to tell him what our strategy was going to be." Nangi smiled again. "Ishii obliged him. Now what we have on tape is visual evidence of Kusunda Ikusa, moral paragon of Nami, passing a great deal of money through an intermediary to Catch Hagawa, a known criminal."

"But that's not what happened," Tomi pointed out. "And Ikusa will be quick to point that out."

"But he won't be quick enough," Nangi said. "You see, on the high moral perch Ikusa has placed himself, there is no room for error. Besides, what will Ikusa say to explain the video away? Whatever lie he uses will be perceived as a cover-up.

"In this case—as it is often—the reality is irrelevant. It is, rather, people's perception of what transpired that counts. The evidence of wrongdoing is before us. That it is an illusion has no meaning. Believe me, the scandal will be real enough, as far as Kusunda Ikusa is concerned."

Shisei took Branding home to her house, because his was sure to be staked out by reporters.

"I want you with me now," he said solemnly. "After what's just happened, I don't want any more surprises."

"Cook," she said, "do you know there's a school in Japan that teaches you to lie with your eyes?"

He looked at her as he began to strip. "I'm going to take a shower," he said. "I feel like I've just jetted in from Hong Kong. I want you in the bathroom with me."

"I won't walk out on you, Cook."

Branding was naked now. He rolled his soiled clothes into a ball. "I don't know where to put these things."

Shisei held out her arms. "Give them to me. I'll have them cleaned."

Branding threw them on the bed.

"You're not going to listen to anything I have to say, are you?"

There was nothing in her voice, no pain, certainly no self-pity, and this is what got to Branding. "You were telling me about this Japanese school," he said, padding into the bathroom.

"Can I join you?" Shisei asked.

He watched her as she took off her clothes. Who teaches women how to do that? Branding wondered. Certainly not their mothers.

"I thought you might be afraid of me," she said.

Branding turned on the water, and soon the bathroom filled with steam. It became uncomfortably warm. He stepped into the shower, kept the door open. Shisei followed him in, shut the door behind her.

"About this school," Branding said. The hot water felt good on his body, sluicing away the dirt, the sweat of fear. God, but he had been frightened when he had seen David Brisling's corpse in the trunk of his car. But not as frightened as when the police had booked him. I couldn't be a criminal, he thought. I haven't the stomach for it.

"The school was in the country," Shisei said. She picked up a bar of soap, began to lather his body. "All its buildings were in the style of a Swiss chalet. I don't know why, except the entire place had the air of fantasy about it. It was called Kinsei no Kumo, Golden Cloud. All collaborative enterprises in Japan need a slogan to be often recited by those involved. Golden Cloud's was, 'Kiyoku Utsukushiku Kanzen,' Pure Beautiful Perfect.

"There were only female students at Golden Cloud, but all the instructors were male. I suppose you could say we were taught acting, although it was nothing like the acting you might think of. Do you remember *kata*, the rules? Well, everything we did at Golden Cloud was according to *kata*. This meant not merely our acting, but our eating, sleeping, bathing. Everything.

"We played only male parts. There were many reasons for this. We were, for instance, made to memorize the life of the great actor, Yoshisawa Ayame, whose concept of acting was to express an ideal. Women actors, he said, could not express the ultimate feminine ideal on stage, because they would automatically rely on their external feminine charms: their lips, their hips, their breasts. This would destroy the ideal. Only a man could create the ideal woman on stage."

"But that's crazy," Branding said.

"Do you think so?" Shisei's soapy hands circled lower and lower on his back. "Why? Don't you realize that an ideal expression is impossible unless it is wholly artificial? The ideal is but an illusion, skillfully sculpted by the artist."

Branding turned around. "Then the same is true for women? Only they can express the male ideal?"

"Yes."

"But you're a female playing a female role."

"I am a graduate," Shisei said. "Not a student. Besides, most of my classmates at Golden Cloud were there because playing male roles allowed them to lose their own femaleness, to become, in a sense, sexless. They knew only too well the servile place waiting for them as women in Japanese society. Golden Cloud allowed them to escape that fate, at least for a time."

"And why were you there?"

"By that time I knew I wanted to become a talento, a celebrity," she said. "I remember watching the marriage of the top two talentos. The media coverage was unprecedented in Japan. Not even the prime minister received that kind of air time. They were treated as if they were royalty. The public adulation was like a wonderful surge of electricity, and I remember thinking that these two perfect people must have entered heaven. They had everything. Everything I wanted."

Shisei's long lashes were heavy with moisture. "The truth is, I went to Golden Cloud to gain a measure of control over others," she said, "because I knew that as a female, I would otherwise have none."

Branding watched the water cascading over Shisei's firm-muscled body. In the small folds and hollows, beads of moisture clung to her flesh. "So this was where you were taught to lie with your eyes," he said. "Did your instructors also teach you to deceive your heart?"

Her head was lifted to his. "Cook—"

He touched her. "If only you wouldn't lie to me."

"Why is the truth so important to you?" Shisei asked.

"The truth is what I have dedicated my life to."

"But all of life is a lie."

"Ah, Shisei, you can't believe that."

"But I do, Cook. I really do. You would, too, if you knew what I knew."

Branding suddenly gripped her shoulders, drew her against him until their lips were almost touching. He looked deep into her eyes, the eyes that had been taught to lie, and said, "Who are you, Shisei? Are you the self-confident lobbyist, slipping artfully through Washington society, playing the game better than almost anyone else? Or are you the concerned environmentalist, wonderfully pure of heart? Or the tormented human painting, kept like an animal at the sufferance of a mad artist? Or the hard-edged little girl sent to Golden Cloud to learn how to submerge her sexuality in order to attain some insane ideal?

"Do you know which one of those people you are, Shisei?" He shook his head. "I don't think so. I don't believe you're any one—or any combination—of those identities.

"I don't think you know who you are. Because somewhere along the way you lost the sense of your own self. You were taught to deceive, of that I have no doubt. The only trouble is, in the end you've deceived only yourself."

Shisei gave a little cry and, twisting from his grasp, collapsed at his feet. Her head hung, the water smashing her hair flat, bringing it like a curtain down around her face.

"Oh, Shisei, don't do that." Branding knelt down beside her, lifted her up.

"Cook," she breathed, "life for me is a lie because the truth is impossible to face."

"Only for right now," Branding assured her. "But you've got to take the first step toward accepting the truth about yourself."

"I cannot."

"If you could tell me the truth about yourself," Branding said, "if you could see that I can accept it, that would be a start."

"No!" She clung to him. "Cook, no. Don't make me!"

"Shisei," he said, hugging her to him, "I can't make you do anything. Although I daresay the opposite has not been true."

Shisei closed her eyes, her heart hammering. "I'm tired, Cook."

Branding turned off the water.

She toweled him off before she began to dry herself. "I think you left some clothes in my closet," she said.

Branding padded into the bedroom, opened the closet door. Inside he found his robe, a fresh pair of underclothes. Shirt and slacks of his were also neatly hung on hangers.

He drew on the robe, tied it. As he did so, he found himself looking at the edge of the closet door. There was a dark patch at head height. It had been wiped clean, but the abrasion of the wood was obviously fresh. He stared at the naked slivers of unpainted wood as if they were an accusing chorus. In his mind he saw again David Brisling's corpse curled in his car trunk, the lethal wound in the back of his head. It had a vee shape, Albemarle had said to him over and over during the interrogation at the police precinct. And tiny pieces of wood were found in the mashed flesh. *Do you know what could have caused that type of wound, Senator? A two-by-four? What's your best guess?* Branding hadn't any. He wondered if he had one now.

His face was still thoughtful as Shisei emerged from the bathroom. She was winding her hair into a thick braid, hesitated when she saw his face.

"Shisei," Branding said quietly, "do you know who murdered David Brisling?"

"Douglas Howe."

"That's what the police think," Branding said.

There was a swath of lamplight on Shisei's face, but Branding could not tell what it revealed. "What's the point of asking? You know I'll only lie to you."

Branding said, "I'm asking you not to. If you feel anything genuine for me in that secret, tortured heart of yours, you'll tell me the truth."

"Cook, I love you."

He shook his head. "I'm not sure what that means right now."

Shisei stood very still, but even at this distance Branding could sense a change come over her. There was a tension, a kind of fluttering of the air between them that made his bowels turn to water. What had she said before? *I thought you might be afraid of me.* If she had murdered Douglas Howe, he would have good reason to be. What would stop her from doing the same to him? But he had no real proof, and never would have. Just a dark, accusatory spot on her closet door and his overactive imagination, which in time he might come to terms with.

After a long time Shisei said, "What would you do if I told you the truth?"

Branding shook his head. "You must tell me because you want to tell me the truth, because you want to start life anew, not because of any reaction I might have."

Shisei's eyes were glowing like amber subjected to the light. She took a deep breath, fighting for *prana*, for equilibrium. The atmosphere in the room seemed to quake, ripples extending outward until they purled against Branding's chest.

"Yes," she whispered. "I know."

Branding gave a tiny sigh, as if he had been holding his breath. He turned away, began slowly preparing the bed for sleep.

Shisei approached him. "Is that all you're going to ask? Don't you want to know more?"

Branding stood up, looked into her face. "I already know more." That tension again, the sweat collecting in his armpits, crawling down the line of his spine.

"I want you to know something, Shisei. I love you. But I'm not yet sure who it is I love. Is it the perfect illusion—one of the many you've conjured up for me? Or is it you—the real you, hidden deep down somewhere with all your weaknesses and flaws?" His eyes never left hers. "I need your help to find out. I'm already well-acquainted with the illusion. Now I need some time with the real Shisei. Tell me. Are you willing to help me?"

Shisei was crying. "I can't believe you're still here. I can't believe I haven't driven you away. Why have you stayed? I can't understand it. The more monstrous things you learn about me, the closer you seem to me. Is that possible? Oh, my God. Oh, my God."

Branding wanted to go to her, to take her in his arms, but he hesitated, sensing that to move at all now would be a mistake. He recalled a vacation out west, talking to a cowboy who had just finished breaking a horse. The cowboy told him that the bronco was at his most dangerous in the moments just before he capitulated, accepting the bit, the direction of the reins, the unfamiliar weight of a human being on his back. *That's when you can get hurt bad,* the cowboy drawled. *'Cause you relax, thinkin' yore work is done, an' you're safe. Let me tell you, bud, that's shore as shit when you git yore neck broke.*

Some similar instinct told Branding now that he was at that critical moment with Shisei. He did not relax, watched, instead, the tears streaming down her face, his heart breaking.

"The truth is—" Shisei stopped, gathered herself, began again. "The truth is, I love a show. I always have. But even more, I love to perform, because I can feel loved then, the collective love of my audience."

She stopped again, and she was so long in continuing that Branding was certain that was all she could squeeze out now. "My brother," Shisei said in a strangled voice, "said that acting would be the death of me."

"I didn't know you had a brother."

"A twin brother." She gave him a wan smile. "There are many things you don't know about me, Cook. Many things I wish now I didn't have to tell you."

"What is it? Do you think I'll leave you when I know?"

Shisei hissed air out of her mouth. "Cook, no one has ever loved you as I love you. No one else will, because no one else can in the way I do. And whatever happens, that at least will never change. I swear to you I'm telling the truth."

"Yes. I know."

"I wish I could believe you."

"Why? I've never lied to you." He held out a hand. "Do you see now how completely you're entangled in the snare of your own deception?"

She leaned heavily against the bed, as if she suddenly had lost the will even to stand up. "Oh, God, what do you want from me? Don't you understand that the truth will destroy me?"

"No," Branding said. "It won't, Shisei. That's just an illusion you're using to frighten yourself. What I want is for you to climb out of the pit you've been living in for Christ knows how many years. I'm offering life, and life only."

Shisei, trembling, said, "I have played the siren with you, and the Judas. Now you ask me to abandon my acting, to give up the roles I have lovingly fashioned, to exist only as myself. I don't know whether I can do that."

"Of course you don't," Branding said. "Because you're a stranger to yourself. Given a choice, don't all humans choose the known over the unknown?"

"But I am not human!" Shisei fairly shouted it, terrified, heartsick that he had at last driven her to this confession, one she had vowed long ago never to make. "I and my brother stand apart from all humankind. We are tanjian. We possess a gift of the mind. We see things, know things— we can do things others cannot."

Branding, stunned, moved on a somnambulist's leaden feet toward where she huddled on the corner of the bed. "You mean you're psychic."

She gave a bitter laugh. "Only in the broadest sense. Not as parlor tricksters, able to tell a stranger's birthdate from holding a possession of his. No, not that. Our gift is far more potent."

Branding sat next to her. He felt her pain as if it were his own. He gave her an encouraging smile. "Is that your secret, the terrible revelation that you thought would make me hate you?"

"No," Shisei breathed. The she turned away from him. "Oh, God, help me." She shivered once, then said, "No. My secret is my twin brother. My bond with him. It was my brother—not the mad artist Zasso, whose name I invented—who imprisoned me, who felt compelled to create upon my back the centerpiece of the dreams that haunted his young life.

"It is my twin brother with whom I have been intimate in ways you could never imagine. It is my twin brother who loves me unto death, who will not let me go, who has destroyed those who would seek to love me as he loves me.

"My twin brother, who is my guardian, my ghost lover, my other half, dark, foreboding, reeking of death."

Branding looked at Shisei spread across the bed, saw the great spider moving, breathing as she breathed, living as she lived, and for the first time he understood the extent of her agony, the nature of the prison without walls in which she was incarcerated.

He moved to touch her. "Shisei—"

"Wait," she said. "There's more. My brother called me yesterday. He's here, in America. In New York City. Something's happened. He's called for me."

"You don't have to go."

"But I do, Cook!" She rolled over. "If you know anything about me, you know that I must. *Kata*, the rules. *Giri*, my duty. These are still the only definitions of my life. Without them, I am nothing."

She sat up. Her eyes were pleading, not for sympathy—that was not in her—but for something akin to understanding. She seemed to be saying, Cook, don't be Western now. Try to think like an Easterner. Be accepting. Be patient.

She held out her arms. "Hold me, Cook. I'm frightened."

"Of your brother?" he asked as he enfolded her in his arms.

"Yes," she whispered. "But now I am just as frightened of myself."

"I think that's a good sign." Branding smelled her damp hair, the faint musk of her skin. It was as heady, as dizzying as throwing yourself into a field of wildflowers. He hugged her to him, feeling at last close to the core of her, that torn and battered part of her that she seemed to despise, and which he knew now that he loved above everything else.

"Cook," she said, and a tremor went through her. "I will have to go. In the morning. First thing."

"Will you tell him about me?"

"I won't have to," Shisei said bleakly. "He will already know."

Branding felt that peculiar sensation run down his spine, as if Shisei's spider were now upon his back. "What will happen?"

"I don't know. My gift does not extend to second sight. I can only feel how powerful your love is. It is like a splendid ache in my heart."

They rocked together, like children locked in the aftermath of a disaster.

"I can't come with you, Shisei," Branding said. "I can't run out on the press. And I have the ASCRA bill coming onto the Senate floor later today. I'm its sponsor; I have to be there. *Kata. Giri.*"

"I understand."

"But I'll be with you, nonetheless." Branding kissed her neck with such tenderness that Shisei began to weep anew.

Her nails dug into the flesh of his back. "Oh, Cook, how I love you!"

When Tomi returned to her office to pick up some notes, she was told by one of the uniforms that someone was waiting for her. She remembered the moment just over a month ago when she had been told that and had then met Tanzan Nangi for the first time.

But as she approached her desk this afternoon, she recognized the man sitting beside it. She detoured, made two cups of tea, brought them to her desk.

"Hello, Scoundrel," she said, handing him a tea. "How the hell are you?" But she could see in his hollowed, frightened eyes how he was.

"*Domo*, Tomi-san," the Scoundrel said. Thank you. He took the tea gratefully, drank it down in three straight thirst-quenching gulps.

"If you want more, you know where the hot plate is," she said.

"Thank you," he said again, and bowed, very formal now, so unlike his grinning, lighthearted self, a Japanese-featured Billy Idol thumbing his nose at the world.

Tomi watched him as he went to get himself more tea, turning over in her mind the change that had come over him.

When he returned, she said, "I must say I'm surprised you've come on your own."

"What?"

"Where's Killan?"

The Scoundrel was so startled he spilled hot tea all over himself.

Tomi gave him a pile of paper napkins so he could brush himself off. "Did you get burned?" she asked.

"It's not so bad," the Scoundrel said.

"I wasn't talking about the tea." His hand came up and their eyes locked. "Why isn't Killan here with you?" She said it softly, the steel inside the glove.

"Killan? Why should she be?"

"Because she's in this thing with you."

"What thing?"

"Stop it!" Tomi said it so sharply that she froze him, the teacup halfway to his lips. "You came here for help. A blind man could tell you're in trouble. So let's save some time. I know about MANTIS, and I know what it can do. While you've been a very bad boy, I've been working with Tanzan Nangi. Do you know him? You should. You tested your MANTIS virus on his computer system." Tomi shook her head. "This is some really bad shit you've fallen into, Seji. I know you, my friend. I know what you're capable of—and what would never occur to you.

"That's how I know that somehow Killan Oroshi is involved. We were all so close once. The Three Musketeers, remember? Haunting movie theaters, hanging out on the Ginza, guzzling beer and pizza."

The Scoundrel cleared his throat. "Long time passing."

"You're telling me, brother." Tomi put her hands on her desk. "Okay. Bottom line. You've come to me for help. I can give it, but only if you're straight with me. The truth and nothing but the truth, so help you John Wayne."

That brought the glimmer of a smile to the Scoundrel's lips, but it soon faded. "You have to understand. Killan's my friend, too. I have an obligation to—"

"We owe her nothing, Seji. Look at her. She's a master manipulator."

"You two just—"

"Forget about us," Tomi said. "Why didn't you come to me before this?"

"Killan said not to."

"Killan." Tomi held herself in check. "I'm your friend, Seji. I would have helped you. I will help you now if you give me the chance."

The Scoundrel's eyes broke from hers. He could not bear to look at her accusatory face. He put his tea aside, rested his face in his hands. "Tomisan, we were almost killed last night. I—I found a tape, electronic ears, surveillance equipment in an abandoned apartment next to mine. The guy—I don't know what happened to him—was spying on me, but also on Killan and Kusunda Ikusa. There's a lot of dirt on it about him. Killan got the idea that we should sell the tape to Ikusa. She told me she could handle him. No sweat.

"Instead, he sent his car after us last night and almost ran us down. For Christ's sake, the fucking thing went up on the sidewalk to get us! If I hadn't put a couple of bullets through the windshield, Killan and I would both be dead!"

"Just hold it," Tomi said. Her heart was hammering so hard she could barely think straight. Could the tape the Scoundrel found have belonged to the Pack Rat? Nangi said that he had been following Ikusa. But if so, how had the Pack Rat come to spy on the Scoundrel? Then she had the connection: Killan Oroshi.

Tomi picked up the phone on her desk, dialed an interoffice extension. "I need a forensics team," she said. She gave the officer the Scoundrel's address and apartment number. "There's an abandoned apartment next door. I want it combed from top to bottom. And this is a red priority. I expect the lab results in twenty-four hours."

Then she dialed another extension. She spoke to the officer on duty, asked him about suspicious car accidents reported within the past twenty-four hours. He told her about a black Mercedes that had smashed into a row of seedy stores in the outskirts of the city, killing two occupants. The odd thing was, the officer said, they'd found bullet holes in the windshield.

Tomi asked if they'd ID'd the victims yet. The officer gave her the names, but they rang no bells. She asked if the names had been run through the computers. "Yes, and because of what we got, we're referring the case to Homicide, your department," he said. "These guys were Yakuza hit men."

Tomi thanked the officer, put down the phone, lost in thought. She looked at the Scoundrel. "You're right," she said. "Kusunda Ikusa tried to have you killed. I'm taking you into protective custody right now. Where's Killan?"

"I—"

Tomi snatched up her bag, came around from behind her desk. "You'd better tell me right now, ace, because tomorrow may be too late."

On the way downstairs she held out her hand. "Give it to me."

And the Scoundrel obediently placed in her hand the audio microcassette he had found in the apartment next to his.

Wherever Kusunda Ikusa looked, he saw his own face replicated as if in a terrible mirror. On the television he saw himself handing Masuto Ishii an envelope stuffed with yen, then Ishii's hand delivering that same envelope to Catch Hagawa. When he turned on the radio, station after station was serving up commentary on the scandal. If he opened a newspaper, he saw his face, along with appropriate photos, reproduced from the damning videotape.

Ikusa thought, I am some kind of animal, trapped in a cage where people come to stare at me, to frown and cluck their tongues in disapproval.

The telephone had begun to ring just after the first news reports were aired. Ikusa's blood ran cold. He knew who was calling him. Nami. Nami would want to exact its own particular brand of retribution. He had had the effrontery to drag Nami into the midst of this scandal, and for that he could not be forgiven. The ties that bound him so tightly to Nami, that had once made him one of the most powerful men in Japan, were now about to strangle him.

Ikusa knew that he could not allow that to happen. He had his own path to take.

In the pouring rain Ikusa slipped out of his house via a side entrance. He was dressed in blue jeans, a UCLA sweatshirt, scuffed Reebok sneakers, and a long, hooded PVC raincoat whose deep pockets were filled with more than his fists. He went unnoticed.

Ikusa walked the few blocks to the subway, went underground. During his trip crosstown he had time to contemplate the fleeting nature of power. How long had he felt invulnerable? He did not know. Time ceased to exist when one was close to being a god. Curious, that. Time and power must be linked in some mysterious equation, he decided, that not even Albert Einstein could fathom.

But there was another, even more interesting element to be considered. Power was so real, so tangible when one had it, so unreal, so ephemeral when one didn't. It occurred to Ikusa, dripping water on the two seats he occupied in the rocketing subway car, that power must then be an illusion. It must exist only in the minds of men if it could be so easily granted and denied.

As Kusunda Ikusa stood in line to get off at his stop, he came to the conclusion that the only real power a man had was to inflict death on his fellow man.

Above ground the sky was black. The rain beat against the sea of opened umbrellas, the shore of the pavement, with a kind of demonic glee.

This is a city of sheep, Ikusa thought, a country of sheep, all moving in one direction with one purpose. Although he walked among them, moved through their bustling midst, he no longer felt a part of them, no longer felt the pride in their oneness—in *his* oneness. Now he was cut adrift, a balloon without anchor or rope, drifting aloft, a child of the invisible winds.

Ikusa paused before a shrine, rang the bell. He invoked the intervention of the Shinto spirit-gods who, it was believed, dwelled everywhere. But he felt nothing; he was cut off from even these elementals, a dead man walking among the living.

That videotape, so villainously, treacherously procured, had stripped Ikusa of *tatemae*, his public image of honor and virtue. Without *tatemae*, which was so vital to him—and to Nami—he was without standing in the community, without face. The living dead.

As he shouldered smaller people aside, he remembered a song he had heard some time ago, part of one of actor Takakura Ken's most popular Yakuza films, which seemed appropriate now to his own situation: *My body drifts and wanders/But in the dim lights of home/I can see mother, but then she fades away.*

Ikusa wept, as one often does at cherry blossom time, when beauty and sadness are epitomized by the fragility of a translucent blossom, so quickly bursting with life, so soon falling from the tree. From home.

How swiftly time passes, Ikusa thought. How abruptly power diminishes. How soon life ends.

Passing his reflection, distorted in a rain-streaked window, Ikusa was appalled at his tears. He had not wept since he was a child, after his first defeat in martial arts competition. Certainly he had not thought of home for many years. He had lacked the time and also, he had to confess, the inclination. As the infusion of power increased, making of him a new man, it had caused him to dismiss his past as unimportant. It was funny now, that was all he could think of.

In the Asakusa district, he came at last to the ferroconcrete building housing an anonymous cheap hotel. Upstairs, he went straight down the featureless hall to the room he wanted and broke down the door. It was not a difficult task for a man of his size and strength.

Inside the room there was no place to hide.

"I had you and that traitor Kikoko followed," Ikusa said to the figure standing in the semidarkness. "But in the end it didn't really matter. I knew you would be hiding like an animal in the dark."

"I thought I'd be safe here," Killan Oroshi said.

"You're not safe with me around," Ikusa said, advancing on her. "You should know by now that you never were."

"But I don't have the tape," Killan said. "I gave it to Seji, and he's taken it to the police."

"I don't care," Ikusa said. "This has gone beyond all that." He came on, big as a tree in the confined space of the tiny hotel room.

Killan moved, her silhouette changing as her arm came up. "Stop right there! I've got a gun!"

"A gun won't stop me, Killan. Nothing you can do can possibly stop me from what I've come here to do." His voice was almost gentle, but it possessed a surety, a finality, that caused her to bite her lip.

Her arms were extended, the elbows locked. Ikusa caught a glimpse of metal gleaming dully in the werelight. "I mean it!"

"So do I," he said.

The rain scratched like a live thing, desperately seeking entrance. The aluminum blinds rattled against the windows, allowing tiny sparks of light into the hotel room, miniature flashes of lightning.

"Stop!" Killan cried. "You're pushing me to the edge!" The hammer of the gun clicked back, a stark, echoey sound. "I know you murdered that man who was spying on us. You bashed him to bits, but I won't let you do that to me. You're not going to get that close."

"You shouldn't have tried to blackmail me, Killan. That was your mistake. I was willing to put up with your tiresome revolutionary cant because I thought I could harness your extraordinary mind. I thought I could channel it into conventional paths. That was my mistake."

"Your mistake was in trying to use me." Killan's voice was filled with contempt. "That's all you know how to do. Use people. Well, how does it feel to be used yourself? You used my father, took his company out from under him, the company he helped my grandfather build from nothing. You destroyed his life, trampled him into the mud, all the while smiling like an innocent baby."

Ikusa frowned. "I thought you hated your father. Was that a lie, too?"

"You were too dense, too full of your own worth to see that I hated you more than I ever could have hated my father." Killan laughed. "You know, you actually did me a favor, you fucker. You made me see my father in a whole new light. With you, I saw his accomplishments, I saw what his company meant to him. In his defeat, his sorrow, I at last came to love him."

"A poor consolation for your death," Ikusa said.

"It's not me who's going to die."

Ikusa lunged for her then. Killan pulled the trigger, and he staggered back a half step. Then he came on. She fired a second time, and something in Ikusa's left hand struck her shoulder.

Killan cried out as she felt the hot pain run down her arm. Blood erupted through her clothes.

Ikusa, too, was bleeding. He had taken one bullet in the chest, another in his hip. But he ignored the pain, his feet set firmly on the path ordained for him from the moment the first news of the scandal broke.

Killan had brought him to this sorry abyss. Stripped of his power, his face, his *tatemae*, he had understood that his sole transgression had been his relationship with her. His hubris had manifested itself in her mocking smile, her passionate embrace, her brilliant, deceiving hand. He had thought, in his arrogance, that he could—as she had said—ride the back of the dragon. But he knew now what he should have understood then: the dragon is too dangerous to be ridden at all.

And this is what he realized at the moment the scandal broke: if he could not ride the dragon, at least he could destroy it. That much power, at least, was left him.

He put his hands around her neck as she struck him across the face with the gun barrel. Blood flowed, blinding him. But he did not need his eyes to accomplish what he had come here to do.

Ikusa squeezed. Killan's scream of anguish was choked off, along with the air. Ikusa saw her jumping like a rag doll. Her muscles spasmed as if with a will of their own. She opened her mouth then snapped it shut, her teeth clashing together.

Slowly, like a balloon—the balloon Ikusa had been—she was deflating, the air seeping out of her. Ikusa felt as heavy as lead. There was a roaring in his ears. His blood had turned to sludge, his pulse drumming in his ears in slow rhythm.

He saw her hands trembling, her face white and staring, and he wanted her to die more than he ever wanted anything else. He saw the gun barrel, but did not believe she had strength enough to pull the trigger. He laughed in her face.

Killan snarled, adrenaline pouring into her system. She could hardly see or move. But that face—his face—laughing, deriding her, mocking her, filled her mind as a harvest moon fills the night sky. She would not give him the satisfaction. She would not be defeated.

Her hands shook so much she did not think she could aim properly. So she did the only thing she could do. She squeezed the trigger.

The explosion was very loud. The gun the Scoundrel had given her for protection bucked in her hands and she was thrown violently backward. She tried to scream but, as in a nightmare, was unable to utter a sound.

She was on her knees. Her right side was completely numb and she felt wet, as if she had soiled herself. Blood was everywhere, a great tree stump in front of her, staring sightlessly at the ceiling with black, button eyes.

Then Killan became aware of a keening in the room, as if a great knife blade had been given the power of speech. Then there were people in the doorway. Familiar faces: the Scoundrel and Tomi Yazawa.

In a moment Killan, so full of pain and dismay, became aware that the keening was coming from herself. She tried to stop it, but she had lost control. She stared upward at them helplessly.

She felt herself being lifted, people speaking to her, but she could not understand what they were saying, did not want to understand. She wanted only to scream and scream and scream. So she did that.

The fire existed still in Senjin's mind: the dark, crackling flames, cleansing the foul air of calumny. They burned longer in his imagination, but did they burn brighter? He thought not.

It was Senjin's birthday. He was twenty-nine, but there was only one other to mark that date: Shisei. He had called her, left a message on her answering machine without giving his name. She was already late. He had expected her to be waiting for him in West Bay Bridge. Why hadn't she been there? He had been so certain that he would see her face, grip her flesh, peer from mind to mind, merge as they had merged for so many years long ago.

He longed to gaze at the canvas he had made of her back while he lay with her, minds entwined, sharing as only they could share. A birthday present.

Senjin had never had his birthday celebrated; there had been no special family dinner, no gathering of friends, no present or even a card to set that day apart from all others of the year. When Senjin had first come upon the practice of gift-giving for a birthday, he was already grown up. He was astounded by the custom, and quickly came to hate it because it made him feel melancholy; instinctively he knew that this must be a weakness thrust upon him by Haha-san which he must fight.

But today Senjin thought that at last he might give himself a birthday present.

Now was the beginning of the end, the last few steps on the road he had been born to tread. *Sensei* had trained him for this moment, though he never could have suspected it. His mind lacked the breadth, the scope of Senjin's own. *Sensei* might be tanjian, he might have the gift, but he was not a *dorokusai*, could not have even an idea what that might mean.

On the other hand, Senjin suspected that Haha-san would. He remembered a day when she took him into town with her. It was a torturous journey, long and, to his mind, boring. He would have preferred to have been with *sensei*. But *sensei* was off on one of the mysterious journeys he undertook periodically, and Shisei was out running an errand for Haha-san.

In the village, Haha-san went to the bank. There, they were seated before a man with a stiff bearing and an even stiffer collar to his black suit. He asked Haha-san some questions about herself, writing down her answers on a square card. Then he gave her a long form to fill out. Senjin watched. When she went to fill in the section marked date of birth, she wrote Senjin and Shisei's instead of her own.

Afterward, out on the village street, Senjin asked her about this.

"Did I?" Haha-san said almost dreamily. She smiled. "Well, it was a natural mistake. Your birthdate was the most vivid day in my life."

It was only years later that Senjin realized what she meant. She had been so wrapped up in her children's rearing—in their lives—that they became her *ikigai*, the meaning of her own life. But as that happened, she invested them with distant, sharp-edged shards of her own personality, fragments of fear, rage, loneliness, and agony: the weaknesses that had already overrun her life.

Senjin put his hand in his pocket, his fingers enclosing the carefully wrapped paper packet of emeralds. They were there, waiting, their power pulsing in his palm. They were six: a bad number, a dangerous, destabilizing number. He knew he was taking a chance carrying them around with him. Given time, they would create the Scorpion, one of the configurations of destruction. Only his own great mass of power made their danger manageable.

He needed to put all the emeralds together, to make the configuration of the nine. Only then would he fulfill his destiny. The last link with Eternity. Invincible, immortal, he would stride across the world, bending it to his whims.

Now, as Senjin studied the converted factory on Greene Street with the sea-green lacquered door, he knew that he must be close to the last of the mystic gems.

That was what he had come for, after all. That and to plunge Nicholas Linnear into a series of hells before he killed him.

But at this moment Senjin's mind was only peripherally aware of Nicholas. He was concentrating on Justine. It was Justine, he was sure, who would unlock the whereabouts of the emeralds. He needed just ten minutes with her to pry the secret out of her brain. And then, when he was finished with her, he would pin her like an insect to a wall.

Obliterated by shadow, Senjin stood silent and unmoving. He saw the apartment's owner, the squat, dangerous-looking Japanese, Conny Tanaka, emerge from the front door, turn right, walk up to Houston Street, where he hailed a cab, got in.

Not ten minutes later, Nicholas Linnear opened the sea-green door, went lightly down the steps, headed south on foot. Senjin was momentarily torn. He thought it would be helpful to know where Nicholas was headed, but the building and what it now housed were too tempting a target. Two days ago Senjin had seen Nicholas going into the front entrance to the Tomkin Industries tower, then later at the Tanaka *dojo*.

Senjin knew of Nicholas's ties to the martial arts school, as well as his other New York hangouts; the Tokyo Metropolitan Police computer was extremely efficient, and what it couldn't provide, interservice intelligence could.

It was Tanaka who had led Senjin home to this block, to this coop that Nicholas and Justine were using as a base. Is this where the last cache of emeralds was?

Now, three days after Nicholas and Justine had come to Manhattan from West Bay Bridge, Senjin was on his stakeout. He had taken a room in a midtown hotel but had never actually stayed there. It was the address he had given to Shisei when his plans had changed so suddenly. The fire had been lighted, the flames had burned hard and high. There was nothing left for Nicholas in West Bay Bridge. Nothing, too, for Senjin.

Senjin kept his eye on the sea-green door. Tanaka had come out and so had Linnear. Which meant Justine was still inside, because two hours before, Senjin had seen the three of them go into the building. There were no other exits or entrances; he had checked thoroughly.

Now, whether Justine was alone or guarded did not matter, Senjin knew that he could get to her—it was merely a matter of how much blood would be spilled.

He held his ground while Nicholas disappeared among the pedestrians. He looked at his watch. Where are you, Shisei? Why haven't you come?

The street was not crowded—at least by Tokyo standards. A Con Edison van was parked midway down the block, the nearby manhole cordoned off with yellow and black strips printed with the words: DANGER! LIVE WIRES! DO NOT CROSS! The back doors were thrown open but the van was empty. Senjin had seen the three men follow one another down the manhole.

It was now nearly two in the afternoon. Senjin had had plenty of time to familiarize himself with all the buildings on the block, then to make a quick trip to the industrial hardware store on the next block.

He quit the shadows, crossed the street. He could hear the voices of the workers below as they drifted up through the open manhole.

Senjin climbed quickly into the van. He emerged a moment later, clad in a spare uniform. Then he walked purposefully to the building next to Tanaka's, picked the lock. He could have rung any one of the half-dozen bells, announced himself as a Con Ed maintenance man, but he did not want to risk some paranoid tenant asking him for ID.

Inside he took an oversized freight elevator, laden with dust, to the top floor, got out. He went swiftly down the corridor to the metal fire door that was the exit to the roof. It was plastered with a red sign that said: CAUTION, EMERGENCY DOOR ONLY. DO NOT OPEN. DOOR IS ALARMED.

Senjin knelt down, located the wire where it entered the metal box on the bar across the door. He made a loop, attached alligator clips to two sections of the wire. Then he snipped the original wire, opened the door as far as his loop would allow. He slipped through, closed the door behind him. It would hide the loop from all but the most discerning eye.

It was broiling on the roof. The black tarmac was soft, almost sticky, and Senjin was careful to cleave to what shadows existed, treading upon tarmac not quite as spongy.

Where the roof of this building ended, the roof of Tanaka's building began. Senjin examined that new field as if it were enemy territory in a war. His eyes took in every shape, color, texture; the length of every shadow, the look of the tarmac—it was different from the roof he was on; it was strewn with sharp-edged bluish gravel. In the center of the roof there was a large, raised skylight made up of small panes of glass surrounded by a painted wooden frame. He suspected that the antiburglar devices would be clustered in and around the skylight.

When he was as satisfied as he could be, he climbed over the brick and terra-cotta wall, into the red zone.

Immediately he froze. His eyes had picked up something in their periphery. He moved his head, bringing the flash into the center of his vision. Now it was gone. He went back to looking at it indirectly.

And he saw the flash again, like sunlight catching a strand of a spider's web. This was similar.

Senjin knelt without in any other way moving. Not three inches in front of him a monofilament wire had been cleverly strung at calf height. It went all around the periphery of the roof. One step and Senjin knew he would have tripped an alarm inside the building.

The obvious answer to the problem was to step over the monofilament. But it was so obvious, Senjin hesitated. Out of the snare and into the real trap, he thought. His head turned this way and that, trying to find out what else was lying in wait for him.

Then he saw it. The electric eyes were cleverly hidden, but he found one, then another. They were at waist height, and any one high-stepping over the monofilament would pass directly through their invisible beam. There was no way for him to disable the electric eyes. Their brain would be within the house, inaccessible to him.

Still in his kneeling position, he measured the height of the monofilament, then nodded to himself. He produced from his pocket a long, coiled length of rope. But it was like no other rope; it was, instead, made of women's hair. It was tremendously tough and resilient, compact, almost weightless, and would not abrade against hard surfaces. Tied to one end was a metal hook.

Senjin produced a two-foot length of what looked like a simple wooden staff. There was nothing simple about it. He gave a quick twist of his wrist, and the staff telescoped out. As it did, its end popped open to form what looked like the talons of an eagle. This was a *shinobi kumade*, the climbing claw.

Senjin attached the hooked end of the special rope to the climbing claw, shoved both underneath the monofilament. The claw brought the hook to the far end of a utility vent where, as Senjin jerked the rope hard, the hook grabbed hold. Senjin lay down on his back, his arms over his head, gripping the rope. Then, hand over hand, he began to pull himself along the tarmac.

His head and shoulders passed beneath the monofilament. He slowed himself, saw that his chest was at the level of the wire. He exhaled, collapsing his lungs. His chest deflated, and he pulled himself all the way through.

He kept going like that, hand over hand, until he was certain he was past the electric-eye beam. Then he knelt, pulled the *shinobi kumade* toward him. He freed the hook from the vent, rolled the rope into a ball, put it away.

Then he went to take a closer look at the skylight.

It was rigged, all right. A pressure-sensitive device was hooked up to the skylight. Any weight on it above that of a pigeon alighting would set off the alarm.

The trigger mechanism was in plain sight. This was not good news. Senjin was not apt to take such situations at face value, especially not after discovering how the roof itself was set up against intruders. He wondered what trigger was lurking in the shadows where he could not see it.

He put that thought aside, went to work disarming the skylight trigger. He froze it with a tiny aerosol of freon, then quickly sprayed it with a

fast-hardening foam sealant similar to the kind used by the marine industry.

He cut the wire at all four corners. Up here it was as quiet as a tomb.
The sounds of the city floated up to him only intermittently: an ambulance's siren, a dog's bark, the brief blare of a horn, followed by the
squeal of a car leaving rubber. He was a cloud, drifting about the jam-
packed earth. Save that a cloud was never so deadly.

Senjin climbed upon the skylight, spread himself out like a starfish. He
used his hands as well as his eyes and ears to seek out the old skylight's
weak points. In time he found one: right down the middle.

He took a long, thin blade, inserted it between the center joints. The
dry wood gave way almost willingly, and he worked the blade up and
down the length of the seam. The wood split, and Senjin rolled away
from the weakened area. He used the blade on the two sides. The wood
here was stronger, but not by much. The skylight should have been
replaced years ago.

Senjin rolled completely off the skylight, lifted a section off just far
enough for him to slip through. He fished the claw of the *shinobi kumade*
around the lip of the skylight housing, let himself down via the telescoped wooden pole.

He paused just within the neck of the skylight. His senses quested
outward, encountered the heat-detecting plate. Any warmblooded living
creature would set it off. The extreme cold of the freon spray would set it
off as well. He pulled out a strip of metallic tape, covered the plate. The
metal was neutral in temperature but shielded the plate from registering
his own body heat as he passed it.

Senjin completed his climb down.

He found himself in what appeared to be a seldom-used attic space.
Once, no doubt, it had housed machinery, but now it appeared to be used
strictly for storage.

Senjin found the stairway down. He listened at the closed door, heard
no movement. He opened the door a crack, listened again. He took a
look. Then he opened the door only as far as he needed to slip out. He
closed it behind him.

He was inside the enemy stronghold. So much closer to Justine.

"I don't know why I let you bring me here," Nangi said.

They could hear the thunder crack and rumble through the canyons of
Tokyo even here inside St. Theresa's.

"I feel nothing when I am here. Nothing."

Rain rattled like sleet against the stained-glass windows, so it appeared that the Virgin at the Crucifixion in the window's center oriel was trembling in her agony.

"Shhh," Umi whispered. "You're disturbing the service."

"What has the service to do with me?" Nangi said. "I am estranged, an orphan in the house of God."

"You are not an orphan," Umi said, close to him, warm against him. "You are merely blind."

"What do you know of God?" he said. "You are a studier of myths, and God cannot well survive myths. Myths are for other religions, the substance of heathen gods."

"Like Buddha?"

Nangi could see she was mocking him, but he did not care. She had a right to be cynical about his religious beliefs. He was not a good Catholic, he realized sadly, otherwise his belief would be unswerving even—especially—during times of doubt and uncertainty.

"Don't mix metaphors," Nangi said shortly. "Buddha is not a god. He's an ideal."

"Or a myth," Umi said. "Like Jesus, the son of God."

"And what of your Spider Woman, spinning her webs across the centuries of the Hopi Indians? Is she also a myth? You seem to believe in her."

"I believe in what is real," Umi said. "Not in what I can see with my eyes or can feel with my hands, but what my mind, expanding into the cosmos, can absorb. There are certain eternal truths, my love. There is a cosmic clock that measures not the passage of time—because time is merely a human illusion—but the ever shifting balance between order and chaos. In the end we must all make that one decision: which side will we fight to preserve?" Umi took his hand. "Once this decision is made, then we will be able to look into the eye of God. And, recognizing the reflection we see there, we will be able to understand the significance of our own existence."

"Are you saying that we are only reflections of Him?" Nangi asked.

Umi squeezed his hand. "You miss the point. We are manifestations only of order or chaos; agents, in some very direct sense. All else is illusion to keep us from discerning the truth. If there is a God, darling, it is he who lives within us."

Nangi recognized in her words quite an accurate description of the human condition. He rubbed his leg, which suffered in the wet weather. He felt calmer at his core, always Umi's gift to him. At last he bowed his head and began to pray.

When he was finished, he said, "I wish I knew where Nicholas was at this moment. I would feel somehow calmer."

"He and I spoke of where he must go," Umi said. "He told me not to tell you. He said you would only worry."

"I am worried now," Nangi said, looking at her.

"He gave me a telephone number." Umi recited it. "There is a man there who knows him as Tik-Tik."

"Yes. Conny Tanaka." Nangi nodded. "Nicholas has told me of him."

Umi said, "I think you should say a prayer for Nicholas."

"My prayers always include him," Nangi said. "He is the child I never had, my legacy. He is ever in my thoughts, bound to me like my own flesh and blood."

"Then pray for him again, Nangi-san. Pray that he will outlive you." Umi's voice lay suspended in the air like smoke. "The *dorokusai* comes for him. This is the ending that has been foretold in many cultures. Before it is over, there will be death and more death."

Senjin existed within Conny Tanaka's coop. He breathed tidally, incidentally, allowing his mind to work. His gift. With it he searched the entire house without ever moving from his spot at the head of the stairway down from the storage attic.

He found Justine. He moved on. There was no one else in the house, but there was a voice.

Nicholas Linnear's voice.

Slipping something dark and heavy over his right hand, Senjin followed the voice, determined to discover its source, as an explorer seeks the headwaters of a winding river.

Senjin flexed his fingers inside the *nekode*. It was a leather war gauntlet used by the ninja of centuries ago. It was studded with short metal spikes. It was so tough that, used in the right manner, it could stop a sword strike in midair.

He went down the stairs.

"Now the spirit is within you, the spirit of grief. Your spirit, bowed before the judgment of Heaven, sinks downward to the earth. It is heavy with gravity's wish. The tenure of eternity grows, freed from the bonds of time. The voices of light have been heard. The hands of sound lie upon your flesh. Here is the judgment of Heaven: I bind you in chains of iron."

Nicholas's voice intoned this litany over and over, as if it were a prayer —or a chant. Senjin froze. He is here, he thought, and I cannot discern him. He is invoking *kokoro*, the heart of tanjian. He is working Tau-tau magic against me. What is his strategy?

"Now the spirit is within you, the spirit of grief."

Senjin set aside the questions that could not yet be answered. He concentrated on Justine, went down the hall, down another flight of stairs.

". . . heavy with gravity's wish."

On the second floor he found her.

"The tenure of eternity grows . . ."

Justine lay on a couch, asleep. The room was not a large one. Nevertheless, it was couched in shadows. The shadows were colored by Nicholas's voice: *"The voices of light have been heard."*

Senjin, a shadow himself, stood at the headwaters of the river, having come as far upstream as he was able. Heavy curtains covered floor-to-ceiling windows. The floor was wooden parquet. Cornices near the ceiling pierced the shadows, thrusting themselves from corners, appearing like lights in the gloom. Persian carpets of black and persimmon were strewn across the floor. Two matching gilt chairs faced each other in empty conversation. Black stereo speakers were almost invisible in two corners of the room. It was from these that Nicholas's voice emerged like a waterfall at a river's source.

"The hands of sound lie upon your flesh."

So he's not here, after all, Senjin thought. He has set this litany of Akshara, the language of eternity, as a guardian while he is gone. He took one step toward the sleeping Justine, and thought, But why would he leave her untended?

He stopped so close to her that he could see her chest moving with her slow, even breathing. She is, indeed, asleep, he thought. But she cannot be alone, unguarded.

"Here is the judgment of Heaven . . ."

Then he considered all the extraordinary precautions he had encountered on the roof, and thought, But they believe that she *is* guarded. Safe from me.

"I bind you with chains of iron."

Justine opened her eyes. She looked at Senjin, sat up. "I know you," she said.

". . . spirit is within you, the spirit of grief."

Justine said, "Why have you followed me here, all the way to America?"

"You don't remember me," Senjin said, moving toward her like a wraith. "You dreamed me, conjured me out of your own pain and loneliness and desire."

"To float," Justine said, "like a cloud above the jam-packed earth."

Senjin touched her, and she shuddered.

"Your spirit, bowed before the judgment of Heaven, sinks downward to the earth."

"That voice," Senjin said, his hand spreading upon her. "Can you turn it off?"

"I hear no voice but yours . . . and mine," she said.

"The tenure of eternity grows, freed from the bonds of time."

Senjin left her for a moment, went behind each speaker, ripped the cables from the wall.

"The voices of light have been heard. The hands of sound lie upon your flesh."

Nicholas's voice did not stop; it seemed to emanate from the walls, the ceiling, the floor, to be inhabiting the very room itself.

"What is it," Justine asked, "I see in your face?"

Then Senjin put his hands on her again. "Where are the emeralds your husband hid?" He asked this in the same tone of voice he had asked the clerk in the hardware store for the aerosol can of freon and the other items he had taken without paying for.

"Wrapped in a box," Justine said.

"What did he do with the box, Justine? Did he bury it?" Senjin asked, closing the distance between them from arm's length to a handsbreadth.

"No. He mailed it."

"Where?"

Here brow furrowed. "I don't know. I—"

"But you *do* know," Senjin urged her. "You saw the address."

"I didn't. I—"

"Think!"

She jumped as his voice changed, charged her.

"Now the spirit is within you—"

"You know, Justine!"

"Yes," Justine said, "I think I do. My husband has an old friend, a trusted friend. Lewis Croaker. Lew lives in Marco Island, Florida now. He owns a fishing boat. He . . . ."

The bones in Senjin's neck cracked as his head swiveled around. That sound!

"The tenure of eternity grows, freed from the bonds of time."

Noises from above. Someone was upstairs. His means of entrance had been discovered.

Senjin closed Justine's eyes with the pads of his thumbs. He lay her back down on the couch. Quickly he crossed the room, drew aside first one curtain then another. There were no windows, just trompe l'oeil paintings depicting a French countryside.

Senjin turned back, went to the door then through it, into the shadows of the hallway but could discern no image, just a black, featureless wall. Nicholas!

He turned, raced down the stairs.

And was plunged into darkness. Senjin stood still, his senses questing outward in ever-widening circles. He ignored the sounds only he could detect, of footsteps on the stairs above him. Nicholas was coming, but his first priority was to get some sense of his environment. He very much wanted this final, inevitable confrontation with Nicholas, but he wanted to do so on territory that was, at worst, neutral.

He found the source of light, activated it. He was surrounded by his own image. Then it was joined by that of Nicholas.

"Now the spirit is within you, the spirit of grief."

There were five of Nicholas, six. Senjin, used to discerning his gift, was at a loss. Since he was unable to see Nicholas's mind, he was unable to tell image from reality.

He turned and Nicholas turned. Or was it the image of Nicholas? There was only one way to find out.

"Your spirit, bowed before the judgment of Heaven, sinks downward to the earth."

Senjin crouched. His wrist flicked once, twice, three times. Glass shattered as blade after blade left his fingertips, entering Nicholas's chest— the image of Nicholas, as it turned out—as one by one he broke the mirrors.

"The voice of light have been heard."

Only one Nicholas; only one Senjin.

"Here I am," Nicholas said, another Nicholas from the one who was constantly intoning, invoking the vibration of *kokoro*, the heart of things, the tanjian field of energy that can be harnessed by ritualized actions and meditative thoughts. "This is what you want."

Senjin leaped, crashed into a mirror. A thousand points of light cascaded over him, a waterfall of sound and image. Then he felt himself whirled around. Other hands were upon him; the touch of a tanjian.

"The hands of sound lie upon your flesh."

Now he understood Nicholas's strategy. He had ignored the incantation—at his own peril! The invocation of the membrane *kokoro* was not to be ignored, ever. The taped chanting had lulled him. He had seen it as a diversion only, beneath all but the most cursory notice. After all, it was Nicholas Linnear he was after, not Nicholas's recorded voice.

And yet the voice had had the same power as if Nicholas were speaking it himself. The membrane *kokoro* responded to repetition and to words of prayer. This Nicholas had accomplished with his tape, even as Senjin was getting what he wanted: the location of the last cache of emeralds.

"Here is the judgment of Heaven . . ."

Senjin put his left leg between Nicholas's, went into the Serpent, an attack stance. From this he wove the Rising Cloud, a strike used from one's knees. All thrust was centered in the small of the back, that area in the opposite side of the body's circumference from the *hara*, the place in the lower belly where all force, all centering energy, resides. In a kneeling position the legs and hips are useless, hence the reliance on the torso.

The Rising Cloud, used from a standing position, surprised Nicholas. Senjin could feel the split instant of his opponent's hesitation, and he struck, using elbows, wrist bones, the sides of his hands.

Nicholas staggered, and Senjin, having regained the initiative, employed the Wounded Dove, using percussive strikes against the nerve meridians in Nicholas's upper arms. It was not Senjin's intention to kill Nicholas quickly, although he felt quite confident that he could do just that had it been his objective. A slow death, by increments—the disabling and death of first friends, then wife, then Nicholas himself—was Senjin's objective.

Then, in two lightning-swift strikes, the initiative changed hands. Nicholas broke through Senjin's attack with the Cross Wind, a downward collapse which took him away from the percussive blows and inside Senjin's defenses.

Senjin's response was to follow Nicholas down onto the floor, to follow up his attack so that there would be no letup. But this was what Nicholas had in mind, and he was ready. The Double Fence used a weak-looking yin posture as a launchpad for a vicious attack.

Nicholas lowered his hands and Senjin followed them, taught, as all tanjian had been, to follow the flow of the hands, not the twist of a shoulder, a turn of the head, a glance of the eyes, which could all be false. Where the hands resided, there would the next attack commence.

Their hands touched, an instantaneous spark of energy. Nicholas's hands covered Senjin's, and Senjin contemptuously thrust them aside. The instant he did this, Nicholas's hands parted, slammed heelfirst into Senjin's unprotected chest.

Senjin reeled backward. His head hit the wall where the last mirror had been, and a shard, razor-sharp, jagged, sliced into his left ear. He jerked his head away, but Nicholas delivered two short, sharp strikes to his sternum, thrusting him back at the shard. It sliced into him again.

Nicholas struck him again, but now Senjin ignored the pain. Lights were flashing in his head and he was having trouble breathing. He needed time to damp down the pain and the bleeding, to bring his mind back into line with Tau-tau.

He twisted so his left shoulder was toward Nicholas, and as Nicholas attacked the shoulder, drove Nicholas's hands into his face with an upward swing. At the same time, he smashed his right knee into Nicholas's lower belly.

Nicholas went to his knees, and Senjin leaped over him, ran up the stairs, back to where Justine lay, entangled in Tau-tau magic. She was Senjin's shield, his power over Nicholas.

"*. . . I bind you in chains of iron.*"

Nangi said, "I want to talk to this man the Scoundrel. He's the key, though I doubt he knows it."

Tomi nodded. She led Nangi into an interrogation room inside the police building in central Tokyo. It had been three days now since Kusunda Ikusa attacked Killan Oroshi in the hotel room, but she wasn't taking any chances with her friend's life. Kusunda Ikusa might be dead, but it was still unclear how many people might be involved. Also, Nangi had been in around-the-clock negotiations with Nami in a monumental psychological tug-of-war over the fate of Sato International and Tomkin Industries.

"You'll find everything you asked for here," she told Nangi, then went to get the Scoundrel.

Her mind was still filled with images of Killan Oroshi and Ikusa. At the moment she burst into the hotel room, her first thought was for her friend's safety. She never should have allowed the Scoundrel to come with her. His own desires were immaterial in the fact of such danger. But Killan had been his responsibility. He hadn't wanted to leave her in the first place, but her antipathy toward Tomi had prevailed. Killan had refused to go with him to deliver the tape—and their confession.

Poor Killan. The sight of her blood-streaked face, the sound of her screaming, haunted Tomi. It was time to tell the Scoundrel what had happened to her.

His face was white and strained, and when he saw her coming to get him, he said, "She's dead, isn't she? Ikusa got to her."

"He certainly tried," Tomi said, nodding for the guard to open the cell door.

The Scoundrel stepped out into the echo-filled corridor. "You mean she's alive? Killan's alive?" He blinked in the harsh fluorescence.

"Yes."

The cell door clanged shut behind him and he jumped. He gave a little, nervous laugh. He looked awful, like a junkie or a condemned man.

"Your perspective changes awfully fast when you're in here," he said as they began to walk down the corridor. "I know you put me here for my protection, but after what I've done, I could imagine myself in here for real." He swallowed hard. "What will happen to me, Tomi?"

"That depends." Tomi saw the desolate look on his face, touched him briefly. "Take it easy. I don't know what laws you've broken, if any."

"Morally—"

"That's another question entirely," Tomi interrupted him. "Policemen aren't empowered to make arrests purely on that score."

The Scoundrel took a deep breath, ran a hand through his stiff platinum hair. "What did you mean by 'That depends'?"

"There's a man here who wants to speak to you. His name is Tanzan Nangi. I know you've heard of him." There was a peculiar twitch to her mouth. Of course the Scoundrel had heard of Tanzan Nangi. It was Nangi's computers at Sato International that the Scoundrel's MANTIS virus had first penetrated. "I think it will be Nangi-san who will ultimately decide your fate."

The Scoundrel groaned, hung his head.

Tomi led her friend into the interrogation room. Nangi snapped off the cassette recorder. He turned to look at Seji Kikoko. "I've just finished playing the tape," he said.

Nangi turned away. He pushed the cassette recorder aside, drew to him a lacquer tray on which sat a pot, three porcelain cups, and a whisk. Nangi took up the whisk. "I've prepared green tea. I thought you might be thirsty. Being inside a prison for any reason is a nasty experience." His hands moved deftly, turning the water and tea leaves to a pale green froth, turning each cup as he did so.

He pushed one cup toward the Scoundrel. "Come, Kikoko-san," Nangi said pleasantly. "Sit. Drink. Relax. We have much to discuss, you and I."

Shisei was given the note by the concierge in the midtown hotel where Senjin had told her he was taking a room.

Sister, where are you? Where have you been? I am waiting for you. I need you.

Shisei read this, as well as the address on Greene Street that ended the note, in the public ladies' room in the hotel lobby. She crumpled the note, flushed it down the toilet.

Then, for three days, Shisei had lived in the hotel room her twin brother had reserved. Three days lying in bed, staring at the ceiling, or sitting on the edge of it, the rumpled sheets in her lap, listening to the muffled voices, the varied psyches living their lives on either side of her.

Every so often, when she thought of it, she ordered room service: hamburgers, french fries, Cokes. She invariably vomited twenty minutes after she gorged herself on these alien and unpalatable meals. The dazed aftermath of her retching was her only solace, because it was then that she felt pain and knew that she was still alive.

Instead of the way she felt most of the time, lying in bed, shivering, the covers pulled up to her chin, or sitting on the edge, the sheets pulled protectively with her whitened fists into her lap. Listening.

Doors slamming, voices raised, the quiet, steady tread of the Jamaican maid who twice daily moved through the hallway outside, always passing by Senjin's room, where Shisei lay or sat or knelt, her forehead against the cool porcelain bowl, DO NOT DISTURB on the doorknob, warning the Jamaican away.

Shisei listened to the voices of arguments, of banal conversations, of children whining or laughing; to inane television shows, soap operas during the day, quiz shows at night; and later, in the darkness, the pantings and moanings, the rhythmic music of human couplings, just beyond the walls, the boundaries of her prison, her limbo, where she waited, impatient, full of anxiety, for the battle inside her to be decided one way or another.

Sister, where are you? Where have you been? I am waiting for you. I need you.

Giri. Duty and independence had gone to war inside Shisei's head. Senjin needed her. She had never before failed to respond when he called for her. But this time was different. When she saw him face to face, he would know without her saying a word about Cotton Branding. Senjin would not allow that relationship to continue. He would seek to terminate it, as he had terminated her relationship with the law student, Jeiji, in the most violent manner.

Shisei rose, went into the bathroom. There were two mirrors there, one a floor-length dressing mirror on the back of the door, the other a makeup mirror over the double sink. By opening the door just so, she could maneuver the mirrors opposite one another. In this way she stared at herself, at the great spider tattooed upon her back.

Senjin's spider: his nightmare and his salvation. It was said that the Demon Woman of Japanese myth had such a spider upon her back. The Demon Woman who was the embodiment of Senjin's only fear. By so marking his twin, Senjin had at once harnessed the threat of the Demon Woman and had bound his sister to him.

It was said, Senjin had told her during one of their mergings, that the Demon Woman was once a fisherman's wife. The fisherman and his father were prosperous. They owned a large boat and, thus, had a crew. It was the wife's duty to rise daily at two in the morning to make the rounds of the crew's houses to make certain they were ready for the boat's departure at three.

Once in a while, in summer, with the moonlight dancing on the water, it was briefly pleasant to feel the cool brush of the night, to imagine herself a mermaid cast upon these rocks.

But mostly she was frightened of the dark walk along the seashore with nothing breathing, nothing stirring but the wind in the stunted, twisted pines. In winter she shivered with the icy cold. And, often, rain lashed at her, soaking her before she had gone a dozen paces.

It was also her duty to gather the other fishermen's wives at the dock when the boat returned, to help with the unloading, sorting, and transporting of the catch to market. In those days this was most often done on their backs. When a crewman fell ill or departed, it was her duty, as well, to find a new man to fill his job.

In bad weather she was sometimes late making her rounds. The rain made the path she took extremely treacherous. There was a half-mile stretch of bare rock. The lichen that spread upon it like fuzz on a baby's scalp grew slippery in rain, or ice, and in her anxiety to complete her wake-up calls, the fisherman's wife would often fall, scraping herself in the process.

She would lie upon the rocks for some time, dazed and in pain. Then the realization that she would be late would flood through her, and she would begin to weep as she gathered herself up, stumbling on into the night.

When she was late, she was sure to be reprimanded by her husband or her father-in-law. They depended on her, they yelled. Was she a simpleton or merely lazy? Why couldn't she complete the simplest tasks?

But she never complained, never thought about an alternative. *Giri.* Her life was defined by duty. Without *giri* she was nothing. She might have been a wild animal rutting in the brush. She must, she thought, be grateful for *giri.* In her adherence to duty lay her humanity.

On one particular night her husband roused her, angry that she had overslept. It was stormy. Rain lashed the shutters of the house, setting them to trembling. The fisherman's wife begged her husband not to take the boat out in such dangerous weather. Now you are a fisherman as well? he shouted. We need the money the catch will bring! How will we live otherwise? Will you support us? Lazy woman! You just want to stay in your warm bed while we do all the work! Do as you are told!

The wife stumbled out into the storm, half running to the first of the crewmen's houses because she was already late. She was halfway through her rounds, shivering and wet, when she saw a figure on the rocks.

Her heart fluttered in her chest and she thought about turning back. But *giri* forestalled her. What would her husband and her father-in-law say if she returned home without having awakened all of the crew?

But she could not bring herself to approach the figure, so she took the longer path that led away from the shoreline. The figure followed her into the woods. The wife, feeling the presence of the figure, picked up her pace. Then, frightened, she began to run. She stumbled over a root, fell into the mud.

She turned, tried to rise. But the figure was already looming over her. It was huge and, as a hand pulled back a cowl, she could see a bearded face, fierce, monstrous, malefic.

The man fell upon her, and his weight almost crushed the wife. She tried to cry out but the man hit her with the flat of his hand, then with his fist. Then he ripped her clothes and, like the beast he was, took her there in the blood-splattered mud.

Wind rattled the trees, rain stung her face. It was as if she were in the middle of a wolf pack. There was a panting all around her, a snuffling, the rank stink of a body too long on the road. And something inside her, battering her over and over, ceaseless as the tide. She slipped into unconsciousness.

A long time later the wife crawled painfully out of the woods. She lifted her head on an unsteady neck, saw the suck and roll of the sea.

On the rocks that were so familiar to her, she collapsed. Lightning illumined her battered face, her bruised, naked body. Her mouth was open, and she gasped rapidly like a landed fish. Blood flowed out of her from many places, onto the rocks. It seeped into the lichen before the rain had a chance to wash it away.

Hours later the fisherman and his father were lashing their boat down against the rising gale. They were alone, having told what crew had straggled down that the weather was too foul to go out.

They were almost finished when they saw approaching them a figure who appeared dressed all in white. But as it came closer, they saw to their astonishment that it was a nude woman. Her skin was the color of snow and she was completely hairless, even between her legs. Her black hair fluttered wildly behind her as if it were composed of serpents. Her face was wide-eyed, demonic. As she confronted them she turned, and they saw upon her back a gigantic spider.

As they watched, dumbfounded, the creature stirred to life, crawling down the buttocks and thighs of the demonic woman. It was gigantic. When it reached the dock it leaped upon them as if it had wings, devouring them whole.

Sated, the insect returned to the woman, climbing again upon her back. Then she turned and, with the strength of ten men, let loose the fishing boat from its moorings, pushing it out from the dock.

Soon the storm took the boat against the black, saw-toothed rocks ringing the shoreline. The boat foundered, went under. Was that the wind that howled so chillingly through the salt-stunted pines? As the waves closed over the fishing boat, the Demon Woman, eyes glowing like coals, turned insubstantial.

In the morning, with the rising sun, all that remained was a pale mist that clung to the lichen-covered rocks, and refused to be dissipated even by the heat of the day.

Shisei lying in bed, staring at the voices beyond the walls in the dark, listening to strangers inhabit Senjin's room, listening to her heartbeat, thum-thum, thum-thum, propel life onward, felt as insubstantial as mist.

Here, in limbo, in purgatory, she had ceased to exist. What existed were the voices in the dark, the strangers moving, speaking, loving, hating, laughing, crying beyond the walls of her dark room, luminous ghosts whom she passively observed, who, in the inertia of her inner struggle, did her living for her.

Sister, where are you? Where have you been? I am waiting for you. I need you.

Giri.
And the Demon Woman's spider etched into her flesh. Senjin's flesh. Wasn't that right? Isn't that what he had taught her when he had mur-

dered Jeiji, her lover, in the Tau-tau ritual that invoked the membrane *kokoro*? The ritual that increased their own power exponentially?

"I have done this for you, Shisei. I love you. I need you. We will be together, always."

But in murdering Jeiji, hadn't Senjin murdered her future?

Giri.

The Demon Woman.

Shisei stood up, the sheet sliding down around her ankles. The voices beyond the walls had ceased.

The spider moved.

When Senjin returned to the room with the trompe l'oeil windows, Justine was gone. The couch lay in the middle of the room, mocking him. Speaker wires that he had ripped from the wall lay like copper-tongued serpents on the black and persimmon Persian carpets.

Senjin held the side of his head, feeling the heat of his own blood, the accelerated beat of his heart. He went to the couch, lay down on it. He could smell Justine's scent, even feel the last vestiges of her warmth. He allowed these things to seep into him, to nourish him as he had allowed Mariko's susurrus to nourish him. But they were not enough. Perhaps, had she been here, Justine's susurrus would have sustained him for his final confrontation with Nicholas Linnear. Perhaps.

Now he would have to call upon the membrane *kokoro*. He would have to begin the meditation without at the same time being able to perform the ritual action that would reinforce his repetitive chanting.

Senjin focused his mind on *kokoro* and began. In a moment his heartbeat slowed. He regulated the flow of his endorphins, cutting his mind free from the pain. Some time later the blood ceased to seep from his wound. A scab began to form.

The healing procedure under way, he began the gathering of power, the channeling of the vibrational energy he drew from *kokoro*, the center of things.

The gathering was not yet complete when his eyes flew open.

Shisei!

She was here. She had come!

Conny Tanaka crouched, saw pieces of himself reflected again and again in a hundred thousand mirrored shards. And dark patches in between. "I see his blood," Conny said. "So this is what happens when the seven of diamonds turns into the ace of spades."

Nicholas, his back against the entryway wall, said, "It wasn't enough." He hurt all over, but the psychic struggle had been far worse than the physical one. "Is Justine all right?"

Conny nodded. "I got her out of the room. She's safe."

"But he got more from her than I thought he would," Nicholas said bitterly. "I gave him too much time with her. It was a terrible risk, but he had to be exposed to the chanting on the tape I gave you to play. I needed the time, and he took it."

"It looks like it weakened him," Conny said. "Just as you suspected."

"But now he knows where the last of So-Peng's emeralds are." Nicholas put his head back against the bare wall. "I can't let him leave here."

Conny looked at Nicholas, at his myriad reflections scattered like stars all around him. "It occurs to me that you never had that intention," he said softly.

Nicholas nodded. "You're right, of course. I just didn't want to have to face it, not if there was a chance it could end differently. Now I know that I must kill him or he will kill me."

"How badly are you hurt?"

"I'll survive," Nicholas said. "For now." He glanced up the stairwell. It was unnaturally quiet in the building. "What's he doing up there, I wonder?" But he could already feel the dark reverberations at *kokoro*, and knew that he was finished. He had so little experience with the tanjian membrane, that in that theater of war, Senjin would surely defeat him. For Nicholas that was the death ground, and he must at all costs stay clear of it. There must be some other way, he thought.

"Okay." Conny rubbed his hands together. "What's Plan B?"

Nicholas looked at his friend, gave him a bleak smile. "There isn't any. I'm out of ideas. This bastard's not going to give up, and I don't think I can stop him."

"You need to rest," Conny said.

"If he gets to me," Nicholas said, "I'll have all the time in the world to rest."

Conny came closer, gave Nicholas some cold tea. "Something happened while you two were at it," Conny said. "I got a call from your friend, Tanzan Nangi. He had a great deal to tell me."

Conny poured more tea, watched as Nicholas drank it down. There was no point in telling Nicholas of the herbs he had stirred into the tea. They would give him strength while they slowed his metabolism, facilitating meditation and the formulation of strategy. He would feel their effects soon enough.

"First of all, Kusunda Ikusa is dead. And they found the tape the Pack Rat made of Ikusa, Killan Oroshi, and this genius, the Scoundrel. It seemed as if the Scoundrel created a supervirus, a computer program that rides piggyback on a software's security program. It gets into the software core and acts as a mole, broadcasting otherwise classified information back to its originator.

"You and Nangi, I'm told, thought that Nami wanted into Sato because of the Sphynx T-PRAM computer chip. To them that was just the gravy. What they really wanted was to be inside the Hive Project. Sato and Tomkin have just signed a deal with Hydrotech-inc for manufacture of certain components for the American Hive Project. Well, according to the Scoundrel, once Nami got control of Sato, they would secrete the Scoundrel's MANTIS supervirus into the components. It would act like a time bomb, inactive until given a prearranged, seemingly innocuous electronic signal. MANTIS would come alive, burrow into the core of the Hive computer and begin sending key data back to Nami."

Nicholas stared at his friend. "Good God. The Hive Project is going to be installed in every section of the United States government: the Pentagon, the National Security Council, the CIA, State Department, FBI, you name it. That would mean Nami would have access to all the secret data this administration has."

Conny nodded. "Pretty neat, huh? Talk about your ultimate mole. The leak would never be found. American security would be irreparably damaged." Conny took a little tea himself. "But here's the real kicker. Nami hired two people to help in their scheme. One is upstairs now, probably bleeding all over my couch. It was his job to disable you permanently so that you wouldn't be able to interfere. Nami was scared to death of you.

"The other person, working the opposite end of the pipeline, is this bastard's twin sister. Her name is Shisei. She was sent over here to somehow link up with the senator—his name's Branding—who's shepherding the Hive Project through the Senate, to make sure the project's funding bill was passed by Congress."

Nicholas nodded, a thoughtful look on his face. "That explains a lot. Most everything, in fact, except why Senjin didn't kill me when he could have the first time we met. If Nami hired him to get rid of me, he had his chance and didn't take it. Why?"

If you die now, if you die too easily, you will never understand. That was what Senjin had said to him in Dr. Hanami's office. Understand what?

Nicholas did not know. Except it was clear that Senjin harbored a personal enmity against Nicholas. But Nicholas was certain that he did not know this man, had never met him before the violent encounter in Dr. Hanami's office.

As he probed deeper into the mystery, Nicholas sank into *Getsumei no michi*. He thought about Senjin's strategy: *Shiro Ninja*, the murder of Dr. Hanami, the surgeon he had coerced into allowing him entrée into the operation on Nicholas's tumor; the murder of Dr. Muku, a clinical psychiatrist who logically might have discovered what Senjin had done to that small piece of Nicholas's brain; the murder of Kyoki, the tanjian who could have helped Nicholas.

None of this fit the profile of an independent ninja operative hired to take out an enemy who might otherwise thwart the greatest international espionage coup ever attempted. This was the strategy of a man driven by a torrent of hate, a strategy meant to disable, to destroy by increments another human being.

Nicholas thanked the great good fortune that had led him to Kansatsu. It was fortuitous karma indeed that Senjin had no knowledge of Kyoki's brother, living high up in the Alps, in sight of the Black Gendarme.

But Senjin's strategy contained another element besides Nicholas's destruction: the possession of So-Peng's mystic emeralds. Are they the connection between us? Nicholas wondered. How he wished he knew more about his grandfather.

He felt Conny's hand on his shoulder and opened his eyes.

"Nick, are you all right?" Conny asked. "I thought for a minute you'd stopped breathing."

"Someone's coming," Nicholas said, rising.

Conny glanced up the staircase.

"Not there," Nicholas said, walking to the front door. He opened it, looked into the exquisite face.

"Hello, Shisei. I am Nicholas Linnear," he said, his will still expanding outward. "But I suppose you already know that."

Shisei looked up into Nicholas's face. "So long the enemy," she said. "I thought my heart would cease to beat when I met you."

They both spoke Japanese, out of some instinct that communication on several levels was essential.

"Come in," Nicholas said. He did not turn his back on her. Over his shoulder he made the introductions with Conny.

Conny cursed in gutter Japanese. "You know who she is, Nick? Why'd you let her in here?"

"I don't think I could have kept her out." Nicholas had not once let go of her eyes with his. "Conny, we're all out of tea."

When they were alone, Nicholas said, "Now you see that you have looked upon the face of the Medusa and you still live."

Neither of them had ceased to move. They circled each other slowly, crunching the glass shards, their images picked up and fired in the crucible of tiny mirrors at their feet.

"Circumstances have changed," Shisei said. "I have not come here to destroy you, or even, I think, to help my brother."

"Then why have you come?" Nicholas asked softly.

"To save myself," Shisei said.

There was more than mere conversation passing between them. Within the interstices of the words, sentences, tiny pauses, silences, their wills met in the center of the room, creating a kind of psychic whirlpool, so that when Conny returned with the tea, he felt so vertiginous he almost dropped the tray he was carrying.

Nicholas heard the clatter, like silverware trembling in an earthquake, and he said, "Stay away, Conny. Leave the tea, but don't come back into this room until it's over."

"But Nick—"

"Do as I tell you, my friend," Nicholas said. "I don't want Justine alone now."

"He's a good friend," Shisei said when Conny had gone. "I envy you."

"I wish we had time to know one another."

"A pity," Shisei agreed. "But there is only time enough to reach some form of accord. I hear the echoes of *kokoro*, the reverberations are strong. It will not be long now before my brother gains all the power he has been yearning for."

"He has stolen six of my emeralds."

"When he gets all of them," Shisei said, "he will truly be invincible. He will create the configuration of the nine. Power beyond imagining will be his. The earth will shudder. He will be one with Eternity, he will walk with the gods. This is what he has wanted all along." She was moving, moving, her body as restless as her psyche. Nicholas wondered whether it was he she did not trust or herself. "But then these emeralds have a history of being stolen. First by So-Peng—"

"My grandfather never stole anything in his life!"

"Perhaps," Shisei said. "Perhaps not. The truth, now, does not matter. What matters is what is in my brother's mind. He and I are descendants of Zhao Hsia, the man whom So-Peng drowned at the base of the waterfall near Gunung Muntahak mountain a century ago."

"I am being attacked by a past I do not know."

"My brother has been taken hostage by that same past."

"You don't expect me to pity him."

"No," Shisei said. "But understanding is essential now. It will not be enough, I think, to meet him in Tau-tau. He has gone beyond even Tau-tau. He has created his own system of magic, most of which even I am unfamiliar with."

"Does he frighten you the way he does me?" Then Nicholas felt the dark pulse, a ripple in the projection of her will, and knew that Senjin frightened his sister. He said, "How can you love that which you fear so?"

"I cannot help myself." Shisei was near to tears. "He is my twin. His flesh is my flesh."

"But his mind is not yours."

"We are like two crystal lanterns," Shisei said, "burning in the darkness. We are the same, yet so very different. This I did not fully realize until today."

"Oh, I think you realized it long before this," Nicholas said. "It took you this long to accept it."

Shisei and Nicholas continued to be locked within the width of the circle they traversed. Yin and yang, dark and light, male and female, soft and hard, but now the definitions were becoming more and more blurred.

"Can you tell me why he kills?" Nicholas asked. "Does it delight him in some unfathomable way?"

"Murder is another means to his end," Shisei said. "When he kills, he does so in the ritualistic way he was taught. The constant reiteration of meditative chants, of ritualized action. This is why he skins his victims. The action combines with the chanting to affect the membrane *kokoro* most powerfully. It is how he draws his strength, why it continues to grow."

Nicholas shuddered. "He must be stopped, Shisei," he said. "There is no other course."

"So that is why I am here."

Nicholas said, "I am a novice at Tau-tau. Without your help, your brother will surely defeat me."

"I know."

Shisei stopped and turned so that her back was to him. She unbuttoned her blouse, let it fall to her waist. She was wearing nothing underneath.

"This is what I am," she said, revealing the great spider. "This is what my brother did to me. This is what he fears. The Demon Woman."

Nicholas went to the tray Conny had left, brought them both tea. They sat cross-legged, facing one another, and drank, silent for only a moment. But the pause was significant, marking a new phase of their engagement.

Nicholas put down his empty cup. "You must go with me, then, to meet Senjin."

"No," Shisei said. "That is for you, and you alone. I can no longer think only of myself now. I have someone more important whom I must protect."

Nicholas did not ask who that person might be. He did not have to. He was contained in the projection of her will: Cotton Branding.

"I must tell you," Nicholas said, "that Nami is finished. Kusunda Ikusa is dead. The MANTIS virus is no longer under his control."

He felt the sense of relief, more profound than words, flooding through her.

"Come here," she said.

When Nicholas was very close to her, Shisei opened her handbag, took out her implements. Swiftly, surely, she set about making up his face. She held in her mind the image she had of the Demon Woman as she strode the storm-swept coastline in search of revenge against not only her men, but all men who in their baseness had treated her as if she were nothing more than an animal. But what also came to her was the visage of her only friend, Kiku, as she had been that night of the moon-viewing festival when she became the Samurai, when Shisei had fallen in love with the perfect male that Kiku had become.

When she was finished, she said, "You look beautiful; you look terrifying. But your hair is wrong. It is a man's hairstyle."

"Wait here," Nicholas said. He disappeared for perhaps thirty seconds.

When he returned, he was dressed in the costume from Conny's Kabuki actor. He carried the elaborate wig. He sat again in front of Shisei, who placed the wig on his head, adjusted it to her satisfaction. When she was finished, she held up a pocket mirror, showed him what he had become.

"It's perfect," Nicholas said, stunned. "Where did you learn this?"

"Do you know Golden Cloud?"

" 'Kiyoku Utsukushiku Kanzan,' " Nicholas recited. "Yes, I know of it." He stared at his reflection. "You have indeed made me Pure, Beautiful, Perfect."

The rolling tones, like a bell around the neck of an approaching itinerant priest, were reaching a crescendo.

"He is coming," Nicholas said. "I must go."

"Now you know what it is he fears," Shisei said. But she had not yet fully betrayed him, her other half, her dark self, her love, her captor, her death, and she knew it. But if she did nothing now, she knew that her coming here was for nothing. Not for her to sit and observe. Her days and nights in her brother's hotel room had told her that.

As Nicholas turned to go, she stopped him with her mind. "Now there is something else," she said, one hand clasping the other. "Something I must give you, something besides my knowledge and my skill, because now I can feel that these things alone will not stop my brother. He is already too strong."

And she slid from her finger the emerald ring Senjin had given her on the day after he had murdered Jeiji, her lover.

"This is a tanjian emerald," she said. "It is the only thing my brother ever gave me. He presented it to me on our birthday, but it was never mine. I suspected it then. I know it now."

Nicholas took the ring with its glowing stone set in platinum, and in that moment he felt what Shisei felt: the power of the Demon Woman.

Turning gracefully as a woman, as Shisei herself would, he went out of the entryway, up the stairs, to look death in the face.

The energy of *kokoro* washed over Senjin, laving him as a mother bathes her infant. Once, he felt another presence at *kokoro*, the center of things, and he reached out almost languidly, already almost a god, exerting godlike power, and the other presence disappeared.

It was Nicholas Linnear, Senjin knew, who had withdrawn when Senjin himself had reached out with the steel coils of his will to embrace *kokoro*. Now that he had successfully cut Nicholas off from the central energy of Tau-tau, Senjin was assured of complete victory.

Senjin sat up. The reverberations at *kokoro* rang in his mind, in his body, setting them to vibrating. Even the tanjian elders at Zhuji cannot milk *kokoro* as I can, he thought. They were afraid to try, afraid that too much pressure on the membrane would cause it to rupture, causing limitless chaos to fill the world. I do not have their fears. I use *kokoro* as I see fit.

He reached out with his mind to enfold Shisei as he had done with *kokoro*, so that she could join in the exhilaration of this victory. He wanted her here, had called for her to join him because now was the time to reclaim the present he had given her: the tanjian emerald he had set into a ring for her.

Shisei had been its guardian without knowing it. When he had stolen it just before he had left the tanjian village of Zhuji, he knew that he must not keep it—at least not initially. The tanjian elders would have used their powers to trace it had he kept it with him. Shisei had never been to Zhuji, had never learned their Tau-tau. They would not find it if she had it.

Senjin could feel her presence, but he needed to be close to her, to merge with her one last time as she gave him the tanjian emerald. Was Nicholas somehow preventing her getting to him?

He went out of the room with the trompe l' oeil windows. His fingertips were sparking with blue flame only he could see: the power of *kokoro*.

Senjin paused at the top of the stairs. He heard the soft pad of feet. He extended his mind outward, felt only a smooth, featureless wall. Nicholas Linnear.

But Shisei was closer. He was smiling as he descended.

Light drifted up to him, indirect but increasing in intensity. Recalling the trick with the mirrors, Senjin prepared himself. Light was Nicholas Linnear's only ally, and Senjin was determined to strip him of it, to send him hurtling into the darkness before he ended his life.

Light shone on the curving staircase, bathing it as a moment before Senjin had bathed in the energy of *kokoro*. Into this confined field climbed the actor turned actress, the male who was female, the yang turned perfect yin: light into dark.

Senjin, at the moment of his ultimate triumph, the moment he had been anticipating, dreaming about, relishing for so many years, the moment when he would free Zhao Hsia from the infamy of defeat, when, by gathering up the stolen tanjian emeralds and murdering the treacherous So-Peng's last ancestor, he would restore honor to his family line, confronted his worst nightmare.

The Demon Woman.

She rose out of the light, entangled within it, blotting it out as she approached: dark-eyed face, at once fierce and maternal, erotic and vindictive.

Haha-san's face.

Senjin screamed or shouted, he did not know which. This was no play that he was taking his intended victims to see, no playacting upon a brilliantly-lit stage where he could observe with fear, loathing, and fascination the visage of the Demon Woman, safe in the confines of the theater, spellbound in the make-believe.

This was real. The Demon Woman, evolved from the mist of the shoreline, had at last come for him.

The shock of recognition lasted perhaps only a second. But it was enough to allow Nicholas to make the first assault, a blinding psychic attack using Akshara, the language of Eternity, taught to him by the tanjian *sensei*, Kansatsu.

Akshara is the center of the universe, Kansatsu had told him. *It is a silence so whole, so complete within itself, that it contains the entire universe. When one expresses oneself with Akshara there is, in a real sense, no need for language. For Akshara was in existence long before there was a need for language. To employ Akshara is to be one with the universal force.*

Still, though Senjin reeled backward on the staircase, his mind ripped by the Akshara assault while he was still paralyzed by the sight of the Demon Woman, he was not destroyed.

As Shisei had intimated, he was already too powerful. And Nicholas knew that he had waited too long, that he had allowed Senjin too much time to gather the forces of *kokoro*, that even Akshara was insufficient to stop him now.

Senjin crashed into the wall of the staircase, whirled down several steps. But now his mind had recovered from the initial shock, and he extended his will like a vise, surrounding the smooth, featureless wall, exerting more and more pressure, pressing inward, inflicting pain, until with a thunderous crash of silence the wall collapsed.

And Senjin was inside Nicholas's last line of defense, in Nicholas's mind, the energy of *kokoro* manifesting itself by tearing Nicholas's psyche apart.

The end was approaching, more rapidly than Nicholas could have imagined. He fell to his knees. His costume ripped, the elaborate wig fell off his head.

He could not breathe, could not move. Thinking was all but obviated by the pressure Senjin was bringing to bear on him. Darkness was descending.

But there was a central core of light that burned in the darkness: a crystal lantern, the essence that Shisei had given him . . .

Now, come to me, my sister, my twin, my love, thought Senjin. Now is when I need you. The dark, sinuous coils of his will expanded outward, touching the smooth wall of Nicholas's psyche.

But the wall was no longer featureless. Its vast curving surface was aglitter with the essence of his twin sister. Shisei rose to meet him, and as Senjin reached out, he was met with a swirl of mist and vengeance.

Shisei! Senjin's mind cried . . .

Nicholas's fingers felt as if they were encased in lead as he fumbled in his pocket. Pain gripped him; he felt his heart thudding heavily in his chest, as if at any moment it might burst.

Then the tanjian emerald Shisei had given him was in his palm, on the tips of his fingers. He exerted the last piece of his will.

And now he felt a power outside himself drawing him and it toward Senjin, faster and faster, as if two unimaginably powerful magnets were about to come together.

They touched . . .

Within the firelight dancing in Senjin's mind was a hollowness. He saw her as if from afar, and he knew with a despair that shriveled his spirit that he had been abandoned, betrayed by the creature he had created. His only love. His ultimate nightmare.

The Demon Woman: Shisei . . .

It was as if the faceted emerald had become a blade, for as it came into contact with Senjin's chest, it cut through skin, muscle, viscera, and bone.

Blood exploded outward, showering Nicholas, the staircase, the walls. Senjin's body arched like a bow. His eyes bugged out, his mouth opened soundlessly. Then all light and life went out of him, just as if some divine hand had extinguished the spark.

Shisei screamed, spun around. She held onto Conny Tanaka's broad shoulders so that she would not collapse. She felt the death of her twin as the earth feels its sun in eclipse.

She gasped once, sharply. She felt ripped asunder, as if she had been eviscerated, a surgeon's cruel scalpel excising in an instant what had been part of her since birth.

Darkness, the utter chill of an endless night. And then, as miraculous as the emergence through winter's frozen soil of the first tender shoot, light and warmth returning.

One heart beating thum-thum, thum-thum, instead of two. Silence where there had been shadowy intimations, calm instead of echoes feverishly ringing. Shisei breathed. At last she was released from the dark, metallic coils of Senjin's will.

"Are you all right?" Conny asked.

"Yes," Shisei managed to get out. "Now."

Immediately Nicholas felt the pain inside him lift. The husk of Senjin Omukae, the *dorokusai*, lay sprawled across the stairs, as inconsequential as ash. The dark reverberations ceased.

Echoes, then silence.

Kokoro was at rest.

SUMMER-AUTUMN, PRESENT

The sun was shining in southwest Florida when Nicholas and Justine drove their convertible rental car across the San Marco Drive causeway onto Marco Island.

Lew Croaker and Alix would have met them at the Fort Myers airport, but they were out on their boat, chartered for the morning.

Nicholas turned onto Collier Boulevard, heading for the dock where Lew's boat was berthed. They went past lavish private homes, surrounded by lush tropical foliage, many with their own boat slips, then condominium developments that fronted the beach against which lapped the warm, gentle waves of the Gulf of Mexico.

Nicholas pulled into a parking space, turned off the engine. For a time neither of them moved. They listened to the wind in the palms, the crying of the gulls, watched the serpentine sweep of the pelicans as they skimmed the diamond-lighted waves, searching for food.

"Justine," Nicholas said. "I'm sorry. At the beginning of all this I closed you out. I thought I was doing the noble thing, that I could protect you from what was happening to me." He took her hand. "But the truth is that I shut you out long before that. I was so happy to be back in Japan that it simply never occurred to me that you could feel differently—that you *must* feel differently. You didn't know the language, the customs were strange, there were few friends of your sex and age to be made and, most of all, you must have missed home."

"Nick—"

"No, let me finish." He watched the salt breeze take her hair, whip it about her face. "Ironically, it was through Senjin that I found you again that I came to understand the core of our estrangement. But then I betrayed you again. I used you to trap Senjin, to blunt his power, which was growing each hour. I put you in danger. It was a calculated risk, I admit, because I put you center stage in a theater of my own making. But—"

Justine's hand on his mouth stopped him. The sun was shining in her eyes, turning them a vivid green. The red motes swam in her left eye like points of fire. "Nick, you must know how deeply I love you. Words mean nothing. But you can look inside my mind—I know that now, after the events of the last few days. You can feel what I feel about you."

She brought his hand up to her mouth, kissed his palm. "I thank God that you've told me what happened, and that it wasn't what I feared. Nick, for a long time I thought you hated me because you blamed me for our daughter's death."

"Justine, how could you—"

"Hush, now. Let me have my say. I was afraid of that because of my own guilt. I projected it onto you, and as we drifted further and further apart, the idea got set in my mind. You never knew, because I couldn't admit it to myself, that I was terrified of having a child. And then when our daughter died, it occurred to me that my fright had somehow killed her."

She drew a lock of hair off her forehead. "And as for Senjin, you did what you had to do. You didn't involve me—Senjin did. You just reacted in the only way you could. No one else could have stopped him, I'm certain of that."

She kissed him hard on the lips. "Now it's over. There's a new life inside me. Our child, Nick. And I'm not afraid anymore. I want it as much as I want you. And very soon I'll need you both, and I know it will be a wonderful feeling."

She rested her head on his shoulder, felt the strength of his arms encircling her. "How I love you," she whispered.

Croaker's boat was just turning past the headland. They could see Alix shading her eyes, straining to make them out. They waved and Alix grinned, waved back.

Ten minutes later, the boat was at its berth. Alix raced down the dock to embrace them both. Lew Croaker was helping his clients off with their catch: an iridescent blue marlin.

He looked different, tan and fit. The constant Florida sun had put a squint in his eyes that looked faintly piratical, and his hair was quite a bit longer than when he had been a NYPD detective.

"Hey, Nick."

"Lew."

They shook hands, then embraced.

Later, on board the *Captain Sumo*, Lew Croaker said, "We're a couple of miles out. How about doing a little fishing for marlin? It's a good day for them."

Nicholas shook his head. "Thanks, but I'd rather relax another way. I've had enough of killing for a while."

Croaker squinted at him. "You haven't turned into some kind of freaking vegetarian in Japan, have you?"

Nicholas laughed. "Jesus, Lew, it's good to see you."

"Yeah. Well, for a while there I thought maybe we'd never see each other again."

"Friends are too important to lose," Nicholas said.

"Hey, buddy, you want to see something?" Croaker dipped into the large cooler on deck, brought out two cans of beer. He tossed one to Nicholas, then lifted the other one in his left hand. The titanium, graphite, and polycarbonate prosthetic the medical geniuses at Todai had grafted onto the stump of his wrist looked like part exotic carapace, part erector set. Croaker had said that at first he had kept it sheathed in a glove, but soon that seemed foolish, especially in a tropical climate.

"Watch this!"

Croaker's left hand squeezed. There was a sound not unlike an explosion. A geyser of frothy beer plumed upward into the clear blue sky. When it came down it drenched them. The left hand opened and a flattened can fell to the deck.

Lew Croaker laughed at the look on Nicholas's face. "Maybe that's something even you can't do," he said good-naturedly.

Inside the cabin, at the helm, Alix said, "Look at them. Like a couple of kids. It's so good to have you and Nick down here, Justine. How long can you stay?"

Justine, looking wistfully at the two boys at play, said, "Not long enough."

Killan woke once to twilight seeping through the open window. Clear liquid dripped into a vein on the inside of her wrist. She saw the silhouette of a figure hunched in a chair. Nothing could be seen of her face, but Killan recognized those old, gnarled hands as the soft light fell upon them. The crooked fingers had lost little of their deftness as they quickly, efficiently folded rice paper back and forth. In no time the hands held a prancing horse. Turning her head slightly, Killan could see a parade of origami animals sitting on the windowsill, lovingly made by her grandmother.

"I'm thirsty." A dusty croak.

Her grandmother rose, placed a porcelain cup against Killan's lips. Tea, tepid, delicious. She drank deeply.

Killan closed her eyes and slept.

When she woke again, daylight was streaming through the window. Her grandmother was sitting in the same spot, her fingers working, working. There were more animals. Killan felt movement beside her, turned her head slowly. Her father was standing over her.

"I'm thirsty." That same dusty croak.

Killan's grandmother rose, but Ken Oroshi said, "I'll get it."

He gave her the tea, and Killan drank it all.

Ken Oroshi said, "I remember feeding you cold tea, just like this, when you were a baby. What fevers you had. Your mother was always frantic with worry."

He put the teacup down. "The doctors have instructed me to tell you that it is a week since they brought you here," he said as soon as he saw that she was finished. "They said that when you woke you might be a little disoriented." His eyes searched her bruised, puffy face. "The police have told me everything."

Not everything, she thought, and closed her eyes.

"The doctors tell me that you're full of painkillers."

"I don't know," she said, in a dry husky voice that cracked. "I don't feel anything." But she wondered at the anxiety in his voice. It must be the company, she thought. Does it make a difference that Kusunda is dead? Nakano is still destroyed.

"I suppose that's good," Ken Oroshi said, "for the time being. I imagine you're wondering about the huskiness in your voice. There was some damage to your vocal chords."

"That's okay," she said. "I'm beginning to like the way I sound."

He cleared his throat, and Killan wondered what it was he wanted. He always wanted something when he spoke to her, even when it was only to rail against her "dangerous" revolutionary friends.

"You know, it occurred to me recently that I never treated you in the same way I treat your brothers. Well, you're my daughter. I always thought that was right and proper. Women have their place in society, an important place, to be sure, but it is not the same as a man's place. This used to be very clear to me."

He shifted on his feet, as if he were suddenly uncomfortable in her presence.

It was a bittersweet homecoming to his beloved Japan for Nicholas. The knowledge that he and Justine might now not stay here permanently was a dark companion that rode on his shoulder. Not that he resented their decision—which had all been worked out in Marco Island. They both had to be happy in Japan, otherwise their relationship was going to suffer. And, Nicholas knew, if it came to that, he could become content with trips to Tokyo every few months.

Nangi, Tomi, and Umi were at Narita Airport when he and Justine cleared Immigration and Customs. Nangi looked haggard but buoyant.

Umi took Nicholas aside. "The ice has begun to melt," she said in her enigmatic way. "I am glad that you have returned. But I sense there is more yet for you to learn."

In the car, Nangi spoke nonstop about the integration of Nakano Industries with Sato International, the ways in which its R&D department would spur revenues and profits in the coming years.

To this flood of good news Nicholas said barely a word. In fact, staring out at the countryside, he often seemed oblivious, displaced.

"Nick, what is it?" Justine said softly. Umi, her eyes closed, seemed lost in prayer or meditation. Nangi and Tomi were talking softly between themselves, and Justine and Nicholas had as much privacy as they could reasonably expect in Japan. "What's troubling you?"

"I still don't know enough about my grandfather," Nicholas said. "Senjin's sister told me he believed that So-Peng was a villain, that he was a murderer, that his mother stole the tanjian emeralds from the elders in Zhuji and that he kept them. I want to know the truth."

"But who is left to tell you the truth?" Justine asked. "No one."

Nicholas, his eyes clouded, shook his head. "Someone knows the truth, Justine."

The Hodaka.

The fifteen days of true summer had come to the upper reaches of the Hodaka in the Japanese Alps. Stark black had turned to subtle shades of gray. The rock formations seemed softer, more forgiving. The snow had lost its brittle crust, and here and there the ice formations were melted to frigid water by the sunlight.

Three days after he and Justine landed in Japan, Nicholas was making his way along the last section of the rough path leading to Kansatsu's mountain retreat.

"Have I come here many times before?" Nicholas asked when his mentor opened the door as he approached.

"I wanted to tell you, since it seemed of some importance to y
have come to an accommodation of sorts. Tanzan Nangi, wh
Nakano, has put pressure on Nami. Since the scandal with Iku
Nami's position has been irreparably undermined. The Emperoı
avowed their policies; he's cut them off completely. Nami had n
but to void the contract Nangi signed. As a consequence, Nangi'
all of Nakano, including the research and development departn
"He's asked me to be Nakano's president. Nangi will be chaiı
course, and I'll report to him. But he has assured me that I wil
good deal of autonomy. I can hire my own people, for instan
company feels like mine again, for the first time in years."

Killan heard something new in her father's voice. Was it humı
wondered.

"Speaking of hiring," Ken Oroshi said. "When you're better,
you to come up to Nakano's offices, take a look around. In fact,
you the grand tour myself. We'll be in our new headquarters, thei
Shinjuku Suiryu Building, where Sato International is. And the F
department is getting its own floor—I'll show you that as well
afterward, perhaps we can go to lunch, talk. I would like that, l

Killan, staring into her father's eyes, nodded, mute.

When he was gone, she closed her eyes again. She heard mo
near her, opened them to see an exquisite origami panda sitting
bed covers. She picked it up, smiled. It was so long since she ha
that, her facial muscles felt strange.

"When the police spoke to your father," Killan's grandmothe
"they played him a tape. I believe you know the one. Whatever he
opened his eyes. He was shocked at what you did—but also I th
was proud of you. For the first time, he saw what it was you w
Perhaps it was the first time for you as well."

Now Killan recognized the new note in her father's voice. It ı
humility; it was respect.

"In any case," her grandmother said, "you have given him hi
back. Now, as is right and proper, he wishes to return the favor."

Killan was silent for some time. At last she stirred, as if in sleep,
the midst of a dream. She said, "Grandma, would you make me ı
keys? I always loved monkeys."

"Yes," the old woman said, lifting a family of three origami monı
from the windowsill. She placed them on her granddaughter's chest
know."

"No," Kansatsu said, smiling. "This meeting will occur only once." He retreated into the gloom of his house. "Enter."

After tea had been made and consumed, Kansatsu said, "In truth, I had no way of knowing whether I would see you again."

"Your gift could not reveal it?"

"Not this time," Kansatsu said. "When it comes to you, I have no second sight." He waited a moment. "Senjin is gone, then."

Nicholas was startled. "You knew his name?"

"I knew *him*, Nicholas. He was once one of my students. That was how I knew the extent of the danger he presented, and I was afraid. But then you came to me here for the first time, trudging up the Hodaka, craning your neck for a sight of your nemesis, the Black Gendarme, and I knew there was hope."

"If you knew Senjin was so dangerous," Nicholas said, "why did you train him?"

"I didn't, in fact, train him." Kansatsu's eyes were hooded, unreadable. "I use the word 'student' purely for convenience. Senjin came here to test me, just as he had tested my brother, Kyoki, before me. I had foreseen Kyoki's death, and consequently knew how I must act with this *dorokusai*.

"At the time he appeared here, he was already far more powerful than I. His mind had conceived of another discipline—which he called Kshira, the language of the sound-light continuum—far more advanced than Tau-tau."

Kansatsu shrugged. "I did what I could. I humored him. This was as much as I could manage with him: I withheld my knowledge of the future and my antipathy toward him. This was why, years later, after he had made you *Shiro Ninja*, he murdered Kyoki and not me. Kyoki had made the mistake of threatening Senjin. Senjin did not consider me an enemy; he did not believe that I would help you even if you knew where to find me. On the contrary, I caused him to believe that he was learning from me during his stay here."

Something in the incense-laden room stirred, hovered at Nicholas's shoulder, making him uneasy. He shook his head. "You knew Senjin would one day murder your brother, yet you did nothing to stop him?"

"Untrue," Kansatsu said. "On the contrary, I did what I could. I created you."

"Me? How is it I could stop Senjin and you couldn't?"

"Because, my dear Nicholas, you are the One. The last male connected with So-Peng. You are the guardian of the tanjian emeralds."

"So it's true, then."

Kansatsu nodded. "As true as anything can be."

"I want to talk to you about my grandfather," Nicholas said. "Was he the murderer, liar, cheat that Senjin believed him to be?"

"Is that at all important?"

"Yes," Nicholas said. "It is to me."

Kansatsu sighed as he rose. "Let us continue this discussion outside on the Hodaka."

They went out, crossing a long, gently sloping shoulder of snow.

"The truth," Kansatsu said. "Down there," pointing into the belly of civilization, "there is no truth. But of course you have discovered that for yourself. Which is why you have made the journey up here." As they walked they left a trail behind them in the snow, a quiet melting that, in the utter silence, could perhaps be discerned. "But let me warn you, Nicholas, that where one finds the truth, it is often dangerous. Often it is better to turn one's back, to walk away and never look back."

"I want to know," Nicholas said. "I have to know."

"Yes," Kansatsu said slowly. "Of course you do." There was an odd note to his voice, as if he were reluctantly, sadly accepting the inevitable.

They crossed the snow shoulder, skirted a black, serpentine ridge of rock from which the snow had been scoured by the constant winds. Below, a four-thousand-foot drop, interrupted only by saw-toothed outcroppings of rock. Above, the sheer, indomitable face of the Black Gendarme impinged upon the purple-blue sky.

Kansatsu stared into a middle distance, at a landscape only he could see, as he began. "It is true that your great-grandmother, So-Peng's mother, fled Zhuji with the mystic emeralds of the tanjian elders. She took sixteen. They were her birthright, bequeathed to her from the moment she came squealing into the world.

"The tanjian, of course, had other emeralds. But they squandered their power, overtaxed *kokoro* with their ambition to put emissaries in other lands. There came a time, therefore, when they needed her emeralds back.

"Toward this end, they concocted a story, fed it to a young tanjian named Zhao Hsia. He was talented but, in this case, particularly impressionable. This was why the elders chose him. They dispatched him to Singapore to bring back the emeralds along with So-Peng, who, they had heard, was a totally untrained tanjian.

"So-Peng's mother was warned and, fearing the worst, she told So-Peng as much as she dared of his heritage. So-Peng did the rest. He sought out Zhao Hsia. They fought. So-Peng prevailed. But at a high price. Before he died, Zhao Hsia told So-Peng that they were half brothers. He had come from the same womb as had So-Peng.

"In the months afterward, knowing that he and his mother would be watched, So-Peng gave over the care of the emeralds to Desaru, the man whose dog's life he had saved on the tiger hunt Tik Po Tak had taken him on. No one else knew of this man or of So-Peng's relationship with him.

"And, true to So-Peng's suspicions, the tanjian elders sent other emissaries to spy on him, to try to get the emeralds back. In this they were unsuccessful. But they managed in their devious ways to murder all of So-Peng's daughters, those offspring whose sex would assure the continuation of the tanjian gift in his family. So-Peng did nothing; he was one man and the tanjian were many. But his blood-friend Tik Po Tak thought otherwise. He sought revenge against the tanjian spies, and was himself killed by them.

"Only when So-Peng's second wife had died, when he had vowed not to take another wife, when they were assured that he would never have a daughter, did the tanjian spies withdraw back to Zhuji in China.

"But So-Peng was a wily fox, and he fooled them all. He discovered a young orphan girl, recognized in her the tanjian gift. He took her in, nurtured her, taught her, loved her more than he ever had loved his own daughters.

"This girl was your mother Cheong. And, through her, So-Peng ensured the continuation of his lineage."

"Then everything that Senjin believed was false."

"Yes."

If you die now, if you die too easily, you will never understand. But it was Senjin who never understood, Nicholas thought. "His hatred, his blood feud with me was for nothing."

Kansatsu stopped at the edge of a ridge. His eyes opened wide and the light, hitting the irises, gave them an iridescent cast. "Oh no. It wasn't for nothing, Nicholas. It brought you to me." Kansatsu smiled, and Nicholas felt again the peculiar stirring at his shoulder, as if another presence were with them. "And not only you: the tanjian emeralds, as well."

"What do you mean?" And still Nicholas did not want to believe it. But at last he looked fully at the presence at his shoulder: the dangerous truth.

"The emeralds in your possession are all that are left," Kansatsu said. "Whoever holds them, holds Eternity in his hand."

Nicholas thought again of Umi's warning to him before he had left for

New York. *The* dorokusai *is close. Closer than you can believe or can imagine. One must focus on the power of the mind. And of illusion.*

Nicholas took a pace backward.

"That will do you no good," Kansatsu said.

"You used Senjin to get to me; then you used me to kill him. He was the only other one who had a chance of getting the emeralds from me."

"I told you that the only truth was here and that it was dangerous."

"You weren't always like this," Nicholas said. "Manipulating people, lives, murdering through proxy. I thought you were incorruptible."

"Corruption is an odd thing," Kansatsu said. "It seems an impossibility until that one moment when it becomes irresistible. Then you tell yourself that it is nothing but giving in to temptation."

"My God, you make it sound like a decision to have an extramarital affair!"

"Well, that is an accurate analogy, don't you think?" Kansatsu said. "I've strayed from the path of Akshara. But consider the reward. Now I will have everything!"

"No," Nicholas raised his fist. "As you've said, you've made your decision. And it is to have nothing."

Nicholas opened his hand. In it lay nine emeralds.

"No!"

It was more than a shout, more even than a scream. In that one syllable was contained the shift in tides that had turned white to black, light into darkness, the righteous into the corrupted, the Way into the snare.

And the snare became the pit.

A humming in the air, a spark and crackle as if of a wood fire or heat lightning.

The emeralds in Nicholas's palm stirred, came to life. They were the nine: the mystic configuration venerated, worshiped by the tanjian since the dawn of time.

The emeralds formed a pattern, complex, three-dimensional. The configuration rose, whirling, into the air of the Hodaka, and with headlong speed rushed at Kansatsu.

They struck him so hard in the face that his features disappeared. For an instant Nicholas could see their glowing facets like a potent constellation of stars embedded in his flesh.

Then the scent of burning flesh arose as if from a pagan pyre.

A scream, echoing through the vast snow-wrapped canyons of the Hodaka, as Kansatsu was blown backward as if from the percussion of a cannon. Flung off the ridge of snowy rock, out into the swirling winds, a black mote in the blue, blue sky.

Dwindling into nothingness.

Nicholas, his heart hammering painfully in his chest, took in huge drafts of air. The terrible fear was still with him: the fear of confronting his mentor—in a very real sense, his father, if only in a spiritual sense; the fear of confronting centuries of arcane power, deceit, and illusion; of having in his possession the means of destroying that power.

He was, indeed, the One. The guardian of the tanjian emeralds. He had fulfilled his destiny.

"*Now* it's over," Nicholas said softly. There was no one there, yet he knew he was speaking directly to his grandfather.

Then he turned, went silently down off the Hodaka. And never looked back at the looming Black Gendarme, inimical, indifferent.

It was just a slab of rock now.

Autumn refused to come to Washington. The leaves on the cherry and plane trees, so lush in midsummer, hung limp and unmoving in the stifling heat. The Potomac seemed gelid, smooth beneath the blanket of oppressive October humidity.

Cotton Branding's ASCRA bill had passed both houses by an overwhelming majority, and there was bipartisan agreement that should the Hive Project pass stringent tests, it would be installed as the one governmental computer system, as early as two years hence.

Branding's popularity spread from coast to coast, and he was making the most of his increased air time. He had been on *Meet the Press* and *Face the Nation*. CNN had run an in-depth piece on him, and he had done exceptionally well on *Firing Line*.

He and Shisei were married in a public ceremony in front of the Lincoln Memorial. The venue itself caused a kind of feverish speculation. What was the senior senator from New York doing getting married in the nation's capital unless there was a political motive?

The media coverage was unprecedented, gaining the lead spot on every TV news-magazine show. Gaily striped tents were filled with laughing people, pop music, and the sound of popping champagne corks. *Forbes* and *Fortune* fought over rights to an exclusive interview with Branding. *Newsweek* put Branding and Shisei on its cover with the headline, "The Golden Couple." *People* ran a cover shot of them kissing at the end of the wedding ceremony. The copy asked the question, "The New Administration?" That same week, *Time*'s cover dubbed them "The New Global Royalty."

Shisei had applied for citizenship, and a month later (because Branding had pulled strings at Immigration) she had taken the oath along with a dozen other immigrants from various nations. The ceremony, which also garnered extensive media coverage, moved her more than she could have imagined.

By October, too, it was clear that Branding had an overwhelming mandate from his party. It seemed likely that after the presidential elections in two years, he would be the one presiding over the installation of the Hive computer from the Oval Office.

That afternoon—a Sunday when Branding and Shisei were finally alone—they had just finished making love. It had been a long and languorous day, the heat from outside seeping into their bare skin as they twined and slept and twined again.

Shisei rose at last, her bladder full, and padded into the bathroom. Beyond, through the open door, was the room they had converted into her study. As she finished, she passed by the open door, saw the red light flashing on her computer. A message was being sent via the modem.

Curious, Shisei went to the computer, punched the code to bring up the message on the screen as it was being transmitted.

She sat down hard on a chair, an icy hand squeezing her insides. For there, blossoming on the screen, was the unmistakable serpentine architecture of the MANTIS virus. But this was a new version, faster, with added elements that carried the information in a stream, curling on the crests of a series of waves.

In a moment the last line of the transmission appeared on the screen, blinking over and over.

MANTIS PERFECTED. IMPLEMENT IMMEDIATELY.

Shisei cleared the screen.

But the new MANTIS was already stored in her computer, as if it were a deadly substance or a genie, slipped into a glass vial, waiting, patient as a god, to be let out.